John Grisham

THE
TESTAMENT

A TIME TO KILL

This edition published in 2000 by Cresset Editions,
an imprint of The Random House Group Ltd,
20 Vauxhall Bridge Road, London SW1V 2SA

Printed and bound in Germany

ISBN 0 09186 959 5

The Testament

ONE

Down to the last day, even the last hour now. I'm an old man, lonely and unloved, sick and hurting and tired of living. I am ready for the hereafter; it has to be better than this.

I own the tall glass building in which I sit, and 97 percent of the company housed in it, below me, and the land around it half a mile in three directions, and the two thousand people who work here and the other twenty thousand who do not, and I own the pipeline under the land that brings gas to the building from my fields in Texas, and I own the utility lines that deliver electricity, and I lease the satellite unseen miles above by which I once barked commands to my empire flung far around the world. My assets exceed eleven billion dollars. I own silver in Nevada and copper in Montana and coffee in Kenya and coal in Angola and rubber in Malaysia and natural gas in Texas and crude oil in Indonesia and steel in China. My company owns companies that produce electricity and make computers and build dams and print paperbacks and broadcast signals to my satellite. I have subsidiaries with divisions in more countries than anyone can find.

I once owned all the appropriate toys – the yachts and jets and blondes, the homes in Europe, farms in Argentina, an island in the Pacific, thoroughbreds, even a hockey team. But I've grown too old for toys.

1

The money is the root of my misery.

I had three families – three ex-wives who bore seven children, six of whom are still alive and doing all they can to torment me. To the best of my knowledge, I fathered all seven, and buried one. I should say his mother buried him. I was out of the country.

I am estranged from all the wives and all the children. They're gathering here today because I'm dying and it's time to divide the money.

I have planned this day for a long time. My building has fourteen floors, all long and wide and squared around a shaded courtyard in the rear where I once held lunches in the sunshine. I live and work on the top floor – twelve thousand square feet of opulence that would seem obscene to many but doesn't bother me in the least. By sweat and brains and luck I built every dime of my fortune. Spending it is my prerogative. Giving it away should be my choice too, but I'm being hounded.

Why should I care who gets the money? I've done everything imaginable with it. As I sit here in my wheelchair, alone and waiting, I cannot think of a single thing I want to buy, or see, or a single place I want to go, or another adventure I want to pursue.

I've done it all, and I'm very tired.

I don't care who gets the money. But I do care very much who does not get it.

Every square foot of this building was designed by me, and so I know exactly where to place everyone for this little ceremony. They're all here, waiting and waiting, though they don't mind. They'd stand naked in a blizzard for what I'm about to do.

The first family is Lillian and her brood – four of my offspring born to a woman who rarely let me touch her. We married young – I was twenty-four and she was eighteen – and so Lillian is old too. I haven't seen

2

her in years, and I won't see her today. I'm sure she's still playing the role of the grieving, abandoned yet dutiful first wife who got traded in for a trophy. She has never remarried, and I'm sure she hasn't had sex in fifty years. I don't know how we reproduced.

Her oldest is now forty-seven, Troy Junior, a worthless idiot who is cursed with my name. As a boy he adopted the nickname of TJ, and still prefers it to Troy. Of the six children gathered here now, TJ is the dumbest, though it's close. He was tossed from college when he was nineteen for selling drugs.

TJ, like the rest, was given five million dollars on his twenty-first birthday. And like the rest, it ran like water through his fingers.

I cannot bear to recount the miserable histories of Lillian's children. Suffice to say they're all heavily in debt and virtually unemployable, with little hope of changing, so my signing of this will is the most critical event in their lives.

Back to the ex-wives. From the frigidity of Lillian, I ran to the steamy passion of Janie, a beautiful young thing hired as a secretary in Accounting but promoted rapidly when I decided I needed her on business trips. I divorced Lillian and married Janie, who was twenty-two years younger than I was and determined to keep me satisfied. She had two children as fast as she could. She used them as anchors to keep me close. Rocky, the younger, was killed in a sports car with two of his buddies, in a wreck that cost me six million to settle out of court.

I married Tira when I was sixty-four. She was twenty-three and pregnant by me with a little monster she named Ramble, for some reason that was never clear to me. Ramble is now fourteen, and already has one arrest for shoplifting and one arrest for possession of marijuana. His oily hair sticks to his neck and falls way down his back, and he adorns himself with rings in his ears, eyebrows, and nose. I'm told he goes to school when he feels like it.

Ramble is ashamed that his father is almost eighty, and his father is ashamed that his son has silver beads pierced through his tongue.

And he, along with the rest of them, expects me to sign my name on this will and make his life better. As large as my fortune is, the money won't last long among these fools.

A dying old man should not hate, but I cannot help it. They are a miserable bunch, all of them. Their mothers hate me, so the children in turn have been taught to hate me too.

They are vultures circling with clawed feet, sharp teeth, and hungry eyes, giddy with the anticipation of unlimited cash.

The soundness of my mind is of great issue now. They think I have a tumor because I say weird things. I babble on incoherently in meetings and on the phone, and my aides behind my back whisper and nod and think to themselves, Yes, it's true. It's the tumor.

I made a will two years ago and left everything to the last live-in, who at the time paraded around my apartment in leopard print panties and nothing else and, yes, I guess I'm crazy about twenty-year-old blondes with all the curves. But she later got the boot. The shredder got the will. I simply got tired.

Three years ago I made a will, just for the hell of it, and left everything to charities, over a hundred of them. I was cursing TJ one day, and he was cursing me, and I told him about this new will. He and his mother and his siblings hired a bunch of crooked lawyers and ran to court in an attempt to have me committed to an institution for treatment and evaluation. This was actually smart on the part of their lawyers because if I'd been judged mentally incompetent my will would have been void.

But I have many lawyers, and I pay them a thousand dollars an hour to manipulate the legal system in my favor. I was not committed, though at the time I was probably a bit off my rocker.

And I have my own shredder, one I've used for all the old wills. They're all gone, eaten by a little machine.

I wear long white robes made of Thai silk, and I shave my head like a monk, and I eat little, so that my body is small and shriveled. They think I'm a Buddhist but in reality I study Zoroaster. They don't know the difference. I can almost understand why they think my mental capacity has diminished.

Lillian and the first family are in the executive conference room on the thirteenth floor, just below me. It's a large room, marble and mahogany, with rich rugs and a long oval table down the center, and it's now filled with very nervous people. Not surprisingly, there are more lawyers than family members. Lillian has a lawyer, and so does each of her four children, except for TJ, who has brought along three to show his importance and make certain all scenarios are properly counseled. TJ has more legal problems than most death row inmates. At one end of the table is a large digital screen which will broadcast the proceedings.

TJ's brother is Rex, age forty-four, my second son, currently married to a stripper. Amber is her name, a poor creature without a brain but with a large fake chest, who, I think, is his third wife. Second or third, but who am I to condemn? She's here, along with the rest of the current spouses and/or live-ins, fidgeting nervously as eleven billion is about to be divided.

Lillian's first daughter, my oldest, is Libbigail, a child I loved desperately until she left for college and

5

forgot about me. Then she married an African and I erased her name from my wills.

Mary Ross was the last child born to Lillian. She's married to a doctor who aspires to be super-rich, but they are heavily in debt.

Janie and the second family wait in a room on the tenth floor. Janie has had two husbands since our divorce many years ago. I'm almost certain she is living alone at the moment. I hire investigators to keep me posted, but not even the FBI could keep track of her bed-hopping. As I mentioned, Rocky, her son, was killed. Her daughter Geena is here with her second husband, a moron with an MBA who is just dangerous enough to take a half a billion or so and masterfully lose it in three years.

And then there's Ramble, slouching in a chair on the fifth floor, licking the gold ring in the corner of his lip, fingering his sticky green hair, scowling at his mother, who had the gall to appear here today with a hairy little gigolo. Ramble expects to get rich today, to be handed a fortune simply because he was sired by me. And Ramble has a lawyer too, a hippie radical sort Tira saw on television and hired right after she laid him. They're waiting, along with the rest.

I know these people. I watch them.

Snead appears from the rear of my apartment. He's been my gofer for almost thirty years now, a round homely little man in a white waistcoat, meek and humble, perpetually bent at the waist as if bowing to the king. Snead stops before me, hands clasped at the belly, as always, head cocked to one side, drippy smile, and says, 'How are you, sir?' in an affected lilt he acquired years back when we were staying in Ireland.

I say nothing, because I'm neither required nor expected to respond to Snead.

'Some coffee, sir?'

6

'Lunch.'

Snead winks with both eyes and bows even deeper, then waddles from the room, his trouser cuffs dragging the floor. He too expects to be made rich when I die, and I suppose he's counting the days like the rest of them.

The trouble with having money is that everybody wants a little of it. Just a slice, a small sliver. What's a million dollars to a man with billions? Give me a million, old boy, and you'll never know the difference. Float me a loan, and we'll both forget about it. Wedge my name in the will somewhere; there's room for it.

Snead's nosy as hell and years ago I caught him picking through my desk, looking, I think, for the current will. He wants me to die because he expects a few million.

What right does he have to expect anything? I should've fired him years ago.

His name is not mentioned in my new will.

He sets a tray before me: an unopened tube of Ritz crackers, a small jar of honey with the plastic seal around the lid, and a twelve-ounce can of Fresca, room temperature. Any variation and Snead would be fired on the spot.

I dismiss him, and dip the crackers in the honey. The final meal.

TWO

I sit and stare through the tinted glass walls. On a clear day, I can see the top of the Washington Monument six miles away, but not today. Today is raw and cold, windy and overcast, not a bad day to die. The wind blows the last of the leaves from their branches and scatters them through the parking lot below.

Why am I worried about the pain? What's wrong with a little suffering? I've caused more misery than any ten people.

I push a button and Snead appears. He bows and pushes my wheelchair through the door of my apartment, into the marble foyer, down the marble hall, through another door. We're getting closer, but I feel no anxiety.

I've kept the shrinks waiting for over two hours.

We pass my office and I nod at Nicolette, my latest secretary, a darling young thing I'm quite fond of. Given some time, she might become number four.

But there is no time. Only minutes.

A mob is waiting – packs of lawyers and some psychiatrists who'll determine if I'm in my right mind. They are crowded around a long table in my conference room, and when I enter, their conversation stops immediately and everybody stares. Snead situates me on one side of the table, next to my lawyer, Stafford.

There are cameras pointing in all directions, and the

technicians scramble to get them focused. Every whisper, every move, every breath will be recorded because a fortune is at stake.

The last will I signed gave little to my children. Josh Stafford prepared it, as always. I shredded it this morning.

I'm sitting here to prove to the world that I am of sufficient mental capacity to make a new will. Once it is proved, the disposition of my assets cannot be questioned.

Directly across from me are three shrinks – one hired by each family. On folded index cards before them someone has printed their names – Dr. Zadel, Dr. Flowe, Dr. Theishen. I study their eyes and faces. Since I am supposed to appear sane, I must make eye contact.

They expect me to be somewhat loony, but I'm about to eat them for lunch.

Stafford will run the show. When everyone is settled and the cameras are ready, he says, 'My name is Josh Stafford, and I'm the attorney for Mr. Troy Phelan, seated here to my right.'

I take on the shrinks, one at a time, eye to eye, glare to glare, until each blinks or looks away. All three wear dark suits. Zadel and Flowe have scraggly beards. Theishen has a bow tie and looks no more than thirty. The families were given the right to hire anyone they wanted.

Stafford is talking. 'The purpose of this meeting is to have Mr. Phelan examined by a panel of psychiatrists to determine his testamentary capacity. Assuming the panel finds him to be of sound mind, then he intends to sign a will which will dispose of his assets upon his death.'

Stafford taps his pencil on a one-inch-thick will lying before us. I'm sure the cameras zoom in for a close-up, and I'm sure the very sight of the document

9

sends shivers up and down the spines of my children and their mothers scattered throughout my building.

They haven't seen the will, nor do they have the right to. A will is a private document revealed only after death. The heirs can only speculate as to what it might contain. My heirs have received hints, little lies I've carefully planted.

They've been led to believe that the bulk of my estate will somehow be divided fairly among the children, with generous gifts to the ex-wives. They know this; they can feel it. They've been praying fervently for this for weeks, even months. This is life and death for them because they're all in debt. The will lying before me is supposed to make them rich and stop the bickering. Stafford prepared it, and in conversations with their lawyers he has, with my permission, painted in broad strokes the supposed contents of the will. Each child will receive something in the range of three hundred to five hundred million, with another fifty million going to each of the three ex-wives. These women were well provided for in the divorces, but that, of course, has been forgotten.

Total gifts to the families of approximately three billion dollars. After the government rakes off several billion the rest will go to charity.

So you can see why they're here, shined, groomed, sober (for the most part), and eagerly watching the monitors and waiting and hoping that I, the old man, can pull this off. I'm sure they've told their shrinks, 'Don't be too hard on the old boy. We want him sane.'

If everyone is so happy, then why bother with this psychiatric examination? Because I'm gonna screw 'em one last time, and I want to do it right.

The shrinks are my idea, but my children and their lawyers are too slow to realize it.

Zadel goes first. 'Mr. Phelan, can you tell us the date, time, and place?'

10

I feel like a first-grader. I drop my chin to my chest like an imbecile and ponder the question long enough to make them ease to the edge of their seats and whisper, 'Come on, you crazy old bastard. Surely you know what day it is.'

'Monday,' I say softly. 'Monday, December 9, 1996. The place is my office.'

'The time?'

'About two-thirty in the afternoon,' I say. I don't wear a watch.

'And where is your office?'

'McLean, Virginia.'

Flowe leans into his microphone. 'Can you state the names and birthdates of your children?'

'No. The names, maybe, but not the birthdates.'

'Okay, give us the names.'

I take my time. It's too early to be sharp. I want them to sweat. 'Troy Phelan, Jr., Rex, Libbigail, Mary Ross, Geena, and Ramble.' I utter these as if they're painful to even think about.

Flowe is allowed a follow-up. 'And there was a seventh child, right?'

'Right.'

'Do you remember his name?'

'Rocky.'

'And what happened to him?'

'He was killed in an auto accident.' I sit straight in my wheelchair, head high, eyes darting from one shrink to the next, projecting pure sanity for the cameras. I'm sure my children and my ex-wives are proud of me, watching the monitors in their little groups, squeezing the hands of their current spouses, and smiling at their hungry lawyers because old Troy so far has handled the preliminaries.

My voice may be low and hollow, and I may look like a nut with my white silk robe, shriveled face, and green turban, but I've answered their questions.

11

Come on, old boy, they're pleading.

Theishen asks, 'What is your current physical condition?'

'I've felt better.'

'It's rumored you have a cancerous tumor.'

Get right to the point, don't you?

'I thought this was a mental exam,' I say, glancing at Stafford, who can't suppress a smile. But the rules allow any question. This is not a courtroom.

'It is,' Theishen says politely. 'But every question is relevant.'

'I see.'

'Will you answer the question?'

'About what?'

'About the tumor.'

'Sure. It's in my head, the size of a golf ball, growing every day, inoperable, and my doctor says I won't last three months.'

I can almost hear the champagne corks popping below me. The tumor has been confirmed!

'Are you, at this moment, under the influence of any medication, drug, or alcohol?'

'No.'

'Do you have in your possession any type of medication to relieve pain?'

'Not yet.'

Back to Zadel: 'Mr. Phelan, three months ago *Forbes* magazine listed your net worth at eight billion dollars. Is that a close estimate?'

'Since when is *Forbes* known for its accuracy?'

'So it's not accurate?'

'It's between eleven and eleven and a half, depending on the markets.' I say this very slowly, but my words are sharp, my voice carries authority. No one doubts the size of my fortune.

Flowe decides to pursue the money. 'Mr. Phelan,

12

can you describe, in general, the organization of your corporate holdings?'

'I can, yes.'

'Will you?'

'I suppose.' I pause and let them sweat. Stafford assured me I do not have to divulge private information here. Just give them an overall picture, he said.

'The Phelan Group is a private corporation which owns seventy different companies, a few of which are publicly traded.'

'How much of The Phelan Group do you own?'

'About ninety-seven percent. The rest is held by a handful of employees.'

Theishen joins in the hunt. It didn't take long to focus on the gold. 'Mr. Phelan, does your company hold an interest in Spin Computer?'

'Yes,' I answer slowly, trying to place Spin Computer in my corporate jungle.

'How much do you own?'

'Eighty percent.'

'And Spin Computer is a public company?'

'That's right.'

Theishen fiddles with a pile of official-looking documents, and I can see from here that he has the company's annual report and quarterly statements, things any semiliterate college student could obtain. 'When did you purchase Spin?' he asks.

'About four years ago.'

'How much did you pay?'

'Twenty bucks a share, a total of three hundred million.' I want to answer these questions more slowly, but I can't help myself. I stare holes through Theishen, anxious for the next one.

'And what's it worth now?' he asks.

'Well, it closed yesterday at forty-three and a half, down a point. The stock has split twice since I bought it, so the investment is now worth around eight-fifty.'

'Eight hundred and fifty million?'

'That's correct.'

The examination is basically over at this point. If my mental capacity can comprehend yesterday's closing stock prices, then my adversaries are certainly satisfied. I can almost see their goofy smiles. I can almost hear their muted hoorahs. Atta boy, Troy. Give 'em hell.

Zadel wants history. It's an effort to test the bounds of my memory. 'Mr. Phelan, where were you born?'

'Montclair, New Jersey.'

'When?'

'May 12, 1918.'

'What was your mother's maiden name?'

'Shaw.'

'When did she die?'

'Two days before Pearl Harbor.'

'And your father?'

'What about him?'

'When did he die?'

'I don't know. He disappeared when I was a kid.'

Zadel looks at Flowe, who's got questions packed together on a notepad. Flowe asks, 'Who is your youngest daughter?'

'Which family?'

'Uh, the first one.'

'That would be Mary Ross.'

'Right –'

'Of course it's right.'

'Where did she go to college?'

'Tulane, in New Orleans.'

'What did she study?'

'Something medieval. Then she married badly, like the rest of them. I guess they inherited that talent from me.' I can see them stiffen and bristle. And I can almost see the lawyers and the current live-ins and/or spouses hide little smiles because no one can argue the fact that I did indeed marry badly.

And I reproduced even more miserably.

Flowe is suddenly finished for this round. Theishen is enamored with the money. He asks, 'Do you own a controlling interest in MountainCom?'

'Yes, I'm sure it's right there in your stack of paperwork. It's a public company.'

'What was your initial investment?'

'Around eighteen a share, for ten million shares.'

'And now it –'

'It closed yesterday at twenty-one a share. A swap and a split in the past six years and the holding is now worth about four hundred million. Does that answer your question?'

'Yes, I believe it does. How many public companies do you control?'

'Five.'

Flowe glances at Zadel, and I'm wondering how much longer this will take. I'm suddenly tired.

'Any more questions?' Stafford asks. We are not going to press them because we want them completely satisfied.

Zadel asks, 'Do you intend to sign a new will today?'

'Yes, that is my intent.'

'Is that the will lying on the table there before you?'

'It is.'

'Does that will give a substantial portion of your assets to your children?'

'It does.'

'Are you prepared to sign the will at this time?'

'I am.'

Zadel carefully places his pen on the table, folds his hands thoughtfully, and looks at Stafford. 'In my opinion, Mr. Phelan has sufficient testamentary capacity at this time to dispose of his assets.' He pronounces this with great weight, as if my perform-ance had them hanging in limbo.

The other two are quick to rush in. 'I have no doubt as to the soundness of his mind,' Flowe says to Stafford. 'He seems incredibly sharp to me.'

'No doubt?' Stafford asks.

'None whatsoever.'

'Dr. Theishen?'

'Let's not kid ourselves. Mr. Phelan knows exactly what he's doing. His mind is much quicker than ours.'

Oh, thank you. That means so much to me. You're a bunch of shrinks struggling to make a hundred thousand a year. I've made billions, yet you pat me on the head and tell me how smart I am.

'So it's unanimous?' Stafford says.

'Yes. Absolutely.' They can't nod their heads fast enough.

Stafford slides the will to me and hands me a pen. I say, 'This is the last will and testament of Troy L. Phelan, revoking all former wills and codicils.' It's ninety pages long, prepared by Stafford and someone in his firm. I understand the concept, but the actual print eludes me. I haven't read it, nor shall I. I flip to the back, scrawl a name no one can read, then place my hands on top of it for the time being.

It'll never be seen by the vultures.

'Meeting's adjourned,' Stafford says, and everyone quickly packs. Per my instructions, the three families are hurried from their respective rooms and asked to leave the building.

One camera remains focused on me, its images going nowhere but the archives. The lawyers and psychiatrists leave in a rush. I tell Snead to take a seat at the table. Stafford and one of his partners, Durban, remain in the room, also seated. When we are alone, I reach under the edge of my robe and produce an envelope, which I open. I remove from it three pages

16

of yellow legal paper and place them before me on the table.

Only seconds away now, and a faint ripple of fear goes through me. This will take more strength than I've mustered in weeks.

Stafford, Durban, and Snead stare at the sheets of yellow paper, thoroughly bewildered.

'This is my testament,' I announce, taking a pen. 'A holographic will, every word written by me, just a few hours ago. Dated today, and now signed today.' I scrawl my name again. Stafford is too stunned to react.

'It revokes all former wills, including the one I signed less than five minutes ago.' I refold the papers and place them in the envelope.

I grit my teeth and remind myself of how badly I want to die.

I slide the envelope across the table to Stafford, and at the same instant I rise from my wheelchair. My legs are shaking. My heart is pounding. Just seconds now. Surely I'll be dead before I land.

'Hey!' someone shouts, Snead I think. But I'm moving away from them.

The lame man walks, almost runs, past the row of leather chairs, past one of my portraits, a bad one commissioned by a wife, past everything, to the sliding doors, which are unlocked. I know because I rehearsed this just hours ago.

'Stop!' someone yells, and they're moving behind me. No one has seen me walk in a year. I grab the handle and open the door. The air is bitterly cold. I step barefoot onto the narrow terrace which borders my top floor. Without looking below, I lunge over the railing.

THREE

Snead was two steps behind Mr. Phelan, and thought for a second that he might catch him. The shock of seeing the old man not only rise and walk but also practically sprint to the door froze Snead. Mr. Phelan hadn't moved that fast in years.

Snead reached the railing just in time to scream in horror, then watched helplessly as Mr. Phelan fell silently, twisting and flailing and growing smaller and smaller until he struck the ground. Snead clenched the railing and stared in disbelief, then he began to cry.

Josh Stafford arrived on the terrace a step behind Snead, and witnessed most of the fall. It happened so quickly, at least the jump; the fall itself seemed to last for an hour. A man weighing a hundred and fifty pounds will drop three hundred feet in less than five seconds, but Stafford later told people the old man floated for an eternity, like a feather whirling in the wind.

Tip Durban got to the railing just behind Stafford, and saw only the body's impact on the brick patio between the front entrance and a circular drive. For some reason Durban held the envelope, which he had absently picked up during the rush to catch old Troy. It felt a lot heavier as he stood in the frigid air, looking down at a scene from a horror film, watching the first onlookers move up to the casualty.

*

Troy Phelan's descent did not reach the level of high drama he had dreamed of. Instead of drifting to the earth like an angel, a perfect swan dive with the silk robe trailing behind, and landing in death before his terror-stricken families, who he'd imagined would be leaving the building at just the right moment, his fall was witnessed only by a lowly payroll clerk, hustling through the parking lot after a very long lunch in a bar. The clerk heard a voice, looked up at the top floor, and watched in horror as a pale naked body tumbled and flapped with what appeared to be a bedsheet gathered at the neck. It landed on its back, on brick, with the dull thud one would expect from such an impact.

The clerk ran to the spot just as a security guard noticed something wrong and bolted from his perch near the front entrance of Phelan Tower. Neither the clerk nor the guard had ever met Mr. Troy Phelan, so neither knew at first upon whose remains they were gazing. The body was bleeding, barefoot, twisted, and naked, and exposed with a sheet bunched at the arms. And it was quite dead.

Another thirty seconds, and Troy would have had his wish. Because they were stationed in a room on the fifth floor, Tira and Ramble and Dr. Theishen and their entourage of lawyers were the first to leave the building. And, therefore, the first to happen upon the suicide. Tira screamed, not from pain nor love nor loss, but from the sheer shock of seeing old Troy splattered on the brick. It was a wretched piercing scream that was heard clearly by Snead, Stafford, and Durban, fourteen floors up.

Ramble thought the scene was rather cool. A child of TV and an addict of video games, he found the gore a magnet. He moved away from his shrieking mother and knelt beside his dead father. The security guard placed a firm hand on his shoulder.

'That's Troy Phelan,' one of the lawyers said as he hovered above the corpse.

'You don't say,' said the guard.

'Wow,' said the clerk.

More people ran from the building.

Janie, Geena, and Cody, with their shrink Dr. Flowe and their lawyers, were next. But there were no screams, no breakdowns. They stuck together in a tight bunch, well away from Tira and her group, and gawked like everyone else at poor Troy.

Radios crackled as another guard arrived and took control of the scene. He called for an ambulance.

'What good will that do?' asked the payroll clerk, who, by virtue of being the first on the scene, assumed a more important role in the aftermath.

'You want to take him away in your car?' asked the guard.

Ramble watched the blood fill in the mortar cracks and run in perfect angles down a gentle slope, toward a frozen fountain and a flagpole nearby.

In the atrium, a packed elevator stopped and opened and Lillian and the first family and their entourage emerged. Because TJ and Rex had once been allowed offices in the building, they had parked in the rear. The entire group turned left for an exit, then someone near the front of the building yelled, 'Mr. Phelan's jumped!' They switched directions and raced through the front door, onto the brick patio near the fountain, where they found him.

They wouldn't have to wait for the tumor after all.

It took Joshua Stafford a minute or so to recover from the shock and start thinking like a lawyer again. He waited until the third and last family was visible below, then asked Snead and Durban to step inside.

The camera was still on. Snead faced it, raised his right hand, and swore to tell the truth, then, fighting tears, explained what he had just witnessed. Stafford opened the envelope and held the yellow sheets of paper close enough for the camera to see.

'Yes, I saw him sign that,' Snead said. 'Just seconds ago.'

'And is that his signature?' Stafford asked.

'Yes, yes it is.'

'Did he declare this to be his last will and testament?'

'He called it his testament.'

Stafford withdrew the papers before Snead could read them. He repeated the same testimony with Durban, then placed himself before the camera and gave his version of events. The camera was turned off, and the three of them rode to the ground to pay their respects to Mr. Phelan. The elevator was packed with Phelan employees, stunned but anxious to have a rare and last glimpse of the old man. The building was emptying. Snead's quiet sobs were muffled in a corner.

Guards had backed the crowd away, leaving Troy alone in his puddle. A siren was approaching. Someone took photographs to memorialize the image of his death, then a black blanket was placed over his body.

For the families, slight twinges of grief soon overcame the shock of death. They stood with their heads low, their eyes staring sadly at the blanket, organizing their thoughts for the issues to come. It was impossible to look at Troy and not think about the money. Grief for an estranged relative, even a father, cannot stand in the way of a half a billion dollars.

For the employees, shock gave way to confusion. Troy was rumored to live up there above them, but very few had ever seen him. He was eccentric, crazy, sick – the rumors covered everything. He didn't like people. There were important vice presidents in the

21

building who saw him once a year. If the company ran so well without him, surely their jobs were secure.

For the psychiatrists – Zadel, Flowe, and Theishen – the moment was filled with tension. You declare a man to be of sound mind, and minutes later he jumps to his death. Yet even a crazy man can have a lucid interval – that's the legal term they repeated to themselves as they shivered in the crowd. Crazy as a bat, but one clear, lucid interval in the midst of the madness, and a person can execute a valid will. They would stand firm with their opinions. Thank God everything was on tape. Old Troy was sharp. And lucid.

And for the lawyers, the shock passed quickly and there was no grief. They stood grim-faced next to their clients and watched the pitiful sight. The fees would be enormous.

An ambulance drove onto the bricks and stopped near Troy. Stafford walked under the barricade and whispered something to the guards.

Troy was quickly loaded onto a stretcher and taken away.

Troy Phelan had moved his corporate headquarters to northern Virginia twenty-two years earlier to escape taxation in New York. He spent forty million on his Tower and grounds, money he saved many times over by being domiciled in Virginia.

He met Joshua Stafford, a rising D.C. lawyer, in the midst of a nasty lawsuit that Troy lost and Stafford won. Troy admired his style and tenacity, and so he hired him. In the past decade, Stafford had doubled the size of his firm and become rich with the money he earned fighting Troy's battles.

In the last years of his life, no one had been closer to Mr. Phelan than Josh Stafford. He and Durban returned to the conference room on the fourteenth floor and locked the door. Snead was sent away with instructions to lie down.

With the camera running, Stafford opened the envelope and removed the three sheets of yellow paper. The first sheet was a letter to him from Troy. He spoke to the camera: 'This letter is dated today, Monday, December 9, 1996. It is handwritten, addressed to me, from Troy Phelan. It has five paragraphs. I will read it in full:

'"Dear Josh: I am dead now. These are my instructions, and I want you to follow them closely. Use litigation if you have to, but I want my wishes carried out.

'"First, I want a quick autopsy, for reasons that will become important later.

'"Second, there will be no funeral, no service of any type. I want to be cremated, with my ashes scattered from the air over my ranch in Wyoming.

'"Third, I want my will kept confidential until January 15, 1997. The law does not require you to immediately produce it. Sit on it for a month.

'"So long. Troy."'

Stafford slowly placed the first sheet on the table, and carefully picked up the second. He studied it for a moment, then said for the camera, 'This is a one-page document purporting to be the last testament of Troy L. Phelan. I will read it in its entirety:

'"The last testament of Troy L. Phelan. I, Troy L. Phelan, being of sound and disposing mind and memory, do hereby expressly revoke all former wills and codicils executed by me, and dispose of my estate as follows:

'"To my children, Troy Phelan, Jr., Rex Phelan, Libbigail Jeter, Mary Ross Jackman, Geena Strong, and Ramble Phelan, I give each a sum of money necessary to pay off all of the debts of each as of today. Any debts incurred after today will not be covered by

23

this gift. If any of these children attempt to contest this will, then this gift shall be nullified as to that child.

"'To my ex-wives, Lillian, Janie, and Tira, I give nothing. They were adequately provided for in the divorces.

"'The remainder of my estate I give to my daughter Rachel Lane, born on November 2, 1954, at Catholic Hospital in New Orleans, Louisiana, to a woman named Evelyn Cunningham, now deceased.'"

Stafford had never heard of these people. He had to catch his breath before plowing ahead.

"'I appoint my trusted lawyer, Joshua Stafford, as executor of this will, and grant unto him broad discretionary powers in its administration.

"'This document is intended to be a holographic will. Every word has been written by my hand, and I hereby sign it.

"'Signed, December 9, 1996, three P.M., by Troy L. Phelan.'"

Stafford placed it on the table and blinked his eyes at the camera. He needed a walk around the building, perhaps a blast of frigid air, but he pressed on. He picked up the third sheet, and said, 'This is a one-paragraph note addressed to me again. I will read it: 'Josh: Rachel Lane is a World Tribes missionary on the Brazil-Bolivia border. She works with a remote Indian tribe in a region known as the Pantanal. The nearest town is Corumbá. I couldn't find her. I've had no contact with her in the last twenty years. Signed, Troy Phelan.'"

Durban turned the camera off, and paced around the table twice as Stafford read the document again and again.

'Did you know he had an illegitimate daughter?'

Stafford was staring absently at a wall. 'No. I drafted eleven wills for Troy, and he never mentioned her.'

24

'I guess we shouldn't be surprised.'

Stafford had declared many times that he had become incapable of being surprised by Troy Phelan. In business and in private, the man was whimsical and chaotic. Stafford had made millions running behind his client, putting out fires.

But he was, in fact, stunned. He had just witnessed a rather dramatic suicide, during which a man confined to a wheelchair suddenly sprang forth and ran. Now he was holding a valid will that, in a few hasty paragraphs, transferred one of the world's great fortunes to an unknown heiress, without the slightest hint of estate planning. The inheritance taxes would be brutal.

'I need a drink, Tip,' he said.

'It's a bit early.'

They walked next door to Mr. Phelan's office, and found everything unlocked. The current secretary and everybody else who worked on the fourteenth floor were still on the ground.

They locked the door behind themselves, and hurriedly went through the desk drawers and file cabinets. Troy had expected them to. He would never have left his private spaces unlocked. He knew Josh would step in immediately. In the center drawer of his desk, they found a contract with a crematorium in Alexandria, dated five weeks earlier. Under it was a file on World Tribes Missions.

They gathered what they could carry, then found Snead and made him lock the office. 'What's in the testament, that last one?' he asked. He was pale and his eyes were swollen. Mr. Phelan couldn't just die like that without leaving him something, some means to survive on. He'd been a loyal servant for thirty years.

'Can't say,' Stafford said. 'I'll be back tomorrow to inventory everything. Do not allow anyone in.'

'Of course not,' Snead whispered, then began weeping again.

Stafford and Durban spent half an hour with a cop on a routine call. They showed him where Troy went over the railing, gave him the names of witnesses, described with no detail the last letter and last will. It was a suicide, plain and simple. They promised a copy of the autopsy report, and the cop closed the case before he left the building.

They caught up with the corpse at the medical examiner's office, and made arrangements for the autopsy.

'Why an autopsy?' Durban asked in a whisper as they waited for paperwork.

'To prove there were no drugs, no alcohol. Nothing to impair his judgment. He thought of everything.'

It was almost six before they made it to a bar in the Willard Hotel, near the White House, two blocks from their office. And it was only after a stiff drink that Stafford managed his first smile. 'He thought of everything, didn't he?'

'He's a very cruel man,' Durban said, deep in thought. The shock was wearing off, but the reality was settling in.

'He *was*, you mean.'

'No. He's still here. Troy's still calling the shots.'

'Can you imagine the money those fools will spend in the next month?'

'It seems a crime not to tell them.'

'We can't. We have our orders.'

For lawyers whose clients seldom spoke to each other, the meeting was a rare moment of cooperation. The largest ego in the room belonged to Hark Gettys, a brawling litigator who'd represented Rex Phelan for a number of years. Hark had insisted on the meeting not long after he returned to his office on Massachusetts

Avenue. He had actually whispered an idea to the attorneys for TJ and Libbigail as they watched the old man being loaded into the ambulance.

It was such a good idea that the other lawyers couldn't argue. They arrived, along with Flowe, Zadel, and Theishen, at Gettys' office after five. A court reporter and two video cameras were waiting.

For obvious reasons, the suicide made them nervous. Each psychiatrist was taken separately, and quizzed at length about his observations of Mr. Phelan just before he jumped.

There was not a scintilla of doubt among the three that Mr. Phelan knew precisely what he was doing, that he was of sound mind, and had more than sufficient testamentary capacity. You don't have to be insane to commit suicide, they emphasized carefully.

When the lawyers, all thirteen of them, had extracted every opinion possible, Gettys broke up the meeting. It was almost 8 P.M.

27

FOUR

According to *Forbes*, Troy Phelan was the tenth richest man in America. His death was a newsworthy event; the manner he chose made it downright sensational.

Outside Lillian's mansion in Falls Church, a cluster of reporters waited on the street for a family spokesman to come forth. They filmed friends and neighbors as they came and went, tossing out banal questions about how the family was doing.

Inside, Phelan's four eldest children gathered with their spouses and their children to receive condolences. The mood was somber when the guests were present. When the guests were gone, the tone changed dramatically. The presence of Troy's grandchildren – eleven of them – forced TJ, Rex, Libbigail, and Mary Ross to at least try and suppress their festive feelings. It was difficult. Fine wine and champagne were served, lots of it. Old Troy wouldn't want them grieving, now would he? The older grandchildren drank more than their parents.

A TV set in the den was kept on CNN, and every half hour they would gather for the latest announcement of Troy's dramatic death. A financial correspondent pieced together a ten-minute segment on the vastness of the Phelan fortune, and everyone smiled.

Lillian kept a stiff upper lip and did a credible job of

being the grieving widow. Tomorrow she would work on the arrangements.

Hark Gettys arrived around ten, and explained to the family that he had spoken to Josh Stafford. There would be no funeral, no service of any type; just an autopsy, a cremation, and a scattering of ashes. It was in writing, and Stafford was prepared to do battle in court to protect his client's wishes.

Lillian didn't give a damn what they did with Troy, nor did her children. But they had to protest and argue with Gettys. It just wasn't right to send him off with no service. Libbigail even managed a small tear and a breaking voice.

'I wouldn't fight this,' Gettys advised gravely. 'Mr. Phelan put it in writing just before his death, and the courts will honor his wishes.'

They came around quickly. No sense wasting a lot of time and money on legal fees. No sense prolonging the grieving. Why make matters worse? Troy always got what he wanted anyway. And they had learned the hard way not to tangle with Josh Stafford.

'We will abide by his wishes,' Lillian said, and the other four nodded sadly behind their mother.

There was no mention of the will and when they might actually see it, though the question was just below the surface. Best to be properly grim for a few more hours, then they could get down to business. Since there would be no wake, no funeral or service, perhaps they might meet as early as tomorrow and discuss the estate.

'Why the autopsy?' asked Rex.

'I have no idea,' Gettys answered. 'Stafford said it was in writing, but even he is not sure.'

Gettys left and they drank some more. The guests stopped coming, so Lillian went to bed. Libbigail and Mary Ross left with their families. TJ and Rex went to the billiards room in the basement, where they locked the door and switched to whiskey. At midnight, they were slapping balls around the table, drunk as sailors, celebrating their fabulous new wealth.

At 8 A.M., the day after the death of Mr. Phelan, Josh Stafford addressed the anxious directors of The Phelan Group. Two years earlier, Josh himself had been placed on the board by Mr. Phelan, but it was not a role he enjoyed.

For the past six years, The Phelan Group had operated quite profitably without much assistance from its founder. For some reason, probably depression, Troy had lost interest in the day-to-day managing of his empire. He became content to simply monitor the markets and the earnings reports.

The current CEO was Pat Solomon, a company man Troy had hired almost twenty years earlier. He was as nervous as the other seven when Stafford entered the room.

There was ample cause for anxiety. Within the company's culture there was a rich body of lore surrounding Troy's wives and his offspring. The vaguest hint that the ownership of The Phelan Group might somehow fall into the hands of those people would terrorize any board.

Josh began by stating Mr. Phelan's desires regarding burial. 'There will be no funeral,' he said somberly. 'Frankly, there is no way to pay your last respects.'

They absorbed this without comment. With the passing of a normal person, such non-arrangements would seem bizarre. But with Troy, it was difficult to be surprised.

'Who will own the company?' Solomon asked.

'I can't say now,' Stafford said, well aware of how evasive and unsatisfactory his answer was. 'Troy signed a will moments before he jumped, and he instructed me to keep it private for a period of time. I cannot, under any circumstances, divulge its contents. At least, not for now.'

'When?'

'Soon. But not now.'

'So it's business as usual?'

'Exactly. This board remains intact; everybody keeps his job. The company does tomorrow what it did last week.'

This sounded fine, but no one believed it. Ownership of the company was about to change hands. Troy had never believed in sharing stock in The Phelan Group. He paid his people well, but he did not buy into the trend of allowing them to own a piece of the company. About 3 percent of the stock was held by a few of his favored employees.

They spent an hour haggling over the wording of a press release, then adjourned for a month.

Stafford met Tip Durban in the lobby, and together they drove to the medical examiner's office in McLean. The autopsy was finished.

The cause of death was obvious. There was no trace of alcohol or drugs of any kind.

And there was no tumor. No sign of cancer. Troy was in good physical health at the time of his death, though slightly malnourished.

Tip broke the silence as they were crossing the Potomac, on the Roosevelt Bridge. 'Did he tell you he had a brain tumor?'

'Yes. Several times.' Stafford drove, though he was oblivious to roads, bridges, streets, cars. How many more surprises did Troy have?

'Why did he lie?'

'Who knows? You're trying to analyze a man who just jumped from a building. The brain tumor made everything urgent. Everybody, including me, thought he was dying. The wackiness made the panel of shrinks seem like a great idea. He set the trap, they rushed in, and now their own psychiatrists are swearing that Troy was perfectly sound. Plus, he wanted sympathy.'

'But he was crazy, wasn't he? He did, after all, take a leap.'

'Troy was weird in a lot of ways, but he knew exactly what he was doing.'

'Why did he jump?'

'Depression. He was a very lonely old man.'

They were on Constitution Avenue, sitting in heavy traffic, both staring at the taillights in front of them and trying to think it through.

'It seems fraudulent,' Durban said. 'He lures them in with the promise of money; he satisfies their psychiatrists, then at the last second he signs a will that completely guts them.'

'It was fraudulent, but this is a will, not a contract. A will is a gift. Under Virginia law, a person is not required to leave a dime to his children.'

'But they'll attack, won't they?'

'Probably. They have lots of lawyers. There's too much money at stake.'

'Why did he hate them so much?'

'He thought they were leeches. They embarrassed him. They fought with him. They never earned an honest dime and went through many of his millions. Troy never planned to leave them anything. He figured that if they could squander millions, then they could waste billions as well. And he was right.'

'How much of the family fighting was his fault?'

'A lot. Troy was a hard man to love. He told me once that he'd been a bad father and a terrible husband. He couldn't keep his hands off women, especially ones who worked for him. He thought he owned them.'

'I remember some claims for sexual harassment.'

'We settled them quietly. And for big bucks. Troy didn't want the embarrassment.'

'Any chance of more unknown heirs out there?'

'I doubt it. But what do I know? I never dreamed he had another heir, and the idea of leaving her everything is something I cannot comprehend. Troy and I spent hours talking about his estate and how to divide it.'

'How do we find her?'

'I don't know. I haven't thought about her yet.'

The Stafford law firm was in a frenzy when Josh returned. By Washington standards, it was considered small – sixty lawyers. Josh was the founder and principal partner. Tip Durban and four others were called partners, which meant Josh listened to them occasionally and shared some of the profits. For thirty years it had been a rough-and-tumble litigation firm, but as Josh approached sixty he spent less time in the courtroom and more time behind his cluttered desk. He could've had a hundred lawyers if he wanted ex-Senators, lobbyists, and regulatory analysts, the usual D.C. lineup. But Josh loved trials and courtrooms, and he hired only young associates who had tried at least ten jury cases.

The average career of a litigator is twenty-five years. The first heart attack usually slows them down enough to delay a second. Josh had avoided burnout by tending to Mr. Phelan's maze of legal needs – securities, antitrust, employment, mergers, and dozens of personal matters.

Three sets of associates waited in the reception room of his large office. Two secretaries shoved memos and phone messages in his direction as he removed his overcoat and settled behind his desk. 'Which is most urgent?' he asked.

'This, I think,' answered a secretary.

It was from Hark Gettys, a man Josh had talked to at least three times a week for the past month. He dialed the number and Hark was immediately on the line. They quickly went through the pleasantries, and Hark got right to the point.

'Listen, Josh, you can imagine how the family is breathing down my neck.'

'I'm sure.'

'They want to see the damned will, Josh. Or at least they want to know what's in it.'

The next few sentences would be crucial, and Josh had plotted them carefully. 'Not so fast, Hark.'

A very slight pause, then, 'Why? Is something the matter?'

'The suicide bothers me.'

'What! What do you mean?'

'Look, Hark, how can a man be of sound mind seconds before he jumps to his death?'

Hark's edgy voice rose an octave, and the words carried even more anxiety. 'But you heard our psychiatrists. Hell, they're on tape.'

'Are they sticking by their opinions, in light of the suicide?'

'Damned right they are!'

'Can you prove this? I'm looking for help here, Hark.'

'Josh, last night we examined our three shrinks again. We drilled them, and they're sticking like glue. Each signed an affidavit eight pages long swearing to the sound mental capacity of Mr. Phelan.'

'Can I see the affidavits?'

'I'll courier them over right now.'

'Please do.' Josh hung up and smiled to no one in particular. The associates were marched in, three sets of bright and fearless young lawyers. They sat around a mahogany table in one corner of the office.

Josh began by summarizing the contents of Troy's

34

handwritten will, and the legal problems it was likely to create. To the first team he assigned the weighty issue of testamentary capacity. Josh was concerned about time, the gap between lucidity and insanity. He wanted an analysis of every case even remotely involving the signing of a will by a person considered crazy.

The second team was dispatched to research holographic wills; specifically, the best ways to attack and defend them.

When he was alone with the third team, he relaxed and sat down. They were the lucky ones, because they would not spend the next three days in the library. 'You have to find a person who, I suspect, does not want to be found.'

He told them what he knew about Rachel Lane. There wasn't much. The file from Troy's desk provided little information.

'First, research World Tribes Missions. Who are they? How do they operate? How do they pick their people? Where do they send them? Everything. Second, there are some excellent private locators in D.C. They're usually ex-FBI and government types who specialize in finding missing people. Select the top two, and we'll make a decision tomorrow. Third, Rachel's mother's name was Evelyn Cunningham, now deceased. Let's put together a bio on her. We're assuming she and Mr. Phelan had a fling that produced a child.'

'Assuming?' asked one of the associates.

'Yes. We take nothing for granted.'

He dismissed them and walked to a room where a small press conference had been arranged by Tip Durban. No cameras, just print media. A dozen reporters sat eagerly around a table, tape recorders and microphones scattered about. They were from large newspapers and well-known financial publications.

The questions began. Yes, there was a last-minute will, but he could not reveal its contents. Yes, there'd been an autopsy, but he couldn't discuss it. The company would continue operating with no changes. He couldn't talk about who the new owners would be.

To no one's surprise, it became obvious that the families had spent the day chatting privately with reporters.

'There's a strong rumor that Mr. Phelan's last will divides his fortune among his six children. Can you confirm or deny this?'

'I cannot. It's just a rumor.'

'Wasn't he dying of cancer?'

'That would go to the autopsy, and I can't comment on that.'

'We've heard that a panel of psychiatrists examined him shortly before his death, and pronounced him mentally sound. Can you confirm this?'

'Yes,' Stafford said, 'this is true.' So they spent the next twenty minutes picking and prying into the mental exam. Josh held his ground, allowing only that Mr. Phelan 'appeared' to be of sound mind.

The financial reporters wanted numbers. Because The Phelan Group was a private company, very tightly held, information had always been hard to come by. This was an opportunity to crack the door, or so they thought. But Josh gave them little.

He excused himself after an hour, and returned to his office, where a secretary informed him that the crematorium had called. Mr. Phelan's remains were ready to be picked up.

FIVE

TJ nursed his hangover until noon, then drank a beer and decided it was time to flex his muscle. He called his principal lawyer to check on the current state of things, and the lawyer cautioned him to be patient. 'This will take a little time, TJ,' the lawyer said.

'Maybe I'm not in the mood to wait,' TJ shot back, his head splitting.

'Give it a few days.'

TJ slammed the phone down and walked to the rear of his dirty condo, where, thankfully, he couldn't find his wife. They had been through three fights already, and it was barely noon. Perhaps she was out shopping, spending a fraction of his new fortune. The shopping didn't bother him now.

'The old goat's dead,' he said out loud. There was no one else around.

His two children were away at college, their tuition paid for by Lillian, who still had some of the money she'd taken from Troy in the divorce decades earlier. So TJ lived alone with Biff, a thirty-year-old divorcée whose two kids lived with their father. Biff had a real estate license and sold darling little starters to newly-weds.

He opened another beer and stared at himself in a full-length mirror in the hall. 'Troy Phelan, Jr.,' he proclaimed. 'Son of Troy Phelan, tenth richest man in

America, net worth of eleven billion, now deceased, survived by his loving wives and loving children, all of whom will love him even more after probate. Yes!'

He decided right then and there that from that day forward, TJ would be ditched and he would go through life as Troy Phelan, Jr. The name was magic.

The condo had a certain smell to it because Biff refused to do housework. She was too busy with her cell phones. The floors were covered with debris but the walls were bare. The furniture was rented from a company that had hired lawyers to recover everything. He kicked a sofa, and yelled, 'Come get this crap! I'll be hiring designers before long.'

He could almost torch the place. Another beer or two, and he might start playing with matches.

He dressed in his best suit, a gray one he'd worn yesterday when Dear Old Dad faced the psychiatrists and performed so wonderfully. Since there would be no funeral, he wouldn't be forced to rush out and buy a new black one. 'Armani, here I come,' he whistled joyfully as he zipped up his pants.

At least he had a BMW. He might live in a dump, but the world would never see it. The world, however, noticed his car, and so he struggled every month to scratch together $680 for the lease. He cursed his condo as he backed away in the parking lot. It was one of eighty new ones wrapped around a shallow pool in an overflow section of Manassas.

He'd been raised better. Life had been soft and luxurious for the first twenty years, and then he received his inheritance. But his five million had disappeared before he reached thirty, and his father despised him for it.

They fought with vigor and regularity. Junior had held various jobs within The Phelan Group, and each ended in disaster. Senior fired him numerous times. Senior had an idea for a venture, and two years later the idea was worth millions. Junior's ideas ended in bankruptcy and litigation.

In recent years the fighting had almost stopped. Neither could change, so they simply ignored each other. But when the tumor appeared, TJ reached out again.

Oh what a mansion he would build! And he knew just the architect, a Japanese woman in Manhattan he'd read about in a magazine. Within a year he'd probably move to Malibu or Aspen or Palm Beach, where he could show the money and be taken seriously.

'What does one do with half a billion dollars?' he asked himself as he sped along the interstate. 'Five hundred million tax-free dollars.' He began to laugh.

An acquaintance managed the BMW-Porsche dealership where he'd leased his car. Junior walked into the showroom like the king of the world, strutting and smiling smugly. He could buy the whole damned place if he wanted. On a salesman's desk he saw the morning paper; a nice bold headline about the death of his father. Not a twinge of grief.

The manager, Dickie, bounded from his office and said, 'TJ, I'm very sorry.'

'Thanks,' Troy Junior said with a brief frown. 'He's better off, you know.'

'My sympathies anyway.'

'Forget it.' They stepped into the office and closed the door.

Dickie said, 'The paper says he signed a will just before he died. Is that true?'

Troy Junior was already looking at the slick brochures for the latest models. 'Yes. I was there. He divided his estate into six pieces, one for each of us.' He said this without looking up, quite casually, as if the money were already in hand, and already becoming a burden.

Dickie's mouth slipped open and he lowered himself into his chair. Was he suddenly in the presence of serious wealth? This guy, the worthless TJ Phelan, now a billionaire? Like everyone else who knew TJ, Dickie assumed the old man had cut him off for good.

'Biff would like a Porsche,' Troy Junior said, still studying the charts. 'A red 911 Carrera Turbo, with both tops.'

'When?'

Troy Junior glared at him. 'Now.'

'Sure, TJ. What about payment?'

'I'll pay for it the same time I pay for my black one, also a 911. How much are they?'

'About ninety thousand each.'

'No problem. When can we take delivery?'

'I'll have to find them first. That should take a day or two. Cash?'

'Of course.'

'When will you get the cash?'

'A month or so. But I want the cars now.'

Dickie caught his breath and did a squirm. 'Look, TJ, I can't turn loose two new cars without some type of payment.'

'Fine. Then we'll look at Jaguars. Biff's always wanted a Jaguar.'

'Come on, TJ.'

'I could buy this entire dealership, you know. I could walk into any bank right now and ask for ten million or twenty million or whatever it would take to buy this place, and they would happily give it to me for sixty days. Do you understand that?'

Dickie's head rocked up and down, his eyes narrow. Yes, he understood. 'How much did he leave you?'

'Enough to buy the bank too. Are you giving me the cars, or shall I go down the street?'

'Let me find them.'

'Smart man,' TJ said. 'Hurry. I'll check back this

afternoon. Get on the phone.' He tossed the brochures on Dickie's desk, and strutted from the office.

Ramble's idea of mourning was to spend the day locked in the basement den smoking pot, listening to rap, ignoring those who knocked or called. His mother granted him an absence from school because of the tragedy; in fact, she excused him for the rest of the week. If she'd had a clue, she would've known he hadn't been to school in a month.

Driving away from Phelan Tower yesterday, his lawyer had told him the money would go into a trust until he was either eighteen or twenty-one, depending on the terms of the will. And though he couldn't touch the money now, he was certainly entitled to a generous allowance.

He would form a band, and with his money they would make albums. He had friends in bands going nowhere because they couldn't afford to rent studio time, but his would be different. His band would be called Ramble, he decided, and he would play bass and sing lead and be chased by the girls. Alternative rock with strong rap influences, something new. Something he was already inventing.

Two floors up, in the study of their spacious home, Tira, his mother, spent the day on the phone chatting with friends who called with their halfhearted condolences. Most of the friends gossiped long enough to ask how much she might be getting from the estate, but she was afraid to guess. She had married Troy in 1982, at the age of twenty-three, and before doing so she signed a thick prenuptial which gave her only ten million and a house in the event of a divorce.

They had split six years earlier. She was down to her last two million.

Her needs were so great. Her friends had beach houses nestled in quiet coves in the Bahamas; she was

41

relegated to luxury hotels. They bought their designer clothes in New York; she picked them up locally. Their children were away in boarding schools, out of the way; Ramble was in the basement and wouldn't come out.

Surely Troy had left her fifty million or so. One percent of his estate would be around a hundred million. One lousy percent. She did the math on a paper napkin as she talked on the phone to her lawyer.

Geena Phelan Strong was thirty and surviving what had evolved into a tumultuous marriage with Cody, husband number two. His family was old money from up East, but so far the money had only been a rumor. She certainly hadn't seen any of it. Cody was beautifully educated – Taft and Dartmouth and an MBA from Columbia – and he considered himself a visionary in the world of commerce. No job could hold him. His talents could not be constricted by the walls of an office. His dreams would not be cramped by the orders and whims of bosses. Cody would be a billionaire, self-made of course, and probably the youngest in history.

But after six years together, Cody had yet to find his niche. In fact, his losses were staggering. There had been a bad gamble on copper futures in 1992 that had taken over a million of Geena's money. And two years later, he was scalded by naked options when the stock market dipped dramatically. Geena left him for four months, but returned after counseling. An idea for 'Snow-Packed Chickens' turned sour, and Cody escaped with a loss of only a half a million.

They spent a lot. Their counselor recommended traveling as a means of therapy, so they'd seen the world. Being young and rich soothed many of their problems, but the money was drying up. The five million Troy gave her on her twenty-first birthday had

42

shrunk to less than a million, and their debts were mounting. The pressure on their marriage had reached the breaking point when Troy leaped from his terrace.

And so they spent a busy morning looking for homes in Swinks Mill, the place of their grandest dreams. Their dreams grew as the day progressed, and by lunch they were making inquiries into homes worth over two million. At two they met an anxious real estate agent, a woman named Lee, with teased hair, gold rings, two cell phones, and a shiny Cadillac. Geena introduced herself as 'Geena Phelan,' with the last name pronounced heavy and uncheated. Evidently, Lee did not read financial publications because the name missed its mark, and well into the third showing Cody was forced to pull her aside and whisper the truth about his father-in-law.

'That rich guy who jumped?' Lee said, hand over mouth. Geena was inspecting a hallway closet with a small sauna tucked into it.

Cody nodded sadly.

By dusk they were looking at an empty home priced at four million five, and the prospective buyers were seriously considering making an offer. Lee rarely saw such wealthy clients, and they'd worked her into a frenzy.

Rex, age forty-four, brother to TJ, was, at the time of Troy's death, the only one of his children under criminal investigation. His troubles stemmed from a bank that failed, with various lawsuits and investigations spinning wildly from it. Bank examiners and the FBI had been making rather fierce inquiries for three years.

To fund his defense, and his expensive lifestyle, Rex had purchased from the estate of a man killed in a gunfight a string of topless bars and strip clubs in the Fort Lauderdale area. The skin business was lucrative;

traffic was always good and cash was easy to skim. Without being overly greedy, he pocketed around twenty-four thousand a month in tax-free dollars, roughly four thousand from each of his six clubs.

The clubs were held in the name of Amber Rockwell, his wife and a former stripper he'd first noticed lurching on a bar one night. In fact, all of his assets were in her name, and this caused him no small amount of anxiety. With the addition of clothing and minus the makeup and kinky shoes, Amber passed herself off as respectable in their Washington circles. Few people knew her past. But she was a whore at heart, and the fact that she owned everything caused poor Rex many sleepless nights.

At the time of his father's death, Rex had lodged against him in excess of seven million dollars' worth of liens and judgments from creditors, business partners, and investors in the bank. And the total was growing. The judgments, though, remained unsatisfied because there was nothing for the creditors to attach. Rex was asset-free; he owned nothing, not even his car. He and Amber leased a condo and matching Corvettes, with all the paperwork in her name. The clubs and bars were owned by an offshore corporation organized by her without a trace of him. Rex so far had proved too slippery to catch.

The marriage was as stable as could be expected from two people with histories of instability; they partied a lot and had wild friends, clingers drawn to the Phelan name. Life was fun, in spite of the financial pressures. But Rex worried fanatically about Amber and her assets. A nasty argument, and she could vanish.

The worrying stopped with Troy's death. The seesaw tilted, and suddenly Rex was on top, his last name finally worth a fortune. He'd sell the bars and clubs, pay off his debts with a wicked swipe, then play with his money. One false move, and she'd be dancing on tables again with wet dollar bills stuck in her G-string.

Rex spent the day with Hark Gettys, his lawyer. He wanted the money quickly, desperately, and he pressured Gettys to call Josh Stafford and ask for a look at the will. Rex made plans, large and ambitious plans for how to handle the money, and Hark would be with him every step of the way. He wanted control of The Phelan Group. His portion of the stock, whatever it might be, added to TJ's and both sisters', would surely give them a majority of voting shares. But was the stock placed in trust, or given outright, or tied up in any one of a hundred devious ways that Troy would certainly enjoy from the grave?

'We have to see that damned will!' he yelled at Hark throughout the day. Hark calmed him with a long lunch and good wine, then they switched to Scotch in the early afternoon. Amber dropped by and found them both drunk, but she wasn't angry. There was no way Rex could anger her now. She loved him more than ever.

SIX

The trip west would be a pleasant respite from the chaos Mr. Phelan created with his leap. His ranch was near Jackson Hole, in the Tetons, where a foot of snow was already on the ground and more was expected. What would Miss Manners say about the scattering of ashes over land covered with snow? Should one wait until the thaw? Or sprinkle them anyway? Josh didn't give a damn. He'd toss them in the face of any natural disaster.

He was being hounded by the lawyers for the Phelan heirs. His cautious comments to Hark Gettys about the old man's testamentary capacity had sent shockwaves through the families, and they were reacting with predictable hysteria. And threats. The trip would be a short vacation. He and Durban could sort through the preliminary research and make their plans.

They left National Airport on Mr. Phelan's Gulfstream IV, a plane Josh had been privileged to fly on only once before. It was the newest of the fleet, and at a price of thirty-five million had been Mr. Phelan's fanciest toy. The summer before they had flown it to Nice, where the old man walked naked on the beach and gawked at young French girls. Josh and his wife had kept their clothes on with the rest of the Americans and sunned by the pool.

A stewardess served them breakfast, then disappeared into the rear galley as they spread their papers on a round table. The flight would take four hours.

The affidavits signed by Drs. Flowe, Zadel, and Theishen were long and verbose, laden with opinions and redundancies that ran on for paragraphs and left not a scintilla of doubt that Troy was of sound and disposing mind and memory. He was downright brilliant, and knew exactly what he was doing in the moments before his death.

Stafford and Durban read the affidavits and enjoyed the humor. When the new will was read, those three experts would be fired, of course, and a half dozen more would be brought in to deliver all sorts of dark and dire suppositions about poor Troy's mental illnesses.

On the subject of Rachel Lane – little had been learned about the world's richest missionary. The investigators hired by the firm were digging furiously.

According to the early research pulled from the Internet, World Tribes Missions was headquartered in Houston, Texas. Founded in 1920, the organization had four thousand missionaries spread around the world working exclusively with native peoples. Its sole purpose and goal was to spread the Christian Gospel to every remote tribe in the world. Obviously, Rachel did not inherit her religious beliefs from her father.

No less than twenty-eight Indian tribes in Brazil were currently being ministered to by World Tribes missionaries, and at least ten in Bolivia. Another three hundred in the rest of the world. Because their target tribes were secluded and detached from modern civilization, the missionaries received exhaustive training in survival, wilderness living, languages, and medical skills.

Josh read with great interest a story written by a missionary who had spent seven years living in a lean-to, in a jungle, trying to learn enough of the primitive tribe's language to communicate. The Indians had had little to do with him. He was, after all, a white man from Missouri who'd backpacked into their village with a vocabulary limited to 'Hello' and 'Thank you.' If he needed a table, he built one. If he needed food, he killed it. Five years passed before the Indians began to trust him. He was well into his sixth year before he told his first Bible story. He was trained to be patient, to build relationships, learn language and culture, and slowly, very slowly, begin to teach the Bible.

The tribe had little contact with the outside world. Life had hardly changed in a thousand years.

What kind of person could possess enough faith and commitment to forsake modern society and enter such a prehistoric world? The missionary wrote that the Indians did not accept him until they realized he wasn't leaving. He had chosen to live with them, forever. He loved them and wanted to be one of them.

So Rachel lived in a hut or a lean-to, and slept on a bed she'd built herself, and cooked over a fire, and ate food she'd grown or trapped and killed, and taught Bible stories to the children and the Gospel to the adults, and knew nothing and certainly cared nothing for the events and worries and pressures of the world. She was very content. Her faith sustained her.

It seemed almost cruel to bother her.

Durban read the same materials and said, 'We may never find her. No phones, no electricity; hell, you have to hike through the mountains to get to these people.'

'We have no choice,' Josh said.

'Have we contacted World Tribes?'

'Later today.'

'What do you tell them?'

'I don't know. But you don't tell them you're

48

looking for one of their missionaries because she's just inherited eleven billion dollars.'

'Eleven billion before taxes.'

'There will be a nice sum left over.'

'So what do you tell them?'

'We tell them there's a pressing legal matter. It's quite urgent, and we must speak to Rachel face to face.'

One of the fax machines on board began humming, and the memos started. The first was from Josh's secretary with a list of the morning's calls – almost all from attorneys for the Phelan heirs. Two were from reporters.

The associates were reporting in, with preliminary research on various aspects of applicable Virginia law. With each page that Josh and Durban read, old Troy's hastily scrawled testament got stronger and stronger.

Lunch was light sandwiches and fruit, again served by the stewardess, who kept to the rear of the cabin and managed to appear only when their coffee cups were empty.

They landed in Jackson Hole in clear weather, with heavy snow plowed to the sides of the runway. They stepped off the plane, walked eighty feet, and climbed onto a Sikorsky S-76C, Troy's favorite helicopter. Ten minutes later they were hovering over his beloved ranch. A stiff wind bounced the chopper, and Durban turned pale. Josh slid open a door, slowly and quite nervously, and a sharp wind blasted him in the face.

The pilot circled at two thousand feet while Josh emptied the ashes from a small black urn. The wind instantly blew them in all directions so that Troy's remains vanished long before they hit the snow. When the urn was empty, Josh retracted his frozen arm and hand and shut the door.

The house was technically a log cabin, with enough massive timbers to give the appearance of something rustic. But at eleven thousand square feet, it was anything but a cabin. Troy had bought it from an actor whose career went south.

A butler in corduroy took their bags and a maid fixed their coffee. Durban admired the stuffed game hanging from the walls while Josh called the office. A fire roared in the fireplace, and the cook asked what they wanted for dinner.

The associate's name was Montgomery, a four-year man who'd been handpicked by Mr. Stafford. He got lost three times in the sprawl of Houston before he found the offices of World Tribes Missions tucked away on the ground floor of a five-story building. He parked his rented car and straightened his tie.

He had talked to Mr. Trill twice on the phone, and though he was an hour late for the appointment it didn't seem to matter. Mr. Trill was polite and soft-spoken but not eager to help. They exchanged the required preliminaries. 'Now, what can I do for you?' Trill asked.

'I need some information about one of your missionaries,' Montgomery said.

Trill nodded but said nothing.

'A Rachel Lane.'

The eyes drifted as if he was trying to place her. 'Name doesn't ring a bell. But then, we have four thousand people in the field.'

'She's working near the border of Brazil and Bolivia.'

'How much do you know about her?'

'Not much. But we need to find her.'

'For what purpose?'

'It's a legal matter,' Montgomery said, with just enough hesitation to sound suspicious.

Trill frowned and pulled his elbows close to his

chest. His small smile disappeared. 'Is there trouble?' he asked.

'No. But the matter is quite urgent. We need to see her.'

'Can't you send a letter or a package?'

'Afraid not. Her cooperation is needed, along with her signature.'

'I assume it's confidential.'

'Extremely.'

Something clicked and Trill's frown softened. 'Excuse me for a minute.' He disappeared from the office, and left Montgomery to inspect the spartan furnishings. The only decoration was a collection of enlarged photos of Indian children on the walls.

Trill was a different person when he returned, stiff and unsmiling and uncooperative. 'I'm sorry, Mr. Montgomery,' he said without sitting. 'We will not be able to help you.'

'Is she in Brazil?'

'I'm sorry.'

'Bolivia?'

'I'm sorry.'

'Does she even exist?'

'I can't answer your questions.'

'Nothing?'

'Nothing.'

'Could I speak to your boss or supervisor?'

'Sure.'

'Where is he?'

'In heaven.'

After a dinner of thick steaks in mushroom sauce, Josh Stafford and Tip Durban retired to the den, where a fire roared. A different butler, a Mexican in a white jacket and starched jeans, served them very old single-malt Scotch from Mr. Phelan's cabinet. Cuban cigars were ordered. Pavarotti sang Christmas songs on a distant stereo.

'I have an idea,' Josh said as he watched the fire. 'We have to send someone to find Rachel Lane, right?'

Tip was in the midst of a lengthy draw from his cigar, so he only nodded.

'And we can't just send anyone. It has to be a lawyer; someone who can explain the legal issues. And it has to be someone from our firm because of confidentiality.'

His jaws filled with smoke, Tip kept nodding.

'So who do we send?'

Tip exhaled slowly, through both his mouth and his nose, and smoke boiled across his face and drifted upward. 'How long will it take?' he finally asked.

'I don't know, but it's not a quick trip. Brazil's a big country, almost as big as the lower forty-eight. And we're talking jungles and mountains. These people are so remote they've never seen a car.'

'I'm not going.'

'We can hire local guides and such, but it still might take a week or so.'

'Don't they have cannibals down there?'

'No.'

'Anacondas?'

'Relax, Tip. You're not going.'

'Thanks.'

'But you see the problem, don't you? We have sixty lawyers, all busy as hell and swamped with more work than we can possibly do. None of us can suddenly drop everything and go find this woman.'

'Send a paralegal.'

Josh didn't like that idea. He sipped his Scotch and puffed his cigar and listened to the flames pop in the fireplace. 'It has to be a lawyer,' he said, almost to himself.

The butler returned with fresh drinks. He inquired

about dessert and coffee, but the guests already had what they wanted.

'What about Nate?' Josh asked when they were alone again.

It was obvious Josh had been thinking about Nate all along, and this slightly irritated Tip. 'You kidding?' he said.

'No.'

They pondered the idea of sending Nate for a while, each working past their initial objections and fears. Nate O'Riley was a partner, a twenty-three-year man who was, at the moment, locked away in a rehab unit in the Blue Ridge Mountains west of D.C. In the past ten years, he had been a frequent visitor to rehab facilities, each time drying out, breaking habits, growing closer to a higher power, working on his tan and tennis game, and vowing to kick his addictions once and for all. And while he swore that each crash was the last one, the final descent to rock bottom, each was always followed by an even harder fall. Now, at the age of forty-eight, he was broke, twice divorced, and freshly indicted for income tax evasion. His future was anything but bright.

'He used to be an outdoor type, didn't he?' Tip asked.

'Oh yeah. Scuba diving, rock climbing, all that crazy stuff. Then the slide began and he did nothing but work.'

The slide had begun in his mid-thirties, at about the time he put together an impressive string of large verdicts against negligent doctors. Nate O'Riley became a star in the medical malpractice game, and also began drinking heavily and using coke. He neglected his family and became obsessive about his addictions – big verdicts, booze, and drugs. He somehow balanced both, but was always on the edge of disaster. Then he lost a case, and fell off the cliff for the first time. The firm hid him in a designer spa until he was sufficiently dried out, and he made an impressive comeback. The first of several.

'When does he get out?' Tip asked, no longer surprised by the idea and liking it more and more.

'Soon.'

But Nate had become a serious addict. He could stay clean for months, even years, but he always crashed. The chemicals ravaged his mind and body. His behavior became quite bizarre, and the rumors of his craziness crept through the firm and ultimately spread through the lawyers' network of gossip.

Almost four months earlier, he had locked himself in a motel room with a bottle of rum and a sack of pills in what many of his colleagues viewed as a suicide attempt.

Josh committed him for the fourth time in ten years.

'It might be good for him,' Tip said. 'You know, to get away for a while.'

SEVEN

On the third day after Mr. Phelan's suicide, Hark Gettys arrived at his office before dawn, already tired but anxious for the day to begin. He'd had a late dinner with Rex Phelan, followed by a couple of hours in a bar, where they fretted over the will and plotted strategy. So his eyes were red and puffy and his head ached, but he was nonetheless moving quickly around the coffeepot.

Hark's hourly rates varied. In the past year, he'd handled a nasty divorce for as little as two hundred dollars an hour. He quoted three-fifty to every prospective client, which was a bit low for such an ambitious D.C. lawyer, but if he got them in the door at three-fifty, he could certainly pad the billing and earn what he deserved. An Indonesian cement company had paid him four hundred and fifty an hour for a small matter, then tried to stiff him when the bill came. He had settled a wrongful death case in which he earned a third of three hundred and fifty thousand. So he was all over the board when it came to fees.

Hark was a litigator in a forty-lawyer firm, a second-tier outfit with a history of infighting and bickering which had hampered its growth, and he longed to open his own shop. Almost half of his annual billings went for the overhead; the way he figured it, the money belonged in his pocket.

At some point during the sleepless night, he'd made the decision to raise his rate to five hundred an hour, and to make it retroactive a week. He'd worked on nothing but the Phelan matter for the past six days, and now that the old man was dead his crazy family was a lawyer's dream.

What Hark desperately wanted was a will contest – a long vicious fight with packs of lawyers filing tons of legal crap. A trial would be wonderful, a high-profile battle over one of the largest estates in America, with Hark in the center. Winning it would be nice, but winning wasn't crucial. He'd make a fortune, and he'd become famous, and that's what modern lawyering was all about.

At five hundred dollars an hour, sixty hours a week, fifty weeks a year, Hark's gross annual billings would be one and a half million. The overhead for a new office – rent, secretaries, paralegals – would be half a million at most, and so Hark could clear a million bucks if he left his miserable firm and opened a new one down the street.

Done. He gulped coffee and mentally said good-bye to his cluttered office. He'd bolt with the Phelan file and maybe one or two others. He'd take his secretary and his paralegal, and he'd do it quickly, before the firm laid claim to any of the Phelan fees.

He sat at his desk, his pulse racing with the anticipation of his spanking new venture, and he thought of all the ways he could start a war with Josh Stafford. There was reason to worry. Stafford had been unwilling to reveal the contents of the new will. He had questioned its validity, in light of the suicide. Hark had been rattled by the change in Stafford's tone immediately after the suicide. Now, Stafford had left town and refused to return calls.

Oh, how he longed for a fight.

At nine, he met with Libbigail Phelan Jeter and

Mary Ross Phelan Jackman, the two daughters from Troy's first marriage. Rex had arranged the meeting, at Hark's insistence. Though both women had lawyers at the moment, Hark wanted them as clients. More clients meant more clout at the bargaining table and in the courtroom, and it also meant he could bill each one of them five hundred an hour for the same work.

The meeting was awkward; neither woman trusted Hark because they didn't trust their brother Rex. TJ had three lawyers of his own, and their mother had another. Why should they join forces when no one else was doing so? With so much money at stake, shouldn't they keep their own lawyers?

Hark pressed but gained little ground. He was disappointed, but later charged ahead with plans to leave his firm immediately. He could smell the money.

Libbigail Phelan Jeter had been a rebellious child who disliked Lillian, her mother, and craved the attention of her father, who was seldom at home. She was nine when her parents divorced.

When she was fourteen, Lillian shipped her away to boarding school. Troy disapproved of boarding schools, as if he knew something about child-rearing, and throughout high school he made an uncharacteristic effort to keep in touch with her. He often told her she was his favorite. She was certainly the brightest.

But he missed her graduation and forgot to send a gift. In the summer before college, she dreamed of ways to hurt him. She fled to Berkeley, ostensibly to study medieval Irish poetry, but in fact she planned to study very little, if at all. Troy hated the idea of her attending college anywhere in California, especially on such a radical campus. Vietnam was ending. The students had won and it was time to celebrate.

She slipped easily into the culture of drugs and casual sex. She lived in a three-story house with a group of students of all races, sexes, and sexual preferences. The combinations changed weekly, as did the numbers. They called themselves a commune, but there was no structure or rules. Money was no problem because most came from wealthy families. Libbigail was known simply as a rich kid from Connecticut. At the time, Troy was worth only a hundred million or so.

With a sense of adventure, she moved along the drug chain until heroin seized her. Her supplier was a jazz drummer named Tino, who had somehow taken up residence in the commune. Tino was in his late thirties, a high school dropout from Memphis, and no one knew exactly how or when he became a member of their group. No one cared.

Libbigail cleaned herself up enough to travel east for her twenty-first birthday, a glorious day for all Phelan children because that was when the old man bestowed The Gift. Troy didn't believe in trusts for his children. If they weren't stable by the age of twenty-one, then why string them along? Trusts required trustees and lawyers and constant fights with the beneficiaries, who resented having their money doled out by accountants. Give them the money, Troy reasoned, let 'em sink or swim.

Most Phelans drowned quickly.

Troy skipped her birthday. He was somewhere in Asia on business. By then he was well into his second marriage, with Janie. Rocky and Geena were little kids, and he'd lost whatever interest he had in his first family.

Libbigail didn't miss him. The lawyers completed the arrangements for The Gift, and she laid up with Tino in a swanky Manhattan hotel for a week, stoned.

Her money lasted for almost five years, a stretch of time that included two husbands, numerous live-ins,

58

two arrests, three lengthy lockdowns in detox units, and a car wreck that almost took her left leg.

Her current husband was an ex-biker she'd met in rehab. He weighed 320 pounds and had a gray frizzy beard that fell to his chest. He went by the name of Spike, and he had actually evolved into a decent sort. He built cabinets in a shop behind their modest home in the Baltimore suburb of Lutherville.

Libbigail's lawyer was a rumpled fellow named Wally Bright, and she went straight to his office after leaving Hark's. She made a full report of everything Hark had said. Wally was a small-timer who advertised quickie divorces on bus benches in the Bethesda area. He'd handled one of Libbigail's divorces and waited a year before he was paid for it. But he'd been patient with her. She was, after all, a Phelan. She would be his ticket to the fat fees he'd never quite been able to command.

In her presence, Wally called Hark Gettys and started a vicious phone fight that raged for fifteen minutes. He stomped around behind his desk, arms flailing, screaming obscenities into the phone. 'I will kill for my client!' he raged at one point, and Libbigail was most impressed.

When he finished, he walked her gently to the door and kissed her on the cheek. He stroked her and patted her and fussed over her. He gave her the attention she had craved all her life. She was not a bad-looking woman; a bit heavy and showing the effects of a hard life, but Wally had seen much worse. Wally had slept with much worse. Given the right moment, Wally might make a move.

EIGHT

Nate's little mountain was covered with six inches of new snow when he was awakened by the stirring sounds of Chopin piped through his walls. Last week it had been Mozart. The week before, he couldn't remember. Vivaldi had been in his recent past, but so much of it was a haze.

As he had done every morning for almost four months, Nate walked to his window and gazed at the Shenandoah Valley spread before him, three thousand feet below. It too was covered with white, and he remembered that it was almost Christmas.

He would be out in time for Christmas. They – his doctors and Josh Stafford – had promised him that much. He thought about Christmas and became saddened by it. There had been some pleasant ones in the not too distant past, when the kids were small and life was stable. But the kids were gone now, either grown or taken away by their mothers, and the last thing Nate wanted was another Christmas in a bar with other miserable drunks singing carols and pretending all was merry.

The valley was white and still, a few cars moving like ants far away.

He was supposed to meditate for ten minutes, either in prayer or with the yoga they'd tried to teach him at

Walnut Hill. Instead he did sit-ups, then went for a swim.

Breakfast was black coffee and a muffin, which he took with Sergio, his counselor/therapist/guru. And for the past four months, Sergio had also been his best friend. He knew everything about the miserable life of Nate O'Riley.

'You have a guest today,' Sergio said.

'Who?'

'Mr. Stafford.'

'Wonderful.'

Any contact with the outside was welcome, primarily because it was so restricted. Josh had visited once a month. Two other friends from the firm had made the three-hour drive from D.C., but they were busy and Nate understood.

Television was prohibited at Walnut Hill because of the beer ads and because so many of the shows and movies glorified drinking, even drugs. Most popular magazines were kept away for the same reasons. It didn't matter to Nate. After four months, he didn't care what was happening at the Capitol or on Wall Street or in the Middle East.

'When?' he asked.

'Late morning.'

'After my workout?'

'Of course.'

Nothing interfered with the workout, a two-hour orgy of sweat and grunting and yelling with a sadistic personal trainer, a sharply toned female Nate secretly adored.

He was resting in his suite, eating a blood orange and watching the valley again, when Josh arrived.

'You look great,' Josh said. 'How much weight have you lost?'

'Fourteen pounds,' Nate said, patting his flat stomach.

61

'Very lean. Maybe I should spend some time here.'

'I highly recommend it. The food is completely fat-free, taste-free, prepared by a chef with an accent. The portions cover half a saucer, couple of bites and you're done. Lunch and dinner take about seven minutes if you chew slowly.'

'For a thousand bucks a day you expect great food.'

'Did you bring me some cookies or something, Josh? Some Chips Ahoy or Oreos? Surely you hid something in your briefcase.'

'Sorry, Nate. I'm clean.'

'Some Doritos or M&M's?'

'Sorry.'

Nate took a bite of his orange. They were sitting next to each other, enjoying the view. Minutes passed.

'How you doing?' Josh asked.

'I need to get out of here, Josh. I'm becoming a robot.'

'Your doc says another week or so.'

'Great. Then what?'

'We'll see.'

'What does that mean?'

'It means we'll see.'

'Come on, Josh.'

'We'll take our time, and see what happens.'

'Can I come back to the firm, Josh? Talk to me.'

'Not so fast, Nate. You have enemies.'

'Who doesn't? But hell, it's your firm. Those guys will go along with whatever you say.'

'You have a couple of problems.'

'I have a thousand problems. But you can't kick me out.'

'The bankruptcy we can work through. The indictment is not so easy.'

No, it was not so easy, and Nate couldn't simply dismiss it. From 1992 to 1995, he had failed to report about sixty thousand dollars in other income.

He tossed the orange peel in a wastebasket, and said, 'So what am I supposed to do? Sit around the house all day?'

'If you're lucky.'

'What's that supposed to mean?'

Josh had to be delicate. His friend was emerging from a black hole. Shocks and surprises had to be avoided.

'Do you think I'm going to prison?' Nate asked.

'Troy Phelan died,' Josh said, and it took Nate a second to change course.

'Oh, Mr. Phelan,' he said.

Nate had had his own little wing in the firm. It was at the end of a long hallway, on the sixth floor, and he and another lawyer and three paralegals and a half-dozen secretaries worked on suing doctors and cared little about the rest of the firm. He certainly knew who Troy Phelan was, but he'd never touched his legal work. 'I'm sorry,' he said.

'So you haven't heard?'

'I hear nothing here. When did he die?'

'Four days ago. Jumped from a window.'

'Without a parachute?'

'Bingo.'

'Couldn't fly.'

'No. He didn't try. I saw it happen. He had just signed two wills – the first prepared by me; the second, and last, handwritten by himself. Then he bolted and jumped.'

'You saw it?'

'Yes.'

'Wow. Musta been a crazy bastard.'

There was a trace of humor in Nate's voice. Nearly four months earlier, he'd been found by a maid in a motel room, his stomach full of pills and rum.

'He left everything to an illegitimate daughter I'd never heard of.'

63

'Is she married? What does she look like?'

'I want you to go find her.'

'Me?'

'Yes.'

'She's lost?'

'We don't know where she is.'

'How much did he –'

'Somewhere around eleven billion, before taxes.'

'Does she know it?'

'No. She doesn't even know he's dead.'

'Does she know Troy's her father?'

'I don't know what she knows.'

'Where is she?'

'Brazil, we think. She's a missionary working with a remote tribe of Indians.'

Nate stood and walked around the room. 'I spent a week there once,' he said. 'I was in college, or maybe law school. It was Carnaval, naked girls dancing in the streets of Rio, the samba bands, a million people partying all night.' His voice trailed away as the nice little memory surfaced and quickly faded.

'This is not Carnaval.'

'No. I'm sure it's not. Would you like some coffee?'

'Yes. Black.'

Nate pressed a button on the wall and announced his order into the intercom. A thousand bucks a day also covered room service.

'How long will I be gone?' he asked, sitting again by the window.

'It's a wild guess, but I'd say ten days. There's no hurry, and she might be hard to find.'

'What part of the country?'

'Western, near Bolivia. This outfit she works for specializes in sending its people into the jungles, where they minister to Indians from the Stone Age. We've done some research, and they seem to take pride in finding the most remote people on the face of the earth.'

'You want me to first find the right jungle, then hike into it in search of the right tribe of Indians, then somehow convince them that I'm a friendly lawyer from the States and they should help me find a woman who probably doesn't want to be found to begin with.'

'Something like that.'

'Might be fun.'

'Think of it as an adventure.'

'Plus, it'll keep me out of the office, right, Josh? Is that it? A diversion while you sort things out.'

'Someone has to go, Nate. A lawyer from our firm has to meet this woman face to face, show her a copy of the will, explain it to her, and find out what she wants to do next. It cannot be done by a paralegal or a Brazilian lawyer.'

'Why me?'

'Because everybody else is busy. You know the routine. You've lived it for more than twenty years. Life at the office, lunch at the courthouse, sleep on the train. Plus, it might be good for you.'

'Are you trying to keep me away from the streets, Josh? Because if you are, then you're wasting your time. I'm clean. Clean and sober. No more bars, no more parties, no more dealers. I'm clean, Josh. Forever.'

Josh nodded along because he was certainly expected to. But he'd been there before. 'I believe you,' he said, wanting to very badly.

The porter knocked and brought their coffee on a silver tray.

After a while, Nate asked, 'What about the indictment? I'm not supposed to leave the country until it's wrapped up.'

'I've talked to the Judge, told him it was pressing business. He wants to see you in ninety days.'

65

'Is he nice?'

'He's Santa Claus.'

'So if I'm convicted, do you think he'll give me a break?'

'That's a year away. Let's worry about it later.'

Nate was sitting at a small table, hunched over his coffee, staring into the cup as he thought of questions. Josh was on the other side, still gazing into the distance.

'What if I say no?' Nate asked.

Josh shrugged as if it didn't matter. 'No big deal. We'll find someone else. Think of it as a vacation. You're not afraid of the jungle, are you?'

'Of course not.'

'Then go have some fun.'

'When would I leave?'

'In a week. Brazil requires a visa, and we'll have to pull some strings. Plus there are some loose ends around here.'

Walnut Hill required at least a week of PreRelease, a period of conditioning before it fed its clients back to the wolves. They had been pampered, sobered, brainwashed, and nudged into emotional, mental, and physical shape. PreRelease braced them for the reentry.

'A week,' Nate repeated to himself.

'About a week, yes.'

'And it'll take ten days.'

'I'm just guessing.'

'So I'll be down there during the holidays.'

'I guess it looks that way.'

'That's a great idea.'

'You want to skip Christmas?'

'Yes.'

'What about your kids?'

There were four of them, two by each wife. One in grad school and one in college, two in middle school.

He stirred his coffee with a small spoon, and said, 'Not a word, Josh. Almost four months here, and not a word from any of them.' His voice ached and his shoulders sagged. He looked quite frail, for a second.

'I'm sorry,' Josh said.

Josh had certainly heard from the families. Both wives had lawyers who'd called to sniff around for money. Nate's oldest child was a grad student at Northwestern who needed tuition money, and he personally had called Josh to inquire not about his father's well-being or whereabouts but, more important, his father's share of the firm's profits last year. He was cocky and rude, and Josh had finally cursed him.

'I'd like to avoid all the parties and holiday cheer,' Nate said, rallying as he got to his bare feet and walked around the room.

'So you'll go?'

'Is it the Amazon?'

'No. It's the Pantanal, the largest wetlands in the world.'

'Piranhas, anacondas, alligators?'

'Sure.'

'Cannibals?'

'No more than D.C.'

'Seriously.'

'I don't think so. They haven't lost a missionary in eleven years.'

'What about a lawyer?'

'I'm sure they would enjoy filleting one. Come on, Nate. This is not heavy lifting. If I weren't so busy, I'd love to go. The Pantanal is a great ecological reserve.'

'I've never heard of it.'

'That's because you stopped traveling years ago. You went into your office and didn't come out.'

'Except for rehab.'

'Take a vacation. See another part of the world.'

Nate sipped coffee long enough to redirect the

conversation. 'And what happens when I get back? Do I have my office? Am I still a partner?'

'Is that what you want?'

'Of course,' Nate said, but with a slight hesitation.

'Are you sure?'

'What else would I do?'

'I don't know, Nate, but this is your fourth rehab in ten years. The crashes are getting worse. If you walked out now, you'd go straight to the office and be the world's greatest malpractice litigator for six months. You'd ignore the old friends, the old bars, the old neighborhoods. Nothing but work, work, work. Before long you'd have a couple of big verdicts, big trials, big pressure. You'd step it up a notch. After a year, there would be a crack somewhere. An old friend might find you. A girl from another life. Maybe a bad jury gives you a bad verdict. I'd be watching every move, but I can never tell when the slide begins.'

'No more slides, Josh. I swear.'

'I've heard it before, and I want to believe you. But what if your demons come out again, Nate? You came within minutes of killing yourself last time.'

'No more crashes.'

'The next one will be the last, Nate. We'll have a funeral and say good-bye and watch them lower you into the ground. I don't want that to happen.'

'It won't, I swear.'

'Then forget about the office. There's too much pressure there.'

The thing Nate hated about rehab was the long periods of silence, or meditation, as Sergio called them. The patients were expected to squat like monks in the semidarkness, close their eyes, and find inner peace. Nate could do the squatting and all that, but behind the closed eyes he was retrying lawsuits, and fighting the IRS, and plotting against his ex-wives, and, most important, worrying about the future. This

68

conversation with Josh was one he'd played out many times.

But his smart retorts and quick comebacks failed him under pressure. Almost four months of virtual solitude had dulled his reflexes. He could manage to look pitiful, and that was all. 'Come on, Josh. You can't just kick me out.'

'You've litigated for over twenty years, Nate. That's about average. It's time to move on to something else.'

'So I'll become a lobbyist, and do lunch with the press secretaries for a thousand little congressmen.'

'We'll find a place for you. But it won't be in the courtroom.'

'I'm not good at doing lunch. I want to litigate.'

'The answer is no. You can stay with the firm, make a lot of money, stay healthy, take up golf, and life will be good, assuming the IRS doesn't send you away.'

For a few pleasant moments the IRS had been forgotten. Now it was back, and Nate sat down again. He squeezed a small pack of honey into his lukewarm coffee; sugar and artificial sweeteners couldn't be allowed in a place as healthy as Walnut Hill.

'A couple of weeks in the Brazilian wetlands is beginning to sound good,' he said.

'So you'll go?'

'Yes.'

Since Nate had plenty of time to read, Josh left him a thick file on the Phelan estate and its mysterious new heir. And there were two books on remote Indians of South America.

Nate read nonstop for eight hours, even neglecting dinner. He was suddenly anxious to leave, to begin his adventure. When Sergio checked on him at ten, he was sitting like a monk in the middle of his bed, papers sprawled around him, lost in another world.

'It's time for me to leave,' Nate said.

'Yes, it is,' Sergio replied. 'I'll start the paperwork tomorrow.'

NINE

The infighting grew worse as the Phelan heirs spent less time talking to each other and more time in their lawyers' offices. A week passed with no will, and no plans to probate. With their fortunes within sight but just out of reach, the heirs became even more agitated. Several lawyers were fired, with more brought in to replace them.

Mary Ross Phelan Jackman fired hers because he wasn't charging enough per hour. Her husband was a successful orthopedic surgeon with lots of business interests. He dealt with lawyers every day. Their new one was a fireball named Grit, who made a noisy entrance into the fray at six hundred dollars per hour.

While the heirs waited, they also incurred massive debt. Contracts were signed for mansions. New cars were delivered. Consultants were hired to do such varied things as design pool houses, locate just the right private jet, and give advice on which thorough-bred to purchase. If the heirs weren't fighting, then they were shopping. Ramble was the exception, but only because he was a minor. He hung out with his lawyer, who was certainly incurring debt on behalf of his client.

Snowball litigation is often commenced with a race to the courthouse. With Josh Stafford refusing to reveal the will, and at the same time dropping mysterious hints about Troy's lack of testamentary capacity, the lawyers for the Phelan heirs finally panicked.

Ten days after the suicide, Hark Gettys went to the Circuit Court of Fairfax County, Virginia, and filed a Petition to Compel the Last Will and Testament of Troy L. Phelan. With all the finesse of an ambitious lawyer to be reckoned with, he tipped a reporter from the *Post*. They chatted for an hour after the filing, some comments off the record, others offered for the glory of the lawyer. A photographer took some pictures.

Oddly, Hark filed his petition on behalf of all Phelan heirs. And he listed their names and addresses as if they were his clients. He faxed them copies when he returned to his office. Within minutes his phone lines were burning.

The *Post's* story the next morning was complemented by a large photo of Hark frowning and rubbing his beard. The story covered even more space than he'd dreamed of. He read it at sunrise in a coffee shop in Chevy Chase, then hurriedly drove to his new office.

A couple of hours later, just after nine, the circuit court clerk's office in Fairfax County was crawling with lawyers, more so than normal. They arrived in tight little packs, spoke in terse sentences to the clerks, and worked hard at ignoring each other. Their petitions were varied but they all wanted the same things – recognition in the Phelan matter, and a look at the will.

Probate matters in Fairfax County were randomly assigned to one of a dozen judges. The Phelan matter landed on the desk of the Honorable F. Parr Wycliff, age thirty-six, a jurist with little experience but lots of ambition. He was thrilled to get such a high-profile case.

Wycliff's office was in the Fairfax County Courthouse, and throughout the morning he monitored the filings in the clerk's office. His secretary hauled in the petitions, and he read them immediately.

When the dust settled below him, he called Josh Stafford to introduce himself. They chatted politely for a few minutes, the usual lawyerly preliminaries, stiff and cautious because weightier matters were coming. Josh had never heard of Judge Wycliff.

'Is there a will?' Wycliff finally asked.

'Yes, Your Honor. There is a will.' Josh chose his words carefully. It was a felony in Virginia to hide a will. If the Judge wanted to know, then Josh would certainly cooperate.

'Where is it?'

'Here in my office.'

'Who is the executor?'

'Me.'

'When do you plan to probate it?'

'My client asked me to wait until January fifteenth.'

'Hmmmm. Any particular reason?'

There was a simple reason. Troy wanted his greedy children to enjoy one last spending spree before he jerked the rug from under them. It was mean and cruel, vintage Troy.

'I have no idea,' Josh said. 'The will is holographic. Mr. Phelan signed it just seconds before he jumped.'

'A holographic will?'

'Yes.'

'Weren't you with him?'

'Yes. It's a long story.'

'Perhaps I should hear it.'

'Perhaps you should.'

Josh had a busy day. Wycliff did not, but he made it sound as though every minute were planned. They agreed to meet for lunch, a quick sandwich in Wycliff's office.

*

Sergio did not like the idea of Nate's trip to South America. After almost four months in a highly structured place like Walnut Hill, where the doors and gates were locked and an unseen guard with a gun watched the road a mile down the mountain, and where TV, movies, games, magazines, and phones were heavily monitored, the reentry into a familiar society was often traumatizing. The notion of a reentry by way of Brazil was more than troubling.

Nate didn't care. He was not at Walnut Hill by court order. Josh had put him there, and if Josh asked him to play hide-and-seek in the jungles, so be it. Sergio could bitch and moan all he wanted.

PreRelease turned into a week from hell. The diet changed from no-fat to low-fat, with such inevitable ingredients as salt, pepper, cheese, and a little butter added to prepare his system for the evils out there. Nate's stomach rebelled, and he lost three more pounds.

'Just an inkling of what's waiting for you down there,' Sergio said smugly.

They fought during therapy, which was common at Walnut Hill. Skin had to be thickened, edges sharpened. Sergio began to distance himself from his patient. It was usually difficult to say good-bye, and Sergio shortened the sessions and became aloof.

With the end in sight, Nate began counting the hours.

Judge Wycliff inquired as to the contents of the will, and Josh politely declined to tell him. They were eating deli sandwiches at a small table in His Honor's small office. The law did not require Josh to reveal what was in the will, at least not now. And Wycliff was slightly out of bounds to ask, but his curiosity was understandable.

'I'm somewhat sympathetic to the petitioners,' he

74

said. 'They have a right to know what's in the will. Why delay it?'

'I'm just following my client's wishes,' Josh replied.

'You have to probate the will sooner or later.'

'Of course.'

Wycliff slid his appointment book up to his plastic plate, and gazed down with a squint over his reading glasses. 'Today is December twentieth. There's no way to assemble everyone before Christmas. How does the twenty-seventh look to you?'

'What do you have in mind?'

'A reading of the will.'

The idea struck Josh, and he almost choked on a dill spear. Gather them all together, the Phelans and their entourages and new friends and hangers-on, and all their merry lawyers, and pack them into Wycliff's courtroom. Make sure the press knows about it. As he crunched on another bite of pickle, and looked at his little black book, he worked hard to suppress a grin. He could hear the gasps and groans, the shockwaves, the utter, bitter disbelief, then the muted cursing. Then, perhaps a sniffle and maybe a sob or two as the Phelans tried to absorb what their beloved father had done to them.

It would be a vicious, glorious, thoroughly unique moment in the history of American law, and Josh suddenly couldn't wait. 'The twenty-seventh is fine with me,' he said.

'Good. I'll notify the parties as soon as I can identify all of them. There are lots of lawyers.'

'It helps if you remember that there are six kids and three ex-wives, so there are nine principal sets of lawyers.'

'I hope my courtroom is big enough.'

Standing room only, Josh almost said. People packed together, with not a sound as the envelope is

75

opened, the will unfolded, the unbelievable words read. 'I suggest you read the will,' Josh said.

Wycliff certainly intended to. He was seeing the same scene as Josh. It would be one of his finest moments, reading a will that disposed of eleven billion dollars.

'I assume the will is somewhat controversial,' the Judge said.

'It's wicked.'

His Honor actually smiled.

TEN

Before his most recent crash, Nate had lived in an aging condo in Georgetown, one he'd leased after his last divorce. But it was gone now, a victim of the bankruptcy. So, literally, there was no place for Nate to spend his first night of freedom.

As usual, Josh had carefully planned the release. He arrived at Walnut Hill on the appointed day with a duffel bag filled with new and neatly pressed J. Crew shorts and shirts for the trip south. He had the passport and the visa, plenty of cash, lots of directions and tickets, a game plan. Even a first-aid kit.

Nate never had the chance to be anxious. He said good-bye to a few members of the staff, but most were busy elsewhere because they avoided departures. He walked proudly through the front door after 140 days of wonderful sobriety; clean, tanned, fit, down 17 pounds to 174, a weight he hadn't known in twenty years.

Josh drove, and for the first five minutes nothing was said. The snow blanketed the pastures, but thinned quickly as they left the Blue Ridge. It was December 22. At a very low volume, the radio played carols.

'Could you turn that off?' Nate finally said.

'What?'

'The radio.'

Josh punched a button, and the music he hadn't heard disappeared.

'How do you feel?' Josh asked.

'Could you pull over at the nearest quick shop?'

'Sure. Why?'

'I'd like to get a six-pack.'

'Very funny.'

'I'd kill for a tall Coca-Cola.'

They bought soft drinks and peanuts at a country store. The lady at the cash register said a cheery 'Merry Christmas,' and Nate could not respond. Back in the car, Josh headed for Dulles, two hours away.

'Your flight goes to São Paulo, where you'll lay over three hours before catching one to a city called Campo Grande.'

'Do these people speak English?'

'No. They're Brazilian. They speak Portuguese.'

'Of course they do.'

'But you'll find English at the airport.'

'How big is Campo Grande?'

'Half a million, but it's not your destination. From there, you'll catch a commuter flight to a place called Corumbá. The towns get smaller.'

'And so do the airplanes.'

'Yes, same as here.'

'For some reason, the idea of a Brazilian commuter flight is not appealing. Help me here, Josh. I'm nervous.'

'Either that or a six-hour bus ride.'

'Keep talking.'

'In Corumbá, you'll meet a lawyer named Valdir Ruiz. He speaks English.'

'Have you talked to him?'

'Yes.'

'Could you understand him?'

'Yes, for the most part. A very nice man. Works for about fifty bucks an hour, if you can believe that.'

'How big is Corumbá?'

'Ninety thousand.'

'So they'll have food and water, and a place to sleep.'

'Yes, Nate, you'll have a room. That's more than you can say for here.'

'Ouch.'

'Sorry. Do you want to back out?'

'Yes, but I'm not going to. My goal at this point is to flee this country before I hear "Jingle Bells" again. I'd sleep in a ditch for the next two weeks to avoid "Frosty the Snowman."'

'Forget the ditch. It's a nice hotel.'

'What am I supposed to do with Valdir?'

'He's looking for a guide to take you into the Pantanal.'

'How? Plane? Helicopter?'

'Boat, probably. As I understand the area, it's nothing but swamps and rivers.'

'And snakes, alligators, piranhas.'

'What a little coward you are. I thought you wanted to go.'

'I do. Drive faster.'

'Relax.' Josh pointed to a briefcase behind the passenger's seat. 'Open that,' he said. 'It's your carry-on bag.'

Nate pulled and grunted. 'It weighs a ton. What's in here?'

'Good stuff.'

It was made of brown leather, new but built to look well used, and large enough to hold a small legal library. Nate sat it on his knees and popped it open. 'Toys,' he said.

'That tiny gray instrument there is the latest high-tech digital phone,' Josh said, proud of the things he'd collected. 'Valdir will have local service for you when you get to Corumbá.'

'So they have phones in Brazil.'

'Lots of them. In fact, telecommunications are booming down there. Everybody has a cell phone.'

'Those poor people. What's this?'

'A computer.'

'What the hell for?'

'It's the latest thing. Look how small.'

'I can't even read the keyboard.'

'You can hook it to the phone and actually get your e-mail.'

'Wow. And I'm supposed to do this in the middle of a swamp with snakes and alligators watching?'

'It's up to you.'

'Josh, I don't even use e-mail at the office.'

'It's not for you. It's for me. I want to keep up with you. When you find her, I want to know immediately.'

'What's this?'

'The best toy in the box. It's a satellite phone. You can use it anywhere on the face of the earth. Keep the batteries charged, and you can always find me.'

'You just said they had a great phone system.'

'Not in the Pantanal. It's a hundred thousand square miles of wetlands, with no towns and very few people. That SatFone will be your only means of communication once you leave Corumbá.'

Nate opened the hard plastic case and examined the glossy little phone. 'How much did this cost you?' he asked.

'Me, not a dime.'

'Okay, how much did it cost the Phelan estate?'

'Forty-four hundred bucks. Worth every penny of it.'

'Do my Indians have electricity?' Nate was flipping through the owner's manual.

'Of course not.'

'Then how am I supposed to keep the batteries charged?'

'There's an extra battery. You'll think of something.'

'So much for a quiet getaway.'

'It's going to be very quiet. You'll thank me for the toys when you get there.'

'Can I thank you now?'

'No.'

'Thanks, Josh. For everything.'

'Don't mention it.'

In the crowded terminal, at a small table across from a busy bar, they sipped weak espresso and read newspapers. Josh was very conscious of the bar; Nate didn't seem to be. The neon Heineken logo was hard to miss.

A tired and skinny Santa Claus ambled by, looking for children to take cheap gifts from his bag. Elvis sang 'Blue Christmas' from a jukebox in the bar. The foot traffic was thick, the noise unnerving, everyone flying home for the holidays.

'Are you okay?' Josh asked.

'Yes, I'm fine. Why don't you leave? I'm sure you have better things to do.'

'I'll stay.'

'Look, Josh, I'm fine. If you think I'm waiting for you to leave so I can dash over there to the bar and guzzle vodka, you're wrong. I have no desire for booze. I'm clean, and very proud of it.'

Josh looked a bit sheepish, primarily because Nate had read his mind. Nate's binges were legendary. If he cracked, there wasn't enough booze in the airport to satisfy him. 'I'm not worried about that,' he said, lying.

'Then go. I'm a big boy.'

They said good-bye at the gate, a warm embrace and promises to call almost on the hour. Nate was anxious to settle into his nest in first class. Josh had a thousand things to do at the office.

Two small, secret precautionary steps had been taken by Josh. First, adjacent seats had been booked for the flight. Nate would have the window; the aisle would remain vacant. No sense having some thirsty executive sitting next to Nate, swilling Scotch and wine. The seats cost over seven thousand dollars each for the round trip, but money was of no concern.

Second, Josh had talked at length with an airline official about Nate's rehab. No alcohol was to be served, under any circumstances. A letter from Josh to the airline was on board, just in case it had to be produced to convince Nate.

A flight attendant served him orange juice and coffee. He wrapped himself in a thin blanket, and watched the sprawl of D.C. disappear below him as the Varig airplane climbed through the clouds.

There was relief in the escape, from Walnut Hill and Sergio, from the city and its grind, from the past troubles with the last wife and the bankruptcy, and from the current mess with the IRS. At thirty thousand feet, Nate had almost decided he would never return.

But every reentry was nerve-racking. The fear of another slide was always there, just beneath the surface. The frightening part now was that there had been so many reentries he felt like a veteran. Like wives and big verdicts, he could now compare them. Would there always be another one?

During dinner, he realized Josh had been working behind the scenes. Wine was never offered. He picked through the food with the caution of one who'd just spent nearly four months enjoying the great lettuces of the world; until a few days ago, no fat, butter, grease, or sugar. The last thing he wanted was a queasy stomach.

He napped briefly, but he was tired of sleeping. As a busy lawyer and late-night prowler, he'd learned to live with little sleep. The first month at Walnut Hill they'd drugged him with pills and he'd slept ten hours a day. He couldn't fight them if he were in a coma.

He assembled his toys in the empty seat next to him, and began reading his collection of owner's manuals. The satellite phone intrigued him, though it was difficult to believe he would actually be forced to use it.

Another phone caught his attention. It was the latest technical gadget in air travel, a sleek little device practically hidden in the wall next to his seat. He grabbed it and called Sergio at home. Sergio was having a late dinner, but happy to hear from him nonetheless.

'Where are you?' he asked.

'In a bar,' Nate replied, his voice low because the lights in the cabin were down.

'Very funny.'

'I'm probably over Miami, with eight hours to go. Just found this phone on board and wanted to check in.'

'So you're okay.'

'I'm fine. Do you miss me?'

'Not yet. You miss me?'

'Are you kidding? I'm a free man, flying off to the jungle for a marvelous adventure. I'll miss you later, okay?'

'Okay. And you'll call if you get in trouble.'

'No trouble, Serge. Not this time.'

'Atta boy, Nate.'

'Thanks, Serge.'

'Don't mention it. Just call me.'

A movie started, but no one was watching. The flight attendant brought more coffee. Nate's secretary was a long-suffering woman named Alice, who'd cleaned up after him for almost ten years. She lived with her sister in an old house in Arlington. He called her next. They'd spoken once in the past four months.

The conversation lasted for half an hour. She was delighted to hear his voice, and learn that he'd been released. She knew nothing about his trip to South America, which was a bit odd because she normally knew everything. But she was reserved on the phone, even cautious. Nate, the trial lawyer, smelled a rat, and attacked as if on cross-examination.

She was still in litigation, still at the same desk, doing pretty much the same thing but for a different lawyer. 'Who?' Nate demanded.

A new guy. A new litigator. Her words were deliberate, and Nate knew that she had been fully briefed by Josh himself. Of course Nate would call her as soon as he was released.

Which office was the new guy in? Who was his paralegal? Where did he come from? How much medical malpractice had he done? Was her assignment with him just temporary?

Alice was sufficiently vague.

'Who's in my office?' he asked.

'No one. It hasn't been touched. Still has little stacks of files in every corner.'

'What's Kerry doing?'

'Staying busy. Waiting for you.' Kerry was Nate's favorite paralegal.

Alice had all the right answers, while revealing little. She was especially mum about the new litigator.

'Get ready,' he said as the conversation ran out of steam. 'It's time for a comeback.'

'It's been dull, Nate.'

He hung up slowly, and played back her words. Something was different. Josh was quietly rearranging his firm. Would Nate get lost in the shuffle? Probably not, but his courtroom days were over.

He would worry about it later, he decided. There

were so many people to call, and so many phones to do it with. He knew a judge who'd kicked booze ten years earlier, and he wanted to check in with his wonderful report from rehab. His first ex-wife deserved a blistering call, but he wasn't in the mood. And he wanted to phone all four of his children and ask why they'd hadn't called or written.

Instead he took a folder from his case and began reading about Mr. Troy Phelan and the business at hand. At midnight, somewhere over the Caribbean, Nate drifted away.

ELEVEN

An hour before dawn, the plane began its descent. He had slept through breakfast, and when he awoke a flight attendant hurriedly brought coffee.

The city of São Paulo appeared, an enormous sprawl that covered almost eight hundred square miles. Nate watched the sea of lights below and wondered how one city could hold twenty million people.

In a rush of Portuguese, the pilot said good morning and then several paragraphs of greetings that Nate missed entirely. The English translation that followed was not much better. Surely he wouldn't be forced to point and grunt his way across the country. The language barrier caused a short bout of anxiety, but it ended when a pretty Brazilian flight attendant asked him to buckle his seat belt.

The airport was hot and swarming with people. He collected his new duffel bag, walked it through customs without so much as a glance from anyone, and rechecked it on Varig to Campo Grande. Then he found a coffee bar with the menu on the wall. He pointed and said, 'Espresso,' and the cashier rang him up. She frowned at his American money, but changed it anyway. One Brazilian real equaled one American dollar. Nate now owned a few reais.

He sipped the coffee while standing shoulder to

shoulder with some rowdy Japanese tourists. Other languages flew around him; German and Spanish mixing with the Portuguese coming over the loudspeakers. He wished he'd bought a phrase book so he could at least understand a word or two.

Isolation settled in, slowly at first. In the midst of multitudes, he was a lonely man. He didn't know a soul. Almost no one knew where he was at that moment, and damned few people cared. Cigarette smoke from the tourists boiled around him, and he walked quickly away, into the main concourse, where he could see the ceiling two levels above and the ground floor below. He began walking through the crowds, aimlessly, carrying the heavy briefcase, cursing Josh for filling it with so much junk.

He heard loud English, and drifted toward it. Some businessmen were waiting near the United counter, and he found a seat near them. It was snowing in Detroit, and they were anxious to get home for Christmas. A pipeline had brought them to Brazil, and before long Nate tired of their drivel. They cured whatever homesickness he felt.

He missed Sergio. After the last rehab, the clinic had placed Nate in a halfway house for a week to ease the reentry. He hated the place and the routine, but with hindsight the idea had merit. You needed a few days to get reoriented. Maybe Sergio was right. He called him from a pay phone, and woke him up. It was six-thirty in São Paulo, but only four-thirty in Virginia.

Sergio didn't mind. It went with the territory.

There were no first-class seats on the flight to Campo Grande, nor any empty ones. Nate was pleasantly surprised to observe that every face was behind the morning news, and a wide variety of papers at that. The dailies were as slick and modern as any in the States, and they were being read by people who had a

87

thirst for the news. Perhaps Brazil wasn't as backward as he thought. These people could read! The airliner, a 727, was clean and newly refurbished. Coca-Cola and Sprite were on the drink cart; he almost felt at home.

Sitting by the window twenty rows back, he ignored the memo on Indians in his lap, and admired the countryside below. It was vast and lush and green, rolling with hills, dotted with cattle farms and criss-crossed with red dirt roads. The soil was a vivid burnt orange, and the roads ran haphazardly from one small settlement to the next. Highways were virtually non-existent.

A paved road appeared, and there was traffic. The plane descended and the pilot welcomed them to Campo Grande. There were tall buildings, a crowded downtown, the obligatory soccer field, lots of streets and cars, and every residence had a red-tiled roof. Thanks to the typical big-firm efficiency, he possessed a memo, one no doubt prepared by the greenest of associates working at three hundred dollars an hour, in which Campo Grande was analyzed as if its presence were crucial to the matters at hand. Six hundred thousand people. A center for cattle trade. Lots of cowboys. Rapid growth. Modern conveniences. Nice to know, but why bother? Nate would not sleep there.

The airport seemed remarkably small for a city its size, and he realized he was comparing everything to the United States. This had to stop. When he stepped from the plane, he was hit with the heat. It was at least ninety degrees. Two days before Christmas, and it was sweltering in the southern hemisphere. He squinted in the brilliance of the sun, and descended the steps with a firm hand on the guardrail.

He managed to order lunch in the airport restaurant, and when it was brought to his table he was pleased to see that it was something he could eat. A grilled chicken sandwich in a bun he'd never seen before, with fries as crisp as those in any fast food joint in the States. He ate slowly while watching the runway in the distance. Halfway through lunch, a twin-engine turbo-prop of Air Pantanal landed and taxied to the terminal. Six people got off.

He stopped chewing as he wrestled with a sudden attack of fear. Commuter flights were the ones you read about and saw on CNN, except that no one back home would ever hear about this one if it went down.

But the plane looked sturdy and clean, even somewhat modern, and the pilots were well-dressed professionals. Nate continued eating. Think positive, he told himself.

He roamed the small terminal for an hour. In a news shop he bought a Portuguese phrase book and began memorizing words. He read travel ads for adventures into the Pantanal – ecotourism, it was called in English. There were cars for rent. A money exchange booth, a bar with beer signs and whiskey bottles lined on a shelf. And near the front entrance was a slender, artificial Christmas tree with a solitary string of lights. He watched them blink to the tune of some Brazilian carol, and despite his efforts not to, Nate thought of his children.

It was the day before Christmas Eve. Not all memories were painful.

He boarded the plane with teeth clenched and spine stiffened, then slept for most of the hour it took to reach Corumbá. The small airport there was humid and packed with Bolivians waiting for a flight to Santa Cruz. They were laden with boxes and bags of Christmas gifts.

He found a cabdriver who spoke not a word of English, but it didn't matter. Nate showed him the words 'Palace Hotel' on his travel itinerary, and they sped away in an old, dirty Mazda.

Corumbá had ninety thousand people, according to

yet another memo prepared by Josh's staff. Situated on the Paraguay River, on the Bolivian border, it had long since declared itself to be the capital of the Pantanal. River traffic and trade had built the city, and kept it going.

Through the heat and swelter of the back of the taxi, Corumbá appeared to be a lazy, pleasant little town. The streets were paved and wide and lined with trees. Merchants sat in the shade of their storefronts, waiting for customers and chatting with each other. Teenagers darted through traffic on scooters. Barefoot children ate ice cream at sidewalk tables.

As they approached the business district, cars bunched together and stopped in the heat. The driver mumbled something, but was not particularly disturbed. The same driver in New York or D.C. would've been near the point of violence.

But it was Brazil, and Brazil was in South America. The clocks ran slower. Nothing was urgent. Time was not as crucial. Take off your watch, Nate told himself. Instead, he closed his eyes and breathed the heavy air.

The Palace Hotel was in the center of downtown, on a street that descended slightly toward the Paraguay River sitting majestically in the distance. He gave the cabbie a handful of reais, and waited patiently for his change. He thanked him in Portuguese, a feeble 'Obrigado.' The cabbie smiled and said something he didn't understand. The doors to the lobby were open, as were all doors facing the sidewalks of Corumbá.

The first words he heard upon entering were being yelled by someone from Texas. A band of roughnecks was in the process of checking out. They had been drinking and were in a festive mood, anxious to get home for the holidays. Nate took a seat near a television and waited for them to clear.

His room was on the eighth floor. For eighteen dollars a day he got a twelve-by-twelve with a narrow

90

bed very close to the floor. If it had a mattress, it was quite thin. No box spring to speak of. There was a desk with a chair, a window unit of AC, a small refrigerator with bottled water, colas, and beer, and a clean bathroom with soap and plenty of towels. Not bad, he told himself. This was an adventure. Not the Four Seasons, but certainly livable.

For half an hour, he tried to call Josh. But the language barrier stopped him. The clerk at the front desk knew enough English to find an outside operator, but from there the Portuguese took over. He tried his new cell phone, but the local service had not been activated.

Nate stretched his tired body the length of his flimsy little bed, and went to sleep.

Valdir Ruiz was a short man with a tiny waist, light brown skin, a small slick head missing most of the hair except for a few strands he kept oiled and combed back. His eyes were black and bunched with wrinkles, the result of thirty years of heavy smoking. He was fifty-two, and at the age of seventeen he'd left home to spend a year with a family in Iowa as a Rotary exchange student. He was proud of his English, though he didn't use it much in Corumbá. He watched CNN and American television most nights in an effort to stay sharp.

After the year in Iowa, he went to college in Campo Grande, then law school in Rio. He reluctantly returned to Corumbá to work in his uncle's small law firm, and to care for his aging parents. For more years than he cared to count, Valdir had endured the languid pace of advocacy in Corumbá, while dreaming of what might have been in the big city.

But he was a pleasant man, happy with life in the way most Brazilians tend to be. He worked efficiently in his small office, just himself and a secretary who answered the phone and did the typing. Valdir liked real estate, the deeds and contracts and such. He never went to court, primarily because courtrooms were not an integral part of practicing law in Brazil. Trials were rare. American-style litigation had not found its way south; in fact, it was still confined to the fifty states. Valdir marveled at the things lawyers did and said on CNN. Why do they clamor for the attention? he often asked himself. Lawyers staging press conferences, and hustling from one talk show to the next chatting about their clients. It was unheard of in Brazil.

His office was three blocks from the Palace Hotel, on a wide shaded lot his uncle had bought decades earlier. Thick trees covered the roof, so regardless of the heat, Valdir kept his windows open. He liked the gentle noise from the street. At three-fifteen, he saw a man he'd never seen before stop and examine his office. The man was obviously a stranger, and an American. Valdir knew it was Mr. O'Riley.

The secretary brought them *cafezinho*, the strong sugary black coffee Brazilians drink all day in tiny cups, and Nate was instantly addicted to it. He sat in Valdir's office, already on a first-name basis, and admired the surroundings: the squeaky ceiling fan above them, the open windows with the muted sounds of the street drifting in, the neat rows of dusty files on the shelves behind Valdir, the scuffed and worn plank floor under them. The office was quite warm, but not uncomfortable. Nate was sitting in a movie, one shot fifty years ago.

Valdir phoned D.C., and got Josh. They talked for a moment, then he handed the phone across the desk. 'Hello, Josh,' Nate said. Josh was obviously relieved to hear his voice. Nate recounted his journey to Corumbá, with emphasis on the fact that he was doing

92

well, still sober, and looking forward to the rest of his adventure.

Valdir busied himself with a file in a corner, trying to appear as if he had no interest in the conversation, but absorbing every word. Why was Nate O'Riley so proud of being sober?

When the phone call was over, Valdir produced and unfolded a large air navigational map of the state of Mato Grosso do Sul, roughly the same size as Texas, and pointed to the Pantanal. It covered the entire northwestern portion of the state, and continued into Mato Grosso to the north and Bolivia to the west. Hundreds of rivers and streams spread like veins through the swampland. It was shaded yellow, and there were no towns or cities in the Pantanal. No roads or highways. A hundred thousand square miles of swamp, Nate recalled from the innumerable memos Josh had packed for him.

Valdir lit a cigarette as they studied the map. He had done some homework. There were four red X's along the western edge of the map, near Bolivia.

'There are tribes here,' he said, pointing to the red marks. 'Guató and Ipicas.'

'How large are they?' Nate asked, leaning close, his first real glimpse at the terrain he was expected to comb in search of Rachel Lane.

'We don't really know,' Valdir replied, his words very slow and precise. He was trying hard to impress the American with his English. 'A hundred years ago, there were many more. But the tribes grow smaller with each generation.'

'How much contact do they have with the outside world?' Nate asked.

'Very little. Their culture hasn't changed in a thousand years. They trade some with the riverboats, but they have no desire to change.'

'Do we know where the missionaries are?'

'It's difficult to say. I talked with the Minister of Health for the state of Mato Grosso do Sul. I know him personally, and his office has a general idea of where the missionaries are working. I also spoke with a representative from FUNAI – it's our Bureau of Indian Affairs.' Valdir pointed to two of the X's. 'These are Guató. There are probably missionaries around here.'

'Do you know their names?' Nate asked, but it was a throwaway question. According to a memo from Josh, Valdir had not been given the name of Rachel Lane. He had been told that the woman worked for World Tribes, but that was it.

Valdir smiled and shook his head. 'That would be too easy. You must understand that there are at least twenty different American and Canadian organizations with missionaries in Brazil. It's easy to get into our country, and it's easy to move around. Especially in the undeveloped areas. No one really cares who's out there and what they're doing. We figure if they're missionaries, then they are good people.'

Nate pointed at Corumbá, then to the nearest red X. 'How long does it take to get from here to there?'

'Depends. By plane, about an hour. By boat, from three to five days.'

'Then where's my plane?'

'It's not that easy,' Valdir said, reaching for another map. He unrolled it and pressed it on top of the first one. 'This is a topographical map of the Pantanal. These are the *fazendas*.'

'The what?'

'*Fazendas*. Large farms.'

'I thought it was all swamp.'

'No. Many areas are elevated just enough to raise cattle. The *fazendas* were built two hundred years ago, and are still worked by the *pantaneiros*. Only a few of the *fazendas* are accessible by boat, so they use small airplanes. The airstrips are marked in blue.'

Nate noticed that there were very few airstrips near the Indian settlements.

Valdir continued, 'Even if you flew into the area, you would then have to use a boat to get to the Indians.'

'How are the airstrips?'

'They're all grass. Sometimes they cut the grass, sometimes they don't. The biggest problem is cows.'

'Cows?'

'Yes, cows like grass. Sometimes it's hard to land because the cows are eating the runway.' Valdir said this with no effort at humor.

'Can't they move the cows?'

'Yes, if they know you're coming. But there are no phones.'

'No phones in the *fazendas*?'

'None. They are very isolated.'

'So I couldn't fly into the Pantanal, then rent a boat to find the Indians?'

'No. The boats are here in Corumbá. As are the guides.'

Nate stared at the map, especially the Paraguay River as it wound and looped its way northward in the direction of the Indian settlements. Somewhere along the river, hopefully in proximity to it, in the midst of this vast wetlands, was a simple servant of God, living each day in peace and tranquillity, thinking little of the future, quietly ministering to her flock.

And he had to find her.

'I'd like to at least fly over the area,' Nate said.

Valdir rerolled the last map. 'I can arrange an airplane and a pilot.'

'What about a boat?'

'I'm working on that. This is the flood season, and

95

most of the boats are in use. The rivers are up. There's more river traffic this time of the year.'

How nice of Troy to kill himself during the flood season. According to the firm's research, the rains came in November and lasted until February, and all of the lowest areas and many of the *fazendas* were under water.

'I must warn you, though,' Valdir said, lighting another cigarette as he refolded the first map, 'air travel is not without risk. The planes are small, and if there's engine trouble, well . . .' His voice trailed away as he rolled his eyes and shrugged as if all hope was lost.

'Well what?'

'There's no place for an emergency landing, no place to put it down. A plane went down a month ago. They found it near a riverbank, surrounded by alligators.'

'What happened to the passengers?' Nate asked, terrified of the answer.

'Ask the alligators.'

'Let's change the subject.'

'More coffee?'

'Yes, please.'

Valdir yelled at his secretary. They walked to a window and watched the traffic. 'I think I have found a guide,' he said.

'Good. Does he speak English?'

'Yes, very well. He's a young man, just out of the army. A fine boy. His father was a river pilot.'

'That's nice.'

Valdir walked to his desk and picked up the phone. The secretary brought Nate another small cup of *cafezinho*, and he sipped it standing in the window. Across the street was a small bar with three tables on the sidewalk under a canopy. A red sign advertised Antartica beer. Two men in shirtsleeves and ties shared a table with a large bottle of Antartica between them. It was a perfect setting – a hot day, a festive mood, a cold drink enjoyed by two friends in the shade.

Nate was suddenly dizzy. The beer sign blurred, the scene came and went, then came back as his heart pounded and his breathing stopped. He touched the windowsill to steady himself. His hands shook, so he placed the *cafezinho* on a table. Valdir was behind him, oblivious, rattling away in Portuguese.

Sweat popped out in neat rows above his eyebrows. He could taste the beer. The slide was beginning. A chink in the armor. A crack in the dam. A rumbling in the mountain of resolve he'd built the last four months with Sergio. Nate took a deep breath, and collected himself. The moment would pass; he knew it would. He'd been here before, many times now.

He picked up the coffee and sipped it furiously as Valdir was hanging up and announcing that the pilot was hesitant to fly anywhere on Christmas Eve. Nate returned to his seat under the squeaking fan. 'Offer him some more money,' he said.

Valdir had been informed by Mr. Josh Stafford that money was no object during this mission. 'He'll call me back in an hour,' he said.

Nate was ready to leave. He produced his brand-new cell phone, and Valdir walked him through the procedure of finding an AT&T operator who spoke English. As a test, he dialed Sergio and got his answering machine. Then he dialed Alice, his secretary, and wished her a Merry Christmas.

The phone worked fine; he was very proud of it. He thanked Valdir and made his way out of the office. They would talk again before the day was over.

He walked toward the river, down just a few blocks from Valdir's, and found a small park where workers were busy arranging chairs for a concert. The late

97

afternoon was humid; his shirt was stained with sweat and stuck to his chest. The little episode back at Valdir's scared him more than he cared to admit. He sat on the edge of a picnic table, and gazed at the great Pantanal lying before him. A mangy teenager appeared from nowhere and offered to sell him marijuana. It was in tiny bags, in a small wooden box. Nate waved him off. Maybe in another life.

A musician began tuning his guitar, and a crowd slowly gathered as the sun sank over the Bolivian mountains not far away.

TWELVE

The money worked. The pilot reluctantly agreed to fly, but insisted that they leave early and be back in Corumbá by noon. He had small children, an angry wife, and it was, after all, Christmas Eve. Valdir promised and soothed, and paid a nice deposit in cash.

A deposit was also paid to Jevy, the guide Valdir had been negotiating with for a week. Jevy was twenty-four, single, a weightlifter with thick arms, and when he bounced into the lobby of the Palace Hotel, he wore a bush hat, denim shorts, black army boots, a tee shirt with no sleeves, and a shiny bowie knife tucked into his belt just in case he might need to skin something. He crushed Nate's hand as he shook it. '*Bom dia,*' he said through a large, wide smile.

'*Bom dia,*' Nate said, gritting his teeth as his fingers cracked. The knife could not be ignored; its blade was eight inches long.

'You speak Portuguese?' Jevy asked.

'No. Just English.'

'No problem,' he said, finally releasing his death grip. 'I speak English.' The accent was thick, but so far Nate had caught every word. 'Learned it in the army,' Jevy said proudly.

Jevy was instantly likable. He took Nate's briefcase and said something smart to the girl behind the desk. She blushed and wanted more.

His truck was a 1978 Ford three-quarter-ton pickup, the largest vehicle Nate had seen so far in Corumbá. It appeared to be jungle-ready, with large tires, a winch on the front bumper, thick grates over the headlights, a black shade tree paint job, no fenders. And no air conditioning.

They roared through the streets of Corumbá, slowing only slightly at red lights, completely ignoring stop signs, and in general bullying cars and motor-cycles, all anxious to avoid Jevy's tank. Either by design or by neglect, the muffler worked badly. The engine was loud, and Jevy felt compelled to talk as he clutched the wheel like a race driver. Nate didn't hear a word. He smiled and nodded like an idiot while holding his position – feet planted on the floor, one hand clenching the window frame, the other holding his briefcase. His heart stopped with each new inter-section.

Evidently the drivers understood a traffic system where the rules of the road, if any, were ignored. There were no accidents, no carnage. Everyone, including Jevy, managed to stop or yield or swerve just in the nick of time.

The airport was deserted. They parked by the small terminal and walked to one end of the tarmac, where four small airplanes were tied down. One was being prepped by the pilot, a man Jevy did not know. Introductions were made in Portuguese. The pilot's name sounded like Milton. He was friendly enough, but it was obvious he'd rather not be flying or working on the day before Christmas.

As the Brazilians talked, Nate examined the aircraft. The first thing he noticed was the need for a paint job, and this in itself concerned him greatly. If the outside was peeling, could the inside be much better? The tires were slick. There were oil stains around the engine compartment. It was an old Cessna 206, single engine.

The fueling took fifteen minutes, and the bright and early start dragged on, with 10 A.M. approaching. Nate withdrew his fancy cell phone from the deep pocket of his khaki shorts, and called Sergio.

He was having coffee with his wife, making plans for last-minute shopping, and Nate was again grateful that he was out of the country, away from the holiday frenzy. It was cold and sleeting along the mid-Atlantic. Nate assured him he was still together; no problems.

He had stopped the slide, he thought. He had awakened with fresh resolve and strength; it had only been a passing moment of weakness. So he didn't mention it to Sergio. He should have, but why worry him now?

As they talked, the sun slipped behind a dark cloud, and a few scattered raindrops fell around Nate. He hardly noticed. He hung up after the standard 'Merry Christmas.'

The pilot announced he was ready. 'Do you feel safe?' Nate asked Jevy as they loaded the briefcase and a backpack.

Jevy laughed, and said, 'No problem. This man has four small children, and a pretty wife, so he says. Why would he risk his life?'

Jevy wanted to take flying lessons, so he volunteered to take the right seat, next to Milton. It was fine with Nate. He sat behind them in a small cramped seat, his belt and shoulder straps fastened as snug as possible. The engine started with some reluctance, too much in Nate's opinion, and the small cabin was an oven until Milton opened his window. The backdraft from the propeller helped them breathe. They taxied and bounced across the tarmac to the end of the runway. Clearance was not a problem because there was no

101

other traffic. When they lifted off, Nate's shirt was stuck to his chest and sweat ran down his neck.

Corumbá was instantly beneath them. It looked prettier from the air, with its neat rows of small houses on streets that all appeared to be smooth and orderly. Downtown was busy now, with cars waiting in traffic and pedestrians darting across the streets. The city was on a bluff with the river below it. They followed the river north, climbing slowly as Corumbá faded behind. There were scattered clouds and light turbulence.

At four thousand feet, the majesty of the Pantanal suddenly appeared as they passed through a large, ominous cloud. To the east and north, a dozen small rivers spun circles around and through each other, going nowhere, linking each marsh to a hundred others. Because of the floods, the rivers were full and in many places ran together. The water had differing shades. The stagnant marshes were dark blue, almost black in some places where the weeds were thick. The deeper ponds were green. The smaller tributaries carried a reddish dirt, and the great Paraguay was full and as brown as malted chocolate. On the horizon, as far as the eye could see, all water was blue and all earth was green.

While Nate looked to the east and north, his two companions were looking to the west, to the distant mountains of Bolivia. Jevy pointed, catching Nate's attention. The sky was darker beyond the mountains.

Fifteen minutes into the flight, Nate saw the first dwelling of any type. It was a farm on the banks of the Paraguay. The house was small and neat, with the mandatory red-tiled roof. White cows grazed in a pasture and drank at the edge of the river. The daily wash hung from a clothesline near the house. No sign of human activity – no vehicles, no TV antenna, no electrical lines. A small square garden with a fence around it was a short walk from the house, down a dirt path. The plane passed through a cloud, and the farm disappeared.

More clouds. They thickened, and Milton dropped to three thousand feet to stay below them. Jevy told him that it was a sightseeing mission, so stay as low as possible. The first Guató settlement was about an hour from Corumbá.

They veered away from the river for a few minutes, and in doing so flew over a *fazenda*. Jevy folded his map, drew a circle around something, and thrust it back to Nate. 'Fazenda da Prata,' he said, then pointed below. On the map, the *fazendas* were all named, as if they were grand estates. On the ground, Fazenda da Prata was not much bigger than the first farm Nate had seen. There were more cows, a couple of small outbuildings, a slightly larger house, and a long straight belt of land that Nate finally realized was the airstrip. There was no river close by, and certainly no roads. Access was only by air.

Milton was increasingly worried about the dark sky to the west. It was moving east, they were moving north, a meeting seemed inevitable. Jevy leaned back and shouted, 'He doesn't like that sky over there.'

Nor did Nate, but he wasn't the pilot. He shrugged because he could think of no other response.

'We'll watch it for a few minutes,' Jevy said. Milton wanted to go home. Nate wanted to at least see the Indian villages. He still held the faint hope that he could somehow fly in to meet Rachel, and perhaps whisk her away to Corumbá, where they could have lunch in a nice café and discuss her father's estate. Faint hopes, and rapidly fading.

A helicopter was not out of the question. The estate could certainly afford it. If Jevy could find the right village, and the right spot to make a landing, Nate would rent a chopper in an instant.

He was dreaming.

Another small *fazenda*, this one a short distance from the Paraguay River. Raindrops began hitting the windows of the plane, and Milton dropped to two thousand feet. An impressive row of mountains was to the left, much nearer, with the river snaking its way through the dense forests at their base.

From over the mountaintops, the storm rushed at them with a fury. The sky was suddenly much darker; the winds jolted the Cessna. It dipped sharply, causing Nate's head to hit the top of the cabin. He was instantly terrified.

'We're turning around,' Jevy shouted back. His voice lacked the calmness Nate would've preferred. Milton was stonefaced, but the cool aviator's sun-shades were gone, and sweat covered his forehead. The plane veered hard to the right, east then south-east, and as it completed its southward turn, a sickening sight awaited them. The sky toward Corumbá was black.

Milton wanted no part of it. He quickly turned east, and said something to Jevy.

'We can't go to Corumbá,' Jevy yelled to the rear seat. 'He wants to look for a *fazenda*. We'll land and wait for the storm to pass.' His voice was high and anxious, his accent much thicker.

Nate nodded as best he could. His head was bobbing and bouncing, and aching from the first crack into the ceiling. And his stomach was beginning to rumble.

For a few minutes it seemed as though the race would be won by the Cessna. Surely, Nate thought, an airplane of any size can outrun a storm. He rubbed the crown of his head, and decided against looking behind them. But the dark clouds were coming from the sides now.

What kind of backward, half-ass pilot takes off

without checking the radar? On the other hand, the radar, if they even had it, was probably twenty years old and unplugged for the holidays.

The rain peppered the aircraft. The winds howled around it. The clouds boiled past it. The storm caught and overtook them, and the small plane was yanked and thrust up and down and pushed from side to side. For a very long two minutes Milton was unable to fly it because of the turbulence. He was riding a bronco, not flying an airplane.

Nate was looking out his window, and seeing nothing, no water or marshes or nice little *fazendas* with long airstrips. He slumped even lower. He locked his teeth and vowed that he would not vomit.

An air pocket dropped the plane a hundred feet in less than two seconds, and all three men yelled something. Nate's was a very loud 'Oh shit!' His Brazilian buddies cursed in Portuguese. The exclamations were wrapped in heavy layers of fear.

There was a break, a very quick one in which the air was still. Milton pushed the control yoke forward and began a nosedive. Nate braced himself with both hands on the back of Milton's seat, and for the first and hopefully only time in his life he felt like a kamikaze pilot. His heart was racing and his stomach was in his throat. He closed his eyes and thought of Sergio, and of the yoga instructor at Walnut Hill who'd taught him prayer and meditation. He tried to meditate and he tried to pray, but it was impossible trapped in a falling airplane. Death was only seconds away.

A thunderclap just above the Cessna stunned them, like a shotgun in a dark room, and it shook them to their bones. Nate's eardrums practically burst.

The dive ended at five hundred feet as Milton fought the winds and leveled off. 'Look for a *fazenda*!' Jevy yelled from the front, and Nate, reluctantly,

105

peeked out the window. The earth below was being pelted by rain and wind. The trees swayed and the small ponds had whitecaps. Jevy scanned a map, but they were hopelessly lost.

The rain came in white sheets that cut visibility to only a few hundred feet. At times, Nate could barely see the ground. They were surrounded by torrents of rain, all being blown sideways by a brutal wind. Their little plane was being tossed about like a kite. Milton fought the controls while Jevy looked desperately in all directions. They were not going down without a fight.

But Nate gave up. If they couldn't see the ground, how could they expect to land safely? The worst of the storm had yet to catch them. It was over.

He would not plea bargain with God. This was what he deserved for the life he had led. Hundreds of people die in plane crashes every year; he was no better.

He caught a glimpse of a river, just under them, and he suddenly remembered the alligators and anacondas. He was horrified by the thought of crash landing in a swamp. He saw himself badly injured but not dead, clinging to life, fighting for survival, trying to get the damned satellite phone to work while at the same time fending off hungry reptiles.

Another thunderclap shook the cabin, and Nate decided to fight after all. He searched the ground in a vain attempt to find a *fazenda*. A flash of lightning blinded them for a second. The engine sputtered and almost stalled, then caught itself and rattled away. Milton dropped to four hundred feet, a safe altitude under normal circumstances. At least there were no hills or mountains to worry about in the Pantanal.

Nate pulled his shoulder harness even tighter, then vomited between his legs. He felt no disgrace in doing so. He felt nothing but utter terror.

Darkness engulfed them. Milton and Jevy yelled back and forth as they bounced and fought to control the airplane. Their shoulders hit and rubbed together. The map was stuck between Jevy's legs, totally useless.

The storm moved under them. Milton descended to two hundred feet, where the ground could be seen in patches. A gust blew them sideways, literally yanking the Cessna to one side, and Nate realized how helpless they were. He saw a white object below, and yelled and pointed, 'A cow! A cow!' Jevy screamed the translation to Milton.

They dropped through the clouds at eighty feet, in a blinding rain, and flew directly over the red roof of a house. Jevy yelled again, and pointed to something on his side of the plane. The airstrip looked to be the length of a nice suburban driveway, dangerous even in good weather. It didn't matter. They had no choice. If they crashed, at least there were people nearby.

They had spotted the strip too late to land with the wind, so Milton muscled the plane around for a landing into the face of the storm. The wind slapped the Cessna around and practically stalled it. The rain reduced visibility to almost nothing. Nate leaned over for a look at the runway, and saw only the water drenching the windshield.

At fifty feet, the Cessna was blown sideways. Milton fought it back into position. Jevy yelled, *'Vaca! Vaca!'* Nate immediately understood that *vaca* meant cow. Nate saw it too. They missed the first one.

In the flash of images before they hit, Nate saw a boy with a stick running through tall grass, soaking wet and frightened. And he saw a cow running away from the airstrip. He saw Jevy brace himself while staring through the windshield, eyes wild, mouth open but no words coming out.

They slammed into the grass, but kept moving forward. It was a landing, not a crash, and in that split second Nate hoped they would not die. Another gust lifted them ten feet into the air, then they hit again.

'*Vaca! Vaca!*'

The propeller ripped into a large, curious, stationary cow. The plane flipped violently, all windows bursting outward, all three men screaming their last words.

Nate woke up sideways, covered in blood, scared beyond words, but very much alive and suddenly aware that it was still raining. The wind howled through the plane. Milton and Jevy were tangled on top of each other, but moving too and trying to get themselves unbuckled.

Nate found a window and stuck his head out. The Cessna was on its side, with a wing cracked and folded under the cabin. Blood was everywhere, but it was from the cow, not the passengers. The rain, still coming down in sheets, was quickly washing it away.

The boy with the stick led them to a small stable near the airstrip. Out of the storm, Milton dropped to his knees and mumbled an earnest little prayer to the Virgin Mary. Nate watched, and sort of prayed along with him.

There were no serious injuries. Milton had a slight cut on his forehead. Jevy's right wrist was swelling. More soreness would come later.

They sat in the dirt for a long time, watching the rain, hearing the wind, thinking of what could've been, saying nothing.

THIRTEEN

The owner of the cow appeared an hour or so later, as the storm began to subside and the rain stopped for a moment. He was barefoot, clad in faded denim shorts and a threadbare Chicago Bulls tee shirt. Marco was his name, and Marco was not filled with holiday cheer.

He sent the boy away, then began a heated discussion with Jevy and Milton about the value of the cow. Milton was more concerned about his airplane, Jevy with his swollen wrist. Nate stood by the window and wondered exactly how it came to be that he was presently in the middle of the Brazilian outback on Christmas Eve in a smelly manger, sore and bruised, covered with the blood of a cow, listening to three men argue in a foreign tongue, and lucky to be alive. There were no clear answers.

Judging by the other cows grazing nearby, they couldn't be worth much. 'I'll pay for the damned thing,' Nate said to Jevy.

Jevy asked the man how much, then said, 'A hundred reais.'

'Does he take American Express?' Nate asked, but the humor missed its mark. 'I'll pay it.' A hundred bucks. He'd pay that much just for Marco to stop griping.

The deal was sealed, and the man became their host. He led them to his house, where lunch was being prepared by a short barefoot woman who smiled and welcomed them profusely. For obvious reasons, guests were unheard of in the Pantanal, and when they realized Nate was from the States they sent for the kids. The boy with the stick had two brothers, and their mother told them to examine Nate because he was an American.

She took the men's shirts and soaked them in a basin filled with soap and rainwater. They ate rice and black beans around a small table, bare-chested and unconcerned about it. Nate was proud of his toned biceps and flat stomach. Jevy had the cut look of a serious weightlifter. Poor Milton showed the signs of rapidly approaching middle age, but clearly didn't care.

The three said little over lunch. The horror of the crash was still fresh. The children sat on the floor beside the table, eating flat bread and rice, watching every move Nate made.

There was a small river a quarter of a mile down the trail, and Marco had a boat with a motor. The Paraguay River was five hours away. Maybe he had enough gasoline, maybe he didn't. But it would be impossible with all three men in the boat.

When the sky cleared, Nate and the children walked to the wrecked plane and removed his briefcase. Along the way he taught them to count to ten in English. And they taught him in Portuguese. They were sweet boys, terribly shy at first but warming to Nate by the minute. It was Christmas Eve, he reminded himself. Did Santa visit the Pantanal? No one seemed to be expecting him.

On a smooth flat stump in the front yard, Nate carefully unpacked and arranged the satellite phone. The receiving dish was a square foot in size, and the phone itself was no larger than a compact laptop. A cord connected the two. Nate turned on the power,

110

punched in his ID and PIN numbers, then slowly turned the dish until it picked up the signal from the Astar-East Satellite, a hundred miles above the Atlantic, hovering somewhere near the equator. The signal was strong, a steady beep confirmed it, and Marco and the rest of his family huddled even closer around Nate. He wondered if they'd ever seen a phone.

Jevy called out the numbers to Milton's home in Corumbá. Nate pressed them slowly, then held his breath and waited. If the call did not work, they were simply stuck with Marco and family for Christmas. The house was small; Nate was assuming he'd sleep in the stable. Perfect.

Plan B was to send Jevy and Marco in the boat. It was almost 1 P.M. Five hours to the Paraguay would put them there just before dark, assuming there was enough gas. Once on the big river, they would then be faced with the task of finding help, and this could take hours. If there wasn't enough gas, they would be stranded deep in the Pantanal. Jevy had not vetoed this plan outright, but no one was pushing it.

There were other factors. Marco was reluctant to leave this late in the day. Normally, when he went to the Paraguay to trade, he left at sunrise. And while there was a chance he could find extra gas from a neighbor an hour away, this was far from certain.

'*Oi*,' came a female voice over the speaker, and everyone smiled. Nate handed the phone to Milton, who said hello to his wife, then slid into a sad narrative about their plight. Jevy whispered a translation to Nate. The children marveled at the English.

The conversation grew tense, then suddenly stopped. 'She's looking for a phone number,' Jevy explained. The number came across, that of a pilot Milton knew. He promised to be home for dinner and hung up.

The pilot wasn't home. His wife said he was in

111

Campo Grande on business, and should return by dark. Milton explained where he was, and she found more phone numbers where her husband might be reached.

'Ask him to talk fast,' Nate said as he punched in another number. 'This battery doesn't last forever.'

No answer to the next number. To the next, the pilot came to the phone and was explaining that his airplane was being repaired when the signal was interrupted.

The clouds were back.

Nate looked at the darkening sky in disbelief. Milton was on the verge of tears.

It was a quick shower, a cool rain the children played in while the adults sat on the porch and watched them in silence.

Jevy had another plan. There was an army base on the edge of Corumbá. He had not been stationed there, but he lifted weights with several of the officers. When the sky was clear again, they returned to the stump and huddled around the phone. Jevy called a friend who found phone numbers.

The army had helicopters. It was, after all, a plane crash. When the second officer answered the phone, Jevy rapidly explained what had happened and asked for help.

Watching Jevy's end of the conversation was torture for Nate. He understood not a word, but the body language told the story. Smiles and frowns, urgings and pleas, frustrating pauses, then the repetition of things already said.

When Jevy finished, he said to Nate, 'He will call his commandant. He wants me to call back in an hour.'

An hour seemed like a week. The sun returned and baked the wet grass. The humidity was thick. Still shirtless, Nate began to feel the stinging of a sunburn.

112

They retired to the shade of a tree to escape the sun. The madam checked on their shirts, which had been left hanging during the last shower and were still wet.

Jevy and Milton had skin several shades darker than Nate's, and they were unconcerned about the sun. It didn't bother Marco either, and the three of them walked to the airplane to inspect the damage. Nate stayed behind, under the tree, where it was safe. The heat of the afternoon was stifling. His chest and shoulders were beginning to stiffen, and the idea of a nap crossed his mind. But the boys had other plans. He finally got their names – Luis was the oldest, the one who'd chased a cow from the airstrip seconds before they landed, Oli was the middle one, and the smallest was Tomas. Using the phrase book he kept in his briefcase, Nate slowly broke the language barrier. Hello. How are you? What is your name? How old are you? Good afternoon. The boys repeated the phrases in Portuguese so Nate could learn the pronunciation, then he made them do it in English.

Jevy returned with maps, and they made the phone call. There appeared to be some interest on the part of the army. Milton pointed to a map and said, 'Fazenda Esperança,' which Jevy repeated with great enthusiasm. It waned, though, seconds later, then he hung up. 'He can't find the commandant,' he said in English, trying to appear hopeful. 'It is, you know, Christmas.'

Christmas in the Pantanal. Ninety-five degrees with humidity even higher. A scorching sun with no sunblock. Bugs and insects with no repellent. Cheerful little kids with no hope of getting toys. No music because there was no electricity. No Christmas tree. No Christmas food, or wine, or champagne.

This is an adventure, he kept telling himself. Where's your sense of humor?

Nate returned the phone to its case and clamped it

113

shut. Milton and Jevy walked to the airplane. Madam went into the house. Marco had something to do in the backyard. Nate went for the shade again, thinking how nice it would be to hear just one verse of 'White Christmas' while sipping a glass of bubbly.

Luis appeared with three of the scrawniest horses Nate had ever seen. One had a saddle, a cruel-looking device made of leather and wood and resting on a bright orange pad, which appeared to be old shag carpet. The saddle was for Nate. Luis and Oli hopped on their bareback horses without the slightest effort; just a skip and a jump and they were mounted, perfectly balanced.

Nate studied his horse. *'Onde?'* he asked. Where?

Luis pointed to a trail. Nate knew from the pointing over lunch and afterward that the trail led to the river where Marco kept his boat.

Why not? It was an adventure. What else was there to do as the hours dragged on? He retrieved his shirt from the clothesline, then managed to mount the poor horse without falling off or hurting himself.

In late October, Nate and some of the other addicts at Walnut Hill had spent a pleasant Sunday on horseback, trailing through the Blue Ridge, taking in the glories of fall. His butt and thighs had ached for a week, but his fear of the beasts had been overcome. Somewhat.

He fought the stirrups until his feet were stuck through them, then clutched the bridle so tight the animal wouldn't move. The boys watched with great amusement, then began trotting away. Nate's horse finally trotted too, a slow rough trot that slapped him in the crotch and bounced him from side to side. Preferring to simply walk, he yanked the bridle and the horse slowed. The boys circled back and walked beside him.

The trail led through a small pasture and around a

bend, so the house was soon out of sight. There was water ahead – a swamp, just like the countless ones Nate had seen from the air. It did not deter the boys, because the trail ran through the middle of it and the horses had crossed it many times before. They never slowed. The water was at first only inches deep, then a foot, then it touched the stirrups. Of course, the boys were barefoot and leather-skinned and completely unconcerned about the water or what might be in it. Nate was wearing his favorite pair of Nikes, which were soon wet.

Piranhas, vicious little fish with razor-sharp teeth, were all over the Pantanal.

He preferred to turn around, but had no idea how to communicate this. 'Luis,' he said, his voice betraying his fears. The boys looked at him without the slightest trace of concern.

When the water was chest-deep on the horses, they slowed a little. A few more steps and Nate saw his feet again. The horses emerged on the other side where the trail resumed.

They passed the remnants of a fence to their left. Then, a dilapidated dwelling. The trail widened into an old roadbed. Many years earlier, the *fazenda* had been more substantial, no doubt with a large cattle operation and many employees.

The Pantanal had been settled over two hundred years earlier, Nate knew from his collection of reading materials, and little had changed. The isolation of the people was astounding. There was no sign of neighbors, or other children, and Nate kept thinking about schools and education. Do the kids flee when they're old enough, to Corumbá to find jobs and spouses? Or do they tend the small farms and raise the next generation of *pantaneiros*? Could Marco and his wife read and write, and if so did they teach their children?

He would ask Jevy these questions. There was more

115

water ahead, a larger swamp with rotted trees bunched together on both sides. And of course the trail ran through the middle of it. It was the flood season, the water was high everywhere. In the dry months, the swamp was a patch of mud, and a novice could follow the trail without fear of being eaten. Come back then, Nate told himself. Small chance.

The horses plodded along like machines, unconcerned about the swamp and the water splashing to their knees. The boys were half-asleep. The pace slowed a bit as the water rose. When Nate's knees were wet, and he was ready to yell something desperate at Luis, Oli pointed very nonchalantly to the right, to a spot where two decayed stumps rose ten feet in the air. Between them lying low in the water was a large black reptile.

'*Jacaré*,' Oli said, sort of over his shoulder as if Nate might want to know. Alligator.

The eyes protruded above the rest of the body, and Nate was certain they were following him specifically. His heart raced and he wanted to cry out, to scream for help. Then Luis turned around and grinned because he knew his guest was terrified. His guest tried to smile as if he were thrilled to finally see one this close.

The horses raised their heads as the water rose. Nate kicked his, under the water, but nothing happened. The alligator slowly lowered himself until nothing could be seen but the eyes, then he pushed forward, in their direction, and disappeared into the black water. Nate yanked his feet from the stirrups and pulled his knees to his chest, so that he teetered on the saddle. The boys said something and began giggling, but Nate didn't care.

Past the middle of the swamp, the water fell to the horses' legs, then their feet. Safely on the other side, Nate relaxed. Then he laughed at himself. He could

116

sell this back home. He had friends who were into extreme vacations – backpackers and whitewater rafters, gorilla trekkers, safari types always trying to outdo the rest with tales of near-death experiences on the other side of the world. Throw in the ecological angle of the Pantanal, and for ten thousand dollars they would gladly hop on a pony and wade through swamps, photographing snakes and alligators along the way.

With no river in sight, Nate decided it was time to turn back. He pointed at his watch, and Luis led them home.

The commandant himself was brought to the phone. He and Jevy traded army talk for five minutes – places they'd been stationed, people they knew – while the battery indicator light blinked faster and the SatFone slowly ran out of gas. Nate pointed; Jevy responded by explaining to the commandant that this was their last chance.

No problem. A chopper was ready; a crew was being scrambled. How bad were the injuries?

Internal, Jevy said, glancing at Milton.

The *fazenda* was forty minutes away by helicopter, according to the army pilots. Give us an hour, the commandant said. Milton smiled for the first time that day.

An hour passed and the optimism faded. The sun was dropping quickly in the west; dusk was approaching. A nighttime rescue was out of the question.

They gravitated to the broken airplane, where Milton and Jevy had worked steadily throughout the afternoon. The fractured wing had been removed, as had the propeller. It was in the grass near the plane, still stained with blood. The right landing brace was bent, but would not require replacement.

The dead cow had been butchered by Marco and

his wife. Its carcass was barely visible in the brush next to the airstrip.

According to Jevy, Milton planned to return by boat as soon as he could find a new wing and propeller. To Nate, this seemed virtually impossible. How could he haul something as bulky as an airplane wing on a boat small enough to navigate the tributaries of the Pantanal, then carry it through the same swamps Nate had seen on horseback?

That was his problem. Nate had other things to worry about.

Madam brought warm coffee and brittle cookies, and they sat in the grass next to the stable and chattered away. Nate's three little shadows sat close to him, afraid he might leave them. Another hour passed.

It was Tomas, the youngest, who heard the humming sound first. He said something, then stood and pointed and the rest of them froze. The sound grew louder, and became the unmistakable whir of a helicopter. They ran to the center of the airstrip and watched the sky.

When it landed, four soldiers jumped from the open bay and ran to the group. Nate knelt among the boys, and gave them each ten reais. '*Feliz Natal*,' he said. Merry Christmas. Then he hugged them quickly, picked up his briefcase, and ran to the helicopter.

Jevy and Nate waved at the little family as they lifted off. Milton was too busy thanking the pilots and soldiers. At five hundred feet, the Pantanal began to stretch to the horizon. It was dark to the east.

And it was dark in Corumbá when they flew over the city a half hour later. It was a beautiful sight – the buildings and houses, the Christmas lights, the traffic. They landed at the army base west of town, on a bluff above the Paraguay River. The commandant met them and received the profuse thanks he so richly deserved. He was surprised at the lack of serious injuries, but happy nonetheless at the success of the mission. He sent them away in an open jeep driven by a young private.

As they entered the city, the jeep made a sudden turn and stopped in front of a small grocery. Jevy walked inside, and returned with three bottles of Brahma beer. He gave one to Milton, and one to Nate.

After a slight hesitation, Nate unscrewed the cap and turned the bottle up. It was very wet, and cold, and thoroughly delicious. And it was Christmas, and what the hell. He could handle it.

Riding in the back of the jeep through the dusty streets, the humid air rushing against his face, cold beer in hand, Nate reminded himself of how lucky he was to be alive.

Nearly four months earlier he had tried to kill himself. Seven hours earlier he had survived a crash landing.

But the day had accomplished nothing. He was no closer to Rachel Lane than he'd been the day before.

The first stop was the hotel. Nate wished them all a Merry Christmas, then went to his room, where he undressed and stood in the shower for twenty minutes.

There were four cans of beer in the refrigerator. He drank them all in an hour, assuring himself with each can that this was not a slide. It would not lead to a crash. Things were under control. He'd cheated death, so why not celebrate with a little Christmas cheer? No one would ever know. He could handle it.

Besides, sobriety had never worked for him. He would prove to himself that he could handle a little alcohol. No problem. A few beers here and there. What was the harm?

FOURTEEN

The phone woke him, but it took a while to get to it.
The beer had no lingering effect, other than guilt, but
the little adventure in the Cessna was taking its toll.
His neck, shoulders, and waist were already dark blue
– neat rows of bruises where the harnesses had held
him in place as the plane slammed into the ground.
There were at least two knots on his skull, the first
from a lick he could remember, the second from one
he could not. His knees had cracked the backs of the
pilots' seats – slight injuries at first, he'd thought, but
their severity had increased during the night. His arms
and neck were sunburned.

'Merry Christmas,' the voice greeted him. It was
Valdir, and it was almost nine.

'Thank you,' Nate said. 'Same to you.'

'Yes. How are you feeling?'

'Fine. Thanks.'

'Yes, well, Jevy called me last night and told me
about the airplane. Milton must be a crazy man to fly
into a storm. I'll never use him again.'

'Neither will I.'

'Are you okay?'

'Yes.'

'Do you need a doctor?'

'No.'

'Jevy said he thought you were okay.'

120

'I'm fine, just a little sore.'

There was a slight pause as Valdir changed speeds. 'We're having a small Christmas party in my home this afternoon. Just my family and a few friends. Would you like to join us?'

There was a stiffness to the invitation. Nate couldn't tell if Valdir was only trying to be polite, or if it was a matter of language and accent.

'That's very kind of you,' he said. 'But I have a lot of reading to do.'

'Are you sure?'

'Yes, thanks.'

'Very well. I have some good news. I rented a boat yesterday, finally.' It didn't take long to leave the party and get to the boat.

'Good. When do I go?'

'Perhaps tomorrow. They're getting it ready. Jevy knows the boat.'

'I'm anxious to get on the river. Especially after yesterday.'

Valdir then launched into a windy narrative of how he'd played hardball with the owner of the boat, a notorious tightwad who had initially demanded a thousand reais per week. They had settled on six hundred. Nate listened but didn't care. The Phelan estate could handle it.

Valdir said good-bye with another Merry Christmas.

His Nikes were still wet, but he put them on anyway, along with running shorts and a tee shirt. He would try to jog, but if the parts wouldn't work then he'd simply walk. He needed fresh air and exercise. Moving slowly around the room, he saw the empty beer cans in the wastebasket.

He would deal with it later. This was not a slide, and it would not lead to a crash. His life had flashed before him yesterday, and that changed things. He could have died. Every day was a gift now, every moment was to be savored. Why not enjoy a few of life's pleasures? Just a little beer and wine, nothing stronger and certainly no narcotics.

This was familiar turf; lies he'd lived before.

He took two Tylenol and covered his exposed skin with sunblock. In the lobby, a Christmas show was on the television but no one was watching, no one was there. The young lady behind the counter smiled and said good morning. The heavy, sticky heat wafted in through the open glass doors. Nate stopped for a quick shot of sweet coffee. The thermos was on the counter, the tiny paper cups stacked neatly beside it, waiting for anyone to pause and enjoy an ounce of *cafezinho*.

Two shots, and he was sweating before he left the lobby. On the sidewalk, he tried to stretch but his muscles were screaming and his joints were locked. The challenge was not running; rather, it was walking without an obvious limp.

But no one was watching. The shops were locked and the streets were empty, as he'd expected them to be. After two blocks, his shirt was already sticking to his back. He was exercising in a sauna.

Avenida Rondon was the last paved street along the bluff above the river. He followed the sidewalk next to it for a long way, limping slightly as the muscles reluctantly loosened a little and the joints stopped grinding. He found the same small park he'd stopped at two days earlier, on the twenty-third, when the crowd gathered for music and carols. Some of the folding chairs were still there. His legs needed rest. He sat on the same picnic table, and glanced about for the mangy teenager who'd tried to sell him drugs.

But there wasn't a soul. He gently rubbed his knees and looked at the great Pantanal, expanding for miles, disappearing on the horizon. Magnificent desolation. He thought of the boys – Luis, Oli, and Tomas – his little buddies with ten reais in their pockets and no way to spend it. Christmas meant nothing to them; every day was the same.

Somewhere in the vast wetlands before him was one Rachel Lane, now just a humble servant of God but about to become one of the richest women in the world. If he actually found her, how would she react to the news of her great fortune? How would she react when she met him, an American lawyer who'd managed to track her down?

The possible answers made him uncomfortable.

For the first time, it occurred to Nate that maybe Troy had been crazy after all. Would a rational, lucid mind give eleven billion dollars to a person who had no interest in wealth? A person practically unknown to everyone, including the one signing the hand-scrawled will? The act seemed insane, much more so now that Nate was sitting above the Pantanal, looking at its wilderness, three thousand miles from home.

Little had been learned about Rachel. Evelyn Cunningham, her mother, was from the small town of Delhi, Louisiana. At the age of nineteen, she moved to Baton Rouge and found a job as a secretary with a company involved in the exploration of natural gas. Troy Phelan owned the company, and during one of his routine visits from New York, he spotted Evelyn. Evidently she had been a beautiful woman, and naive in her small-town upbringing. Ever the vulture, Troy struck quickly, and within a few months Evelyn found herself pregnant. This was in the spring of 1954.

In November of that year, Troy's people at the home office quietly arranged for Evelyn to be admitted to the Catholic Hospital in New Orleans, where Rachel was born on the second. Evelyn never saw her child.

With plenty of lawyers and lots of pressure, Troy arranged for the quick, private adoption of Rachel by a minister and his wife in Kalispell, Montana. He was buying copper and zinc mines in the state, and had contacts through his companies there. The adoptive parents did not know the identities of the biological ones.

Evelyn didn't want the child, nor did she want anything further to do with Troy Phelan. She took ten thousand dollars and returned to Delhi, where, typically, rumors of her sins were waiting for her. She moved in with her parents, and they waited patiently for the storm to pass. It did not. With the cruelty that is peculiar to small towns, Evelyn found herself an outcast among the people she most needed. She rarely left the house, and with time retreated even farther, to the darkness of her bedroom. It was there, in the hidden gloom of her own little world, that Evelyn began to miss her daughter.

She wrote letters to Troy, none of which were answered. A secretary hid them and filed them away. Two weeks after his suicide one of Josh's investigators found them buried in Troy's personal archives in his apartment.

As the years passed Evelyn sank deeper into her own abyss. The rumors became sporadic but never went away. The appearance of her parents at church or at the grocery always prompted stares and whispers, and they eventually withdrew too.

Evelyn killed herself on November 2, 1959, on Rachel's fifth birthday. She drove her parents' car to the edge of town, and jumped off a bridge.

The obituary and the story of her death in the local paper found their way to Troy's office in New Jersey, where they were also filed away and hidden.

Very little had been learned about Rachel's childhood. The Reverend and Mrs. Lane moved twice, from Kalispell to Butte, then from Butte to Helena. He died of cancer when Rachel was seventeen. She was an only child.

124

For reasons no one but Troy could explain, he decided to reenter her life as she was finishing high school. Perhaps he felt some measure of guilt. Perhaps he was worried about her college education and how she would afford it. Rachel knew she was adopted, but had never expressed an interest in knowing her real parents.

The specifics were unknown, but Troy met Rachel sometime in the summer of 1972. Four years later, she graduated from the University of Montana. Gaps appeared thereafter, huge voids in her history that no investigation had been able to fill.

Nate suspected that only two people could properly document the relationship. One was dead; the other was living like an Indian somewhere out there, on the banks of one of a thousand rivers.

He tried to jog for a block, but quit in pain. Walking was difficult enough. Two cars passed, people were stirring. The roar approached quickly from behind and was upon him before he could react. Jevy slammed on the brakes next to the sidewalk. '*Bom dia*,' he yelled above the engine.

Nate nodded. '*Bom dia.*'

Jevy turned the switch and the engine died. 'How do you feel?'

'Sore. And you?'

'No problem. The girl at the desk said you were running. Let's go for a ride.'

Nate preferred jogging in pain to riding with Jevy, but the traffic was light and the streets were safer.

They drove through downtown, with his chauffeur still thoroughly ignoring all lights and stop signs. Jevy never looked around as they sped through intersections.

'I want you to see the boat,' Jevy said at one point. If he was sore and stiff from the crash landing, he didn't show it. Nate only nodded.

There was a boatyard of sorts on the east end of town, at the foot of the bluff, on a small inlet where the water was murky and oil-stained. A sad collection of boats rocked gently in the river – some had been scrapped decades earlier, others were rarely used. Two were obviously cattle boats, with their decks sectioned into muddy wooden pens.

'There it is,' Jevy said as he pointed in the general direction of the river. They parked on the street and walked down the bank. There were several fishing boats, small and low in the water, and their owners were either coming or going. Nate couldn't tell. Jevy yelled at two of them, and they retorted with something humorous.

'My father was a boat captain,' Jevy explained. 'I was here every day.'

'Where is he now?' Nate asked.

'He drowned in a storm.'

Wonderful, thought Nate. The storms get you both in the air and on the water.

A sagging sheet of plywood bridged the dirty water and led to their boat. They stopped at the edge of the bank to admire the vessel, the *Santa Loura*. 'How do you like it?' Jevy asked.

'I don't know,' Nate replied. It was certainly nicer than the cattle boats. Someone was hammering in the back of it.

A coat of paint would help tremendously. The boat was at least sixty feet long, with two decks and a bridge at the top of the steps. It was larger than Nate had expected.

'It's just me, right?' he asked.

'Right.'

'No other passengers?'

'No. Just you, me, and a deckhand who can also cook.'

'What's his name?'

'Welly.'

The plywood creaked but didn't break. The boat dipped a little as they jumped on board. Barrels of diesel fuel and water lined the bow. Through a door and two steps down, and they were in the cabin, which had four bunks, each with white sheets and a thin layer of foam rubber as a mattress. Nate's sore muscles flinched at the thought of a week on one of those. The ceiling was low, the windows shut, and the first major problem was the fact that there was no air conditioning. The cabin was an oven.

'We'll get a fan,' Jevy said, reading his mind. 'It's not so bad when the boat is moving.' This was impossible to believe. Shuffling sideways, they moved along the narrow walkway toward the rear of the boat, passing along the way a kitchen with a sink and a propane stove, the engine room, and finally a small bathroom. In the engine room a grimy, shirtless man was sweating profusely and staring at a wrench in his hand as if it had offended him.

Jevy knew the man, and managed to say the wrong thing, because sharp words suddenly filled the air. Nate retreated to the rear walkway, where he found a small aluminum boat tied to the *Santa Loura*. It had paddles and an outboard motor, and Nate suddenly had a vision of himself and Jevy scooting across shallow water, darting through weeds and trunks, dodging alligators, chasing another dead end. The adventure was growing.

Jevy laughed and the tension eased. He walked to the rear of the boat and said, 'He needs an oil pump. The store is closed today.'

'What about tomorrow?' Nate asked.

'No problem.'

'What's this little boat for?'

'Lots of things.'

They climbed the grated steps to the bridge, where

Jevy inspected the wheel and engine switches. Behind the bridge was a small open room with two bunks; Jevy and the deckhand would take turns sleeping there. And farther behind was a deck, about fifteen square feet in size and shaded with a bright green canopy. Stretched the length of the deck was a comfortable-looking hammock, which immediately caught Nate's attention.

'This is yours,' Jevy said with a smile. 'You will have lots of time to read and sleep.'

'How nice,' Nate said.

'This boat is sometimes used for tourists, usually Germans, who want to see the Pantanal.'

'Have you worked as the captain on this boat?'

'Yes, a couple of times. Several years ago. The owner is not a pleasant man.'

Nate carefully sat on the hammock, then swung his damaged legs around until he was fully fitted into it. Jevy gave him a push, then left to have another chat with the mechanic.

FIFTEEN

Lillian Phelan's dreams of a cozy Christmas dinner were shattered when Troy Junior arrived late and drunk and in the midst of a nasty fight with Biff. They came in separate cars, each driving new Porsches of different colors. The shouting spread as Rex, who'd also had a few drinks, chastised his older brother for ruining their mother's Christmas. The house was full. Lillian's four children – Troy Junior, Rex, Libbigail, and Mary Ross – were there, as well as all eleven grandchildren, along with an assortment of their friends, most of whom had not been specifically invited by Lillian.

The Phelan grandchildren, like their parents, had attracted new pals and confidants since Troy's passing.

Until Troy Junior's arrival, it had been a delightful celebration of Christmas. Never had so many fabulous gifts been exchanged. The Phelan heirs bought for each other and for Lillian without regard to cost – designer clothing, jewelry, electronic gadgets, even art. For a few hours, the money brought out the best in them. Their generosity knew no bounds.

In only two days the will would be read.

Libbigail's husband Spike, the ex-biker she'd met in rehab, attempted to intervene in the rift between Troy Junior and Rex, and in the process got himself cursed by Troy Junior, who reminded him that he was a 'fat hippie whose brain had been fried by LSD.' This offended Libbigail, who called Biff a slut. Lillian ran to her bedroom and locked the door. The grandchildren and their entourages drifted to the basement, where someone had stashed a cooler of beer.

Mary Ross, arguably the most reasonable and certainly the least volatile of the four, convinced her brothers and Libbigail to stop yelling and find separate corners between rounds. They drifted off into little groups; some in the den, some in the living room. An uneasy ceasefire settled in.

The lawyers hadn't helped matters. They now worked in teams as they represented what they claimed to be the best interests of each Phelan heir. And they also spent hours conniving and figuring ways to get a larger piece of the pie. Four very distinct little armies of lawyers – six if you counted Geena's and Ramble's – all working feverishly. The more time the Phelan heirs spent with their lawyers, the more they distrusted each other.

After an hour of peace, Lillian emerged and surveyed the truce. Saying nothing, she went to the kitchen and finished preparing dinner. A buffet now made sense. They could eat in shifts, come in groups and fill their plates and retire to the safety of their corners.

And so the first Phelan family enjoyed a quiet Christmas dinner after all. Troy Junior ate ham and sweet potatoes by himself at the bar near the rear patio. Biff ate with Lillian in the kitchen. Rex and his wife Amber, the stripper, enjoyed turkey in the bedroom with a football game on. Libbigail, Mary Ross, and their husbands ate on TV trays in the den.

And the grandchildren and their groupies took frozen pizza to the basement, where the beer was flowing.

The second family had no Christmas at all, at least not together. Janie had never been fond of the holiday, and so she fled the country, to Klosters in Switzerland, where the pretty people from Europe gathered to be seen and ski. She took with her a bodybuilder named Lance, who at twenty-eight was half her age, but happy to be along for the ride.

Her daughter Geena was forced to spend Christmas with in-laws in Connecticut, normally a bleak and gloomy prospect, but things had changed dramatically. For Geena's husband Cody, it was a triumphant return to the family's aging country estate near Waterbury.

The Strong family once had a fortune built in shipping, but after centuries of mismanagement and inbreeding the money had practically dried up. The name and the pedigree still guaranteed acceptance to the right schools and the proper clubs, and a Strong wedding still received a lengthy announcement. But the trough was only so wide and long, and too many generations had been eating from it.

They were an arrogant bunch, proud of their name and accent and bloodlines, and on the surface unconcerned about the dwindling family money. They had careers in New York and Boston. They spent what they earned because the family fortune had always been their safety net.

The last Strong with any vision had evidently seen the end and established trusts for education, thick trusts written by squads of lawyers, impenetrable trusts clad with iron and able to withstand the desperate assaults from future Strongs. The assaults came; the trusts held firm, and any young Strong was still guaranteed a fine education. Cody boarded at Taft, was an average student at Dartmouth, then received an MBA from Columbia.

His marriage to Geena Phelan had not been well

received by the family, primarily because it was her second. The fact that her estranged father was worth, at the time of the wedding, six billion dollars helped ease her entry into the clan. But she would always be looked down on because she was a divorcée and poorly educated at non-Ivy League schools, and also because Cody was a bit odd.

But they were all there to greet her on Christmas Day. She had never seen so many smiles from people she detested; so many stiff little hugs and awkward pecks on the cheeks and pats on the shoulder. She hated them even more for their phoniness.

A couple of drinks, and Cody began talking. The men grouped around him in the den and it wasn't long before someone asked, 'How much?'

He frowned as if the money was already a burden. 'Probably half a billion,' he said, the perfect delivery of a line he'd rehearsed in front of his bathroom mirror.

Some of the men gasped. Others grimaced because they knew Cody, and they were all Strongs, and they knew they would never see a dime of it. They all quietly seethed with envy. Word filtered out from the group and before long the women scattered around the house were whispering about the half a billion. Cody's mother, a prim and shriveled little woman whose wrinkles cracked when she smiled, was appalled by the obscenity of the fortune. 'It's new money,' she said to a daughter. New money earned by a scandalous old goat with three wives and a string of bad children, not a one of whom had attended an Ivy League school.

· New or old, the money was much envied by the younger women. They could see the jets and beach houses and fabulous family gatherings on distant islands, and trust funds for nieces and nephews, and perhaps even outright gifts of cash.

The money thawed the Strongs, thawed them to a

warmness they had never shown to an outsider, thawed them to the point of melting. It taught them openness and love, and made for a warm, cozy Christmas.

Late in the afternoon, as the family gathered around the table for the traditional dinner, it began to snow. What a perfect Christmas, all the Strongs said. Geena hated them more than ever.

Ramble spent the holiday with his lawyer, at six hundred dollars an hour, though the billing would be hidden as only lawyers can hide such things.

Tira likewise had left the country with a young gigolo. She was on a beach somewhere, topless and probably bottomless too, and completely unconcerned with what her fourteen-year-old son might be doing.

The lawyer, Yancy, was single, twice divorced, and had twin eleven-year-old sons from his second marriage. The boys were exceptionally bright for their age; Ramble was painfully slow for his, so they had a great time playing video games in the bedroom while Yancy watched football alone.

His client was set to receive the obligatory five million dollars on his twenty-first birthday, and given the client's level of maturity and direction at home, the money wouldn't even last as long as it had for the other Phelan offspring. But Yancy wasn't concerned with a meager five million; hell, he'd make that much in fees off Ramble's cut from the will.

Yancy had other worries. Tira had hired a new law firm, an aggressive one near the Capitol, one with all the right connections. She was only an ex-wife, not an offspring, and her portion would be much smaller than anything Ramble received. The new lawyers of course realized this. They were pressuring Tira to ditch Yancy and steer young Ramble into their corner. Fortunately, the mother didn't care much for the child, and Yancy was doing a splendid job of manipulating child away from mother.

The laughter of the boys was music to his ears.

SIXTEEN

Late in the afternoon, he stopped at a small deli a few blocks from the hotel. He was roaming the sidewalks, saw that the deli was open, and walked into it with the hope of finding a beer. Nothing but a beer, maybe two. He was alone on the far side of the world. It was Christmas and he had no one to share it with. A wave of loneliness and depression fell hard upon Nate, and he began to slide. Self-pity seized him.

He saw the rows of bottles of liquor, all full and unopened, whiskeys and gins and vodkas, lined up like pretty little soldiers in bright uniforms. His mouth was instantly dry, even parched. His jaw dropped and his eyes closed. He grabbed the counter so he wouldn't waver, and his entire face contorted with pain as he thought about Sergio back at Walnut Hill and Josh and the ex-wives and the ones he'd hurt so many times when he crashed. Thoughts spun wildly and he was about to faint when the little man said something. Nate glowered at him, bit his lip, and pointed at the vodka. Two bottles, eight reais.

Every crash had been different. Some were slow in building, a drink here, a snort there, a crack in the dam followed by more. Once he'd actually driven himself to a detox center. Another time he'd awakened strapped to a bed with an IV in his wrist. With the last crash, a maid had found him in a cheap motel room, thirty bucks a day, comatose.

He clutched the paper sack and walked with a purpose to his hotel, stepping around a group of sweaty little boys dribbling a soccer ball on the sidewalk. So lucky are the children, he thought. No burdens, no baggage. Tomorrow's just another game.

It would be dark in an hour, and Corumbá was gently coming to life. The sidewalk cafés and bars were opening, a few cars moved about. At the hotel, live music from the pool drifted through the lobby, and for a second Nate was tempted to get a table for one last song.

But he didn't. He went to his room, where he locked the door and filled a tall plastic cup with ice. He placed the bottles side by side, opened one, slowly poured the vodka over the ice, and vowed not to stop until both were empty.

Jevy was waiting for the parts merchant when he arrived at eight. The sun was up and unfiltered by clouds. The sidewalks were hot to the touch.

There was no oil pump, at least not one for a diesel engine. The merchant made two calls, and Jevy roared away in his pickup. He drove to the edge of Corumbá where a boat dealer ran a salvage yard cluttered with the remains of dozens of scrapped vessels. In the engine shop a parts boy produced a well-used oil pump, covered with oil and grease and wrapped in a dirty shop rag. Jevy gladly paid twenty reais for it.

He drove to the river and parked near the water's edge. The *Santa Loura* hadn't moved. He was pleased to see that Welly had arrived. Welly was a novice deckhand, not yet eighteen, who claimed he could cook, pilot, guide, clean, navigate, and perform any and all other services required. Jevy knew he was lying,

136

but such bravado was not uncommon among boys looking for work on the river.

'Have you seen Mr. O'Riley?' Jevy asked.

'The American?' asked Welly.

'Yes, the American.'

'No. No sign of him.'

A fisherman in a wooden boat yelled something at Jevy, but he was preoccupied with other matters. He bounced across the plywood onto the boat, where the banging had started again in the rear. The same grimy mechanic was wrestling with the engine. He hovered over it in a half-crouch, shirtless and dripping with sweat. The engine room was suffocating. Jevy handed him the oil pump and he inspected it with his short stubby fingers.

The engine was a five-cylinder in-line diesel, with the pump at the bottom of the crankcase, just below the edge of the grated floor. The mechanic shrugged as if Jevy's purchase might indeed do the trick, then he maneuvered his belly around the manifold, dropped slowly to his knees, and bent low with the top of his head resting on the exhaust.

He grunted something, and Jevy handed him a wrench. The replacement pump was slowly fitted into place. Jevy's shirt and shorts were soaked within minutes.

With both men wedged tightly into the engine room, Welly decided to appear and ask if he was needed. No, in fact he was not. 'Just watch for the American,' Jevy said, wiping sweat from his forehead.

The mechanic cursed and flung wrenches for half an hour, then declared the pump ready for use. He started the engine, and spent a few minutes monitoring the oil pressure. He finally smiled, then gathered his tools.

Jevy drove downtown to the hotel to find Nate. The shy girl at the front desk had not seen Mr.

O'Riley. She phoned his room and no one answered. A maid walked by the desk and got herself quizzed. No, to her knowledge, he had not left the room. Reluctantly, the girl gave Jevy a key.

The door was locked but unchained, and Jevy entered slowly. The first odd thing he noticed was the empty bed with its disheveled sheets. Then he saw the bottles. One was empty and lying on its side on the floor; the other was half-filled. The room was very cool, the air conditioner running at full speed. He saw a bare foot, then stepped closer to see Nate, lying naked, wedged between the bed and the wall with a sheet pulled down and wrapped around his knees. Jevy gently kicked his foot, and the leg jerked.

At least he wasn't dead.

Jevy spoke to him and jabbed his shoulder, and after a few seconds a grunt was heard. A low, painful emission. Squatting on the bed, Jevy carefully clasped his hands under the nearest armpit and pulled Nate up from the floor, away from the wall, and managed to roll him onto the bed, where he quickly covered his privates with a sheet.

Another painful groan. Nate was on his back with one foot hanging off the bed, eyes swollen and still closed, hair wild, his breathing slow and labored. Jevy stood at the end of the bed and stared at him.

The maid and the girl from the front desk appeared at the crack in the door, and Jevy waved them away. He locked it, and picked up the empty bottle.

'It's time to go,' he said, and received no response whatsoever. Perhaps he should call Valdir, who in turn would report to the Americans who'd sent this poor drunk to Brazil. Maybe later.

'Nate!' he said loudly. 'Speak to me!'

No response. If he didn't rally soon, Jevy would call a doctor. A bottle and a half of vodka in one night could kill a man. Maybe his system was poisoned and he needed a hospital.

In the bathroom he soaked a towel with cold water, then wrapped it around Nate's neck. Nate began to squirm, and he opened his mouth in an effort to speak. 'Where am I?' he grunted, his tongue thick and sticky.

'In Brazil. In your hotel room.'

'I'm alive.'

'More or less.'

Jevy took an edge of the towel and wiped Nate's face and eyes. 'How do you feel?' he asked.

'I want to die,' Nate said, reaching for the towel. He took it, eased it into his mouth, and began sucking on it.

'I'll get some water,' Jevy said. He opened the refrigerator and removed a bottle of water. 'Can you lift your head?' he asked.

'No,' Nate grunted.

Jevy dripped water onto Nate's lips and tongue. Some of it rolled down his cheeks and into the towel. He didn't care. His head was splitting and pounding and his first thought was exactly how in hell did he wake up.

An eye opened, the right one, barely. The lids on the left were still matted together. Light scalded his brain and a wave of nausea rolled from his knees to his throat. With surprising suddenness, he flipped to one side, then rocked on all fours as the vomit shot forth.

Jevy jumped back, then went for another towel. He lingered in the bathroom, listening to the gagging and coughing. The sight of a naked man on his hands and knees in the middle of a bed puking his guts out was something he could do without. He turned on the shower and adjusted the water.

His deal with Valdir paid him a thousand reais to take Mr. O'Riley into the Pantanal, find the person he was searching for, then deliver him back to Corumbá.

It was good money, but he wasn't a nurse and he wasn't a baby-sitter. The boat was ready. If Nate couldn't answer the bell without an escort, then Jevy would move along to the next job.

There was a break in the nausea, and Jevy man-handled Nate into the bathroom, into the shower, where he crumpled onto the plastic floor. 'I'm sorry,' he said over and over. Jevy left him there, to drown for all he cared. He folded the sheets and tried to clean the mess, then he went downstairs for a pot of strong coffee.

It was almost two when Welly heard them coming. Jevy parked on the bank, his huge truck scattering rocks and waking fishermen as it roared to a stop. There was no sign of the American.

Then a head slowly lifted itself from somewhere in the cab. The eyes were covered with thick shades, and a cap was pulled as low as possible. Jevy opened the passenger door and helped Mr. O'Riley onto the rocks. Welly walked to the truck and grabbed Nate's bag and briefcase from the back. He wanted to meet Mr. O'Riley, but the timing was bad. He was quite ill, with bleached skin that was soaked with sweat, and he was too weak to walk on his own. Welly followed them to the edge of the water and helped guide them along the rickety plywood walkway onto the boat. Jevy practically carried Mr. O'Riley up the steps to the bridge, then along the catwalk to the small deck, where the hammock was waiting. He shoveled him into it.

When they returned to the deck, Jevy started the engine and Welly pulled the ropes. 'What's wrong with him?' Welly asked.

'He's drunk.'

'But it's only two o'clock.'

'He's been drunk for a long time.'

140

The *Santa Loura* eased away from the shore, and, moving upriver, slowly made its way past Corumbá.

Nate watched the city go by. The roof above him was a thick, green worn canvas stretched over a metal frame anchored to the deck by four poles. Two of these supported his hammock, which had rocked a bit just after the launch. The nausea crept back. He tried not to move. He wanted everything to be perfectly still. The boat moved gently upstream. The river was smooth. There was no wind at the moment, so Nate was able to lie deep in his hammock and stare at the dark green canvas above him and try to ponder things. The pondering was difficult, though, because his head spun and ached. Concentration was a challenge.

He had called Josh from his room just before checking out. With ice packs on his neck and a wastebasket between his feet he had dialed the number and tried mightily to sound normal. Jevy hadn't told Valdir. Valdir hadn't told Josh. No one knew but Nate and Jevy, and they had agreed to keep it that way. There was no alcohol on the boat, and Nate had promised sobriety until they returned. How was he supposed to find a drink in the Pantanal?

If Josh was worried, his voice didn't convey it. The firm was still closed for Christmas, et cetera, but he was busy as hell. The usual.

Nate said that he was doing just fine. The boat was adequate and now properly repaired. They were anxious to set sail. When he hung up he vomited again. And then he showered again. Then Jevy helped him to the elevator and through the lobby.

The river bent slightly and turned again, and Corumbá disappeared. The boat traffic around the city thinned as their journey gained momentum. Nate's vantage point gave him a view of the wake and of the muddy brown water bubbling behind them. The

141

Paraguay was less than a hundred yards wide and narrowed quickly around the bends. They passed a rickety boat laden with green bananas, and two small boys waved.

The steady knock of the diesel failed to stop, as Nate had hoped, but it became a low hum, a constant vibration throughout the entire vessel. There was no choice but to accept it. He tried swinging in the hammock, a gentle swing as a breeze crept through. The nausea was gone.

Don't think about Christmas, and home and children and broken memories, and don't think about your addictions. The crash is over, he told himself. The boat was his treatment center. Jevy was his counselor. Welly was his nurse. He'd dry out in the Pantanal, then never drink again.

How many times could he lie to himself?

The aspirin Jevy had given him wore off, and his head pounded again. He lapsed into a near-sleep, and awoke when Welly appeared with a bottle of water and a bowl of rice. He ate it with a spoon, his hands shaking so badly he spilled the rice on his shirt and in the hammock. It was warm and salty, and he ate every grain.

'*Mais?*' Welly asked.

Nate shook his head no, then sipped the water. He sank into the hammock and tried to nap.

SEVENTEEN

After a few false starts, the jet lag and fatigue and the aftereffects of the vodka caught up with him. The rice helped too, and Nate fell into a hard deep sleep. Welly checked on him every hour. 'He's snoring,' he reported to Jevy in the wheelhouse.

The sleep was dreamless. His nap lasted four hours as the *Santa Loura* inched ahead in the general direction of north, against the current and the wind. Nate awoke to the steady beat of the diesel and the sensation that the boat was not really moving. He rose gently in the hammock and peeked over the edge and studied the riverbank for signs of progress. The vegetation was dense. The river appeared completely uninhabited. There was a wake behind the boat and by staring at a tree he could tell that, yes, they were in fact going somewhere. But very slowly. The water was up because of the rains; navigation was easier but traffic upstream was not as fast.

The nausea and headaches were gone, but movements were still delicate. He began the challenge of removing himself from the hammock, primarily because he needed to urinate. He managed to safely place his feet on the deck without incident, and as he paused for a moment Welly appeared like a mouse and handed him a small cup of coffee.

Nate took the warm cup, cradled it and sniffed it.

Nothing had ever smelled better. '*Obrigado*,' he said. Thanks.

'*Sim*,' Welly said with an even brighter smile.

Nate sipped the precious sweet coffee and tried not to return Welly's stare. The kid was dressed in the standard river garb; old gym shorts, old tee shirt, and cheap rubber sandals that protected the soles of scarred and hardened feet. Like Jevy and Valdir, and most of the Brazilians he'd met so far, Welly had black hair and dark eyes, semi-Caucasian features, and a shade of brown skin that was lighter than some, darker than others, but a shade all his own.

I'm alive and sober, Nate thought, sipping. I have once again touched briefly the edge of hell and survived. I've bottomed, I've crashed, I've stared at the blurred image of my face and welcomed death, yet here I am sitting and breathing. Twice in three days I have uttered my last words. Maybe it's not my time.

'*Mais?*' Welly asked, nodding at the empty cup.

'*Sim*,' Nate replied, and handed it to him. Two steps and he was gone.

Stiff from the plane wreck and shaky from the vodka, Nate pulled himself up and stood unaided in the center of the deck, wobbly and bent at the knees. But he was able to stand, and this alone meant everything. Recovery was nothing but a series of small steps, small victories. String them together with no stumbles and no defeats and you're treated. Never cured, just treated or rehabbed or sanitized for a while. He'd done the puzzle before; celebrate every little piece.

Then the flat bottom of the boat brushed a sandbar, jolting it, and Nate fell hard against the hammock. It flipped him onto the deck, where his head cracked on a wooden plank. He scrambled to his feet and clutched the railing with one hand while rubbing his skull with the other. No blood, just a small knot, just

144

another little wound to the flesh. But the blow woke him, and when his eyes cleared, he moved slowly along the railing to the small cramped bridge, where Jevy sat on a stool, one hand draped over the wheel.

The quick Brazilian smile, then, 'How do you feel?' 'Much better,' Nate said, almost ashamed. But shame was an emotion Nate had abandoned years earlier. Addicts know no shame. You disgrace yourself so many times you become immune to it.

Welly bounced up the steps with coffee in both hands. He gave one to Nate and the other to Jevy, then took his perch on a narrow bench next to the captain.

The sun was beginning to fall behind the distant mountains of Bolivia, and clouds were forming to the north, directly in front of them. The air was light and much cooler. Jevy found his tee shirt and put it on. Nate feared another storm, but the river wasn't wide. Surely they could land the damned boat and tie it to a tree.

They approached a little square house, the first dwelling Nate had seen since Corumbá. There were signs of life: a horse and a cow, wash on the line, a canoe near the water. A man with a straw hat, a bona fide *pantaneiro*, stepped onto the porch and gave them a lazy wave.

Past the house, Welly pointed to a spot where thick undergrowth spilled into the river. '*Jacarés*,' he said. Jevy looked but seemed not to care. He'd seen a million alligators. Nate had seen only one, from the back of a horse, and as he gazed at the slimy reptiles watching them from the mud he was struck by how much smaller they appeared from the deck of a boat. He preferred the distance.

Something told him, though, that before his journey was over he would once again get too close for comfort. The johnboat trailing behind the *Santa Loura* would have to be used in their search for Rachel Lane.

He and Jevy would navigate small rivers, dodge undergrowth, wade through dark and weedy waters. Surely there would be *jacarés* and other species of vicious reptiles waiting for lunch.

But, oddly, Nate didn't care at the moment. So far in Brazil he'd proved himself quite resistant. It was an adventure, and his guide seemed fearless.

Grasping the handrail, he managed the steps down with great care, then shuffled along the narrow walkway past the cabin and the kitchen, where Welly had a pot on the propane stove. The diesel roared in the engine room. The last stop was the rest room, a small closet with a toilet, a dirty sink in a corner, and a flimsy showerhead swinging back and forth inches above his head. He relieved himself while studying the cord for the shower. He backed away and pulled it. Warm water with a slight brownish tint came down with sufficient force. It was obviously river water, scooped from an unlimited supply and presumably unfiltered. There was a wire basket above the door for a towel and a change of clothes, so you had to strip and somehow straddle the toilet while pulling the shower rope with one hand and bathing with the other.

What the hell, thought Nate. There simply wouldn't be many showers.

He looked in the pot on the stove and found it filled with rice and black beans and wondered if every meal would be the same. But he didn't really care. Food was not an issue with him. At Walnut Hill they dried you out while gently starving you. His appetite had shrunk months earlier.

He sat on the steps to the bridge, his back to the captain and Welly, and watched the river grow dark. In the dusk the wildlife prepared itself for the night. Birds flew low over the water, moving from tree to tree, looking for one last minnow or fish for the night.

They called to each other as the boat passed, their chants and shrieks rising well above the steady drone of the diesel. Water splashed along the banks as alligators moved about. Perhaps there were snakes in there too, large anacondas bedding down, but Nate preferred not to think about them. He felt quite safe on the *Santa Loura*. The breeze was slight and warmer now, and blowing at them. The storm had not materialized.

Time was racing somewhere else, but in the Pantanal time was of no consequence. He was slowly adjusting to it. He thought of Rachel Lane. What would the money do to her? No one, regardless of his level of faith and commitment, could remain the same. Would she leave with him, and go to the States to tend to her father's estate? She could always return to her Indians. How would she greet the news? How would she react to the sight of an American lawyer who'd tracked her down?

Welly strummed an old guitar and Jevy added some low and unrefined vocals. Their duet was pleasant, almost soothing; the song of simple men who lived by the day and not by the minute. Men who gave little thought to tomorrow and none for what may or may not happen next year. He envied them, at least while they were singing.

It was quite a comeback for a man who'd tried to drink himself to death a day earlier. He was enjoying the moment, happy to be alive, looking forward to the rest of his adventure. His past was truly in another world, light years away, in the cold wet streets of Washington.

Nothing good could happen there. He'd proved clearly that he could not stay clean living there, knowing the same people, doing the same work, ignoring the same old habits until he crashed. He would always crash.

147

Welly started a solo that snapped Nate away from his past. It was a slow mournful ballad that lasted until the river was completely dark. Jevy switched on two small floodlights, one on each side of the bow. The river was easy to navigate. It rose and fell with the seasons and never attained much depth. The boats were shallow and flat on the bottom, and built to take sandbars that sometimes got in the way. Jevy hit one just after dark, and the *Santa Loura* stopped moving. He reversed the engine, then thrust it forward, and after five minutes of this maneuvering they were free again. The boat was unsinkable.

In a corner of the cabin, not far from the four bunks, Nate ate alone at a table that was bolted to the floor. Welly served him the beans and rice, along with boiled chicken and an orange. He drank cold water from a bottle. A bulb on a light cord swung above his food. The cabin was hot and unventilated. Welly had suggested sleeping in the hammock.

Jevy arrived with a navigational map of the Pantanal. He wanted to plot their progress, and so far there had been little. They were indeed inching up the Paraguay, with only a tiny gap between their current position and Corumbá.

'The water is high,' Jevy explained. 'We'll go much faster on the return.'

The return was not something Nate had thought much about. 'No problem,' he said. Jevy pointed in various directions and made some more calculations. 'The first Indian village is in this area,' he said, pointing to a spot that looked weeks away, given their current pace.

'Guató?'

'*Sim*. Yes. I think we should go there first. If she is not there, then maybe someone knows where she is.'

'How long before we get there?'

'Two, maybe three days.'

148

Nate shrugged. Time had stopped. His wristwatch was in his pocket. His collection of hourly, daily, weekly, monthly planners was long forgotten. His trial calendar, the one great inviolate map of his life, had been tucked away in some secretary's drawer. He had cheated death, and so every day now was a gift.

'I have lots of reading,' he said.

Jevy carefully refolded the map. 'Are you okay?' he asked.

'I'm fine. I feel good.'

There was a lot more Jevy wanted to ask. Nate was not ready for a confessional. 'I'm fine,' he said again. 'This little trip will be good for me.'

He read for an hour at the table, under the swaying light, until he realized he was soaked with sweat. From his bunk he gathered insect repellent, a flashlight, and a stack of Josh's memos, and carefully made his way to the bow, then up the steps to the wheelhouse, where Welly was in command and Jevy was catching a nap. He sprayed his arms and legs, then crawled into the hammock, squirming and adjusting until his head was properly elevated above his butt. When things were perfectly balanced, and the hammock swung gently with the flow of the river, Nate clicked on his flashlight and began reading again.

EIGHTEEN

It was a simple hearing, a reading of a will, but the details were crucial. F. Parr Wycliff had thought of little else during his Christmas holiday. Every seat in his courtroom would be filled, with more spectators packed three deep against the walls. He'd worried so much that the day after Christmas he had walked around his empty courtroom pondering where to seat everyone.

And, typically, the press was out of control. They wanted cameras inside, and he had vehemently refused. They wanted cameras in the hallway peering in through the small square windows in the doors, and he said no. They wanted preferred seating; again, no. They wanted interviews with him, and he was stiff-arming them at the moment.

The lawyers too were showing their asses. Some wanted the entire hearing closed to the world, others wanted it televised, for obvious reasons. Some wanted the file sealed, others wanted copies of the will faxed over for their perusal. There were motions for this and that, requests to have seating here and there, concerns about who would be allowed inside the courtroom and who would not. Several of the lawyers went so far as to suggest that they be allowed to open and read the will. It was quite thick, you know, and they might be forced to explain some of the more intricate provisions as they read along.

Wycliff arrived early and met with the extra deputies he'd requested. They followed him, along with his secretary and his law clerk, around the courtroom as he made seat assignments and tested the sound system and counted chairs. He was very concerned with the details. Someone said a television news crew was attempting to set up camp down the hall, and he quickly dispatched a deputy to retake the area.

With the courtroom secure and organized, he retired to his office to tend to other matters. Concentration was difficult. Never again would his daily calendar promise such excitement. Quite selfishly, he hoped that the will of Troy Phelan was scandalously controversial; that it stripped money from one ex-family and awarded it to another. Or perhaps it screwed all of his crazy children and made someone else rich. A long nasty will contest would certainly liven up Wycliff's rather mundane career in probate. He'd be the center of the storm, one that would no doubt rage for years, with eleven billion at stake.

He was certain this would happen. Alone, with his door locked, he spent fifteen minutes ironing his robe.

The first spectator was a reporter who arrived just after eight, and because he was the first he received the full treatment from the jumpy security detail blocking the double doors to the courtroom. He was greeted gruffly, asked to produce a picture ID and sign a sheet for journalists, got his steno pad inspected as if it were a grenade, then was directed through the metal detector, where two thick guards were obviously disappointed when no sirens erupted as he passed through. He was grateful he did not get strip-searched. Once inside, he was led down the center aisle by yet another uniformed officer to a spot two rows from the

151

front. He was relieved to get a seat. The courtroom was empty.

The hearing was set for ten, and by nine a nice crowd had assembled in the foyer outside the courtroom. Security was taking its time with the paperwork and the searches. A line formed down the hall.

Some of the lawyers for the Phelan heirs arrived in a rush and became instantly irritated with the delay in getting into the courtroom. Harsh words were exchanged; threats were made and received by the lawyers and by the deputies. Someone sent for Wycliff, but he was polishing his boots and didn't want to be disturbed. And, like a bride before the wedding, he didn't want to be seen by the guests. The heirs and the lawyers were given priority, and this eased the tense situation.

The courtroom slowly filled. Tables were placed in a U-shape, with the Judge's bench at the open end, so that His Honor could look down from his perch and see everyone: lawyers, heirs, spectators. To the left of the bench, in front of the jury box, was a long table where the Phelans were being placed. Troy Junior was first, with Biff in tow. They were directed to a spot nearest the bench, where they sat and huddled with three lawyers from their legal team while working desperately to appear somber and at the same time ignore everyone else in the courtroom. Biff was furious because the security detail had confiscated her cell phone. She couldn't make real estate calls.

Ramble was next. For the occasion he had neglected his hair, which still bore streaks of lime green and hadn't been washed in two weeks. His rings were in full glory – ear, nose, eyebrow. Black leather jacket with no sleeves, temporary tattoos on his skinny arms. Ragged jeans; old boots. Surly attitude. He caught the attention of the journalists when he walked down the aisle. He was coddled and fussed over every step of the way by Yancy, his aging hippie lawyer, who had somehow managed to hang on to his prized client.

Yancy took a quick look at the seating scheme, and asked to sit as far away from Troy Junior as possible. The deputy complied and put them at the end of a temporary table facing the bench. Ramble sank into his chair, green hair hanging over the back of it. The spectators watched him in horror – this thing was about to inherit a half a billion dollars? The potential for mayhem seemed limitless.

Geena Phelan Strong was next with her husband Cody and two of their lawyers. They gauged the distance between Troy Junior and Ramble, then split the difference and sat as far away from both as possible. Cody was particularly burdened and earnest and immediately began reviewing some important papers with one of his lawyers. Geena just gawked at Ramble; she couldn't believe they were half-brother and -sister.

Amber the stripper made a grand entrance in a short skirt and low-cut blouse that gave away most of her expensive breasts. The deputy escorting her down the aisle couldn't believe his good fortune. He chatted her up along the way, eyes glued to the edge of her blouse. Rex followed behind in a dark suit, carrying a bulky briefcase as if he had serious work today. Behind him was Hark Gettys, still the noisiest advocate of the bunch. Hark brought with him two of his new associates; his firm was growing by the week. Since Amber and Biff weren't speaking, Rex quickly intervened and pointed to a spot between Ramble and Geena.

The tables were filling; the gaps were closing. Before long some of the Phelans would be sitting close to each other.

Ramble's mother Tira brought two young men of about the same age. One had tight jeans and a hairy chest; the other was well groomed in dark pinstripes. She was sleeping with the gigolo. The lawyer would get his on the back-end.

Another gap was filled. On the other side of the bar, the courtroom was alive with the hum of gossip and speculation. 'No wonder the old man jumped,' one reporter said to another as they examined the Phelans.

The Phelan grandchildren were forced to sit with the spectators and common folk. They huddled with their small entourages and support groups and giggled nervously as fate was about to swing their way.

Libbigail Jeter arrived with her husband Spike, the three-hundred-twenty-pound ex-biker, and they waddled down the aisle, as out of place as anyone, though they'd seen their share of courtrooms. They followed Wally Bright, their yellow page lawyer. Wally wore a spotted raincoat that dragged the floor, scuffed wing tips, and a polyester tie that was twenty years old, and if the spectators had voted right then he would've easily won the award for the worst-dressed lawyer. He carried his papers in an expandable file, one that had been used for countless divorces and other matters. For some reason, Bright had never purchased a briefcase. He'd finished tenth in his class in night school.

They went straight for the widest gap, and as they were taking their seats Bright began the noisy process of removing his raincoat. The ragged hem of it brushed against the neck of one of Hark's nameless associates, an earnest young man already bothered by Bright's body odor.

'If you don't mind!' he said sharply, swinging a backhand toward Bright, and missing. The words cracked through the tense and edgy air. Heads jerked around the tables as important documents were instantly ignored. Everybody hated everybody.

'Sorry!' Bright responded with great sarcasm. Two

154

deputies moved forward to intervene if necessary. But the raincoat found a place under the table without further incident, and Bright finally managed to seat himself, next to Libbigail, with Spike sitting on the other side stroking his beard and staring at Troy Junior as if he'd love to slap him.

Few people in the courtroom expected the brief skirmish to be the last among the Phelans.

You die with eleven billion, and people care about your last will and testament. Especially if there's a chance that one of the world's great fortunes is about to be fed to the vultures. The tabloids were there, along with the local papers and all the important financial magazines. The three rows Wycliff had designated for the press were full by nine-thirty. The journalists had a delightful time watching the Phelans gather in front of them. Three artists worked feverishly; the panorama before them was rich with inspiration. The punk with the green hair received more than his share of sketches.

Josh Stafford made his appearance at nine-fifty. Tip Durban was with him, along with two other members of the firm and a couple of paralegals to round out the team. Stern and somber-faced, they took seats at their table, a rather spacious one compared to the cramped quarters holding all the Phelans and all their lawyers. Josh placed a single thick file in front of him, and all eyes were immediately upon it. Inside was what appeared to be a document, almost two inches thick and very similar to what old Troy had signed on video just nineteen days earlier.

They couldn't help staring at it. Everyone but Ramble. Virginia law allowed heirs to receive early distributions if the estate was liquid and there was no concern about the payment of debts and taxes. Estimates from the Phelan lawyers ranged from a low of ten million per heir, all the way to Bright's guess of fifty million. Bright in his entire life had never seen fifty thousand.

At ten the deputies locked the doors, and upon some unseen cue Judge Wycliff emerged from an opening behind the bench, and the room was silent. He eased into the chair, his crisp robe settling around him, and smiled. 'Good morning,' he said into the microphone.

Everyone smiled back. To his great satisfaction, the room was filled to capacity. A quick deputy count revealed eight armed and ready. He studied the Phelans; there were no gaps left. Some of their lawyers were practically touching one another.

'Are all of the parties present?' he asked. Heads shook from around the tables.

'I need to identify everyone,' he said, reaching for papers. 'The first petition was filed by Rex Phelan.' Before the words settled, Hark Gettys was on his feet, clearing his throat.

'Your Honor, I'm Hark Gettys,' he boomed toward the bench. 'And I represent Mr. Rex Phelan.'

'Thank you. You may keep your seat.'

He went around the tables, methodically taking names of the heirs and the lawyers. All the lawyers. The reporters scribbled them as fast as the Judge. Six heirs in all, three ex-wives. Everyone was present.

'Twenty-two lawyers,' Wycliff mumbled to himself.

'Do you have the will, Mr. Stafford?' he asked.

Josh stood, holding a different file. 'I do.'

'Would you please take the witness stand?'

Josh made his way around the tables and past the court reporter to the witness stand, where he raised his right hand and swore to tell the truth.

'You represented Troy Phelan?' Wycliff asked.

'I did. For a number of years.'

'Did you prepare a will for him?'

'I prepared several.'

156

'Did you prepare his last will?'

There was a pause, and as it grew longer the Phelans inched closer.

'No, I did not,' Josh said slowly, looking at the vultures. The words were soft, but they cut through the air like thunder. The Phelan lawyers reacted much more quickly than the Phelan heirs, several of whom weren't sure what to make of it. But it was serious, and unexpected. Another layer of tension settled around the tables. The courtroom grew even quieter.

'Who prepared his last will and testament?' Wycliff asked, like a bad actor reading a script.

'Mr. Phelan himself.'

It wasn't so. They had seen the old man sit at the table with lawyers all around him, and the three shrinks – Zadel, Flowe, and Theishen – directly across the table. He'd been declared sane on the spot, and seconds later had taken a thick will prepared by Stafford and one of his associates, declared it to be his, and signed it.

There was no dispute about this.

'Oh my God,' Hark Gettys said, under his breath but loud enough for everyone to hear.

'When did he sign it?' Wycliff asked.

'Moments before he jumped to his death.'

'Is it handwritten?'

'It is.'

'Did he sign it in your presence?'

'He did. There were other witnesses. The signing was also videotaped.'

'Please hand me the will.'

Josh deliberately withdrew a single envelope from the file and passed it up to His Honor. It looked awfully small. There was no way it contained enough language to convey to the Phelans what was rightfully theirs.

'What the hell is this?' Troy Junior hissed at the nearest lawyer. But the lawyer couldn't respond.

The envelope held only one sheet of yellow paper. Wycliff removed it slowly for all to see, unfolded it carefully, then studied it for a moment.

Panic seized the Phelans, but there was nothing they could do. Had the old man screwed them one last time? Was the money slipping away? Maybe he had changed his mind and given them even more. Around the tables they nudged and elbowed their lawyers, all of whom were remarkably quiet.

Wycliff cleared his throat and leaned a bit closer to the microphone. 'I'm holding here a one-page document purporting to be a will handwritten by Troy Phelan. I will read it straight through:

'"The last testament of Troy L. Phelan. I, Troy L. Phelan, being of sound and disposing mind and memory, do hereby expressly revoke all former wills and codicils executed by me, and dispose of my estate as follows:

'"To my children, Troy Phelan, Jr., Rex Phelan, Libbigail Jeter, Mary Ross Jackman, Geena Strong, and Ramble Phelan, I give each a sum of money necessary to pay off all the debts of each as of today. Any debts incurred after today will not be covered by this gift. If any of these children attempt to contest this will, then this gift shall be nullified as to that child."'

Even Ramble heard the words, and understood them. Geena and Cody started crying softly. Rex leaned forward, elbows on the table, face buried in his hands, his mind numb. Libbigail looked past Bright to Spike and said, 'That son of a bitch.' Spike concurred. Mary Ross covered her eyes as her lawyer rubbed her knee. Her husband rubbed the other one. Only Troy Junior managed a poker face, but not for much longer.

There was more damage yet to come. Wycliff wasn't finished. '"To my ex-wives, Lillian, Janie, and Tira, I

158

give nothing. They were adequately provided for in the divorces."'

At that moment, Lillian, Janie, and Tira were wondering what the hell they were doing in the courtroom. Had they really expected to receive more cash from a man they hated? They felt the stares and tried to hide among their lawyers.

The reporters and journalists were downright giddy. They wanted to take notes, but they were afraid of missing a single word. Some couldn't help but grin.

"'The remainder of my estate I give to my daughter Rachel Lane, born on November, 2, 1954, at Catholic Hospital in New Orleans, Louisiana, to a woman named Evelyn Cunningham, now deceased.'"

Wycliff paused, though not for dramatic effect. With only two small paragraphs left, the damage was done. The eleven billion had been given to an illegitimate heir he'd not read about. The Phelans sitting before him had been stripped. He couldn't help but look at them.

"'I appoint my trusted lawyer, Joshua Stafford, as executor of this will, and grant unto him broad discretionary powers in its administration.'"

For the moment they had forgotten about Josh. But there he sat, in the box like the innocent witness of a car wreck, and they glared at him with as much hatred as possible. How much had he known? Was he a conspirator? No doubt he could've done something to prevent this.

Josh fought to keep a straight face.

"'This document is intended to be a holographic will. Every word has been written by my hand, and I hereby sign it.'" Wycliff lowered it and said, 'The testament was signed by Troy L. Phelan at three P.M. on December 9, 1996.'

He laid it down, and looked around the courtroom, the epicenter. The quake was ending and now it was

159

time for the aftershocks. The Phelans sat low in their seats, some rubbing eyes and foreheads, others staring wildly at the walls. For the moment, all twenty-two lawyers were incapable of speech.

The shocks rippled through the rows of spectators, where, oddly, a few smiles could be seen. Ah, it was the media, suddenly anxious to race from the room and start reporting.

Amber sobbed loudly, then caught herself. She'd met Troy only once, and he'd made a crude advance. Her grief was not for the loss of a loved one. Geena cried quietly, as did Mary Ross. Libbigail and Spike chose to curse instead. 'Don't worry,' Bright said, waving them off as if he could remedy this injustice in a matter of days.

Biff glared at Troy Junior, and the seeds of a divorce were planted. Since the suicide, he'd been especially arrogant and condescending to her. She'd tolerated it for obvious reasons, but no longer. She relished the first fight, one that would no doubt begin just a few feet outside the courtroom doors.

Other seeds were planted. For the thick-skinned lawyers, the surprise was received, absorbed, then shaken off as instinctively as a duck shakes off water. They were about to get rich. Their clients were heavily in debt with no relief in sight. They had no choice but to contest the will. Litigation would rage for years.

'When do you anticipate probating the will?' Wycliff asked Josh.

'Within a week.'

'Very well. You may step down.'

Josh returned to his seat, triumphant, as the lawyers began shuffling papers and pretending everything was fine.

'We are adjourned.'

160

NINETEEN

There were three fights in the hallway after adjournment. Fortunately, none involved Phelans fighting Phelans. Those would come later.

A mob of reporters waited outside the courtroom doors as the Phelans were consoled inside by their lawyers. Troy Junior was the first to exit, and he was immediately surrounded by a pack of wolves, several with microphones in the attack position. He was hungover to begin with, and now that he was half a billion dollars poorer he was in no mood to talk about his father.

'Are you surprised?' some idiot asked, from behind a microphone.

'Damned right,' he said, trying to walk through the group.

'Who is Rachel Lane?' asked another.

'I guess she's my sister,' he snapped.

A skinny little boy with stupid eyes and a bad complexion stopped directly in front of him, thrust a tape recorder in his face, and asked, 'How many illegitimate children did your father have?'

Troy Junior instinctively shoved the tape recorder back at him. It landed sharply just above his nose, and as he fell back Troy Junior launched a wild left hook that popped him in the ear and knocked him down. In

161

the commotion, a deputy pushed Troy Junior in another direction and they made a quick escape.

Ramble spit on another reporter, who had to be restrained by a colleague who reminded him the kid was underage.

The third skirmish happened when Libbigail and Spike lumbered out of the courtroom behind Wally Bright. 'No comment!' Bright yelled at the horde closing ranks around them. 'No comment! Please get out of the way!'

Libbigail, who was crying, tripped over a TV cable and tumbled into a reporter, who also fell. There were shouts and curses, and as the reporter was on all fours and getting to his feet, Spike kicked him in the ribs. He squealed and fell flat again, and as he was thrashing about trying to get up, his foot caught the edge of Libbigail's dress, and she slapped him for good measure. Spike was about to slaughter him when a deputy intervened.

Deputies broke up each fight, always siding with the Phelans over the reporters. They helped rush the beleaguered heirs and their lawyers down the stairs, through the lobby, and out of the building.

Lawyer Grit, who represented Mary Ross Phelan Jackman, was overcome by the sight of so many reporters. The First Amendment seized him, or at least his own rudimentary understanding of it, and he felt compelled to speak freely. With his arm around his distraught client, he grimly offered their reaction to the surprise will. It was obviously the work of a demented man. How else could you explain the passing of such a great fortune to an unknown heir? His client adored her father, loved him deeply, worshiped him, and as Grit babbled on and on about the incredible love between father and daughter, Mary Ross finally took the hint and began crying. Grit himself appeared on the verge of tears. Yes, they would fight. They would battle this grave injustice to the U.S. Supreme Court. Why? Because this was not the work of the Troy Phelan they knew. Bless his heart. He loved his children, and they loved him. Theirs was an incredible bond, forged through tragedy and hardship. They would fight because their beloved father was not himself when he scribbled this ghastly document.

Josh Stafford was in no hurry to leave. He spoke quietly to Hark Gettys and some of the attorneys from the other tables. He promised to send them copies of the hideous will. Things were initially cordial but hostilities were growing by the minute. A reporter he knew from the *Post* was waiting in the hall, and Josh spent ten minutes with him while saying nothing. Of particular interest was Rachel Lane; her history and whereabouts. There were lots of questions, but Josh had no answers.

Surely Nate would find her before anyone else.

The story grew. It shot from the courthouse on the waves of the latest telecommunications gadgets and hi-tech hardware. The reporters scrambled with cell phones and laptops and pagers, talking without thinking.

The major wires began running the news twenty minutes after adjournment, and an hour later the first round-the-clock news-gab-a-thon broke into its running series of repetitive stories to go live to a reporter in front of a camera outside the courthouse. 'Stunning news here . . .' she began and then told the story, getting most of it right.

Seated in the rear of the courtroom was Pat Solomon, the last person selected by Troy to run The Phelan Group. He'd been CEO for six years, six very uneventful and very profitable years.

He left the courthouse without being recognized by

163

any reporter. As he rode away, in the back of his limo, Solomon attempted to analyze Troy's last bombshell. He was not shocked by it. After working for Troy for twenty years nothing surprised him. The reaction of his idiot children and their lawyers was comforting. Solomon had once been assigned the impossible task of finding within the company a job that Troy Junior could perform without causing a dip in quarterly profits. It had been a nightmare. Spoiled, immature, badly educated, and lacking basic management skills, Troy Junior had run roughshod through an entire division in Minerals before Solomon was given the green light from above to sack him.

A few years later, a similar episode involved Rex and his pursuit of his father's approval and money. In the end, Rex had gone to Troy in an effort to remove Solomon.

The wives and other children had butted in for years, but Troy had held fast. His private life was a fiasco, but nothing hampered his beloved company.

Solomon and Troy had never been close. In fact, no one, perhaps with the exception of Josh Stafford, had ever managed to become a confidant. The parade of blondes had shared the obvious intimacies, but Troy had no friends. And as he withdrew and declined both physically and mentally, those who ran the company sometimes whispered about its ownership. Surely Troy would not leave it to his children.

He hadn't, at least not the usual suspects.

The board was waiting, on the fourteenth floor, in the same conference room where Troy had produced his testament, then taken flight. Solomon described the scene in the courtroom, and his colorful narrative became humorous. Thoughts of the heirs gaining control had caused great discomfort among the board. Troy Junior had let it be known that he and his

164

siblings had the votes to seize a majority, and that he planned to clean house and show some real profits.

They wanted to know about Janie, wife number two. She'd worked for the company as a secretary until her promotion to mistress, then to wife, and after reaching the top she had been particularly abusive to many of the employees. Troy banned her from the corporate headquarters.

'When she left she was crying,' Solomon said happily.

'And Rex?' asked a director, the chief financial officer who had once been fired by Rex in an elevator.

'Not a happy boy. He's under investigation, you know.'

They talked about most of the children and all of the wives, and the meeting grew festive.

'I counted twenty-two lawyers,' Solomon said with a smile. 'Talk about a sad bunch.'

Since it was an informal board meeting, Josh's absence was of no consequence. The head of Legal declared the will to be a stroke of great luck after all. They had to worry about only one, unknown heir, as opposed to six idiots.

'Any idea where this woman is?'

'None,' answered Solomon. 'Maybe Josh knows.'

By late afternoon, Josh had been forced from his office and had retreated to a small library in the basement of his building. His secretary stopped counting phone messages at a hundred and twenty. The lobby off the main entrance had been crammed with reporters since late morning. He'd left behind strict instructions with his secretaries that no one should disturb him for an hour. So the knock on the door was especially aggravating.

'Who is it?' he shot at the door.

'It's an emergency, sir,' answered a secretary.

'Come in.'

Her head entered just far enough to look him in the face and say, 'It's Mr. O'Riley.' Josh stopped rubbing his temples and actually smiled. He glanced around the room and remembered there were no phones. She took two steps and placed a portable on the table, then disappeared.

'Nate,' he said into the receiver.

'That you, Josh?' came the reply. The volume was fine but the words were a little scratchy. The reception was better than most car phones.

'Yes, can you hear me, Nate?'

'Yes.'

'Where are you?'

'I'm on the satellite, on the back of my little yacht, floating down the Paraguay River. Can you hear me?'

'Yes, fine. Are you okay, Nate?'

'I'm wonderful, having a ball, just a little boat trouble.'

'What kind of trouble?'

'Well, the propeller snagged a line of old rope, and the engine choked down. My crew is attempting to unravel it. I'm supervising.'

'You sound great.'

'It's an adventure, right, Josh?'

'Of course. Any sign of the girl?'

'Not a chance. We're a couple of days away at best, and now we're floating backward. I'm not sure we'll ever get there.'

'You have to, Nate. We read the will this morning in open court. The whole world will soon be looking for Rachel Lane.'

'I wouldn't worry about that. She's safe.'

'I wish I were with you.'

The edge of a cloud nipped the signal. 'What did you say?' Nate asked, louder.

'Nothing. So you'll see her in a couple of days, huh.'

'If we're lucky. The boat runs around the clock, but we're going upriver, and it's the rainy season so the rivers are full and the currents are strong. Plus, we're not exactly sure where we're going. Two days is very optimistic, assuming we get the damned propeller fixed.'

'So the weather's bad,' Josh said, almost at random. There wasn't much to discuss. Nate was alive and well and moving in the general direction of the target.

'It's hot as hell and it rains five times a day. Other than that it's lovely.'

'Any snakes?'

'A couple. Anacondas longer than the boat. Lots of alligators. Rats as big as dogs. They call them *capivaras*. They live at the edge of the rivers among the alligators, and when these people get hungry enough they kill them and eat them.'

'But you have plenty of food?'

'Oh yes. Our cargo is black beans and rice. Welly cooks them for me three times a day.'

Nate's voice was sharp and filled with adventure.

'Who's Welly?'

'My deckhand. Right now he's under the boat in twelve feet of water, holding his breath and cutting rope from the prop. Like I said, I'm supervising.'

'Stay out of the water, Nate.'

'Are you kidding? I'm on the upper deck. Look, I gotta run. I'm using juice and I haven't found a way to recharge these batteries.'

'When will you call again?'

'I'll try and wait until after I find Rachel Lane.'

'Good idea. But call if you have trouble.'

'Trouble? Why would I call you, Josh? There's not a damned thing in the world you can do.'

'You're right. Don't call.'

TWENTY

The storm hit at dusk, as Welly was boiling rice in the kitchen and Jevy was watching the river grow dark. The wind woke Nate, a sudden howling blast that shook the hammock and snapped him to his feet. Thunder and lightning followed. He walked to Jevy's side and looked north into a vast blackness. 'A big storm,' Jevy said, seemingly indifferent.

Shouldn't we park this thing? Nate thought. At least find shallow water? Jevy didn't appear concerned; his nonchalance was somewhat comforting. When the rain started, Nate went below for his rice and beans. He ate in silence with Welly in the corner of the cabin. The bulb above them swayed as the wind rocked the boat. Heavy raindrops battered the windows.

On the bridge, Jevy put on a yellow poncho stained with grease and fought the rain hitting him sharply in the face. The tiny wheelhouse had no windows. The two floodlights attempted to show the way through the darkness, but revealed no more than fifty feet of churning water in front of them. Jevy knew the river well, and he'd been through worse storms.

Reading was difficult with the boat swaying and rolling. After a few minutes of it, Nate felt sick. In his bag he found a knee-length poncho with a hood. Josh had thought of everything. Clutching the railings, he slowly made his way up the stairs where Welly sat huddled next to the wheelhouse, drenched.

The river bent to the east, toward the heart of the Pantanal, and when they turned, the wind caught them broadside. The boat rocked and threw Nate and Welly hard into the railings. Jevy braced himself with the door of the wheelhouse, his thick arms holding himself in place and maintaining control.

The gusts became relentless, one after the other, only seconds apart, and the *Santa Loura* stopped moving upstream. The storm shoved it toward shore. The rain pellets were hard and cold now, and poured down upon them in sheets. Jevy found a long flashlight in a box beside the wheel, and gave it to Welly.

'Find the bank!' he yelled, his voice struggling over the howling wind and heavy rain.

Nate grappled along the railings to a spot next to Welly because he too wanted to see where they might be headed. But the beam caught nothing but rain, rain so thick it looked like fog swirling above the water.

Then lightning came to their aid. A flash, and they saw the dense black growth of the riverbank not far away. The wind was pushing them toward it. Welly shouted and Jevy yelled something back just as another gust slammed into the boat and tipped it violently to its starboard side. The sudden jolt knocked the flashlight out of Welly's hand and they watched it disappear into the water.

Crouched on the walkway, clutching the railing, soaked and shivering, it occurred to Nate that one of two things was about to happen. And neither was within their control. First, the boat was going to capsize. If it didn't, then they were about to be shoved into the side of the river, into the quagmire where the reptiles lived. He was only slightly scared until he thought about the papers.

Under no circumstances could the papers be lost.

He suddenly stood, just as the boat tipped again, and he almost went over the rail. 'I have to go below!' he yelled to Jevy, who was gripping the wheel. The captain was scared too.

With his back to the wind, Nate crept down the grated steps. The deck was slick with diesel fuel. A drum had tipped over and was leaking. He tried to lift it, but it would take two men. He ducked into the cabin, flung his poncho in a corner, and went for his briefcase under the cot. The wind slammed into the boat. It pitched and caught Nate with his hands free. He landed hard against the wall with his feet above his head.

There were two things he couldn't lose, he decided. First, the papers; second, the SatFone. Both were in the briefcase, which was new and nice but certainly not waterproof. He clutched it across his chest and lay on his bunk while the *Santa Loura* rode out the storm.

The knocking stopped. He hoped Jevy had killed the engine with a switch. He could hear their footsteps directly above him. We're about to hit the bank, he thought, and it's best for the prop to be disengaged. Surely it wasn't engine trouble.

The lights went out. Complete darkness.

Lying there in the dark, swaying with the pitch and roll, waiting for the *Santa Loura* to crash into the riverbank, Nate had a horrible thought. If she refused to sign the acknowledgment and/or the waiver, a return trip might be necessary. Months down the road, or maybe years, someone, probably Nate himself, would be forced to trek back up the Paraguay and inform the world's richest missionary that things were finalized and the money was hers.

He'd read that missionaries took furloughs – long breaks in their work when they returned to the States and recharged their batteries. Why couldn't Rachel take a furlough, maybe even fly home with him, and hang around long enough for Daddy's mess to get cleaned up? For eleven billion, that seemed the least she could do. He'd suggest it to her, if he ever got the chance to meet her.

There was a crash, and Nate was tossed to the floor. They were in the brush.

The *Santa Loura* was flat-bottomed, built, like all the boats in the Pantanal, to scrape across sandbars and take the hits of river debris. After the storm, Jevy started the engine and for half an hour worked the boat back and forth, slowly dislodging it from the sand and mud. When they were free, Welly and Nate cleared the deck of limbs and brush. Their search of the boat found no new passengers, no snakes or *jacarés*. During a quick coffee break, Jevy told the story of an anaconda that had found its way on board, years ago. Attacked a sleeping deckhand.

Nate said he didn't particularly care for snake stories. His search was slow and deliberate.

The clouds went away and a beautiful half-moon appeared above the river. Welly brewed a pot of coffee. After the violence of the storm, the Pantanal seemed determined to be perfectly still. The river was as smooth as glass. The moon guided them, disappearing when they turned with the river, but always there when they headed north again.

Because Nate was half-Brazilian now, he wore no wristwatch. Time mattered little. It was late, probably midnight. The rain had battered them for four hours.

Nate slept a few hours in the hammock, and awakened just after dawn. He found Jevy snoring on his bunk in the tiny cabin behind the wheelhouse. Welly was at the wheel, himself half-asleep. Nate sent him for coffee and took the helm of the *Santa Loura*.

The clouds were back, but no rain was in sight. The

171

river was littered with limbs and leaves, the rubble and remains from last night's storm. It was wide and there was no traffic, so Nate the skipper sent Welly to the hammock for a nap while he commanded the vessel.

It beat the hell out of a courtroom. Shirtless, shoeless, sipping sweet coffee while leading an expedition into the heart of the world's largest swamp. In the glory days, he would've been racing to a trial somewhere, juggling ten things at once, phones stuck in every pocket. He didn't really miss it; no lawyer in his right mind really missed the courtroom. But he would never admit that.

The boat practically guided itself. With Jevy's binoculars, he watched the shoreline for *jacarés*, snakes, and *capivaras*. And he counted tuiuius, the tall, white, long-necked bird with a red head that had become the symbol of the Pantanal. There were twelve in one flock on a sandbar. They stood still and watched the boat go by.

The captain and his sleepy crew steamed northward, as the sky turned orange and the day began. Deeper and deeper into the Pantanal, uncertain where their journey would lead them.

TWENTY-ONE

The coordinator of South American Missions was a woman named Neva Collier. She was born in an igloo in Newfoundland, where her parents had worked for twenty years among the Inuit natives. She herself had spent eleven years working in the mountains of New Guinea, so she knew firsthand the trials and challenges of the nine hundred or so people whose activities she coordinated.

And she was the only person who knew that Rachel Porter had once been Rachel Lane, illegitimate daughter of Troy Phelan. After med school, Rachel had changed names in an effort to erase as much of her past as possible. She had no family; both adoptive parents had died. No siblings. No aunts, uncles, or cousins. At least none that she knew. She had only Troy, and she was desperate to remove him from her life. After completing the World Tribes seminary, Rachel had confided her secrets to Neva Collier.

The higher-ups at World Tribes knew Rachel had secrets, but not a history that would impede her yearning to serve God. She was a doctor, a graduate of their seminary, a dedicated and humble servant of Christ who was eager to enter the mission field. They promised never to divulge anything about Rachel, including her exact location in South America.

Sitting in her small neat office in Houston, Neva

read the extraordinary account of the reading of Mr. Phelan's will. She had been following the story since the suicide.

Communication with Rachel was a slow process. They exchanged mail twice a year, in March and in August, and Rachel usually called once a year from a pay phone in Corumbá when she went there for supplies. Neva had spoken to her the year before. Her last furlough had been in 1992. After six weeks she'd abandoned it and returned to the Pantanal. She had no interest in being in the United States, she had confided in Neva. It was not her home. She belonged with her people.

Judging from the lawyers' comments in the article, the issue was far from settled. Neva put the file away and decided to wait. At the appropriate time, whenever that might be, she would inform her governing board of Rachel's old identity.

She hoped that moment would never come. But how, exactly, does one hide eleven billion dollars?

No one really expected the lawyers to agree on where to meet. Each firm insisted on choosing the site of the summit. The fact that they agreed to actually get together, on such short notice, was monumental.

So they met at a hotel, the Ritz in Tysons Corner, in a banquet room where tables had been hastily wedged together in a perfect square. When the door was finally closed, there were close to fifty people in the room, for every firm felt obliged to bring along extra associates and paralegals and even secretaries to impress.

The tension was almost visible. No Phelans were present, only their legal teams.

Hark Gettys called the meeting to order, and did the wise thing of cracking a very funny joke. Like humor in the courtroom, where people were anxious and not expecting comedy, the laughter was loud and healthy.

He suggested they go around the table and let one lawyer per Phelan heir say what was on his or her mind. He would go last.

An objection was lodged. 'Who exactly are the heirs?'

'The six Phelan children,' Hark responded.

'What about the three wives?'

'They're not heirs. They're ex-wives.'

This upset the attorneys for the wives, and after a heated battle they threatened to walk out. Someone suggested allowing them to speak anyway, and this solved the problem.

Grit, the feisty litigator hired by Mary Ross Phelan Jackman and her husband, stood and made a plea for war. 'We have no choice but to challenge the will,' he said. 'There was no undue influence, so we have to prove the old buzzard was crazy. Hell, he jumped to his death. And he gave one of the world's great fortunes to some unknown heir. Sounds crazy to me. We can find psychiatrists who'll testify.'

'What about the three who examined him before he jumped?' someone shot from across the table.

'That was stupid,' Grit snarled back. 'It was a setup, and you guys fell for it.'

This upset Hark and the other lawyers who had agreed on the mental exam. 'Perfect hindsight,' Yancy said, and that stalled Grit for the moment.

The legal team for Geena and Cody Strong was headed by a woman named Langhorne, who was tall and thick and wore an Armani dress. She had once been a professor at Georgetown Law and when she addressed the group she did so with the air of one who knew everything. Point one: There were only two grounds for contesting a will in Virginia – undue influence and lack of mental capacity. Since no one knew Rachel Lane, it was safe to assume she had little or no contact with Troy. Therefore, it would be

175

difficult if not impossible to prove she somehow unduly influenced him when he made his last will. Point two: Lack of testamentary capacity was their only hope. Point three: Forget fraud. Sure he lured them into the mental exam under false pretenses, but a will cannot be attacked on the grounds of fraud. A contract yes, a will no. They had already done the research and she had the cases, if anyone cared.

She worked from a brief of some sort, and was impeccably prepared. No less than six others from her firm huddled behind her in support.

Point four: The mental exam would be very difficult to crack. She'd seen the video. They would probably lose the war, but they could get paid for the battle. Her conclusion: Challenge the will with a fury, and hope for a lucrative out-of-court settlement.

Her lecture lasted for ten minutes, and covered little new ground. She was tolerated without interruption because she was female and the chip was almost visible.

Wally Bright, he of the night school, was next, and in sharp contrast to Ms. Langhorne, he raged and railed at injustice in general. Nothing was prepared – no brief, no notes, no thoughts about what he would say next, just a lot of hot air by a brawler who perpetually flew by the seat of his pants.

Two of Lillian's lawyers stood at the same time, and appeared to be joined at the hip. Both wore black suits, and had the pale faces of estate lawyers who rarely saw the sun. One would start a sentence and the other would finish it. One would ask a rhetorical question, the other had the answer. One mentioned a file, the other pulled it from a briefcase. The tag team was efficient, to the point, and repeated in succinct fashion what had already been said.

A consensus was quickly emerging. Fight, for (a) there was little to lose, (b) there was nothing else to do, and (c) it was the only way to force a settlement. Not to mention (d), wherein they would get paid handsomely by the hour for fighting.

Yancy was particularly forceful in urging the use of litigation. And rightly so. Ramble was the only minor among the heirs, and had no debts to speak of. The trust that would pay him five million on his twenty-first had been established decades earlier, and could not be revoked. With five million guaranteed, Ramble was in far better shape financially than any of his siblings. With nothing to lose, why not sue for more?

An hour passed before someone mentioned the contest clause in the will. The heirs, excluding Ramble, ran the risk of losing what little Troy left them if they contested the will. This issue was given slight treatment by the lawyers. They had already decided to fight the will, and they knew their greedy clients would follow their advice.

A lot was not being said. The litigation would be cumbersome to begin with. The wisest and most cost-efficient course would be to select one firm with experience to act as chief trial counsel. The others could take a step back, still protect their clients, and be kept abreast of every development. Such a strategy would require two things: (1) cooperation, and (2) the voluntary downsizing of most of the egos in the room.

It was never mentioned during the three-hour meeting.

Through no grand scheme of their own – schemes require cooperation – the lawyers had managed to divide the heirs so that no two shared the same firm. Through skillful manipulation that is not taught in law school but acquired naturally thereafter, the lawyers had convinced the clients to spend more time talking to them than to their fellow heirs. Trust was not a virtue known to the Phelans, nor to their attorneys.

It was shaping up to be one long chaotic lawsuit.

Not one brave voice suggested the will be left alone. There was not the slightest interest in following the wishes of the man who'd actually made the fortune they now conspired to carve up.

During the third or fourth trip around the tables, an effort was made to determine the level of debt held by each of the six heirs at the time of Mr. Phelan's death. But the effort fizzled under a barrage of legal nitpicking.

'Are the debts of spouses included?' asked Hark, attorney for Rex, whose wife Amber the stripper owned the skin clubs and had her name on most of the debts.

'What about obligations to the IRS?' asked the attorney for Troy Junior, who'd been having tax trouble for fifteen years.

'My clients have not authorized me to divulge financial information,' said Langhorne, who with that dire declaration effectively iced the issue.

The reluctance confirmed what everybody knew – the Phelan heirs were up to their ears in loans and mortgages.

All the lawyers, being lawyers, were deeply concerned about publicity, and how their fight would be portrayed by the media. Their clients were not simply a bunch of spoiled, greedy children who'd been cut out by their father. But they feared the press might take this posture. Perceptions were crucial.

'I suggest we hire a public relations firm,' Hark announced. It was a wonderful idea, one that several others immediately seized as their own. Hire a pro to paint the Phelan heirs as the brokenhearted children who'd loved a man who had little time for them. An eccentric, philandering, half-crazy . . . Yes! That was it! Make Troy the bad guy. And make their clients the victims!

The idea bloomed and the fiction spread happily

178

around the tables until someone asked just exactly how they would pay for such services.

'They're horribly expensive,' said a lawyer, who happened to be charging six hundred dollars an hour for himself and four hundred an hour for each of his three useless associates.

The idea lost steam quickly until Hark offered the lame suggestion that each firm could front some expense money. The meeting grew incredibly quiet. Those who'd had so much to say about everything were now captivated by the magical language of briefs and old cases.

'We can talk about this later,' Hark said, attempting to save face. No doubt the idea would never be mentioned again.

They then discussed Rachel, and where she might be. Should they retain a top-notch security firm to locate her? Almost every lawyer happened to know one. The idea was quite appealing and received more attention than it should have. What lawyer wouldn't want to represent the chosen heir?

But they decided against looking for Rachel, primarily because they couldn't agree on what they would do if they found her. She would surface soon enough, no doubt with her own entourage of lawyers.

The meeting ended on a pleasant note. The lawyers gave themselves the outcome they wanted. They left with plans to immediately call their clients and proudly report how much progress was made. They could say unequivocally that it was the combined wisdom of all the Phelan lawyers that the will should be attacked with a vengeance.

TWENTY-TWO

The river rose throughout the day, slowly leaving its banks in some places, swallowing sandbars, rising into the thick brush, flooding the small muddy yards of houses they passed once every three hours. The river carried more and more debris – weeds and grass, limbs and saplings. As it grew wider it grew stronger, and the currents running against the boat slowed them even more.

But no one was watching the clock. Nate had been politely relieved of his captain's duties after the *Santa Loura* was struck by a wayward tree trunk, one he never saw. No damage, but the jolt sent Jevy and Welly scurrying to the wheelhouse. He returned to his own little deck with the hammock stretched through the center, and there he spent the morning reading and watching wildlife.

Jevy joined him for coffee. 'So what do you think of the Pantanal?' he asked. They sat next to each other on a bench with their arms through the railing and their bare feet dangling over the side of the boat.

'It's pretty magnificent.'

'Do you know Colorado?'

'I've been there, yes.'

'During the rainy season, the rivers in the Pantanal overflow. The flooded area is the size of Colorado.'

'Have you been to Colorado?'

'Yes. I have a cousin there.'

'Where else have you been?'

'Three years ago, my cousin and I rode a big bus, a Greyhound, across the country. We were in every state but six.'

Jevy was a poor Brazilian boy of twenty-four. Nate was twice his age and for most of his career had had plenty of money. Yet Jevy had seen much more of the United States than Nate.

When the money was good, though, Nate had always traveled to Europe. His favorite restaurants were in Rome and Paris.

'When the floods stop,' Jevy continued, 'we have the dry season. Grasslands, marshes, more lagoons and swamps than anyone can count. The cycle – the flooding and the dry season – produces more wildlife than any place in the world. We have six hundred and fifty species of birds here, more than Canada and the U.S. combined. At least two hundred and sixty species of fish. Snakes, caiman, alligators, even giant otters live in the water.'

As if on cue, he pointed to a thicket at the edge of a small forest. 'Look, it's a deer,' he said. 'We have lots of deer. And lots of jaguars, giant anteaters, *capivaras*, tapirs, and macaws. The Pantanal is filled with wildlife.'

'You were born here?'

'I took my first breath in the hospital in Corumbá, but I was born on these rivers. This is my home.'

'You told me your father was a river pilot.'

'Yes. When I was a small boy I began going with him. Early in the morning, when everybody was asleep, he would allow me to take the wheel. I knew all the main rivers by the time I was ten.'

'And he died on the river.'

'Not this, but the Taquiri, to the east. He was

guiding a boat of German tourists when a storm hit them. The only survivor was a deckhand.'

'When was this?'

'Five years ago.'

Forever the trial lawyer, Nate had a dozen more questions about the accident. He wanted the details – details win lawsuits. But he said, 'I'm sorry,' and let it go.

'They want to destroy the Pantanal,' Jevy said.

'Who?'

'Lots of people. Big companies that own big farms. To the north and east of the Pantanal they are clearing large sections of land for farms. The main crop is *soja*, which you call soybeans. They want to export it. The more forests they clear, the more runoff collects in the Pantanal. Sediment rises each year in our rivers. Their farm soil is not good, so the companies use many sprays and fertilizers to grow crops. We get the chemicals. Many of the big farms dam up rivers to create new pastures. This upsets the flooding cycle. And mercury is killing our fish.'

'How does mercury get here?'

'Mining. To the north, they mine gold, and they do it with mercury. It runs into the rivers, the rivers eventually run into the Pantanal. Our fish swallow it and die. Everything gets dumped into the Pantanal. Cuiabá is a city of a million people to the east. It has no waste treatment. Guess where its sewage goes.'

'Doesn't the government help?'

Jevy managed a bitter laugh. 'Have you heard of Hidrovia?'

'No.'

'It's a big ditch, to be cut through the Pantanal. It is supposed to link Brazil, Bolivia, Paraguay, Argentina, and Uruguay. It is supposed to save South America. But it will drain the Pantanal. And our government is supporting it.'

Nate almost said something pious about environmental responsibility, then remembered that his countrymen were the biggest energy hogs the world had ever seen. 'It's still beautiful,' he said.

'It is.' Jevy finished his coffee. 'Sometimes I think it's too big for them to destroy.'

They passed a narrow inlet where more water entered the Paraguay. A small herd of deer waded through the floodwaters, nibbling at green vines, oblivious to the noise from the river. Seven deer, two of which were spotted fawns.

'There is a small trading post a few hours away,' Jevy said, getting to his feet. 'We should be there before dark.'

'What are we shopping for?'

'Nothing, I guess. Fernando is the owner, and he hears everything on the river. Maybe he will know something about missionaries.'

Jevy emptied his cup into the river and stretched his arms. 'Sometimes he has beer for sale. *Cerveja*.'

Nate kept his eyes on the water.

'I think we should not buy any,' Jevy said, and walked away.

Fine with me, thought Nate. He drained his cup, sucking down the grounds and grains of sugar.

A cold brown bottle, perhaps Antartica or Brahma, the two brands he'd already sampled in Brazil. Excellent beer. A favorite haunt had been a college bar near Georgetown with 120 foreign beers on the menu. He'd tried them all. They served roasted peanuts by the basket and expected you to throw the hulls on the floor. When his pals from law school were in town they always met at the bar and reminisced about the old days. The beer was ice cold, the peanuts hot and salty, the floor cracked with hulls when you walked, and the girls were young and loose. The place had been there forever, and during each trip through rehab and sobriety it was the bar Nate missed most.

He began to sweat, though the sun was hidden and there was a cool breeze. He buried himself in the hammock and prayed for sleep, a deep hard coma that would take him past their little stop and into the night. The sweating worsened until his shirt was soaked. He started a book about the demise of the Brazilian Indians, then tried to sleep again.

He was wide awake when the engine was throttled down and the boat moved close to the bank. There were voices, then a gentle bump as they docked at the trading post. Nate slowly removed himself from the hammock and returned to the bench, where he sat.

It was a country store of sorts, built on stilts – a tiny building, made of unpainted boards with a tin roof and a narrow porch where, not surprisingly, a couple of locals were lounging with cigarettes and tea. A smaller river circled behind it and disappeared into the Pantanal. A large fuel tank was braced to the side of the building.

A flimsy pier jutted into the river to dock the boats. Jevy and Welly eased along the pier, carefully, because the currents were strong. They chatted with the *pantaneiros* on the porch, then went through the open door.

Nate had vowed to remain on the boat. He went to the other side of the deck, sat on the opposite bench, stuck his arms and legs through the rail, and watched the full width of the river go by. He would stay up on the deck, on the bench, with his arms and legs locked in the rail. The coldest beer in the world couldn't pull him away.

As he had learned, there was no such thing as a short visit in Brazil. Especially on the river, where visits were rare. Jevy bought thirty gallons of diesel fuel

184

to replace what had been lost in the storm. The engine started.

'Fernando says there is a woman missionary. She works with the Indians.' Jevy handed him a bottle of cold water. They were moving again.

'Where?'

'He's not sure. There are some settlements to the north, near Bolivia. But the Indians don't move on the river, so he doesn't know much about them.'

'How far is the nearest settlement?'

'We should be close by morning. But we can't take this boat. We must use the little one.'

'Sounds like fun.'

'You remember Marco, the farmer whose cow was killed by our plane?'

'Sure I do. He had three little boys.'

'Yes. He was there yesterday,' Jevy said, pointing to the store, which was disappearing around a bend. 'He comes once a month.'

'Were the boys with him?'

'No. It's too dangerous.'

What a small world. Nate hoped the boys had spent the money he'd given them for Christmas. He watched the store until it was out of sight.

Perhaps on the return leg he'd be well enough to stop and have a cool one. Just a couple, to celebrate their successful journey. He crawled back into the safety of his hammock, and cursed himself for his weakness. In the wilderness of a gigantic swamp he had had a near brush with alcohol, and for hours his thoughts had been consumed with nothing else. The anticipation, the fear, the sweating, and the scheming of ways to get a drink. Then the near miss, the escape through no strength of his own, and now in the aftermath the fantasy of renewing his romance with alcohol. A few drinks would be fine because then he could stop. That was his favorite lie.

He was just a drunk. Run him through a designer rehab clinic at a thousand bucks a day, and he was still an addict. Run him through AA in the basement of a church on Tuesday nights, and he was still a drunk.

His addictions gripped him, and desperation settled around Nate. He was paying for the damned boat; Jevy worked for him. If he insisted that they turn around and go straight to the store, they would do so. He could buy all the beer Fernando owned, load it on ice below the deck, and sip Brahma all the way to Bolivia. And there wasn't a damned thing anyone could do about it.

Like a mirage, Welly appeared with a smile and a cup of fresh coffee. '*Vou cozinhar,*' he said. I'm going to cook.

Food would help, Nate thought. Even another platter of beans, rice, and boiled chicken. Food would satisfy his tastes, or least divert his attention from other cravings.

He ate slowly, on the upper deck, alone and in the dark, swatting thick mosquitoes away from his face. When he was finished, he sprayed repellent from his neck to his bare feet. The seizure was over, only slight aftershocks gripped him. He could no longer taste beer or smell the peanuts from his favorite bar.

He retreated to his sanctuary. It was raining again, a quiet rain with no wind or thunder. Josh had sent along four books for his reading pleasure. All the briefs and memos had been read and reread. Nothing remained but the books. He'd already read half of the thinnest one.

He burrowed deep in the hammock and went back to reading the sad history of the native people of Brazil.

When the Portuguese explorer Pedro Alvares Cabral first stepped on Brazilian soil, on the coast of Bahia, in

186

April of 1500, the country had five million Indians, scattered among nine hundred tribes. They spoke 1,175 languages, and except for the usual tribal skirmish they were peaceful people.

After five centuries of getting themselves 'civilized' by Europeans, the Indian population had been decimated. Only 270,000 survived, in 206 tribes using 170 languages. War, murder, slavery, territorial losses, diseases – no method of exterminating Indians had been neglected by those from civilized cultures.

It was a sick and violent history. If the Indians were peaceful and tried to cooperate with the colonists, they were subject to strange diseases – smallpox, measles, yellow fever, influenza, tuberculosis – for which they had no natural defenses. If they did not cooperate, they were slaughtered by men using weapons more sophisticated than arrows and poison darts. When they fought back and killed their attackers, they were branded as savages.

They were enslaved by miners, ranchers, and rubber barons. They were driven from their ancestral homes by any group with enough guns. They were burned at the stake by priests, hunted by armies and gangs of bandits, raped at will by any able-bodied man with the desire, and slaughtered with impunity. At every point in history, whether crucial or insignificant, when the interests of native Brazilians conflicted with those of white people, the Indians had lost.

You lose for five hundred years, and you expect little from life. The biggest problem facing some modern-day tribes was the suicide of its young people.

After centuries of genocide, the Brazilian government finally decided it was time to protect its 'noble savages.' Modern-day massacres had brought international condemnation, so bureaucracies were established and laws were passed. With self-righteous fanfare, some tribal lands were returned to the natives

187

and lines were drawn on government maps declaring them to be safe zones.

But the government was also the enemy. In 1967, an investigation into the agency in charge of Indian affairs shocked most Brazilians. The report revealed that agents, land speculators, and ranchers – thugs who either worked for the agency or had the agency working for them – had been systematically using chemical and bacteriological weapons to wipe out Indians. They issued clothing to the Indians that was infected with smallpox and tuberculosis germs. With airplanes and helicopters, they bombed Indian villages and land with deadly bacteria.

And in the Amazon Basin and other frontiers, ranchers and miners cared little for lines on maps.

In 1986, a rancher in Rondônia used crop dusters to spray nearby Indian land with deadly chemicals. He wanted to farm the land, but first had to eliminate the inhabitants. Thirty Indians died, and the rancher was never prosecuted. In 1989, a rancher in Mato Grosso offered rewards to bounty hunters for the ears of murdered Indians. In 1993, gold miners in Manaus attacked a peaceful tribe because they would not leave their land. Thirteen Indians were murdered, and no one was ever arrested.

In the 1990s, the government had aggressively sought to open up the Amazon Basin, a land of vast natural resources to the north of the Pantanal. But the Indians were still in the way. The majority of those surviving inhabited the Basin; in fact, it was estimated that as many as fifty jungle tribes had been lucky enough to escape contact with civilization.

Now civilization was on the attack again. The abuse of Indians was growing as miners and loggers and ranchers pushed deep into the Amazon, with the support of the government.

188

The history was fascinating, if depressing. Nate read for four hours nonstop and finished the book.

He walked to the wheelhouse and drank coffee with Jevy. The rain had stopped.

'Will we be there by morning?' he asked.

'I think so.'

The lights from the boat rocked gently up and down with the current. It seemed as though they were hardly moving.

'Do you have any Indian blood?' Nate asked, after some hesitation. It was a personal matter, one that in the United States no one would dare ask.

Jevy smiled without taking his gaze from the river. 'All of us have Indian blood. Why do you ask?'

'I've been reading the history of Indians in Brazil.'

'So what do you think?'

'It's pretty tragic.'

'It is. Do you think the Indians have been treated badly here?'

'Of course they have.'

'What about in your country?'

For some reason, General Custer was the first thought. At least the Indians had won something. And we didn't burn them at the stake, or spray them with chemicals, or sell them into slavery. Did we? What about all those reservations? Land everywhere.

'Not much better, I'm afraid,' he said in defeat. It was not a discussion he wanted.

After a long silence, Nate eased down to the toilet. When he finished his work there, he pulled the chain above it and left the small room. Light brown river water ran into the toilet bowl and flushed the waste through a tube and sent it directly into the river.

TWENTY-THREE

It was still dark when the engine stopped and woke Nate. He touched his left wrist and remembered he wasn't wearing a watch. He listened as Welly and Jevy moved below him. They were at the rear of the boat, talking quietly.

He was proud of himself for another sober morning, another clean day for the books. Six months earlier, every wake-up had been a blur of swollen eyes, cobwebbed thoughts, seared mouth, arid tongue, bitter breath, and the great daily question of 'Why did I do it?' He often vomited in the shower, sometimes inducing it himself to get it over with. After the shower, there was always the dilemma of what to have for breakfast. Something warm and oily to settle the stomach, or perhaps a bloody mary to settle the nerves? Then he was off to work, always at his desk by eight to begin another brutal day as a litigator.

Every morning. No exceptions. In the final days of his last crash he had gone weeks without a clear morning. Out of desperation he'd seen a counselor, and when asked if he could recall the last day he'd stayed sober, he admitted he could not.

He missed the drinking, but not the hangovers.

Welly pulled the johnboat to the port side of the *Santa Loura*, and tied it closely. They were loading it when Nate crept down the steps. The adventure was moving into a new phase. Nate was ready for a change of scenery.

It was overcast and threatening more rain. The sun finally broke through at about six. Nate knew because he'd rearmed himself with a watch.

A rooster crowed. They were docked near a small farmhouse, their bow tied to a timber that once held a pier. Westward, to their left, a much smaller river met the Paraguay.

The challenge was to pack the boat without overloading it. The smaller tributaries they were about to encounter were flooded; banks would not always be visible. If the boat sat too low in the water, they might run aground, or worse, damage the prop of the outboard. There was only one motor on the johnboat, no backup, just a couple of paddles that Nate studied from the deck as he drank his coffee. The paddles would work, he decided, especially if wild Indians or hungry animals were in pursuit.

Three five-gallon gas tanks were arranged neatly in the center of the boat. 'These should give us fifteen hours,' Jevy explained.

'That's a long time.'

'I'd rather be safe.'

'How far away is the settlement?'

'I'm not sure.' He pointed to the house. 'The farmer there said four hours.'

'Does he know the Indians?'

'No. He doesn't like Indians. Says he never sees them on the river.'

Jevy packed a small tent, two blankets, two mosquito nets, a rain fly for the tent, two buckets to dip out rainfall, and his poncho. Welly added a box of food and a case of bottled water.

Seated on his bunk in the cabin, Nate took the copy of the will, the acknowledgment, and the waiver from his briefcase, folded them together, and placed them

191

in a letter-sized envelope. An official Stafford Law Firm envelope. Since there were no Ziploc bags or garbage liners on board, he wrapped the envelope in a twelve-inch square section he cut from the hem of his poncho. He taped the seams with duct tape, and after examining his handiwork declared his package to be waterproof. Then he taped it to his tee shirt, across his chest, and covered it with a light denim pullover.

There were copies of the papers in his briefcase, which he would leave behind. And since the *Santa Loura* seemed much more secure than the johnboat, he decided to leave the SatFone too. He double-checked the papers and the phone, then locked the briefcase and left it on his bunk. Today could be the day, he thought to himself. There was a nervous excitement in finally meeting Rachel Lane.

Breakfast was a quick roll with butter on the deck, standing above the johnboat and watching the clouds. Four hours meant six or eight in Brazil, and Nate was anxious to cast off. The last item Jevy loaded into the boat was a clean shiny machete with a long handle. 'This is for the anacondas,' he said, laughing. Nate tried to ignore it. He waved good-bye to Welly, then huddled over his last cup of coffee as they floated with the river until Jevy started the outboard.

Mist settled just above the water, and it was cool. Since leaving Corumbá Nate had observed the river from the safety of the top deck; now he was practically sitting on it. He glanced around and saw no life jackets. The river slapped the hull. Nate kept a wary eye on the mist, watching for debris; a nice fat tree trunk with a jagged end and the johnboat was history.

They went crosscurrent until they entered the mouth of the tributary that would take them to the Indians. The water there was much calmer. The outboard whined and left a boiling wake. The Paraguay disappeared quickly.

192

On Jevy's river map the tributary was officially labeled as the Cabixa. Jevy had never navigated it before, because there had been no need. It coiled like string out of Brazil and into Bolivia, and apparently went nowhere. At its mouth it was eighty feet wide at most, and narrowed to about fifty as they followed it. It had flooded in some places; in others the brush along the banks was thicker than the Paraguay.

Fifteen minutes in, Nate checked his watch. He would time everything. Jevy slowed the boat as they approached the first fork, the first of a thousand. A river of the same size branched to the left, and the captain was faced with the decision of which route would keep them on the Cabixa. They kept to the right, but somewhat slower, and soon entered a lake. Jevy stopped the motor. 'Hold on,' he said, and stood on the gas tanks, gazing at the floodwaters that encircled them. The boat was perfectly still. A ragged row of scrub trees caught his attention. He pointed and said something to himself.

Exactly how much guesswork was involved Nate couldn't tell. Jevy had studied his maps and had lived on these rivers. They all led back to the Paraguay. If they took a wrong turn and got lost, surely the currents would eventually lead them back to Welly.

They followed the scrub trees and flooded thickets that, in the dry season, made up the riverbank, and soon they were in the middle of a shallow stream with limbs overhead. It didn't look like the Cabixa, but a quick glance at the captain's face revealed nothing but confidence.

An hour into the journey they approached the first dwelling – a mud-splattered little hut with a red-tiled roof. Three feet of water covered the bottom of it, and there was no sign of humans or animals. Jevy slowed so they could talk.

'In the flood season, many people in the Pantanal

move to higher ground. They load up their cows and kids and leave for three months.'

'I haven't seen higher ground.'

'There's not much of it. But every *pantaneiro* has a place to go this time of the year.'

'What about the Indians?'

'They move around too.'

'Wonderful. We don't know where they are, and they like to move around.'

Jevy chuckled and said, 'We'll find them.'

They floated by the hut. It had no doors or windows. Not much to come home to.

Ninety minutes, and Nate had completely forgotten about being eaten when they rounded a bend and came close to a pack of alligators sleeping in a pile in six inches of water. The boat startled them and upset their nap. Tails slapped and water splashed. Nate glanced at the machete, just in case, then laughed at his own foolishness.

The reptiles did not attack. They watched the boat ease past.

No animals for the next twenty minutes. The river narrowed again. The banks squeezed together so close that trees from both sides touched each other above the water. It was suddenly dark. They were floating through a tunnel. Nate checked his watch. The *Santa Loura* was two hours away.

As they zigzagged through the marshes, they caught glimpses of the horizon. The mountains of Bolivia were looming, getting closer, it seemed. The water widened, the trees cleared, and they entered a large lake with more than a dozen little rivers twisting into it. They circled slowly the first time, then even slower the second. All the tributaries looked the same. The Cabixa was one of a dozen, and the captain had not a clue.

Jevy stood on the gas tanks and surveyed the flood

while Nate sat motionless. A fisherman was in the weeds on the other side of the lake. Finding him would be their only luck of the day.

He was sitting patiently in a small, handmade canoe, one carved from a tree a very long time ago. He wore a ragged straw hat that hid most of his face. When they were only a few feet away, close enough to inspect him, Nate noticed that he was fishing without the benefit of a pole or a rod. No stick of any sort. The line was wrapped around his hand.

Jevy said all the right things in Portuguese, and handed him a bottle of water. Nate just smiled and listened to the soft slurring sounds of the strange language. It was slower than Spanish, almost as nasal as French.

If the fisherman was happy to see another human in the middle of nowhere, he certainly didn't show it. Where could the poor man live?

Then they started pointing, in the general direction of the mountains, though by the time they finished the little man had encompassed the entire lake with his bearings. They chatted some more, and Nate got the impression Jevy was extracting every scrap of information. It could be hours before they saw another face. With the swamps and rivers swollen, navigation was proving difficult. Two and a half hours in, and they were already lost.

A cloud of small black mosquitoes swept over them, and Nate scrambled for the repellent. The fisherman watched him with curiosity.

They said good-bye and paddled away, drifting with the slight wind. 'His mother was an Indian,' Jevy said.

'That's nice,' Nate replied, hammering mosquitoes.

'There's a settlement a few hours from here.'

'A few hours?'

'Three maybe.'

They had fifteen hours of fuel, and Nate planned to

count every minute of it. The Cabixa began again near an inlet where another, very identical river also left the lake. It widened, and they were off, at full throttle.

Nate moved lower in the boat, and found a spot on the bottom between the box of food and the buckets, with his back to the bench. From there the mist couldn't spray his head. He was contemplating a nap when the motor sputtered. The boat lurched and slowed. He kept his eyes on the river, afraid to turn around and look at Jevy.

Engine trouble was not something he had spent time worrying about, yet. Their journey had enough little perils already. It would take days of backbreaking labor to paddle back to Welly. They would be forced to sleep in the boat, eat what they'd brought until the food ran out, dip water from it during the rains, and hope like hell they could find their little fishing buddy to point them to safety.

Suddenly Nate was terrified.

Then they were off again, the motor howling as if nothing had happened. It became a routine; every twenty minutes or so, just as Nate was about to doze off, the steady strain of the motor would break. The bow would dip. Nate would quickly look at the edges of the river to inspect the wildlife. Jevy would curse in Portuguese, fiddle with the choke and the throttle, and then things would be fine for another twenty minutes or so.

They had lunch – cheese, saltines, and cookies – under a tree in a small fork as rain fell around them.

'That little fisherman back there,' Nate said. 'Does he know the Indians?'

'Yes. About once a month they go to the Paraguay to trade with a boat. He sees them.'

'Did you ask him if he'd ever seen a female missionary?'

'I did. He has not. You are the first American he's ever seen.'

'Lucky guy.'

The first sign of the settlement came at almost seven hours. Nate saw a thin line of blue smoke rising above the trees, near the foot of a hill. Jevy was certain they were in Bolivia. The ground was higher and they were close to the mountains. The flooded areas were behind them.

They came to a gap in the trees and in a clearing were two canoes. Jevy guided the johnboat to the clearing. Nate quickly jumped ashore, anxious to stretch his legs and feel the earth.

'Stay close,' Jevy warned as he switched gas tanks in the boat. Nate looked at him. Their eyes met, and Jevy nodded to the trees.

An Indian was watching them. A male, brown-skinned, bare-chested, with a straw skirt of some sort hanging from his waist, no visible weapon. The fact that he was unarmed helped immensely because Nate was at first terrified of him. The Indian had long black hair and red stripes on his forehead, and if he'd been holding a spear Nate would've surrendered without a word.

'Is he friendly?' he asked without taking his eyes off the man.

'I think so.'

'Does he speak Portuguese?'

'I don't know.'

'Why don't you go find out?'

'Relax.'

Jevy stepped from the boat. 'He looks like a cannibal,' he whispered. The attempt at humor didn't work.

They took a few steps toward the Indian, and he took a few steps toward them. All three stopped with a

197

nice gap in the center. Nate was tempted to raise the palm of his hand and say, 'Howdy.'

'*Fala português?*' Jevy said with a nice smile.

The Indian pondered the question for a long time, and it became painfully obvious that he did not speak Portuguese. He looked young, probably not yet twenty, and just happened to be near the river when he heard their outboard.

They examined each other from twenty feet as Jevy considered his options. There was a movement in the brush behind the Indian. Along the tree line, three of his tribesmen emerged, all mercifully weaponless. Outnumbered and trespassing, Nate was ready to bolt. They weren't particularly large, but they had the home-field advantage. And they weren't friendly folks, no smiles or hellos.

A young female suddenly appeared from the trees and stood next to the first Indian. She too was brown and bare-chested, and Nate tried not to stare. '*Falo,*' she said.

Speaking slowly, Jevy explained what they were up to, and asked to see their tribal leader. She translated his words and relayed them to the men, who huddled and talked grimly among themselves.

'Some want to eat us now,' Jevy said under his breath. 'Some want to wait until tomorrow.'

'Very funny.'

When the men finished their deliberations they reported to the woman. She then told the intruders that they must wait, by the river, while news of their arrival was duly reported to the higher-ups. This suited Nate just fine, but Jevy was a bit perturbed by it. He asked if a woman missionary lived with them.

You must wait, she said.

The Indians vanished into the woods.

'What do you think?' Nate asked when they were gone. Neither he nor Jevy had moved an inch. They stood in grass ankle-high and looked at the trees, thick woods from which Nate was certain they were being watched.

'They catch diseases from outsiders,' Jevy explained. 'That's why they are careful.'

'I'm not touching anybody.'

They retreated to the boat, where Jevy busied himself by cleaning the spark plugs. Nate removed both of his shirts and inspected the contents of his makeshift waterproof pouch. The papers were still dry.

'Those papers are for the woman?' Jevy asked.

'Yes.'

'Why? What has happened to her?'

The rigid rules governing client confidentiality seemed less constricting at that moment. They were life and death in practice, but sitting in a boat deep in the Pantanal, with no other American even remotely near, the rules could be bent. And why not? Who could Jevy tell? What harm could come from a little gossip?

Per Josh's strict instructions to Valdir, Jevy had been told only that there was an important legal matter back home that required them to find Rachel Lane.

'Her father died a few weeks ago. He left her a lot of money.'

'How much?'

'Several billion.'

'Billion?'

'That's right.'

'He was very wealthy.'

'Yes, he was.'

'Did he have other children?'

'Six, I think.'

'Did he give them several billion?'

'No. He gave them very little.'

'Why did he give her so much?'

'No one knows. It was a surprise.'

'Does she know her father is dead?'

'No.'

'Did she love her father?'

'I doubt it. She was illegitimate. It looks as though she tried to run away from him, and from everything else. Wouldn't you say so?' Nate waved his arm at the Pantanal as he said this.

'Yes. It's a very good place to hide. Did he know where she was when he died?'

'Not exactly. He knew she was a missionary working with the Indians somewhere around here.'

Jevy ignored the spark plug in his hand and absorbed the news. He had many questions. The lawyer's breach of confidentiality was growing wider.

'Why would he leave such a fortune to a child who didn't love him?'

'Maybe he was crazy. He jumped out of a window.'

This was more than Jevy could handle at one moment. He squinted his eyes and looked at the river, deep in thought.

TWENTY-FOUR

The Indians were Guató, longtime residents who lived like their ancestors and preferred no contact with outsiders. They grew their food in small patches, fished the rivers, and hunted with bows and arrows.

Evidently, they were a deliberate people. After an hour, Jevy smelled smoke. He climbed a tree near the boat, and when he was forty feet up he saw the roofs of their huts. He asked Nate to join him.

Nate had not been in a tree in forty years, but at the moment there was nothing else to do. He made the climb with less ease than Jevy, and finally came to rest on a frail branch. He hugged the trunk with one arm.

They could see the tops of three huts – thick straw laid in neat rows. The blue smoke rose between two of the huts, from a point they couldn't see.

Could he be that close to Rachel Lane? Was she there now, listening to her people and deciding what to do? Would she send a warrior to fetch them, or would she herself simply walk through the woods and say hello?

'It's a small settlement,' Nate said, trying not to move.

'There could be more huts.'

'What do you think they're doing?'

'Talking. Just talking.'

'Well I hate to bring this up, but we need to make a

201

move. We left the boat eight and a half hours ago. I'd like to see Welly before dark.'

'No problem. We'll go back with the current. Plus I know the way. It will be much faster.'

'You're not worried?'

Jevy shook his head as if he hadn't given a thought to shooting down the Cabixa in the dark. Nate certainly had. Of particular concern were the two large lakes they had encountered, each with various tributaries, all of which appeared identical in the daylight.

His plan was to simply say hello to Ms. Lane, give her a bit of history, cover the required legalities, show her the paperwork, answer the basic questions, get her signature, thank her, and complete the meeting as soon as possible. He was worried about the time of day, and the sputtering motor, and the trip back to the *Santa Loura*. She would probably want to talk, or maybe she wouldn't. Maybe she would say very little and want them to leave and never come back.

Back on the ground, he had settled into the boat for a nap when Jevy saw the Indians. He said something and pointed, and Nate looked at the woods.

They slowly approached the river, in a line behind their leader, the oldest Guató they'd seen so far. He was stocky with an ample belly, and he carried a long stick of some sort. It didn't appear to be sharp or dangerous. It had pretty feathers near the tip, and Nate surmised that it was probably just a ceremonial spear.

The leader quickly sized up the two intruders, and directed his comments at Jevy.

Why are you here? he asked in Portuguese. His face wasn't friendly, but there was no aggression in his presence. Nate studied the spear.

We are looking for an American missionary, a woman, Jevy explained.

202

Where are you from? The chief asked this while glancing at Nate.

Corumbá.

And him? All eyes were on Nate.

He's an American. He needs to find the woman.

Why does he need to find the woman?

It was the first hint that the Indians might know of Rachel Lane. Was she hiding back there somewhere, in the village or maybe in the woods, listening?

Jevy went through a windy narrative explaining how Nate had traveled great distances and almost lost his life. It was an important matter among the Americans, nothing he, Jevy, or the Indians would ever understand.

Is she in danger?

No. None.

She is not here.

'He says she's not here,' Jevy said to Nate.

'Tell him I think he's a lying bastard,' Nate said, softly.

'I don't think so.'

Have you ever seen a woman missionary around here? Jevy asked.

The leader shook his head. No.

Have you ever heard of one?

At first, there was no response. His eyes narrowed as he stared at Jevy, sizing him up, as if to say, Can this man be trusted? Then, a slight nod.

Where is she? Jevy asked.

With another tribe.

Where?

He said he wasn't sure, but he began pointing anyway. Somewhere off to the north and west, he said, with his spear waving across half the Pantanal.

'Guató?' Jevy asked.

He frowned and shook his head, as if she lived among undesirables. 'Ipicas,' he said with scorn.

203

How far away?

A day.

Jevy attempted to pin him down on the time, but soon learned that hours meant nothing to the Indians. A day wasn't twenty-four hours and it wasn't twelve. It was simply a day. He tried the concept of half a day, and made progress.

'Twelve to fifteen hours,' he said to Nate.

'But that's in one of those little canoes, right?' Nate whispered.

'Yes.'

'So how fast can we get there?'

'Three or four hours. If we can find it.'

Jevy retrieved two maps and spread them on the grass. The Indians were very curious. They squatted close to their leader.

To find out where they were going, they first had to determine where they were. And this took a bad turn when the leader informed Jevy that the river that brought them in was not, in fact, the Cabixa. They had taken a wrong turn at some point after meeting the fisherman, and stumbled onto the Guató. Jevy took the news hard, and whispered it to Nate.

Nate took it even harder. He was trusting Jevy with his life.

Fancy-colored navigational maps meant little to the Indians. They were soon ignored as Jevy began drawing his own. He started with the unnamed river lying before them, and, chatting constantly with the chief, slowly made his way to the north. The chief received input from two young men. The two, he explained to Jevy, were excellent fishermen and traveled occasionally to the Paraguay.

'Hire them,' Nate whispered.

Jevy tried, but in the course of negotiations learned that the two had never seen the Ipicas, didn't particularly want to, didn't know exactly where they were, and didn't understand the concept of working and getting paid for it. Plus the chief didn't want them to leave.

The route went from one river to the next, twisting northward, until the chief and his fishermen could no longer agree on where to go next. Jevy compared his drawing to his maps.

'We've found her,' he said to Nate.

'Where?'

'There is a settlement of Ipicas here,' he said, pointing to a map. 'South of Porto Indio, at the edge of the mountains. Their directions take us close to it.'

Nate leaned lower and examined the markings. 'How do we get there?'

'I think we go back to the boat, and go north a half a day on the Paraguay. Then we use the little boat again to get to the settlement.'

The Paraguay looped relatively close to their target, and traveling to it on the *Santa Loura* struck Nate as a splendid idea. 'How many hours in the little boat?' Nate asked.

'Four, more or less.'

'More or less' covered everything in Brazil. The distance, though, looked less than what they had covered since early morning.

'Then what are we waiting for?' Nate asked, standing and smiling at the Indians.

Jevy began saying thanks to their hosts, while folding his maps. Now that they were leaving, the Indians loosened up and wanted to be hospitable. They offered food, which Jevy declined. He explained that they were suddenly in a hurry, since they planned to return to the big river before dark.

Nate grinned at them as he backtracked to the river. They wanted to see the boat. They stood at the edge of the water, watching with great curiosity as Jevy adjusted the motor. When he started it, they took a step back.

The river, whatever it was named, looked entirely different going in the other direction. As they approached the first bend, Nate glanced over his shoulder and saw the Guató, still standing in the water.

The time was almost 4 P.M. With luck, they could make it past the large lakes before dark, then onto the Cabixa. Welly would be waiting, with beans and rice. As Nate did these quick calculations, he felt the first raindrops.

The flaw in the motor was not dirty spark plugs. It shut down completely fifty minutes into the return leg. The boat drifted with the current while Jevy removed the cover and attacked the carburetor with a screwdriver. Nate asked if he could help, and was quickly informed that he could not. At least not with the engine. He could, however, take a bucket and begin dipping out the rainwater. And he could take a paddle and keep them in the center of the river, whatever it was named.

He did both. The current kept them moving, although at a much slower pace than Nate preferred. The rain was intermittent. The river grew shallow as they approached a sharp curve, but Jevy was too busy to notice. The boat gained speed, and the rapids shoved it toward a thicket of dense brush.

'I need some help here,' Nate said.

Jevy grabbed a paddle. He turned the boat so the bow would hit and it wouldn't flip. 'Hold on!' he said as they rammed into the thicket. Vines and branches flew around Nate and he fought them with his paddle.

A small snake dropped into the boat just over Nate's shoulder. He didn't see it. Jevy scooped it up with his paddle and flung it into the river. It was best not to mention it.

They battled the current for a few minutes, as well as battling each other. Nate somehow managed to push water in all the wrong directions. His enthusiasm for paddling kept the boat precariously close to rolling.

When they were free again, away from the brush and the wildlife, Jevy confiscated both paddles and found a new job for Nate. He asked him to stand over the motor, holding his poncho wide to keep the rain off the carburetor. So Nate hovered, sort of like an angel with his arms spread, one foot on a gas tank, one foot on the side of the boat, frozen with fear.

Twenty minutes dragged by, as they drifted aimlessly down the narrow river. The Phelan estate could purchase every shiny new outboard motor in Brazil, and here Nate was watching an amateur mechanic try to patch one that was older than he was.

Jevy bolted the top on it, then worked with the throttle for an eternity. He yanked the starter rope, as Nate found himself saying a prayer. On the fourth pull, the miracle happened. The engine howled, though not as smoothly as before. It missed and sputtered, and Jevy adjusted throttle cables without much luck.

'We'll have to go slower,' he reported, without looking at Nate.

'Fine. As long as we know where we are.'

'No problem.'

The storm crept over the mountains of Bolivia, then roared into the Pantanal, much like the one that had almost killed them in the airplane. Nate was sitting low in the boat, under the safety of his poncho, watching the river to the east, searching for something familiar, when he felt the first gust of wind. And the rain suddenly fell harder. He slowly turned and looked behind him. Jevy had already seen it, but said nothing.

The sky was dark gray, almost black. Clouds boiled low to the ground so that the mountains could not be seen. The rain began to drench them. Nate felt completely exposed and helpless.

There was nowhere to hide, no safe harbor to dock at and ride out the storm. There was nothing but water around them, water for miles in all directions. They were in the middle of a flood, with only the tops of the brush and a few trees to guide them through the rivers and swamps. They would stay in the boat because they had no choice.

A gale swept in behind them, driving the boat forward as the rain pelted their backs. The sky darkened. Nate wanted to curl up under his aluminum bench, clutch his floatable cushion, and hide as much as possible under his poncho. But the water was accumulating around his feet. The supplies were getting wet. He took his bucket and began shoveling rainwater.

They came to a fork that Nate was certain they had not passed earlier, then to a junction of rivers they could barely see through the rain. Jevy reduced the throttle to survey the waters, then hit the gas and took a sharp right as if he knew precisely where he was going. Nate was convinced they were lost.

After a few minutes, the river disappeared into a thicket of rotted trees – a memorable sight they had not seen earlier. Jevy quickly turned the boat around. Now they raced into the storm, and it was a terrifying sight. The sky was black. The current was churning with whitecaps.

Back at the junction, they talked for a moment, shouting through the wind and rain, then selected another river.

Just before dark they passed through a large flooded plain, a temporary lake that looked vaguely similar to the place where they'd found the fisherman in the weeds. He wasn't around.

Jevy selected a tributary, one of several, and proceeded as if he navigated this corner of the Pantanal every day. Then lightning came and for a while they could almost see where they were going. The rain slackened. The storm was slowly leaving them.

Jevy stopped the motor and studied the edges of the river.

'What are you thinking?' Nate asked. There had been very little conversation during the storm. They were lost, that much was certain. But Nate would not force Jevy to admit it.

'We should make camp,' Jevy said. It was more of a suggestion than a plan.

'Why?'

'Because we have to sleep somewhere.'

'We can take turns napping in the boat,' Nate said. 'It's safer here.' He said this with the confidence of a seasoned river guide.

'Maybe. But I think we should stop here. We might get lost if we keep going in the dark.'

We've been lost for three hours, Nate wanted to say.

Jevy guided the boat to a bank with some growth. They drifted downriver, staying close to the shore and watching the shallow waters with their flashlights. Two little red dots glowing just above the surface meant an alligator was watching too, but thankfully they saw none. They anchored by tying a guide rope to a limb ten feet from the bank.

Dinner was semidry saltines, canned little fish that Nate had never experienced, bananas and cheese.

When the winds stopped, the mosquitoes arrived. Repellent was passed back and forth. Nate rubbed it on his neck and face, even his eyelids and his hair. The tiny bugs were quick and vicious and moved in small black clouds from one end of the boat to the other.

209

Though the rain had stopped, neither man removed his poncho. The mosquitoes tried fiercely, but they could not penetrate the plastic.

Around 11 P.M. the sky cleared somewhat, but there was no moon. The current gently rocked the boat. Jevy offered to hold the first watch, and Nate tried his best to get comfortable enough to doze. He propped his head on the tent, and stretched his legs. A gap opened in his poncho and a dozen mosquitoes rushed forth, chewing him at the waist. Something splashed, perhaps a reptile. The aluminum boat was not designed for reclining.

Sleep was out of the question.

TWENTY-FIVE

Flowe, Zadel, and Theishen, the three psychiatrists who had examined Troy Phelan only weeks earlier and had presented the unified opinion, both on video and later in long affidavits, that he was of sound mind, were fired. Not only were they fired, they were rebuked by the Phelan lawyers as nuts, even crackpots.

New psychiatrists were found. Hark bought the first one, at three hundred bucks an hour. He found him in a magazine for trial lawyers, in the classifieds, among the ads for everything from accident reconstructionists to X-ray analysts. He was Dr. Sabo, retired from active practice and now willing to sell his testimony. One brief look at the behavior of Mr. Phelan and he ventured the preliminary opinion that he clearly lacked testamentary capacity. Jumping from a window was not the act of a clear and lucid mind. And leaving an eleven-billion-dollar fortune to an unknown heir was evidence of a deeply disturbed person.

Sabo relished the idea of working on the Phelan case. Refuting the opinions of the first three psychiatrists would be challenging. The publicity was seductive – he'd never had a famous case. And the money would pay for a trip to the Orient.

All of the Phelan lawyers were scrambling to undo the testimony of Flowe, Zadel, and Theishen. The only way to discredit them was to find new experts with new opinions.

Fat hourly rates yielded to contingencies. The heirs wouldn't be able to pay the hefty monthly fees they were about to incur, so their lawyers graciously agreed to simplify matters by taking percentages. The range was staggering, though no firm would ever divulge its cut. Hark wanted 40 percent, but Rex berated him for his greediness. They finally agreed on 25 percent. Grit squeezed 25 percent out of Mary Ross Phelan Jackman.

The clear victor was Wally Bright, the street fighter, who insisted on an even deal with Libbigail and Spike. He would get half of their settlement.

In the mad scramble before they filed their suits, not a single Phelan heir asked if they were doing the right thing. They trusted their lawyers, and besides, everybody else was contesting the will. No one could afford to be left out. There was so much at stake.

Because Hark had been the loudest of the Phelan lawyers, he caught the attention of Snead, Troy's longtime gofer. No one had noticed Snead in the aftermath of the suicide. He'd been forgotten in the stampede to the courthouse. His employment had been terminated. And when the will was read, Snead himself was sitting in the courtroom, his face disguised with sunglasses and a hat, recognized by no one. He had left in tears.

He hated the Phelan children because Troy hated them. Over the years, Snead had been forced to do all sorts of unpleasant things to protect Troy from his families. Snead had arranged abortions, and had bribed cops when the boys were caught with drugs. He had lied to the wives to protect the mistresses, and when the mistresses became wives, then poor Snead lied to them too, to protect the girlfriends.

212

In return for his good work, the children and wives had called him a fag.

And in return for a career of faithful service, Mr. Phelan left him nothing. Not a cent. He'd been paid well over the years, and had some money in mutuals, but not enough to survive on. He had sacrificed everything for his job and his master. He'd been denied a normal life because Mr. Phelan expected him to be on duty every hour of the day. A family had been out of the question. He had no real friends to speak of.

Mr. Phelan had been his friend, his confidant, the only person Snead could trust.

Over the years, there had been many promises made by the old man about taking care of Snead. He knew for a fact that he'd been named in one will. He'd seen the document himself. He would inherit a million bucks upon Mr. Phelan's death. At the time, Troy had a net worth of three billion, and Snead remembered thinking how small a million seemed. As the old man got richer, Snead imagined his own bequest growing with each will.

He'd occasionally asked about the matter, subtle, gentle inquiries made at just the right moments, he thought. But Mr. Phelan had cursed him and threatened to cut him out completely. 'You're as bad as my children,' he had said, crushing poor Snead.

Somehow he'd gone from a million to zero, and he was bitter about it. He would be forced to join the enemies simply because he had no choice.

He found the new office of Hark Gettys & Associates near Dupont Circle. The receptionist explained that Mr. Gettys was very busy. 'So am I,' Snead replied rudely. Because he'd been so close to Troy, he had spent most of his life around lawyers. They were always busy.

'Give him this,' he said, handing her an envelope.

213

'It's quite urgent. I'll wait over there for ten minutes, then I'll walk down the street to the next law office.'

Snead took a seat and stared at the floor. Cheap new carpet. The receptionist hesitated for a moment, then disappeared through a door. The envelope held a small handwritten note that read: 'I worked for Troy Phelan for thirty years. I know everything. Malcolm Snead.'

Hark appeared in a flash, holding the note, smiling goofily as if friendliness would impress Snead. They practically ran down the hall to a large office, the receptionist behind them. No, Snead did not want coffee, tea, water, or a cola. Hark slammed the door and locked it.

The office smelled of fresh paint. The desk and shelves were new and the woods didn't match. Boxes of files and junk were stacked along the walls. Snead took his time examining the details. 'Just move in?' he said.

'Couple of weeks ago.'

Snead hated the place, and he wasn't sure about the lawyer either. He wore a cheap wool suit, much less expensive than the one Snead was wearing.

'Thirty years, huh?' Hark said, still holding the note.

'That's right.'

'Were you with him when he jumped?'

'No. He jumped alone.'

A fake laugh, then the smile returned. 'I mean, were you in the room?'

'Yes. I almost caught him.'

'Must've been terrible.'

'It was. Still is.'

'Did you see him sign the will, the last one?'

'I did.'

'Did you see him write the damned thing?'

Snead was perfectly prepared to lie. The truth

214

meant nothing because the old man had lied to him. What was there to lose?

'I saw a lot of things,' he said. 'And I know a lot more. This visit is about nothing but money. Mr. Phelan promised that he would take care of me in his will. There were many promises, all broken.'

'So you're in the same boat as my client,' Hark said.

'I hope not. I despise your client and his miserable siblings. Let's get that straight on the front end.'

'I think it's straight.'

'No one was closer to Troy Phelan than I. I saw and heard things no one else can testify to.'

'So you wanna be a witness?'

'I am a witness, an expert. And I'm very expensive.'

Their eyes locked for a second. The message was delivered and received.

'The law says that laymen cannot render opinions as to the mental capacity of one executing a will, but you can certainly testify as to specific acts and deeds that prove an unsound mind.'

'I know all this,' Snead said rudely.

'Was he crazy?'

'He was or he wasn't. Doesn't matter to me. I can go either way.'

Hark had to stop and contemplate this. He scratched his face and studied the wall.

Snead decided to help him. 'This is the way I see it. Your boy got screwed, along with his brother and sisters. They each got five million bucks when they turned twenty-one, and we know what they did with the money. Since they're all heavily in debt, they have no choice but to contest the will. No jury's gonna feel sorry for them, though. They're a bunch of greedy losers. It'll be a tough case to win. But you and the other legal eagles will attack the will, and you'll create this huge mess of a lawsuit that quickly gets in the tabloids because there's eleven billion at stake. Since you don't have much of a case, you hope for a settlement before you go to trial.'

'You catch on quick.'

'No. I watched Mr. Phelan for thirty years. Anyway, the size of your settlement depends on me. If my recall is clear and detailed, then perhaps my old boss lacked testamentary capacity when he wrote the will.'

'Then your memory comes and goes.'

'My memory is whatever I want it to be. There's no one to question it.'

'What do you want?'

'Money.'

'How much?'

'Five million.'

'That's a lot.'

'It's nothing. I'll take it from this side, or the other. It doesn't matter.'

'How am I supposed to get five million bucks to you?'

'Don't know. I'm not a lawyer. I figure you and your cronies can conjure up some dirty little plan.'

There was a long pause as Hark began the conjuring. He had a lot of questions, but suspected he wouldn't get a lot of answers. At least not now.

'Any more witnesses?' he asked.

'Only one. Her name is Nicolette. She was Mr. Phelan's last secretary.'

'How much does she know?'

'Depends. She can be bought.'

'You've already talked to her.'

'Every day. We're a package.'

'How much for her?'

'She'll be covered in the five million.'

'A real bargain. Anybody else?'

'No one of consequence.'

Hark closed his eyes and massaged both temples. 'I

don't object to your five million,' he said, pinching his nose. 'I just don't know how we can funnel it to you.'

'I'm sure you'll think of something.'

'Give me some time, okay? I need to think about this.'

'I'm in no hurry. I'll give you a week. If you say no, then I'll go to the other side.'

'There is no other side.'

'Don't be so certain.'

'You know something about Rachel Lane?'

'I know everything,' Snead said, then left the office.

TWENTY-SIX

The first streaks of dawn brought no surprises. They were tied to a tree at the edge of a small river that looked like all the others they'd seen. The clouds were heavy again; the light of day came slowly.

Breakfast was a small box of cookies, the last of the rations Welly had packed for them. Nate ate slowly, wondering with each bite when he might eat again.

The current was strong, so they drifted with it as the sun rose. The only sound was the rush of the water. They were conserving gas and delaying the moment when Jevy would be forced to try and start the motor.

They drifted into a flooded area where three streams met, and for a few moments sat in the stillness.

'I guess we're lost, aren't we?' Nate said.

'I know exactly where we are.'

'Where?'

'We're in the Pantanal. And all rivers run to the Paraguay.'

'Eventually.'

'Yes, eventually.' Jevy removed the top cover of the motor and wiped the moisture from the carburetor. He adjusted the throttle, checked the oil, then tried to start the motor. On the fifth pull, the motor caught and sputtered, then quit.

I will die here, Nate said to himself. I'll either

drown, starve, or be eaten, but it is here, in this immense swamp, that I will breathe my last.

To their surprise, they heard a shout. The voice was high, like that of a young girl. The sputtering of the motor had attracted the attention of another human. The voice came from a weedy marsh along the bank of a converging stream. Jevy yelled and a few seconds later the voice yelled back.

A kid of no more than fifteen came through the weeds in a tiny canoe, hand-carved from the trunk of a tree. With a homemade paddle he cut through the water with amazing ease and speed. '*Bom dia,*' he said with a wide smile. The little face was brown and square, and probably the most beautiful Nate had seen in years. He threw a rope and the two boats were attached.

A long lazy conversation ensued, and after a while Nate was agitated. 'What's he saying?' he snapped at Jevy.

The kid looked at Nate, and Jevy said, '*Americano.*'

'He says we're a great distance from the Cabixa River,' Jevy said.

'I could've told you that.'

'He says the Paraguay is a half a day to the east.'

'By canoe, right?'

'No, by plane.'

'Funny. How long will it take us?'

'Four hours, more or less.'

Five, maybe six hours. And that was with a properly running motor. It would take a week if they were forced to paddle.

The Portuguese resumed, in no particular hurry. The canoe was empty except for a roll of fishing line wrapped around a tin can, and a jar of mud which Nate assumed contained worms or some type of bait. What did he know about fishing? He scratched his mosquito bites.

A year ago he'd been skiing in Utah with the boys. The drink of the day had been some type of tequila concoction, which, typically, Nate consumed with gusto until he passed out. The hangover had lasted for two days.

There was a flourish in the chatter, and suddenly they were pointing. Jevy looked at him as he spoke.

'What is it?' Nate asked.

'The Indians are not far away.'

'How far?'

'One hour, maybe two.'

'Can he take us there?'

'I know the way.'

'I'm sure you do. But I'd feel better if he'd tag along.'

It was a slight affront to Jevy's pride, but under the circumstances he could not argue. 'He may want a little money.'

'Whatever.' If the kid only knew. The Phelan estate on one side of the table, and this skinny little *pantaneiro* on the other. Nate smiled at the mental picture. How about a fleet of canoes, with rods and reels and depth finders? Just name it, son, and it's yours.

'Ten reais,' Jevy said, after brief negotiations.

'Fine.' For about ten bucks, they would be delivered to Rachel Lane.

A plan was devised. Jevy tilted the outboard so that the prop was out of the water, and they began paddling. They followed the boy in the canoe for twenty minutes until they entered a small shallow stream with rapid currents. Nate withdrew his paddle, caught his breath, and wiped sweat from his face. His heart was pounding and his muscles were already tired. The clouds were breaking up, so the sun was bearing down.

Jevy went to work on the motor. Luckily it started,

220

and kept running, and they followed the boy, his canoe easily outpacing them and their sputtering outboard.

It was almost one when they found the higher ground. The floodwaters gradually disappeared, so that the rivers were lined with thick brush and the trees were dense. The kid was somber and, oddly, concerned with the position of the sun.

Just up there, he told Jevy. Just around the bend. He seemed afraid to go further.

I'll stop here, he said. I need to return home.

Nate handed him the money, and they thanked him. He headed back with the current and disappeared quickly. They plowed ahead, the outboard halting and struggling at half-speed, but getting them there nonetheless.

The river ran into a forest where the trees hung low over the water, so low that they weaved together above and formed a tunnel that blocked out light. It was dark, and the uneven hum of their motor resounded from the banks. Nate had the eerie suspicion that they were being watched. He could almost feel the arrows being aimed at him. He braced for an attack of deadly blow darts by savages dressed in war paint and trained to kill anyone with a white face.

But they saw children first, happy little brown bodies splashing in the water. The tunnel ended near a settlement.

The mothers were bathing too, just as completely naked as their children, and thoroughly unconcerned about it. At first, they retreated to the bank when they saw the johnboat. Jevy killed the engine and began talking and smiling as they drifted in. An older girl ran away, in the direction of the settlement.

'*Fala português?*' Jevy asked the crowd of four

women and seven children. They just stared. The smaller ones hid behind their mothers. The women were short, with thick bodies and small breasts.

'Are they friendly?' Nate asked.

'The men will tell us.'

The men arrived within minutes, three of them, also short, thick, and muscular. Thankfully, their privates were covered with small leather pouches.

The oldest one claimed to speak Jevy's language, but his Portuguese was rudimentary at best. Nate stayed in the boat, where things appeared to be safe, while Jevy leaned on a tree near the water and tried to make himself understood. The Indians crowded around Jevy, who was a foot taller than the men.

After a few minutes of repetition and hand gestures, Nate said, 'Translation please.'

The Indians looked at Nate.

'*Americano*,' Jevy explained, and another conversation ensued.

'What about the woman?' Nate asked.

'We haven't got that far yet. I'm still trying to convince them not to burn you alive.'

'Try harder.'

More Indians arrived. Their huts were visible a hundred yards away, near the edge of a forest. Upriver, a half-dozen canoes were tied to the bank. The children became bored. They slowly left their mothers and waded close to the boat to inspect it. They were also intrigued by the man with the white face. Nate smiled and winked and before long got a grin. If Welly hadn't been so damned cheap with the cookies, Nate would've had something to share with them.

The conversation poked along. The Indian doing the talking would periodically turn to his pals and make a report, and inevitably his words caused great concern. Their language was a series of primal grunts and strains, all delivered with as little lip movement as possible.

'What's he saying?' Nate growled.

'I don't know,' Jevy replied.

A little boy placed his hand on the edge of the boat, and studied Nate with black pupils as big as quarters. Very softly he said, 'Hello.' Nate knew they were in the right place.

No one heard the boy but Nate. He leaned forward, and softly said, 'Hello.'

'Good-bye,' the boy said, without moving. Rachel had taught him at least two English words.

'What is your name?' Nate asked, his voice a whisper.

'Hello,' he repeated.

Under the tree, the translating was making the same progress. The male Indians were huddling in animated conversation while the women said nothing.

'What about the woman?' Nate repeated.

'I asked. They have no answer.'

'What does that mean?'

'I'm not sure. I think she's here, but they are reluctant for some reason.'

'Why would they be reluctant?'

Jevy frowned and looked away. How was he supposed to know?

They talked some more, then the Indians left en masse – men first, then the women, then the children. They trooped single file to the settlement, disappearing from view.

'Did you make them mad?'

'No. They want to have a meeting of some kind.'

'Do you think she's here?'

'I think so.' Jevy took his seat in the boat and prepared himself for a nap. It was almost one, in whatever time zone they happened to be in. Lunch was over and done with without so much as a soggy saltine.

The hike began around three. They were led by a small group of young men away from the river, along the dirt path to the village, through the huts where everyone stood still and watched, then away again, along another path into the woods.

It's a death march, thought Nate. They're taking us into the jungle for some Stone Age blood ritual. He followed Jevy, who loped along in a confident gait. 'Where the hell are we going?' he hissed, like a prisoner of war afraid to offend his captors.

'Relax.'

The woods opened to a clearing, and they were near the river again. The leader suddenly stopped, and pointed. At the edge of the water, an anaconda stretched in the sun. He was black with yellow markings on his underside. His girth was at least a foot at its widest. 'How long is he?' Nate asked.

'Six or seven meters. Finally, you see an anaconda,' Jevy said.

Nate's knees buckled and his mouth was dry. He had been joking about the snakes. The sight of a real one, long and massive, was truly amazing.

'Some Indians worship snakes,' Jevy said.

Then what are our missionaries doing? Nate thought. He would ask Rachel about this practice.

The mosquitoes seemed to bother only him. The Indians were immune. Jevy never swatted. Nate slapped his own flesh and scratched until he drew blood. His repellent was in the boat, along with his tent and machete and everything else he owned at the moment, no doubt being examined by the children.

The hike was adventurous for the first half hour,

then the heat and the insects made things monotonous. 'How far are we going?' Nate asked, not really expecting an answer with any accuracy.

Jevy said something to the point man, who said something in return. 'Not far,' came the reply. They crossed another trail, then a wider one. There was traffic in the area. Soon they saw the first hut, then smelled smoke.

When they were two hundred yards away, the leader pointed to a shaded area near the river. Nate and Jevy were led to a bench made of hollow cane poles lashed together with string. They were left there with two guards while the others reported to the village.

As time passed, the two guards grew weary and decided to take a nap. They leaned against the trunk of a tree, and were soon asleep.

'I guess we could escape,' Nate said.

'To where?'

'Are you hungry?'

'Sort of. Are you?'

'No, I'm stuffed,' Nate said. 'I ate seven thin cookies nine hours ago. Remind me to slap Welly when I see him.'

'I hope he is okay.'

'Why shouldn't he be? He's swinging in my hammock, drinking fresh coffee, safe and dry and well fed.'

They wouldn't have brought them this far if Rachel wasn't nearby. As Nate rested on the bench and stared at the tops of the huts in the distance, he had many questions about her. He was curious about her appearance – her mother was supposed to have been a beautiful woman. Troy Phelan had a good eye for women. What kind of clothes would she wear? The Ipicas she ministered to were naked. How long since she'd seen civilization? Was he the first American to ever visit the village?

225

How would she react to his presence? And to the money?

As time dragged along, Nate became more anxious about meeting her.

Both of the guards were asleep when there was movement from the settlement. Jevy tossed a pebble at them and whistled quietly. They jumped to their feet and resumed their positions.

The weeds along the trail were knee-high, and from the distance they could see a patrol moving their way, along the path. Rachel was with them; she was coming. There was a light yellow shirt in the midst of the brown-skinned chests, and a lighter face under a straw hat. From a hundred yards, Nate could see her.

'We've found our girl,' he said.

'Yes, I think we have.'

They took their time. Three young men were in front, and three behind. She was slightly taller than the Indians, and carried herself with an easy elegance. She could've been out for a walk among the flowers. There was no hurry.

Nate watched every step. She was very slender, with wide bony shoulders. She began looking in their direction as they grew closer. Nate and Jevy stood to meet her.

The Indians stopped at the edge of the shade, but Rachel kept walking. She removed her hat. Her hair was brown and half-gray, and very short. She stopped a few feet from Jevy and Nate.

'*Boa tarde, senhor,*' she said to Jevy, then looked at Nate. Her eyes were dark blue, almost indigo. No wrinkles, no makeup. She was forty-two years old and aging quite well, with the soft glow of one who knew little stress.

'*Boa tarde.*'

She didn't offer to shake hands, nor did she give her name. The next move belonged to them.

'My name is Nate O'Riley. I'm an attorney from Washington.'

'And you?' she said to Jevy.

'I'm Jevy Cardozo, from Corumbá. I'm his guide.'

She looked them up and down with a slight grin. The moment was not at all unpleasant for her. She was enjoying the encounter.

'What brings you here?' she asked. It was American English with no accent, no trace of Louisiana or Montana, just the flat, precise, inflectionless English from Sacramento or St. Louis.

'We heard the fishing was good,' Nate said.

No response. 'He makes bad jokes,' Jevy said, apologizing.

'Sorry. I'm looking for Rachel Lane. I have reason to believe you and she are one and the same.'

She absorbed this without changing expressions. 'Why do you want to find Rachel Lane?'

'Because I'm a lawyer, and my firm has an important legal matter with Rachel Lane.'

'What kind of legal matter?'

'I can tell no one but her.'

'I'm not Rachel Lane. I'm sorry.'

Jevy sighed and Nate's shoulders slumped. She saw every movement, every reaction, every twitch. 'Are you hungry?' she asked them.

They both nodded. She called the Indians and gave them instructions. 'Jevy,' she said, 'go with these men into the village. They will feed you, and give you enough food for Mr. O'Riley here.'

They sat on the bench, in the darkening shade, watching in silence as the Indians took Jevy to the village. He turned around once, just to make sure Nate was okay.

TWENTY-SEVEN

She didn't seem as tall away from the Indians. And she had avoided whatever the women ate that made them thick. Her legs were thin and long. She wore leather sandals, which seemed odd in a culture where no one had shoes. Where did she get them? And where did she get her yellow short-sleeved shirt and khaki shorts? Oh, the questions he had.

Her clothing was simple and well worn. If she wasn't Rachel Lane, then surely she knew where Rachel was.

Their knees almost touched. 'Rachel Lane ceased to exist many years ago,' she said, gazing at the village in the distance. 'I kept the name Rachel, but dropped the Lane. It must be serious or you wouldn't be here.' She spoke softly and slowly, no syllable missed and each carefully weighed.

'Troy's dead. He killed himself three weeks ago.'

She lowered her head slightly, closed her eyes, and appeared to be praying. It was a brief prayer, followed by a long pause. Silence didn't bother her. 'Did you know him?' she finally asked.

'I met him once, years ago. Our firm has many lawyers, and I personally never worked on Troy's business. No, I didn't know him.'

'Neither did I. He was my earthly father, and I've

228

spent many hours praying for him, but he was always a stranger.'

'When did you last see him?' Nate's words too were softer and slower. She had a soothing effect.

'Many years ago. Before I went to college . . . How much do you know about me?'

'Not much. You don't leave much of a trail.'

'Then how did you find me?'

'Troy helped. He tried to find you before he died, but couldn't. He knew you were a missionary with World Tribes, and that you were in this general part of the world. The rest was up to me.'

'How could he have known that?'

'He had an awful lot of money.'

'And that's why you're here.'

'Yes, that's why I'm here. We need to talk business.'

'Troy must've left me something in his will.'

'You could say that.'

'I don't want to talk business. I want to chat. Do you know how often I hear English?'

'Rarely, I would imagine.'

'I go to Corumbá once a year for supplies. I phone the home office, and for about ten minutes I speak English. It's always frightening.'

'Why?'

'I'm nervous. My hands shake as I hold the phone. I know the people I'm talking to, but I'm afraid I will use the wrong words. Sometimes I even stutter. Ten minutes a year.'

'You're doing a fine job now.'

'I'm very nervous.'

'Relax. I'm a swell guy.'

'But you've found me. I was seeing a patient just an hour ago when the boys came to tell me that an American was here. I ran to my hut and started praying. God gave me strength.'

'I come in peace for all mankind.'

'You seem like a nice man.'

If you only knew, thought Nate. 'Thanks. You, uh, said something about seeing a patient.'

'Yes.'

'I thought you were a missionary.'

'I am. I'm also a doctor.'

And Nate's specialty was suing doctors. It was neither the time nor the place for a discussion about medical malpractice. 'That's not in my research.'

'I changed my name after college, before med school and seminary. That's probably where the trail ended.'

'Exactly. Why did you change your name?'

'It's complicated, at least it was then. It doesn't seem important now.'

A breeze settled in from the river. It was almost five. The clouds over the forest were dark and low. She saw him glance at his watch. 'The boys are bringing your tent here. This is a good place to sleep tonight.'

'Thanks, I guess. We'll be safe, won't we?'

'Yes. God will protect you. Say your prayers.'

At that moment, Nate planned to pray like a preacher. The proximity to the river was of particular concern. He could shut his eyes and see that anaconda slithering up to his tent.

'You do pray, don't you, Mr. O'Riley?'

'Please call me Nate. Yes, I pray.'

'Are you Irish?'

'I'm a mutt. More German than anything else. My father had Irish ancestors. Family history has never interested me.'

'What church do you attend?'

'Episcopal.' Catholic, Lutheran, Episcopal, it didn't matter. Nate hadn't seen the inside of a church since his second wedding.

His spiritual life was a subject he preferred to avoid. Theology was not his long suit, and he didn't want to discuss it with a missionary. She paused, as usual, and he changed directions. 'Are these Indians peaceful?'

'For the most part. The Ipicas are not warriors, but they do not trust white people.'

'What about you?'

'I've been here eleven years. They have accepted me.'

'How long did it take?'

'I was lucky because there was a missionary couple here before me. They had learned the language and translated the New Testament. And I'm a doctor. I made friends fast when I helped the women through childbirth.'

'Your Portuguese sounded pretty good.'

'I'm fluent. I speak Spanish, Ipica, and Machiguenga.'

'What is that?'

'The Machiguenga are natives in the mountains of Peru. I was there for six years. I had just become comfortable with the language when they evacuated me.'

'Why?'

'Guerrillas.'

As if snakes and alligators and diseases and floods weren't enough.

'They kidnapped two missionaries in a village not far from me. But God saved them. They were released unharmed four years later.'

'Any guerrillas around here?'

'No. This is Brazil. The people are very peaceful. There are some drug runners, but nobody comes this deep into the Pantanal.'

'Which brings up an interesting point. How far away is the Paraguay River?'

'This time of the year, eight hours.'

'Brazilian hours?'

She smiled at this. 'You've learned that time is slower here. Eight to ten hours, American time.'

'By canoe?'

'That's how we travel. I used to have a boat with a motor. But it was old, and it eventually wore out.'

'How long does it take if you have a boat with a motor?'

'Five hours, more or less. It's the flood season, and it's easy to get lost.'

'So I've learned.'

'The rivers run together. You'll need to take one of the fishermen with you when you leave. There's no way you'll find the Paraguay without a guide.'

'And you go once a year?'

'Yes, but I go in the dry season, in August. It's cooler then, not as many mosquitoes.'

'You go alone?'

'No. I get Lako, my Indian friend, to travel with me to the Paraguay. It takes about six hours by canoe when the rivers are down. I'll wait for a boat, then catch a ride to Corumbá. I'll stay for a few days, do my business, then catch a boat back.'

Nate thought of how few boats he'd seen on the Paraguay. 'Just any boat?'

'Usually a cattle boat. The captains are good about taking passengers.'

She travels by canoe because her old boat wore out. She bums rides on cattle boats to visit Corumbá, her only contact with civilization. How would the money change her? Nate asked himself. The question seemed impossible to answer.

He would tell her tomorrow, when the day was fresh, when he was rested and fed and they had hours to deal with the issues. Figures appeared at the edge of the settlement – men walking in their direction.

'Here they are,' she said. 'We eat just before dark, then we go to sleep.'

232

'I guess there's nothing to do afterward.'

'Nothing we can discuss,' she said quickly, and it was funny.

Jevy appeared with a group of Indians, one of whom handed Rachel a small square basket. She passed it to Nate, who removed a small loaf of hard bread.

'This is manioc,' she said. 'It's our main food.'

And evidently their only food, at least for that meal. Nate was into his second loaf when they were joined by Indians from the first village. They brought the tent, mosquito net, blankets, and bottled water from the boat.

'We're staying here tonight,' Nate said to Jevy.

'Says who?'

'It's the best spot,' Rachel said. 'I would offer you a place in the village, but the leader must first approve a visit by white men.'

'That would be me,' Nate said.

'Yes.'

'And not him?' He nodded at Jevy.

'He went for food, not to sleep. The rules are complicated.'

This struck Nate as funny – primitive natives yet to discover clothing but following a complicated system of rules.

'I would like to leave by noon tomorrow,' Nate said to her.

'That too will be up to the leader.'

'You mean we can't leave when we want?'

'You will leave when he says you can leave. Don't worry.'

'Are you and the chief close?'

'We get along.'

She sent the Indians back to the village. The sun had disappeared over the mountains. The shadows from the forest were engulfing them.

For a few minutes, Rachel watched as Jevy and Nate

struggled with the tent. It looked quite small rolled up in its case, and expanded just a little as they hooked the poles together. Nate wasn't sure it would hold Jevy, let alone the both of them. Fully erected, it was waist-high, pitched sharply from the sides, and painfully small for two grown men.

'I'm going,' she announced. 'You will be fine here.'

'Promise?' Nate said, with sincerity.

'I can have a couple of boys stand watch if you like.'

'We'll be fine,' Jevy said.

'What time do you folks wake up around here?' Nate asked.

'An hour before sunrise.'

'I'm sure we'll be awake,' Nate said, glancing at the tent. 'Can we meet early? We have a lot to discuss.'

'Yes. I'll send some food out at daybreak. Then we'll chat.'

'That would be nice.'

'Say your prayers, Mr. O'Riley.'

'I will.'

She stepped into the darkness and was gone. For a moment, Nate could see her silhouette winding along the trail, then nothing. The village was lost in the blackness of the night.

They sat on the bench for hours, waiting for the air to cool, dreading the moment when they would be forced to pack themselves into the tent and sleep back to back, both smelly and sweaty. There was no choice. The tent, flimsy as it was, would protect them from mosquitoes and other insects. It would also keep out things that crawled.

They talked about the village. Jevy told Indian stories, all of which ended in the death of someone. He finally asked, 'Did you tell her about the money?'

'No. I'll do that tomorrow.'

234

'You've seen her now. What will she think about the money?'

'I have no idea. She's happy here. It seems cruel to upset her life.'

'Then give me the money. It won't upset my life.'

They followed the pecking order. Nate crawled into the tent first. He'd spent the previous night watching the sky from the bottom of the boat, so the fatigue hit fast.

When he was snoring, Jevy slowly unzipped the tent door, and nudged here and there until he had a spot. His pal was unconscious.

TWENTY-EIGHT

After nine hours of sleep, the Ipicas arose before dawn to begin their day. The women built small cooking fires outside their huts, then left with the children for the river, to collect water and to bathe. As a rule, they waited until first light to walk the dirt trails. It was prudent to see what lay before them.

In Portuguese, the snake was known as an *urutu*. The Indians called it a *bima*. It was common around the waterways of southern Brazil, and often fatal. The girl's name was Ayesh, age seven, helped into the world by the white missionary. Ayesh was walking in front of her mother instead of behind, as was the custom, and she felt the *bima* squirm under her bare foot.

It struck her below the ankle as she screamed. By the time her father got to her, she was in shock and her right foot had doubled in size. A boy of fifteen, the fastest runner in the tribe, was dispatched to get Rachel.

There were four small Ipica settlements along two rivers that met in a fork very near the spot where Jevy and Nate had stopped. The distance from the fork to the last Ipica hut was no more than five miles. The settlements were distinct and self-contained little tribes, but they were all Ipicas, with the same language, heritage, and customs. They socialized and intermarried.

236

Ayesh lived in the third settlement from the fork. Rachel was in the second, the largest. The runner found her as she was reading scriptures in the small hut where she'd lived for eleven years. She quickly checked her supplies and filled her small medical bag.

There were four poisonous snakes in their part of the Pantanal, and at various times Rachel had had the antivenin for each. But not this time. The runner told her the snake was a *bima*. Its antivenin was manufactured by a Brazilian company, but she had been unable to find it during her last trip to Corumbá. The pharmacies there had less than half the medicines she needed.

She laced her leather boots and left with her bag. Lako and two other boys from her village joined her as she jogged away, through the tall weeds and into the woods.

According to Rachel's statistics, there were eighty-six adult females, eighty-one adult males, and seventy-two children in the four settlements, a total of 239 Ipicas. When she began working with the Ipicas eleven years earlier, there had been 280. Malaria took the weak ones every few years. An outbreak of cholera killed twenty in one village in 1991. If Rachel hadn't insisted on a quarantine, most of the Ipicas would've been wiped out.

With the diligence of an anthropologist, she kept records of births, deaths, weddings, family trees, illnesses, and treatments. Most of the time she knew who was having an extramarital affair, and with whom. She knew every name in every village. She had baptized Ayesh's parents in the river where they bathed.

Ayesh was small and thin, and she would probably die because there was no medicine. The antivenin was readily available in the States and in the larger cities of

237

Brazil, and not terribly expensive. Her small budget from World Tribes would cover it. Three injections in six hours and death could be prevented. Without it, the child would become violently ill with nausea, then a fever would hit, followed by a coma, then death.

It had been three years since the Ipicas had seen a death by snakebite. And for the first time in two years, Rachel had no antivenin.

Ayesh's parents were Christians, new saints struggling with a new religion. About a third of the Ipicas had been converted. Because of the work of Rachel and her predecessors, half of them could read and write.

She prayed as she trotted behind the boys. She was lean and tough. She walked several miles a day and ate little. The Indians admired her stamina.

Jevy was washing himself in the river when Nate unzipped the mosquito fly and extricated himself from the tent. He still carried bruises from the plane crash. Sleeping in the boat and on the ground did little to ease the soreness. He stretched his back and legs, aching all over, feeling every one of his forty-eight years. He could see Jevy, waist-deep in water that looked much clearer than the rest of the Pantanal.

I'm lost, Nate whispered to himself. I'm hungry. I have no toilet paper. He gingerly touched his toes as he summed up his sad inventory.

It was an adventure, dammit! It was time for all lawyers to charge into the new year with resolutions to bill more hours, win bigger verdicts, cut more overhead, take home more money. He'd made those vows for years, and now they seemed silly.

With a little luck, he'd sleep in his hammock tonight, swinging in the breeze, sipping coffee. To the best of his recollection, Nate had never before longed for black beans and rice.

Jevy returned as a patrol of Indians arrived from the village. The chief wanted to see them. 'He wants to have bread,' Jevy said as they walked away.

'Bread's fine. Ask if they have bacon and eggs.'

'They eat a lot of monkey.'

He didn't appear to be kidding. At the edge of the village, a group of children stood waiting for a look at the strangers. Nate offered them all a frozen smile. He'd never felt so white in his life, and he wanted to be liked. Some naked mothers gawked from the first hut. When he and Jevy entered the wide common area, everyone stopped and stared.

Small fires were burning out; breakfast was over. The smoke hung like fog over the roofs, and made the humid air even stickier. It was a few minutes after seven, and already very hot.

The village architect had done a fine job. Each dwelling was perfectly square with a thatched roof angled steeply, almost to the ground. Some were larger than others, but the design never varied. They circled the settlement in an oval-shaped ring, all facing a large flat area – the town square. In the center were four large structures – two circular and two rectangular – and all had the same thick straw roofs.

The chief was waiting for them. Not surprisingly, his home was the largest hut in the village. And he was the largest Indian of the lot. He was young, and lacked the heavy wrinkles across the forehead and the thick belly the older men carried with pride. He stood and gave Nate a look that would have horrified John Wayne. An older warrior did the interpreting, and within minutes Nate and Jevy were asked to sit near the fire, where the chief's naked wife was preparing breakfast.

When she bent over, her breasts swung about, and poor Nate couldn't help but stare, if only for a long second. There was nothing particularly sexy about the naked woman or her breasts. It was just the fact that she could be so naked and so unconcerned about it.

Where was his camera? The boys around the office would never believe it without proof.

She handed Nate a wooden plate covered with a serving of what appeared to be boiled potatoes. He glanced at Jevy, who gave a quick nod as if he knew everything about Indian cuisine. She served the chief last, and when he began eating with his fingers, so did Nate. It was a cross between a turnip and a redskin potato, with very little taste.

Jevy talked while he ate, and the chief enjoyed the conversation. After a few sentences, Jevy would translate things into English and pass them along.

The village never flooded. They had been there for more than twenty years. The soil was good. They preferred not to move, but sometimes the soil forced them to. His father had been a chief too. The chief, according to the chief, was the wisest, smartest, and fairest of them all, and he could not engage in extramarital affairs. Most of the other men did, but not the chief.

Nate suspected there was little else to do but fool around.

The chief had never seen the Paraguay River. He preferred hunting over fishing, thus spent more time in the woods than on the rivers. He'd learned basic Portuguese from his father and from the white missionaries.

Nate ate, listened, and watched the village for any sign of Rachel.

She wasn't there, the chief explained. She was in the next village tending to a child who'd been bitten by a snake. He wasn't sure when she would return.

Just wonderful, thought Nate.

'He wants us to stay here tonight, in the village,' Jevy said. The wife was refilling their plates.

240

'Didn't know we were staying,' Nate said.

'He says we are.'

'Tell him I'll think about it.'

'You tell him.'

Nate cursed himself for not bringing the SatFone. Josh was surely pacing the floor of his office right now, worried sick. They had not talked in almost a week.

Jevy said something slightly humorous that upon translation became downright funny. The chief roared with laughter, and soon everyone else was laughing too. Including Nate, who laughed at himself for laughing with the Indians.

They declined an invitation to go hunting. A patrol of young men led them back to the first village, to their boat. Jevy wanted to clean the spark plugs again and fiddle with the carburetor. Nate had nothing else to do.

Lawyer Valdir took the early call from Mr. Stafford. The pleasantries took only seconds.

'I haven't heard from Nate O'Riley in days,' Stafford said.

'But he has one of those phones,' Valdir said, on the defensive, as if it was his duty to protect Mr. O'Riley.

'Yes, he does. That's what worries me. He can call anytime, from anywhere.'

'Can he use the phone in bad weather?'

'No. I suppose not.'

'We've had many storms down here. It is, after all, the rainy season.'

'You haven't heard from your boy?'

'No. They are together. The guide is very good. The boat is very good. I'm sure they are well.'

'Then why hasn't he called?'

'I can't answer. But the skies have not been clear. Perhaps he cannot use his phone.'

They agreed that Valdir would call at once if

something was heard from the boat. Valdir walked to his open window and looked at the busy streets of Corumbá. The Paraguay River was just down the hill. Stories were legion of people who entered the Pantanal and never came back. It was part of the lore, and the lure.

Jevy's father had piloted the rivers for thirty years, and his body was never recovered.

Welly found the law office an hour later. He had not met Mr. Valdir, but he knew from Jevy that the lawyer was paying for the expedition.

'It's very important,' he told the secretary. 'It is urgent.'

Valdir heard the ruckus and appeared from his office. 'Who are you?' he demanded.

'My name is Welly. Jevy hired me as a deckhand on the *Santa Loura*.'

'The *Santa Loura*!'

'Yes.'

'Where is Jevy?'

'He's still in the Pantanal.'

'Where is the boat?'

'It sank.'

Valdir realized the boy was tired and frightened. 'Sit down,' he said, and the secretary ran to get water. 'Tell me everything.'

Welly clutched the arms of his chair, and spoke rapidly. 'They left in the johnboat to find the Indians, Jevy and Mr. O'Riley.'

'When?'

'I don't know. A few days ago. I was to stay with the *Santa Loura*. A storm hit, the biggest storm ever. It blew the boat free in the middle of the night, then rolled it over. I was thrown into the water and picked up later by a cattle boat.'

'When did you arrive here?'

'Only a half hour ago.'

The secretary brought a glass of water. Welly thanked her and asked for coffee. Valdir leaned on her desk and watched the poor kid. He was dirty and smelled like cow manure.

'So the boat is gone?' Valdir said.

'Yes. I'm sorry. There was nothing I could do. I have never seen such a storm.'

'Where was Jevy during the storm?'

'Somewhere on the Cabixa River. I fear for him.'

Valdir walked to his office, where he closed the door and returned to his window. Mr. Stafford was three thousand miles away. Jevy could survive in a small boat. No sense jumping to conclusions.

He decided not to call for a few days. Give Jevy time, and surely he would return to Corumbá.

The Indian stood in the boat and braced himself by clutching Nate's shoulder. There was no noticeable improvement in the motor's performance. It continued to sputter and miss, and at full throttle had less than half the power it had when they left the *Santa Loura*.

They passed the first settlement, and the river bent and looped almost to the point of going in circles. Then it forked, and the Indian pointed. Twenty minutes later, their little tent came into view. They docked where Jevy had bathed earlier in the day. They broke camp and moved their belongings into the village, where the chief wanted them.

Rachel had not returned.

Because she was not one of them, her hut was not in the oval. It was a hundred feet away, nearer to the edge of the forest, alone. It appeared to be smaller than any of the others, and when Jevy inquired about this, the Indian who'd been assigned to them explained that it was because she had no family. The

243

three of them – Nate, Jevy, and their Indian – spent two hours under a tree at the edge of the village, watching the daily routine while waiting for Rachel.

The Indian had learned Portuguese from the Coopers, the missionary couple who had come before Rachel. And he had a few words of English he intermittently tried on Nate. The Coopers had been the first white people any of the Ipicas had ever seen. Mrs. Cooper died of malaria and Mr. Cooper went back to wherever he came from.

The men were hunting and fishing, he explained to his guests, and the younger ones were no doubt sneaking around seeing their girlfriends. The women had the hard work – cooking, baking, cleaning, watching the children. But labor was at a languid pace. If time moved slower south of the equator, then there was no clock at all among the Ipicas.

The doors to the huts remained open, and children ran from one to the other. Young girls braided their hair in the shade, while their mothers worked over the fires.

Cleanliness was an obsession. The dirt of the common areas was swept with straw brooms. The exteriors of the huts were tidy and neat. The women and children bathed three times a day in the river; twice for the men, and never with the women. Everybody was naked but some things were private.

Late in the afternoon, the men gathered outside the men's house, the larger of the two rectangular buildings in the center. They worked on their hair for a while – cutting and cleaning – then began to wrestle. The matchups were one on one and toe to toe, with the object being to throw the opponent to the ground. It was a rough game, but with strict rules and smiles afterward. The chief settled any disputes. The women watched from their doorways with only a passing interest, as if they were expected to. Little boys imitated their fathers.

And Nate sat on a block of wood, under a tree, watching a drama from another age, and wondering, not for the first time, where he was.

TWENTY-NINE

Few of the Indians around Nate knew the girl's name was Ayesh. She was only a child and she lived in another village. They all knew, though, that a girl had been bitten. They gossiped about it throughout the day while they kept their own children closer at hand.

Word came during dinner that the girl had died. A messenger arrived in a rush and delivered the news to the chief, and it swept through the huts in a matter of minutes. Mothers gathered their little ones even closer.

Dinner resumed until there was movement along the main trail. Rachel was returning with Lako and the other men who'd been with her all day. As she entered the village, the eating and the chatting stopped as everyone stood and stared. They lowered their heads as she walked by their huts. She smiled at some, whispered to others, paused long enough to say something to the chief, then continued to her hut, followed by Lako, whose limp was worse.

She passed near the tree where Nate and Jevy and their Indian had spent most of the afternoon, but she didn't see them. She wasn't looking. She was tired and suffering and seemed anxious to get home.

'What do we do now?' Nate asked Jevy, who passed the question along in Portuguese.

'We wait,' came the reply.

'Surprise, surprise.'

Lako found them as the sun was falling behind the mountains. Jevy and the Indian went to eat leftovers. Nate followed the boy along the trail to Rachel's dwelling. She was standing in the door, drying her face with a hand towel. Her hair was wet and she had changed clothes.

'Good evening, Mr. O'Riley,' she said, in the same low, slow tone that betrayed nothing.

'Hello, Rachel. Please call me Nate.'

'Sit over there, Nate,' she said, pointing to a short square stump remarkably similar to the one he'd been perched upon for the past six hours. It was in front of the hut, near a ring of rocks where she made her fires. He sat, his rear still numb.

'I'm sorry about the little girl,' Nate said.

'She is with the Lord.'

'Her poor parents aren't.'

'No. They are grieving. It's very sad.'

She sat in the doorway, arms folded over her knees, eyes lost in the distance. The boy stood guard under a nearby tree, almost unseen in the darkness.

'I would invite you into my home,' she said. 'But it would not be proper.'

'No problem here.'

'Only married people can be alone indoors at this time of the day. It's a custom.'

'When in Rome, do like the Romans.'

'Rome is very far away.'

'Everything is very far away.'

'Yes it is. Are you hungry?'

'Are you?'

'No. But then I don't eat much.'

'I'm fine. We need to talk.'

'I'm sorry about today. I'm sure you understand.'

'Of course.'

'I have some manioc and some juice if you'd like.'

'No, really, I'm okay.'

247

'What did you do today?'

'Oh, we met with the chief, had breakfast at his table, hiked back to the first village, got the boat, worked on it, set up our tent behind the chief's hut, then waited for you.'

'The chief liked you?'

'Evidently. He wants us to stay.'

'What do you think of my people?'

'They're all naked.'

'They always have been.'

'How long did it take to get accustomed to it?'

'I don't know. A couple of years. It gradually grows on you, like everything else. I was homesick for three years, and there are times now when I would like to drive a car, eat a pizza, and see a good movie. But you adjust.'

'I can't begin to imagine.'

'It's a matter of calling. I became a Christian when I was fourteen years old, and I knew then that God wanted me to be a missionary. I didn't know exactly where, but I put my faith in Him.'

'He picked a helluva spot.'

'I enjoy your English, but please don't swear.'

'Sorry. Can we talk about Troy?' The shadows were falling fast. They were ten feet apart and could still see each other, but the blackness would soon separate them.

'Suit yourself,' she said, with a weary air of resignation.

'Troy had three wives and six children, six that we knew about. You, of course, were a surprise. He didn't like the other six, but evidently was quite fond of you. He left them virtually nothing, just enough to cover their debts. Everything else was given to Rachel Lane, born out of wedlock on November 2, 1954, at Catholic Hospital in New Orleans, to a woman named

248

Evelyn Cunningham, now deceased. That Rachel would be you.'

The words fell heavy in the thick air; there were no other sounds. Her silhouette absorbed them, and, as usual, she thought before she spoke. 'Troy wasn't fond of me. We hadn't seen each other in twenty years.'

'That's not important. He left his fortune to you. No one had a chance to ask why because he jumped out of a window after signing his last testament. I have a copy for you.'

'I don't want to see it.'

'And I have some other papers which I'd like you to sign, maybe tomorrow, first thing, when we can see. Then I can be on my way.'

'What kind of papers?'

'Legal stuff, all for your benefit.'

'You're not concerned about my benefit.' Her words were much quicker and sharper, and Nate was stung by the rebuke.

'That's not true,' he replied weakly.

'Sure it is. You don't know what I want, or need, or like, or dislike. You don't know me, Nate, so how can you know what will or will not benefit me?'

'Okay, you're right. I don't know you, you don't know me. I'm here on behalf of your father's estate. It is still very hard for me to believe that I am actually sitting in the dark outside a hut, in a primitive Indian village, lost in a swamp the size of Colorado, in a third world country I've never seen before, talking to a very lovely missionary who just happens to be the richest woman in the world. Yes, you're right, I don't know what benefits you. But it is very important for you to see these papers, and to sign them.'

'I'm not signing anything.'

'Oh, come on.'

'I have no interest in your papers.'

'You haven't seen them yet.'

249

'Tell me about them.'

'They're formalities. My firm has to probate your father's estate. All of the heirs named in his will must inform the court, either in person or in writing, that they have been notified of the proceedings, and have been given the opportunity to take part. It's required by the law.'

'And if I refuse?'

'Honestly, I haven't thought about that. It's so routine that everybody simply cooperates.'

'So I submit myself to the court in . . .?'

'Virginia. The probate court there takes jurisdiction over you, even though you're absent.'

'I'm not sure if I like that idea.'

'Fine, then hop in the boat and we'll go to Washington.'

'I'm not leaving.' And with that a long silence ensued, a pause made even quieter by the darkness that now engulfed them. The boy was perfectly still under the tree. The Indians were settling in their huts, with no noise except for the cry of an infant.

'I'll get us some juice,' she almost whispered, then moved into the house. Nate stood and stretched his tender body, and slapped at mosquitoes. His repellent was in his tent.

There was a small light of some sort flickering through the house. Rachel held a clay pot with a flame in the center. 'These are leaves from that tree over there,' she explained as she sat it on the ground by the door. 'We burn them to keep mosquitoes away. Sit here, close to it.'

Nate did as he was told. She returned with two cups filled with a liquid he could not see. 'It's *macajuno*, similar to orange juice.' They sat together on the ground, almost touching, with their backs resting against the hut, the burning pot not far from their feet.

'Speak softly,' she said. 'Voices carry in the dark,

and the Indians are trying to sleep. They are also very curious about us.'

'They can't understand anything.'

'Yes, but they will listen anyway.'

Soap had not touched his body in days, and he was suddenly concerned with his hygiene. He took a small sip, then another.

'Do you have a family?' she asked.

'I've had a couple. Two marriages, two divorces, four children. I now live alone.'

'Divorce is so easy, isn't it?'

Nate took a very small sip of the warm liquid. He had thus far managed to avoid the raging diarrhea that struck so many foreigners. Surely the murky liquid was harmless.

Two Americans alone in the wilderness. With so much to talk about, why couldn't they avoid divorce?

'Actually, they were quite painful.'

'But we move on. We marry, then divorce. Find someone else, marry, then divorce. Find someone else.'

'We?'

'I'm just using the pronoun. Civilized people. Educated, complicated people. The Indians never divorce.'

'They haven't seen my first wife either.'

'She was unpleasant?'

Nate exhaled and took another drink. Indulge her, he told himself. She's desperate for conversation with one of her own.

'I'm sorry,' she said. 'I'm not prying. It's not important.'

'She was not a bad person, not in the early years. I worked hard, drank even harder. When I wasn't at the office, I was in a bar. She became resentful, then mean, then vicious. Things spiraled out of control and we grew to hate each other.'

251

The little confessional was over in a flash, and it was enough for both of them. His marital debris seemed so irrelevant then and there.

'You've never married?' he asked.

'No.' She took a sip. She was left-handed, and when she raised the cup her elbow touched Nate's. 'Paul never married, you know.'

'Paul who?'

'The Apostle Paul.'

'Oh, that Paul.'

'Do you read the Bible?'

'No.'

'I thought I was in love once, in college. I wanted to marry him, but the Lord led me away.'

'Why?'

'Because the Lord wanted me here. The boy I loved was a good Christian, but he was weak physically. He would have never survived on the mission field.'

'How long will you stay here?'

'I don't plan to leave.'

'So the Indians will bury you?'

'I suppose. It's not something I worry about.'

'Do most World Tribes missionaries die in the field?'

'No. Most retire and go home. But then, they have families to bury them.'

'You'd have lots of family and friends if you went home now. You'd be quite famous.'

'That's another good reason to stay here. This is home. I don't want the money.'

'Don't be foolish.'

'I'm not foolish. Money means nothing to me. That should be obvious.'

'You don't even know how much it is.'

'I haven't asked. I went about my work today with no thought of the money. I'll do the same tomorrow, and the next day.'

'It's eleven billion, give or take.'

'Is that supposed to impress me?'

'It got my attention.'

'But you worship money, Nate. You're part of a culture where everything is measured by money. It's a religion.'

'True. But sex is pretty important too.'

'Okay, money and sex. What else?'

'Fame. Everybody wants to be a celebrity.'

'It's a sad culture. People live in a frenzy. They work all the time to make money to buy things to impress other people. They're measured by what they own.'

'Am I included?'

'Are you?'

'I suppose.'

'Then you're living without God. You're a very lonely person, Nate, I can sense it. You don't know God.'

He squirmed and considered a quick defense, but the truth disarmed him. He had no weapons, no punches, no foundation to stand on. 'I believe in God,' he said, truthfully but weakly.

'It's easy to say that,' she said, her words still slow and soft. 'And I don't doubt you. But saying is one thing, living is another matter. That crippled boy under the tree over there is Lako. He's seventeen, small for his age, and always sick. His mother told me he was born early. Lako is the first to catch every disease that comes our way. I doubt if he'll live to be thirty. Lako doesn't care. Lako became a Christian several years ago, and he has the sweetest spirit of anyone here. He talks to God all day long; in fact he's probably praying right now. He has no worries, no fears. If he has a problem, he goes straight to God and leaves it there.'

Nate looked at the darkness under the tree where Lako was praying, but saw nothing.

She continued, 'That little Indian has nothing on this earth, but he's storing riches in heaven. He knows that when he dies he'll spend eternity in heaven with his creator. Lako is a wealthy boy.'

'What about Troy?'

'I doubt if Troy believed in Christ when he died. If not, then he's burning in hell right now.'

'You don't believe that.'

'Hell is a very real place, Nate. Read the Bible. Right now Troy would give his eleven billion for a drink of cold water.'

Nate was ill-equipped to argue theology with a missionary, and he knew it. He said nothing for a while, and she took the cue. Minutes passed as the last infant fell asleep in the village. The night was perfectly black and still, no moon or stars, the only light coming from the thin yellow flame near their feet.

Very gently, she touched him. She patted him three times on his arm, and said, 'I'm sorry. I shouldn't have said that you are lonely. How would I know?'

'It's okay.'

She kept her fingers on his arm, as if desperate to touch something.

'You are a good person, aren't you, Nate?'

'No, I am actually not a good person. I do lots of bad things. I am weak, and fragile, and I don't want to talk about it. I didn't come here to find God. Finding you was hard enough. I'm required by law to give you these papers.'

'I'm not signing the papers and I don't want the money.'

'Come on –'

'Please don't beg. My decision is final. Let's not talk about the money.'

'But the money is the only reason I'm here.'

She removed her fingers, but managed to lean an

inch or two closer so that their knees were touching. 'I'm sorry you came. You've wasted a trip.'

Another gap in the conversation. He needed to relieve himself, but the thought of stepping three feet in any direction was horrifying.

Lako said something and startled Nate. He was less than ten feet away, still unseen.

'He needs to go to his hut,' she said, rising to her feet. 'Follow him.'

Nate unfolded himself and slowly stood, joints popping and muscles reluctantly stretching. 'I would like to leave tomorrow.'

'Good. I'll speak to the chief.'

'It won't be a problem, will it?'

'Probably not.'

'I need thirty minutes of your time, to at least go over the papers and show you a copy of the will.'

'We can talk. Good night.'

He practically breathed down the back of Lako's neck as they shuffled along the short trail and into the village.

'Over here,' Jevy whispered in the dark. He had somehow managed to secure the use of two hammocks on the small porch of the men's building. Nate asked how. Jevy promised to explain in the morning.

Lako vanished in the night.

THIRTY

F. Parr Wycliff was in his courtroom, running late with a docket of dull motion hearings. Josh waited in the Judge's office with the video. He paced the floor of the cluttered room, gripping his cell phone, his mind in another hemisphere. There was still no word from Nate.

Valdir's assurances seemed well rehearsed – the Pantanal is a big place, the guide is very good, the boat is large, the Indians move about, the Indians do not wish to be found, everything is fine. He would call when he heard from Nate.

Josh had considered the idea of a rescue. But getting to Corumbá seemed enough of a challenge; penetrating the Pantanal to find a missing lawyer seemed impossible. Still, he could go there and sit with Valdir until they heard something.

He was working twelve hours a day, six days a week, and the Phelan matter was about to explode. Josh barely had time for lunch, let alone a trip to Brazil.

He tried Valdir on his cell phone, but the line was busy.

Wycliff entered the office, apologizing and removing his robe at the same time. He wanted to impress a powerful lawyer like Stafford with the importance of his docket.

It was just the two of them. They watched the first

256

part of the video without comment. It began with old Troy sitting in his wheelchair, Josh adjusting the microphone in front of him, and the three psychiatrists with their pages of questions. The exam lasted twenty-one minutes, and ended with the unanimous opinions that Mr. Phelan knew exactly what he was doing. Wycliff couldn't suppress a grin.

The room cleared. The camera directly across from Troy was kept on. He whipped out the holographic will, and signed it four minutes after the mental exam had ended.

'This is where he jumps,' Josh said

The camera didn't move. It caught Troy as he suddenly pushed back from the table and stood. He disappeared off-screen as Josh and Snead and Tip Durban watched in disbelief for a second, then bolted after the old man. The footage was quite dramatic.

Five and a half minutes elapse, the camera records nothing but empty chairs and voices. Then poor Snead takes the seat where Troy sat. He's visibly shaken and on the verge of tears, but manages to tell the camera what he just witnessed. Josh and Tip Durban do the same thing.

Thirty-nine minutes of video.

'How are they going to unravel that?' Wycliff asked when it was over. It was a question with no answer. Two of the heirs – Rex and Libbigail – had already filed petitions to contest the will. Their lawyers – Hark Gettys and Wally Bright respectively – had managed to attract significant attention and get themselves interviewed and photographed by the press.

The other heirs would quickly follow suit. Josh had spoken with most of their lawyers, and the scramble for the courthouse was in process.

'Every discredited shrink in the country wants a piece of this,' Josh said. 'There will be lots of opinions.'

257

'Does the suicide worry you?'

'Sure it does. But he planned everything so carefully, even his death. He knew precisely how and when he wanted to die.'

'What about the other will? The thick one he signed first.'

'He didn't sign it.'

'But I saw him. It's on the video.'

'No. He scrawled the name Mickey Mouse.'

Wycliff was taking notes on a legal pad, and his hand stopped in mid-sentence. 'Mickey Mouse?' he repeated.

'Here's where we are, Judge. From 1982 until 1996, I prepared eleven wills for Mr. Phelan. Some were thick, others were thin, and they disposed of his fortune in more ways than you can imagine. The law says that with each new will, the old one has to be destroyed. So I would bring the new will to his office, we'd spend two hours nitpicking our way through it, then he'd sign it. I kept the wills in my office, and I always brought the last one along. Once he signed the new one, we – Mr. Phelan and I – would feed the old one through a shredder he kept near his desk. It was a ceremony that he enjoyed immensely. He'd be happy for a few months, then one of his kids would make him mad, and he'd start talking about changing his will.

'If the heirs can prove that he lacked sufficient mental capacity when he executed the handwritten will, then there is no other will. They were all destroyed.'

'In which case he died without a will,' Wycliff added.

'Yes, and, as you well know, under Virginia law his estate is then divided among his children.'

'Seven children. Eleven billion dollars.'

'Seven that we know about. Eleven billion seems to be fairly accurate. Wouldn't you attack the will?'

A big nasty will contest was exactly what Wycliff wanted. And he knew that the lawyers, including Josh Stafford, would get even richer from the war.

But the battle needed two sides, and so far only one had surfaced. Someone had to defend Mr. Phelan's last testament.

'Any word from Rachel Lane?' he asked.

'No, but we're looking.'

'Where is she?'

'We think she's a missionary somewhere in South America. But we haven't found her. We have people down there.' Josh realized he was using the word 'people' quite loosely.

Wycliff was gazing at the ceiling, deep in thought. 'Why would he give eleven billion to an illegitimate daughter who is a missionary?'

'I can't answer that, Judge. He surprised me so many times that I became jaded.'

'Sounds a little crazy, doesn't it?'

'It's strange.'

'Did you know about her?'

'No.'

'Could there be other heirs?'

'Anything is possible.'

'Do you think he was unbalanced?'

'No. Weird, eccentric, whimsical, mean as hell. But he knew what he was doing.'

'Find the girl, Josh.'

'We're trying.'

The meeting involved only the chief and Rachel. From where Nate sat, on the porch under his hammock, he could see their faces and hear their voices. The chief was bothered by something in the clouds. He would talk, then listen to Rachel, then raise his eyes slowly upward as if anticipating death from the skies. It was obvious to Nate that the chief not only listened to Rachel but also sought her advice.

Around them, the morning meal was winding down as the Ipicas prepared for another day. The hunters gathered in small groups at the men's house to sharpen their arrows and string their bows. The fishermen laid out their nets and lines. The young women began the day-long task of keeping the dirt properly swept around their huts. Their mothers were leaving for the gardens and fields near the forest.

'He thinks it's going to storm,' Rachel explained when the meeting was over. 'He says you can go, but he will not send a guide. It's too dangerous.'

'Can we make it without a guide?' Nate asked.

'Yes,' Jevy said, and Nate shot him a look that conveyed many thoughts.

'It would not be wise,' she said. 'The rivers run together. It's easy to get lost. Even the Ipicas have lost fishermen during the rainy season.'

'When might the storm be over?' Nate asked.

'We'll have to wait and see.'

Nate breathed deeply as his shoulders sagged. He was sore and tired, covered with mosquito bites, hungry, sick of his little adventure, and worried that Josh was worried. His mission so far had been a failure. He wasn't homesick because there was nothing at home. But he wanted to see Corumbá again, with its cozy little cafés and nice hotels and lazy streets. He wanted another opportunity to be alone, clean and sober and unafraid of drinking himself to death.

'I'm sorry,' she said.

'I really need to get back. There are people at the office waiting to hear from me. This has already taken much longer than expected.'

She listened but she really didn't care. A few worried people in a law office in D.C. didn't concern her that much.

'Can we talk?' he asked.

'I have to go to the next village for the funeral of the little girl. Why don't you go with me? We will have plenty of time to talk.'

Lako led the way, his right foot twisted in, so that with each step he dipped to the left, then jerked himself to the right. It was painful to watch. Rachel followed him, then Nate, laden with a cloth bag she'd brought. Jevy stayed well behind them, afraid he might overhear their conversation.

Beyond the oval ring of huts, they passed small square patches of farmland, now abandoned and overrun with scrub brush. 'The Ipicas grow their food on small plots which they carve out of the jungle,' she explained. Nate was close behind her, trying to keep up. She took long strides with her wiry legs. A two-mile hike through the woods was child's play. 'They are hard on the soil, and after a few years it stops producing. They abandon it, nature reclaims it, and they dig farther into the jungle. In the long run, the soil returns to normal and no harm is done. Land means everything to the Indians. It is their life. Most of it has been taken away by the civilized folks.'

'Sounds familiar.'

'Yes, it does. We decimate their population with bloodshed and disease, and take away their land. Then we put them on reservations and can't understand why they're not happy about it.'

She said hello to two naked little ladies tilling soil near the trail. 'The women get the hard work,' Nate observed.

'Yes. But the work is easy compared to childbirth.'

'I'd rather watch them work.'

The air was humid, but free of the smoke that hung eternally over the village. When they entered the woods, Nate was already sweating.

261

'So tell me about yourself, Nate,' she said over her shoulder. 'Where were you born?'

'This could take a while.'

'Just hit the high points.'

'There are more low ones.'

'Come on, Nate. You wanted to talk, let's talk. The hike takes half an hour.'

'I was born in Baltimore, oldest of two sons, parents divorced when I was fifteen, high school at St. Paul, college at Hopkins, law school at Georgetown, then I never left D.C.'

'Was it a happy childhood?'

'I suppose. Lots of sports. My father worked for National Brewery for thirty years, and he always had tickets to the Colts and Orioles. Baltimore is a great city. Are we going to talk about your childhood?'

'If you like. It wasn't very happy.'

What a surprise, thought Nate. This poor woman has never had a chance at happiness.

'Did you want to be a lawyer when you grew up?'

'Of course not. No kid in his right mind wants to be a lawyer. I was going to play for the Colts or the Orioles, maybe both.'

'Did you go to church?'

'Sure. Every Christmas and Easter.'

The trail almost disappeared and they were wading through stiff weeds. Nate walked while watching her boots, and when he couldn't see them, he said, 'This snake that killed the girl, what kind is it?'

'It's called a *bima*, but don't worry.'

'Why shouldn't I worry?'

'Because you're wearing boots. It's a small snake that bites below the ankle.'

'The big one will find me.'

'Relax.'

'What about Lako up there? He's never worn shoes.'

'Yes, but he sees everything.'

262

'I take it the *bima* is quite deadly.'

'It can be, but there is an antivenin. I've actually had it here before, and if I'd had it yesterday, the little girl wouldn't have died.'

'Then if you had lots of money you could buy lots of antivenin. You could stock your shelves with all the medicines you need. You could buy a nice little outboard to take you to Corumbá and back. You could build a clinic and a church and a school, and spread the Gospel all over the Pantanal.'

She stopped and turned abruptly. They were face to face. 'I've done nothing to earn the money, and I didn't know the man who made it. Please don't mention it again.' Her words were firm, but her face gave no hint of frustration.

'Give it away. Give it all to charity.'

'It's not mine to give.'

'It'll be squandered. Millions will go to the lawyers, and what's left will be divided among your siblings. And, believe me, you don't want that. You have no idea of the misery and heartache these people will cause if they get the money. What they don't waste they'll pass down to their kids, and the Phelan money will pollute the next generation.'

She took his wrist and squeezed it. Very slowly she said, 'I don't care. I'll pray for them.'

Then she turned and started walking again. Lako was far ahead. Jevy could barely be seen behind them. They hiked in silence through a field near a stream, then entered a patch of tall thick trees. The limbs and branches were woven together to form a dark canopy. The air was suddenly cool.

'Let's take a break,' she said. The stream curved through the woods and the trail crossed it in a bed of blue and orange rocks. She knelt by the water and splashed her face.

263

'You can drink this,' she said. 'It comes from the mountains.'

Nate squatted near her and felt the water. It was cold and clear.

'This is my favorite spot,' she said. 'I come here almost every day to bathe, to pray, to meditate.'

'It's hard to believe we're in the Pantanal. It's much too cool.'

'We're on the very edge of it. The mountains of Bolivia are not far away. The Pantanal begins somewhere near here and stretches east forever.'

'I know. We flew over it trying to find you.'

'Oh you did?'

'Yes, it was a short flight, but I had a good view of the Pantanal.'

'And you didn't find me?'

'No. We flew into a storm and had to make an emergency landing. I got lucky and walked away. I'll never get near another small airplane.'

'There's no place to land around here.'

They took off their socks and boots and dipped their feet into the stream. They sat on the rocks and listened as the water trickled by. They were alone; neither Lako nor Jevy were within eyesight.

'When I was a little girl in Montana, we lived in a small town where my father, my adoptive father, was a minister. Not far from the edge of town was a little creek, about the size of this. And there was a place, under some tall trees, similar to these, where I would go and put my feet in the water and sit for hours.'

'Were you hiding?'

'Sometimes.'

'Are you hiding now?'

'No.'

'I think you are.'

'No, you are wrong. I have perfect peace, Nate. I surrendered my will to Christ many years ago, and I

264

follow wherever He leads. You think I'm lonely – you're wrong. He is with me every step of the way. He knows my thoughts, my needs, and He takes away my fears and worries. I am completely and perfectly at peace in this world.'

'I've never heard that before.'

'You said last night that you are weak and fragile. What does that mean?'

Confession was good for the soul, Sergio had told him during therapy. If she wanted to know, then he would try and shock her with the truth.

'I'm an alcoholic,' he said, almost proudly, the way he'd been trained to admit it during rehab. 'I've hit the bottom four times in the past ten years, and I came out of detox to make this trip. I cannot say for sure that I will never drink again. I've kicked cocaine three times, and I think, though I'm not certain, that I will never touch the stuff again. I filed for bankruptcy four months ago, while in rehab. I'm currently under indictment for income tax evasion, and stand a fifty-fifty chance of going to jail and losing my license to practice law. You know about the two divorces. Both women dislike me, and they've poisoned my children. I've done a fine job of wrecking my life.'

There was no noticeable pleasure or relief in laying himself bare.

She took it without flinching. 'Anything else?' she asked.

'Oh yes. I've tried to kill myself at least twice – twice that I can recall. Once last August that landed me in rehab. Then just a few days ago in Corumbá. I think it was Christmas night.'

'In Corumbá?'

'Yes, in my hotel room. I almost drank myself to death with cheap vodka.'

'You poor man.'

'I'm sick, okay. I have a disease. I've admitted it many times to many counselors.'

'Have you ever confessed it to God?'

'I'm sure He knows.'

'I'm sure He does. But He won't help unless you ask. He is omnipotent, but you have to go to Him, in prayer, in the spirit of forgiveness.'

'What happens?'

'Your sins will be forgiven. Your slate will be wiped clean. Your addictions will be taken away. The Lord will forgive all of your transgressions, and you will become a new believer in Christ.'

'What about the IRS?'

'That won't go away, but you'll have the strength to deal with it. Through prayer you can overcome any adversity.'

Nate had been preached at before. He had surrendered to Higher Powers so many times he could almost deliver the sermons. He had been counseled by ministers and therapists and gurus and shrinks of every stripe and variety. Once, during a three-year stretch of sobriety, he actually worked as a counselor for AA, teaching the twelve-point recovery plan to other alcoholics in the basement of an old church in Alexandria. Then he crashed.

Why shouldn't she try to save him? Wasn't it her calling in life to convert the lost?

'I don't know how to pray,' he said.

She took his hand and squeezed it firmly. 'Close your eyes, Nate. Repeat after me: Dear God, Forgive me of my sins, and help me to forgive those who have sinned against me.' Nate mumbled the words and squeezed her hand even harder. It sounded vaguely similar to the Lord's Prayer. 'Give me strength to overcome temptations, and addictions, and the trials ahead.' Nate kept mumbling, kept repeating her words, but the little ritual was confusing. Prayer was easy for Rachel because she did so much of it. For him, it was a strange rite.

'Amen,' she said. They opened their eyes but kept their hands together. They listened to the water as it rushed gently over the rocks. There was an odd sensation as his burdens seemed to be lifted; his shoulders felt lighter, his head clearer, his soul was less troubled. But Nate carried so much baggage he wasn't certain which loads had been taken away and which remained.

He was still frightened by the real world. It was easy to be brave deep in the Pantanal where the temptations were few, but he knew what awaited him at home.

'Your sins are forgiven, Nate,' she said.

'Which ones? There are so many.'

'All of them.'

'It's too easy. There's a lot of wreckage back there.'

'We'll pray again tonight.'

'It will take more for me than most folks.'

'Trust me, Nate. And trust God. He's seen worse.'

'I trust you. It's God who's got me worried.'

She squeezed his hand even tighter, and for a long still moment they watched the water bubble around them. Finally, she said, 'We need to go.' But they didn't move.

'I've been thinking about this burial, this little girl,' Nate said.

'What about it?'

'Will we see her body?'

'I suppose. It will be hard to miss.'

'Then I'd rather not. Jevy and I will go back to the village and wait.'

'Are you sure, Nate? We could talk for hours.'

'I don't want to see a dead child.'

'Very well. I understand.'

He helped her to her feet, though she certainly

didn't need assistance. They held hands until she reached for her boots. As usual, Lako materialized from nowhere, and they were off, soon lost in the dark woods.

He found Jevy asleep under a tree. They picked their way along the trail, watching for snakes with every step, and slowly returned to the village.

THIRTY-ONE

The chief wasn't much of a weatherman. The storm never materialized. It rained twice during the day as Nate and Jevy fought the tedium by napping in their borrowed hammocks. The showers were brief, and after each the sun returned to bake the dampened soil and raise the humidity. Even in the shade, moving only when necessary, the two men sweltered in the heat.

They watched the Indians whenever there was activity, but the work and play ebbed and flowed with the heat. When the sun was out in full force the Ipicas retreated to their huts or to the shade trees behind them. During the brief showers the children played in the rain. When the sun was blocked by clouds, the women ventured out to do their chores and go to the river.

After a week in the Pantanal, Nate was numbed by the listless pace of life. Each day appeared to be an exact copy of the one before. Nothing had changed in centuries.

Rachel returned in mid-afternoon. She and Lako went straight to the chief and reported on events in the other village. She spoke to Nate and Jevy. She was tired and wanted a quick nap before they discussed business.

What's another hour to be killed? thought Nate. He

watched her walk away. She was lean and tough and could probably run marathons.

'What are you looking at?' Jevy asked with a grin.

'Nothing.'

'How old is she?'

'Forty-two.'

'How old are you?'

'Forty-eight.'

'Has she been married?'

'No.'

'Do you think she's ever been with a man?'

'Why don't you ask her?'

'Do you?'

'I really don't care.'

They fell asleep again, sleeping because there was nothing else to do. In a couple of hours the wrestling would start, then dinner, then darkness. Nate dreamed of the *Santa Loura*, a humble vessel at best, but with each passing hour the boat grew finer. In his dreams it was fast becoming a sleek, elegant yacht.

When the men began to gather to fix their hair and prepare for their games, Nate and Jevy eased away. One of the larger Ipicas yelled at them, and with teeth flashing issued what seemed to be an invitation to come wrestle. Nate scooted away even faster. He had a sudden image of himself getting flung about the village by some squatty little warrior, genitals flying everywhere. Jevy wanted no part of the action either. Rachel rescued them.

She and Nate left the huts and walked toward the river, to their old spot on the narrow bench under the trees. They sat close, their knees touching again.

'You were wise not to go,' she said. Her voice was tired. The nap had failed to revive her.

'Why?'

'Every village has a doctor. He's called a *shalyun*,

and he cooks herbs and roots for his remedies. He also calls forth spirits to help with all sorts of problems.'

'Ah, the old medicine man.'

'Something like that. More of a witch doctor. There are lots of spirits in the Indian world, and the *shalyun* supposedly directs their traffic. Anyway, the *shalyun* are my natural enemies. I am a threat to their religion. They are always on the attack. They persecute the Christian believers. They prey on new converts. They want me to leave and so they are always lobbying the chiefs to run me off. It's a daily struggle. In the last village down the river, I had a small school where I taught reading and writing. It was for the believers, but it was also open to anyone. A year ago we had a bout of malaria and three people died. The local *shalyun* convinced the chief down there that the disease was a punishment on the village because of my school. It's now closed.'

Nate just listened. Her courage, already admirable, was reaching new heights. The heat and languid pace of life had lured him into the belief that all was at peace among the Ipicas. No visitor would suspect a war was raging over souls.

'The parents of Ayesh, the girl who died, are Christians, and very strong in their faith. The *shalyun* spread the word that he could've saved the girl, but the parents didn't call on him. They, of course, wanted me to treat her. The *bima* snake has been around forever, and there are home remedies that the *shalyun* brew up. I've never seen one work. After she died yesterday, and after I left, the *shalyun* called some spirits forth and held a ceremony in the center of the village. He blamed me for her death. And he blamed God.'

Her words were pouring forth, faster than normal, as if she wanted to hurry and use her English one more time.

'During the burial today, the *shalyun* and a few troublemakers began chanting and dancing nearby. The poor parents were completely overcome with grief and humiliation. I couldn't finish the service.' Her voice cracked, just slightly, and she bit her lip.

Nate patted her arm. 'It's okay. It's over.'

Crying was not something she could do in front of the Indians. She had to be strong and stoic, filled with faith and courage under all circumstances. But she could cry with Nate, and he would understand. He expected it.

She wiped her eyes and slowly collected her emotions. 'I'm sorry,' she said.

'It's okay,' Nate said again, anxious to help. The tears of a woman melted the facade of coolness, whether in a bar or sitting by a river.

There was hollering in the village. The wrestling had started. Nate had a quick thought about Jevy. Surely he had not succumbed to the temptation of playing with the boys.

'I think you should go now,' she said abruptly, breaking the silence. Her emotions were under control, her voice was back to normal.

'What?'

'Yes, now. Very soon.'

'I'm anxious to go, but what's the rush? It'll be dark in three hours.'

'There is reason to worry.'

'I'm listening.'

'I think I saw a case of malaria in the other village today. Mosquitoes carry it and it spreads quickly.'

Nate began scratching and was ready to hop in the boat, then he remembered his pills. 'I'm safe. I'm taking chloro-something.'

'Chloroquine?'

'That's it.'

'When did you start?'

'Two days before I left the States.'

'Where are the pills now?'

'I left them on the big boat.'

She shook her head with disapproval. 'You're supposed to take them before, during, and after the trip.' Her tone was medically authoritative, as if death could be imminent.

'And what about Jevy?' she asked. 'Is he taking the pills?'

'He was in the army. I'm sure he's okay.'

'I'm not going to argue, Nate. I've already spoken to the chief. He sent two fishermen out this morning before sunrise. The flooded waters are tricky for the first two hours, then the navigation becomes familiar. He will provide three guides in two canoes, and I'll send Lako to handle the language. Once you're on the Xeco River, it's a straight shot to the Paraguay.'

'How far away is that?'

'The Xeco is about four hours away. The Paraguay, six. And you're going with the current.'

'Whatever. You seem to have everything planned.'

'Trust me, Nate. I've had malaria twice, and you don't want it. The second time almost killed me.'

It had never occurred to Nate that she might die. The Phelan estate would be chaotic enough with Rachel hiding in the jungles and rejecting the paperwork. If she died, it would take years to settle things.

And he admired her greatly. She was everything he wasn't – strong and brave, grounded in faith, happy with simplicity, certain of her place in the world and the hereafter. 'Don't die, Rachel,' he said.

'Death is not something I fear. For a Christian, death is a reward. But do pray for me, Nate.'

'I'm going to pray more, I promise.'

'You're a good man. You have a good heart and a good mind. You just need some help.'

'I know. I'm not very strong.'

273

He had the papers in a folded envelope in his pocket. He pulled them out. 'Can we at least discuss these?'

'Yes, but only as a favor to you. I figure you've come this far, the least I can do is have our little law chat.'

'Thank you.' He handed her the first sheet, a copy of Troy's one-page will. She read it slowly, struggling with parts of the handwriting. When she finished, she asked, 'Is this a legal will?'

'So far.'

'But it's so primitive.'

'Handwritten wills are valid. Sorry, it's the law.'

She read it again. Nate noticed the shadows falling along the tree line. He had become afraid of the dark, both on land and on water. He was anxious to leave.

'Troy didn't care for his other offspring, did he?' she said with amusement.

'You wouldn't either. But then I doubt if he was much of a father.'

'I remember the day my mother told me about him. I was seventeen. It was late summer. My father had just died of cancer, and life was pretty bleak. Troy had somehow found me and was bugging my mother to visit. She told me the truth about my biological parents, and it meant nothing to me. I didn't care about those people. I'd never known them, and had no desire to meet them. I found out later that my birth mother killed herself. How do you figure that, Nate? Both of my real parents killed themselves. Is there something in my genes?'

'No. You're much stronger than they were.'

'I welcome death.'

'Don't say that. When did you meet Troy?'

'A year went by. He and my mother became phone pals. She became convinced his motives were good, and so one day he came to our house. We had cake and tea, then he left. He sent money for college. He

274

began pressuring me to take a job with one of his companies. He started acting like a father, and I grew to dislike him. Then my mother died, and the world caved in around me. I changed my name and went to med school. I prayed for Troy over the years, the same way I pray for all the lost people I know. I assumed he had forgotten about me.'

'Evidently not,' Nate said. A black mosquito landed on his thigh, and he slapped with enough violence to crack lumber. If it carried malaria, the insect would spread it no further. A red outline of a handprint appeared on his flesh.

He gave her the waiver and the acknowledgment. She read them carefully and said, 'I'm not signing anything. I don't want the money.'

'Just keep them, okay. Pray over them.'

'Are you making fun of me?'

'No. I just don't know what to do next.'

'I can't help you. But I will ask one favor.'

'Sure. Anything.'

'Don't tell anyone where I am. I beg you, Nate. Please protect my privacy.'

'I promise. But you have to be realistic.'

'What do you mean?'

'The story is irresistible. If you take the money, then you're probably the richest woman in the world. If you decline it, then the story is even more compelling.'

'Who cares?'

'Bless your heart. You're protected from the media. We have nonstop news now, twenty-four hours of endless coverage of everything. Hours and hours of news programs, news magazines, talking heads, late-breaking stories. It's all junk. No story is too small to be tracked down and sensationalized.'

'But how can they find me?'

'That's a good question. We got lucky because Troy

had picked up your trail. To our knowledge, though, he told no one.'

'Then I'm safe, right? You can't tell. The lawyers in your firm can't tell.'

'That's very true.'

'And you were lost when you arrived here, right?'

'Very lost.'

'You have to protect me, Nate. This is my home. These are my people. I don't want to run again.'

HUMBLE MISSIONARY IN JUNGLE SAYS NO TO ELEVEN-BILLION-DOLLAR FORTUNE

What a headline. The vultures would invade the Pantanal with helicopters and amphibious landing craft to get the story. Nate felt sorry for her.

'I'll do what I can,' he said.

'Do I have your word?'

'Yes, I promise.'

The send-off party was led by the chief himself, followed by his wife, then a dozen men, then Jevy followed by at least ten more men. They snaked along the trail, headed for the river. 'It's time to go,' she said.

'I guess so. You're sure we'll be safe in the dark.'

'Yes. The chief is sending his best fishermen. God will protect you. Say your prayers.'

'I will.'

'I'll pray for you every day, Nate. You're a good person with a good heart. You're worth saving.'

'Thank you. You wanna get married?'

'I can't.'

'Sure you can. I'll take care of the money, you take care of the Indians. We'll get a bigger hut and throw away our clothes.'

They both laughed, and they were still smiling when the chief got to them. Nate stood to say hello or good-bye or something, and for a second his vision was gone. A surge of dizziness rolled from his chest through his head. He caught himself, cleared his vision, and glanced at Rachel to see if she had noticed.

She had not. His eyelids began to ache. The joints at his elbows were throbbing.

There was a flourish of grunts in Ipica, and everyone stepped to the river. Food was placed in Jevy's boat and in the two narrow canoes the guides and Lako would use. Nate thanked Rachel, who in turn thanked the chief, and when all the right farewells were finished it was time to go. Standing ankle-deep in water, Nate hugged her gently, patting her on the back and saying, 'Thanks.'

'Thanks for what?'

'Oh, I don't know. Thanks for creating a fortune in legal fees.'

She smiled and said, 'I like you, Nate, but I couldn't care less about the money and the lawyers.'

'I like you too.'

'Please don't come back.'

'Don't worry.'

Everyone was waiting. The fishermen were already on the river. Jevy had his paddle, anxious to shove off.

Nate took a step into the boat, and said, 'We could honeymoon in Corumbá.'

'Good-bye, Nate. Just tell your people you never found me.'

'I will. So long.' He pushed away, and swung himself into the boat, where he sat down hard, his head spinning again. As they drifted away, he waved at Rachel and the Indians, but the figures were blurred together.

Pushed by the current, the canoes glided over the water, the Indians paddling in perfect tandem. They wasted no effort and no time. They were in a hurry. The motor started on the third pull, and they soon caught the canoes. When Jevy throttled down, the motor sputtered but did not quit. At the first turn in the river, Nate glanced over his shoulder. Rachel and the Indians hadn't moved.

He was sweating. With clouds shielding the sun, and with a nice breeze in his face, Nate realized that he was sweating. His arms and legs were wet. He rubbed his neck and forehead and looked at the dampness on his fingers. Instead of praying as he had promised, he mumbled, 'Oh shit. I'm sick.'

The fever was low, but coming fast. The breeze chilled him. He huddled on his seat and looked for something else to wear. Jevy noticed him, and after a few minutes said, 'Nate, are you okay?'

He shook his head no, and pain shot from his eyes to his spine. He wiped drainage from his nose.

After two bends in the river, the trees grew thin and the ground was lower. The river widened, then spilled into a flooded lake with three decaying trees in the center of it. Nate knew they had not passed the trees on the way in. They were taking a different route out. Without the current, the canoes slowed a little but still cut through the water with amazing quickness. The guides did not study the lake. They knew exactly where they were going.

'Jevy, I think I have malaria,' Nate said. His voice was hoarse; his throat already sore.

'How do you know?' Jevy lowered the throttle for a second.

'Rachel warned me. She saw it in the other village yesterday. That's why we left when we did.'

'Do you have a fever?'

'Yes, and I'm having trouble seeing things.'

Jevy stopped the boat and yelled at the Indians, who were almost out of sight. He moved empty gas tanks and the remnants of their supplies, then quickly unrolled the tent. 'You will get chills,' he said as he

278

worked. The boat rocked back and forth as he moved around.

'Have you had malaria?'

'No. But most of my friends have died from it.'

'What!'

'Bad joke. It doesn't kill many, but you will be very sick.'

Moving gently, keeping his head as still as possible, Nate crawled behind his seat and lay in the center of the boat. A bedroll was his pillow. Jevy spread the lightweight tent over him and anchored it with two empty gas tanks.

The Indians were beside them, curious about what was happening. Lako inquired in Portuguese. Nate heard the word malaria spoken by Jevy, and it caused mumblings in Ipica. Then they were off.

The boat seemed faster. Maybe it was because Nate was lying on the bottom of it, feeling it slice through the water. An occasional branch or limb that Jevy didn't see jolted Nate, but he didn't care. His head ached and throbbed like no hangover he'd ever experienced. His muscles and joints hurt too much to move. And he was growing colder. The chills were starting.

There was a low rumble in the distance. Nate thought it might be thunder. Wonderful, he thought. That's precisely what we need now.

The rains stayed away. The river turned once to the west, and Jevy saw the orange and yellow remnants of a sunset. Then it turned back to the east, to the approaching darkness across the Pantanal. Twice the canoes slowed as the Ipicas conferred about which fork to take. Jevy kept their boat a hundred feet or so behind, but as darkness settled in he followed closer. He couldn't see Nate buried under the tent, but he knew his friend was suffering. Jevy actually once knew a man who died from malaria.

Two hours into the journey, the guides led them through a bewildering series of narrow streams and quiet lagoons, and when they emerged into a broader river the canoes slowed for a moment. The Indians needed a rest. Lako called to Jevy and explained that they were now safe, that they had just gone through the difficult part and the rest should be easy. The Xeco was about two hours away, and it led straight to the Paraguay.

Can we make it alone? Jevy asked. No, came the reply. There were still forks to deal with, plus the Indians knew a spot on the Xeco that would not be flooded. There they would sleep.

How is the American? Lako asked. Not well, Jevy replied.

The American heard their voices, and he knew the boat was not moving. The fever burned him from head to toe. His flesh and clothes were soaked, and the aluminum under him was wet as well. His eyes were swollen shut, his mouth so dry it hurt to open it. He heard Jevy asking him something in English, but he could not answer. Consciousness came and went.

In the darkness, the canoes moved more slowly. Jevy trailed closer, at times using his flashlight to help the guides study the forks and tributaries. At half-throttle, his unsteady outboard settled into a constant whine. They stopped just once, to eat a loaf of bread and drink juice, and to relieve themselves. They latched the three craft together and floated for ten minutes.

Lako was concerned about the American. What shall I tell the missionary about him? he asked Jevy. Tell her he has malaria.

Lightning in the distance ended their brief dinner and rest. The Indians set off again, paddling as hard as ever. They had not seen solid ground in hours. There was no place to land and ride out a storm.

The motor finally quit. Jevy switched to his last full tank, and started it again. At half-throttle, he had enough fuel for about six hours, long enough to find the Paraguay. There would be traffic there, and houses, and at some point, the *Santa Loura*. He knew the exact spot where the Xeco emptied into the Paraguay. Going downriver, they should find Welly by dawn.

The lightning followed, but did not catch them. Each flash made the guides work harder. But they began to tire. At one point, Lako grabbed a side of the johnboat, another Ipica held the other, Jevy held the flashlight above his head, and they plowed forward like a barge.

The trees and brush grew thicker and the river widened. There was solid ground on both sides. The Indians were chattering more, and when they entered the Xeco the paddling stopped. They were exhausted and ready to stop. It's three hours past their bedtime, Jevy thought. They found their spot and landed.

Lako explained that he had been the missionary's assistant for many years. He'd seen lots of malaria; he'd even had it himself three times. He eased the tent off Nate's head and chest, and touched his forehead. A very high fever, he told Jevy, who was holding the flashlight, standing in mud, and anxious to get back in the boat.

There's nothing you can do, he said as he completed his diagnosis. The fever will go away, then there will be another attack in forty-eight hours. He was disturbed by the swollen eyes, something he'd never seen before with malaria.

The oldest guide began talking to Lako and pointing to the dark river. The translation to Jevy was to keep it in the center, ignore the small divides, especially the ones to the left, and in two hours he should find the Paraguay. Jevy thanked them profusely, and took off.

The fever didn't die. An hour later, Jevy checked Nate and his face was still burning. He was curled into a fetal position, semiconscious and mumbling incoherently. Jevy forced water into his mouth, then poured the rest over his face.

The Xeco was wide and easy to navigate. They passed a house, the first they'd seen in a month, it seemed. Like a lighthouse beckoning a wayward ship, the moon broke through the clouds and lit the waters in front of them.

'Can you hear me, Nate?' Jevy said, not loud enough to be heard. 'Our luck is changing.'

He followed the moon to the Paraguay.

THIRTY-TWO

The boat was a *chalana*, a floating shoe box, thirty feet long, eight feet wide, flat-bottomed, and used to haul cargo through the Pantanal. Jevy had captained dozens of them. He saw the light coming around a bend, and when he heard the knock of the diesel, he knew precisely what kind of boat it was.

And he knew the captain, who was sleeping on his bunk when the deckhand stopped the *chalana*. It was almost 3 A.M. Jevy tied his johnboat to the bow and hopped on board. They fed him two bananas while he gave them a quick summary of what he was doing. The deckhand brought sweet coffee. They were headed north to Porto Indio, to the army base there to trade with the soldiers. They could spare five gallons of gas. Jevy promised to pay them back in Corumbá. No problem. Everybody helps on the river.

More coffee, and some sugared wafers. Then he asked about the *Santa Loura*, and Welly. 'It's at the mouth of the Cabixa,' Jevy told them, 'docked where the old pier used to be,' he said.

They shook their heads. 'It wasn't there,' the captain said. The deckhand agreed. They knew the *Santa Loura*, and they had not seen it. It would have been impossible to miss.

'It has to be there,' Jevy said.

'No. We passed the Cabixa at noon yesterday. There was no sign of the *Santa Loura*.'

Perhaps Welly had taken it a few miles into the Cabixa to look for them. He had to be worried sick. Jevy would forgive him for moving the *Santa Loura*, but not before a tongue lashing.

The boat would be there, he was certain. He sipped more coffee and told them about Nate and the malaria. There were fresh rumors in Corumbá about waves of the disease sweeping through the Pantanal. Jevy had heard these all of his life.

They filled a tank from a barrel on board the *chalana*. As a general rule, river traffic during the rainy season was three times faster downstream than up. A johnboat with a good motor should reach the Cabixa in four hours, the trading post in ten, Corumbá in eighteen. The *Santa Loura*, if and when they found it, would take longer, but at least they would have hammocks and food.

Jevy's plan was to stop and rest briefly on the *Santa Loura*. He wanted to get Nate into a bed, and he would use the SatFone to call Corumbá and talk to Valdir. Valdir in turn could find a good doctor who would know what to do when they reached home.

The captain gave him another box of wafers and a paper cup of coffee. Jevy promised to find them in Corumbá next week. He thanked them and unhitched his boat. Nate was alive, but motionless. The fever had not broken.

The coffee quickened Jevy's pulse and kept him awake. He played with the throttle, raising it until the engine began to sputter, then backing down before it died. As the darkness faded, a heavy mist fell upon the river.

He arrived at the mouth of the Cabixa an hour after dawn. The *Santa Loura* was not there. Jevy docked at the old pier and went to find the owner of the only nearby house. He was in his stable, milking a cow. He remembered Jevy, and told the story of the storm that took away the boat. The worst storm ever. It happened in the middle of the night, and he didn't see much. The wind was so fierce that he, his wife, and his child hid under a bed.

'Where did it sink?' Jevy asked.

'I don't know.'

'What about the boy?'

'Welly? I don't know.'

'Haven't you talked to anyone else? Has anyone seen the boy?'

No one. He had not spoken with anyone off the river since Welly disappeared in the storm. He was very sad about everything, and for good measure offered the opinion that Welly was probably dead.

Nate was not. The fever dipped significantly, and when he awoke he was cold and thirsty. He opened his eyes with his fingers, and saw only the water around him, the brush on the bank, and the farmhouse.

'Jevy,' he said, his throat raw, his voice weak. He sat up and worked on his eyes for a few minutes. Nothing focused. Jevy did not answer. Every part of his body ached – muscles, joints, the blood pumping through his brain. There was a hot rash on his neck and chest, and he scratched it until the skin broke. He was sickened by his own odor.

The farmer and his wife followed Jevy back to the boat. They didn't have a drop of gasoline, and this irritated their visitor.

'How are you, Nate?' he asked, stepping into the boat.

'I'm dying.' He exhaled the words.

Jevy felt his forehead, then gently touched the rash. 'Your fever's down.'

'Where are we?'

'We're at the Cabixa. Welly is not here. The boat sank in a storm.'

'Our luck continues,' Nate said, then grimaced as pain shot through his head. 'Where is Welly?'

'I don't know. Can you make it to Corumbá?'

'I'd rather just go ahead and die.'

'Lie down, Nate.'

They left the bank with the farmer and his wife standing ankle-deep in mud, waving but getting ignored.

Nate sat for a while. The wind felt good against his face. Before long, though, he was cold again. A chill shuttered through his chest, and he lowered himself gently under the tent. He tried to pray for Welly, but thoughts lasted only for seconds. He simply couldn't believe he'd caught malaria.

Hark planned the brunch in great detail. It was in a private dining room of the Hay-Adams Hotel. There were oysters and eggs, caviar and salmon, champagne and mimosas. By eleven they were all there, dressed casually, and laying into the mimosas.

He had assured them the meeting was of the utmost importance. It had to be kept confidential. He'd found the one witness who could win the case for them.

Only the lawyers for the Phelan children were invited. The Phelan wives had not yet contested the will, and there seemed little enthusiasm on their part for getting involved. Their legal position was very weak. Judge Wycliff had hinted off the record to one of their lawyers that he would not look favorably upon frivolous suits by the ex-wives.

Frivolous or not, the six children had wasted no time contesting the will. All six had rushed into the fray, all with the same basic claim – that Troy Phelan lacked mental capacity when he signed his last testament.

A maximum of two lawyers per heir were allowed at the meeting, and preferably one, if possible. Hark was alone, representing Rex. Wally Bright was alone, representing Libbigail. Yancy was the only lawyer Ramble knew. Grit was there for Mary Ross. Madam Langhorne, the former professor of law, was there for Geena and Cody. Troy Junior had hired and fired three firms since his father's death. His latest lawyers were from a firm of four hundred. Their names were Hemba and Hamilton, and they introduced themselves to the loose-knit confederation.

Hark closed the door and addressed the group. He gave a short biography of Malcolm Snead, a man he'd been meeting with almost daily. 'He was with Mr. Phelan for thirty years,' he said gravely. 'Maybe he helped him write his last will. Maybe he is prepared to say the old man was completely nuts at the time.'

The lawyers were surprised by the news. Hark watched their happy faces for a moment, then said, 'Or, maybe he is prepared to say he knew nothing of the handwritten will and that Mr. Phelan was perfectly rational and lucid the day he died.'

'How much does he want?' asked Wally Bright, cutting to the chase.

'Five million dollars. Ten percent now, the rest upon settlement.'

Snead's fee did not faze the lawyers. There was so much at stake. In fact, his greed seemed rather modest.

'Our clients, of course, do not have the money,' Hark said. 'So if we want to purchase his testimony, then it's up to us. For about eighty-five thousand per heir, we can sign a contract with Mr. Snead. I'm convinced he will deliver testimony that will either win the case or force a settlement.'

The range of wealth in the room was broad. Wally Bright's office account was overdrawn. He owed back taxes. At the other end of the spectrum, the firm where Hemba and Hamilton worked had partners earning more than a million bucks a year.

'Are you suggesting we pay a lying witness?' Hamilton asked.

'We don't know if he's lying,' Hark responded. He could anticipate every question. 'No one knows. He was alone with Mr. Phelan. There are no witnesses. The truth will be whatever Mr. Snead wants it to be.'

'This sounds shady,' Hemba added.

'You have a better idea?' Grit growled. He was into his fourth mimosa.

Hemba and Hamilton were big-firm lawyers, unaccustomed to the dirt and grime from the streets. Not that they or their ilk were beyond corruption, but their clients were rich corporations that used lobbyists for legal bribery to land fat government contracts and hid money in Swiss accounts for foreign despots, all with the help of their trusty lawyers. But because they were big-firm lawyers they quite naturally looked down upon the type of unethical behavior being suggested by Hark, and condoned by Grit and Bright and the other ham-and-eggers.

'I'm not sure our client will agree to this,' Hamilton said.

'Your client will jump at it,' Hark said. It was almost humorous to drape ethics over TJ Phelan. 'We know him better than you. The question is whether you're willing to do it.'

'Are you suggesting we, the lawyers, front the initial five hundred thousand?' Hemba asked, his tone one of contempt.

'Exactly,' Hark said.

'Then our firm would never go along with such a scheme.'

'Then your firm is about to be replaced,' Grit

288

chimed in. 'Keep in mind, you're the fourth bunch in a month.'

In fact, Troy Junior had already threatened to fire them. They grew quiet and listened. Hark had the floor.

'To avoid the embarrassment of asking each of us to cough up the cash, I have found a bank willing to loan five hundred thousand dollars for a year. All we need is six signatures on the loan. I've already signed.'

'I'll sign the damned thing,' Bright said in a burst of machismo. He was fearless because he had nothing to lose.

'Let me get this straight,' Yancy said. 'We pay Snead the money first, then he talks. Right?'

'Right.'

'Shouldn't we hear his version first?'

'His version needs some work. That's the beauty of the deal. Once we pay him, he's ours. We get to shape his testimony, to structure it to suit ourselves. Keep in mind, there are no other witnesses, maybe with the exception of a secretary.'

'How much does she cost?' asked Grit.

'She's free. She's included in Snead's package.'

How many times in a career would you get the chance to rake off a percentage of the country's tenth largest fortune? The lawyers did the math. A little risk here, a gold mine later.

Madam Langhorne surprised them by saying, 'I'll recommend to my firm that we take the deal. But this has to be a graveyard secret.'

'Graveyard,' repeated Yancy. 'We could all be disbarred, probably indicted. Suborning perjury is a felony.'

'You're missing the point,' Grit said. 'There can be no perjury. The truth is defined by Snead and Snead alone. If he says he helped write the will, and at the

289

time the old man was nuts, then who in the world can dispute it? It's a brilliant deal. I'll sign.'

'That makes four of us,' Hark said.

'I'll sign,' Yancy said.

Hemba and Hamilton were squirming. 'We'll have to discuss it with our firm,' Hamilton said.

'Do we have to remind you boys that all of this is confidential?' Bright said. It was comical, the street fighter from night school chiding the law review editors on ethics.

'No,' Hemba said. 'You don't have to remind us.'

Hark would call Rex, tell him about the deal, and Rex would then call his brother TJ and inform him that his new lawyers were screwing up the deal. Hemba and Hamilton would be history within forty-eight hours.

'Move quickly,' Hark warned them. 'Mr. Snead claims to be broke, and is perfectly willing to cut a deal with the other side.'

'Speaking of which,' Langhorne said, 'do we know any more about who's on the other side? We're all contesting the will. Someone has to be its proponent. Where is Rachel Lane?'

'Evidently she's hiding,' Hark said. 'Josh has assured me that they know where she is, that they are in contact with her, and that she will hire lawyers to protect her interests.'

'For eleven billion, I would hope so,' added Grit.

They pondered the eleven billion for a moment, each dividing it by various magnitudes of the number six, then applying their own personal percentages. Five million for Snead seemed such a reasonable sum.

Jevy and Nate limped to the trading post early in the afternoon. The outboard was missing badly and low on gas. Fernando, the owner of the store, was in a hammock on the porch, trying to avoid the scorching sun. He was an old man, a rugged veteran of the river who'd known Jevy's father.

Both men helped Nate from the boat. He was burning with fever again. His legs were numb and weak, and the three of them inched carefully along the narrow pier and up the steps to the porch. When they folded him into the hammock, Jevy delivered a quick review of the past week. Fernando missed nothing on the river.

'The *Santa Loura* sank,' he said. 'There was a big storm.'

'Have you seen Welly?' Jevy asked.

'Yes. He was pulled from the river by a cattle boat. They stopped here. He told me the story. I'm sure he's in Corumbá.'

Jevy was relieved to hear that Welly was alive. The loss of the boat, however, was tragic news. The *Santa Loura* was one of the finer boats in the Pantanal. It went down under his watch.

Fernando was studying Nate as they talked. Nate could barely hear their words. He certainly couldn't understand them. Not that he cared.

'This is not malaria,' Fernando said, touching the rash on Nate's neck. Jevy moved to the hammock and looked at his friend. His hair was matted and wet, his eyes still swollen shut.

'What is it?' he asked.

'Malaria doesn't produce a rash like this. Dengue does.'

'Dengue fever?'

'Yes. It's similar to malaria—fever and chills, sore muscles and joints, spread by mosquitoes. But the rash means it's dengue.'

'My father had it once. He was a very sick man.'

'You need to get him to Corumbá, as quickly as possible.'

'Can I borrow your motor?'

291

Fernando's boat was docked under the rickety building. His outboard wasn't as rusty as Jevy's, and it had five more horsepower. They scurried around, swapping motors and filling tanks, and after an hour in the hammock, comatose, poor Nate was shuffled back down the pier and laid into the boat under the tent. He was too sick to realize what was happening.

It was almost two-thirty. Corumbá was nine to ten hours away. Jevy left Valdir's phone number with Fernando. On rare occasions a boat on the Paraguay would have a radio. If Fernando happened to encounter one, Jevy wanted him to contact Valdir with the news.

He sped away at full throttle, quite proud to once again have a boat that sliced through the water with speed. The wake boiled behind him.

Dengue fever could be fatal. His father had been deathly ill for a week, with blinding headaches and fevers. His eyes hurt so badly that his mother kept him in a dark room for days. He was a tough river man, accustomed to injuries and pain, and when Jevy heard him moaning like a child he knew his father was dying. The doctor visited every other day, and finally the fever broke.

He could see Nate's feet from under the tent, nothing else. Surely he wouldn't die.

THIRTY-THREE

He woke once, but couldn't see. He woke again and it was dark. He tried to say something to Jevy about water, just a small drink, and maybe a bite of bread. But his voice was gone. Speaking required effort and movement, especially when trying to yell over the howl of the engine. His joints pulled him tightly into a knot. He was welded to the aluminum shell of the boat.

Rachel lay beside him under the smelly tent, her knees also pulled close and just touching his, same as when they sat together on the ground in front of her hut, and later on the bench under the tree by the river. A cautious little contact from a woman starved for the innocent feeling of flesh. She had lived among the Ipicas for eleven years, and their nakedness kept a distance between themselves and any civilized person. A simple hug was complicated. Where do you hold? Where do you pat? How long do you squeeze? Surely she'd never touched any of the males.

He wanted to kiss her, if only on the cheek, because she had obviously gone years without such affection. 'When was your last kiss, Rachel?' he wanted to ask her. 'You've been in love. How physical was it?'

But he kept his questions to himself, and instead they talked about people they didn't know. She'd had a piano teacher whose breath was so bad the ivory keys turned yellow. He'd had a lacrosse coach who was paralyzed from the waist down because he cracked his spine in a lacrosse game. A girl in her church got pregnant, and her father condemned her from the pulpit. She killed herself a week later. He'd lost a brother to leukemia.

He rubbed her knees and she seemed to like it. But he would go no further. It wouldn't pay to get fresh with a missionary.

She was there to keep him from dying. She'd fought malaria twice herself. The fevers rise and fall, the chills hit like ice in the belly, then fade away. The nausea comes in waves. Then there is nothing for hours. She patted his arm and promised he was not going to die. She tells everybody this, he thought. Death would be welcome.

The touching stopped. He opened his eyes and reached for Rachel, but she was gone.

Jevy heard the delirium twice. Each time he stopped the boat and pulled the tent off Nate. He forced water into his mouth, and poured it gently through his sweating hair.

'We're almost there,' he said over and over. 'Almost there.'

The first lights of Corumbá brought tears to his eyes. He had seen them many times when returning from excursions into the northern Pantanal, but they had never been so welcome. They flickered on the hill in the distance. He counted them until they blurred together.

It was almost 11 P.M. when he jumped into the shallow water and pulled his rig onto the broken concrete. The boat dock was deserted. He ran up the hill to a pay phone.

Valdir was watching television in his pajamas, smoking his last cigarette of the night and ignoring his cranky wife, when the phone rang. He answered it without getting up, then jumped to his feet.

'What is it?' she asked, as he ran to the bedroom.

'Jevy's back,' he answered over his shoulder.

'Who's Jevy?'

Passing by her on the way out, he said, 'I'm going to the river.' She couldn't have cared less.

Driving across the city, he called a doctor friend, who had just gone to bed, and cajoled him into meeting them at the hospital.

Jevy was pacing along the dock. The American was sitting on a rock, his head resting on his knees. Without a word, they gently shuffled him into the backseat, and took off, gravel flying behind them.

Valdir had so many questions he didn't know where to start. The harsh words could wait. 'When did he get sick?' he asked in Portuguese. Jevy sat next to him, rubbing his eyes, trying to stay awake. His last sleep had been with the Indians. 'I don't know,' he said. 'The days all run together. It's dengue fever. The rash comes on the fourth or fifth day, and I think he's had it for two days. I don't know.'

They were racing through downtown, ignoring lights and signs. The sidewalk cafés were closing. There was little traffic.

'Did you find the woman?'

'We did.'

'Where?'

'She's close to the mountains. I think she's in Bolivia. A day south of Porto Indio.'

'Was she on the map?'

'No.'

'Then how did you find her?'

No Brazilian could ever admit to being lost, especially a seasoned guide like Jevy. It would hurt his self-esteem, and perhaps his business. 'We were in a flooded region where maps mean nothing. I found a fisherman who helped us. How's Welly?'

'Welly's fine. The boat's gone.' Valdir was much more concerned about the boat than about its deck-hand.

'I've never seen such storms. We've been hit with three of them.'

'What did the woman say?'

'I don't know. I didn't really talk to her.'

'Was she surprised to see you?'

'She didn't seem to be. She was pretty cool. I think she liked our friend back there.'

'How did their meeting go?'

'Ask him.'

Nate was curled tightly in the backseat, hearing nothing. And Jevy was supposed to know nothing, so Valdir didn't press. The lawyers could talk later, as soon as Nate was able.

A wheelchair was waiting at the curb when they arrived at the hospital. They poured Nate into it, and followed the orderly along the sidewalk. The air was warm and sticky, still very hot. On the front steps, a dozen maids and assistants in white uniforms smoked cigarettes and chatted quietly. The hospital had no air conditioning.

The doctor friend was brusque and all business. The paperwork would be done in the morning. They pushed Nate through the empty lobby, along a series of hallways and into a small exam room where a sleepy nurse took him. With Jevy and Valdir watching in a corner, the doctor and nurse stripped the patient bare. The nurse washed him with alcohol and white cloths. The doctor studied the rash, which began at his chin and stopped at his waist. He was covered with mosquito bites, many of which he'd scratched into little red sores. They checked his temperature, blood pressure, heart rate.

'Looks like dengue fever,' the doctor said after ten minutes. He then rattled off a list of details for the nurse, who hardly listened because she'd done it before. She began washing Nate's hair.

Nate mumbled something, but it had nothing to do with anyone present. His eyes were still swollen shut; he hadn't shaved in a week. He would've been at home in a gutter outside a bar.

'The fever is high,' the doctor said. 'He's delirious. We'll start an IV with antibiotics and painkillers, lots of water, maybe a little food later.'

The nurse placed a heavy gauze bandage over Nate's eyes, then strapped it down with tape from ear to ear. She found a vein and started the IV. She pulled a yellow gown from a drawer and dressed him.

The doctor checked his temperature again. 'It should begin falling soon,' he told the nurse. 'If not, call me at home.' He glanced at his watch.

'Thanks,' Valdir said.

'I'll see him early in the morning,' the doctor said, and left them there.

Jevy lived on the edge of town, where the houses were small, the streets unpaved. He fell asleep twice as Valdir drove him home.

Mrs. Stafford was shopping for antiques in London. The phone rang a dozen times before Josh grabbed it. The digital gave the time as 2:20 A.M.

'This is Valdir,' the voice announced.

'Oh yes, Valdir.' Josh rubbed his hair and blinked his eyes. 'This better be good.'

'Your boy is back.'

'Thank God.'

'He's very sick, though.'

'What! What's the matter with him?'

'He has dengue fever, similar to malaria. Mosquitoes carry it. It is not uncommon here.'

'I thought he had shots for everything.' Josh was on his feet, bent at the waist, pulling his hair now.

'There is no shot for dengue.'

'He's not going to die, is he?'

'Oh no. He's in the hospital. I have a good friend who is a doctor, and he's taking care of him. He says your boy will be fine.'

'When can I talk to him?'

'Maybe tomorrow. He has a high fever and he's unconscious.'

'Did he find the woman?'

'Yes.'

Atta boy, thought Josh. He exhaled in relief and sat on the bed. So she's really out there. 'Give me his room number.'

'Well, they don't have phones in the rooms.'

'It's a private room, isn't it? Come on, Valdir, money is no problem here. Tell me he's being taken care of.'

'He is in good hands. But the hospital is a little different from yours.'

'Should I come down there?'

'If you wish. It's not necessary. You can't change the hospital. He has a good doctor.'

'How long will he be there?'

'A few days. We should know more in the morning.'

'Call me early, Valdir. I mean it. I have to talk to him as soon as possible.'

'Yes, I will call early.'

Josh went to the kitchen for ice water. Then he paced around his den. At three, he gave up, made a pot of strong coffee, and went to his office in the basement.

Because he was a rich American, they cut no corners. Nate got pumped into his veins the best drugs available from the pharmacy. The fever dipped a little,

298

the sweating stopped. The pain vanished, washed away by a tide of the finest American-made chemicals. He was snoring heavily as the nurse and an orderly rolled him to his room, two hours after his arrival.

He would share the room for the night with five others. Mercifully, he was blindfolded and comatose. He couldn't see the open sores, the uncontrolled shaking of the old man next to him, the lifeless shriveled creature across the room. He couldn't smell the waste.

THIRTY-FOUR

Though he held no assets in his own name, and had been on the financial ropes for most of his adult life, Rex Phelan had a talent for numbers. It was one of the very few things he inherited from his father. He was the only Phelan heir with both the aptitude and the stamina to read all six of the petitions contesting Troy's will. When he finished, he realized that six law firms were basically duplicating each other's work. In fact, some of the legalese sounded as if it had been borrowed from the last petition, or the next one.

Six firms fighting the same fight, and each wanting an exorbitant piece of the pie. It was time for a little familial harmony. He decided to begin with his brother TJ, who was the easiest target because his lawyers were clinging to their ethics.

The two brothers agreed to meet in secret; their wives hated each other and discord could be avoided if the women simply didn't know. Rex told Troy Junior on the phone that it was time to bury the hatchet. Economics demanded it.

They met for breakfast in a suburban pancake house, and after a few minutes of waffles and football talk the edge was off. Rex got down to business by telling the Snead story. 'This is enormous,' he gushed. 'It could literally make or break our case.' He layered the story, slowing building to the promissory note the lawyers wanted to sign, all lawyers except for Troy Junior's. 'Your attorneys are screwing up the deal,' he said grimly, eyes darting around as if spies were grazing at the egg and bacon bar.

'Son of a bitch wants five million?' Troy Junior said, still in disbelief over Snead.

'It's a bargain. Look, he's willing to say he was the only person with Dad when he wrote the will. Whatever it takes to strike it down. He only wants half a million now. We can screw him out of the rest of it later.'

This appealed to Troy Junior. And changing law firms was certainly nothing new to him. If he'd been candid, he would have admitted that Hemba and Hamilton's firm was intimidating. Four hundred lawyers. Marble foyers. Art on the wall. Somebody was paying for their good taste.

Rex switched gears. 'Have you read the six petitions?' he asked.

Troy Junior chomped a strawberry and shook his head no. He hadn't even read the one filed on his behalf. Hemba and Hamilton had discussed it with him, and he'd signed it, but it was thick and Biff had been waiting in the car.

'Well I've read them, slowly and carefully, and they're all the same. We have six law firms doing the same work, all attacking the same will. It's absurd.'

'I've been thinking about that,' Troy Junior added helpfully.

'And all six expect to get rich when we settle. How much are your boys getting?'

'How much is Hark Gettys getting?'

'Twenty-five percent.'

'Mine wanted thirty. We agreed on twenty.' There was a quick flash of pride because Troy Junior had outnegotiated Rex.

'Let's play with the numbers,' Rex continued.

'Hypothetically, let's say we hire Snead, he says all the right things, we got our shrinks, the mess gets stirred up, and the estate wants to settle. Let's say each heir gets, I don't know, say twenty million. That's forty at this table. Five goes to Hark. Four goes to your boys. That's nine, so we get thirty-one.'

'I'll take it.'

'Me too. But if we take your boys out of the picture, and join up, then Hark will cut his fee. We don't need all these lawyers, TJ. They're just riding each other's backs and waiting to pounce on our money.'

'I hate Hark Gettys.'

'Fine. Let me deal with him. I'm not asking you to be friends.'

'Why don't we fire Hark and stick with my guys?'

'Because Hark found Snead. Because Hark found the bank that'll loan the money to buy Snead. Because Hark is willing to sign the papers and your boys are too ethical. This is a nasty business, TJ. Hark understands it.'

'He strikes me as being a crooked bastard.'

'Yes! And he's our crook. If we join forces, his take goes from twenty-five to twenty. If we can bring in Mary Ross, then he'll cut it to seventeen-five. Libbigail, down to fifteen.'

'We'll never get Libbigail.'

'There's always a chance. If the three of us are on board, she might listen.'

'What about that thug she's married to?' Troy Junior actually asked the question with complete sincerity. He was talking to his brother, who was married to a stripper.

'We'll take 'em one at a time. Let's cut our deal, then we go see Mary Ross. Her lawyer is that Grit guy, and he doesn't strike me as being too sharp.'

'There's no sense fighting,' Troy Junior said sadly.

'It'll cost us a bloody fortune. It's time for a truce.'

'Mom will be proud.'

The high ground on the Xeco had been used by the Indians for decades. It was a camp for fishermen who sometimes stayed the night, and it was a stopping place for river traffic. Rachel and Lako, and another tribesman named Ten, huddled under a lean-to with a straw roof and waited for the storm to pass. The roof leaked and the wind blew the rain sideways at their faces. The canoe was at their feet, dragged from the Xeco after battling the storm for a horrifying hour. Rachel's clothing was soaked, but at least the rain-water was warm. The Indians wore no clothing, except for a string around their waists and a leather covering over their privates.

She once had a wooden boat with an old motor. It had belonged to the Coopers, her predecessors. When there was gasoline, she used it on the rivers between the four Ipica settlements. And it would take her to Corumbá in two very long days, four on the return.

The motor had finally quit, and there was no money for a new one. Each year when she submitted her modest budget to World Tribes, she prayerfully requested a new outboard, or at least a good used one. She had found one in Corumbá for three hundred dollars. But budgets were tight around the world. Her allotments went for medical supplies and Bible literature. Keep praying, she was told. Maybe next year.

She accepted this without question. If the Lord meant for her to have a new outboard, then she would have one. The questions of if and when were left for Him. They were not for her to worry about.

Without a boat, she traveled between the villages on foot, almost always with Lako limping at her side. And once each August she convinced the chief to loan her a canoe and a guide for the journey to the Paraguay. There, she would wait for a cattle boat or a *chalana* headed south. Two years before, she had waited for three days, sleeping in the stable of a small *fazenda* on the river. In three days she went from a stranger to a friend to a missionary as the farmer and his wife became Christians under her teachings and prayer.

She would stay with them tomorrow, and wait for a boat to Corumbá.

The wind howled through the lean-to. She held Lako's hand and they prayed, not for their safety, but for the health of their friend Nate.

Breakfast was served to Mr. Stafford at his desk – cereal and fruit. He refused to leave the office, and when he declared that he would in fact hole up there all day, both of his secretaries scurried to rearrange no less than six meetings. A bagel at ten, at the desk. He called Valdir and was told that he was out of the office, in a meeting somewhere across town. Valdir had a cell phone. Why hadn't he called?

An associate delivered a two-page summary of dengue, taken from the Internet. The associate said he was needed in court, and asked if Mr. Stafford had any more medical work for him. Mr. Stafford did not see the humor.

Josh read the summary with his bagel. It was in all-caps, double-spaced with one-inch margins, about a page and a half long. A Stafford Memo. Dengue fever is a viral infection common throughout the tropical regions of the world. It is spread by a mosquito known as the Aedes, which prefers to bite during the day. The first sign is tiredness, followed quickly by a severe headache behind the eyes, then a mild fever that soon turns into an intense one with sweating and nausea and vomiting. As the fever rises, the muscles in the calves and back begin to ache. The fever is also known as 'breakbone fever' because of the brutal muscle and joint pains. A rash appears after all other symptoms are present. The fever may break for a day or so, but it usually returns with increased intensity. After about a week, the infection wanes and the danger is gone. There is no cure and no vaccine. It takes a month of rest and liquids to return to normal.

And that's a mild case. Dengue can progress into dengue hemorrhagic fever or dengue shock syndrome, both of which are sometimes fatal, especially in children.

Josh was prepared to send Mr. Phelan's jet to Corumbá to collect Nate. On board would be a doctor and a nurse, and anything else that might be needed.

'It's Mr. Valdir,' a secretary said through the intercom. No other calls were being taken.

He was at the hospital. 'I've just checked on Mr. O'Riley,' he said slowly, precisely. 'He is okay. But he is not very conscious.'

'Can he talk?' Josh asked.

'No. Not now. They are giving him drugs for his pain.'

'Does he have a good doctor?'

'The best. A friend of mine. The doctor's with him now.'

'Ask him when Mr. O'Riley will be able to fly home. I will send a private jet and a doctor to Corumbá.'

There was a conversation in the background. 'Not soon,' Valdir reported. 'He will need rest when he leaves the hospital.'

'When will he leave the hospital?'

Another conversation. 'He can't say right now.'

Josh shook his head and flung the remnants of his bagel into the wastebasket. 'Did you say anything to Mr. O'Riley?' he growled at Valdir.

'No. I think he's asleep.'

'Listen, Mr. Valdir, it is very important that I talk to him as soon as possible, okay?'

'I understand this. But you must be patient.'

'I'm not a patient man.'

'I understand this. But you must try.'

'Call me this afternoon.'

Josh slammed the phone down and began pacing. It had been an unwise decision to send Nate, fragile and unstable as he was, into the dangers of the tropics. Convenience had been the reason. Send him away for a couple of weeks more, keep him busy elsewhere while the firm sorts out his mess. There were four lesser partners in his firm besides Nate, four Josh had handpicked and hired and mentored and listened to on some matters of management. Tip was one, and he was the sole voice of support for Nate. The other three wanted him gone.

Nate's secretary had been reassigned. A rising associate had been borrowing his office lately, and was said to have found a home.

If dengue fever didn't get poor Nate, the IRS was waiting.

The IV bag emptied silently around the middle of the day, though no one bothered to check it. Several hours later Nate woke up. His head was light, and at peace, with no fever. He was stiff but not sweating. He felt the heavy gauze over his eyes, felt the tape holding it there, and after some thought decided to have a look. His left arm held the IV, so he began picking at the tape with the fingers of his right hand. He was aware of voices in another room, and steps on a hard floor. People were busy down the hall. Closer, someone was moaning in a low, steady, painful voice.

He slowly worked the tape from his skin and hair, and cursed the person who'd stuck it there. He laid the bandage to one side; it hung over his left ear. His first image was peeling paint, a dull shade of faded yellow on the wall just above him. The lights were off, rays of sun drifted in from a window. The paint on the ceiling was cracked too, large black gaps shrouded with cobwebs and dust. A rickety fan dropped from the center and wobbled as it spun.

Two feet caught his attention, two old, gnarled, scarred feet layered with wounds and calluses from toes to soles, sticking in the air, and when he lifted his head slightly he saw that they belonged to a shriveled little man whose bed almost touched his. He appeared dead.

The moaning came from the wall near the window. This poor guy was just as small and just as shriveled. He sat in the middle of his bed, arms and legs folded and tucked into a ball, and suffered his affliction in a trance.

The smell was of old urine, human waste, and heavy antiseptic all mixed into one thick odor. Nurses laughed down the hall. The paint was peeling on every wall. There were five beds besides Nate's, all of the rollaway variety, parked here and there with little effort at order.

His third roommate was by the door. He was naked except for a wet diaper, and his body was covered with open red sores. He too appeared dead, and Nate certainly hoped he was. For his own good.

There were no buttons to push, no emergency cord or intercom, no way to summon help except for yelling, and this might wake the dead. These creatures might arise and want to visit with him.

He wanted to run, to swing his feet off the bed, onto the floor, rip the IV from his arm, and sprint for freedom. He would take his chances on the street. Surely there couldn't be as much disease out there. Any place was better than this leper's ward.

But his feet were like bricks. Nate tried mightily to lift them, one at a time, but they barely moved.

Nate sunk his head to his pillow, closed his eyes, and thought about crying. I am in a hospital in a third world country, he said over and over. I left Walnut Hill, a thousand bucks a day, pushbutton everything, carpet, showers, therapists at my beck and call.

The man with the sores grunted, and Nate sank even lower. Then he carefully took the gauze and placed it over his eyes, and he taped it just like before, only tighter this time.

THIRTY-FIVE

Snead arrived for the meeting with a contract of his own, one he had prepared without the aid of a lawyer. Hark read it, and had to admit that it was not a bad job of drafting. It was titled Contract for Expert Witness Services. Experts give opinions. Snead would deal primarily with the facts, but Hark didn't care what the contract said. He signed it, and handed over a certified check for half a million. Snead took it delicately, examined every word, then folded it and tucked it away in his coat pocket. 'Now where do we start?' he said with a smile.

There was so much to cover. The other Phelan lawyers wanted to be present. Hark had time only for a primer. 'In general terms,' he said, 'what was the old man's frame of mind the morning he died?'

Snead squirmed and twisted and frowned as if in deep thought. He really wanted to say the right things. He felt as though he had four-point-five million riding on him now. 'He was out of his mind,' he said, the words hanging in the air while he waited for approval.

Hark nodded. So far so good. 'Was this unusual?'

'No. In his last days he was hardly rational.'

'How much time did you spend with him?'

'Off and on, twenty-four hours a day.'

'Where did you sleep?'

'My room was down the hall, but he had a buzzer

for me. I was on call around the clock. He would sometimes get up in the middle of the night and want juice or a pill. He simply pushed a button, the buzzer rang me, and I fetched whatever he wanted.'

'Who else lived with him?'

'No one.'

'Who else did he spend time with?'

'Perhaps young Nicolette, the secretary. He fancied her.'

'Did he have sex with her?'

'Would it help our case?'

'Yes.'

'Then they were screwing like rabbits.'

Hark couldn't help but smile. The allegation that Troy was chasing his last secretary would surprise no one.

It hadn't taken long for them to find the same sheet to sing from. 'Look, Mr. Snead, this is what we want. We need the quirks, the little oddities, the glaring lapses, the strange things he said and did that when taken as a whole will convince anyone he was not of sound mind. You have time. Sit down and begin writing. Put the pieces together. Have a chat with Nicolette, make sure they were having sex, listen to what she says.'

'She'll say anything we need.'

'Good. Then rehearse, and make sure there are no gaps that other lawyers can find. Your stories must hold together.'

'There's no one to contradict them.'

'No one? No limo driver or maid or ex-lover or maybe another secretary?'

'He had all those, sure. But no one lived on the fourteenth floor but Mr. Phelan and myself. He was a very lonely man. And quite crazy.'

'Then how did he perform so well for the three psychiatrists?'

Snead thought about this for a moment. Fiction failed him. 'What would you guess?' he asked.

'I would guess that Mr. Phelan knew the examination would be difficult because he knew he was slipping, and so he asked you to prepare lists of anticipated questions, and that you and Mr. Phelan spent that morning reviewing such simple matters as the day's date, he couldn't keep it straight, and the names of children, names he'd virtually forgotten, where they went to college, whom they were married to, etcetera, then you covered questions about his health. I would guess that after you had drilled him on these basics, you spent at least two hours prompting him on his holdings, the structure of The Phelan Group, the companies he owned, the acquisitions he'd made, the closing prices of certain stocks. He relied on you more and more for financial news, and so this came easy for you. It was tedious for the old man, but you were determined to keep him sharp just before you wheeled him in for the exam. Does this sound familiar?'

Snead liked it immensely. He was awed by the lawyer's gift of creating lies on the spot. 'Yes, yes, that's it! That's how Mr. Phelan snowed the psychiatrists.'

'Then work on it, Mr. Snead. The more you work on your stories, the better witness you'll be. The lawyers on the other side will come after you. They will attack your testimony and call you a liar, so you must be ready. Write everything down, so you'll always have a record of your stories.'

'I like that idea.'

'Dates, times, places, incidents, oddities. Everything, Mr. Snead. Same for Nicolette. Make her write it down.'

'She doesn't write well.'

'Help her. It's up to you, Mr. Snead. You want the rest of the money, then earn it.'

'How much time do I have?'

'We, the other lawyers and myself, would like to video you in a few days. We'll hear your stories, pepper you with questions, then watch your performance. I'm sure we'll want to change some things. We'll coach you along, maybe do more videos. When things are perfect, then you'll be ready for your deposition.'

Snead left in a hurry. He wanted to put the money in the bank, and buy a new car. Nicolette needed one too.

A night orderly on his rounds noticed the empty bag. The handprinted instructions on the back of it said that the fluids should not be interrupted. He took it to the pharmacy, where a part-time student nurse remixed the chemicals and gave the bag back to the orderly. There were rumors around the hospital about the rich American patient.

In his sleep, Nate was refortified with drugs he didn't need.

When Jevy found him before breakfast, he was half-awake, eyes still covered because he preferred the darkness. 'Welly's here,' Jevy whispered.

The nurse on duty helped Jevy roll the bed from the room, down the hall, and into a small courtyard where there was sunshine. The nurse turned a crank and half the bed inclined. She removed the gauze and tape, and Nate never flinched. He slowly opened his eyes and tried to focus. Jevy, just inches away, said, 'The swelling is down.'

'Hello, Nate,' Welly said. He was hovering on the other side. The nurse left them.

'Hello, Welly,' Nate said, his words deep, slow, thick. He was groggy, but happy. How well he knew the feeling of being stoned.

Jevy patted his forehead and announced, 'The fever is gone too.' The Brazilians smiled at each other, relieved that they had not killed the American during their excursion into the Pantanal.

'What happened to you?' Nate asked Welly, trying to clip his words and not sound like a drunk. Jevy passed along the question in Portuguese. Welly was instantly animated, and began his long narrative about the storm and the sinking of the *Santa Loura*. Jevy stopped him every thirty seconds for the translation. Nate listened while trying to keep his eyes open, but he floated in and out of the scene.

Valdir found them there. He greeted Nate warmly, delighted that their guest was sitting up in bed and looking better. He whipped out a cell phone, and as he punched numbers he said, 'You must talk to Mr. Stafford. He is quite anxious.'

'I'm not sure I . . .' Nate's words trailed off as he drifted.

'Here, sit up, it's Mr. Stafford,' Valdir said, handing him the phone and puffing up his pillow. Nate took the phone and said, 'Hello.'

'Nate!' came the reply. 'Is that you!'

'Josh.'

'Nate, tell me you're not going to die. Please tell me.'

'I'm not sure,' Nate said. Valdir gently pushed the phone closer to Nate's head, and helped him hold it in place. 'Speak louder,' he whispered. Jevy and Welly stepped back.

'Nate, did you find Rachel Lane?' Josh yelled into the phone.

Nate rallied for a second. He frowned hard, trying to concentrate. 'No,' he said.

'What!'

'Her name's not Rachel Lane.'

'What the hell is it?'

313

Nate thought hard for a second, then fatigue hit him. He slumped a bit, still trying to remember her name. Maybe she never told him her last name. 'I don't know,' he mumbled, his lips barely moving. Valdir pressed the phone harder.

'Nate, talk to me! Did you find the right woman?'

'Oh yes. Everything's okay down here, Josh. Relax.'

'What about the woman?'

'She's lovely.'

Josh hesitated for a second, but he couldn't waste any time. 'That's nice, Nate. Did she sign the papers?'

'I can't think of her name.'

'Did she sign the papers?'

There was a long pause as Nate's chin dropped to his chest and he appeared to be napping. Valdir nudged his arm and tried to move his head with the phone. 'I really liked her,' Nate suddenly babbled. 'A lot.'

'You're stoned, aren't you, Nate? They've got you on painkillers, right?'

'Yep.'

'Look, Nate, call me when your head is clear, okay?'

'I don't have a phone.'

'Then use Valdir's. Please call me, Nate.'

His head nodded and his eyes closed. 'I asked her to marry me,' he said into the phone, then his chin fell for the last time.

Valdir took the phone and walked to a corner. He tried to describe Nate's condition.

'Do I need to come down there?' Josh yelled for the third or fourth time.

'That is not necessary. Please be patient.'

'I'm tired of you telling me to be patient.'

'I understand.'

'Get him well, Valdir.'

'He is fine.'

'No he's not. Call me later.'

★

314

Tip Durban found Josh standing in the window of his office, staring at the cluster of buildings that composed his view. Tip closed the door, took a seat, and asked, 'What did he say?'

Josh kept staring out the window. 'He said he found her, that she's lovely, and that he asked her to marry him.' There was no trace of humor in his voice.

Tip found it humorous nonetheless. When it came to women, Nate culled little, especially between divorces. 'How is he?'

'Feeling no pain, pumped full of painkillers, semi-conscious. Valdir said the fever is gone and he looks much better.'

'So he's not going to die?'

'It appears not.'

Durban began chuckling. 'That's our boy Nate. Never met a skirt he didn't like.'

When Josh turned around he looked quite amused. 'It's beautiful,' he said. 'Nate's bankrupt. She's only forty-two, probably hasn't seen a white man in years.'

'Nate wouldn't care if she was as ugly as sin. She happens to be the richest woman in the world.'

'I'm not surprised, now that I think about it. I thought I was doing him a favor sending him off on an adventure. It never occurred to me he would try to seduce a missionary.'

'You think he hit on her?'

'Who knows what they did in the jungle.'

'I doubt it,' Tip added on second thought. 'We know Nate, but we don't know her. It takes two.'

Josh sat on the edge of his desk, still amused, grinning at the floor. 'You're right. I'm not sure she would go for Nate. There's a lot of baggage.'

'Did she sign the papers?'

'We didn't get that far. I'm sure she did or he wouldn't have left her.'

'When is he coming home?'

315

'As soon as he can travel.'

'Don't be so sure. For eleven billion, I might stick around for a while.'

THIRTY-SIX

The doctor found his patient snoring in the shade of the courtyard, still sitting up in bed, mouth open, gauze removed, head fallen to one side. His friend from the river was napping on the ground nearby. He studied the IV bag and stopped the flow. He touched Nate's forehead and felt no fever.

'Senhor O'Riley,' he said loudly as he tapped the patient's shoulder. Jevy jumped to his feet. The doctor did not speak English.

He wanted Nate to return to his room, but when this was translated by Jevy it was not well received. Nate pleaded with Jevy and Jevy begged the doctor. Jevy had seen the other patients, the open sores, the seizures and dying men just down the hall, and he promised the doctor he would sit right there in the shade with his friend until dark. The doctor relented. He really didn't care.

Across the courtyard was a small separate ward with thick black bars sunk in cement. Patients wandered out from time to time to gawk through the bars into the courtyard. They could not escape. A screamer appeared late in the morning, and took offense at the presence of Nate and Jevy across the way. He had brown spotted skin and red patchy hair, and looked as crazy as he was. He clasped two bars, stuck his face between them, and began yelling. His voice was shrill

317

and echoed around the courtyard and down the halls.

'What's he saying?' Nate asked. The lunatic's yelling startled him, and helped clear his head.

'I can't understand a word. He's insane.'

'They have me in the same hospital with the crazy people?'

'Yes. Sorry. It's a small town.'

The yelling intensified. A nurse from the safe side appeared and shouted for him to be quiet. He lashed back at her with language that made her run away. Then he refocused on Nate and Jevy. He squeezed the bars until his knuckles were white, and began hopping as he screamed.

'Poor guy,' Nate said.

The screaming turned to wailing, and after a few minutes of nonstop racket a male nurse appeared behind the man and attempted to lead him away. He didn't want to go, and a short scuffle ensued. With witnesses, the nurse was firm but cautious. The man's hands, however, were glued around the bars and could not be removed. The wailing turned to shrieking as the nurse tugged from behind.

Finally, the nurse gave up and disappeared. The screamer pulled down his pants and began peeing through the bars, laughing loudly as he aimed in the general direction of Nate and Jevy, who were out of range. While his hands were off the bars, the nurse suddenly attacked from the rear, grabbing him in a full nelson and dragging him away. Once he was out of sight, the yelling ceased immediately.

When the daily drama was over and the courtyard was once again quiet, Nate said, 'Jevy, get me out of here.'

'What do you mean?'

'Get me out of here. I feel fine. The fever is gone, my strength is returning. Let's go.'

'We can't leave until the doctor releases you. And

318

you have that,' he added, pointing to the IV in Nate's left forearm.

'This is nothing,' Nate said as he quickly slid the needle from his arm and yanked the IV free. 'Find me some clothes, Jevy. I'm checking out.'

'You don't know dengue. My father had it.'

'It's over. I can feel it.'

'No, it's not. The fever will return, and it will be worse. Much worse.'

'I don't believe that. Take me to a hotel, Jevy, please. I'll be fine there. I'll pay you to stay with me, and if the fever returns you can feed me pills. Please, Jevy.'

Jevy was standing at the foot of the bed. He glanced around as if someone might understand their English. 'I don't know,' he said, waivering. It was not such a bad idea.

'I'll pay you two hundred dollars to get me some clothes and take me to a hotel. And I'll pay you fifty dollars a day to guard me until I'm okay.'

'It's not about money, Nate. I'm your friend.'

'And I'm your friend, Jevy. And friends help friends. I can't go back to that room. You saw those poor sick people in there. They're all rotting and dying and pissing all over themselves. It smells like human waste. The nurses don't care. The doctors don't check on you. The insane asylum is just over there. Please, Jevy, get me out of here. I'll pay you good money.'

'Your money went down with the *Santa Loura*.'

That stopped him cold. Nate had not even thought about the *Santa Loura*, and his belongings – his clothes, money, passport, and briefcase with all the gadgets and papers Josh had sent. There had been few lucid moments since leaving Rachel, just a few clear intervals during which he had thought about living and dying. Never about tangible things or assets. 'I can get plenty of money, Jevy. I'll wire it in from the States. Please help me.'

Jevy knew that dengue was rarely fatal. Nate's bout with it appeared to be under control, though the fever would surely return. No one could blame him for wanting to escape the hospital. 'Okay,' he said, glancing around again. No one was near them. 'I'll return in a few minutes.'

Nate closed his eyes and contemplated his lack of a passport. And he had no cash, not a dime. No clothes, no toothbrush. No SatFone, cell phone, no calling cards. And matters weren't much better at home. From the ruins of his personal bankruptcy, he could expect to keep his leased car, his clothing and modest furniture, and the money put away in his IRA. Nothing else. The lease on his small condo in Georgetown had been surrendered during rehab. There was no place to go when he returned. No family to speak of. His two older kids were distant and unconcerned. The two middle schoolers from the second marriage had been taken far away by their mother. He hadn't seen them in six months, and had scarcely thought about them at Christmas.

On his fortieth birthday, Nate had won a $10 million verdict against a doctor who failed to diagnose cancer. It was the largest verdict of his career, and when the appeals were finished two years later the firm collected over $4 million in fees. Nate's bonus that year had been $1.5 million. He was a millionaire for a few months, until he bought the new house. There were furs and diamonds, cars and trips, some shaky investments. Then he started seeing a college girl who loved cocaine, and the wall cracked. He crashed hard and spent two months locked away. His second wife left with the money, then came back briefly without it.

He'd been a millionaire, and now he imagined how he looked from the roof of the courtyard – sick, alone, broke, under indictment, afraid of the return home, and terrified of the temptations there.

His quest to find Rachel had kept him focused. There was excitement in the hunt. Now that it was over, and he was flat on his back again, he thought of Sergio and rehab and addictions and all the trouble waiting for him. Darkness was looming again.

He couldn't spend the rest of his life riding *chalanas* up and down the Paraguay with Jevy and Welly, far removed from booze and drugs and women, oblivious to his legal troubles. He had to go back. He had to face the music one more time.

A piercing squawk jolted him from his daydreams. The red-headed screamer was back.

Jevy rolled the bed under a veranda, then down a hallway headed toward the front of the hospital. He stopped by a janitor's closet, and helped the patient out of bed. Nate was weak and shaky, but determined to escape. Inside the closet, he ripped off the gown and put on a pair of baggy soccer shorts, a red tee shirt, the obligatory rubber sandals, a denim cap, and a pair of plastic sunshades. Though he looked the part, he did not feel the least bit Brazilian. Jevy had spent little on his outfit. He was adjusting the cap when he fainted.

Jevy heard him hit the door. He quickly opened it, and found Nate slumped in a pile with buckets and mops rattling around. He clutched him under the arms and dragged him back to the bed. He rolled him into it and covered him with the sheet.

Nate opened his eyes and said, 'What happened?'

'You fainted,' came the reply. The bed was moving; Jevy was behind him. They passed two nurses who didn't seem to notice them. 'This is a bad idea,' Jevy said.

'Just keep going.'

They parked near the lobby. Nate crawled out of

bed, felt faint again, and began walking. Jevy placed a heavy arm around his shoulder and steadied him by clutching his bicep. 'Take it easy,' Jevy kept saying. 'Nice and slow.'

No stares from the admissions clerks, nor the sick people trying to get in. No odd looks from the nurses and orderlies smoking on the front steps. The sun hit Nate hard and he leaned on Jevy. They crossed the street to where Jevy's massive Ford was parked.

They narrowly avoided death at the first intersection. 'Could you please drive slower,' Nate snapped. He was sweating and his stomach was rolling.

'Sorry,' Jevy said, and the truck slowed considerably.

With charm and the promise of future payment, Jevy cajoled a double room out of the young girl at the front desk of the Palace Hotel. 'My friend is sick,' he whispered to her, nodding at Nate, who certainly appeared ill. Jevy didn't want the pretty lady to get the wrong idea. They had no bags.

In the room, Nate collapsed on the bed. The little escape had tired him immensely. Jevy found the rerun of a soccer game on TV, but after five minutes was bored. He left to continue his flirting.

Nate tried twice to get an international operator. He had a vague recollection of hearing Josh's voice on the phone, and he suspected that a follow-up was needed. On the second attempt, he got an earful of Portuguese. When she tried English, he thought he caught the words 'calling card.' He hung up and went to sleep.

The doctor called Valdir. Valdir found Jevy's truck parked on the street outside the Palace Hotel, and he found Jevy in the pool sipping a beer.

Valdir squatted at the edge of the pool. 'Where is Mr. O'Riley?' he asked. His irritation was obvious.

322

'Upstairs in his room,' Jevy answered, then took another sip.

'Why is he here?'

'Because he wanted to leave the hospital. Do you blame him?'

Valdir's only surgery had been in Campo Grande, four hours away. No one with money would ever voluntarily submit themselves to the hospital in Corumbá. 'How is he?'

'I think he's fine.'

'Stay with him.'

'I don't work for you anymore, Mr. Valdir.'

'Yes, but there is the matter of the boat.'

'I can't raise it. I didn't sink it. A storm did. What do you want me to do?'

'I want you to watch Mr. O'Riley.'

'He needs money. Can you wire it in for him?'

'I suppose.'

'And he needs a passport. He lost everything.'

'Just watch him. I'll take care of the details.'

The fever returned quietly during the night, warming his face as he slept, taking its time as it built momentum for the havoc to come. Its calling card was a row of tiny pellets of sweat lined perfectly above the eyebrows, then sweat in the hair that rested on the pillow. It simmered while he slept, stewing, preparing to erupt. It sent tremors, little waves of chills, through his body, but he was fatigued and there were the remnants of so many chemicals that he kept sleeping. It built pressure behind his eyes, so that when he did open them he would want to scream. It drained the fluids from his mouth.

Nate finally groaned. He felt the vicious pounding of a jackhammer between his temples. When he opened his eyes, death awaited him. He was in a pool

323

of sweat, his face on fire, his knees and elbows bending in pain. 'Jevy,' he whispered. 'Jevy!'

Jevy hit the switch for the table lamp between them, and Nate groaned even louder. 'Turn that off!' he said. Jevy ran to the bathroom and found a less direct source of light. For the ordeal, he had purchased bottled water, ice, aspirin, over-the-counter pain medications, and a thermometer. He thought he was prepared.

An hour passed and Jevy counted every minute of it. The fever climbed to 102; the chills came in waves so violent that the small bed rattled and shook on the floor. When Nate wasn't shaking, Jevy stuffed pills in his mouth and poured down water. He soaked his face with wet towels. Nate suffered in silence, bravely gritting his teeth so that the pain was quiet. He was determined to suffer through the fevers in the relative luxury of the small hotel room. Every time he wanted to scream, he remembered the cracked plaster and smells of the hospital.

At 4 A.M., the fever climbed to 103, and Nate began to drift away. His knees almost touched his chin. His arms were wrapped around his calves. He held himself tightly. Then a chill would hit and untangle him as his body shuddered.

The last temperature reading was 105, and Jevy knew at some point his friend would go into shock. He finally panicked, not from the temperature, but from the sight of sweat dripping from the bedsheets onto the floor. His friend had suffered enough. There were better drugs at the hospital.

He found a janitor asleep on the third floor, and together they dragged Nate to the elevator, through the empty lobby, and to his truck. He called Valdir at 6 A.M., waking him.

When Valdir finished cursing Jevy, he agreed to call the doctor.

THIRTY-SEVEN

The treatment was phoned in from the doctor's bed. Fill the IV bag with lots of goodies, poke the needle in his arm, try to find a better room. The rooms were full, so they simply left him in the hall of the men's ward, near a messy desk they called the nurses' station. At least they couldn't ignore him. Jevy was asked to leave. There was nothing he could do but wait.

At one point in the morning, during a lull in other activities, an orderly appeared with a pair of scissors. He cut off the new gym shorts and the new red tee shirt, and replaced them with another yellow gown. In the process Nate lay naked on the bed for five full minutes, in plain view of everyone passing by. No one noticed; Nate certainly didn't care. The sheets were changed because they were soaked. The rags that had been the shorts and shirt were thrown away, and once again Nate O'Riley had no clothes.

If he shook too much or moaned too loud, the nearest doctor or nurse or orderly would gently open the IV. And when he was snoring too loud, someone would close it a little.

A cancer death created an opening. Nate was rolled into the nearest room where he was parked between a worker who'd just lost a foot and a man dying from kidney failure. The doctor saw him twice during the day. The fever wavered between 102 and 104. Valdir stopped by late in the afternoon for a chat but Nate was not awake. He reported the day's events to Mr. Stafford, who was not pleased.

'The doctor says this is normal,' Valdir said, speaking into his cell phone in the hallway. 'Mr. O'Riley will be fine.'

'Don't let him die, Valdir,' Josh growled from America.

Money was being wired. They were working on the passport.

Once again the IV bag dripped itself empty, and no one noticed. Hours passed and the drugs gradually wore off. It was pitch dark, the middle of the night, and there was no movement from the other three beds when Nate finally shook off the cobwebs of his coma and showed signs of life. He could barely see his roommates. The door was open and there was a faint light down the hallway. No voices, no feet shuffling by.

He touched his gown – drenched from the sweat – and realized he was again naked underneath. He rubbed his swollen eyes and tried to straighten his cramped legs. His forehead was very hot. He was thirsty and could not remember his last meal. He tried not to move for fear of waking those around him. Surely a nurse would stop by soon.

The sheets were wet, so when the chills began again there was no way to get warm. He shook and vibrated, rubbing his arms and legs, his teeth clapping together. After the chills stopped, he tried to sleep and managed a few naps as the night wore on, but when it was darkest the fever rose again. His temples pounded so hard that Nate began to cry. He wrapped the pillow around his head and squeezed as hard as he could.

In the darkness of the room, a silhouette entered and moved from bed to bed, finally stopping beside

Nate's. She watched him flounder and fight under the sheets, his low moans muffled by the pillow. She touched him gently on the arm. 'Nate,' she whispered.

Under normal circumstances, he would have been startled. But hallucinating had become a common symptom. He lowered the pillow to his chest and tried to focus on the figure.

'It's Rachel,' she whispered.

'Rachel?' he whispered, his breathing labored. He tried to sit up, then tried to open his eyes with his fingers. 'Rachel?'

'I'm here, Nate. God sent me to protect you.'

He reached for her face and she took his hand. She kissed his palm. 'You are not going to die, Nate,' she said. 'God has plans for you.'

He could say nothing. Slowly his eyes adjusted and he could see her. 'It's you,' he said. Or was it another dream?

He reclined again, resting his head on the pillow, relaxing as his muscles unclenched themselves and his joints became loose. He closed his eyes, but still held her hand. The pounding behind his eyes faded. The heat left his forehead and face. The fever had sapped his strength, and he drifted away again, into a deep sleep induced not by chemicals but by sheer exhaustion.

He dreamed of angels – white-robed young maidens floating in the clouds above him, there to protect him, humming hymns he'd never heard but that somehow seemed familiar.

He left the hospital at noon the next day, armed with his doctor's orders and accompanied by Jevy and Valdir. There was no trace of fever, no rash, just a little soreness in the joints and muscles. He insisted on leaving, and the doctor readily concurred. The doctor was happy to be rid of him.

The first stop was a restaurant where he consumed a large bowl of rice and a plate of boiled potatoes. He avoided the steaks and chops. Jevy did not. They were both still hungry from their adventure. Valdir sipped coffee, smoked his cigarettes, and watched them eat.

No one had seen Rachel come and go at the hospital. Nate had whispered the secret to Jevy, who had inquired of the nurses and maids. After lunch, Jevy left them and began roaming downtown on foot, searching for her. He went to the river where he talked to deckhands on the last cattle boat. She had not traveled with them. The fishermen hadn't seen her. No one seemed to know anything about the arrival of a white woman from the Pantanal.

In Valdir's office, alone, Nate dialed the number of the Stafford Law Firm, a number he had trouble remembering. They pulled Josh out of a meeting. 'Talk to me, Nate,' he said. 'How are you?'

'The fever is gone,' he said, rocking in Valdir's easy chair. 'I feel fine. A little sore and tired, but I feel good.'

'You sound great. I want you home.'

'Give me a couple of days.'

'I'm sending a jet down, Nate. It will leave tonight.'

'No. Don't do that, Josh. That's not a good idea. I'll get there whenever I want.'

'Okay. Tell me about the woman, Nate.'

'We found her. She is the illegitimate daughter of Troy Phelan, and she has no interest in the money.'

'So how did you talk her into taking it?'

'Josh, you don't talk this woman into anything. I tried, got nowhere, so I stopped.'

'Come on, Nate. Nobody walks away from this kind of money. Surely you talked some sense into her.'

'Not even close, Josh. She is the happiest person I've ever met, perfectly content to spend the rest of her life working among her people. It's where God wants her to be.'

'She signed the papers though?'

'Nope.'

There was a long pause as Josh absorbed it. 'You must be kidding,' he finally said, barely audible in Brazil.

'Nope. Sorry, boss. I tried my best to convince her to at least sign the papers, but she wouldn't budge. She'll never sign them.'

'Did she read the will?'

'Yes.'

'And you told her it was eleven billion dollars?'

'Yep. She lives alone in a hut with a thatched roof, no plumbing, no electricity, simple food and clothes, no phones or faxes, and no concern about the things she's missing. She's in the Stone Age, Josh, right where she wants to be, and money would change that.'

'It's incomprehensible.'

'I thought so too, and I was there.'

'Is she bright?'

'She's a doctor, Josh, an M.D. And she has a degree from a seminary. She speaks five languages.'

'A doctor?'

'Yeah, but we didn't talk about medical practice litigation.'

'You said she was lovely.'

'I did?'

'Yeah, on the phone two days ago. I think you were stoned.'

'I was, and she is.'

'So you liked her?'

'We became friends.' It would serve no purpose to tell Josh that she was in Corumbá. Nate hoped to find her quickly, and, while in civilization, try to discuss Troy's estate.

329

'It was quite an adventure,' Nate said. 'To say the least.'

'I've lost sleep worrying about you.'

'Relax. I'm still in one piece.'

'I wired five thousand dollars. Valdir has it.'

'Thanks, boss.'

'Call me tomorrow.'

Valdir invited him to dinner, but he declined. He collected the money and left on foot, loose again on the streets of Corumbá. His first stop was a clothing store where he bought underwear, safari shorts, plain white tee shirts, and hiking boots. By the time he hauled his new wardrobe four blocks to the Palace Hotel, Nate was exhausted. He slept for two hours.

Jevy found no trace of Rachel. He watched the crowds on the busy streets. He talked to the river people he knew so well, and heard nothing about her arrival. He walked through the lobbies of the downtown hotels and flirted with the receptionists. No one had seen an American woman of forty-two traveling alone.

As the afternoon wore on, Jevy doubted his friend's story. Dengue makes you see things, makes you hear voices, makes you believe in ghosts, especially in the night. But he kept searching.

Nate roamed too, after his nap and another meal. He walked slowly, pacing himself, trying to keep in the shade and always with a bottle of water in hand. He rested on the bluff above the river, the majesty of the Pantanal spread before him for hundreds of miles.

Fatigue hit him hard, and he limped back to the hotel for another rest. He slept again, and when he awoke Jevy was tapping on the door. They had promised to meet for dinner at seven. It was after eight, and when Jevy entered the room he immediately began looking for empty bottles. There were none.

They ate roasted chicken at a sidewalk café. The

night was alive with music and foot traffic. Couples with small children bought ice cream and drifted back home. Teenagers moved in packs with no apparent destination. The bars spilled outdoors, to the edges of the streets. Young men and women moved from one bar to the next. The streets were warm and safe; no one seemed concerned about getting shot or mugged.

At a nearby table, a man drank a cold Brahma beer from a brown bottle, and Nate watched every sip.

After dessert, they said good-bye and promised to meet early for another day of searching. Jevy went one direction, Nate another. He was rested, and tired of beds.

Two blocks away from the river, and the streets were quieter. The shops were closed; the homes were dark; traffic was lighter. Ahead, he saw the lights of a small chapel. That, he said almost aloud, is where she'll be.

The front door was wide open, so from the sidewalk Nate could see rows of wooden pews, the empty pulpit, the mural of Christ on the cross, and the backs of a handful of worshipers leaning forward in prayer and meditation. The organ music was low and soft, and it pulled him in. He stopped in the door and counted five people scattered among the pews, no two sitting together, no one with even the slightest resemblance to Rachel. Under the mural, the organ bench was empty. The music came from a speaker.

He could wait. He had the time; she might appear. He shuffled along the back row and sat alone. He studied the crucifixion, the nails through His hands, the sword in His side, the agony in His face. Did they really kill Him in such a dreadful manner? Along the way, at some point in his miserable secular life, Nate had read or heard the basic stories of Christ: the virgin birth, thus Christmas; the walking on the water; maybe another miracle or two; was he swallowed by

331

the whale or was that someone else? And then the betrayal by Judas; the trial before Pilate; the crucifixion, thus Easter, and, finally, the ascension into heaven.

Yes, Nate knew the basics. Perhaps his mother had told him. Neither of his wives had been churchgoers, though number two was Catholic and they did midnight mass at Christmas every other year.

Three more stragglers came from the street. A young man with a guitar appeared from a side door and went to the pulpit. It was exactly nine-thirty. He strummed a few chords and began singing, his face glowing with words of faith and praise. A tiny little woman one pew up clapped her hands and sang along.

Maybe the music would draw Rachel. She had to crave real worship in a church with wooden floors and stained glass, with fully clothed people reading Bibles in a modern language. Surely she visited the churches when she was in Corumbá.

When the song was finished, the young man read some scripture and began teaching. His Portuguese was the slowest Nate had encountered so far in his little adventure. Nate was mesmerized by the soft, slurring sounds, and the unhurried cadence. Though he understood not a word, he tried to repeat the sentences. Then his thoughts drifted.

His body had purged the fevers and chemicals. He was well fed, alert, rested. He was his old self again, and that suddenly depressed him. The present was back, hand in hand with the future. The burdens he'd left with Rachel had found him again, found him then and there in the chapel. He needed her to sit with him, to hold his hand and help him pray.

He hated his weaknesses. He named them one by one, and was saddened by the list. The demons were waiting at home – the good friends and the bad friends, the haunts and habits, the pressures he

332

couldn't stand anymore. Life could not be lived with the likes of Sergio at a thousand bucks a day. And life could not be lived free on the streets.

The young man was praying, his eyes clenched tightly, his arms waving gently upward. Nate closed his eyes too, and called God's name. God was waiting.

With both hands, he clenched the back of the pew in front of him. He repeated the list, mumbling softly every weakness and flaw and affliction and evil that plagued him. He confessed them all. In one long glorious acknowledgment of failure, he laid himself bare before God. He held nothing back. He unloaded enough burdens to crush any three men, and when he finally finished Nate had tears in his eyes. 'I'm sorry,' he whispered to God. 'Please help me.'

As quickly as the fever had left his body, he felt the baggage leave his soul. With one gentle brush of the hand, his slate had been wiped clean. He breathed a massive sigh of relief, but his pulse was racing.

He heard the guitar again. He opened his eyes and wiped his cheeks. Instead of seeing the young man in the pulpit, Nate saw the face of Christ, in agony and pain, dying on the cross. Dying for him.

A voice was calling Nate, a voice from within, a voice leading him down the aisle. But the invitation was confusing. He felt many conflicting emotions. His eyes were suddenly dry.

Why am I crying in a small hot chapel, listening to music I don't understand, in a town I'll never see again? The questions poured forth, the answers elusive.

It was one thing for God to forgive his astounding array of iniquities, and Nate certainly felt as though his burdens were lighter. But it was a far more difficult step to expect himself to become a follower.

As he listened to the music, he became bewildered. God couldn't be calling him. He was Nate O'Riley –

boozer, addict, lover of women, absent father, miserable husband, greedy lawyer, swindler of tax money. The sad list went on and on.

He was dizzy. The music stopped and the young man prepared for another song. Nate hurriedly left the chapel. As he turned a corner, he glanced back, hoping to see Rachel, but also to make sure God hadn't sent someone to follow him.

He needed someone to talk to. He knew she was in Corumbá, and he vowed to find her.

THIRTY-EIGHT

The *despachante* is an integral part of Brazilian life. No business, bank, law firm, medical group, or person with money can operate without the services of a *despachante*. He is a facilitator extraordinaire. In a country where the bureaucracy is sprawling and antiquated, the *despachante* is the guy who knows the city clerks, the courthouse crowd, the bureaucrats, the customs agents. He knows the system and how to grease it. No official paper or document is obtained in Brazil without waiting in long lines, and the *despachante* is the guy who'll stand there for you. For a small fee, he'll wait eight hours to renew your auto inspection, then affix it to your windshield while you're busy at the office. He'll do your voting, banking, packaging, mailing – the list has no end.

No bureaucratic obstacle is too intimidating.

Firms of *despachantes* display their names in windows just like lawyers and doctors. They're in the yellow pages. The job requires no formal training. All one needs is a quick tongue, patience, and a lot of brass.

Valdir's *despachante* in Corumbá knew another one in São Paulo, a powerful one with high contacts, and for a fee of two thousand dollars a new passport would be delivered.

*

Jevy spent the next few mornings at the river, helping a friend repair a *chalana*. He watched everything and heard the gossip. Not a word about the woman. By noon on Friday, he was convinced she had not arrived in Corumbá, at least not in the past two weeks. Jevy knew all the fishermen, captains, and deckhands. And they loved to talk. If an American woman who lived with the Indians suddenly arrived in town, they would know it.

Nate searched until the end of the week. He walked the streets, watched the crowds, checked out hotel lobbies and sidewalk cafés, looked at the faces, and saw no one even remotely resembling Rachel.

At one on his last day, he stopped at Valdir's office and collected his passport. They said good-bye like old friends, and promised to see each other soon. Both knew it would never happen. At two, Jevy drove him to the airport. They sat in the departure lounge for half an hour, watching as the only plane was unloaded, then prepped for reboarding. Jevy wanted to spend time in the United States, and needed Nate's help. 'I'll need a job,' he said. Nate listened with sympathy, not certain if he himself was still employed.

'I'll see what I can do.'

They talked about Colorado and the West and places Nate had never been. Jevy was in love with the mountains, and after two weeks in the Pantanal Nate understood this. When it was time to go, they embraced warmly and said farewell. Nate walked across the hot pavement to the plane, carrying his entire wardrobe in a small gym bag.

The turbo-prop with twenty seats landed twice before it reached Campo Grande. There, the passengers boarded a jet for São Paulo. The lady in the seat next to him ordered a beer from the drink cart. Nate studied the can less than ten inches away. Not anymore, he told himself. He closed his eyes and asked God to give him strength. He ordered coffee.

The flight to Dulles left at midnight. It would arrive in D.C. at nine the next morning. His search for Rachel had taken him out of the country for almost three weeks.

He wasn't sure where his car was. He had no place to live, and no means to get one. But he couldn't worry. Josh would take care of the details.

The plane dropped through the clouds at nine thousand feet. Nate was awake, sipping coffee, dreading the streets of home. The streets were cold and white. The earth was blanketed by a heavy snow. It was lovely for a few minutes as they approached Dulles, then Nate remembered how much he hated the winter. He wore a thin pair of trousers, no socks, cheap sneakers, and a fake Polo shirt he'd paid six dollars for in the Saõ Paulo airport. He had no coat.

He would sleep somewhere that night, probably in a hotel, unsupervised in D.C. for the first time since August 4, the night he'd staggered into a suburban motel room. It had happened at the bottom of a long, pathetic crash. He'd worked hard to forget it.

But that was the old Nate, and now there was a new one. He was forty-eight years old, thirteen months away from fifty, and ready for a different life. God had fortified him, and strengthened his resolve. He had thirty years left. They wouldn't be spent clutching empty bottles. Nor would they be spent on the run.

Snowplows raced about as they taxied to the terminal. The runways were wet and flurries were still falling. When Nate stepped off the plane into the tunnel, winter hit him and he thought of the humid streets of Corumbá. Josh was waiting at the baggage claim, and of course he had an extra overcoat.

'You look awful,' were his first words.

337

'Thanks.' Nate grabbed the coat and put it on.

'You're skinny as a rail.'

'You wanna lose fifteen pounds, find the right mosquito.'

They moved with a mob toward the exits, bodies jostling and bumping, a shove here, a push there, the throng squeezing tighter to fit through doors. Welcome home, he said to himself.

'You're traveling light,' Josh said, pointing at his gym bag.

'My worldly possessions.'

With no socks or gloves, Nate was freezing on the curb by the time Josh found him with the car. The snowstorm had hit during the night, and had attained the status of a blizzard. Against the buildings the drifts had reached two feet.

'It was ninety-three yesterday in Corumbá,' Nate said as they left the airport.

'Don't tell me you miss it.'

'I do. Suddenly, I do.'

'Look, Gayle is in London. I thought you could stay at our place for a couple of days.'

Josh's house could sleep fifteen. 'Sure, thanks. Where's my car?'

'In my garage.'

Of course it was. It was a leased Jaguar, and it no doubt had been properly serviced, washed, and waxed, and the monthly payments were current. 'Thanks, Josh.'

'I put your furnishings in a mini-storage. Your clothes and personal effects are packed in the car.'

'Thanks.' Nate was not at all surprised.

'How do you feel?'

'I'm fine.'

'Look, Nate, I've read about dengue fever. It takes a month to fully recover. Level with me.'

A month. It was the opening jab in the fight over

338

Nate's future with the firm. Take another month, old boy. Maybe you're too ill to work. Nate could write the script.

But there would be no fight.

'I'm a little weak, that's all. I'm sleeping a lot, drinking a lot of liquids.'

'What kind of liquids?'

'Get right to the point, don't you?'

'I always do.'

'I'm clean, Josh. Relax. No stumbles.'

Josh had heard that many times. The exchange had been a bit sharper than both men wanted, so they rode in silence for a while. The traffic was slow.

The Potomac was half-frozen with large chunks of ice floating slowly toward Georgetown. Stalled in traffic on the Chain Bridge, Nate announced, matter-of-factly, 'I'm not going back to the office, Josh. Those days are over.'

There was no visible reaction from Josh. He could've been disappointed because an old friend and fine litigator was calling it quits. He could've been delighted because a major headache was quietly leaving the firm. He could've been indifferent because Nate's exit was probably inevitable. The tax evasion mess would ultimately cost him his license anyway.

So he simply asked, 'Why?'

'Lots of reasons, Josh. Let's just say I'm tired.'

'Most litigators burn out after twenty years.'

'So I've heard.'

Enough of the retirement talk. Nate's mind was made up, and Josh didn't want to change it. The Super Bowl was two weeks away, and the Redskins were not in it. They seized the topic of football, as men usually do when they have to keep the conversation going in the midst of weightier matters.

Even under a heavy layer of snow, the streets looked mean to Nate.

★

The Staffords owned a large house in Wesley Heights, in Northwest D.C. They also had a cottage on the Chesapeake and a cabin in Maine. The four kids were grown and scattered. Mrs. Stafford preferred to travel while her husband preferred to work.

Nate retrieved some warm clothes from the trunk of his car, then enjoyed a hot shower in the guest quarters. The water pressure was weaker in Brazil. The shower in his hotel room was never hot, and never cold. The bars of soap were smaller. He compared the things around him. He was amused at the thought of the shower on the *Santa Loura*, a cord above the toilet that, when pulled, delivered lukewarm river water from a shower head. He was tougher than he thought; the adventure had taught him that much.

He shaved and then worked on his teeth, going about his habits with great deliberation. In many ways, it was nice to be home.

Josh's office in his basement was larger than the one downtown, and just as cluttered. They met there for coffee. It was time to debrief. Nate began with the ill-fated effort to find Rachel by air, the crash landing, the dead cow, the three little boys, the bleakness of Christmas in the Pantanal. With great detail, he recounted the story of his ride on the horse, and the encounter in the swamp with the curious alligator. Then the rescue by helicopter. He said nothing about the binge on Christmas night; it would serve no purpose and he was terribly ashamed of it. He described Jevy, Welly, the *Santa Loura*, and the trip north. When he and Jevy were lost in the johnboat, he remembered being frightened but too busy to be consumed with fear. Now, in the safety of civilization, their wanderings seemed terrifying.

Josh was astounded by the adventure. He wanted to apologize for sending Nate into such a treacherous place, but the excursion had obviously been exciting.

The alligators grew as the narrative continued. The lone anaconda, sunning by the river, was joined by another that swam near their boat.

Nate described the Indians, their nakedness and bland food and languid lives, the chief and his refusal to let them leave.

And Rachel. At that point in the debriefing, Josh took his legal pad and began writing notes. Nate portrayed her in great detail, from her soft slow voice to her sandals and hiking boots. Her hut and medicine bag, Lako and his limp, and the way the Indians looked at her when she walked by. He told the story of the child who died from the snakebite. He relayed what little of her history she'd given him.

With the precision of a courtroom veteran, Nate covered everything about Rachel that he'd gathered on his visit. He used her exact words when talking about the money and the paperwork. He remembered her comment about how primitive Troy's handwritten will looked.

Nate recounted what little he remembered of their retreat from the Pantanal. And he downplayed the horror of dengue fever. He had survived, and that in itself surprised him.

A maid brought soup and hot tea for lunch. 'Here's where we are,' Josh said after a few spoonfuls. 'If she rejects the gift under Troy's will, then the money remains in his estate. If, however, the will is found to be invalid for any reason, then there is no will.'

'How can the will be invalid? They had psychiatrists talking to him minutes before he jumped.'

'Now there are more psychiatrists, well paid and with different opinions. It'll get messy. All of his prior wills were shredded. If it's one day found that he died with no valid will, then his children, all seven of them, will share equally in his estate. Since Rachel doesn't

341

want a share, then hers will be divided by the other six.'

'Those fools will get a billion dollars each.'

'Something like that.'

'What are the chances of striking down his will?'

'Not good. I'd rather have our case than theirs, but things can change.'

Nate walked around the room, nibbling on a saltine, weighing the issues. 'Why fight for the validity of the will if Rachel declines everything?'

'Three reasons,' Josh said quickly. As usual, he had analyzed everything from all possible angles. There was a master plan, and it would be revealed to Nate piece by piece. 'First, and most important, my client prepared a valid will. It gave away his assets exactly as he wanted. I, as his lawyer, have no choice but to fight to protect the integrity of the will. Second, I know how Mr. Phelan felt about his children. He was horrified that they would somehow get their hands on his money. I share his feelings about them, and I shudder to think what would happen if they got a billion each. Third, there's always a chance Rachel will change her mind.'

'Don't count on it.'

'Look, Nate, she's only human. She has those papers with her. She'll wait a few days and start to think about them. Maybe thoughts of wealth have never entered her mind, but at some point she has to think of all the good things she could do with the money. Did you explain trusts and charitable foundations to her?'

'I barely know what those are myself, Josh. I was a litigator, remember?'

'We're gonna fight to protect Mr. Phelan's will, Nate. Problem is, the biggest seat at the table is empty. Rachel needs representation.'

'No she doesn't. She's oblivious.'

342

'The litigation can't proceed until she has a lawyer.'

Nate was no match for the master strategist. The black hole opened from nowhere, and he was already falling into it. He closed his eyes and said, 'You must be kidding.'

'No. And we can't delay much longer. Troy died a month ago. Judge Wycliff is desperate to know the whereabouts of Rachel Lane. Six lawsuits have been filed contesting the will, and there's a lot of pressure behind them. Everything gets reported in the papers. If we give any hint that Rachel plans to decline the bequest, then we lose control. The Phelan heirs and their lawyers go crazy. The Judge suddenly loses interest in upholding Troy's last testament.'

'So I'm her lawyer?'

'There's no way around it, Nate. If you're quitting, that's fine, but you have to take one last case. Just sit at the table and protect her interests. We'll do the heavy lifting.'

'But there's a conflict. I'm a partner in your firm.'

'It's a minor conflict because our interests are the same. We – the estate and Rachel – have the same goal of protecting the will. We sit at the same table. And technically, we can claim you left the firm last August.'

'There's a lot of truth in that.'

Both acknowledged the sad truth. Josh sipped his tea, his eyes never leaving Nate. 'At some point we go to Wycliff and tell him that you found Rachel, that she plans to make no appearance at this time, that she's not sure what to do, but that she wants you to protect her interests.'

'Then we'll be lying to the Judge.'

'It's a small lie, Nate, and he'll thank us for it later. He's anxious to start proceedings, but he can't until he hears from Rachel. If you're her lawyer, the war begins. I'll do the lying.'

'So I'm a one-man office working on my last case.'

'Right.'

'I'm leaving town, Josh. I'm not staying.' Nate said this, then he laughed. 'Where would I stay?'

'Where are you going?'

'I don't know. I haven't thought that far ahead.'

'I have an idea.'

'I'm sure you do.'

'Take my cottage on Chesapeake Bay. We don't use it in the wintertime. It's at St. Michaels, two hours away. You can drive in when you're needed, and stay here. Again, Nate, we'll do the work.'

Nate studied the bookshelves for a while. Twenty-four hours earlier he'd been eating a sandwich on a park bench, in Corumbá, watching the pedestrians and waiting for Rachel to appear. He had vowed to never again voluntarily step into a courtroom.

But he grudgingly admitted that the plan had its strong points. He certainly couldn't imagine a better client. The case would never go to trial. And with the money at stake he could at least earn a living for a few months.

Josh finished his soup and moved to the next item on the list. 'I propose a fee of ten thousand dollars a month.'

'That's generous, Josh.'

'I think we can squeeze it from the old man's estate. With no overhead, it'll get you back on your feet.'

'Until . . .'

'Right, until we settle with the IRS.'

'Any word from the Judge?'

'I call him occasionally. We had lunch last week.'

'So he's your buddy?'

'We've known each other for a long time. Forget jail, Nate. The government will settle for a big fine and a five-year suspension of your law license.'

'They can have my law license.'

'Not yet. We need it for one more case.'

344

'How long will the government wait?'

'A year. It's not a priority.'

'Thanks, Josh.' Nate was tired again. The all-night flight, the ravages of the jungle, the mental jousting with Josh. He wanted a warm soft bed in a dark room.

THIRTY-NINE

At six Sunday morning, Nate finished another hot shower, his third in twenty-four hours, and began making plans for a quick departure. One night in the city, and he was anxious to leave. The cottage on the bay was calling him. D.C. had been his home for twenty-six years, and since the decision to leave had been made, he was eager to move on.

With no address, moving was easy. He found Josh in the basement, at his desk, on the phone with a client in Thailand. As Nate listened to one-half of the conversation about natural gas deposits, he was quite happy to be leaving the practice of law. Josh was twelve years older, a very rich man, and his idea of fun was to be at his desk at six-thirty on a Sunday morning. Don't let it happen to me, Nate said to himself, but he knew it wouldn't. If he went back to the office, he would return to the grind. Four rehabs meant a fifth was somewhere down the road. He wasn't as strong as Josh. He'd be dead in ten years.

There was an element of excitement in walking away. Suing doctors was a nasty business, one he could do without. Nor would he miss the stress of a high-powered office. He'd had his career, his triumphs. Success had brought him nothing but misery; he couldn't handle it. Success had thrown him in the gutter.

Now that the horror of jail had been removed, he could enjoy a new life.

He left with a trunkload of clothes, leaving the rest in a box in Josh's garage. The snow had stopped, but the plows were still catching up. The streets were slick, and after two blocks it occurred to Nate that he had not held the wheel of a car in over five months. There was no traffic, though, and he crept along Wisconsin into Chevy Chase, then onto the Beltway where the ice and snow had been cleared.

Alone, in his own fine car, he began to feel like an American again. He thought of Jevy in his loud, dangerous Ford truck, and wondered how long he would last on the Beltway. And he thought of Welly, a kid so poor his family owned no car. Nate planned to write letters in the days to come, and he would send one to his buddies in Corumbá.

The phone caught his attention. He picked it up; it appeared to be working. Of course Josh had made sure the bills were paid. He called Sergio at home, and they talked for twenty minutes. He got scolded for not calling sooner. Sergio had been worried. He explained the situation with telephone service in the Pantanal. Things were going in a different direction, there were some unknowns, but his adventure was continuing. He was leaving the profession and avoiding jail.

Sergio never asked about sobriety. Nate certainly sounded clean and strong. He gave him the number at the cottage, and they promised to have lunch soon.

He called his oldest son at Northwestern, in Evanston, and left a message on the recorder. Where would a twenty-three-year-old grad student be at 7 A.M. on a Sunday morning? Not at early mass. Nate didn't want to know. Whatever his son was doing, he would never screw up as badly as his father. His daughter was twenty-one, an on-again off-again student at Pitt. Their last conversation had been about tuition, a day

347

before Nate checked into the motel room with a bottle of rum and a sack full of pills.

He couldn't find her phone number.

Their mother had remarried twice since leaving Nate. She was an unpleasant person whom he called only when absolutely necessary. He would wait a couple of days, then ask her for their daughter's phone number.

He was determined to make the painful trip west, to Oregon, to at least see his two youngest children. Their mother had remarried too, remarkably to another lawyer, but one who evidently lived a clean life. He would ask them for forgiveness, and try to establish the frail beginnings of a relationship. He wasn't sure how to do this, but he vowed to try.

In Annapolis, he stopped at a café and had breakfast. He listened to the weather predictions from a group of rowdy regulars in a booth, and he mindlessly scanned the *Post*. From the headlines and late-breaking stories, Nate saw nothing that interested him in the least. The news never changed: trouble in the Middle East, trouble in Ireland; scandals in Congress; the markets were up then down; an oil spill; another AIDS drug; guerrillas killing peasants in Latin America; turmoil in Russia.

His clothes hung loose on him, so he ate three eggs with bacon and biscuits. A shaky consensus emerged from the booth that more snow was on the way.

He crossed the Chesapeake on the Bay Bridge. The highways on the eastern shore had not been plowed well. The Jaguar skidded twice, and he slowed down. The car was a year old, and he couldn't remember when the lease expired. His secretary had handled the paperwork. He'd picked the color. He decided to get rid of it as soon as possible and find an old four-wheel drive. The fancy lawyer's car had once seemed so important. Now he had no need for it.

At Easton, he turned onto State Route 33, a road with two inches of loose snow still resting on the blacktop. Nate followed the tracks of other vehicles, and soon passed through sleepy little settlements with harbors filled with sailboats. The shores of the Chesapeake were covered with heavy snow; its waters were deep blue.

St. Michaels had a population of thirteen hundred. Route 33 became Main Street for a few blocks as it ran through the town. There were shops and stores on both sides, old buildings side by side, all well preserved and ready for the postcard.

Nate had heard of St. Michaels all his life. There was a maritime museum, an oyster festival, an active harbor, dozens of quaint little bed-and-breakfasts which attracted city folks for long weekends. He passed the post office and a small church, where the Rector was shoveling snow from the front steps.

The cottage was on Green Street, two blocks off Main, facing north with a view of the harbor. It was Victorian, with twin gables, and a long front porch that wrapped around to the sides. Painted slate blue, with white and yellow trim, the house had snow drifts almost to the front door. The front lawn was small, the driveway under two feet of snow. Nate parked at the curb and fought his way to the porch. He flipped on lights inside as he walked to the rear. In a closet by the back door, he found a plastic shovel.

He spent a wonderful hour cleaning the porch, clearing the drive and sidewalk, working his way back to his car.

Not surprisingly, the house was richly decorated with period pieces, and it was tidy and organized. Josh said a maid came every Wednesday to dust and clean. Mrs. Stafford stayed there for two weeks in the spring and one in the fall. Josh had slept there three nights in the past eighteen months. There were four bedrooms and four baths. Some cottage.

But there was no coffee to be found, and this presented the first emergency of the day. Nate locked the doors and headed for town. The sidewalks were clear and wet from melting snow. According to the thermometer in the window of the barbershop, the temperature was thirty-five degrees. The shops and stores were closed. Nate studied their windows as he ambled along. Ahead, the church bells began.

According to the bulletin handed to Nate by the elderly usher, the Rector was Father Phil Lancaster, a short, wiry little man with thick horn-rimmed glasses and curly hair that was red and gray. He could've been thirty-five or fifty. His flock for the eleven o'clock service was old and thin, no doubt hampered by the weather. Nate counted twenty-one people in the small sanctuary, and that included Phil and the organist. There were many gray heads.

It was a handsome church, with a vaulted ceiling, pews and floors of dark wood, four windows of stained glass. When the lone usher took his seat in the back pew, Phil rose in his black robe and welcomed them to Trinity Church, where everyone was at home. His voice was high and nasal, and he needed no microphone. In his prayer he thanked God for snow and winter, for the seasons given as reminders that He was always in control.

They struggled through the hymns and prayers. When Father Phil preached he noticed Nate, the sole visitor, sitting in the next to last row. They exchanged smiles, and for one scary moment Nate was afraid he was about to be introduced to the small crowd.

His sermon was on the subject of enthusiasm, an odd choice given the average age of his congregation. Nate struggled hard to pay attention, but began to drift. His thoughts returned to the little chapel in Corumbá, with the front doors open, the windows up, the heat drifting through, the dying Christ suffering on the cross, the young man with the guitar.

Careful not to offend Phil, he managed to keep his eyes fixed on the globe of a dim light on the wall behind and above the pulpit. Given the thickness of the preacher's eyeglasses, he figured his disinterest would go unnoticed.

Sitting in the warm little church, finally safe from the uncertainties of his great adventure, safe from fevers and storms, safe from the dangers of D.C., safe from his addictions, safe from spiritual extinction, Nate realized that for the first time in memory he was at peace. He feared nothing. God was pulling him in some direction. He wasn't certain where, but he wasn't afraid either. Be patient, he told himself.

Then he whispered a prayer. He thanked God for sparing his life, and he prayed for Rachel, because he knew she was praying for him.

The serenity made him smile. When the prayer was over, he opened his eyes and saw that Phil was smiling at him.

After the benediction, they filed past Phil at the front door, each complimenting him on the sermon and mentioning some brief bit of church news. The line moved slowly; it was a ritual. 'How's your aunt?' Phil asked one of his flock, then listened carefully as the aunt's latest affliction was described. 'How's that hip?' he asked another. 'How was Germany?' He clutched their hands and bent forward to hear every word. He knew what was on their minds.

Nate waited patiently at the end of the line. There was no hurry. He had nothing else to do. 'Welcome,' Father Phil said as he grabbed Nate by the hand and arm. 'Welcome to Trinity.' He squeezed so tightly Nate wondered if he were the first guest in years.

'I'm Nate O'Riley,' he said, then added, 'From Washington,' as if that would help define him.

'So nice to have you with us this morning,' Phil said, his big eyes dancing behind the glasses. Up close, the wrinkles revealed that he was at least fifty. His head had more gray curls than red.

'I'm staying in the Stafford cottage for a few days,' Nate said.

'Yes, yes, a lovely home. When did you arrive?'

'This morning.'

'Are you alone?'

'Yes.'

'Well, then you must join us for lunch.'

The aggressive hospitality made Nate laugh. 'Well, uh, thanks, but –'

Phil was all smiles too. 'No, I insist. My wife makes a lamb stew every time it snows. It's on the stove now. We have so few guests in the wintertime. Please, the parsonage is just behind the church.'

Nate was in the hands of a man who'd shared his Sunday table with hundreds. 'Really, I was just stopping by, and I –'

'It's our pleasure,' Phil said, already tugging at Nate's arm and leading him back toward the pulpit. 'What do you do in Washington?'

'I'm a lawyer,' Nate said. A complete answer would get complicated.

'What brings you here?'

'It's a long story.'

'Oh wonderful! Laura and I love stories. Let's have a long lunch and tell stories. We'll have a grand time.' His enthusiasm was irresistible. Poor guy was starved for fresh conversation. Why not? thought Nate. There was no food in the cottage. All stores appeared to be closed.

They passed the pulpit and went through a door leading to the rear of the church. Laura was turning off

352

lights. 'This is Mr. O'Riley, from Washington,' Phil said loudly to his wife. 'He's agreed to join us for lunch.'

Laura smiled and shook Nate's hand. She had short gray hair and looked at least ten years older than her husband. If a sudden guest at the table surprised her, it wasn't evident. Nate got the impression it happened all the time. 'Please call me Nate,' he said.

'Nate it is,' Phil announced, peeling off his robe.

The parsonage was adjacent to the church lot, facing a side street. They carefully stepped through the snow. 'How was my sermon?' Phil asked her as they stepped onto the porch.

'Excellent, dear,' she said without a trace of enthusiasm. Nate listened and smiled, certain that every Sunday for years Phil had asked the same question, at the same place and time, and received the same answer.

Any hesitation about staying for lunch vanished when he stepped into the house. The rich, heavy aroma of the lamb stew wafted through the den. Phil poked at the orange coals in the fireplace while Laura prepared the meal.

In the narrow dining room between the kitchen and the den, a table had been set for four. Nate was pleased that he had accepted their invitation, not that he'd had the chance to decline it.

'We're so glad you're here,' Phil said as they took their seats. 'I had a hunch we might have a guest today.'

'Whose place is that?' Nate asked, nodding to the empty setting.

'We always set four places on Sunday,' Laura said, and let the explanation go at that. They held hands as Phil thanked God again for the snow and the seasons, and for the food. He concluded with, 'And keep us ever mindful of the needs and wants of others.' Those words triggered something in Nate's memory. He'd heard them before, many, many years before.

As the food was passed around, there was the usual talk about the morning. They averaged forty at the eleven o'clock service. The snow had indeed kept people away. And there was a flu bug on the peninsula. Nate complimented them on the simple beauty of the sanctuary. They had been in St. Michaels for six years. Not long into the lunch, Laura said, 'You have a nice tan for January. You didn't get that in Washington?'

'No. I just returned from Brazil.' They both stopped eating and leaned closer. The adventure was on again. Nate took a large spoonful of stew, which was thick and delicious, then began the story.

'Please eat,' Laura said every five minutes or so. Nate took a bite, chewed slowly, then proceeded. He referred to Rachel only as 'the daughter of a client.' The storms grew fiercer, the snakes longer, the boat smaller, the Indians less friendly. Phil's eyes danced with amazement as Nate went from chapter to chapter.

It was the second time Nate had told the story since his return. Other than a slight exaggeration here and there, he kept to the facts. And it amazed even him. It was a remarkable story to tell, and his hosts got a long, rich version of it. They wedged in questions whenever they could.

When Laura cleared the table and served brownies for dessert, Nate and Jevy had just arrived at the first Ipica settlement.

'Was she surprised to see you?' Phil asked when Nate described the scene with the band of Indians leading the woman out of the village to meet them.

'Not really,' Nate said. 'She seemed to know we were coming.'

Nate did his best to describe the Indians and their

Stone Age culture, but words failed to deliver the right images. He ate two brownies, clearing his plate with large bites during brief gaps in the narrative.

They pushed their plates away and had coffee. Sunday lunch for Phil and Laura was more about conversation than eating. Nate wondered who'd been the last guest lucky enough to be invited in for stories and food.

It was hard to downplay the horrors of dengue, but Nate tried gamely. A couple of days in the hospital, some medication, and he was back on his feet. When he finished, the questions began. Phil wanted to know everything about the missionary – her denomination, her faith, her work with the Indians. Laura's sister had lived in China for fifteen years, working in a church hospital, and this became the source of more stories.

It was almost three o'clock when Nate made it to the door. His hosts would have gladly sat at the table or in the den and talked until dark, but Nate needed a walk. He thanked them for their hospitality, and when he left them waving on the porch he felt as though he'd known them for years.

It took an hour to walk St. Michaels. The streets were narrow and lined with homes a hundred years old. Nothing was out of place, no stray dogs, vacant lots, abandoned buildings. Even the snow was neat – carefully shoveled so that the streets and sidewalks were clear and no neighbor was offended. Nate stopped at the pier and admired the sailboats. He had never set foot on one.

He decided he wouldn't leave St. Michaels until he was forced. He would live in the cottage, and remain there until Josh politely evicted him. He would save his money, and when the Phelan matter was over he would find some way to hang on.

Near the harbor he stumbled on to a small grocery about to close for the day. He bought coffee, canned

355

soup, saltines, and oatmeal for breakfast. There was a display of bottled beer by the counter. He smiled at it, happy those days were behind him.

FORTY

Grit got himself fired by fax and by e-mail, a first for his office. Mary Ross did it to him, early Monday morning, after a tense weekend with her brothers.

Grit did not exit gracefully. He faxed her back and submitted a bill for his services to date – 148 hours at $600 per, for a total of $88,800. His hourly billings were to be applied against his percentage upon settlement or other favorable outcome. Grit didn't want $600 an hour. Grit wanted a piece of the pie, a healthy fraction of his client's cut, the 25 percent he'd negotiated. Grit wanted millions, and as he sat in his locked office, staring at the fax, he found it impossible to believe that his fortune had slipped away. He truly believed that after a few months of hardball litigation, the Phelan estate would settle with the children. Throw twenty million at each of the six, watch them attack it like hungry dogs, and there wouldn't be the slightest dent in the Phelan fortune. Twenty million to his client was five million to him, and Grit, alone, had to confess that he'd already thought of several ways to spend it.

He called Hark's office to curse him, but was told Mr. Gettys was too busy at the moment.

Mr. Gettys now had three of the four heirs from the first family. His percentage had dropped from twenty-five to twenty, and now to seventeen-five. But his upside potential was enormous.

Mr. Gettys walked into his conference room a few minutes after ten and greeted the remaining Phelan lawyers, gathered there for an important meeting. He cheerfully said, 'I have an announcement. Mr. Grit is no longer involved in this case. His ex-client, Mary Ross Phelan Jackman, has asked me to represent her, and, after much consideration, I have agreed to do so.'

His words hit like small bombs around the conference table. Yancy stroked his scraggly beard and wondered what method of coercion had been used to pry the woman away from Grit's tentacles. He felt somewhat safe, though. Ramble's mother had used every means possible to lure the kid to another lawyer. But the kid hated his mother.

Madam Langhorne was surprised, especially since Hark had just added Troy Junior as a client. But after the brief shock, she felt secure. Her client, Geena Phelan Strong, detested her older half-brothers and - sisters. Surely she wouldn't throw in with their lawyer. Nonetheless, a power lunch was needed. She would call Geena and Cody when the meeting was over. They'd dine at the Promenade near the Capitol, and maybe catch a glimpse of a powerful subcommittee vice chairman.

The back of Wally Bright's neck turned scarlet with the news. Hark was raiding clients, chasing ambulances. Only Libbigail remained from the first family, and Wally Bright would kill Hark if he tried to steal her. 'Stay away from my client, okay?' he said loudly and bitterly, and the entire room froze.

'Relax.'

'Relax, my ass. How can we relax when you're stealing clients?'

'I didn't steal Mrs. Jackman. She called me. I didn't call her.'

'We know the game you're playing, Hark. We're not stupid.' Wally said this while looking at his fellow lawyers. They certainly didn't consider themselves to be stupid, but they weren't so sure about Wally. Truth was, no one could trust anyone. There was simply too much money at stake to assume that the lawyer next to you would not pull out a knife.

They led Snead in, and this changed the focus of the discussion. Hark introduced him to the group. Poor Snead looked like a man facing a firing squad. He sat at the end of the table, with two video cameras aimed at him. 'This is just a rehearsal,' Hark assured him. 'Relax.' The lawyers pulled out legal pads covered with questions, and they inched closer to Snead.

Hark walked behind him, patted him on the shoulder, and said, 'Now, when you give your deposition, Mr. Snead, the lawyers for the other side will be allowed to interrogate you first. So for the next hour or so, you are to assume that we are the enemy. Okay?'

It certainly wasn't okay with Snead, but he'd taken their money. He had to play along.

Hark picked up his legal pad and began asking questions, simple things about his birth, background, family, school, easy stuff that Snead handled well and relaxed with. Then the early years with Mr. Phelan, and a thousand questions that seemed completely irrelevant.

After a bathroom break, Madam Langhorne took the baton and grilled Snead about the Phelan families, the wives, the kids, the divorces, and mistresses. Snead thought it was a lot of unnecessary dirt, but me lawyers seemed to enjoy it.

'Did you know about Rachel Lane?' Langhorne asked.

Snead pondered this for a moment, then said, 'I haven't thought about that.' In other words, help me with the answer. 'What would you guess?' he asked Mr. Gettys.

Hark was quick with the fiction. 'I would guess that you knew everything about Mr. Phelan, especially his women and their offspring. Nothing escaped you. The old man confided everything in you, including the existence of his illegitimate daughter. She was ten or eleven when you went to work for Mr. Phelan. He tried to reach out to her over the years but she would have nothing to do with him. I would guess that this hurt him deeply, that he was a man who got whatever he wanted, and when Rachel spurned him his pain turned to anger. I would guess that he disliked her immensely. Thus, for him to leave her everything was an act of sheer insanity.'

Once again, Snead marveled at Hark's ability to spin tales so quickly. The other lawyers were impressed too. 'What do you think?' Hark asked them.

They nodded their approvals. 'Better get him all the background on Rachel Lane,' Bright said.

Snead then repeated for the cameras the same story Hark had just told, and in doing so showed a passable skill at expanding on a theme. When he finished, the lawyers couldn't suppress their pleasure. The worm would say anything. And there was no one to contradict it.

When Snead was asked a question that needed assistance, he responded by saying, 'Well, I haven't thought about that.' The lawyers would then reach out to help. Hark, who seemed to anticipate Snead's weaknesses, usually had a quick narrative at hand. Often, though, the other lawyers chimed in with their little plots, all anxious to display their skills at lying.

Layer upon layer was fabricated, and fine-tuned, carefully molded to ensure that Mr. Phelan was out of his mind the morning he scrawled his last testament. Snead was coached by the lawyers, and he proved quite easy to lead. In fact, he was so coachable the lawyers worried that he might say too much. His credibility could not be damaged. There could be no holes in his testimony.

For three hours they built his story, then for two hours they tried to tear it down with relentless cross-examination. They didn't feed him lunch. They sneered at him and called him a liar. At one point Langhorne had him near tears. When he was exhausted and ready to collapse, they sent him home with the pack of videos and instructions to study them over and over.

He wasn't ready to testify, they told him. His stories weren't airtight. Poor Snead drove home in his new Range Rover, tired and bewildered, but also determined to practice his lies until the lawyers applauded him.

Judge Wycliff enjoyed the quiet little lunches in his office. As usual, Josh picked up sandwiches from a Greek deli near Dupont Circle. He unpacked them, along with iced tea and pickles, on the small table in a corner. They huddled over their food, at first talking about how busy they were, then quickly getting around to the Phelan estate. Something was up, or Josh wouldn't have called.

'We found Rachel Lane,' he said.

'Wonderful. Where?' The relief in Wycliff's face was obvious.

'She made us promise not to tell. At least not now.'

'Is she in the country?' The Judge forgot about his corned beef on kaiser.

'No. She's in a very remote spot in the world, and quite content to stay there.'

'How did you find her?'

'Her lawyer found her.'

'Who's her lawyer?'

'A guy who used to work in my firm. Name's Nate O'Riley, a former partner. Left us back in August.'

Wycliff narrowed his eyes and considered this. 'What a coincidence. She hires a former partner of the law firm her father used.'

'There's no coincidence. As the attorney for the estate, I had to find her. I sent Nate O'Riley. He found her, she hired him. It's really pretty simple.'

'When does she make her appearance?'

'I doubt if she'll do it in person.'

'What about the acknowledgment and waiver?'

'They're coming. She's very deliberate, and, frankly, I'm not sure what her plans are.'

'We have a will contest, Josh. The war has already erupted. Things can't wait. This court must have jurisdiction over her.'

'Judge, she has legal representation. Her interests will be protected. Let's fight. We'll start discovery, and see what the other side has.'

'Can I talk to her?'

'It's impossible.'

'Come on, Josh.'

'I swear. Look, she's a missionary in a very remote place, in a different hemisphere. That's all I can tell you.'

'I want to see Mr. O'Riley.'

'When?'

Wycliff walked to his desk and grabbed the nearest appointment book. He was so busy. Life was regulated by a docket calendar, a trial calendar, a motion calendar. His secretary kept an office calendar. 'How about this Wednesday?'

'Fine. For lunch? Just the three of us, off the record.'

'Sure.'

Lawyer O'Riley had planned to read and write

362

throughout the morning. His plans were diverted, though, with a phone call from the Rector. 'Are you busy?' Father Phil asked, his strong voice resonating over the phone.

'Well, no, not really,' Nate said. He was sitting in a deep leather chair, under a quilt, beside the fire, sipping coffee and reading Mark Twain.

'Are you sure?'

'Of course I'm sure.'

'Well, I'm at the church, working in the basement, doing some remodeling, and I need a hand. I thought you might be bored, you know, since there's not much to do here in St. Michaels, at least not in the winter. It's supposed to snow again today.'

The lamb stew crossed Nate's mind. There was plenty of it left over. 'I'll be there in ten minutes.'

The basement was directly under the sanctuary. Nate heard hammering as he carefully descended the shaky steps. It was an open room, long and wide with a low ceiling. A remodeling project had been under way for a long time, with no end in sight. The general plan appeared to be a series of small rooms against the outer walls, with an open space in the center. Phil stood between two sawhorses, tape measure in hand, sawdust on his shoulders. He wore a flannel shirt, jeans, boots, and would've easily passed for a carpenter.

'Thanks for coming,' he said with a big smile.

'You're welcome. I was bored,' Nate said.

'I'm hanging wallboard,' he said, waving his arm at the construction. 'It's easier if there are two people. Mr. Fuqua used to help, but he's eighty now and his back is not what it used to be.'

'What are you building?'

'Six classrooms for Bible study. This center area will be a fellowship hall. I started two years ago. Our budget doesn't allow much in the way of new projects, so I'm doing it myself. Keeps me in shape.'

Father Phil hadn't been in shape in years. 'Point me in the right direction,' Nate said. 'And remember I'm a lawyer.'

'Not a lot of honest work, huh?'

'No.'

They each took an end of a sheet of wallboard and wrestled it across the floor to the current classroom in progress. The sheet was four feet by six, and as they lifted it into place Nate realized that it was indeed a job for two people. Phil grunted and frowned and bit his tongue, and when the piece fit the puzzle, he said, 'Now just hold it right there.' Nate pressed the board against the two by four studs while Phil quickly tacked it into place with sheetrock nails. Once secure, he drove six more nails into the studs, and admired his handiwork. Then he produced a tape and began to measure the next open space.

'Where did you learn to be a carpenter?' Nate asked as he watched with interest.

'It's in my blood. Joseph was a carpenter.'

'Who's he?'

'The father of Jesus.'

'Oh, that Joseph.'

'Do you read the Bible, Nate?'

'Not much.'

'You should.'

'I'd like to start.'

'I can help you, if you want.'

'Thanks.'

Phil scribbled dimensions on the wallboard they had just installed. He measured carefully, then remeasured. Before long, Nate realized why the project was taking so long. Phil took his time and believed in a vigorous regimen of coffee breaks.

After an hour, they walked up the stairs to the main

floor, to the Rector's office, which was ten degrees warmer than the basement. Phil had a pot of strong coffee on a small burner. He poured two cups and began scanning the rows of books on the shelves. 'Here's a wonderful daily devotional guide, one of my favorites,' he said, gently removing the book, wiping it as if it were covered in dust, then handing it to Nate. It was a hardback with the dust jacket intact. Phil was particular about his books.

He selected another, and handed it to Nate. 'This is a Bible study for busy people. It's very good.'

'What makes you think I'm busy?'

'You're a lawyer in Washington, aren't you?'

'Technically, but those days are about to be over.'

Phil tapped his fingertips together, and looked at Nate as only a minister can. His eyes said, 'Keep going. Tell me more. I'm here to help.'

So Nate unloaded some of his troubles, past and present, with emphasis on the pending showdown with the IRS and the imminent loss of his law license. He would avoid jail, but be required to pay a fine he couldn't afford.

Nonetheless, he wasn't unhappy about the future. In fact, he was relieved to be leaving the profession.

'What will you do?' Phil asked.

'I have no idea.'

'Do you trust God?'

'Yes, I think so.'

'Then relax. He'll show you the way.'

They talked long enough to stretch the morning to the lunch hour, then walked next door and feasted once again on the lamb stew. Laura joined them late. She taught kindergarten and only had thirty minutes for lunch.

Around two, they made it back to the basement, where they reluctantly resumed their labor. Watching

Phil work, Nate became convinced that the project would not be finished in his lifetime. Joseph may have been a fine carpenter, but Father Phil belonged in the pulpit. Every open space on the wall had to be measured, remeasured, pondered over, looked at from various angles, then measured again. The sheet of wallboard destined to fill the open space went through the same procedures. Finally, after enough pencil markings to confuse an architect, Phil, with great trepidation, took the electric saw and cut the wallboard. They carried the sheet to the open space, tacked it, then secured it. The fit was always perfect, and with each one Phil seemed genuinely relieved.

Two classrooms appeared to be finished and ready for paint. Late in the afternoon, Nate decided that tomorrow he would become a painter.

FORTY-ONE

Two days of pleasant labor yielded little progress in the chilly basement of Trinity Church. But much coffee was consumed, the lamb stew was finally finished, some paint and wallboard fell into place, and a friendship was built.

Nate was scraping paint from his fingernails Tuesday night when the phone rang. It was Josh, calling him back to the real world. 'Judge Wycliff wants to see you tomorrow,' he said. 'I tried to call earlier.'

'What does he want?' Nate asked, his voice flat with dread.

'I'm sure he'll have questions about your new client.'

'I'm really busy, Josh. I'm into remodeling, painting, and sheetrock, stuff like that.'

'Oh really.'

'Yeah, I'm doing the basement of a church. Time is of the essence.'

'Didn't know you had such talents.'

'Do I have to come, Josh?'

'I think so, pal. You agreed to take this case. I've already told the Judge. You're needed, old boy.'

'When and where?'

'Come to my office at eleven. We'll ride over together.'

'I don't want to see the office, Josh. It's all bad memories. I'll just meet you at the courthouse.'

'Fine. Be there at noon. Judge Wycliff's office.'

Nate put a log on the fire and watched the snow flurries float across the porch. He could put on a suit and tie and carry a briefcase around. He could look and talk the part. He could say 'Your Honor' and 'May it please the court,' and he could yell objections and grill witnesses. He could do all the things a million others did, but he no longer considered himself a lawyer. Those days were gone, thank God.

He could do it once more, but only once. He tried to convince himself it was for his client, for Rachel, but he knew she didn't care.

He still hadn't written her, though he'd planned the letter many times. The one to Jevy had required two hours of hard work, for a page and a half.

After three days in the snow, he missed the humid streets of Corumbá, with the lazy pedestrian traffic, the outdoor cafés, the pace of life that said everything could wait until tomorrow. It was snowing harder by the minute. Maybe it's another blizzard, he thought, and the roads will be closed, and I won't have to go after all.

More sandwiches from the Greek deli, more pickles and tea. Josh prepared the table as they waited for Judge Wycliff. 'Here's the court file,' he said, handing a bulky red binder to Nate. 'And here's your response,' he said, handing over a manila file. 'You need to read and sign this as soon as possible.'

'Has the estate filed an answer?' Nate asked.

'Tomorrow. The answer of Rachel Lane is in there, already prepared, just waiting for your signature.'

'There's something wrong here, Josh. I'm filing an answer to a will contest on behalf of a client who doesn't know it.'

'Send her a copy.'

'To where?'

'To her only known address, that of World Tribes Missions in Houston, Texas. It's all in the file.'

Nate shook his head in frustration at Josh's preparations. He felt like a pawn on a gameboard. The Answer of the Proponent, Rachel Lane, was four pages long and denied, both generally and specifically, the allegations set forth in the six petitions challenging the will. Nate read the six petitions while Josh worked his cell phone.

When all the rash allegations and legalese were pared down, it was a simple case: Did Troy Phelan know what he was doing when he wrote his last testament? The trial would be a circus though, with the lawyers trotting in psychiatrists of every sort and species. Employees, ex-employees, old girlfriends, janitors, maids, chauffeurs, pilots, bodyguards, doctors, prostitutes, anybody who'd spent five minutes with the old man would be hauled in to testify.

Nate didn't have the stomach for it. The file grew heavier as he read. It would fill a room when the war was finally over.

Judge Wycliff made his usual fussy entrance at twelve-thirty, apologizing for being so busy while yanking off his robe. 'You're Nate O'Riley,' he said, thrusting forth a hand.

'Yes, Judge, a pleasure to meet you.'

Josh managed to disengage himself from the cell phone. They squeezed around the small table and began eating. 'Josh tells me you found the richest woman in the world,' Wycliff said, smacking his food.

'Yes, I did. About two weeks ago.'

'And you can't tell me where she is?'

'She begged me not to. I promised.'

'Will she appear and testify at the appropriate time?'

'She won't have to,' Josh explained. Of course he

369

had a brief, a Stafford Memo, in his file on the issue of her presence during the lawsuit. 'If she knows nothing about Mr. Phelan's mental capacity, she can't be a witness.'

'But she's a party,' Wycliff said.

'Yes she is. But her presence can be excused. We can litigate without her.'

'Excused by whom?'

'You, Your Honor.'

'I plan to file a motion at the appropriate time,' Nate said, 'asking the court to allow the trial to be held without her presence.' Josh smiled across the table. Atta boy, Nate.

'I guess we'll worry about it later,' Wycliff said. 'I'm more concerned about discovery. Needless to say, the contestants are quite anxious to move ahead.'

'The estate will file its answer tomorrow,' Josh said. 'We're ready for battle.'

'What about the proponent?'

'I'm still working on her answer,' Nate said somberly, as if he'd labored days on it. 'But I can file it tomorrow.'

'Are you ready for discovery?'

'Yes sir.'

'When can we expect the waiver and acknowledgment from your client?'

'I'm not sure.'

'Technically, I don't have jurisdiction over her until I receive them.'

'Yes, I understand. I'm sure they'll be here soon. Her mail service is very slow.'

Josh smiled at his protégé.

'You actually found her, showed her a copy of the will, explained the waiver and acknowledgment, and agreed to represent her?'

'Yes sir,' Nate said, but only because he had to.

'Will you put that in an affidavit for the file?'

'That's a bit unusual, isn't it?' Josh asked.

'Maybe, but if we start discovery without her waiver and acknowledgment, I want some record in the file showing that she has been contacted and knows what we're doing.'

'Good idea, Judge,' Josh said, as if the idea had been his to start with. 'Nate will sign it.'

Nate nodded and took a large bite of his sandwich, hoping they would let him eat without being forced to tell more lies.

'Was she close to Troy?' Wycliff asked.

Nate chewed as long as he could before answering. 'We're off the record here, aren't we?'

'Of course. This is just gossip.'

Yes, and gossip can win and lose lawsuits. 'I don't think they were that close. She hadn't seen him in years.'

'How did she react when she read the will?'

Wycliff's tone was indeed gossipy and chatty, and Nate knew the Judge wanted all the details. 'She was surprised, to say the least,' he said dryly.

'I'll bet. Did she ask how much?'

'Eventually, yes. I think she was overwhelmed, as anyone would be.'

'Is she married?'

'No.'

Josh realized the questions about Rachel could go on for a while. And the questions were dangerous. Wycliff could not know, at least not at that point, that Rachel had no interest in the money. If he kept digging, and if Nate kept telling the truth, something would slip. 'You know, Judge,' he said, gently steering the conversation in another direction, 'this is not a complicated case. Discovery shouldn't take forever. They're anxious. We're anxious. There's a pile of money sitting on the table and everybody wants it. Why can't we fast-track discovery and set a trial date?'

371

Speeding litigation along in a probate matter was unheard of. Estate lawyers were paid by the hour. Why hurry?

'That's interesting,' Wycliff said. 'What do you have in mind?'

'Have a discovery conference as soon as possible. Get all the lawyers in one room, make each produce a list of potential trial witnesses and documents. Designate thirty days for all depositions, and set a trial date ninety days away.'

'That's awfully fast.'

'We do it in federal court all the time. It works. The boys on the other side will jump at it because their clients are all broke.'

'What about you, Mr. O'Riley? Is your client anxious to get the money?'

'Wouldn't you be anxious, Judge?' Nate asked.

And they all laughed.

When Grit finally penetrated Hark's line of phone defenses, his first words were, 'I'm thinking about going to the Judge.'

Hark pressed the record button on his phone, and said, 'Good afternoon to you, Grit.'

'I might tell the Judge the truth, that Snead has sold his testimony for five million dollars, and nothing he says is the truth.'

Hark laughed just loud enough for Grit to hear. 'You can't do that, Grit.'

'Of course I can.'

'You're not very bright, are you. Listen to me, Grit, and listen good. First, you signed the note along with the rest of us, so you're implicated in any wrongdoing you allege. Second, and most important, you know about Snead because you were involved in the case as an attorney for Mary Ross. That's a confidential relationship. If you divulge any information learned as

372

her attorney, then you breach the confidentiality. If you do something stupid, she will file a complaint with the bar, and I'll hound your ass into disbarment. I'll take your license, Grit, do you understand that?'

'You're scum, Gettys. You stole my client.'

'If your client was happy, then why was she looking for another lawyer?'

'I'm not finished with you.'

'Don't do anything stupid.'

Grit slammed the phone down. Hark enjoyed the moment, then went back to work.

Nate drove alone into the city, over the Potomac River, past the Lincoln Memorial, moving with the traffic, in no hurry. Flurries hit his windshield, but the heavier snow had not materialized. At a red light on Pennsylvania, he looked in his rearview mirror and saw the building, clustered among a dozen others, where he had spent most of the past twenty-three years. His office window was six floors up. He could barely see it.

On M Street into Georgetown, he began to see the hangouts – the old bars and joints where he'd passed long dark hours with people he couldn't remember anymore. He could, however, remember the names of the bartenders. Every pub had a story. In the drinking days, a hard day at the office or in the courtroom had to be softened with a few hours of alcohol. He couldn't go home without it. He turned north on Wisconsin and saw a bar where he'd once fought a college boy, a kid drunker than himself. A sleazy co-ed had prompted the dispute. The bartender sent them outside for the fisticuffs. Nate had worn a Band-Aid into court the next morning.

And there was a small café where he'd bought enough cocaine to almost kill himself. The narcs raided it when he was in recovery. Two stockbroker buddies went to jail.

He'd spent his glory days on those streets, while his wives were waiting and his kids were growing up without him. He was ashamed of the misery he'd caused. As he left Georgetown, he vowed never to return.

At the Stafford home, he loaded his car again with more clothes and personal items, then left in a hurry.

In his pocket was a check for ten thousand dollars, the first month's retainer. The IRS wanted sixty thousand in back taxes. The fine would be at least that much too. He owed his second wife about thirty thousand in past-due child support, monthly obligations racked up while he recovered with Sergio.

His bankruptcy did not discharge these debts. He conceded that his financial future was indeed bleak. The younger children cost him three thousand a month each in support. The two older ones were almost as expensive with tuition and room and board. He could live off the Phelan money for a few months, but the way Josh and Wycliff were talking the trial would be held sooner rather than later. When the estate was finally closed, Nate would go before a federal judge, plead guilty to tax evasion, and surrender his license.

Father Phil was teaching him not to worry about the future. God would take care of His own.

Once again, Nate wondered if God was getting more than He bargained for.

Since he was incapable of writing on anything but a legal pad, with its wide lines and broad margins, Nate took one and tried to begin a letter to Rachel. He had the address of World Tribes in Houston. He would mark the envelope 'Personal and Confidential,' address it to Rachel Lane, and attach an explanatory note: To Whom It May Concern.

Someone at World Tribes knew who and where she was. Perhaps someone knew Troy was her father. Maybe this someone put two and two together, and now knew that their Rachel was the beneficiary.

Nate was also assuming Rachel would contact World Tribes, if she had not already done so. She'd been in Corumbá when she'd come to the hospital. It was reasonable to believe she'd called Houston and told someone about his visit.

She had mentioned her annual budget with World Tribes. There had to be a method of corresponding by mail. If his letter got in the right hands in Houston, then maybe it would find the right place in Corumbá.

He wrote the date, then 'Dear Rachel:'

An hour passed while he watched the fire and tried to think of words that would sound intelligent. Finally, he opened the letter with a paragraph about snow. Did she miss it from her childhood? What was it like in Montana? There was a foot on the ground outside his window.

He was compelled to confess that he was acting as her lawyer, and once he fell into the rhythm of legalese, the letter took off. He explained as simply as he could what was happening with the lawsuit.

He told her about Father Phil, and the church and its basement. He was studying the Bible and enjoying it. He was praying for her.

When he finished, the letter was three pages long, and Nate was quite proud of himself. He reread it twice, and declared it to be worthy of sending. If it somehow made it to her hut, he knew that she would read it again and again, and give not the slightest thought to any shortcomings in style.

Nate longed to see her again.

FORTY-TWO

One reason for the sluggish progress of the church's basement was Father Phil's penchant for sleeping late. Laura said she left home each weekday morning at eight, for kindergarten, and more often than not the Rector was still buried under the blankets. He was a night owl, he said in self-defense, and he loved to watch old black-and-white movies after midnight.

So when he called at seven-thirty Friday morning, Nate was somewhat surprised. 'Have you seen the *Post?*' he asked.

'I don't read newspapers,' Nate replied. He had broken the habit during rehab. Phil, on the other hand, read five a day. They were a good source of material for his sermons.

'Perhaps you should,' he said.

'Why?'

'There's a story about you.'

Nate put on his boots and trudged two blocks to a coffee shop on Main Street. There was a nice story on the front page of Metro about the finding of the lost heir of Troy Phelan. Papers had been filed late the day before in the Circuit Court of Fairfax County in which she, acting through her attorney, a Mr. Nate O'Riley, disputed the allegations of those contesting her late father's will. Since there wasn't much to say about her, the story dwelt on her attorney. According to his affidavit, also filed in court, he had tracked down Rachel Lane, showed her a copy of the handwritten will, discussed the various legal issues with her, and had somehow managed to become her lawyer. There was no indication of exactly where Ms. Lane was.

Mr. O'Riley was a former partner in the Stafford Law Firm; had once been a prominent trial lawyer; had left the firm in August; filed for bankruptcy in October; been indicted in November; and a final disposition of his tax evasion charges was still pending. The IRS claimed he beat them out of sixty thousand dollars. For good measure, the reporter mentioned the useless fact that he had been divorced twice. To complete the humiliation, a bad photo ran with the story, one of Nate with a drink in his hand at a D.C. bar function several years earlier. He studied the grainy image of himself, eyes glowing, cheeks darkened with alcohol, goofy smile as if he were mixing and mingling with people he enjoyed. It was embarrassing, but it was another life.

Of course no story could be complete without a quick recital of the messy statistics of Troy's life and death – three wives, seven known children, eleven billion or so in assets, his last flight from fourteen floors up.

Mr. O'Riley could not be found for comment. Mr. Stafford had nothing to say. The lawyers for the Phelan heirs had evidently said so much already that they were not asked to comment again.

Nate folded the paper and returned to the cottage. It was eight-thirty. He had an hour and a half before construction commenced in the basement.

The bloodhounds now knew his name, but finding his scent would be difficult. Josh had arranged for his mail to be routed to a post office box in D.C. He had a new office phone number, one for Nathan F. O'Riley,

377

Attorney-at-Law. The calls were answered by a secretary in Josh's office who filed away the messages.

In St. Michaels, only the Rector and his wife knew who he was. Rumor had it that he was a wealthy lawyer from Baltimore writing a book.

Hiding was addictive. Maybe that was why Rachel did it.

Copies of Rachel Lane's response were mailed to all the Phelan lawyers, who, as a group, were electrified by the news. She was indeed alive, and willing to fight, though her choice of lawyer was somewhat puzzling. O'Riley's reputation was accurate – an efficient litigator with flashes of brilliance who couldn't handle the pressure. But the Phelan lawyers, along with Judge Wycliff, suspected Josh Stafford was calling the shots. He'd rescued O'Riley from rehab, cleaned him up, put the file in his hands, and pointed him toward the courthouse.

The Phelan lawyers met Friday morning at Ms. Langhorne's place, a modern building packed among many on Pennsylvania Avenue, in the business district. Her firm was a wanna-be – with forty lawyers it wasn't big enough to attract blue-chip clients, but the leadership was very ambitious. The furnishings were showy and pretentious, the trappings of a bunch of lawyers desperate for the big time.

They had decided to meet once a week, each Friday at eight, for no more than two hours, to discuss the Phelan litigation and plot strategy. The idea had been Langhorne's. She had realized that she would have to be the peacemaker. The boys were busy strutting and fighting. And there was too much money to be lost in a trial where the contestants, all on one side of the room, were knifing each other in the back.

It appeared, at least to her, that the raiding was over. Her clients, Geena and Cody, were sticking.

Yancy seemed to have Ramble adequately collared. Wally Bright was practically living with Libbigail and Spike. Hark had the other three – Troy Junior, Rex, and Mary Ross – and seemed content with his harvest. The dust was settling around the heirs. Relationships were becoming familiar. The issues had been defined. The lawyers knew they had better work as a team or lose the case.

Number one was Snead. They had spent hours watching the videos of his first effort, and each had prepared lengthy notes of ways to improve his performance. The fabricating was shameless. Yancy, in years past an aspiring screenwriter, had actually written a fifty-page script for Snead, filled with enough bald allegations to make poor Troy appear thoroughly brainless.

Number two was Nicolette, the secretary. They would hammer her in a few days on video, and there were certain things she needed to say. Bright had the idea that perhaps the old man had had a stroke during sex with her just hours before he faced the three psychiatrists, and this was something both Nicolette and Snead could testify to. A stroke would mean diminished mental capacity. It was a decent idea, generally well received, and it prompted a lengthy discussion about the autopsy. They had not yet seen a copy of it. Poor guy was splattered on the bricks, with terrible trauma to his head, as one would expect. Could the autopsy reveal a stroke?

Number three was their own experts. Grit's shrink had made a hasty exit with the attorney, so they were down to four, one per firm. Four was not an unmanageable number at trial, in fact, four could be persuasive, especially if they all reached the same conclusions but by different routes. They agreed that they should also rehearse the testimony of their psychiatrists, grilling them and trying to make them crack under pressure.

Number four was other witnesses. They had to find others who were around the old man in his last days. Snead could help them there.

The last item of business was the appearance of Rachel Lane and her lawyer. 'There is nothing in the file signed by this woman,' Hark said. 'She's a recluse. No one knows where she is, except for her lawyer and he's not telling. It took a month to find her. She has signed nothing. Technically the court does not have jurisdiction. It's obvious to me that this woman is reluctant to come forward.'

'So are some lottery winners,' Bright inserted. 'They want to keep it quiet, otherwise every bum in the neighborhood's beating on the door.'

'What if she doesn't want the money?' Hark asked, and the room was stunned.

'That's crazy,' Bright said on instinct, his words trailing away as he considered the impossible.

While they were scratching their heads, Hark pushed forward. 'It's just a thought, but one we should consider. Under Virginia law, a bequest in a will can be renounced. The gift remains in the estate, subject to the remainder provisions. If this will is struck down, and if there are no other wills, then the seven children of Troy Phelan take all. Since Rachel Lane wants nothing, then our clients divide the estate.'

Dizzying calculations raced through their heads. Eleven billion, less estate taxes, divided by six. Then apply the appropriate percentages, and serious wealth was possible. Fees of seven figures became fees of eight figures.

'That's a bit far-fetched,' Langhorne said slowly, her brain still burning with the math.

'I'm not so sure,' Hark said. It was obvious he knew more than the rest. 'A waiver is a very simple document to execute. Are we expected to believe Mr. O'Riley traveled to Brazil, found Rachel Lane, told her about Troy, got himself hired, but did not get a simple signature on a short document that would give the court jurisdiction? Something's going on here.'

Yancy was the first to say, 'Brazil?'

'Yes. He just returned from Brazil.'

'How do you know this?'

Hark slowly reached into a file and removed some papers. 'I have a very good investigator,' he said, and the room was silent. 'Yesterday, after I received her answer and O'Riley's affidavit, same as you, I called the investigator. In three hours, he learned the following: On December twenty-second, Nate O'Riley left Dulles on Varig Flight 882 nonstop to São Paulo. From there he flew Varig Flight 146 to Campo Grande, and then he took an Air Pantanal commuter to a small city called Corumbá, arriving on the twenty-third. He stayed almost three weeks and then he returned to Dulles.'

'Maybe it was a vacation,' Bright mumbled. He was as amazed as the rest of them.

'Maybe, but I doubt it. Mr. O'Riley spent last fall in rehab, not for the first time. He was in the tank when Troy jumped. He was released on the twenty-second, same day he left for Brazil. His trip had only one purpose, and that was to find Rachel Lane.'

'How do you know all this?' Yancy had to ask.

'It's not that difficult, really. Especially the flight information. Any good hacker can get it.'

'How did you know he was in rehab?'

'Spies.'

There was a long silence as they digested this. They simultaneously despised Hark and admired him. He seemed to always have information they didn't, yet he was on their side now. They were a team.

'It's just leverage,' he said. 'We go full speed ahead

with discovery. We attack the will with a vengeance. We say nothing about the court's lack of jurisdiction over Rachel Lane. If she doesn't show either in person or by waiver, then it's an excellent indication that she doesn't want the money.'

'I'll never believe that,' Bright said.

'That's because you're a lawyer.'

'What are you?'

'The same, just not as greedy. Believe it or not, Wally, there are people in this world who are not motivated by money.'

'There are about twenty of them,' Yancy said. 'And they're all my clients.'

A little laughter broke the tension.

Before adjourning, they once again forced each other to agree that everything they said was confidential. Each meant it, but no one completely trusted the other. The news about Brazil was especially delicate.

FORTY-THREE

The envelope was brown and slightly larger than legal-sized. Beside the World Tribes address in Houston were the words, in bold black print: For Rachel Lane, Missionary in South America, Personal and Confidential.

It was received by the mail clerk, examined for a few moments, then sent upstairs to a supervisor. Its journey continued throughout the morning until it landed, still unopened, on the desk of Neva Collier, Coordinator of South American Missions. She gaped at it in disbelief – no one knew Rachel Lane was a World Tribes missionary. No one but her.

Evidently, those who'd passed it along did not make the connection between the name on the envelope and the name in the recent news. It was Monday morning, the offices were slow and quiet.

Neva locked her door. Inside was a letter, addressed: 'To Whom It May Concern,' and a smaller, sealed envelope. She read the letter aloud, astounded by the fact that someone knew even the partial identity of Rachel Lane.

To Whom It May Concern:
Enclosed is a letter to Rachel Lane, one of your missionaries in Brazil. Please forward it to her, unopened.

I met Rachel about two weeks ago. I found her in the Pantanal, living among the Ipicas, where, as you know, she has been for eleven years now. The purpose of my visit was a pending legal matter.

For your information, she is doing well. I promised Rachel that I would not, under any circumstances, tell anyone of her location. She does not wish to be disturbed with any more legal matters, and I agreed to her request.

She does need money for a new boat and motor, and also additional funds for medicines. I will gladly forward a check to your organization for these expenses; just give me directions.

I plan to write Rachel again, though I have no idea how she gets her mail. Could you please drop me a line and let me know this letter was received and that her letter was forwarded to her? Thanks.

It was signed Nate O'Riley. At the bottom of the letter was a phone number in St. Michaels, Maryland, and an address at a law firm in Washington.

Corresponding with Rachel was a very simple matter. Twice a year, on March 1 and on August 1, World Tribes sent packages to the post office in Corumbá. Included were medical supplies, Christian literature, and anything else that she might need or want. The post office agreed to hold the August packages for thirty days, and if they went unclaimed they were to be returned to Houston. This had never happened. In August of every year, Rachel made her annual trek to Corumbá, at which time she called the home office and practiced her English for ten minutes. She collected her packages and returned to the Ipicas. In March, after the rainy season, the packages were sent upriver on a *chalana* and dropped off at a *fazenda* near the mouth of the Xeco River. Lako would retrieve them eventually. The March packages were always smaller than the August ones.

In eleven years, Rachel had never received a personal letter, at least not through World Tribes.

Neva copied the phone number and address on a notepad, then hid the letter in a drawer. She would send it in a month or so, along with the usual supplies for March.

They worked for almost an hour cutting two by fours for the next little classroom. The floor was covered with sawdust. Phil had some in his hair. The screech of the saw still rang in their ears. It was time for coffee. They sat on the floor, their backs to the wall, near a portable heater. Phil poured strong latte from a thermos.

'You missed a great sermon yesterday,' he said with a grin.

'Where?'

'What do you mean, where? Here of course.'

'What was the subject?'

'Adultery.'

'For it or against it?'

'Against it, as always.'

'I wouldn't think that'd be much of a problem with your congregation.'

'I give the sermon once a year.'

'Same sermon?'

'Yes, but always fresh.'

'When was the last time one of your members had a problem with adultery?'

'Couple of years ago. One of our younger members thought her husband had another woman in Baltimore. He traveled there once a week on business, and she noticed that he returned home a different person. He had more energy, more enthusiasm for life. This would last for two or three days, then he was his usual cranky self again. She became convinced he had fallen in love.'

'Cut to the chase.'

'He was seeing a chiropractor.'

Phil laughed loudly through his nose, a strange cackle that was infectious and usually funnier than the punch line. When the humor passed, they sipped in unison. Then Phil asked, 'In your other life, Nate, did you ever have a problem with adultery?'

'None whatsoever. It wasn't a problem, it was a way of life. I chased anything that walked. Every semiattractive woman was nothing but a potential quickie. I was married, but I never thought that I was committing adultery. It wasn't sin; it was a game. I was a sick puppy, Phil.'

'I shouldn't have asked.'

'No, confession is good for the soul. I'm ashamed of the person I used to be. The women, booze, drugs, bars, fights, divorces, neglected children – I was a mess. I wish I had those days back. But it's important now to remember how far I've come.'

'You have many good years left, Nate.'

'I hope so. I'm just not sure what to do.'

'Be patient. God will lead you.'

'Of course, at the rate we're going, I could have a very long career right here.'

Phil smiled but didn't erupt with a cackle. 'Study your Bible, Nate, and pray. God needs people like you.'

'I suppose.'

'Trust me. It took me ten years to find God's will. I ran for a while, then I stopped and listened. Slowly, he led me into the ministry.'

'How old were you?'

'I was thirty-six when I entered the seminary.'

'Were you the oldest one?'

'No. It's not uncommon to see people in their forties in seminary. Happens all the time.'

'How long does it take?'

'Four years.'

'That's worse than law school.'

'It wasn't bad at all. In fact, it was quite enjoyable.'

'Can't say that for law school.'

They worked for another hour, then it was time for lunch. The snow had finally melted, all of it, and there was a crab house down the road in Tilghman that Phil enjoyed. Nate was anxious to buy lunch.

'Nice car,' Phil said as he belted himself in. Sawdust shook from his shoulder onto the spotless leather seat of the Jaguar. Nate couldn't have cared less.

'It's a lawyer's car, leased of course because I couldn't afford to pay cash for it. Eight hundred bucks a month.'

'Sorry.'

'I'd love to unload it and get me a nice little Blazer or something.'

Route 33 narrowed as they left town, and they were soon winding along the bay.

He was in bed when the phone rang, but not asleep. Sleep was an hour away. It was only ten, but his body was still accustomed to the routine of Walnut Hill, his trip south notwithstanding. And at times he felt some residual fatigue from the dengue.

It was difficult to believe that for most of his professional life he often worked until nine or ten at night, then had dinner in a bar and drinks until one. He grew weary just thinking about it.

Since the phone seldom rang, he grabbed it quickly, certain it was trouble. A female voice said, 'Nate O'Riley, please.'

'This is Nate O'Riley.'

'Good evening, sir. My name is Neva Collier, and I received a letter from you for our friend in Brazil.'

The covers flew off as Nate jumped from the bed. 'Yes! You got my letter?'

'We did. I read it this morning, and I will send Rachel's letter to her.'

'Wonderful. How does she get mail?'

'I send it to Corumbá, at certain times of the year.'

'Thank you. I'd like to write her again.'

'That's fine, but please don't put her name on the envelopes.'

It occurred to Nate that it was nine o'clock in Houston. She was calling from home, and this seemed more than odd. The voice was pleasant enough, but tentative.

'Is something wrong?' he asked.

'No, except that no one here knows who she is. No one but me. Now with your involvement, there are two people in the world who know where she is and who she is.'

'She swore me to secrecy.'

'Was she difficult to find?'

'You could say that. I wouldn't worry about others finding her.'

'But how did you do it?'

'Her father did it. You know about Troy Phelan?'

'Yes. I'm clipping news stories.'

'Before he left this world, he tracked her to the Pantanal. I have no idea how he did it.'

'He had the means.'

'Yes he did. We knew generally where she was, and I went down there, hired a guide, got lost, and found her. Do you know her well?'

'I'm not sure anyone knows Rachel well. I speak to her once a year in August, from Corumbá. She tried a furlough five years ago, and I had lunch with her one day. But no, I don't know her that well.'

'Have you heard from her recently?'

'No.'

Rachel had been in Corumbá two weeks earlier. He knew this for a fact because she had come to the hospital. She had spoken to him, touched him, and then vanished along with his fevers. But she hadn't called the home office? How strange.

'She is doing well,' he said. 'Very much at home with her people.'

'Why did you track her down?'

'Someone had to. Do you understand what her father did?'

'I'm trying to.'

'Someone had to notify Rachel, and it had to be a lawyer. I just happened to be the only one in our firm with nothing better to do.'

'And now you're representing her?'

'You are paying attention, aren't you?'

'We may have more than a passing interest. She is one of us, and she is, shall we say, out of the loop.'

'That would be an understatement.'

'What does she plan to do about her father's estate?'

Nate rubbed his eyes and paused to slow the conversation. The nice lady on the other end was stepping over the line. He doubted if she realized it. 'I don't want to be rude, Ms. Collier, but I can't discuss with you things Rachel and I talked about pertaining to her father's estate.'

'Of course not. I wasn't trying to pry. It's just that I'm not sure what World Tribes should do at this point.'

'Nothing. You have no involvement unless Rachel asks you to step in.'

'I see. So I'll just follow events in the newspapers.'

'I'm sure the proceedings will be well documented.'

'You mentioned certain things she needs down there.'

Nate told her the story of the little girl who died because Rachel had no antivenin. 'She can't find enough medical supplies in Corumbá. I'd love to send her whatever she needs.'

'Thank you. Send the money to my attention at World Tribes, and I'll make sure she gets the supplies. We have four thousand Rachels around the world, and our budgets get stretched.'

'Are the others as remarkable as Rachel?'

'Yes. They are chosen by God.'

They agreed to keep in touch. Nate could send all the letters he wanted. Neva would ship them to Corumbá. If either one heard from Rachel, he or she would call the other.

Back in bed, Nate replayed the phone call. The things that weren't said were amazing. Rachel had just learned from him that her father had died and left her one of the world's great fortunes. She then sneaked into Corumbá because she knew from Lako that Nate was very ill. And then she left, without calling anyone at World Tribes to discuss the money.

When he left her on the riverbank, he was convinced that she had no interest in the money. Now he was convinced even more.

FORTY-FOUR

The deposition derby began on Monday, February 17, in a long bare room in the Fairfax County Courthouse. It was a witness room, but Judge Wycliff had pulled strings and reserved it for the last two weeks of the month. At least fifteen people were scheduled to be deposed, and the lawyers had been unable to agree on places and times. Wycliff had intervened. The depositions would be taken in an orderly fashion, one after the other, hour after hour, day after day, until finished. Such a marathon was rare, but then, so were the stakes. The lawyers had shown an amazing ability to clear their calendars for the discovery phase of the Phelan matter. Trials had been postponed; other depositions wiggled out of; important deadlines delayed yet again; briefs shoved off on other partners; vacations happily put off until summer. Associates were sent to handle lesser chores. Nothing was as important as the Phelan mess.

For Nate, the prospect of spending two weeks in a room crowded with lawyers, grilling witnesses, was a misery just short of hell itself.

If his client didn't want the money, why should he care who got it?

His attitude changed somewhat when he met the Phelan heirs.

The first deponent was Mr. Troy Phelan, Jr. The

court reporter swore him to honesty, but with his shifty eyes and reddened cheeks, he lost credibility within seconds of being seated at the head of the table. A video camera at the other end zoomed in on his face.

Josh's staff had prepared hundreds of questions for Nate to hammer him with. The work and research had been done by a half-dozen associates, people Nate would never meet. But he could've handled it himself, off the cuff, with no preparation whatsoever. It was just a deposition, a fishing trip, and Nate had been there a thousand times.

Nate introduced himself to Troy Junior, who gave him a nervous smile, much like the inmate looking at the executioner. 'This is not going to be painful, is it?' he seemed to ask.

'Are you currently under the influence of any illegal drugs, prescription drugs, or alcohol?' Nate began pleasantly, and this rankled the Phelan lawyers on the other side of the table. Only Hark understood. He had taken almost as many depositions as Nate O'Riley.

The smile vanished. 'I am not,' Troy Junior snapped. His head was pounding from a hangover, but he was currently sober.

'And you understand that you have just sworn to tell the truth?'

'Yes.'

'Do you understand what perjury is?'

'I certainly do.'

'Which one is your lawyer?' Nate asked, waving at the crowd opposite.

'Hark Gettys.'

The arrogance of Mr. O'Riley rankled the attorneys again, this time Hark included. Nate hadn't bothered to learn which lawyers were attached to which client. His disdain for the entire group was offensive.

Within the first two minutes, Nate had established a

nasty tone for the day. There was little doubt that he distrusted Troy Junior immensely, and perhaps the guy was under the influence. It was an old trick.

'How many wives have you had?'

'How many have you had?' Junior shot back, then looked at his lawyer for approval. Hark was studying a sheet of paper.

Nate kept his cool. Who knew what the Phelan lawyers had been saying behind his back? He did not care.

'Let me explain something to you, Mr. Phelan,' Nate said without the slightest irritation. 'I will go over this very slowly, so listen carefully. I am the lawyer, you are the witness. Do you follow me so far?'

Troy Junior slowly nodded.

'I ask the questions, you give the answers. Do you understand that?'

The witness nodded again.

'You don't ask questions, and I don't give answers. Understand?'

'Yep.'

'Now, I don't think you'll have trouble with the answers if you'll pay attention to the questions. Okay?'

Junior nodded again.

'Are you still confused?'

'Nope.'

'Good. If you get confused again, please feel free to consult with your attorney. Am I getting through?'

'I understand.'

'Wonderful. Let's try it again. How many wives have you had?'

'Two.'

An hour later they finished with his marriages, his children, his divorce. Junior was sweating and wondering how long his deposition would last. The Phelan lawyers were staring blankly at sheets of paper and asking themselves the same thing. Nate, however, had yet to look at the pages of questions prepared for him. He could peel the skin off any witness simply by staring at his eyes and using one question to lead to another. No detail was too small for him to investigate. Where was your first wife's high school, college, first job? Was it her first marriage? Give us her employment history. Let's talk about the divorce. How much was your child support? Did you pay all of it?

For the most part it was useless testimony, evoked not for the sake of information, but rather to annoy the witness and put him on notice that the skeletons could be summoned from the closet. He filed the lawsuit. He had to suffer the scrutiny.

His employment history took them to the brink of lunch. He stumbled badly when Nate grilled him about his various jobs for his father's companies. There were dozens of witnesses who could be called to rebut his version of how useful he'd been. With each job, Nate asked for the names of all his co-workers and supervisors. The trap was laid. Hark saw it coming and called time-out. He stepped into the hall with his client and lectured him about telling the truth.

The afternoon session was brutal. Nate asked about the five million dollars he'd received on his twenty-first birthday, and the entire wall of Phelan lawyers seemed to stiffen.

'That was a long time ago,' Troy Junior said with an air of resignation. After four hours with Nate O'Riley, he knew the next round would be painful.

'Well, let's try to remember,' Nate said with a smile. He showed no signs of fatigue. In fact, he'd been there so many times he actually seemed anxious to grind through the details.

His acting was superb. He hated being there and tormenting people he hoped he'd never see again. The more questions Nate asked, the more determined he was to start a new career.

'How was the money given to you?' he asked.

'It was initially placed in an account in a bank.'

'You had access to the account?'

'Yes.'

'Did anyone else have access to the account?'

'No. Just me.'

'How did you get money out of the account?'

'By writing checks.'

And write them he did. His first purchase had been a brand-new Maserati, dark blue. They talked about the damned car for fifteen minutes.

Troy Junior never returned to college after receiving the money, not that any of the schools he'd attended were anxious to have him back. He simply partied, though this came not in the form of a confession. Nate hammered him about his employment from ages twenty-one to thirty, and slowly extricated enough facts to reveal that Troy Junior did not work at all for those nine years. He played golf and rugby, traded cars with gusto, spent a year in the Bahamas and a year in Vail, lived with an amazing assortment of women before finally marrying number one at the age of twenty-nine, and indulged himself in grand style until the money ran out.

Then the prodigal son crawled to his father and asked for a job.

As the afternoon wore on, Nate began to envision the havoc this witness would sow upon himself and those around him if he got his sticky fingers on the Phelan fortune. He would kill himself with the money.

At 4 P.M., Troy Junior asked to be excused for the day. Nate refused. During the break that followed, a note was sent to Judge Wycliff down the hall. While they waited, Nate looked at Josh's questions for the first time.

The return message instructed that the proceedings keep going.

A week after Troy's suicide, Josh had hired a security firm to conduct an investigation into the Phelan heirs. The probe was more financial than personal. Nate skimmed the highlights while the witness smoked in the hall.

'What kind of car are you driving now?' Nate asked when they resumed. The exam took yet another direction.

'A Porsche.'

'When did you buy it?'

'I've had it awhile.'

'Try to answer the question. When did you buy it?'

'Couple of months ago.'

'Before or after your father's death?'

'I'm not real sure. Before, I think.'

Nate lifted a sheet of paper. 'What day did your father die?'

'Lemme see. It was a Monday, uh, December the ninth, I think.'

'Did you buy the Porsche before or after December the ninth?'

'Like I said, I think it was before.'

'Nope, wrong again. On Tuesday, December tenth, did you go to Irving Motors in Arlington and purchase a black Porsche Carrera Turbo 911 for ninety thousand dollars, give or take?' Nate asked the question while reading from the sheet of paper.

Troy Junior squirmed and fidgeted yet again. He looked at Hark, who shrugged as if to say, 'Answer the question. He's got the paperwork.'

'Yes, I did.'

'Did you buy any other cars that day?'

'Yes.'

'How many?'

'A total of two.'

'Two Porsches?'

'Yes.'

'For a total of nearly one hundred and eighty thousand dollars?'

'Something like that.'

'How did you pay for them?'

'I haven't.'

'So the cars were gifts from Irving Motors?'

'Not exactly. I bought them on credit.'

'You qualified for credit?'

'Yes, at Irving Motors anyway.'

'Do they want their money?'

'Yes, you could say that.'

Nate picked up more papers. 'In fact, they've filed suit to recover either the money or the cars, haven't they?'

'Yes.'

'Did you drive the Porsche to the deposition today?'

'Yes. It's in the parking lot.'

'Let me get this straight. On December tenth, the day after your father died, you went to Irving Motors and bought two expensive cars, on some type of credit, and now, two months later, you haven't paid a dime and are being sued. Correct?'

The witness nodded.

'This is not the only lawsuit, is it?'

'No,' Troy Junior said in defeat. Nate almost felt sorry for him.

A rental company was suing for nonpayment on a furniture lease. American Express wanted over fifteen thousand. A bank sued Troy Junior a week after the reading of his father's will. Junior had fast-talked it into a loan of twenty-five thousand dollars, secured by nothing but his name. Nate had copies of all the litigation, and they trudged through the details of each lawsuit.

At five, another argument occurred. Another note was sent to Wycliff. The Judge appeared himself and

397

asked about their progress. 'When do you think you'll finish with this witness?' he asked Nate.

'There's no end in sight,' Nate said, staring at Junior, who was in a trance and praying for liquor.

'Then work until six,' Wycliff said.

'Can we start at eight in the morning?' Nate asked, as if they were going to the beach.

'Eight-thirty,' His Honor decreed, then left.

For the last hour, Nate peppered Junior with random questions on many subjects. The deponent had no clue where his interrogator was going, and Junior was being led by a master. Just as they settled on one topic and he began to feel comfortable, Nate changed course and hit him with something new.

How much money did he spend from December 9 to December 27, the day the will was read? What did he buy his wife for Christmas, and how did he pay for the gifts? What did he buy for his children? Back to the five million, did he put any of the money in stocks or bonds? How much money did Biff earn last year? Why did her first husband get custody of her kids? How many lawyers had he hired and fired since his father died? And on and on.

At precisely six, Hark stood and announced the deposition was being adjourned. Ten minutes later, Troy Junior was in a bar in a hotel lobby two miles away.

Nate slept in the Stafford guest room. Mrs. Stafford was somewhere in the house, but he never saw her. Josh was in New York on business.

The second day of questioning started on time. The cast was the same, though the lawyers were dressed much more casually. Junior wore a red cotton sweater.

Nate recognized the face of a drunk – the red eyes, the puffy flesh around them, the pink cheeks and nose, the sweat above the brows. The face had been his for years. Treating the hangover was as much a part of the morning as the shower and the dental floss. Take some pills, drink lots of water and strong coffee. If you're gonna be stupid you gotta be tough.

'You realize that you're still under oath, Mr. Phelan?' he began.

'I do.'

'Are you under the influence of any drugs or alcohol?'

'No sir, I am not.'

'Good. Let's go back to December the ninth, the day your father died. Where were you when he was examined by the three psychiatrists?'

'I was in his building, in a conference room with my family.'

'And you watched the entire examination, didn't you?'

'I did.'

'There were two color monitors in the room, right? Each twenty-six inches wide?'

'If you say so. I didn't measure them.'

'But you could certainly see them, couldn't you?'

'Yes.'

'Your view was unobstructed?'

'I had a clear view, yes.'

'And you had a clear reason to watch your father closely?'

'I did.'

'Did you have any trouble hearing him?'

'No.'

The lawyers knew where Nate was going. It was an unpleasant aspect of their case, but one that could not be avoided. Each of the six heirs would be led down this path.

'So you watched and heard the entire exam?'

'I did.'

'You missed nothing?'

'I missed nothing.'

'Of the three psychiatrists, Dr. Zadel had been hired by your family, correct?'

'That's correct.'

'Who found him?'

'The lawyers.'

'You trusted your lawyers to hire the psychiatrist?'

'Yes.'

For ten minutes, Nate quizzed him on exactly how they came to select Dr. Zadel for such a crucial exam, and in the process got what he wanted. Zadel was hired because he had excellent credentials, came highly recommended, and was very experienced.

'Were you pleased with the way he handled the exam?' Nate asked.

'I suppose.'

'Was there something you didn't like about Dr. Zadel's performance?'

'Not that I recall.'

The trip to the edge of the cliff continued as Troy Junior admitted that he was pleased with the exam, pleased with Zadel, happy with the conclusions reached by all three doctors, and left the building with no doubt that his father knew what he was doing.

'After the exam, when did you first doubt your father's mental stability?' Nate asked.

'When he jumped.'

'On December the ninth?'

'Right.'

'So you had doubts immediately.'

'Yes.'

'What did Dr. Zadel say to you when you expressed these doubts?'

'I didn't talk to Dr. Zadel.'

'You didn't?'

'No.'

'From December ninth to December twenty-seventh, the day the will was read in court, how many times did you talk to Dr. Zadel?'

'I don't remember any.'

'Did you see him at all?'

'No.'

'Did you call his office?'

'No.'

'Have you seen him since December the ninth?'

'No.'

Having walked him to the edge, it was time for the shove. 'Why did you fire Dr. Zadel?'

Junior had been prepped to some degree. 'You'll have to ask my lawyer that,' he said, and hoped Nate would just go away for a while.

'I'm not deposing your lawyer, Mr. Phelan. I'm asking you why Dr. Zadel was fired.'

'You'll have to ask the lawyers. It's part of our legal strategy.'

'Did the lawyers discuss it with you before Dr. Zadel was fired?'

'I'm not sure. I really can't remember.'

'Are you pleased that Dr. Zadel no longer works for you?'

'Of course I am.'

'Why?'

'Because he was wrong. Look, my father was a master con man, okay. He bluffed his way through the exam, same way he did all of his life, then jumped out of the window. He snowed Zadel and the other shrinks. They fell for his act. He was obviously off his rocker.'

'Because he jumped?'

'Yes, because he jumped, because he gave his money to some unknown heir, because he made no effort to shield his fortune from estate taxes, because he'd been crazy as hell for some time. Why do you think we had the exam to begin with? If he hadn't been nuts, would we have needed three shrinks to check him out before he signed his will?'

'But the three shrinks said he was okay.'

'Yeah, and they were dead wrong. He jumped. Sane people don't fly out of windows.'

'What if your father had signed the thick will and not the handwritten one? And then he jumped? Would he be crazy?'

'We wouldn't be here.'

It was the only time during the two-day ordeal that Troy Junior fought to a draw. Nate knew to move on, then to come back later.

'Let's talk about Rooster Inns,' he announced, and Junior's shoulders fell three inches. It was just another one of his bankrupt ventures, nothing more or less. But Nate had to have every little detail. One bankruptcy led to another. Each failure prompted questions about other doomed enterprises.

Junior's had been a sad life. Though it was hard to be sympathetic, Nate realized that the poor guy had never had a father. He had longed for Troy's approval, and never received it. Josh had told him that Troy had taken great delight when his children's ventures collapsed.

The lawyer freed the witness at five-thirty, day two. Rex was next. He'd waited in the hall throughout the day, and was highly agitated at being put off again.

Josh had returned from New York. Nate joined him for an early dinner.

FORTY-FIVE

Rex Phelan had spent most of the previous day on the cell phone in the hallway while his brother was roughed up by Nate O'Riley. Rex had been in enough lawsuits to know that litigation meant waiting: waiting for lawyers, judges, witnesses, experts, trial dates, and appeals courts, waiting in hallways for your turn to give testimony. When he raised his right hand and swore to tell the truth, he already despised Nate.

Both Hark and Troy Junior had warned him of what was to come. The lawyer could get under your skin and fester there like a boil.

Again, Nate started with inflammatory questions, and within ten minutes the room was tense. For three years, Rex had been the target of an FBI investigation. A bank had failed in 1990; Rex had been an investor and director. Depositors lost money. Borrowers lost their loans. Litigation had been raging for years with no end in sight. The president of the bank was in jail, and those close to the epicenter thought Rex would be next. There was enough dirt to keep Nate going for hours.

For fun, he continually reminded Rex that he was under oath. There was also a very good chance the FBI would see his deposition.

It was mid-afternoon before Nate worked his way to the strip bars. Rex owned six of them – held in his wife's name – in the Fort Lauderdale area. He'd bought them from a man killed in a gunfight. They were simply irresistible as subjects of conversation. Nate took them one by one – Lady Luck, Lolita's, Club Tiffany, et cetera – and asked a hundred questions. He asked about the girls, the strippers, where they came from, how much they earned, did they use drugs, what drugs, did they touch the customers, and on and on. He asked question after question about the economics of the skin business. After three hours of carefully painting a portrait of the sleaziest business in the world, Nate asked, 'Didn't your current wife work in one of the clubs?'

The answer was yes, but Rex couldn't just blurt it out. His throat and neck flashed red and for a moment he appeared ready to lunge across the table.

'She was a bookkeeper,' he said with a clenched jaw.

'She ever do any dancing, on the tables?'

Another pause, as Rex squeezed the table with his fingers. 'She certainly did not.' It was a lie, and everyone in the room knew it.

Nate flipped through some papers searching for the truth. They watched him carefully, half-expecting him to pull out a photo of Amber in a G-string and kinky heels.

They adjourned at six again, with the promise of more tomorrow. When the video camera was off and the court reporter was busy putting away her equipment, Rex stopped at the door, pointed at Nate, and said, 'No more questions about my wife, okay?'

'That's impossible, Rex. All assets are in her name.' Nate waved some papers at him, as if he had all their records. Hark shoved his client through the door.

Nate sat alone for an hour, skimming notes, flipping pages, wishing he were in St. Michaels sitting on the porch of the cottage with a view of the bay. He needed to call Phil.

This is your last case, he kept telling himself. And you're doing it for Rachel.

By noon of the second day, the Phelan lawyers were openly discussing whether Rex's deposition would take three days or four. He had over seven million dollars in liens and judgments filed against him, yet the creditors couldn't execute because all assets were in the name of his wife, Amber, the ex-stripper. Nate took each judgment, laid it on the table, examined it from every conceivable angle and direction, then placed it back in the file where it might stay and it might not. The tedium was unnerving everyone but Nate, who somehow kept an earnest demeanor as he plodded ahead.

For the afternoon session he selected the topic of Troy's leap and the events leading up to it. He followed the same line he'd used on Junior, and it was obvious Hark had prepped Rex. His answers to the questions about Dr. Zadel were rehearsed, but adequate. Rex hung with the party line – the three psychiatrists were simply wrong because Troy jumped minutes later.

More familiar territory was covered when Nate grilled him about his dismal employment career with The Phelan Group. Then they spent two painful hours wasting the five million Rex had received as his inheritance.

At five-thirty, Nate abruptly said he was finished, and walked out of the room.

Two witnesses in four days. Two men laid bare on video, and it wasn't a pretty sight. The Phelan lawyers went to their separate cars and drove away. Perhaps the worst was behind them, perhaps not.

Their clients had been spoiled as children, ignored by their father, cast into the world with fat checking accounts at an age when they were ill-equipped to handle money, and expected to prosper. They had

405

made bad choices, but all blame ultimately went back to Troy. That was the considered judgment of the Phelan lawyers.

Libbigail was led in early Friday morning and placed in the seat of honor. Her hair was of a style quite similar to a crew cut, with the sides peeled to the skin and an inch of gray on top. Cheap jewelry hung from her neck and wrists so that when she raised her hand to be sworn there was a racket at her elbow.

She looked at Nate in horror. Her brothers had told her the worst.

But it was Friday, and Nate wanted out of the city more than he wanted food when he was hungry. He smiled at her and began with easy background questions. Kids, jobs, marriages. For thirty minutes, all was pleasant. Then he began to probe into her past. At one point, he asked, 'How many times have you been through rehab for drugs and alcohol?'

The question shocked her, so Nate said, 'I've done it four times myself, so don't be ashamed.' His candor disarmed her.

'I really can't remember,' she said. 'But I've been clean for six years.'

'Wonderful,' said Nate. One addict to another. 'Good for you.'

From that point on, the two talked about things as if they were alone. Nate had to pry, and he apologized for doing so. He asked about the five million, and with no small amount of humor she told tales of good drugs and bad men. Unlike her brothers, Libbigail had found stability. His name was Spike, the ex-biker who'd also been detoxed into submission. They lived in a small house in the suburbs of Baltimore.

'What would you do if you got one sixth of your father's estate?' Nate asked.

'Buy lots of things,' she said. 'Same as you. Same as

anybody else. But I would be smart with the money this time. Real smart.'

'What's the first thing you'd buy?'

'The biggest Harley in the world, for Spike. Then a nicer house, not a mansion though.' Her eyes danced as she spent the money.

Her deposition lasted less than two hours. Her sister, Mary Ross Phelan Jackman, followed her, and likewise looked at Nate as if he had fangs. Of the five adult Phelan heirs, Mary Ross was the only one still married to her first spouse, though he had a prior wife. He was an orthopedist. She was dressed tastefully, with nice jewelry.

The early questions revealed the standard prolonged college experience, but without arrests, addictions, or expulsions. She'd taken her money and lived in Tuscany for three years, then Nice for two. At twenty-eight, she married the doctor, had two girls, one now seven, the other five. It was unclear how much of the five million was left. The doctor handled their investments, so Nate figured they were practically broke. Wealthy, but heavily in debt. Josh's background on Mary Ross showed a massive home with imported cars stacked in the driveway, a condo in Florida, and an estimated income by the doc of $750,000 a year. He was paying $20,000 a month to a bank, his part of the residual damage from a failed partnership that tried to corner the car wash business in northern Virginia.

The doctor also had an apartment in Alexandria where he kept a mistress. Mary Ross and her husband were rarely seen together. Nate decided not to discuss these matters. He was suddenly in a hurry, but careful not to show it.

Ramble slouched into the room after the lunch break, his lawyer Yancy leading and pointing and fussing over him, obviously terrified now that his client was expected to carry on an intelligent conversation.

The kid's hair was bright red now, and it sort of matched his zits. No portion of his face had gone unmutilated – rings and studs littered and scarred his features. The collar of his black leather jacket was turned up, James Dean style, so that it touched the earrings dangling from his lobes.

After a few questions, it was obvious the kid was as stupid as he looked. Since he had not yet had the opportunity to squander his money, Nate left him alone. They established that he seldom went to school, lived alone in the basement, had never held a job for which he was paid, liked to play the guitar, and planned to be a serious rock star real soon. His new band was aptly called the Demon Monkeys, but he wasn't sure they would record under that name. He played no sports, had never seen the inside of a church, spoke to his mother as little as possible, and preferred to watch MTV whenever he was awake and not playing his music.

It would take a billion dollars in therapy to straighten out this poor kid, Nate thought. He finished with him in less than an hour.

Geena was the last witness of the week. Four days after her father's death, she and her husband Cody had signed a contract to purchase a home for $3.8 million. When Nate assaulted her with this information right after she was sworn, she began to stutter and stammer and look at her lawyer, Ms. Langhorne, who was equally surprised. Her client had not told her about the contract.

'How did you plan to pay for the home?' Nate asked.

The answer was obvious but she couldn't confess it. 'We have money,' she said defensively, and this opened a door that Nate went barging through.

'Let's talk about your money,' he said with a smile.

'You're thirty years old. Nine years ago you received five million dollars, didn't you?'

'I did.'

'How much of it is left?'

She struggled with the answer for a long time. The answer was not so simple. Cody had made a lot of money. They had invested some, spent a lot, it was all co-mingled, so you couldn't just look at their balance sheet and say there was X amount left from the five million. Nate gave her the rope, and she slowly hung herself.

'How much money do you and your husband have today in your checking accounts?' he asked.

'I'd have to look.'

'Guess, please. Just give me an estimate.'

'Sixty thousand dollars.'

'How much real estate do you own?'

'Just our home.'

'What is the value of your home?'

'I'd have to get it appraised.'

'Guess, please. Just a ballpark figure.'

'Three hundred thousand.'

'And how much is your mortgage?'

'Two hundred thousand.'

'What is the approximate value of your portfolio?'

She scribbled some notes and closed her eyes. 'Approximately two hundred thousand dollars.'

'Any other significant assets?'

'Not really.'

Nate did his own calculations. 'So in nine years, your five million dollars has been reduced to something in the range of three hundred to four hundred thousand dollars. Am I correct?'

'Surely not. I mean, it seems so low.'

'So tell us again how you were going to pay for this new home?'

'Through Cody's work.'

'What about your dead father's estate? Ever think about that?'

'Maybe a little.'

'Now you've been sued by the seller of the house, haven't you?'

'Yes, and we've countersued. There are a lot of issues.'

She was shifty and dishonest, glib and quick with the half-truth. Nate thought she might be the most dangerous Phelan yet. They walked through Cody's ventures, and it was quickly apparent where the money had gone. He'd lost a million gambling on copper futures in 1992. He'd put half a million into 'Snow-Packed Chickens,' and lost it all. An indoor worm farm in Georgia took six hundred thousand dollars when a heat wave cooked the bait.

They were two immature kids living a pampered life with someone else's money, and dreaming of the big score.

Near the end of her deposition, with Nate still feeding her all the rope she wanted, she testified with a straight face that her involvement in the will contest had nothing to do with money. She loved her father deeply, and he loved her, and if he'd had his right mind he would have taken care of his children in his will. To give it all to a stranger was strong evidence of his illness. She was there fighting to protect the reputation of her father.

It was a well-rehearsed little oration, and it convinced no one. Nate let it slide. It was five o'clock, Friday afternoon, and he was tired of fighting.

As he left the city and fought the heavy traffic on Interstate 95 to Baltimore, his thoughts were on the Phelan heirs. He had pried into their lives, to the point of embarrassment. He felt sympathy for them, for the way they were raised, for the values they were never

410

taught, for their hollow lives revolving around nothing but money.

But Nate was convinced that Troy knew exactly what he was doing when he scrawled his testament. Serious money in the hands of his children would cause unmitigated chaos and untold misery. He left his fortune to Rachel, who had no interest in it. He excluded the others, whose lives were consumed by it.

Nate was determined to uphold the validity of Troy's last testament. But he was also very much aware that the final distribution of the estate would not be determined by anyone in the northern hemisphere.

It was late when he arrived in St. Michaels, and as he passed Trinity Church he wanted to stop, go inside, kneel and pray, and ask God to forgive him for the sins of the week. Confession and a hot bath were needed after five days of depositions.

FORTY-SIX

As a harried big-city professional, Nate had never been introduced to the ritual of sitting. Phil, on the other hand, was an accomplished practitioner. When a parishioner was ill, he was expected to visit and sit with the family. If there was a death, he would sit with the widow. If a neighbor stopped by, regardless of the time, he and Laura would sit and chat. Sometimes they practiced the art by themselves, on the porch, in the swing, alone. Two elderly gentlemen in his congregation expected Phil to stop by once a week and simply sit for an hour while they dozed by the fire. Conversation was nice, but not required. It was perfectly fine to just sit and enjoy the stillness.

But Nate caught on quickly. He sat with Phil on the front steps of the Stafford cottage, both men wearing heavy sweaters and gloves, and sipping hot cocoa Nate had prepared in the microwave. They gazed at the bay before them, at the harbor and the choppy waters beyond. Conversation crept up occasionally, but there was a lot of silence. Phil knew his friend had suffered a bad week. By now, Nate had told him most of the details of the Phelan mess. Theirs was a confidential relationship.

'I'm planning a road trip,' Nate announced quietly. 'Wanna come?'

'To where?'

'I need to see my kids. I have two younger ones, Austin and Angela, in Salem, Oregon. I'll probably go there first. My older son is a grad student at Northwestern in Evanston, and I have a daughter in Pittsburgh. It'll be a nice little tour.'

'How long?'

'There's no rush. A couple of weeks. I'm driving.'

'When did you see them last?'

'It's been over a year since I've seen Daniel and Kaitlin, the two from my first marriage. I took the two younger ones to an Orioles game last July. I got drunk and didn't remember driving back to Arlington.'

'Do you miss them?'

'Sure, I guess. Truth is, I never spent much time with them. I know so little about them.'

'You were working hard.'

'I was, and I was drinking even harder. I was never at home. On those rare occasions when I could take off, I would go to Vegas with the boys, or golfing or deep-sea fishing in the Bahamas. I never took the kids.'

'You can't change that.'

'No, I can't. Why don't you come with me? We could talk for hours.'

'Thanks, but I can't leave. I've finally built some momentum in the basement. I'd hate to lose it.'

Nate had seen the basement earlier in the day. There was evidence of momentum.

Phil's only child was a twenty-something drifter who'd flunked out of college and fled to the West Coast. Laura had let it slip that they had no idea where the kid was. He hadn't called home in over a year.

'Do you expect the trip to be successful?' Phil asked.

'I'm not sure what to expect. I want to hug my kids and apologize for being such a lousy father, but I'm not sure how that's supposed to help them now.'

'I wouldn't do that. They know you've been a lousy

413

father. Flogging yourself won't help. But it's important to be there, to take the first step in building new relationships.'

'I was such a miserable failure for my kids.'

'You can't beat yourself up, Nate. You're allowed to forget the past. God certainly has. Paul murdered Christians before he became one, and he didn't flail himself for what he'd been before. Everything is forgiven. Show your kids what you are now.'

A small fishing boat backed away from the harbor, and turned into the bay. It was the only blip on their screen, and they watched with rapt attention. Nate thought of Jevy and Welly, back on the river now, guiding a *chalana* loaded with produce and wares, the steady knock of the diesel pushing them deep into the Pantanal. Jevy would have the wheel, Welly would be strumming his guitar. All the world was at peace.

Later, long after Phil had gone home, Nate huddled by the fire and began another letter to Rachel. It was his third. He dated it, Saturday, February 22. 'Dear Rachel,' he began. 'I have just spent a very unpleasant week with your brothers and sisters.'

He talked about them, beginning with Troy Junior and ending three pages later with Ramble. He was honest about their shortcomings and the damage they would inflict on themselves and others if they got the money. And he was sympathetic too.

He was sending a check to World Tribes for five thousand dollars for a boat, a motor, and medical supplies. There was plenty more if she needed. The interest on her fortune was about two million dollars a day, he informed her, so a lot of good things could be done with the money.

Hark Gettys and his conspirators at law blundered badly when they terminated the services of Drs. Flowe, Zadel, and Theishen. The lawyers had rebuked

414

the doctors, and offended them, and caused irreparable damage.

The new batch of psychiatrists had the benefit of Snead's newly fabricated testimony upon which to create their opinions. Flowe, Zadel, and Theishen did not. When Nate deposed them Monday, he followed the same script with all three. He began with Zadel, and showed him the video of the examination of Mr. Phelan. He asked him if he had any reason to alter his opinions. Zadel, as expected, said no. The video happened before the suicide. The eight-page affidavit was prepared just hours afterward, at the insistence of Hark and the other Phelan lawyers. Zadel was asked by Nate to read the affidavit to the court reporter.

'Do you have any reason to change any of the opinions set out in that affidavit?' Nate asked.

'I do not,' Zadel said, looking at Hark.

'Today is February twenty-fourth, more than two months after your examination of Mr. Phelan. Is it your opinion today that he had sufficient mental capacity to execute a valid will?'

'It is,' Zadel answered, smiling at Hark.

Flowe and Theishen smiled too, each genuinely happy to turn the screws on the lawyers who'd hired them and fired them. Nate showed each of them the video, asked them the same questions, and received the same answers. Each read his affidavit into the record. They adjourned at four, Monday afternoon.

At eight-thirty sharp, Tuesday morning, Snead was escorted into the room and placed in the chair of honor. He wore a dark suit with a bow tie which gave him a brainy aura that was undeserved. The lawyers had carefully selected his wardrobe. They'd been molding and programming Snead for weeks, and the poor man doubted if he could utter a spontaneous or honest word. Every syllable had to be right. He had to project an air of confidence, yet avoid even the slightest hint of arrogance. He and he alone defined reality, and it was crucial that his stories were believable.

Josh had known Snead for many years. He was a servant whom Mr. Phelan often talked of getting rid of. Of the eleven wills Josh had prepared for Troy Phelan, only one mentioned the name of Malcolm Snead. A gift of a million dollars had been designated for him, a gift revoked months later with yet another will. Mr. Phelan had removed Snead's name precisely because Snead had inquired as to how much he might expect to receive.

Snead had been too preoccupied with the money to suit his master. His name on the witness list for the contestants meant only one thing – money. He was being paid to testify, and Josh knew it. Two weeks of simple surveillance had discovered a new Range Rover, a newly leased condo in a building where the prices started at eighteen hundred dollars a month, and a trip to Rome, first class.

Snead faced the video camera and was somewhat comfortable. He felt as though he'd been looking at one for a year. He'd spent all of Saturday and half of Sunday in Hark's office, getting himself grilled again. He'd watched the videos of himself for hours. He'd written dozens of pages of fiction on the final days of Troy Phelan. He'd rehearsed with Nicolette the bimbo.

Snead was ready. The lawyers had anticipated questions about the money. If asked whether he was being paid to testify, Snead was trained to lie. It was that simple. There was no way around it. Snead had to lie about the half a million bucks already in hand, and he had to lie about the promise of $4.5 million upon settlement or other favorable outcome. He had to lie about the existence of the contract between himself

416

and the lawyers. Since he was lying about Mr. Phelan he could certainly lie about the money.

Nate introduced himself and then asked, quite loudly, 'Mr. Snead, how much are you being paid to testify in this case?'

Snead's lawyers thought the question would be, 'Are you being paid?' not, 'How much?' Snead's rehearsed answer was a simple 'No, I certainly am not!' But to the question still ringing around the room he had no quick response. Hesitation sank him. He seemed to gasp as he looked wildly at Hark, whose spine had become rigid and his stare frozen like a deer's.

Snead had been warned that Mr. O'Riley had done his homework and seemed to know everything before he asked the questions. In the long painful seconds that followed, Mr. O'Riley frowned at him, cocked his head sideways, and lifted some papers.

'Come on, Mr. Snead, I know you're being paid. How much?'

Snead cracked his knuckles hard enough to break them. Beads of sweat popped out in the creases of his forehead. 'Well, I, uh, I'm not –'

'Come on, Mr. Snead. Did you or did you not purchase a new Range Rover last month?'

'Well, yes, as a matter of –'

'And you leased a two-bedroom condo at Palm Court?'

'Yes I did.'

'And you just returned from ten days in Rome, didn't you?'

'I did.'

He knew everything! The Phelan lawyers shrank in their seats, each cowering lower, ducking their heads so the ricocheting bullets wouldn't strike them.

'So how much are you being paid?' Nate asked angrily. 'Keep in mind you're under oath!'

'Five hundred thousand dollars,' Snead blurted out. Nate stared at him in disbelief, his jaw dropping slowly. Even the court reporter froze.

A couple of the Phelan lawyers managed to exhale, slightly. As horrible as the moment was, it could certainly have been bloodier. What if Snead had panicked even more and confessed to the entire five million?

But it was a very small comfort. At the moment, the news that they had paid a witness a half a million dollars seemed fatal to their cause.

Nate shuffled papers as if he needed some document. The words still echoed through all the ears in the room.

'I take it you have already received this money?' Nate asked.

Unsure whether he was supposed to lie or go straight, Snead simply said, 'Yes.'

On a hunch, Nate asked, 'Half a million now, how much later?'

Anxious to begin the lying, Snead answered, 'Nothing.' It was a casual denial, one that appeared believable. The other two Phelan lawyers were able to breathe.

'Are you sure about that?' Nate asked. He was fishing. He could ask Snead if he'd been convicted of grave-robbing if he wanted to.

It was a game of high-stakes chicken, and Snead held firm. 'Of course I'm sure,' he said with enough indignation to seem plausible.

'Who paid you this money?'

'The lawyers for the Phelan heirs.'

'Who signed the check?'

'It came from a bank, certified.'

'Did you insist they pay you for your testimony?'

'I guess you could say that.'

'Did you go to them, or did they come to you?'

418

'I went to them.'

'Why did you go to them?'

Finally, they seemed to be approaching familiar territory. There was a general relaxing on the Phelan side of the table. The lawyers began to scribble notes.

Snead crossed his legs under the table and frowned intelligently at the camera. 'Because I was with Mr. Phelan before he died, and I knew the poor man was out of his mind.'

'How long had he been out of his mind?'

'All day.'

'When he woke up, he was crazy?'

'When I fed him breakfast, he did not know my name.'

'What did he call you?'

'Nothing, he just grunted at me.'

Nate leaned on his elbows and ignored the paper-work around him. This was a jousting match, and he actually enjoyed it. He knew where he was going, but poor Snead did not.

'Did you see him jump?'

'Yes.'

'And fall?'

'Yes.'

'And hit the ground?'

'Yes.'

'Were you standing near him when he was examined by the three psychiatrists?'

'Yes.'

'And this was about two-thirty in the afternoon, right?'

'Yes, as I recall.'

'And he'd been crazy all day, right?'

'I'm afraid so, yes.'

'How long did you work for Mr. Phelan?'

'Thirty years.'

'And you knew everything about him, right?'

419

'As much as one person can know about another.'

'So you knew his lawyer, Mr. Stafford?'

'Yes, I'd met him many times.'

'Did Mr. Phelan trust Mr. Stafford?'

'I suppose.'

'I thought you knew everything.'

'I'm sure he trusted Mr. Stafford.'

'Was Mr. Stafford sitting by his side during the mental examination?'

'He was.'

'What was Mr. Phelan's mental state during the exam, in your opinion?'

'He was unsound, uncertain of where he was and what he was doing.'

'You're sure about this?'

'I am.'

'Who did you tell?'

'It wasn't my job to tell.'

'Why not?'

'I would've been fired. Part of my job was to keep my mouth shut. It's called discretion.'

'You knew Mr. Phelan was going to sign a will dividing his vast fortune. At the same time he was of unsound mind, yet you didn't tell his lawyer, a man he trusted?'

'It wasn't my job.'

'Mr. Phelan would've fired you?'

'Immediately.'

'Then what about after he jumped? Who did you tell then?'

'No one.'

'Why not?'

Snead took a breath and recrossed his legs. He was rallying nicely, he thought. 'It was a matter of privacy,' he said gravely. 'I considered my relationship with Mr. Phelan to be confidential.'

'Until now. Until they offered you half a million bucks, right?'

Snead could think of no quick reply, and Nate didn't offer much of a chance. 'You're selling not only your testimony but also your confidential relationship with Mr. Phelan, right, Mr. Snead?'

'I'm trying to undo an injustice.'

'How noble. Would you be undoing it if they weren't paying you?'

Snead managed to utter a shaky 'Yes,' and Nate erupted in laughter. He laughed loud and long and did so while looking at the solemn and partially hidden faces of the Phelan lawyers. He laughed directly at Snead. He stood and walked along his end of the table, chuckling to himself. 'What a trial,' he said, then sat down again.

He glanced at some notes, then continued, 'Mr. Phelan died on December the ninth. His will was read on December the twenty-seventh. During the interval, did you tell anyone that he was of unsound mind when he signed his will?'

'No.'

'Of course not. You waited until after the will was read, then, realizing you had been cut out, decided to go to the lawyers and strike a deal, didn't you, Mr. Snead?'

The witness answered, 'No,' but Nate ignored him.

'Was Mr. Phelan mentally ill?'

'I'm not an expert in that field.'

'You said he was out of his mind. Was this a permanent condition?'

'It came and went.'

'How long had it been coming and going?'

'For years.'

'How many years?'

'Ten maybe. It's just a guess.'

'In the last fourteen years of his life, Mr. Phelan

421

executed eleven wills, one of which left you a million dollars. Did you ever think of telling anyone then that he was of unsound mind?'

'It wasn't my job to tell.'

'Did he ever see a psychiatrist?'

'Not to my knowledge.'

'Did he ever see any mental health professional?'

'Not to my knowledge.'

'Did you ever suggest to him that he seek professional help?'

'It wasn't my job to suggest such things.'

'If you'd found him lying on the floor having a seizure would you have suggested to someone that perhaps he needed help?'

'Of course I would have.'

'If you'd found him coughing blood, would you have told someone?'

'Yes.'

Nate had a memo two inches thick with summaries of Mr. Phelan's holdings. He flipped to a page at random and asked Snead if he knew anything about Xion Drilling. Snead struggled mightily to remember, but his mind had been so overloaded with new data that it failed him. Delstar Communications? Again, Snead grimaced but could not make the connection.

The fifth company Nate mentioned rang a bell. Snead proudly informed the lawyer that he knew the company. Mr. Phelan had owned it for quite some time. Nate had questions about sales, products, holdings, earnings, an endless list of financial statistics. Snead answered nothing right.

'How much did you know about Mr. Phelan's holdings?' Nate asked repeatedly. Then he asked questions about the structure of The Phelan Group. Snead had memorized the basics, but the smaller details escaped him. He could name no mid-level manager. He did not know the name of the company's accountants.

Nate hammered him relentlessly about the things he didn't know. Late in the afternoon, with Snead weary and punch-drunk, Nate, in the midst of the millionth question about financials, asked, with no warning, 'Did you sign a contract with the lawyers when you took the half a million?'

A simple 'No' would have sufficed, but Snead was caught off guard. He hesitated, looked at Hark then looked at Nate, who was again shuffling through papers as if he had a copy of the contract. Snead hadn't lied in two hours, and wasn't quick.

'Uh, of course not,' he stuttered, and convinced no one.

Nate saw the untruth, and let it go. There were other ways to obtain a copy of the contract.

The Phelan lawyers met in a dark bar to lick their wounds. Snead's dismal performance seemed even worse after two rounds of stiff drinks. He could be propped up some for trial, but the fact that he'd been paid so much would forever taint his testimony.

How did O'Riley know? He was so certain Snead had been paid.

'It was Grit,' Hark said. Grit, they all repeated to themselves. Surely Grit hadn't gone to the other side.

'That's what you get for stealing his client,' Wally Bright said after a long silence.

'Shut up,' Ms. Langhorne said.

Hark was too tired to fight. He finished his drink and ordered another. In the flood of testimony, the other Phelan lawyers had forgotten about Rachel. There was still no official record of her in the court file.

FORTY-SEVEN

The deposition of Nicolette the secretary lasted eight
minutes. She gave her name, address, and brief
employment history, and the Phelan lawyers on the
other side settled into their chairs to await the details
of her sexual escapades with Mr. Phelan. She was
twenty-three, with few qualifications beyond a slender
body, nice chest, and a pretty face with sandy blond
hair. They couldn't wait to hear her spend a few hours
talking about sex.

Getting right to the point, Nate asked, 'Did you
ever have sex with Mr. Phelan?'

She tried to appear embarrassed by the question,
but said yes anyway.

'How many times?'

'I didn't count them.'

'For how long?'

'Usually ten minutes.'

'No, I mean for how long a period of time. Starting
in what month and ending when?'

'Oh, I only worked there five months.'

'Roughly twenty weeks. On the average, how many
times each week did you have sex with Mr. Phelan?'

'Two times I guess.'

'So about forty times?'

'I guess. That sounds like a lot, doesn't it?'

'Not to me. Did Mr. Phelan take his clothes off when you guys did it?'

'Sure. We both did.'

'So he was completely naked?'

'Yes.'

'Did he have any visible birthmarks on his body?'

When witnesses concoct lies, they often miss the obvious. So do their lawyers. They become so consumed with their fiction that they overlook a fact or two. Hark and the guys had access to the Phelan wives – Lillian, Janie, Tira – any one of whom could have told them that Troy had a round purple birthmark the size of a silver dollar at the very top of his right leg, near the hip, just below the waist.

'Not that I recall,' Nicolette answered.

The answer surprised Nate, and then it didn't. He could've easily believed that Troy was doing his secretary, something he'd done for decades. And he could just as easily have believed Nicolette was lying.

'No visible birthmarks?' Nate asked again.

'None.'

The Phelan lawyers were stricken with fear. Could another star witness be melting before their eyes?

'No further questions,' Nate said, and left the room to refill his coffee.

Nicolette looked at the lawyers. They were staring at the table, wondering exactly where the birthmark was.

After she left, Nate slid an autopsy photo across the table to his bewildered enemies. He didn't say a word, didn't need to. Old Troy was on the slab, nothing but withered and battered flesh with the birthmark staring out from the photo.

They spent the rest of Wednesday and all day Thursday with the four new psychiatrists who'd been hired to say that the three old ones really didn't know what they were doing. Their testimony was predictable and repetitive – people with sound minds do not jump out of windows.

As a group they were less distinguished than Flowe, Zadel, and Theishen. A couple were retired and picked up a few retainers here and there as professional testifiers. One taught at a crowded community college. One eked out a living in a small office in the suburbs.

But they weren't paid to be impressive; rather, their purpose was simply to muddy the water. Troy Phelan was known to be erratic and eccentric. Four experts said he didn't have the mental capacity to execute a will. Three said he did. Keep the issues dense and tangled and hope those supporting the will would one day grow weary and settle. If not, it would be up to a jury of laymen to sift through the medical jargon and make sense of the conflicting opinions.

The new experts were paid well to stick to their convictions, and Nate didn't try to change them. He had deposed enough doctors to know not to argue medicine with them. Instead, he dwelt on their credentials and experience. He made them watch the video and criticize the first three psychiatrists.

When they adjourned Thursday afternoon, fifteen depositions had been completed. Another round was scheduled for late March. Wycliff was planning a trial for the middle of July. The same witnesses would testify again, but in open court with spectators watching and jurors weighing every word.

Nate fled the city. He went west through Virginia, then south through the Shenandoah Valley. His mind was numb from nine days of hardball probing into the intimate lives of others. At some undefined point in his life, pushed by his work and his addictions, he had lost his decency and shame. He had learned to lie, cheat, deceive, hide, badger, and attack innocent witnesses without the slightest twinge of guilt.

But in the quiet of his car and the darkness of the night, Nate was ashamed. He had pity for the Phelan children. He felt sorry for Snead, a sad little man just trying to survive. He wished he hadn't attacked the new experts with such vigor.

His shame was back, and Nate was pleased. He was proud of himself for feeling so ashamed. He was human after all.

At midnight, he stopped at a cheap motel near Knoxville. There was heavy snow in the Midwest, in Kansas and Iowa. Lying in bed with his atlas, he mapped a trail through the Southwest.

He slept the second night in Shawnee, Oklahoma; the third in Kingman, Arizona; the fourth in Redding, California.

The kids from his second marriage were Austin and Angela, twelve and eleven respectively, seventh and sixth grades. He'd last seen them in July, three weeks before the last crash, when he took them to an Orioles game. The pleasant outing later turned into another ugly scene. Nate had drunk six beers at the game – the kids counted because their mother told them to – and he drove the two hours from Baltimore to Arlington under the influence.

At the time, they were moving to Oregon with their mother, Christi, and her second husband, Theo. The game was to be Nate's last visit with them for some time, and instead of dwelling on good-byes Nate got plastered. He fought with his ex-wife in the driveway while the children watched, all too familiar with the scene. Theo had threatened him with a broom handle. Nate woke up in his car, parked in the handicapped zone of a McDonald's, an empty six-pack on the seat.

When they met fourteen years earlier, Christi was

the headmistress of a private school in Potomac. She was on a jury. Nate was one of the lawyers. She wore a short black skirt on the second day of the trial, and the litigation practically stopped. Their first date was a week later. For three years Nate stayed clean, long enough to get remarried and have the two kids. When the dam started cracking, Christi was scared and wanted to run. When it burst, she fled with the children and didn't return for a year. The marriage endured ten chaotic years.

She was working at a school in Salem. Theo was with a small law firm there. Nate had always believed that he ran them out of Washington. He couldn't blame them for fleeing to the other coast.

He called the school from his car near Medford, four hours away, and was put on hold for five minutes; time, he was certain, for her to lock her door and collect her thoughts. 'Hello,' she finally said.

'Christi, it's me, Nate,' he said, feeling silly identifying his voice to a woman he'd lived with for ten years.

'Where are you?' she asked, as if an attack were imminent.

'Near Medford.'

'In Oregon?'

'Yes. I'd like to see the kids.'

'Well, when?'

'Tonight, tomorrow, I'm in no hurry. I've been on the road for a few days, just seeing the country. I have no itinerary.'

'Well, sure, Nate. I guess we can work something out. But the kids are very busy, you know, school, ballet, soccer.'

'How are they?'

'They're doing very well. Thanks for asking.'

'And you? How's life treating you?'

'I'm fine. We love Oregon.'

'I'm doing well too. Thanks for asking. I'm clean

428

and sober, Christi, really. I've finally kicked the booze and drugs for good. Looks like I'll be leaving the practice of law, but I'm doing really well.'

She'd heard it before. 'That's good, Nate.' Her words were cautious. She was planning two sentences in advance.

They agreed to have dinner the following night, enough time for her to prepare the kids and fix up the house and allow Theo to decide what his role should be. Enough time to rehearse and plan exits.

'I won't get in the way,' Nate promised, before hanging up.

Theo decided to work late and skip the reunion. Nate hugged Angela tightly. Austin just shook hands. The one thing he vowed not to do was gush about how much they'd grown. Christi loitered in her bedroom for an hour as the father was reintroduced to his children.

Nor would he bury them with apologies about things he couldn't change. They sat on the floor of the den and talked about school, and ballet, and soccer. Salem was a pretty town, much smaller than D.C., and the kids had adjusted well, with lots of friends, a good school, nice teachers.

Dinner was spaghetti and salad, and it lasted for one hour. Nate told tales from the jungles of Brazil as he took them on his journey to find the missing client. Evidently, Christi had not seen the right newspapers. She knew nothing of the Phelan matter.

At seven sharp, he said he had to go. They had homework, and school came early. 'I have a soccer game tomorrow, Dad,' Austin said, and Nate's heart almost stopped. He couldn't remember the last time he'd been called Dad.

'It's at the school,' Angela said. 'Could you come?'

The little ex-family shared an awkward moment as

each of them glanced at the other. Nate had no idea what to say.

Christi settled the issue by saying, 'I'll be there. We could talk.'

'Of course I'll be there,' he said. The children hugged him as he left. Driving away, Nate suspected Christi wanted to see him two days in a row to examine his eyes. She knew the signs.

Nate stayed in Salem for three days. He watched the soccer game and was overcome with pride in his son. He got himself invited back to dinner, but agreed to come only if Theo would join them. He had lunch with Angela and her friends at school.

After three days, it was time to leave. The kids needed their normal routines back, without the complications Nate brought. Christi was tired of pretending nothing had ever happened between them. And Nate was getting attached to his children. He promised to call and e-mail and see them soon.

He left Salem with a broken heart. How low could a man sink to lose such a wonderful family? He remembered almost nothing of his kids when they were smaller – no school plays, Halloween costumes, Christmas mornings, trips to the mall. Now they were practically grown, and another man was raising them.

He turned east, and drifted with the traffic.

While Nate was meandering through Montana, thinking of Rachel, Hark Gettys filed a motion to dismiss her answer to the will contest. His reasons were clear and obvious, and he supported his attack with a twenty-page brief he'd worked on for a month. It was March 7, almost three months after the death of Mr. Phelan, not quite two months after the entry of Nate O'Riley into the matter, nearly three weeks into discovery, four months before the trial, and the court still did not have jurisdiction over Rachel Lane. But

430

for the allegations of her attorney, there'd been no sign of her. No document in the official court file had her signature on it.

Hark referred to her as the 'phantom party.' He and the other contestants were litigating against a shadow. The woman stood to inherit eleven billion dollars. The least she could do was sign a waiver and follow the law. If she'd gone to the trouble to hire a lawyer, she could certainly subject herself to the jurisdiction of the court.

The passage of time was benefiting the heirs greatly, though it was hard for them to be patient while dreaming of such wealth. Each week that passed with no word from Rachel was further proof that she had no interest in the proceedings. At the Friday morning meetings, the Phelan lawyers reviewed discovery, talked about their clients, and plotted trial strategy. But they spent most of their time speculating why Rachel had not made an official appearance. They were enthralled with the ridiculous notion that she might not want the money. It was absurd, yet it somehow managed to surface every Friday morning.

The weeks were turning into months. The lottery winner was not claiming her prize.

There was another significant reason for putting pressure on the defenders of Troy's testament. His name was Snead. Hark, Yancy, Bright, and Langhorne had watched their star witness's deposition until it was memorized, and they were not confident of his ability to sway jurors. Nate O'Riley had made a fool out of him, and that was only in a deposition. Imagine how sharp the daggers would be at trial, in front of a jury made up primarily of middle-class folks struggling to pay their monthly bills. Snead pocketed a half a million to tell his story. It would be a hard sell.

The problem with Snead was obvious. He was lying, and liars eventually get caught in court. After Snead stumbled so badly in the deposition, the lawyers were terrified of presenting him to a jury. Another lie or two exposed to the world, and their case was down the toilet.

The birthmark had rendered Nicolette completely useless as a witness.

Their own clients were not particularly sympathetic. With the exception of Ramble, who was the scariest of all, each had been handed five million dollars with which to get a start. None of the jurors would earn that much in a lifetime. Troy's children could whine about being raised by an absent father, but half the jurors would be from broken homes.

The battle of the shrinks would be hard to call, but it was the segment of the trial that worried them the most. Nate O'Riley had been shredding doctors in courtrooms for more than twenty years. Their four substitutes could not withstand his brutal cross-examinations.

To avoid a trial, they had to settle. To settle, they had to find a weakness. Rachel Lane's apparent lack of interest was more than sufficient, and certainly their best shot.

Josh reviewed the Motion to Dismiss with admiration. He loved the legal maneuvering, the ploys and tactics, and when someone, even an opponent, got it right, he silently applauded. Everything about Hark's move was perfect – the timing, the rationale, the superbly argued brief.

The contestants had a weak case, but their problems were small compared to Nate's. Nate had no client. He and Josh had managed to keep this quiet for two months, but the ruse had run its course.

FORTY-EIGHT

Daniel, his oldest child, insisted on meeting him in a pub. Nate found the place after dark, two blocks off the campus, on a street lined with bars and clubs. The music, the flashing beer signs, the co-eds yelling across the street – it was all too familiar. It was Georgetown just a few months ago, and none of it appealed to him. A year earlier he would've been yelling back, chasing them from one bar to the other, believing he was still twenty and able to go all night.

Daniel was waiting in a cramped booth, along with a girl. Both were smoking. Each had two longneck bottles sitting on the table in front of them. Father and son shook hands because anything more affectionate would make the son feel uncomfortable.

'This is Stef,' Daniel said, introducing the girl. 'She's a model,' he added quickly, proving to his old man that he was chasing a high caliber of woman.

For some reason, Nate had hoped they could spend a few hours alone. It was not going to happen.

The first thing he noticed about Stef was her gray lipstick, applied heavily to the thick and pouty lips, lips that scarcely cracked when she gave him the obligatory half-smile. She was certainly plain and gaunt enough to be a model. Her arms were as skinny as broom handles. Though Nate couldn't see them, he knew her bony legs ran to her armpits, and without a doubt there were at least two tattoos burned into the flesh around her ankles.

Nate disliked her immediately, and got the impression the feeling was mutual. No telling what Daniel had told her.

Daniel had finished college at Grinnell a year earlier, then spent the summer in India. Nate had not seen him in thirteen months. He had not gone to his commencement, had not sent a card or a gift, had not bothered to call with congratulations. There was enough tension at the table without the mannequin puffing smoke and looking at Nate with a completely blank stare.

'You wanna beer?' Daniel asked when a waiter got close. It was a cruel question, a quick little shot designed to inflict pain.

'No, just water,' Nate said. Daniel yelled at the waiter, then said, 'Still on the wagon, huh?'

'Always,' Nate said with a smile, trying to deflect the arrows.

'Have you fallen off since last summer?'

'No. Let's talk about something else.'

'Dan tells me you've been through rehab,' Stef said, smoke drifting from her nostrils. Nate was surprised she was able to start and finish a sentence. Her words were slow, her voice as hollow as her eye sockets.

'I have, several times. What else has he told you?'

'I've done rehab,' she said. 'But only once.' She seemed proud of her accomplishment, yet saddened by her lack of experience. The two beer bottles in front of her were empty.

'That's nice,' Nate said, dismissing her. He couldn't pretend to like her, and in a month or two she'd have another serious love.

'How's school?' he asked Daniel.

'What school?'

'Grad school.'

'I dropped out.' His words were edgy and strained. There was pressure behind them. Nate was involved in the dropping out; he just wasn't exactly sure how and why. His water arrived. 'Have you guys eaten?' he asked.

Stef avoided food and Daniel wasn't hungry. Nate was starving but didn't want to eat alone. He glanced around the pub. Pot was being smoked somewhere in another corner. It was a rowdy little dump, the kind of place he'd loved in a not too distant life.

Daniel lit another cigarette, a Camel with no filter, the worst cancer sticks on the market, and he blasted a cloud of thick smoke at the cheap beer chandelier hanging above them. He was angry and tense.

The girl was there for two reasons. She would prevent harsh words and maybe a fight. Nate suspected his son was broke, that he wanted to lash out at his father for his lack of support, but that he was afraid to do so because the old man was fragile and had been prone to crack and go off the deep end. Stef would throttle his anger and his language.

The second reason was to make the meeting as brief as possible.

It took about fifteen minutes to figure this out.

'How's your mother?' he asked.

Daniel attempted to smile. 'She's fine. I saw her Christmas. You were gone.'

'I was in Brazil.'

A co-ed in tight jeans walked by. Stef inspected her from top to bottom, her eyes finally showing some life. The girl was even skinnier than Stef. How did emaciation become so cool?

'What's in Brazil?' Daniel asked.

'A client.' Nate was tired of the stories from his adventure.

'Mom says you're in some kind of trouble with the IRS.'

435

'I'm sure that pleases your mother.'

'I guess. She didn't seem bothered by it. You going to jail?'

'No. Could we talk about something else?'

'That's the problem, Dad. There is nothing else, nothing but the past and we can't go there.'

Stef, the referee, rolled her eyes at Daniel, as if to say, 'That's enough.'

'Why did you drop out of school?' Nate asked, anxious to get it over with.

'Several reasons. It got boring.'

'He ran out of money,' Stef said, helpfully. She gave Nate her best blank look.

'Is that true?' Nate asked.

'That's one reason.'

Nate's first instinct was to pull out his checkbook and solve the kid's problems. That's what he'd always done. Parenting for him had been one long shopping trip. If you can't be there, send money. But Daniel was now twenty-three, a college grad, hanging around with the likes of Ms. Bulimia over there, and it was time for him to sink or swim on his own.

And the checkbook wasn't what it used to be.

'It's good for you,' Nate said. 'Work for a while. It'll make you appreciate school.'

Stef disagreed. She had two friends who'd dropped out and pretty much fallen off the face of the earth. As she prattled on, Daniel withdrew to his corner of the booth. He drained his third bottle. Nate had all sorts of lectures about alcohol, but he knew how phony they'd sound.

After four beers, Stef was bombed and Nate had nothing else to say. He scribbled his phone number in St. Michaels on a napkin and gave it to Daniel. 'This is where I'll be for the next couple of months. Call me if you need me.'

'See you, Pop,' Daniel said.

'Take care.'

Nate stepped into the frigid air and walked toward Lake Michigan.

Two days later he was in Pittsburgh for his third and final reunion, one that did not occur. He'd spoken twice to Kaitlin, his daughter from marriage number one, and the details were clear. She was to meet him for dinner at 7:30 P.M., in front of the restaurant in the lobby of his hotel. Her apartment was twenty minutes away. She paged him at 8:30 with the news that a friend had been involved in an auto accident, and that she was at the hospital where things looked bad.

Nate suggested they have lunch the following day. Kaitlin said that wouldn't work because the friend had a head injury, was on life support, and she planned to stay with her there until she was stable. With his daughter in full retreat, Nate asked where the hospital was located. At first she didn't know, then she wasn't sure, then upon further thought a visit was not a good idea because she couldn't leave the bedside.

He ate in his room, at a small table next to the window, with a view of downtown. He picked at his food and thought of all the possible reasons his daughter didn't want to see him. A ring in her nose? A tattoo on her forehead? Had she joined a cult and shaved her head? Had she gained a hundred pounds or lost fifty? Was she pregnant?

He tried to blame her so he wouldn't be forced to face the obvious. Did she hate him that much?

In the loneliness of the hotel room, in a city where he knew no one, it was easy to pity himself, to suffer once again through the mistakes of his past.

He grabbed the phone and got busy. He called Father Phil to check on things in St. Michaels. Phil had been bothered by the flu, and since it was chilly in the church basement Laura wouldn't let him work

437

there. How wonderful, thought Nate. Though many uncertainties lay in his path, the one constant, at least for the near future, would be the promise of steady work in the basement of Trinity Church.

He called Sergio for their weekly pep session. The demons were well in hand, and he felt surprisingly under control. His hotel room had a mini-bar, and he had not been near it.

He called Salem and had a pleasant chat with Angela and Austin. Odd how the younger kids wanted to talk while the older ones did not.

He called Josh, who was in his basement office, thinking about the Phelan mess. 'You need to come home, Nate,' he said. 'I have a plan.'

FORTY-NINE

Nate wasn't invited to the first round of peace talks. There were a couple of reasons for his absence. First, Josh arranged the summit, so it was therefore held on his turf. Nate had thus far avoided his old office and wanted this to continue. Second, the Phelan lawyers viewed Josh and Nate as allies, and rightfully so. Josh wanted the role of peacemaker, the intermediary. To gain trust from one side, he had to ignore the other, if only for a short while. His plan was to meet with Hark et al., then with Nate, then back and forth for a few days if necessary until a deal was struck.

After a lengthy session of pleasantries and chitchat, Josh asked for their attention. They had lots of territory to cover. The Phelan lawyers were anxious to get started.

A settlement can happen in seconds, during a recess in a heated trial when a witness stumbles, or when a new CEO wants to start fresh and unload nagging litigation. And a settlement can take months, as the lawsuit inches toward a trial date. As a whole, the Phelan lawyers dreamed of a quickie, and the meeting in Josh's suite was the first step. They truly believed they were about to become millionaires.

Josh began by diplomatically offering his opinion that their case was rather flimsy. He knew nothing about his client's plans to whip out a holographic will

439

and create chaos, but it was a valid will nonetheless. He had spent two hours with Mr. Phelan the previous day finishing the other new will, and he was prepared to testify that he knew exactly what he was doing. He would also testify, if necessary, that Snead was nowhere in the picture when they met.

The three psychiatrists who examined Mr. Phelan had been carefully chosen by Phelan's children and ex-wives, and their lawyers, and had impeccable credentials. The four now on retainer were flaky. Their résumés were thin. The battle of the experts would be won by the original three, in his opinion.

Wally Bright had on his best suit, which wasn't saying much. He took this criticism with a clenched jaw, bottom lip between his teeth so he wouldn't say something stupid, and he took useless notes on a legal pad because that's what everybody else was doing. It was not his nature to sit back and accept such disparagement, even from a renowned lawyer like Josh Stafford. But he would do anything for the money. The month before, February, his little office generated twenty-six hundred dollars in fees, and consumed the usual four thousand in overhead. Wally took home nothing. Of course, most of his time had been spent on the Phelan matter.

Josh skated onto thin ice when he summarized the testimony of their clients. 'I've watched the videos of their depositions,' he said sadly. 'Frankly, with the exception of Mary Ross, I think they will make terrible witnesses at trial.'

Their lawyers took this in stride. This was a settlement conference, not a trial.

He didn't dwell on the heirs. The less said the better. Their lawyers knew they would get butchered before the jury.

'That brings us to Snead,' he said. 'I've watched his deposition too, and, frankly, if you call him as a

440

witness at trial it will be a terrible mistake. In my opinion, in fact, it will border on legal malpractice.'

Bright, Hark, Langhorne, and Yancy huddled even closer over their legal pads. Snead was a dirty word among them. They'd fought over who was to blame for botching it so badly. They'd lost sleep fretting over the man. They were half a million down, and as a witness he was worthless.

'I've known Snead for almost twenty years,' Josh said, then spent fifteen minutes effectively portraying him as a butler of marginal talents, a gofer who was not always reliable, a servant Mr. Phelan often talked of firing. They believed every word of it.

So much for Snead. Josh managed to gut their star witness without even mentioning the fact that he'd been bribed with five hundred thousand dollars to tell his story.

And so much for Nicolette too. She was lying along with her buddy Snead.

They had been unable to locate other witnesses. There were some disgruntled employees, but they wanted no part of a trial. Their testimony was tainted anyway. There were two rivals from the business world who'd been wiped out trying to compete with Troy. But they knew nothing about his mental capacity.

Their case was not very strong, Josh concluded. But everything's risky with a jury.

He talked about Rachel Lane as if he'd known her for years. Not too many specifics, but enough general-izations to convey the impression that Josh knew her well. She was a lovely lady who lived a very simple life, in another country, and was not the type of person who understood litigation. She ran from controversy. She despised confrontation. And she'd been closer to old Troy than most people knew.

Hark wanted to ask if Josh had ever met her. Ever seen her? Ever heard her name before he read the will?

441

But it was neither the time nor the place for discord. Money was about to be laid upon the table, and Hark's percentage was seventeen point five.

Ms. Langhorne had researched the town of Corumbá, and was wondering again what an American woman, age forty-two, could possibly be doing in such a place. She and Hark, behind the backs of Bright and Yancy, had quietly become confidants. They had talked at length about leaking the whereabouts of Rachel Lane to certain reporters. The press would certainly find her down there, in Corumbá. They'd smoke her out, and in the process the world would learn what she planned to do with the money. If, as they hoped and dreamed, she didn't want it, then their clients could press for all the money.

It was a risk, and they were still talking about it.

'What does Rachel Lane plan to do with all this money?' Yancy asked.

'I'm not sure,' Josh said, as if he and Rachel discussed it every day. 'She'll probably keep a little, and give most of it to charity. In my opinion, that's why Troy did what he did. He figured that if your clients got the money, it wouldn't last ninety days. By leaving it to Rachel, he knew it would be passed on to those in need.'

There was a long pause in the conversation when Josh finished with this. Dreams slowly crumbled. Rachel Lane indeed existed, and she was not going to decline the money.

'Why hasn't she made an appearance?' Hark finally asked.

'Well, you have to know this woman to answer that question. Money means nothing to her. She did not expect to be named in her father's will. Then, suddenly, she finds out that she has inherited billions. She's still in shock.'

Another long pause as the Phelan lawyers doodled

442

on their pads. 'We are prepared to litigate to the Supreme Court, if necessary,' Langhorne said. 'Does she realize this could take years?'

'She does,' Josh replied. 'And that's one reason she would like to explore settlement possibilities.'

Now they were making progress.

'Where do we start?' asked Wally Bright.

It was a difficult question. On one side of the table was a pot of gold worth eleven billion or so. Estate taxes would take more than half, leaving five to play with. On the other side were the Phelan heirs, all of whom were broke with the exception of Ramble. Who would throw out the first figure? How much would it be? Ten million per heir? Or a hundred?

Josh had it planned. 'Let's start with the will,' he said. 'Assuming it's held to be valid, it contains clear language terminating any gift to any heir who challenges it. That would apply to your clients. Therefore, you start from a position of zero. Then, the will gives to each of your clients a sum of money equal to their debts as of the day of Mr. Phelan's death.' Josh lifted another sheet of paper and studied it for a second. 'According to what we've learned so far, Ramble Phelan has no debts, yet. Geena Phelan Strong had debts of four hundred twenty thousand on December ninth. Libbigail and Spike had debts of around eighty thousand. Mary Ross and her doctor husband had debts of nine hundred thousand. Troy Junior had discharged most of his in one bankruptcy or another, but still owed a hundred and thirty thousand. Rex, as we know, wins the prize. He and his lovely wife Amber owed, on December ninth, a total of seven point six million dollars. Any problem with these numbers?'

No. The numbers were accurate. It was the next number that concerned them.

'Nate O'Riley has been in contact with his client.

To settle this matter, she will offer each of the six heirs ten million dollars.'

The lawyers had never calculated and scribbled so fast. Hark had three clients; 17.5 percent gave him a fee of $5.25 million. Geena and Cody had agreed on a 20 percent cut for Langhorne, so her little firm would collect $2 million. Same for Yancy, subject to court approval because Ramble was still a minor. And Wally Bright, a street hustler who scratched out a living by advertising quickie divorces on bus benches, would collect half of the $10 million under his unconscionable contract with Libbigail and Spike.

Wally reacted first. Though his heart was frozen and his esophagus clamped shut, he managed to say, with some measure of brass, 'No way my client will settle for less than fifty million.'

The others shook their heads too. They frowned and tried to appear disgusted with the paltry sum being offered, while in fact they were already spending the money.

Wally Bright couldn't write fifty million and get the zeros in the correct places. But he managed to throw the figure out like a Vegas high-roller.

They had agreed before the meeting that if money was discussed, they would go no lower than fifty million per heir. This sounded fine, before the meeting. Now, the ten million on the table looked awfully good.

'That's about one percent of the estate,' Hark said.

'You can look at it that way,' Josh said. 'In fact, there are many ways to look at it. But I prefer to start at zero, which is where you are now, and work up, rather than look at the entire estate and work down.'

But Josh also wanted their trust. They kicked the numbers around for a while, then he said, 'No, personally, if I represented one of the heirs, I wouldn't take ten million.'

They froze and listened intently.

'She is not a greedy woman. I think Nate O'Riley could convince her to settle at twenty million per heir.'

The fees doubled – over ten million for Hark. Four million for Langhorne and Yancy. Poor Wally, at ten now, was suddenly struck with diarrhea and asked to leave the meeting.

Nate was happy and busy painting door trim when his cell phone buzzed. Josh made him keep the damned thing within reach.

'If it's for me, take a number,' Father Phil said. He was measuring a complicated corner for the next piece of wallboard.

It was Josh. 'It couldn't have gone better,' he announced. 'I stopped at twenty million, they want fifty.'

'Fifty?' Nate said in disbelief.

'Yeah, but they're already spending the money. I'll bet at least two of them are at the Mercedes dealer right now.'

'Who'll spend it faster? Lawyers or clients?'

'I'd bet on the lawyers. Look, I just talked to Wycliff. The meeting is for Wednesday at three, in his office. We should wrap it up by then.'

'I can't wait,' Nate said, and folded the phone. Time for a coffee break. They sat on the floor, backs to a wall, and sipped warm latte.

'They wanted fifty?' Phil asked. By now, he knew the details. Alone in the basement, the two had kept few secrets as they drifted through their labors. Conversation was more important than progress. Phil was clergy. Nate was a lawyer. Everything said was covered by some manner of confidential privilege.

'It's a nice starting place,' Nate said. 'But they'll take a lot less.'

'You expect it to be settled?'

445

'Sure. We'll meet on Wednesday with the Judge. He'll apply more pressure. By then the lawyers and their clients will be counting the money.'

'So when do you leave?'

'Friday, I guess. You wanna come?'

'I can't afford it.'

'Sure you can. My client will foot the bill. You can be my spiritual adviser for the trip. Money is no object.'

'It wouldn't be right.'

'Come on, Phil. I'll show you the Pantanal. You can meet my pals Jevy and Welly. We'll go for a boat ride.'

'You haven't made it sound very appealing.'

'It's not dangerous. There's quite a tourist business in the Pantanal. It's a great ecological preserve. Seriously, Phil, if you're interested I can make it happen.'

'I don't have a passport,' he said and sipped his coffee. 'Plus I have so much work to do here.'

Nate would be gone for a week, and he somehow liked the fact that the basement would look the same when he returned.

'Mrs. Sinclair is expected to die any day now,' Phil said quietly. 'I can't be gone.'

The church had been waiting for Mrs. Sinclair to die for at least a month. Phil was fearful about a trip to Baltimore. Nate knew he would never leave the country.

'So you're gonna see her again,' Phil said.

'Yes, I am.'

'Are you excited?'

'I don't know. I look forward to seeing her, but I'm not sure she wants to see me. She's very happy and wants no part of this world. She will resent more of the legal stuff.'

'Then why do it?'

'Because there's nothing to lose. If she rejects the

446

money again, we're in the same position as now. The other side gets everything.'

'And that's a disaster.'

'Yes. It would be difficult to find a group of people less equipped to handle serious money than the Phelan heirs. They'll kill themselves with it.'

'Can't you explain this to Rachel?'

'I tried. She has no interest in hearing it.'

'So she's not going to change her mind?'

'No. Never.'

'And the trip down is a waste of time?'

'I'm afraid so. But at least we'll try.'

FIFTY

With the exception of Ramble, all of the Phelan heirs insisted on being either in the courthouse or within a rock's throw during the meeting. Each had a cell phone, as did each lawyer inside Wycliff's office.

Much sleep had been lost by the clients and their lawyers.

How often does one become an instant millionaire? At least twice for the Phelan heirs, and they vowed to themselves that they would be much wiser this time around. They would never get another chance.

They walked the hallways of the courthouse, waiting. They smoked outside by the front doors. They kept warm in their cars in the parking lot, fidgeting. They checked their watches, tried to read newspapers, chatted nervously when they bumped into each other.

Nate and Josh sat on one side of the room. Josh of course wore an expensive dark suit. Nate wore a denim shirt with specks of white paint on the collar. No tie. Jeans and hiking boots rounded out his ensemble.

Wycliff first addressed the Phelan lawyers across the room. He informed them that he was not inclined to dismiss the answer of Rachel Lane, at least not at that time. There was too much at stake to cut her from the proceedings. Mr. O'Riley was doing a fine job of representing her interests; therefore the lawsuit would proceed as scheduled.

The purpose of the meeting was to explore settlement, something every judge wanted for every case. Wycliff was still enthralled with the vision of a long, nasty, high-profile trial, but he could never admit it. It was his duty to push, prod, and cajole the parties into a settlement.

Prodding and cajoling would not be necessary.

His Honor had reviewed all the pleadings and documents, and he'd watched every minute of every deposition. He recapped the evidence as he viewed things, and offered the grave conclusion to Hark, Bright, Langhorne, and Yancy that, in his learned opinion, they didn't have much of a case.

They took it well. It came as no surprise. Money was on the table and they were anxious to get to it. Insult us all you want, they said to themselves, but let's hurry along to the money.

On the other hand, Wycliff was saying, you never know what a jury will do. He spoke as if he empaneled juries every week, which he did not. And the lawyers knew it.

He asked Josh to recap the initial settlement conference of Monday, two days earlier. 'I want to know exactly where we are,' he said.

Josh was brief. The bottom line was simple. The heirs wanted fifty million dollars each. Rachel, the sole major beneficiary, was offering twenty million only to settle, without admitting the other side had a valid case.

'That's a substantial gap,' Wycliff observed.

Nate was bored but tried to appear sharp. These were high-powered settlement negotiations involving one of the greatest self-made fortunes in the world. Josh had scolded him for his appearance. He didn't care. He kept himself interested by watching the faces of the lawyers across the room. They were an edgy bunch, not anxious or worried, but animated and desperate to learn how much they would be getting. Their eyes were keen and quick; their hand movements impulsive.

How much fun it would be to abruptly stand, announce Rachel wasn't offering a dime to settle, and storm out of the room. They would sit in shock for a few seconds, then they would chase him like hungry dogs.

When Josh finished, Hark spoke for the group. He had notes and he'd spent time on his remarks. He got their attention by admitting that the development of their case had not followed the course they'd wanted. Their clients were not good witnesses. The current psychiatrists were not as solid as the first three. Snead was not reliable. He admitted all this, and his sincerity was admirable.

Instead of arguing legal theories, Hark dwelt on people. He talked about their clients, the Phelan children, and he admitted that on the surface they were not a sympathetic bunch. But once you got past the surface, and you got to know them the way their lawyers had, you realized they simply never had a chance. As children they were rich and spoiled, raised in privilege by nannies who came and went, thoroughly ignored by their father, who was either in Asia buying factories or living at the office with his latest secretary. Hark did not intend to disparage the dead, but Mr. Phelan was what he was. Their mothers were an odd collection, but they too had endured the hell of life with Troy.

The Phelan children had not been raised in normal families. They had not been taught the lessons most children learn from their parents. Their father was a great businessman whose approval they craved but never received. Their mothers busied themselves with clubs and causes and the art of shopping. Their father's idea of providing his children with a proper start in life was simply to give each five million dollars when he or she turned twenty-one. This was much too late, and it was much too early. The money couldn't provide the wisdom, guidance, and love they needed as children. And they had clearly proved that they weren't ready for the responsibilities of new wealth.

The gifts had been disastrous, yet they had also brought maturity. Now, with the benefit of the years, the Phelan children looked back at their mistakes. They were embarrassed by how foolish they'd been with the money. Imagine waking up one day like the prodigal son, as Rex had once done at the age of thirty-two – divorced, broke, and standing before a judge who was about to jail him for nonpayment of child support. Imagine sitting in jail for eleven days while your brother, also broke and divorced, tried to convince your mother to bail you out. Rex said he spent his time behind bars trying to recount where the money had gone.

Life has been hard for the Phelan children. Many of their wounds were self-inflicted, but many had been inevitable because of their father.

The final act of neglect by their father had been his handwritten will. They would never understand the malice of the man who'd spurned them as children, chastised them as adults, and erased them as heirs.

Hark concluded by saying, 'They are Phelans, Troy's own flesh and blood, for better or for worse, and they certainly deserve a fair portion of their father's estate.'

When Hark finished he sat down, and the room was silent. It was a heart-felt plea, and Nate and Josh, even Wycliff, were moved by it. It would never play to a jury because he couldn't admit in open court that his clients had no case. But for the moment and the setting, Hark's little oration was just perfect.

Nate supposedly held the money, at least that was his part of the game. He could haggle and squeeze, bluff and dicker for an hour and trim a few million from the fortune. But he was simply in no mood to do so. If Hark could shoot straight, so could he. It was all a ruse anyway.

'What's your bottom line?' he asked Hark, their eyes locking like radar.

'I'm not sure we have a bottom line. I think fifty million per heir is reasonable. I know it sounds like a lot, and it is, but look at the size of the estate. After taxes, we're still only talking about five percent of the money.'

'Five percent is not very much,' Nate said, then let the words hang between them. Hark was watching him, but the others were not. They were hunched over their legal pads, pens ready for the next round of calculations.

'It really isn't,' Hark said.

'My client will agree to fifty million,' Nate said. At the moment, his client was probably teaching Bible songs to small children under the shade of a tree by the river.

Wally Bright had just earned a fee of twenty-five million dollars, and his first impulse was to bolt across the room and kiss Nate's feet. But instead he frowned with intelligence and made careful notes, notes he couldn't read.

Josh knew it was coming, of course, his bean counters had done the math, but Wycliff did not. A settlement had just occurred, no trial would be held. He had to appear pleased. 'Well, then,' he said, 'do we have a settlement?'

Out of nothing but sheer habit, the Phelan lawyers

engaged in one last huddle. They grouped around Hark and tried to whisper, but words failed them.

'It's a deal,' Hark announced, twenty-six million dollars richer.

Josh just happened to have the rough draft of a settlement agreement. They began filling in the blanks, when suddenly the Phelan lawyers remembered their clients. They asked to be excused, then ran into the hallway, cell phones appearing from every pocket. Troy Junior and Rex were waiting by a soft drink machine on the first floor. Geena and Cody were reading newspapers in an empty courtroom. Spike and Libbigail were sitting in their old pickup down the street. Mary Ross was in her Cadillac in the parking lot. Ramble was at home in the basement, door locked, headphones on, in another world.

The settlement would not be complete until signed and approved by Rachel Lane. The Phelan lawyers wanted it to be strictly confidential. Wycliff agreed to seal the court file. After an hour the agreement was complete. It was signed by each of the Phelan heirs and their lawyers. It was signed by Nate.

Only one signature was left. Nate informed them that it would take him a few days to get it.

If they only knew, he thought as he left the courthouse.

Friday afternoon, Nate and the Rector left St. Michaels in the lawyer's leased car. The Rector drove so he could get used to it. Nate napped in the passenger's seat. As they crossed the Bay Bridge, Nate woke up and read the final settlement agreement to Phil, who wanted all the details.

The Phelan Group Gulfstream IV was waiting at the Baltimore-Washington airport. It was sleek and shiny, big enough to haul twenty people anywhere in the world. Phil wanted a better look, so they asked the pilots for a tour. No problem. Whatever Mr. O'Riley wanted. The cabin was all leather and wood, with sofas, recliners, a conference table, several television screens. Nate would've been happy to travel like a normal person, but Josh had insisted.

He watched Phil drive away, then reboarded the plane. In nine hours he would be in Corumbá.

The trust agreement was deliberately thin, in as few words as possible, and with words as short and as plain as the drafters of such impossible instruments could invent. Josh had made them rewrite it numerous times. If Rachel had the slightest inclination to sign it, then it was imperative she be able to grasp its meaning. Nate would be there to do the explaining, but he knew she had little patience with such matters.

The assets she received under her father's last will and testament would be placed in a trust, named the Rachel Trust, for lack of anything more creative. The principal would remain intact for ten years, with only the interest and earnings available for charitable giving. After ten years, 5 percent of the principal per year, in addition to the interest and earnings, could be spent at the discretion of the trustees. The annual disbursements were to be used for a variety of charitable purposes, with emphasis on the mission work of World Tribes. But the language was so loose that the trustees could use the money for almost any benevolent cause. The original trustee was Neva Collier, at World Tribes, and she had the authority to appoint up to a dozen other trustees to help with the work. The trustees would govern themselves and report to Rachel, if she wanted.

If Rachel so desired, she would never see or touch the money. The trust would be set up with the assistance of attorneys chosen by World Tribes.

It was such a simple solution.

It would take only a signature, one quick Rachel

Lane or whatever her last name was. One signature on the trust, one on the settlement agreement, and the Phelan estate could be closed in due course with no more fireworks. Nate could move on, face his troubles, take his medicine, and begin rebuilding his life. He was anxious to get started.

If she refused to sign the trust and the settlement, then Nate needed her signature on a document of renunciation. She could decline the gift, but she had to notify the court.

A renunciation would render Troy's testament worthless. It would be valid, but not operable. The assets would have no place to go, so the effect would be the same as if he'd died with no will. The law would divide the estate into six shares, one for each of his heirs.

How would she react? He wanted to think she would be delighted to see him, but he wasn't convinced of that. He remembered her waving to his boat as he left, just before the dengue hit. She was standing among her people, waving him away, saying good-bye forever. She did not want to be bothered with the things of the world.

FIFTY-ONE

Valdir was waiting at the Corumbá airport when the Gulfstream taxied to the small terminal. It was 1 A.M.; the airport was deserted, only a handful of small planes were at the far end of the tarmac. Nate glanced at them, and wondered if Milton's had ever returned from the Pantanal.

They greeted each other like old friends. Valdir was impressed with how healthy Nate looked. When they last saw each other, Nate was reeling from dengue fever and looked like a skeleton.

They drove away in Valdir's Fiat, windows down, the warm muggy air blowing in Nate's face. The pilots would follow in a taxi. The dusty streets were empty. No one moved about. Downtown, they stopped in front of the Palace Hotel. Valdir handed him a key. 'Room two-twelve,' he said. 'I'll see you at six.'

Nate slept four hours, and was waiting on the sidewalk when the morning sun peeked between the buildings. The sky was clear, and that was one of the first things he took note of. The rainy season had ended a month earlier. Cooler weather was approaching, though in Corumbá the daytime high seldom dipped below seventy-five degrees.

In his heavy satchel he had the paperwork, a camera, a new SatFone, a new cell phone, a pager, a quart of the strongest insect repellent known to

456

modern chemistry, a small gift for Rachel, and two changes of clothes. All limbs were covered; thick khakis over the legs, long sleeves over the arms. He might get uncomfortable and sweat a little, but no insect would penetrate his armor.

At 6 A.M. sharp Valdir arrived, and they sped away to the airport. The town was slowly coming to life.

Valdir had rented the helicopter from a company in Campo Grande for a thousand dollars an hour. It could hold four passengers, came with two pilots, and had a range of three hundred miles.

Valdir and the pilots had studied Jevy's maps of the Xeco River and the tributaries that filled it. With the floods down, the Pantanal was much easier to navigate, both on water and from the air. Rivers were in their banks. Lakes were back within their shores. *Fazendas* were above water and could be found on aerial maps.

As Nate loaded his satchel into the helicopter, he tried not to think of his last flight over the Pantanal. Odds were in his favor. No way he would crash on successive flights.

Valdir preferred to stay behind, close to a phone. He did not enjoy flying, especially in a helicopter, especially over the Pantanal. The sky was calm and cloudless when they lifted off. Nate wore a seat belt, shoulder harness, and helmet. They followed the Paraguay out of Corumbá. Fishermen waved at them. Small boys knee-deep in river water stopped and stared upward. They flew over a *chalana* loaded with bananas, headed north, in their direction. Then another rickety *chalana* headed south.

Nate adjusted to the racket and vibration of the aircraft. He listened with his earphones as the pilots chatted back and forth in Portuguese. He remembered the *Santa Loura*, and his hangover the last time he'd left Corumbá headed north.

457

They climbed to two thousand feet and leveled off. Thirty minutes into the flight, Nate saw Fernando's trading post at the edge of the river.

He was amazed at the difference in the Pantanal from one season to the next. It was still an endless variety of swamps, lagoons, and rivers spinning wildly in all directions, but it was much greener now that the floods had receded.

They stayed above the Paraguay. The skies remained clear and blue under Nate's watchful eyes. He recalled the crash in Milton's plane on Christmas Eve. The storm had boiled over the mountains in an instant.

Dropping to a thousand feet as they circled, the pilots began pointing as if they'd found their target. Nate heard the word Xeco, and saw a tributary enter the Paraguay. He, of course, remembered nothing about the Xeco River. During his first encounter with it, he'd been curled under a tent at the bottom of the boat, wanting to die. They turned west and left the main river, twisting with the Xeco, heading for the mountains of Bolivia. The pilots became more occupied with things below. They were searching for a blue and yellow *chalana*.

On the ground, Jevy heard the distant thumping of the chopper. He quickly lit an orange flare and sent it flying. Welly did the same. The flares burned bright and left a trail of blue and silver smoke. Within minutes, the chopper came into view. It circled slowly.

Jevy and Welly had used machetes to cut a clearing in a patch of dense shrub, fifty yards from the edge of the river. The ground had been under water just a month earlier. The chopper rocked and swayed and slowly lowered itself to the ground.

After the blades stopped, Nate jumped out and hugged his old pals. He hadn't seen them in more than two months, and the fact that he was even there was a surprise to all three.

Time was precious. Nate feared storms, darkness, floods, and mosquitoes, and he wanted to move as quickly as possible. They walked to the *chalana* at the river. Next to it was a long, clean johnboat, which appeared to be waiting for its maiden voyage. Attached to it was a brand-new outboard, all compliments of the Phelan estate. Nate and Jevy quickly loaded themselves into it, said good-bye to Welly and the pilots, and sped off.

The settlements were two hours away, Jevy explained, yelling over the motor. He and Welly had arrived yesterday afternoon with the *chalana*. The river had become too small even for it, so they had docked it near land flat enough to handle the helicopter. Then they had ventured on with the johnboat, eventually going near the first settlement. He had recognized the approach, but turned around before the Indians heard them.

Two hours, maybe three. Nate hoped it wouldn't be five. He would not, under any circumstances, sleep on the ground, or in a tent, or a hammock. No skin would be exposed to the dangers of the jungle. The horrors of dengue were too fresh.

If they were unable to find Rachel, then he would return to Corumbá in the chopper, have a nice dinner with Valdir, sleep in a bed, then try again tomorrow. The estate could buy the damned helicopter if necessary.

But Jevy seemed confident, which was not unusual. They slashed through the water, the bow bouncing as the powerful motor sped them along. How nice to have an outboard that whined in one long, efficient, uninterrupted roar. They were invincible.

Nate was mesmerized once again with the Pantanal; the alligators thrashing in the shallow waters as they

459

flew by, the birds dipping low over the river, the magnificent isolation of the place. They were in too deep to see *fazendas*. They were searching for people who'd been there for centuries.

Twenty-four hours earlier he'd been sitting on the porch of the cottage, under a quilt, sipping coffee, watching the boats drift into the bay, waiting for Father Phil to call and say he was headed for the basement. It took an hour in the boat to fully adjust to where he was.

The river did not look familiar. The last time they had found the Ipicas they were very lost, and scared, wet, hungry, and relying on the guidance of a young fisherman. The waters were up, the landmarks hidden from them.

Nate watched the sky as if he expected bombs to fall. The first sign of a dark cloud, and he would bolt.

Then a bend in the river looked vaguely familiar, maybe they were close. Would she greet him with a smile, and a hug, and want to sit in the shade and chat in English? Any chance she'd missed him, or even thought about him? Had she received the letters? It was mid-March, her packages were supposed to be there. Did she have her new boat by now, and all the new medicines?

Or would she run? Would she huddle with the chief and ask him to protect her, to get rid of the American for the last time? Would Nate even get the chance to see her?

He would be firm, much tougher than last time. It wasn't his fault Troy had made such a ridiculous will, nor could he help the fact that she was his illegitimate daughter. She couldn't change things either, and it was not asking too much for a little cooperation. Either agree to the trust, or sign the renunciation. He would not leave without her signature.

She could turn her back on the world, but she

would always be the daughter of Troy Phelan. That in itself required some small measure of cooperation. Nate practiced his arguments out loud. Jevy couldn't hear him.

He would tell her about her siblings. He would paint a dreadful picture of what would happen if they received the entire fortune. He would list the worthwhile causes she could advance if she simply signed the trust. He practiced and practiced.

The trees on both sides grew thicker and leaned over the river where they touched. Nate recognized the tunnel. 'Up there,' Jevy said, pointing ahead to the right, to the spot where they had first seen the children swimming in the river. He throttled down, and they eased by the first settlement without seeing a single Indian. When the huts were out of sight, the river forked and the streams became smaller.

It was familiar territory. They zigzagged deeper into the woods, the river looping almost in circles, the mountains occasionally visible through clearings. At the second settlement, they stopped near the large tree where they'd slept the first night, back in January. They stepped ashore in the same spot where Rachel had stood when she'd waved good-bye, just as the dengue was calling. The bench was there, its cane poles lashed tightly together.

Nate was watching the village while Jevy was tying off the boat. A young Indian ran along the trail toward them. Their outboard had been heard.

He spoke no Portuguese, but through grunts and hand signals conveyed the message that they were to stay there, by the river, until further orders. If he recognized them, he didn't show it. He appeared scared.

And so they took their places on the bench and waited. It was almost 11 A.M. There was a lot to talk

461

about. Jevy'd been busy on the rivers, running *chalanas* with goods and supplies into the Pantanal. He occasionally captained a tourist boat, where the money was better.

They talked about Nate's last visit, how they'd raced in from the Pantanal with Fernando's borrowed motor, the horrors of the hospital, their efforts to find Rachel in Corumbá.

'I tell you,' Jevy said, 'I have listened much on the river, and the lady did not come. She was not in the hospital. You were dreaming, my friend.'

Nate wasn't about to argue. He wasn't sure himself.

The man who owned the *Santa Loura* had been slandering Jevy around town. It sank on his watch, but everyone knew the storm did it. The man was a fool anyway.

As Nate expected, the conversation soon swung around to Jevy's future in the States. Jevy had applied for a visa, but needed a sponsor and a job. Nate bobbed and weaved, and slid enough punches to keep his friend confused. He couldn't muster the courage to tell him that he too would soon be looking for work.

'I'll see what I can do,' he said.

Jevy had a cousin in Colorado who was also looking for a job.

A mosquito circled Nate's hand. His first impulse was to crush it with a violent slap, but instead he watched to gauge the effectiveness of his super-repellent. When it tired of surveying its target, it made a sudden nosedive toward the back of his right hand. But two inches away, it suddenly stopped, pulled away, and vanished. Nate smiled. His ears, neck, and face were lathered with the oil.

The second attack of dengue usually causes hemorrhaging. It's much worse than the first, and often fatal. Nate O'Riley would not be a victim.

They faced the village as they talked, and Nate

watched every move. He expected to see Rachel stride elegantly between the huts and along the path to greet them. By now, she knew the white man was back.

But did she know it was Nate? What if the Ipica had not recognized them, and Rachel was terrified that someone else had found her?

Then they saw the chief slowly walking toward them. He carried a long ceremonial spear and was followed by an Ipica Nate recognized. They stopped at the edge of the trail, a good fifty feet from the bench. They were not smiling; in fact, the chief looked particularly unpleasant. In Portuguese, he asked, 'What do you want?'

'Tell him we want to see the missionary,' Nate said, and Jevy translated it.

'Why?' came the reply.

Jevy explained that the American had traveled a great distance to be there, and that it was very important to see the woman. The chief again asked, 'Why?'

Because they have things to discuss, big things that neither Jevy nor the chief would understand. It was very important or else the American wouldn't be there.

Nate remembered the chief as a loud character with a quick smile, a big laugh, and a trigger temper. Now his face had little expression. From fifty feet his eyes looked hard. He had once insisted they sit by his fire and share his breakfast. Now he stood as far away as possible. Something was wrong. Something had changed.

He told them to wait, then left again, slowly making his way back to the village. Half an hour passed. By now Rachel knew who they were, the chief would have told her. And she was not coming to meet them.

A cloud passed in front of the sun, and Nate watched it closely. It was puffy and white, not the least bit threatening, but it scared him nonetheless. Any thunder in the distance, and he'd be ready to move. They ate some wafers and cheese while sitting in the boat.

The chief whistled for them and interrupted their snack. He was alone, coming from the village. They met halfway, and followed him for a hundred feet, then changed directions and moved behind the huts on another trail. Nate could see the common area of the village. It was deserted, not a single Ipica wandering about. No children playing. No young ladies raking the dirt around the dwellings. No women cooking and cleaning. Not a sound. The only movement was the drifting smoke of their fires.

Then he saw faces in the windows, little heads peeking through doors. They were being watched. The chief kept them away from the huts as if they were carrying diseases. He turned onto another trail, one that led through the woods for a few moments. When they emerged into a clearing, they were across from Rachel's hut.

There was no sign of her. The chief led them past the front door, and to the side, where, under the thick shade trees, they saw the graves.

FIFTY-TWO

The matching white crosses were made of wood and had been carefully cut and polished by the Indians, then lashed together with string. They were small, less than a foot tall, and stuck into the fresh dirt at the far end of both graves. There was no writing on them, nothing to indicate who had died, or when.

It was dark under the trees. Nate put his satchel on the ground between the graves, and sat on it. The chief began talking softly and quickly.

'The woman is on the left. Lako is on the right. They died on the same day, about two weeks ago,' Jevy translated. More words from the chief, then, 'Malaria has killed ten people since we left,' Jevy said.

The chief delivered a long narrative without stopping for any translating. Nate heard the words, yet heard nothing. He looked at the mound of dirt to the left, a neat pile of black soil laid in a perfect little rectangle, carefully bordered by shaved limbs four inches round. Buried there was Rachel Lane, the bravest person he'd ever known because she had absolutely no fear of death. She welcomed it. She was at peace, her soul finally with the Lord, her body forever lying among the people she loved.

And Lako was with her, his heavenly body cured of defects and afflictions.

The shock came and went. Her death was tragic,

but then it wasn't. She wasn't a young mother and wife who left a family behind. She didn't have a wide circle of friends who'd rush to mourn her passing. Only a handful of people in her native land would ever know she was gone. She was an oddity among the people who'd buried her.

He knew her well enough to know she wouldn't want anyone grieving. She wouldn't approve of tears, and Nate had none to give her. For a few moments he stared at her grave in disbelief, but reality soon set in. This was not an old friend with whom he'd shared many moments. He'd barely known her. His motives in finding her had been purely selfish. He had invaded her privacy, and she had asked him not to return.

But his heart ached anyway. He'd thought about her every day since he'd left the Pantanal. He'd dreamed of her, felt her touch, heard her voice, remembered her wisdom. She had taught him to pray, and given him hope. She was the first person in decades to see anything good in him.

He had never met anyone like Rachel Lane, and he missed her greatly.

The chief was quiet. 'He says we can't stay very long,' Jevy said.

'Why not?' Nate asked, still staring at her grave.

'The spirits are blaming us for the malaria. It arrived when we came the first time. They are not happy to see us.'

'Tell him his spirits are a bunch of clowns.'

'He has something to show you.'

Slowly, Nate stood and faced the chief. They walked through the door of her hut, bending at the knees to get through. The floor was dirt. There were two rooms. The front room had furniture too primitive to believe, a chair made of cane pole and lashings, a sofa with stumps for legs and straw for cushions. The back room was a bedroom and a kitchen. She slept in

466

a hammock like the Indians. Under the hammock, on a small table, was a plastic box that once held medical supplies. The chief pointed to the box and began speaking.

'There are things in there for you to see,' Jevy translated.

'For me?'

'Yes. She knew she was dying. She asked the chief to guard her hut. If an American came, then show him the box.'

Nate was afraid to touch it. The chief picked it up and gave it to him. He backed out of the room and sat on the sofa. The chief and Jevy stepped outside.

His letters never made it, at least they were not in the box. There was a Brazilian identification badge, one required of every non-Indian in the country. There were three letters from World Tribes. Nate didn't read them because at the bottom of the box he saw her will.

It was in a white, legal-sized envelope and had a Brazilian name engraved for the return address. On it, she had neatly printed the words: Last Testament of Rachel Lane Porter.

Nate stared at it in disbelief. His hands shook as he carefully opened it. Folded inside were two sheets of white letter-sized paper, stapled together. On the first sheet, in large letters across the top she had printed, again, Last Testament of Rachel Lane Porter.

It read:

I, Rachel Lane Porter, child of God, resident of His world, citizen of the United States, and being of sound mind, do hereby make this as my last testament.

1. I have no prior testaments to revoke. This is my first and last. Every word is written by my hand. This is intended to be a holographic will.

467

2. I have in my possession a copy of the last testament of my father, Troy Phelan, dated December 9, 1996, in which he gives me the bulk of his estate. I am attempting to pattern this will after his.

3. I do not reject or decline that portion of his estate due me. Nor do I wish to receive it. Whatever his gift is to me, I want it placed in a trust.

4. The earnings from the trust are to be used for the following purposes: a) to continue the work of World Tribes missionaries around the world, b) to spread the Gospel of Christ, c) to protect the rights of indigenous peoples in Brazil and South America, d) to feed the hungry, heal the sick, shelter the homeless, and save the children.

5. I appoint my friend Nate O'Riley to manage the trust, and I grant him broad discretionary powers in its administration. I also appoint him as executor of this testament.

Signed, the sixth day of January 1997, at Corumbá, Brazil.

RACHEL LANE PORTER

He read it again, and again. The second sheet was typed and in Portuguese. It would have to wait for a moment.

He studied the dirt between his feet. The air was sticky and perfectly still. The world was silent, not a sound from the village. The Ipicas were still hiding from the white man and his plagues.

Do you sweep dirt? To make it neat and clean? What happens when it rains and the straw roof leaks? Does it puddle and turn to mud? On the wall facing him were handmade shelves filled with books – Bibles, devotionals, studies in theology. The shelves were slightly uneven, tilting an inch or two to the right.

This was her home for eleven years.

He read it again. January 6 was the day he walked

out of the hospital in Corumbá. She wasn't a dream. She'd touched him and told him he wouldn't die. Then she had written her will.

The straw rustled under him as he moved. He was in a trance when Jevy poked his head through the door and said, 'The chief wants us to leave.'

'Read this,' Nate said, handing him the two sheets of paper with the second one on top. Jevy stepped forward to catch the light from the door. He read slowly, then said, 'Two people here. The first is a lawyer, who says that he saw Rachel Lane Porter sign her testament in his office, in Corumbá. She was mentally okay. And she knew what she was doing. His signature is officially marked by a, what do you say –'

'A notary.'

'Yes, a notary. The second, here on the bottom, is the lawyer's secretary, who, it looks like, says the same things. And the notary certifies her signature too. What does this mean?'

'I'll explain later.'

They stepped into the sunlight. The chief had his arms folded over his chest – his patience was almost gone. Nate removed his camera from the satchel and began taking pictures of the hut and the graves. He made Jevy hold her will while squatting by her grave. Then Nate held it as Jevy took photos. The chief would not agree to have his picture taken with Nate. He kept as much distance as possible. He grunted, and Jevy was afraid he might erupt.

They found the trail and headed for the woods, again staying away from the village. As the trees grew thicker, Nate stopped and turned for one last look at her hut. He wanted to take it with him, to lift it somehow and transport it to the States, to preserve it as a monument so that the millions of people she would touch could have a place to visit and say thanks. And her grave too. She deserved a shrine.

469

That's the last thing she would want. Jevy and the chief were out of sight, so Nate hurried ahead.

They made it to the river without infecting anyone. The chief grunted something at Jevy as they got in the boat. 'He says for us not to come back,' Jevy said.

'Tell him he has nothing to worry about.'

Jevy said nothing, but instead started the engine and backed away from the bank.

The chief was already walking away, toward his village. Nate wondered if he missed Rachel. She'd been there for eleven years. She seemed to have considerable influence over him, but she had not been able to convert him. Did he mourn her passing, or was he relieved that his gods and his spirits now had free rein? What would happen to the Ipicas who had become Christians, now that she was gone?

He remembered the *shalyuns*, the witch doctors in the villages who hounded Rachel. They were celebrating her death. And assailing her converts. She had fought a good fight, now she was resting in peace.

Jevy stopped the motor and guided the boat with a paddle. The current was slow, the water smooth. Nate carefully opened the SatFone and arranged it on a bench. The sky was clear, the signal strong, and within two minutes he had Josh's secretary scurrying to find her boss.

'Tell me she signed that damned trust, Nate,' were his first words. He was yelling into the phone.

'You don't have to yell, Josh. I can hear you.'

'Sorry. Tell me she signed it.'

'She signed a trust, but not ours. She's dead, Josh.'

'No!'

'Yes. She died two weeks ago. Malaria. She left a holographic will, just like her father.'

'Do you have it!?'

'Yes. It's safe. Everything goes into a trust. I'm the trustee and executor.'

470

'Is it valid?'

'I think so. It's written entirely in her hand, signed, dated, witnessed by a lawyer in Corumbá and his secretary.'

'Sounds valid to me.'

'What happens now?' Nate asked. He could see Josh standing behind his desk, eyes closed in concentration, one hand holding the phone, the other patting his hair. He could almost hear him plotting over the phone.

'Nothing happens. His will is valid. Its bequests are carried out.'

'But she's dead.'

'His estate is transferred to hers. Happens all the time in car wrecks when one spouse dies one day, then the other dies the next. The bequests go from estate to estate.'

'What about the other heirs?'

'The settlement stands. They get their money, or what's left of it after the lawyers take their cuts. The heirs are the happiest people on the face of the earth, with the possible exception of their lawyers. There's nothing for them to attack. You have two valid wills. Looks like you've just become a career trustee.'

'I have broad discretionary powers.'

'You have a lot more than that. Read it to me.'

Nate found it deep in his satchel, and read it, very slowly, word for word.

'Hurry home,' Josh said.

Jevy absorbed every word too, though he appeared to be watching the river. When Nate hung up and put the phone away, Jevy asked, 'The money is yours?'

'No. The money goes into a trust.'

'What is a trust?'

'Think of it as a big bank account. It sits in the bank, protected, earning interest. The trustee decides where the interest goes.'

Jevy still wasn't convinced. He had many questions,

471

and Nate sensed his confusion. It was not the time for a primer on the Anglo version of wills, estates, and trusts.

'Let's go,' Nate said.

The motor started again, and they flew across the water, roaring around curves, a wide wake spraying behind them.

They found the *chalana* late in the afternoon. Welly was fishing. The pilots were playing cards on the back of the boat. Nate called Josh again, and told him to retrieve the jet from Corumbá. He wouldn't be needing it. He would take his time coming home.

Josh objected, but that was all he could do. The Phelan mess had been settled. There was no real rush.

Nate told the pilots to contact Valdir when they returned, then sent them on their way.

The crew of the *chalana* watched the chopper disappear like an insect, then cast off. Jevy was at the wheel. Welly sat below, at the front of the boat, his feet dangling inches above the water. Nate found a bunk and tried to nap. But the diesel was next door. Its steady knock prevented sleep.

The vessel was a third the size of the *Santa Loura*, even the bunks were shorter. Nate lay on his side and watched the riverbanks go by.

Somehow she'd known he wasn't a drunk anymore, that his addictions were gone, that the demons who'd controlled his life had been forever locked away. She had seen something good in him. Somehow she knew he was searching. She'd found his calling for him. God told her.

Jevy woke him after dark. 'We have a moon,' he said. They sat on the front of the boat, Welly at the wheel just behind them, following the light of a full moon as the Xeco snaked its way toward the Paraguay.

'The boat is slow,' Jevy said. 'Two days to Corumbá.'

Nate smiled. He didn't care if it took a month.

472

AUTHOR'S NOTE

The Pantanal region of Brazil, in the states of Mato Grosso and Mato Grosso do Sul, is a land of great natural beauty and a fascinating place to visit. I hope I haven't portrayed it as one big swamp, fraught with danger. It is not. It's an ecological gem that attracts many tourists, most of whom survive. I've been there twice, and look forward to going back.

Carl King, my friend and a Baptist missionary in Campo Grande, took me deep into the Pantanal. I'm not sure how much of his information was accurate, but we had a wonderful time for four days counting alligators, photographing wildlife, looking for anacondas, eating black beans and rice, telling stories, all from a boat that somehow grew smaller. Many thanks to Carl for the adventure.

Thanks also to Rick Carter, Gene McDade, Penny Pynkala, Jonathan Hamilton, Fernando Catta-Preta, Bruce Sanford, Marc Smirnoff, and Estelle Laurence. And thanks, as always, to David Gernert for poring over the manuscript and making the book better.

A TIME TO KILL

To Renée,

A woman of uncommon beauty,
A fiercely loyal friend,
A compassionate critic,
A doting mother,

A perfect wife.

AUTHOR'S NOTE

Since I am prone to start projects that never quite get finished, my goal when I began writing this book was simply to complete it. I could envision a neat pile of typed pages over in the corner of my office, and one day I would be able to point to it with some measure of pride and explain to clients and friends that it was a novel I had written. Surely, somewhere in the deep recesses of my mind, I dreamed of getting it published, but I honestly can't remember such thoughts, at least not when I started writing. It would become my first prolonged effort at fiction.

I began in the fall of 1984, just three years out of law school and still very wet behind the ears. In those early days of my legal career I spent many hours in courtrooms, watching good lawyers try their cases. I have always been fascinated by courtrooms—still am. People discuss things in open court that they wouldn't dare mention outside their homes. The greatest dramas occur not on screens or stages, but in countless courtrooms across this country.

One day I stumbled upon a horrible trial in which a young girl testified against the man who brutally raped her. It was a gut-wrenching experience for me, and I was only a spectator. One moment she was courageous, the next pitifully frail. I was mesmerized. I could not imagine the nightmare she and her family had been through. I wondered what I would do if she were my daughter. As I watched her suffer before the jury, I wanted personally to shoot the rapist. For one brief yet interminable moment, I wanted to be her father. I wanted justice. There was a story there.

I became obsessed with the idea of a father's retribution. What would a jury of average and ordinary people do to such a father? Naturally there would be a great deal of sympathy, but would there be enough for an acquittal? The idea for this novel emerged over a three-month period in which I thought of little else.

I wrote the first chapter in longhand on a legal pad, and asked Renée, my wife, to read it. She was impressed, and said she would like to read the second chapter. A month later I gave her chapters two and three, and she said she was hooked. Renée reads five or six novels a week—mysteries, suspense, thrillers, espionage, all sorts of fiction—and she has little patience with a story that doesn't work.

I approached the writing of this book much like a hobby, an hour here and an hour there, with a somewhat disciplined effort to write at least a page a day. I never abandoned it. I remember a four-week period in which nothing was written. I occasionally skipped a day, but for the most part I plowed ahead with blind diligence. I thought the story was wonderful, but I wasn't sure about the writing. Renée liked it, so I kept going.

After a year, I was amazed at how quickly the pages had piled up, and I realized that the book was half finished. My original goal was forgotten, and I caught myself thinking of publishing contracts and royalty statements and fancy lunches with agents and editors—the dreams of every unpublished novelist.

Three years after I started, Renée read the last chapter and we shipped it off to New York. The working title was *Deathknell,* a bad idea that was scrapped as soon as the manuscript landed in the office of my new agent, Jay Garon. Jay had seen the first three chapters, and immediately sent me a contract of representation. Sixteen other agents had passed, as well as a dozen publishers. Jay took the manuscript, and told me to start writing another book. I followed his advice.

A year passed and nothing happened. I was deep into the writing of *The Firm* when Jay called in April 1988 with the wonderful news that this book would indeed be published. Bill Thompson at Wynwood Press had read the manuscript and immediately bought it. Under his guidance, I worked through countless revisions and found a new title, *A Time to Kill.* I think it was the sixth or seventh one I decided on. I'm not good with titles.

Wynwood printed 5,000 copies and published the book in June 1989. It sold well within a hundred miles of home, but was neglected by the rest of the world. There was no paperback deal, no foreign rights. But it was a first novel, and most of them are ignored. Better things were just around the corner.

I finished *The Firm* in 1989, and sent it to Jay. Doubleday/Dell bought it, and when it was published in hardcover in March 1991, my writing career took a dramatic turn. The success of *The Firm* has aroused new interest in *A Time to Kill.*

There's a lot of autobiography in this book. I no longer practice law, but for ten years I did so in a manner very similar to Jake Brigance. I represented people, never banks or insurance companies or big corporations. I was a street lawyer. Jake and I are the same age. I played quarterback in high school, though not very well. Much of what he says and does is what I think I would say and do under the circumstances. We both drive Saabs. We've both felt the unbearable pressure of murder trials, which is something I tried to capture in the story. We've both lost sleep over clients and vomited in courthouse rest rooms.

This one came from the heart. It's a first novel, and at times it rambles, but I wouldn't change a word if given the chance.

Oxford, Mississippi
January 30, 1992

1

Billy Ray Cobb was the younger and smaller of the two rednecks. At twenty-three ie was already a three-year veteran of the state penitentiary at Parchman. Possession, with intent to sell. He was a lean, tough little punk who had survived prison by somehow maintaining a ready supply of drugs that he sold and sometimes gave to the blacks and the guards for protection. In the year since his release he had continued to prosper, and his small-time narcotics business had elevated him to the position of one of the more affluent rednecks in Ford County. He was a businessman, with employees, obligations, deals, everything but taxes. Down at the Ford place in Clanton he was known as the last man in recent history to pay cash for a new pickup truck. Sixteen thousand cash, for a custom-built, four-wheel drive, canary yellow, luxury Ford pickup. The fancy chrome wheels and mudgrip racing tires had been received in a business deal. The rebel flag hanging across the rear window had been stolen by Cobb from a drunken fraternity boy at an Ole Miss football game. The pickup was Billy Ray's most prized possession. He sat on the tailgate drinking a beer, smoking a joint, watching his friend Willard take his turn with the black girl.

Willard was four years older and a dozen years slower. He was generally a harmless sort who had never been in serious trouble and had never been seriously employed. Maybe an occasional fight with a night in jail, but nothing that would distinguish him. He called himself a pulpwood cutter, but a bad back customarily kept him out of the woods. He had hurt his back working on an offshore rig somewhere in the Gulf, and the oil company paid him a nice settlement, which he lost when his ex-wife cleaned him out. His primary vocation was that of a part-time employee of Billy Ray Cobb, who didn't pay much but was liberal with his dope. For the first time in years Willard could always get his hands on something. And he always needed something. He'd been that way since he hurt his back.

She was ten, and small for her age. She lay on her

elbows, which were stuck and bound together with yellow nylon rope. Her legs were spread grotesquely with the right foot tied tight to an oak sapling and the left to a rotting, leaning post of a long-neglected fence. The ski rope had cut into her ankles and the blood ran down her legs. Her face was bloody and swollen, with one eye bulging and closed and the other eye half open so she could see the other white man sitting on the truck. She did not look at the man on top of her. He was breathing hard and sweating and cursing. He was hurting her.

When he finished, he slapped her and laughed, and the other man laughed in return, then they laughed harder and rolled around the grass by the truck like two crazy men, screaming and laughing. She turned away from them and cried softly, careful to keep herself quiet. She had been slapped earlier for crying and screaming. They promised to kill her if she didn't keep quiet.

They grew tired of laughing and pulled themselves onto the tailgate, where Willard cleaned himself with the little nigger's shirt, which by now was soaked with blood and sweat. Cobb handed him a cold beer from the cooler and commented on the humidity. They watched her as she sobbed and made strange, quiet sounds, then became still. Cobb's beer was half empty, and it was not cold anymore. He threw it at the girl. It hit her in the stomach, splashing white foam, and it rolled off in the dirt near some other cans, all of which had originated from the same cooler. For two six-packs now they had thrown their half-empty cans at her and laughed. Willard had trouble with the target, but Cobb was fairly accurate. They were not ones to waste beer, but the heavier cans could be felt better and it was great fun to watch the foam shoot everywhere.

The warm beer mixed with the dark blood and ran down her face and neck into a puddle behind her head. She did not move.

Willard asked Cobb if he thought she was dead. Cobb opened another beer and explained that she was not dead because niggers generally could not be killed by kicking and beating and raping. It took much more, something like a knife or a gun or a rope to dispose of a nigger. Although he had never taken part in such a killing, he had lived with a

bunch of niggers in prison and knew all about them. They
were always killing each other, and they always used a
weapon of some sort. Those who were just beaten and raped
never died. Some of the whites were beaten and raped, and
some of them died. But none of the niggers. Their heads
were harder. Willard seemed satisfied.

Willard asked what he planned to do now that they
were through with her. Cobb sucked on his joint, chased it
with beer, and said he wasn't through. He bounced from the
tailgate and staggered across the small clearing to where she
was tied. He cursed her and screamed at her to wake up,
then he poured cold beer in her face, laughing like a crazy
man.

She watched him as he walked around the tree on her
right side, and she stared at him as he stared between her
legs. When he lowered his pants she turned to the left and
closed her eyes. He was hurting her again.

She looked out through the woods and saw something
—a man running wildly through the vines and underbrush. It
was her daddy, yelling and pointing at her and coming desperately to save her. She cried out for him, and he disappeared. She fell asleep.

When she awoke one of the men was lying under the tailgate, the other under a tree. They were asleep. Her arms
and legs were numb. The blood and beer and urine had
mixed with the dirt underneath her to form a sticky paste
that glued her small body to the ground and crackled when
she moved and wiggled. Escape, she thought, but her mighti-
est efforts moved her only a few inches to the right. Her feet
were tied so high her buttocks barely touched the ground.
Her legs and arms were so deadened they refused to move.

She searched the woods for her daddy and quietly
called his name. She waited, then slept again.

When she awoke the second time they were up and
moving around. The tall one staggered to her with a small
knife. He grabbed her left ankle and sawed furiously on the
rope until it gave way. Then he freed the right leg, and she
curled into a fetal position with her back to them.

Cobb strung a length of quarter-inch ski rope over a

limb and tied a loop in one end with a slip knot. He grabbed
her and put the noose around her head, then walked across
the clearing with the other end of the rope and sat on the
tailgate, where Willard was smoking a fresh joint and grinning at Cobb for what he was about to do. Cobb pulled the
rope tight, then gave a vicious yank, bouncing the little nude
body along the ground and stopping it directly under the
limb. She gagged and coughed, so he kindly loosened the
rope to spare her a few more minutes. He tied the rope to
the bumper and opened another beer.

They sat on the tailgate drinking, smoking, and staring
at her. They had been at the lake most of the day, where
Cobb had a friend with a boat and some extra girls who were
supposed to be easy but turned out to be untouchable. Cobb
had been generous with his drugs and beer, but the girls did
not reciprocate. Frustrated, they left the lake and were driving to no place in particular when they happened across the
girl. She was walking along a gravel road with a sack of
groceries when Willard nailed her in the back of the head
with a beer can.

"You gonna do it?" asked Willard, his eyes red and
glazed.

Cobb hesitated. "Naw, I'll let you do it. It was your
idea."

Willard took a drag on his joint, then spit and said,
"Wasn't my idea. You're the expert on killin' niggers. Do it."

Cobb untied the rope from the bumper and pulled it
tight. It peeled bark from the limb and sprinkled fine bits of
elm around the girl, who was watching them carefully now.
She coughed.

Suddenly, she heard something—like a car with loud
pipes. The two men turned quickly and looked down the dirt
road to the highway in the distance. They cursed and scrambled around, one slamming the tailgate and the other running toward her. He tripped and landed near her. They
cursed each other while they grabbed her, removed the rope
from her neck, dragged her to the pickup and threw her over
the tailgate into the bed of the truck. Cobb slapped her and
threatened to kill her if she did not lie still and keep quiet.
He said he would take her home if she stayed down and did
as told; otherwise, they would kill her. They slammed the

doors and sped onto the dirt road. She was going home. She passed out.

Cobb and Willard waved at the Firebird with the loud pipes as it passed them on the narrow dirt road. Willard checked the back to make sure the little nigger was lying down. Cobb turned onto the highway and raced away.

"What now?" Willard asked nervously.

"Don't know," Cobb answered nervously. "But we gotta do something fast before she gets blood all over my truck. Look at her back there, she's bleedin' all over the place."

Willard thought for a minute while he finished a beer. "Let's throw her off a bridge," he said proudly.

"Good idea. Damned good idea." Cobb slammed on the brakes. "Gimme a beer," he ordered Willard, who stumbled out of the truck and fetched two beers from the back.

"She's even got blood on the cooler," he reported as they raced off again.

———————————

Gwen Hailey sensed something horrible. Normally she would have sent one of the three boys to the store, but they were being punished by their father and had been sentenced to weed-pulling in the garden. Tonya had been to the store before by herself—it was only a mile away—and had proven reliable. But after two hours Gwen sent the boys to look for their little sister. They figured she was down at the Pounders' house playing with the many Pounders kids, or maybe she had ventured past the store to visit her best friend, Bessie Pierson.

Mr. Bates at the store said she had come and gone an hour earlier. Jarvis, the middle boy, found a sack of groceries beside the road.

Gwen called her husband at the paper mill, then loaded Carl Lee, Jr., into the car and began driving the gravel roads around the store. They drove to a settlement of ancient shotgun houses on Graham Plantation to check with an aunt. They stopped at Broadway's store a mile from Bates Grocery and were told by a group of old black men that she had not been seen. They crisscrossed the gravel roads and dusty field roads for three square miles around their house.

Cobb could not find a bridge unoccupied by niggers with fishing poles. Every bridge they approached had four or five niggers hanging off the sides with large straw hats and cane poles, and under every bridge on the banks there would be another group sitting on buckets with the same straw hats and cane poles, motionless except for an occasional swat at a fly or a slap at a mosquito.

He was scared now. Willard had passed out and was of no help, and he was left alone to dispose of the girl in such a way that she could never tell. Willard snored as he frantically drove the gravel roads and county roads in search of a bridge or ramp on some river where he could stop and toss her without being seen by half a dozen niggers with straw hats. He looked in the mirror and saw her trying to stand. He slammed his brakes, and she crashed into the front of the bed, just under the window. Willard ricocheted off the dash into the floorboard, where he continued to snore. Cobb cursed them both equally.

Lake Chatulla was nothing more than a huge, shallow, man-made mudhole with a grass-covered dam running exactly one mile along one end. It sat in the far southwest corner of Ford County, with a few acres in Van Buren County. In the spring it would hold the distinction of being the largest body of water in Mississippi. But by late summer the rains were long gone, and the sun would cook the shallow water until the lake would dehydrate. Its once ambitious shorelines would retreat and move much closer together, creating a depthless basin of reddish brown water. It was fed from all directions by innumerable streams, creeks, sloughs, and a couple of currents large enough to be named rivers. The existence of all these tributaries necessarily gave rise to a good number of bridges near the lake.

It was over these bridges the yellow pickup flew in an all-out effort to find a suitable place to unload an unwanted passenger. Cobb was desperate. He knew of one other bridge, a narrow wooden one over Foggy Creek. As he approached, he saw niggers with cane poles, so he turned off a side road and stopped the truck. He lowered the tailgate, dragged her out, and threw her in a small ravine lined with kudzu.

Carl Lee Hailey did not hurry home. Gwen was easily excited, and she had called the mill numerous times when she thought the children had been kidnapped. He punched out at quitting time, and made the thirty-minute drive home in thirty minutes. Anxiety hit him when he turned onto his gravel drive and saw the patrol car parked next to the front porch. Other cars belonging to Gwen's family were scattered along the long drive and in the yard, and there was one car he didn't recognize. It had cane poles sticking out the side windows, and there were at least seven straw hats sitting in it.

Where were Tonya and the boys?

As he opened the front door he heard Gwen crying. To his right in the small living room he found a crowd huddled above a small figure lying on the couch. The child was covered with wet towels and surrounded by crying relatives. As he moved to the couch the crying stopped and the crowd backed away. Only Gwen stayed by the girl. She softly stroked her hair. He knelt beside the couch and touched the girl's shoulder. He spoke to his daughter, and she tried to smile. Her face was bloody pulp covered with knots and lacerations. Both eyes were swollen shut and bleeding. His eyes watered as he looked at her tiny body, completely wrapped in towels and bleeding from ankles to forehead.

Carl Lee asked Gwen what happened. She began shaking and wailing, and was led to the kitchen by her brother. Carl Lee stood and turned to the crowd and demanded to know what happened.

Silence.

He asked for the third time. The deputy, Willie Hastings, one of Gwen's cousins, stepped forward and told Carl Lee that some people were fishing down by Foggy Creek when they saw Tonya lying in the middle of the road. She told them her daddy's name, and they brought her home.

Hastings shut up and stared at his feet.

Carl Lee stared at him and waited. Everyone else stopped breathing and watched the floor.

"What happened, Willie?" Carl Lee yelled as he stared at the deputy.

Hastings spoke slowly, and while staring out the window repeated what Tonya had told her mother about the white men and their pickup, and the rope and the trees, and being hurt when they got on her. Hastings stopped when he heard the siren from the ambulance.

The crowd filed solemnly through the front door and waited on the porch, where they watched the crew unload a stretcher and head for the house.

The paramedics stopped in the yard when the front door opened and Carl Lee walked out with his daughter in his arms. He whispered gently to her as huge tears dripped from his chin. He walked to the rear of the ambulance and stepped inside. The paramedics closed the door and carefully removed her from his embrace.

2 Ozzie Walls was the only black sheriff in Mississippi. There had been a few others in recent history, but for the moment he was the only one. He took great pride in that fact, since Ford County was seventy-four percent white and the other black sheriffs had been from much blacker counties. Not since Reconstruction had a black sheriff been elected in a white county in Mississippi.

He was raised in Ford County, and he was kin to most of the blacks and a few of the whites. After desegregation in the late sixties, he was a member of the first mixed graduating class at Clanton High School. He wanted to play football nearby at Ole Miss, but there were already two blacks on the team. He starred instead at Alcorn State, and was a defensive tackle for the Rams when a knee injury sent him back to Clanton. He missed football, but enjoyed being the high sheriff, especially at election time when he received more white votes than his white opponents. The white kids loved him because he was a hero, a football star who had played on TV and had his picture in magazines. Their parents respected him and voted for him because he was a tough cop who did not discriminate between black punks and white punks. The white politicians supported him because, since he became the sheriff, the Justice Department stayed out of Ford County. The blacks adored him because he was Ozzie, one of their own.

He skipped supper and waited in his office at the jail for Hastings to report from the Hailey house. He had a suspect. Billy Ray Cobb was no stranger to the sheriff's office. Ozzie knew he sold drugs—he just couldn't catch him. He also knew Cobb had a mean streak.

The dispatcher called in the deputies, and as they reported to the jail Ozzie gave them instructions to locate, but not arrest, Billy Ray Cobb. There were twelve deputies in all —nine white and three black. They fanned out across the county in search of a fancy yellow Ford pickup with a rebel flag in the rear window.

When Hastings arrived he and the sheriff left for the Ford County hospital. As usual, Hastings drove and Ozzie gave orders on the radio. In the waiting room on the second floor they found the Hailey clan. Aunts, uncles, grandparents, friends, and strangers crowded into the small room and some waited in the narrow hallway. There were whispers and quiet tears. Tonya was in surgery.

Carl Lee sat on a cheap plastic couch in a dark corner with Gwen next to him and the boys next to her. He stared at the floor and did not notice the crowd. Gwen laid her head on his shoulder and cried softly. The boys sat rigidly with their hands on knees, occasionally glancing at their father as if waiting on words of reassurance.

Ozzie worked his way through the crowd, quietly shaking hands and patting backs and whispering that he would catch them. He knelt before Carl Lee and Gwen. "How is she?" he asked. Carl Lee did not see him. Gwen cried louder and the boys sniffed and wiped tears. He patted Gwen on the knee and stood. One of her brothers led Ozzie and Hastings out of the room into the hall, away from the family. He shook Ozzie's hand and thanked him for coming.

"How is she?" Ozzie asked.

"Not too good. She's in surgery and most likely will be there for a while. She's got broken bones and a bad concussion. She's beat up real bad. There's rope burns on her neck like they tried to hang her."

"Was she raped?" he asked, certain of the answer.

"Yeah. She told her momma they took turns on her and hurt her real bad. Doctors confirmed it."

"How's Carl Lee and Gwen?"

"They're tore up pretty bad. I think they're in shock. Carl Lee ain't said a word since he got here."

Ozzie assured him they would find the two men, and it wouldn't take long, and when they found them they would be locked up someplace safe. The brother suggested he should hide them in another jail, for their own safety.

Three miles out of Clanton, Ozzie pointed to a gravel driveway. "Pull in there," he told Hastings, who turned off the highway and drove into the front yard of a dilapidated house trailer. It was almost dark.

Ozzie took his night stick and banged violently on the front door. "Open up, Bumpous!"

The trailer shook and Bumpous scrambled to the bathroom to flush a fresh joint.

"Open up, Bumpous!" Ozzie banged. "I know you're in there. Open up or I'll kick in the door."

Bumpous yanked the door open and Ozzie walked in. "You know, Bumpous, evertime I visit you I smell somethin' funny and the commode's flushin'. Get some clothes on. I gotta job for you."

"W-what?"

"I'll explain it outside where I can breathe. Just get some clothes on and hurry."

"What if I don't want to?"

"Fine. I'll see your parole officer tomorrow."

"I'll be out in a minute."

Ozzie smiled and walked to his car. Bobby Bumpous was one of his favorites. Since his parole two years earlier, he had led a reasonably clean life, occasionally succumbing to the lure of an easy drug sale for a quick buck. Ozzie watched him like a hawk and knew of such transactions, and Bumpous knew Ozzie knew; therefore, Bumpous was usually most eager to help his friend, Sheriff Walls. The plan was to eventually use Bumpous to nail Billy Ray Cobb for dealing, but that would be postponed for now.

After a few minutes he marched outside, still tucking his shirttail and zipping his pants. "Who you lookin' for?" he demanded.

"Billy Ray Cobb."

"That's no problem. You can find him without me."

"Shut up and listen. We think Cobb was involved in a rape this afternoon. A black girl was raped by two white men, and I think Cobb was there."

"Cobb ain't into rape, Sheriff. He's into drugs, remember?"

"Shut up and listen. You find Cobb and spend some time with him. Five minutes ago his truck was spotted at Huey's. Buy him a beer. Shoot some pool, roll dice, whatever. Find out what he did today. Who was he with? Where'd he go? You know how he likes to talk, right?"

"Right."

"Call the dispatcher when you find him. They'll call me. I'll be somewhere close. You understand?"

"Sure, Sheriff. No problem."

"Any questions?"

"Yeah. I'm broke. Who's gonna pay for this?"

Ozzie handed him a twenty and left. Hastings drove in the direction of Huey's, down by the lake.

"You sure you can trust him?" Hastings asked.

"Who?"

"That Bumpous kid."

"Sure I trust him. He's proved very reliable since he was paroled. He's a good kid tryin' to go straight, for the most part. He supports his local sheriff and would do anything I ask."

"Why?"

"Because I caught him with ten ounces of pot a year ago. He'd been outta jail about a year when I caught his brother with an ounce, and I told him he was lookin' at thirty years. He started cryin' and carryin' on, cried all night in his cell. By mornin' he was ready to talk. Told me his supplier was his brother, Bobby. So I let him go and went to see Bobby. I knocked on his door and I could hear the commode flushin'. He wouldn't come to the door, so I kicked it in. I found him in his underwear in the bathroom tryin' to unstop the commode. There was dope all over the place. Don't know how much he flushed, but most of it was comin' back out in the overflow. Scared him so bad he wet his drawers."

"You kiddin'?"

"Nope. The kid pissed all over himself. He was a sight standin' there with wet drawers, a plunger in one hand, dope in the other, and the room fillin' up with commode water."

"What'd you do?"

"Threatened to kill him."

"What'd he do?"

"Started cryin'. Cried like a baby. Cried 'bout his momma and prison and all this and that. Promised he'd never screw up again."

"You arrest him?"

"Naw, I just couldn't. I talked real ugly to him and threatened him some more. I put him on probation right there in his bathroom. He's been fun to work with ever since."

They drove by Huey's and saw Cobb's truck in the gravel parking lot with a dozen other pickups and four-wheel drives. They parked behind a black church on a hill up the highway from Huey's, where they had a good view of the honky tonk, or tonk, as it was affectionately called by the patrons. Another patrol car hid behind some trees at the other end of the highway. Moments later Bumpous flew by and wheeled into the parking lot. He locked his brakes, spraying gravel and dust, then backed next to Cobb's truck. He looked around and casually entered Huey's. Thirty minutes later the dispatcher advised Ozzie that the informant had found the subject, a male white, at Huey's, an establishment on Highway 305 near the lake. Within minutes two more patrol cars were hidden close by. They waited.

"What makes you so sure it's Cobb?" Hastings asked.

"I ain't sure. I just got a hunch. The little girl said it was a truck with shiny wheels and big tires."

"That narrows it down to two thousand."

"She also said it was yellow, looked new, and had a big flag hangin' in the rear window."

"That brings it down to two hundred."

"Maybe less than that. How many of those are as mean as Billy Ray Cobb?"

"What if it ain't him?"

"It is."

"If it ain't?"

"We'll know shortly. He's got a big mouth, 'specially when he's drinkin'."

For two hours they waited and watched pickups come and go. Truck drivers, pulpwood cutters, factory workers, and farmhands parked their pickups and jeeps in the gravel and strutted inside to drink, shoot pool, listen to the band, but mainly to look for stray women. Some would leave and walk next door to Ann's Lounge, where they would stay for a few minutes and return to Huey's. Ann's Lounge was darker both inside and out, and it lacked the colorful beer signs and live music that made Huey's such a hit with the locals. Ann's

was known for its drug traffic, whereas Huey's had it all—
music, women, happy hours, poker machines, dice, dancing,
and plenty of fights. One brawl spilled through the door into
the parking lot, where a group of wild rednecks kicked and
clawed each other at random until they grew winded and
returned to the dice table.

"Hope that wasn't Bumpous," observed the sheriff.

The restrooms inside were small and nasty, and most of
the patrons found it necessary to relieve themselves between
the pickups in the parking lot. This was especially true on
Mondays when ten-cent beer night drew rednecks from four
counties and every truck in the parking lot received at least
three sprayings. About once a week an innocent passing motorist would get shocked by something he or she saw in the
parking lot, and Ozzie would be forced to make an arrest.
Otherwise, he left the places alone.

Both tonks were in violation of numerous laws. There
was gambling, drugs, illegal whiskey, minors, they refused to
close on time, etc. Shortly after he was elected the first time
Ozzie made the mistake, due in part to a hasty campaign
promise, of closing all the honky tonks in the county. It was a
horrible mistake. The crime rate soared. The jail was
packed. The court dockets multiplied. The rednecks united
and drove in caravans to Clanton, where they parked around
the courthouse on the square. Hundreds of them. Every
night they invaded the square, drinking, fighting, playing
loud music, and shouting obscenities at the horrified town
folk. Each morning the square resembled a landfill with cans
and bottles thrown everywhere. He closed the black tonks
too, and break-ins, burglaries, and stabbings tripled in one
month. There were two murders in one week.

Finally, with the city under siege, a group of local ministers met secretly with Ozzie and begged him to ease up on
the tonks. He politely reminded them that during the campaign they had insisted on the closings. They admitted they
were wrong and pleaded for relief. Yes, they would support
him in the next election. Ozzie relented, and life returned to
normal in Ford County.

Ozzie was not pleased that the establishments thrived in
his county, but he was convinced beyond any doubt that his

law-abiding constituents were much safer when the tonks were open.

At ten-thirty the dispatcher radioed that the informant was on the phone and wanted to see the sheriff. Ozzie gave his location, and a minute later they watched Bumpous emerge and stagger to his truck. He spun tires, slung gravel, and raced toward the church.

"He's drunk," said Hastings.

He wheeled through the church parking lot and came to a screeching stop a few feet from the patrol car. "Howdy, Sheriff!" he yelled.

Ozzie walked to the pickup. "What took so long?"

"You told me to take all night."

"You found him two hours ago."

"That's true, Sheriff, but have you ever tried to spend twenty dollars on beer when it's fifty cents a can?"

"You drunk?"

"Naw, just havin' a good time. Could I have another twenty?"

"What'd you find out?"

" 'Bout what?"

"Cobb!"

"Oh, he's in there all right."

"I know he's in there! What else?"

Bumpous quit smiling and looked at the tonk in the distance. "He's laughin' about it, Sheriff. It's a big joke. Said he finally found a nigger who was a virgin. Somebody asked how old she was, and Cobb said eight or nine. Everybody laughed."

Hastings closed his eyes and dropped his head. Ozzie gritted his teeth and looked away. "What else did he say?"

"He's bad drunk. He won't remember any of it in the mornin'. Said she was a cute little nigger."

"Who was with him?"

"Pete Willard."

"Is he in there?"

"Yep, they're both laughin' about it."

"Where are they?"

"Left-hand side, next to the pinball machines."

Ozzie smiled. "Okay, Bumpous. You did good. Get lost."

Hastings called the dispatcher with the two names. The dispatcher relayed the message to Deputy Looney, who was parked in the street in front of the home of County Judge Percy Bullard. Looney rang the doorbell and handed the judge two affidavits and two arrest warrants. Bullard scribbled on the warrants and returned them to Looney, who thanked His Honor and left. Twenty minutes later Looney handed the warrants to Ozzie behind the church.

At exactly eleven, the band quit in mid-song, the dice disappeared, the dancers froze, the cue balls stopped rolling, and someone turned on the lights. All eyes followed the big sheriff as he and his men swaggered slowly across the dance floor to a table by the pinball machines. Cobb, Willard, and two others sat in a booth, the table littered with empty beer cans. Ozzie walked to the table and grinned at Cobb.

"I'm sorry, sir, but we don't allow niggers in here," Cobb blurted out, and the four burst into laughter. Ozzie kept grinning.

When the laughing stopped, Ozzie said, "You boys havin' a good time, Billy Ray?"

"We was."

"Looks like it. I hate to break things up, but you and Mr. Willard need to come with me."

"Where we goin'?" Willard asked.

"For a ride."

"I ain't movin'," Cobb vowed. With that, the other two scooted from the booth and joined the spectators.

"I'm placin' you both under arrest," Ozzie said.

"You got warrants?" Cobb asked.

Hastings produced the warrants, and Ozzie threw them among the beer cans. "Yeah, we got warrants. Now get up."

Willard stared desperately at Cobb, who sipped a beer and said, "I ain't goin' to jail."

Looney handed Ozzie the longest, blackest nightstick ever used in Ford County. Willard was panic-stricken. Ozzie cocked it and struck the center of the table, sending beer and cans and foam in all directions. Willard bolted upright, slapped his wrists together and thrust them at Looney, who was waiting with the handcuffs. He was dragged outside and thrown into a patrol car.

Ozzie tapped his left palm with the stick and grinned at

Cobb. "You have the right to remain silent. Anything you say will be used against you in court. You have the right to a lawyer. If you can't afford one, the state'll furnish one. Any questions?"

"Yeah, what time is it?"

"Time to go to jail, big man."

"Go to hell, nigger."

Ozzie grabbed his hair and lifted him from the booth, then drove his face into the floor. He jammed a knee into his spine and slid his nightstick under his throat, and pulled upward while driving the knee deeper into his back. Cobb squealed until the stick began crushing his larynx.

The handcuffs were slapped into place, and Ozzie dragged him by his hair across the dance floor, out the door, across the gravel and threw him into the back seat with Willard.

News of the rape spread quickly. More friends and relatives crowded into the waiting room and the halls around it. Tonya was out of surgery and listed as critical. Ozzie talked to Gwen's brother in the hall and told of the arrests. Yes, they were the ones, he was sure.

3 Jake Brigance rolled across his wife and staggered to the small bathroom a few feet from his bed, where he searched and groped in the dark for the screaming alarm clock. He found it where he had left it, and killed it with a quick and violent slap. It was 5:30 A.M., Wednesday, May 15.

He stood in the dark for a moment, breathless, terrified, his heart pounding rapidly, staring at the fluorescent numbers glowing at him from the face of the clock, a clock he hated. Its piercing scream could be heard down the street. He flirted with cardiac arrest every morning at this time when the thing erupted. On occasion, about twice a year, he was successful in shoving Carla onto the floor, and she would maybe turn it off before returning to bed. Most of the time, however, she was not sympathetic. She thought he was crazy for getting up at such an hour.

The clock sat on the windowsill so that Jake was required to move around a bit before it was silenced. Once up, Jake would not permit himself to crawl back under the covers. It was one of his rules. At one time the alarm was on the nightstand, and the volume was reduced. Carla would reach and turn it off before Jake heard anything. Then he would sleep until seven or eight and ruin his entire day. He would miss being in the office by seven, which was another rule. The alarm stayed in the bathroom and served its purpose.

Jake stepped to the sink and splashed cold water on his face and hair. He switched on the light and gasped in horror at the sight in the mirror. His straight brown hair shot in all directions, and the hairline had receded at least two inches during the night. Either that or his forehead had grown. His eyes were matted and swollen with the white stuff packed in the corners. A seam in a blanket left a bright red scar along the left side of his face. He touched, then rubbed it and wondered if it would go away. With his right hand he pushed his hair back and inspected the hairline. At thirty-two, he had no gray hair. Gray hair was not the problem. The problem was pattern baldness, which Jake had richly inherited from both sides of his family. He longed for a full, thick hairline beginning an inch above his eyebrows. He still had plenty of hair, Carla told him. But it wouldn't last long at the rate it was disappearing. She also assured him he was as handsome as ever, and he believed her. She had explained that a receding hairline gave him a look of maturity that was essential for a young attorney. He believed that too.

But what about old, bald attorneys, or even mature, middle-aged bald attorneys? Why couldn't the hair return after he grew wrinkles and gray sideburns and looked very mature?

Jake pondered these things in the shower. He took quick showers, and he shaved and dressed quickly. He had to be at the Coffee Shop at 6:00 A.M.—another rule. He turned on lights and slammed and banged drawers and closet doors in an effort to arouse Carla. This was the morning ritual during the summer when she was not teaching school. He had explained to her numerous times that she had all day to catch up on any lost sleep, and that these early moments should be spent together. She moaned and tunneled deeper under the covers. Once dressed, Jake jumped on the bed with all fours and kissed her in the ear, down the neck, and all over the face until she finally swung at him. Then he yanked the covers off the bed and laughed as she curled up and shivered and begged for the blankets. He held them and admired her dark, tanned, thin, almost perfect legs. The bulky nightshirt covered nothing below the waist, and a hundred lewd thoughts danced before him.

About once a month this ritual would get out of hand. She would not protest, and the blankets would be jointly removed. On those mornings Jake undressed even quicker and broke at least three of his rules. That's how Hanna was conceived.

But not this morning. He covered his wife, kissed her gently, and turned out the lights. She breathed easier, and fell asleep.

Down the hall he quietly opened Hanna's door and knelt beside her. She was four, the only child, and there would be no others. She lay in her bed surrounded by dolls and stuffed animals. He kissed her lightly on the cheek. She was as beautiful as her mother, and the two were identical in

looks and manners. They had large bluish-gray eyes that
could cry instantly, if necessary. They wore their dark hair
the same way—had it cut by the same person at the same
time. They even dressed alike.

Jake adored the two women in his life. He kissed the
second one goodbye and went to the kitchen to make coffee
for Carla. On his way out he released Max, the mutt, into the
backyard, where she simultaneously relieved herself and
barked at Mrs. Pickle's cat next door.

Few people attacked the morning like Jake Brigance.
He walked briskly to the end of the driveway and got the
morning papers for Carla. It was dark, clear, and cool with
the promise of summer rapidly approaching.

He studied the darkness up and down Adams Street,
then turned and admired his house. Two homes in Ford
County were on the National Register of Historic Places,
and Jake Brigance owned one of them. Although it was
heavily mortgaged, he was proud of it nonetheless. It was a
nineteenth-century Victorian built by a retired railroad man
who died on the first Christmas Eve he spent in his new
home. The facade was a huge, centered gable with hipped
roof over a wide, inset front porch. Under the gable a small
portico covered with bargeboard hung gently over the porch.
The five supporting pillars were round and painted white
and slate blue. Each column bore a handmade floral carving,
each with a different flower—daffodils, irises, and sunflow-
ers. The railing between the pillars was filled with lavish
lacework. Upstairs, three bay windows opened onto a small
balcony, and to the left of the balcony an octagonal tower
with stained-glass windows protruded and rose above the
gable until it peaked with an iron-crested finial. Below the
tower and to the left of the porch, a wide, graceful veranda
with ornamental railing extended from the house and served
as a carport. The front panels were a collage of gingerbread,
cedar shingles, scallops, fish scales, tiny intricate gables, and
miniature spindles.

Carla had located a paint consultant in New Orleans,
and the fairy chose six original colors—mostly shades of
blue, teal, peach, and white. The paint job took two months
and cost Jake five thousand dollars, and that did not include
the countless hours he and Carla had spent dangling from

ladders and scraping cornices. And although he was not wild about some of the colors, he had never dared suggest repainting.

As with every Victorian, the house was gloriously unique. It had a piquant, provocative, engaging quality derived from an ingenuous, joyous, almost childlike bearing. Carla had wanted it since before they married, and when the owner in Memphis finally died and the estate was closed, they bought it for a song because no one else would have it. It had been abandoned for twenty years. They borrowed heavily from two of the three banks in Clanton, and spent the next three years sweating and doting over their landmark. Now people drove by and took pictures of it.

The third local bank held the mortgage on Jake's car, the only Saab in Ford County. And a red Saab at that. He wiped the dew from the windshield and unlocked the door. Max was still barking and had awakened the army of bluejays that lived in Mrs. Pickle's maple tree. They sang to him and called farewell as he smiled and whistled in return. He backed into Adams Street. Two blocks east he turned south on Jefferson, which two blocks later ran dead end into Washington Street. Jake had often wondered why every small Southern town had an Adams, a Jefferson, and a Washington, but no Lincoln or Grant. Washington Street ran east and west on the north side of the Clanton square.

Because Clanton was the county seat it had a square, and the square quite naturally had a courthouse in the center of it. General Clanton had laid out the town with much thought, and the square was long and wide and the courthouse lawn was covered with massive oak trees, all lined neatly and spaced equally apart. The Ford County courthouse was well into its second century, built after the Yankees burned the first one. It defiantly faced south, as if telling those from the North to politely and eternally kiss its ass. It was old and stately, with white columns along the front and black shutters around the dozens of windows. The original red brick had long since been painted white, and every four years the Boy Scouts added a thick layer of shiny enamel for their traditional summer project. Several bond issues over the years had allowed additions and renovations.

The lawn around it was clean and neatly trimmed. A crew from the jail manicured it twice a week.

Clanton had three coffee shops—two for the whites and one for the blacks, and all three were on the square. It was not illegal or uncommon for whites to eat at Claude's, the black cafe on the west side. And it was safe for the blacks to eat at the Tea Shoppe, on the south side, or the Coffee Shop on Washington Street. They didn't, however, since they were told they could back in the seventies. Jake ate barbecue every Friday at Claude's, as did most of the white liberals in Clanton. But six mornings a week he was a regular at the Coffee Shop.

He parked the Saab in front of his office on Washington Street and walked three doors to the Coffee Shop. It had opened an hour earlier and by now was bustling with action. Waitresses scurried about serving coffee and breakfast and chatting incessantly with the farmers and mechanics and deputies who were the regulars. This was no white-collar cafe. The white collars gathered across the square at the Tea Shoppe later in the morning and discussed national politics, tennis, golf, and the stock market. At the Coffee Shop they talked about local politics, football, and bass fishing. Jake was one of the few white collars allowed to frequent the Coffee Shop. He was well liked and accepted by the blue collars, most of whom at one time or another had found their way to his office for a will, a deed, a divorce, a defense, or any one of a thousand other problems. They picked at him and told crooked lawyer jokes, but he had a thick skin. They asked him to explain Supreme Court rulings and other legal oddities during breakfast, and he gave a lot of free legal advice at the Coffee Shop. Jake had a way of cutting through the excess and discussing the meat of any issue. They appreciated that. They didn't always agree with him, but they always got honest answers. They argued at times, but there were never hard feelings.

He made his entrance at six, and it took five minutes to greet everyone, shake hands, slap backs, and say smart things to the waitresses. By the time he sat at his table his favorite girl, Dell, had his coffee and regular breakfast of toast, jelly, and grits. She patted him on the hand and called him honey and sweetheart and generally made a fuss over him. She griped and snapped at the others, but had a different routine for Jake.

He ate with Tim Nunley, a mechanic down at the Chevrolet place, and two brothers, Bill and Bert West, who worked at the shoe factory north of town. He splashed three drops of Tabasco on his grits and stirred them artfully with a slice of butter. He covered the toast with a half inch of homemade strawberry jelly. Once his food was properly prepared, he tasted the coffee and started eating. They ate quietly and discussed how the crappie were biting.

In a booth by the window a few feet from Jake's table, three deputies talked among themselves. The big one, Marshall Prather, turned to Jake and asked loudly, "Say, Jake, didn't you defend Billy Ray Cobb a few years ago?"

The cafe was instantly silent as everyone looked at the lawyer. Startled not by the question but by its response, Jake swallowed his grits and searched for the name.

"Billy Ray Cobb," he repeated aloud. "What kind of case was it?"

"Dope," Prather said. "Caught him sellin' dope about four years ago. Spent time in Parchman and got out last year."

Jake remembered. "Naw, I didn't represent him. I think he had a Memphis lawyer."

Prather seemed satisfied and returned to his pancakes. Jake waited.

Finally he asked, "Why? What's he done now?"

"We picked him up last night for rape."

"Rape!"

"Yeah, him and Pete Willard."

"Who'd they rape?"

"You remember that Hailey nigger you got off in that murder trial a few years ago?"

"Lester Hailey. Of course I remember."

"You know his brother Carl Lee?"

"Sure. Know him well. I know all the Haileys. Represented most of them."

"Well, it was his little girl."

"You're kidding?"

"Nope."

"How old is she?"

"Ten."

Jake's appetite disappeared as the cafe returned to normal. He played with his coffee and listened to the conversation change from fishing to Japanese cars and back to fishing. When the West brothers left, he slid into the booth with the deputies.

"How is she?" he asked.

"Who?"

"The Hailey girl."

"Pretty bad," said Prather. "She's in the hospital."

"What happened?"

"We don't know everything. She ain't been able to talk much. Her momma sent her to the store. They live on Craft Road behind Bates Grocery."

"I know where they live."

"Somehow they got her in Cobb's pickup and took her out in the woods somewhere and raped her."

"Both of them?"

"Yeah, several times. And they kicked her and beat her real bad. Some of her kinfolks didn't know her, she was beat so bad."

Jake shook his head. "That's sick."

"Sure is. Worst I've ever seen. They tried to kill her. Left her for dead."

"Who found her?"

"Buncha niggers fishin' down by Foggy Creek. Saw her floppin' out in the middle of the road. Had her hands tied behind her. She was talkin' a little—told them who her daddy was and they took her home."

"How'd you know it was Billy Ray Cobb?"

"She told her momma it was a yellow pickup truck with a rebel flag hangin' in the rear window. That's about all Ozzie needed. He had it figured out by the time she got to the hospital."

Prather was careful not to say too much. He liked Jake, but he was a lawyer and he handled a lot of criminal cases.

"Who is Pete Willard?"

"Some friend of Cobb's."

"Where'd y'all find them?"

"Huey's."

"That figures." Jake drank his coffee and thought of Hanna.

"Sick, sick, sick," Looney mumbled.

"How's Carl Lee?"

Prather wiped syrup from his mustache. "Personally, I don't know him, but I ain't ever heard anything bad about him. They're still at the hospital. I think Ozzie was with them all night. He knows them real well, of course, he knows all those folks real well. Hastings is kin to the girl somehow."

"When's the preliminary hearing?"

"Bullard set it for one P.M. today. Ain't that right, Looney?"

Looney nodded.

"Any bond?"

"Ain't been set yet. Bullard's gonna wait till the hearing. If she dies, they'll be lookin' at capital murder, won't they?"

Jake nodded.

"They can't have a bond for capital murder, can they, Jake?" Looney asked.

"They can but I've never seen one. I know Bullard won't set a bond for capital murder, and if he did, they couldn't make it."

"If she don't die, how much time can they get?" asked Nesbit, the third deputy.

Others listened as Jake explained. "They can get life sentences for the rape. I assume they will also be charged with kidnapping and aggravated assault."

"They already have."

"Then they can get twenty years for the kidnapping and twenty years for the aggravated assault."

"Yeah, but how much time will they serve?" asked Looney.

Jake thought a second. "They could conceivably be paroled in thirteen years. Seven for the rape, three for the kidnapping, and three for the aggravated assault. That's assuming they're convicted on all charges and sentenced to the maximum."

"What about Cobb? He's got a record."

"Yeah, but he's not habitual unless he's got two prior convictions."

"Thirteen years," Looney repeated, shaking his head.

Jake stared through the window. The square was coming to life as pickups full of fruits and vegetables parked next to the sidewalk around the courthouse lawn, and the old farmers in faded overalls neatly arranged the small baskets of tomatoes and cucumbers and squash on the tailgates and hoods. Watermelons from Florida were placed next to the dusty slick tires, and the farmers left for an early-morning meeting under the Vietnam monument, where they sat on benches and chewed Red Man and whittled while they caught up on the gossip. They're probably talking about the rape, Jake thought. It was daylight now, and time for the office. The deputies were finished with their food, and Jake excused himself. He hugged Dell, paid his check, and for a second thought of driving home to check on Hanna.

At three minutes before seven, he unlocked his office and turned on the lights.

Carl Lee had difficulty sleeping on the couch in the waiting room. Tonya was serious but stable. They had seen her at midnight, after the doctor warned that she looked bad. She did. Gwen had kissed the little bandaged face while Carl Lee stood at the foot of the bed, subdued, motionless, unable to do anything but stare blankly at the small figure surrounded by machines, tubes, and nurses. Gwen was later sedated and taken to her mother's house in Clanton. The boys went home with Gwen's brother.

The crowd had dispersed around one, leaving Carl Lee alone on the couch. Ozzie brought coffee and doughnuts at two, and told Carl Lee all he knew about Cobb and Willard.

Jake's office was a two-story building in a row of two-story buildings overlooking the courthouse on the north side of the square, just down from the Coffee Shop. The building was built by the Wilbanks family back in the 1890s, back when they owned Ford County. And there had been a Wilbanks practicing law in the building from the day it was built until 1979, the year of the disbarment. Next door to the east was an insurance agent Jake had sued for botching a claim for Tim Nunley, the mechanic down at the Chevrolet place. To the west was the bank with the mortgage on the Saab. All the buildings around the square were two-story brick except the banks. The one next door had also been built by the Wilbankses and had just two floors, but the one on the southeast corner of the square had three floors, and the newest one, on the southwest corner, had four floors.

Jake practiced alone, and had since 1979, the year of the disbarment. He liked it that way, especially since there was no other lawyer in Clanton competent enough to practice with him. There were several good lawyers in town, but most were with the Sullivan firm over in the bank building with four floors. Jake detested the Sullivan firm. Every lawyer detested the Sullivan firm except those in it. There were eight in all, eight of the most pompous and arrogant jerks Jake had ever met. Two had Harvard degrees. They had the big farmers, the banks, the insurance companies, the railroads, everybody with money. The other fourteen lawyers in the county picked up the scraps and represented people— living, breathing human souls, most of whom had very little money. These were the "street lawyers"—those in the trenches helping people in trouble. Jake was proud to be a street lawyer.

His offices were huge. He used only five of the ten rooms in the building. Downstairs there was a reception room, a large conference room, a kitchen, and a smaller storage and junk room. Upstairs, Jake had his vast office and another smaller office he referred to as the war room. It had no windows, no telephones, no distractions. Three offices sat empty upstairs and two downstairs. In years past these had been occupied by the prestigious Wilbanks firm, long before the disbarment. Jake's office upstairs, *the* office, was immense; thirty by thirty with a ten-foot hardwood ceiling, hardwood floors, huge fireplace, and three desks—his work desk, a small conference desk in one corner, and a rolltop desk in another corner under the portrait of William Faulkner. The antique oak furniture had been there for almost a century, as had the books and shelves that covered one wall. The view of the square and courthouse was impressive, and could be enhanced by opening the French doors and walking onto a small balcony overhanging the sidewalk next to Washington Street. Jake had, without a doubt, the finest office in Clanton. Even his bitter enemies in the Sullivan firm would concede that much.

For all the opulence and square footage, Jake paid the sum of four hundred dollars a month to his landlord and former boss, Lucien Wilbanks, who had been disbarred in 1979.

For decades the Wilbanks family ruled Ford County. They were proud, wealthy people, prominent in farming, banking, politics, and especially law. All the Wilbanks men were lawyers, and were educated at Ivy League schools. They founded banks, churches, schools, and several served in public office. The firm of Wilbanks & Wilbanks had been the most powerful and prestigious in north Mississippi for many years.

Then came Lucien. He was the only male Wilbanks of his generation. There was a sister and some nieces, but they were expected only to marry well. Great things were expected of Lucien as a child, but by the third grade it was evident he would be a different Wilbanks. He inherited the law firm in 1965 when his father and uncle were killed in a plane crash. Although he was forty, he had just recently, several months prior to their deaths, completed his study of the law by correspondence courses. Somehow he passed the bar exam. He took control of the firm and clients began disappearing. Big clients, like insurance companies, banks, and farmers, all left and went to the newly established Sullivan firm. Sullivan had been a junior partner in the Wilbanks firm until Lucien fired him and evicted him, after which he left with the other junior partners and most of the clients. Then Lucien fired everyone else—associates, secretaries, clerks—everyone but Ethel Twitty, his late father's favorite secretary.

Ethel and John Wilbanks had been very close through the years. In fact she had a younger son who greatly resembled Lucien. The poor fellow spent most of his time in and out of various nut houses. Lucien jokingly referred to him as his retarded brother. After the plane crash, the retarded brother appeared in Clanton and started telling folks he was the illegitimate son of John Wilbanks. Ethel was humiliated, but couldn't control him. Clanton seethed with scandal. A

lawsuit was filed by the Sullivan firm as counsel for the retarded brother seeking a portion of the estate. Lucien was
furious. A trial ensued, and Lucien vigorously defended his
honor and pride and family name. He also vigorously defended his father's estate, all of which had been left to Lucien and his sister. At trial the jury noted the striking resemblance between Lucien and Ethel's son, who was several
years younger. The retarded brother was strategically seated
as close as possible to Lucien. The Sullivan lawyers instructed him to walk, talk, sit, and do everything just like
Lucien. They even dressed him like Lucien. Ethel and her
husband denied the boy was any kin to the Wilbanks, but the
jury felt otherwise. He was found to be an heir of John
Wilbanks, and was awarded one third of the estate. Lucien
cursed the jury, slapped the poor boy, and was carried
screaming from the courtroom and taken to jail. The jury's
decision was reversed and dismissed on appeal, but Lucien
feared more litigation if Ethel ever changed her story. Thus,
Ethel Twitty remained with the Wilbanks firm.

Lucien was satisfied when the firm disintegrated. He
never intended to practice law like his ancestors. He wanted
to be a criminal lawyer, and the old firm's clientele had become strictly corporate. He wanted the rapes, the murders,
the child abuses, the ugly cases no one else wanted. He
wanted to be a civil rights lawyer and litigate civil liberties.
But most of all, Lucien wanted to be a radical, a flaming
radical of a lawyer with unpopular cases and causes, and lots
of attention.

He grew a beard, divorced his wife, renounced his
church, sold his share of the country club, joined the
NAACP and ACLU, resigned from the bank board, and in
general became the scourge of Clanton. He sued the schools
because of segregation, the governor because of the prison,
the city because it refused to pave streets in the black section, the bank because there were no black tellers, the state
because of capital punishment, and the factories because
they would not recognize organized labor. He fought and
won many criminal cases, and not just in Ford County. His
reputation spread, and a large following developed among
blacks, poor whites, and the few unions in north Mississippi.
He stumbled into some lucrative personal injury and wrong-

ful death cases. There were some nice settlements. The firm, he and Ethel, was more profitable than ever. Lucien did not need the money. He had been born with it and never thought about it. Ethel did the counting.

The law became his life. With no family, he became a workaholic. Fifteen hours a day, seven days a week, Lucien practiced law with a passion. He had no other interests, except alcohol. In the late sixties he noticed an affinity for Jack Daniel's. By the early seventies he was a drunk, and when he hired Jake in 1978 he was a full-fledged alcoholic. But he never let booze interfere with his work; he learned to drink and work at the same time. Lucien was always half drunk, and he was a dangerous lawyer in that condition. Bold and abrasive by nature, he was downright frightening when he was drinking. At trial he would embarrass the opposing attorneys, insult the judge, abuse the witnesses, then apologize to the jury. He respected no one and could not be intimidated. He was feared because he would say and do anything. People walked lightly around Lucien. He knew it and loved it. He became more and more eccentric. The more he drank, the crazier he acted, then people talked about him even more, so he drank even more.

Between 1966 and 1978 Lucien hired and disposed of eleven associates. He hired blacks, Jews, Hispanics, women, and not one kept the pace he demanded. He was a tyrant around the office, constantly cursing and berating the young lawyers. Some quit the first month. One lasted two years. It was difficult to accept Lucien's craziness. He had the money to be eccentric—his associates did not.

He hired Jake in 1978 fresh from law school. Jake was from Karaway, a small town of twenty-five hundred, eighteen miles west of Clanton. He was clean-cut, conservative, a devout Presbyterian with a pretty wife who wanted babies. Lucien hired him to see if he could corrupt him. Jake took the job with strong reservations because he had no other offers close to home.

A year later Lucien was disbarred. It was a tragedy for those very few who liked him. The small union at the shoe factory north of town had called a strike. It was a union Lucien had organized and represented. The factory began hiring new workers to replace the strikers, and violence followed. Lucien appeared on the picket line to rally his people. He was drunker than normal. A group of scabs attempted to cross the line and a brawl erupted. Lucien led the charge, was arrested and jailed. He was convicted in city court of assault and battery and disorderly conduct. He appealed and lost, appealed and lost.

The State Bar Association had grown weary of Lucien over the years. No other attorney in the state had received as many complaints as had Lucien Wilbanks. Private reprimands, public reprimands, and suspensions had all been used, all to no avail. The Complaints Tribunal and Disciplinary Committee moved swiftly. He was disbarred for outrageous conduct unbecoming a member of the bar. He appealed and lost, appealed and lost.

He was devastated. Jake was in Lucien's office, the big office upstairs, when word came from Jackson that the Supreme Court had upheld the disbarment. Lucien hung up the phone and walked to the doors overlooking the square. Jake watched him closely, waiting for the tirade. But Lucien said nothing. He walked slowly down the stairs, stopped and stared at Ethel, who was crying, and then looked at Jake. He opened the door and said, "Take care of this place. I'll see you later."

They ran to the front window and watched him speed away from the square in his ragged old Porsche. For several months there was no word from him. Jake labored diligently on Lucien's cases while Ethel kept the office from chaos. Some of the cases were settled, some left for other lawyers, some went to trial.

Six months later Jake returned to his office after a long day in court and found Lucien asleep on the Persian rug in the big office. "Lucien! Are you all right?" he asked.

Lucien jumped up and sat in the big leather chair behind the desk. He was sober, tanned, relaxed.

"Jake, my boy, how are you?" he asked warmly.

"Fine, just fine. Where have you been?"

"Cayman Islands."

"Doing what?"

"Drinking rum, lying on the beach, chasing little native girls."

"Sounds like fun. Why did you leave?"

"It got boring."

Jake sat across the desk. "It's good to see you, Lucien."

"Good to see you, Jake. How are things around here?"

"Hectic. But okay, I guess."

"Did you settle Medley?"

"Yeah. They paid eighty thousand."

"That's very good. Was he happy?"

"Yes, seemed to be."

"Did Cruger go to trial?"

Jake looked at the floor. "No, he hired Fredrix. I think it's set for trial next month."

"I should've talked to him before I left."

"He's guilty, isn't he?"

"Yes, very. It doesn't matter who represents him. Most defendants are guilty. Remember that." Lucien walked to the French doors and gazed at the courthouse. "What are your plans, Jake?"

"I'd like to stay here. What are your plans?"

"You're a good man, Jake, and I want you to stay. Me, I don't know. I thought about moving to the Caribbean, but I won't. It's a nice place to visit, but it gets old. I have no plans really. I may travel. Spend some money. I'm worth a ton, you know."

Jake agreed. Lucien turned and waved his arms around the room. "I want you to have all this, Jake. I want you to stay here and keep some semblance of a firm going. Move into this office; use this desk that my grandfather brought from Virginia after the Civil War. Keep the files, cases, clients, books, everything."

"That's very generous, Lucien."

"Most of the clients will disappear. No reflection on you —you'll be a great lawyer someday. But most of my clients have followed me for years."

Jake didn't want most of his clients. "How about rent?"

"Pay me what you can afford. Money will be tight at first, but you'll make it. I don't need money, but you do."

"You're being very kind."

"I'm really a nice guy." They both laughed awkwardly. Jake quit smiling. "What about Ethel?"

"It's up to you. She's a good secretary who's forgotten more law than you'll ever know. I know you don't like her, but she would be hard to replace. Fire her if you want to. I don't care."

Lucien headed for the door. "Call me if you need me. I'll be around. I want you to move into this office. It was my father's and grandfather's. Put my junk in some boxes, and I'll pick it up later."

Cobb and Willard awoke with throbbing heads and red, swollen eyes. Ozzie was yelling at them. They were in a small cell by themselves. Through the bars to the right was a cell where the state prisoners were held awaiting the trip to Parchman. A dozen blacks leaned through the bars and glared at the two white boys as they struggled to clear their eyes. To the left was a smaller cell, also full of blacks. Wake up, Ozzie yelled, and stay quiet, or he would integrate his jail.

Jake's quiet time was from seven until Ethel arrived at eight-thirty. He was jealous with this time. He locked the front door, ignored the phone, and refused to make appointments. He meticulously planned his day. By eight-thirty he would have enough work dictated to keep Ethel busy and quiet until noon. By nine he was either in court or seeing clients. He would not take calls until eleven, when he methodically returned the morning's messages—all of them. He never delayed returning a phone call—another rule. Jake worked systematically and efficiently with little wasted time. These habits he had not learned from Lucien.

At eight-thirty Ethel made her usual noisy entrance downstairs. She made fresh coffee and opened the mail as she had every day for the past forty-one years. She was sixty-four and looked fifty. She was plump, but not fat, well kept, but not attractive. She chomped on a greasy sausage and biscuit brought from home and read Jake's mail.

Jake heard voices. Ethel was talking to another woman. He checked his appointment book—none until ten.

"Good morning, Mr. Brigance," Ethel announced through the intercom.

"Morning, Ethel." She preferred to be called Mrs.

Twitty. Lucien and everyone else called her that. But Jake
had called her Ethel since he had fired her shortly after the
disbarment.

"There's a lady here to see you."

"She doesn't have an appointment."

"Yes, sir, I know."

"Make one for tomorrow morning after ten-thirty. I'm
busy now."

"Yes, sir. But she says it's urgent."

"Who is it?" he snapped. It was always urgent when
they dropped in unannounced, like dropping by a funeral
home or a Laundromat. Probably some urgent question
about Uncle Luke's will or the case set for trial in three
months.

"A Mrs. Willard," Ethel replied.

"First name?"

"Earnestine Willard. You don't know her, but her son's
in jail."

Jake saw his appointments on time, but drop-ins were
another matter. Ethel either ran them off or made appointments for the next day or so. Mr. Brigance was very busy, she
would explain, but he could work you in day after tomorrow.
This impressed people.

"Tell her I'm not interested."

"But she says she must find a lawyer. Her son has to be
in court at one this afternoon."

"Tell her to see Drew Jack Tyndale, the public defender.
He's good and he's free."

Ethel relayed the message. "But, Mr. Brigance, she
wants to hire you. Someone told her you're the best criminal
lawyer in the county." The amusement was obvious in
Ethel's voice.

"Tell her that's true, but I'm not interested."

Ozzie handcuffed Willard and led him down the hall to his
office in the front section of the Ford County jail. He removed the handcuffs and seated him in a wooden chair in
the center of the cramped room. Ozzie sat in the big chair
across the desk and looked down at the defendant.

"Mr. Willard, this here is Lieutenant Griffin with the

Mississippi Highway Patrol. Over here is Investigator Rady with my office, and this here is Deputy Looney and Deputy Prather, whom you met last night but I doubt if you remember it. I'm Sheriff Walls."

Willard jerked his head fearfully to look at each one. He was surrounded. The door was shut. Two tape recorders sat side by side near the edge of the sheriff's desk.

"We'd like to ask you some questions, okay?"

"I don't know."

"Before I start, I wanna make sure you understand your rights. First of all, you have the right to remain silent. Understand?"

"Uh huh."

"You don't have to talk if you don't want to, but if you do, anything you say can and will be used against you in court. Understand?"

"Uh huh."

"Can you read and write?"

"Yeah."

"Good, then read this and sign it. It says you've been advised of your rights."

Willard signed. Ozzie pushed the red button on one of the tape recorders.

"You understand this tape recorder is on?"

"Uh huh."

"And it's Wednesday, May 15, at eight forty-three in the mornin'."

"If you say so."

"What's your full name?"

"James Louis Willard."

"Nickname?"

"Pete. Pete Willard."

"Address?"

"Route 6, Box 14, Lake Village, Mississippi."

"What road?"

"Bethel Road."

"Who do you live with?"

"My momma, Earnestine Willard. I'm divorced."

"You know Billy Ray Cobb?"

Willard hesitated and noticed his feet. His boots were

back in the cell. His white socks were dirty and did not hide his two big toes. Safe question, he thought.

"Yeah, I know him."

"Was you with him yesterday?"

"Uh huh."

"Where were y'all?"

"Down at the lake."

"What time did you leave?"

" 'Bout three."

"What were you drivin'?"

"I wasn't."

"What were you ridin' in?"

Hesitation. He studied his toes. "I don't think I wanna talk no more."

Ozzie pushed another button and the recorder stopped. He breathed deeply at Willard. "You ever been to Parchman?"

Willard shook his head.

"You know how many niggers at Parchman?"

Willard shook his head.

" 'Bout five thousand. You know how many white boys are there?"

"No."

" 'Bout a thousand."

Willard dropped his chin to his chest. Ozzie let him think for a minute, then winked at Lieutenant Griffin.

"You got any idea what those niggers will do to a white boy who raped a little black girl?"

No response.

"Lieutenant Griffin, tell Mr. Willard how white boys are treated at Parchman."

Griffin walked to Ozzie's desk and sat on the edge. He looked down at Willard. "About five years ago a young white man in Helena County, over in the delta, raped a black girl. She was twelve. They were waiting on him when he got to Parchman. Knew he was coming. First night about thirty blacks tied him over a fifty-five-gallon drum and climbed on. The guards watched and laughed. There's no sympathy for rapists. They got him every night for three months, and then killed him. They found him castrated, stuffed in the drum."

Willard cringed, then threw his head back and breathed heavily toward the ceiling.

"Look, Pete," Ozzie said, "we're not after you. We want Cobb. I've been after that boy since he left Parchman. I want him real bad. You help us get Cobb and I'll help you as much as I can. I ain't promisin' nothin', but me and the D.A. work close together. You help me get Cobb, and I'll help you with the D.A. Just tell us what happened."

"I wanna lawyer," Willard said.

Ozzie dropped his head and groaned. "What's a lawyer gonna do, Pete? Get the niggers off of you? I'm tryin' to help you and you're bein' a wiseass."

"You need to listen to the sheriff, son. He's trying to save your life," Griffin said helpfully.

"There's a good chance you could get off with just a few years here in this jail," Rady said.

"It's much safer than Parchman," Prather said.

"Choice is yours, Pete," Ozzie said. "You can die at Parchman or stay here. I'll even consider makin' you a trusty if you behave."

Willard dropped his head and rubbed his temples. "Okay, okay."

Ozzie punched the red button.

"Where'd you find the girl?"

"Some gravel road."

"Which road?"

"I don't know. I's drunk."

"Where'd you take her?"

"I don't know."

"Just you and Cobb?"

"Yeah."

"Who raped her?"

"We both did. Billy Ray went first."

"How many times?"

"I don't remember. I's smokin' weed and drinkin'."

"Both of you raped her?"

"Yeah."

"Where'd you dump her?"

"Don't remember. I swear I don't remember."

Ozzie pushed another button. "We'll type this up and get you to sign it."

Willard shook his head. "Just don't tell Billy Ray."

"We won't," promised the sheriff.

4 Percy Bullard fidgeted nervously in the leather chair behind the huge, battered oak desk in the judge's chambers behind the courtroom, where a crowd had gathered to see about the rape. In the small room next door the lawyers gathered around the coffee machine and gossiped about the rape.

Bullard's small black robe hung in a corner by the window that looked north over Washington Street. His size-six feet were wearing jogging shoes that barely touched the floor. He was a small, nervous type who worried about preliminary hearings and every other routine hearing. After thirteen years on the bench he had never learned to relax. Fortunately, he was not required to hear big cases; those were for the Circuit Court judge. Bullard was just a County Court judge, and he had reached his pinnacle.

Mr. Pate, the ancient courtroom deputy, knocked on the door.

"Come in!" Bullard demanded.

"Afternoon, Judge."

"How many blacks out there?" Bullard asked abruptly.

"Half the courtroom."

"That's a hundred people! They don't draw that much for a good murder trial. Whatta they want?"

Mr. Pate shook his head.

"They must think we're trying these boys today."

"I guess they're just concerned," Mr. Pate said softly.

"Concerned about what? I'm not turning them loose. It's just a preliminary hearing." He quieted and stared at the window. "Is the family out there?"

"I think so. I recognize a few of them, but I don't know her parents."

"How about security?"

"Sheriff's got ever deputy and ever reserve close to the courtroom. We checked everbody at the door."

"Find anything?"

"No, sir."

"Where are the boys?"

"Sheriff's got them. They'll be here in a minute."

The judge seemed satisfied. Mr. Pate laid a handwritten note on the desk.

"What is it?"

Mr. Pate inhaled deeply. "It's a request from a TV crew from Memphis to film the hearing."

"What!" Bullard's face turned red and he rocked furiously in the swivel chair. "Cameras," he yelled. "In my courtroom!" He ripped the note and threw the pieces in the direction of the trash can. "Where are they?"

"In the rotunda."

"Order them out of the courthouse."

Mr. Pate left quickly.

Carl Lee Hailey sat on the row next to the back. Dozens of relatives and friends surrounded him in the rows of padded benches on the right side of the courtroom. The benches on the left side were empty. Deputies milled about, armed, apprehensive, keeping a nervous watch on the group of blacks, and especially on Carl Lee, who sat bent over, elbows on knees, staring blankly at the floor.

Jake looked out his window across the square to the rear of the courthouse, which faced south. It was 1:00 P.M. He had skipped lunch, as usual, and had no business across the street, but he did need some fresh air. He hadn't left the building all day, and although he had no desire to hear the details of the rape, he hated to miss the hearing. There had to be a crowd in the courtroom because there were no empty parking spaces around the square. A handful of reporters and photographers waited anxiously near the rear of the courthouse by the wooden doors where Cobb and Willard would enter.

The jail was two blocks off the square on the south side, down the highway. Ozzie drove the car with Cobb and Willard in the back seat. With a squad car in front and one behind, the procession turned off Washington Street into the short driveway leading under the veranda of the courthouse. Six deputies escorted the defendants past the reporters, through the doors, and up the back stairs to the small room just outside the courtroom.

Jake grabbed his coat, ignored Ethel, and raced across the street. He ran up the back stairs, through a small hall outside the jury room, and entered the courtroom from a side door just as Mr. Pate led His Honor to the bench.

"All rise for the court," Mr. Pate shouted. Everyone stood. Bullard stepped to the bench and sat down.

"Be seated," he yelled. "Where are the defendants? Where? Bring them in then."

Cobb and Willard were led, handcuffed, into the courtroom from the small holding room. They were unshaven, wrinkled, dirty, and looked confused. Willard stared at the large group of blacks while Cobb turned his back. Looney removed the handcuffs and seated them next to Drew Jack Tyndale, the public defender, at the long table where the defense sat. Next to it was a long table where the county prosecutor, Rocky Childers, sat taking notes and looking important.

Willard glanced over his shoulder and again checked on the blacks. On the front row just behind him sat his mother and Cobb's mother, each with a deputy for protection. Willard felt safe with all the deputies. Cobb refused to turn around.

From the back row, eighty feet away, Carl Lee raised his head and looked at the backs of the two men who raped his daughter. They were mangy, bearded, dirty-looking strangers. He covered his face and bent over. The deputies stood behind him, backs against the wall, watching every move.

"Now listen," Bullard began loudly, "This is just a preliminary hearing, not a trial. The purpose of a preliminary hearing is to determine if there is enough evidence that a crime has been committed to bind these defendants over to the grand jury. The defendants can even waive this hearing if they want to."

Tyndale stood. "No sir, Your Honor, we wish to proceed with the hearing."

"Very well. I have copies of affidavits sworn to by Sheriff Walls charging both defendants with rape of a female under the age of twelve, kidnapping, and aggravated assault. Mr. Childers, you may call your first witness."

"Your Honor, the State calls Sheriff Ozzie Walls."

Jake sat in the jury box, along with several other attorneys, all of whom pretended to be busy reading important materials. Ozzie was sworn and sat in the witness chair to the left of Bullard, a few feet from the jury box.

"Would you state your name?"

"Sheriff Ozzie Walls."

"You're the sheriff of Ford County?"

"Yes."

"I know who he is," Bullard mumbled as he flipped through the file.

"Sheriff, yesterday afternoon, did your office receive a call about a missing child?"

"Yes, around four-thirty."

"What did your office do?"

"Deputy Willie Hastings was dispatched to the residence of Gwen and Carl Lee Hailey, the parents of the girl."

"Where was that?"

"Down on Craft Road, back behind Bates Grocery."

"What did he find?"

"He found the girl's mother, who made the call. Then drove around searchin' for the girl."

"Did he find her?"

"No. When he returned to the house, the girl was there. She'd been found by some folks fishin', and they took her home."

"What shape was the girl in?"

"She'd been raped and beaten."

"Was she conscious?"

"Yeah. She could talk, or mumble, a little."

"What did she say?"

Tyndale jumped to his feet. "Your Honor, please, I know hearsay is admissible in a hearing like this, but this is triple hearsay."

"Overruled. Shut up. Sit down. Continue, Mr. Childers."

"What did she say?"

"Told her momma it was two white men in a yellow pickup truck with a rebel flag in the window. That's about all. She couldn't say much. Had both jaws broken and her face kicked in."

"What happened then?"

"The deputy called an ambulance and she was taken to the hospital."

"How is she?"

"They say she's critical."

"What happened then?"

"Based on what I knew at the time I had a suspect in mind."

"So what'd you do?"

"I located an informant, a reliable informant, and placed him in a beer joint down by the lake."

Childers was not one to dwell on details, especially in front of Bullard. Jake knew it, as did Tyndale. Bullard sent every case to the grand jury, so every preliminary was a formality. Regardless of the case, the facts, the proof, regardless of anything, Bullard would bind the defendant over to the grand jury. If there was insufficient proof, let the grand jury turn them loose, not Bullard. He had to be reelected, the grand jury did not. Voters got upset when criminals were cut loose. Most defense lawyers in the county waived the preliminary hearings before Bullard. Not Jake. He viewed such hearings as the best and quickest way to look at the prosecution's case. Tyndale seldom waived a preliminary hearing.

"Which beer joint?"

"Huey's."

"What'd he find out?"

"Said he heard Cobb and Willard, the two defendants over there, braggin' 'bout rapin' a little black girl."

Cobb and Willard exchanged stares. Who was the informant? They remembered little from Huey's.

"What'd you find at Huey's?"

"We arrested Cobb and Willard, then we searched a pickup titled in the name of Billy Ray Cobb."

"What'd you find?"

"We towed it in and examined it this mornin'. Lot of blood stains."

"What else?"

"We found a small T-shirt covered with blood."

"Whose T-shirt?"

"It belonged to Tonya Hailey, the little girl who was raped. Her daddy, Carl Lee Hailey, identified it this mornin'."

Carl Lee heard his name and sat upright. Ozzie stared

straight at him. Jake turned and saw Carl Lee for the first time.

"Describe the truck."

"New yellow Ford half-ton pickup. Big chrome wheels and mud tires. Rebel flag in the rear window."

"Owned by who?"

Ozzie pointed at the defendants. "Billy Ray Cobb."

"Does it match the description given by the girl?"

"Yes."

Childers paused and reviewed his notes. "Now, Sheriff, what other evidence do you have against these defendants?"

"We talked to Pete Willard this mornin' at the jail. He signed a confession."

"You did what!" Cobb blurted. Willard cowered and looked for help.

"Order! Order!" shouted Bullard as he banged his gavel. Tyndale separated his clients.

"Did you advise Mr. Willard of his rights?"

"Yes."

"Did he understand them?"

"Yes."

"Did he sign a statement to that effect?"

"Yes."

"Who was present when Mr. Willard made his statement?"

"Me, two deputies, my investigator, Rady, and Lieutenant Griffin with the Highway Patrol."

"Do you have the confession?"

"Yes."

"Please read it."

The courtroom was still and silent as Ozzie read the short statement. Carl Lee stared blankly at the two defendants. Cobb glared at Willard, who picked dirt off his boots.

"Thank you, Sheriff," Childers said when Ozzie finished. "Did Mr. Willard sign the confession?"

"Yes, in front of three witnesses."

"The State has nothing further, Your Honor."

Bullard shouted, "You may cross-examine, Mr. Tyndale."

"I have nothing at this time, Your Honor."

Good move, thought Jake. Strategically, for the defense, it was best to stay quiet at preliminary hearings. Just listen, take notes, let the court reporter record the testimony, and stay quiet. The grand jury would see the case anyway, so why bother? And never allow the defendants to testify. Their testimony would serve no purpose and haunt them at trial. Jake knew they would not testify because he knew Tyndale.

"Call your next witness," demanded the Judge.

"We have nothing further, Your Honor."

"Good. Sit down. Mr. Tyndale, do you have any witnesses?"

"No, Your Honor."

"Good. The court finds there is sufficient evidence that numerous crimes have been committed by these defendants, and the court orders Mr. Cobb and Mr. Willard to be held to await action by the Ford County grand jury, which is scheduled to meet on Monday, May 27. Any questions?"

Tyndale rose slowly. "Yes, Your Honor, we would request the court to set a reasonable bond for these de—"

"Forget it," snapped Bullard. "Bail will be denied as of now. It's my understanding that the girl is in critical condition. If she dies, there will of course be other charges."

"Well, Your Honor, in that case, I would like to request a bail hearing a few days from now, in the hopes that her condition improves."

Bullard studied Tyndale carefully. Good idea, he thought. "Granted. A bail hearing is set for next Monday, May 20, in this courtroom. Until then the defendants will remain in the custody of the Ford County sheriff. Court's adjourned."

Bullard rapped the gavel and disappeared. The deputies swarmed around the defendants, handcuffed them, and they too disappeared from the courtroom, into the holding room, down the back stairs, past the reporters, and into the squad car.

The hearing was typical for Bullard—less than twenty minutes. Justice could be very swift in his courtroom.

Jake talked to the other lawyers and watched the crowd file silently through the enormous wooden doors at the rear of the courtroom. Carl Lee was in no hurry to leave, and motioned for Jake to follow him. They met in the rotunda.

Carl Lee wanted to talk, and he excused himself from the crowd and promised to meet them at the hospital. He and Jake walked down the winding staircase to the first floor.

"I'm truly sorry, Carl Lee," Jake said.

"Yeah, me too."

"How is she?"

"She'll make it."

"How's Gwen?"

"Okay, I guess."

"How about you?"

They walked slowly down the hall toward the rear of the courthouse. "It ain't sunk in yet. I mean, twenty-four hours ago everthing was fine. Now look at us. My little girl's layin' up in the hospital with tubes all over her body. My wife's crazy and my boys are scared to death, and all I think about is gettin' my hands on those bastards."

"I wish I could do something, Carl Lee."

"All you can do is pray for her, pray for us."

"I know it hurts."

"You gotta little girl, don't you, Jake?"

"Yeah."

Carl Lee said nothing as they walked in silence. Jake changed the subject. "Where's Lester?"

"Chicago."

"What's he doing?"

"Workin' for a steel company. Good job. Got married."

"You're kidding? Lester, married?"

"Yeah, married a white girl."

"White girl! What's he want with a white girl?"

"Aw, you know Lester. Always an uppity nigger. He's on his way home now. Be in late tonight."

"What for?"

They stopped at the rear door. Jake asked again: "What's Lester coming in for?"

"Family business."

"Y'all planning something?"

"Nope. He just wants to see his niece."

"Y'all don't get excited."

"That's easy for you to say, Jake."

"I know."

"What would you plan, Jake?"

"What do you mean?"

"You gotta little girl. Suppose she's layin up in the hospital, beat and raped. What would you do?"

Jake looked through the window of the door and could not answer. Carl Lee waited.

"Don't do anything stupid, Carl Lee."

"Answer my question. What would you do?"

"I don't know. I don't know what I'd do."

"Lemme ask you this. If it was your little girl, and if it was two niggers, and you could get your hands on them, what would you do?"

"Kill them."

Carl Lee smiled, then laughed. "Sure you would, Jake, sure you would. Then you'd hire some big-shot lawyer to say you's crazy, just like you did in Lester's trial."

"We didn't say Lester was crazy. We just said Bowie needed killing."

"You got him off, didn't you?"

"Sure."

Carl Lee walked to the stairs and looked up. "This how they get to the courtroom?" he asked without looking at Jake.

"Who?"

"Those boys."

"Yeah. Most of the time they take them up those stairs. It's quicker and safer. They can park right outside the door here, and run them up the stairs."

Carl Lee walked to the rear door and looked through the window at the veranda. "How many murder trials you had, Jake?"

"Three. Lester's and two more."

"How many were black?"

"All three."

"How many you win?"

"All three."

"You pretty good on nigger shootin's, ain't you?"

"I guess."

"You ready for another one?"

"Don't do it, Carl Lee. It's not worth it. What if you're convicted and get the gas chamber? What about the kids? Who'll raise them? Those punks aren't worth it."

"You just told me you'd do it."

Jake walked to the door next to Carl Lee. "It's different with me. I could probably get off."

"How?"

"I'm white, and this is a white county. With a little luck I could get an all-white jury, which will naturally be sympathetic. This is not New York or California. A man's supposed to protect his family. A jury would eat it up."

"And me?"

"Like I said, this ain't New York or California. Some whites would admire you, but most would want to see you hang. It would be much harder to win an acquittal."

"But you could do it, couldn't you, Jake?"

"Don't do it, Carl Lee."

"I have no choice, Jake. I'll never sleep till those bastards are dead. I owe it to my little girl, I owe it to myself, and I owe it to my people. It'll be done."

They opened the doors, walked under the veranda and down the driveway to Washington Street, across from Jake's office. They shook hands. Jake promised to stop by the hospital tomorrow to see Gwen and the family.

"One more thing, Jake. Will you meet me at the jail when they arrest me?"

Jake nodded before he thought. Carl Lee smiled and walked down the sidewalk to his truck.

5 Lester Hailey married a Swedish girl from Wisconsin, and although she still professed love for him, Lester suspected the novelty of his skin was beginning to fade. She was terrified of Mississippi, and flatly refused to travel south with Lester even though he assured her she would be safe. She had never met his family. Not that his people were anxious to meet her—they were not. It was not uncommon for Southern blacks to move north and marry white girls, but no Hailey had ever mixed. There were many Haileys in Chicago; most were kin, and all married black. The family was not impressed with Lester's blonde wife. He drove to Clanton in his new Cadillac, by himself.

It was late Wednesday night when he arrived at the hospital and found some cousins reading magazines in the second-floor waiting room. He embraced Carl Lee. They had not seen each other since the Christmas holidays, when half the blacks in Chicago trooped home to Mississippi and Alabama.

They stepped into the hall, away from the relatives. "How is she?" Lester asked.

"Better. Much better. Might go home this weekend."

Lester was relieved. When he left Chicago eleven hours earlier she had been near death, according to the cousin who had called and scared him from bed. He lit a Kool under the NO SMOKING sign and stared at his big brother. "You okay?"

Carl Lee nodded and glanced down the hall.

"How's Gwen?"

"Crazier than normal. She's at her momma's. You come by yourself?"

"Yeah," Lester answered defensively.

"Good."

"Don't get smart. I didn't drive all day to hear crap about my wife."

"Okay, okay. You still got gas?"

Lester smiled and chuckled. He had been plagued by stomach gas since the day he married the Swede. She prepared dishes he couldn't pronounce, and his system behaved violently. He longed for collards, peas, okra, fried chicken, barbecue pork, and fatback.

They found a small waiting room on the third floor with folding chairs and a card table. Lester bought two cups of stale, thick coffee from a machine and stirred the powdered cream with his finger. He listened intently as Carl Lee detailed the rape, the arrests, and the hearing. Lester found some napkins and diagrammed the courthouse and the jail. It had been four years since his murder trial, and he had trouble with the drawings. He had spent only a week in jail, prior to posting bond, and had not visited the place since his acquittal. In fact, he had left for Chicago shortly after his trial. The victim had relatives.

They made plans and discarded them, plotting well past midnight.

———

At noon Thursday Tonya was removed from intensive care and placed in a private room. She was listed as stable. The doctors relaxed, and her family brought candy, toys, and flowers. With two broken jaws and a mouthful of wire, she could only stare at the candy. Her brothers ate most of it. They clung to her bed and held her hand, as if to protect and reassure. The room stayed full of friends and strangers, all patting her gently and saying how sweet she was, all treating her as someone special, someone who had been through this horrible thing. The crowd moved in shifts, from the hall into her room, and back into the hall, where the nurses watched carefully.

The wounds hurt, and at times she cried. Every hour the nurses cleared a path through the visitors and found the patient for a dose of painkiller.

That night in her room, the crowd hushed as the Memphis station talked about the rape. The television showed pictures of the two white men, but she couldn't see very well.

———

The Ford County Courthouse opened at 8:00 A.M. and closed at 5:00 P.M. every day except Friday, when it closed at four-thirty. At four-thirty on Friday Carl Lee was hiding in a first-floor restroom when they locked the courthouse. He sat on a toilet and listened quietly for an hour. No janitors. No one. Silence. He walked through the wide, semidark hall to the rear doors, and peeked through the window. No one in sight. He listened for a while. The courthouse was deserted. He turned and looked down the long hall, through the rotunda and through the front doors, two hundred feet away.

He studied the building. The two sets of rear doors opened to the inside into a large, rectangular entrance area. To the far right was a set of stairs, and to the left was an identical stairway. The open area narrowed and led into the hall. Carl Lee pretended to be on trial. He grabbed his hands behind him, and touched his back to the rear door. He walked to his right thirty feet to the stairs; up the stairs, ten steps, then a small landing, then a ninety-degree turn to the left, just like Lester said; then, ten more steps to the holding room. It was a small room, fifteen by fifteen, with nothing but a window and two doors. One door he opened, and walked into the huge courtroom in front of the rows of padded pews. He walked to the aisle and sat in the front row. Surveying the room, he noticed in front of him the railing, or bar, as Lester called it, which separated the general public from the area where the judge, jury, witnesses, lawyers, defendants, and clerks sat and worked.

He walked down the aisle to the rear doors and examined the courtroom in detail. It looked much different from Wednesday. Back down the aisle, he returned to the holding room and tried the other door, which led to the area behind the bar where the trial took place. He sat at the long table where Lester and Cobb and Willard had sat. To the right was another long table where the prosecutors sat. Behind the tables was a row of wooden chairs, then the bar with swinging gates on both ends. The judge sat high and lordly behind the elevated bench, his back to the wall under the faded portrait of Jefferson Davis, frowning down on everyone in the room. The jury box was against the wall to Carl Lee's right, to the judge's left, under the yellow portraits of other forgotten Confederate heroes. The witness stand was next to the bench, but lower, of course, and in front of the jury. To Carl Lee's left, opposite the jury box, was a long, enclosed workbench covered with large red docket books.

Clerks and lawyers usually milled around behind it during a trial. Behind the workbench, through the wall, was the holding room.

Carl Lee stood, still as though handcuffed, and walked slowly through the small swinging gate in the bar, and was led through the first door into the holding room; then down the steps, ten of them, through the narrow, shadowy stairway; then he stopped. From the landing halfway down the steps, he could see the rear doors of the courthouse and most of the entrance area between the doors and the hall. At the foot of the stairs, to the right, was a door that he opened and found a crowded, junky janitor's closet. He closed the door and explored the small room. It turned and ran under the stairway. It was dark, dusty, crowded with brooms and buckets and seldom used. He opened the door slightly and looked up the stairs.

For another hour he roamed the courthouse. The other rear stairway led to another holding room just behind the jury box. One door went to the courtroom, the other to the jury room. The stairs continued to the third floor, where he found the county law library and two witness rooms, just as Lester said.

Up and down, up and down, he traced and retraced the movements to be made by the men who raped his daughter.

He sat in the judge's chair and surveyed his domain. He sat in the jury box and rocked in one of the comfortable chairs. He sat in the witness chair and blew into the microphone. It was finally dark at seven when Carl Lee raised a window in the restroom next to the janitor's closet, and slid quietly through the bushes and into the darkness.

———

"Who would you report it to?" Carla asked as she closed the fourteen-inch pizza box and poured some more lemonade.

Jake rocked slightly in the wicker swing on the front porch and watched Hanna skip rope on the sidewalk next to the street.

"Are you there?" she asked.

"No."

"Who would you report it to?"

"I don't plan to report it," he said.

"I think you should."

"I think I shouldn't."

"Why not?"

His rocking gained speed and he sipped the lemonade. He spoke slowly. "First of all, I don't know for sure that a crime is being planned. He said some things any father would say, and I'm sure he's having thoughts any father would have. But as far as actually planning a crime, I don't think so. Secondly, what he said to me was said in confidence, just as if he was a client. In fact, he probably thinks of me as his lawyer."

"But even if you're his lawyer, and you know he's planning a crime, you have to report it, don't you?"

"Yes. If I'm certain of his plans. But I'm not."

She was not satisfied. "I think you should report it."

Jake did not respond. It wouldn't matter. He ate his last bite of crust and tried to ignore her.

"You want Carl Lee to do it, don't you?"

"Do what?"

"Kill those boys."

"No, I don't." He was not convincing. "But if he did, I wouldn't blame him because I'd do the same thing."

"Don't start that again."

"I'm serious and you know it. I'd do it."

"Jake, you couldn't kill a man."

"Okay. Whatever. I'm not going to argue. We've been through it before."

Carla yelled at Hanna to move away from the street. She sat next to him in the swing and rattled her ice cubes. "Would you represent him?"

"I hope so."

"Would the jury convict him?"

"Would you?"

"I don't know."

"Well, think of Hanna. Just look at that sweet little innocent child out there skipping rope. You're a mother. Now think of the little Hailey girl, lying there, beaten, bloody, begging for her momma and daddy—"

"Shut up, Jake!"

He smiled. "Answer the question. You're on the jury. Would you vote to convict the father?"

She placed her glass on the windowsill and suddenly became interested in her cuticles. Jake smelled victory.

"Come on. You're on the jury. Conviction or acquittal?"

"I'm always on the jury around here. Either that or I'm being cross-examined."

"Convict or acquit?"

She glared at him. "It would be hard to convict."

He grinned and rested his case.

"But I don't see how he could kill them if they're in jail."

"Easy. They're not always in jail. They go to court and they're transported to and from. Remember Oswald and Jack Ruby. Plus, they get out if they can make bail."

"When can they do that?"

"Bonds will be set Monday. If they bond out, they're loose."

"And if they can't?"

"They remain in jail until trial."

"When is the trial?"

"Probably late summer."

"I think you should report it."

Jake bolted from the swing and went to play with Hanna.

6

K. T. Bruster, or Cat Bruster, as he was known, was, to his knowledge, the only one-eyed black millionaire in Memphis. He owned a string of black topless joints in town, all of which he operated legally. He owned blocks of rental property, which he operated legally, and he owned two churches in south Memphis, which were also operated legally. He was a benefactor for numerous black causes, a friend of the politicians, and a hero to his people.

It was important for Cat to be popular in the community because he would be indicted again and tried again, and in all likelihood acquitted again by his peers, half of whom were black. The authorities had found it impossible to convict Cat of killing people and of selling such things as women, cocaine, stolen goods, credit cards, food stamps, untaxed liquor, guns, and light artillery.

He had one eye with him. The other one was somewhere in a rice paddy in Vietnam. He lost it the same day in 1971 that his buddy Carl Lee Hailey was hit in the leg. Carl Lee carried him for two hours before they found help. After the war he returned to Memphis and brought with him two pounds of hashish. The proceeds went to buy a small saloon on South Main, and he almost starved before he won a whore in a poker game with a pimp. He promised her she could quit whoring if she would take off her clothes and dance on his tables. Overnight he had more business than he could seat, so he bought another bar, and brought in more dancers. He found his niche in the market, and within two years he was a very wealthy man.

His office was above one of his clubs just off South Main between Vance and Beale, in the roughest part of Memphis. The sign above the sidewalk advertised Bud and breasts, but much more was for sale behind the black windows.

Carl Lee and Lester found the lounge—Brown Sugar—around noon, Saturday. They sat at the bar, ordered Bud, and watched the breasts.

"Is Cat in?" Carl Lee asked the bartender when he walked behind them. He grunted and returned to the sink, where he continued his beer mug washing. Carl Lee glanced at him between sips and dance routines.

"Another beer!" Lester said loudly without taking his eyes off the dancers.

"Cat Bruster here?" Carl Lee asked firmly when the bartender brought the beer.

"Who wants to know?"

"I do."

"So."

"So me and Cat are good friends. Fought together in 'Nam."

"Name?"

"Hailey. Carl Lee Hailey. From Mississippi."

The bartender disappeared, and a minute later emerged from between two mirrors behind the liquor. He motioned for the Haileys, who followed him through a small door, past the restrooms and through a locked door up the stairs. The office was dark and gaudy. The carpet on the floor was gold, on the walls, red, on the ceiling, green. A green shag ceiling. Thin steel bars covered the two blackened windows, and for good measure a set of heavy, dusty, burgundy drapes hung from ceiling to floor to catch and smother any sunlight robust enough to penetrate the painted glass. A small, ineffective chrome chandelier with mirror panes rotated slowly in the center of the room, barely above their heads.

Two mammoth bodyguards in matching three-piece black suits dismissed the bartender and seated Lester and Carl Lee, and stood behind them.

The brothers admired the furnishings. "Nice, ain't it?" Lester said. B.B. King mourned softly on a hidden stereo.

Suddenly, Cat entered from a hidden door behind the marble and glass desk. He lunged at Carl Lee. "My man! My man! Carl Lee Hailey!" He shouted and grabbed Carl Lee. "So good to see you, Carl Lee! So good to see you!"

Carl Lee stood and they bearhugged. "How are you, my man!" Cat demanded.

"Doin' fine, Cat, just fine. And you?"

"Great! Great! Who's this?" He turned to Lester and threw a hand in his chest. Lester shook it violently.

"This here's my brother, Lester," Carl Lee said. "He's from Chicago."

"Glad to know you, Lester. Me and the big man here are mighty tight. Mighty tight."

"He's told me all about you," Lester said. Cat admired Carl Lee. "My, my, Carl Lee. You lookin' good. How's the leg?"

"It's fine, Cat. Tightens up sometimes when it rains, but it's fine."

"We mighty tight, ain't we?"

Carl Lee nodded and smiled. Cat released him. "You fellas want a drink?"

"No thanks," said Carl Lee.

"I'll take a beer," said Lester. Cat snapped his fingers and a bodyguard disappeared. Carl Lee fell into his chair and Cat sat on the edge of his desk, his feet dangling and swinging like a kid on a pier. He grinned at Carl Lee, who squirmed under all the admiration.

"Why don't you move to Memphis and go to work for me?" Cat said. Carl Lee knew it was coming. Cat had been offering him jobs for ten years.

"No thanks, Cat. I'm happy."

"And I'm happy for you. What's on your mind?"

Carl Lee opened his mouth, hesitated, crossed his legs and frowned. He nodded, and said, "Need a favor, Cat. Just a small favor."

Cat spread his arms. "Anything, big man, anything you want."

"You remember them M-16's we used in 'Nam? I need one of them. As quick as possible."

Cat recoiled his arms and folded them across his chest. He studied his friend. "That's a bad gun. What kinda squirrels you huntin' down there?"

"It ain't for squirrels."

Cat analyzed them both. He knew better than to ask why. It was serious, or Carl Lee wouldn't be there. "Semi?"

"Nope. The real thing."

"You talkin' some cash."

"How much?"

"It's illegal as hell, you know?"

"If I could buy it at Sears I wouldn't be here."

Cat grinned again. "When do you need it?"

"Today."

The beer arrived and was served to Lester. Cat moved behind his desk, to his orange vinyl captain's chair. "Thousand bucks."

"I got it."

Cat was mildly surprised, but didn't show it. Where did this simple small-town Mississippi nigger find a thousand dollars? Must have borrowed it from his brother.

"Thousand for anyone else, but not for you, big man."

"How much?"

"Nothin', Carl Lee, nothin'. I owe you somethin' worth much more than money."

"I'll be glad to pay for it."

"Nope. I won't hear it. The gun's yours."

"That's mighty kind, Cat."

"I'd give you fifty of them."

"Just need one. When can I get it?"

"Lemme check." Cat phoned someone and mumbled a few sentences into the receiver. The orders given, he hung up and explained it would take about an hour.

"We can wait," Carl Lee said.

Cat removed the patch from his left eye and wiped the empty socket with a handkerchief. "I gotta better idea." He snapped at the bodyguards. "Get my car. We'll drive over and pick it up."

They followed Cat through a secret door and down a hall. "I live here, you know." He pointed. "Through that door is my pad. Usually keep some naked women around."

"I'd like to see it," Lester volunteered.

"That's okay," said Carl Lee.

Farther down the hall Cat pointed to a thick, black, shiny iron door at the end of a short hallway. He stopped as if to admire it. "That's where I keep my cash. Post a guard in there around the clock."

"How much?" Lester asked with a sip of beer.

Cat glared at him and continued down the hall. Carl Lee frowned at his brother and shook his head. Where the hall ended they climbed a narrow stairway to the fourth floor. It was darker, and somewhere in the darkness Cat found a button on a wall. They waited silently for a few seconds until the wall opened and revealed a bright elevator with red carpet and a NO SMOKING sign. Cat pushed another button.

"You gotta walk up to catch the elevator goin' down," he said with amusement. "Security reasons." They nodded approval and admiration.

It opened in the basement. One of the bodyguards waited by the open door of a clean white stretch limo, and Cat invited his guests in for a ride. They moved slowly past a row of Fleetwoods, several more limos, a Rolls, and an assortment of European luxury cars. "They're all mine," he said proudly.

The driver honked and a heavy door rolled up to reveal a one-way side street. "Drive slow," Cat yelled to the chauffeur and the bodyguard way up front. "I wanna show you fellas around some."

Carl Lee had received the tour a few years earlier during his last visit to Cat. There were rows of beaten and paintless shacks that the great man referred to as rental properties. There were ancient red-bricked warehouses with blackened or boarded windows and no clue as to what was stored inside. There was a church, a prosperous church, and a few blocks away, another one. He owned the preachers too, he said. There were dozens of corner taverns with open doors and groups of young blacks sitting on benches outside drinking quart bottles of Stag beer. He pointed proudly to a burned-out building near Beale and told with great zeal the story of a competitor who had attempted to gain a foothold in the topless business. He had no competitors, he said. And then there were the clubs, places with names like Angels and Cat's House and Black Paradise, places where a man could go for good drink, good food, good music, naked women, and possibly more, he said. The clubs had made him a very rich man. Eight of them in all.

They were shown all eight. Plus what seemed like most of the real estate in south Memphis. At the dead end of a nameless street near the river, the driver turned sharply between two of the red-bricked warehouses and drove through a narrow alley until a gate opened to the right. Past the gate a door opened next to a loading dock and the limo disappeared into the building. It stopped and the bodyguard got out.

"Keep your seats," Cat said.

The trunk opened, then shut. In less than a minute the limo was again cruising the streets of Memphis.

"How 'bout lunch?" Cat asked. Before they answered he yelled at the driver, "Black Paradise. Call and tell them I'm comin' for lunch.

"Got the best prime rib in Memphis, right here in one of my clubs. Course you won't read about it in the Sunday paper. I've been shunned by the critics. Can you imagine?"

"Sounds like discrimination," Lester said.

"Yeah, I'm sure it is. But I don't use that until I'm indicted."

"We ain't read about you lately, Cat," Carl Lee said.

"It's been three years since my last trial. Tax evasion. Feds spent three weeks puttin' on proof, and the jury stayed out twenty-seven minutes and returned with the two most precious words in the Afro-English language—'Not guilty.' "

"I've heard them myself," Lester said.

A doorman waited under the canopy at the club, and a set of matching bodyguards, different bodyguards, escorted the great one and his guests to a private booth away from the dance floor. Drinks and food were served by a squad of waiters. Lester switched to Scotch and was drunk when the prime rib arrived. Carl Lee drank iced tea and swapped war stories with Cat.

When the food was gone, a bodyguard approached and whispered to Cat. He grinned and looked at Carl Lee. "Y'all in the red Eldorado with Illinois plates?"

"Yeah. But we left it at the other place."

"It's parked outside . . . in the trunk."

"What?" said Lester. "How—"

Cat roared and slapped him on the back. "Don't ask, my man, don't ask. It's all taken care of, my man. Cat can do anything."

————————

As usual, Jake worked Saturday morning, after breakfast at the Coffee Shop. He enjoyed the tranquility of his office on Saturday—no phones, no Ethel. He locked the office, ignored the phone, and avoided clients. He organized files, read recent decisions from the Supreme Court and planned strategy if a trial was approaching. His best thoughts and ideas came during quiet Saturday mornings.

At eleven he phoned the jail. "Sheriff in?" he asked the dispatcher.

"Lemme check," came the reply.

Moments passed before the sheriff answered. "Sheriff Walls," he announced.

"Ozzie, Jake Brigance. How are you?"

"Fine, Jake. You?"

"Fine. Will you be there for a while?"

"Coupla hours. What's up?"

"Not much. Just need to talk for a minute. I'll be there in thirty minutes."

"I'll be waitin'."

Jake and the sheriff had a mutual like and respect for each other. Jake had roughed him up a few times during cross-examinations, but Ozzie considered it business and nothing personal. Jake campaigned for Ozzie, and Lucien financed the campaigns, so Ozzie didn't mind a few sarcastic and pointed questions during trial. He liked to watch Jake at trial. And he liked to kid him about *the game*. In 1969, when Jake was a sophomore quarterback at Karaway, Ozzie was a senior all-conference, all-state tackle at Clanton. The two rivals, both undefeated, met in the final game at Clanton for the conference championship. For four long quarters Ozzie terrorized the Karaway offense, which was much smaller and led by a gutsy but battered sophomore quarterback. Late in the fourth quarter, leading 44–0, Ozzie broke Jake's leg on a blitz.

For years now he had threatened to break the other one. He always accused Jake of limping and asked about the leg.

"What's on your mind, buddy?" Ozzie asked as they sat in his small office.

"Carl Lee. I'm a little worried about him."

"What way?"

"Look, Ozzie, whatever we say here is said in confidence. I don't want anyone to know about this conversation."

"You sound serious, Jake."

"I am serious. I talked to Carl Lee Wednesday after the hearing. He's out of his mind, and I understand that. I would be too. He was talking about killing the boys, and he sounded serious. I just think you ought to know."

"They're safe, Jake. He couldn't get to them if he wanted to. We've had some phone calls, anonymous of course, with all kinds of threats. Black folks are bad upset. But the boys're safe. They're in a cell by themselves, and we're real careful."

"That's good. I haven't been hired by Carl Lee, but I've represented all the Haileys at one time or another and I'm sure he considers me to be his lawyer, for whatever reason. I feel a responsibility to let you know."

"I'm not worried, Jake."

"Good. Let me ask you something. I've got a daughter, and you've got a daughter, right?"

"Got two of them."

"What's Carl Lee thinking? I mean, as a black father?"

"Same thing you'd be thinkin'."

"And what's that?"

Ozzie reared back in his chair and crossed his arms. He thought for a moment. "He's wonderin' if she's okay, physically, I mean. Is she gonna live, and if she does, how bad is she hurt. Can she ever have kids? Then he's wonderin' if she's okay mentally and emotionally, and how will this affect her for the rest of her life. Thirdly, he wants to kill the bastards."

"Would you?"

"It's easy to say I would, but a man don't know what he'd do. I think my kids need me at home a whole lot more than Parchman needs me. What would you be thinkin', Jake?"

"About the same, I guess. I don't know what I'd do. Probably go crazy." He paused and stared at the desk. "But I might seriously plan to kill whoever did it. It'd be mighty hard to lie down at night knowing he was still alive."

"What would a jury do?"

"Depends on who's on the jury. You pick the right jury and you walk. If the D.A. picks the right jury you get the gas. It depends strictly on the jury, and in this county you can pick the right folks. People are tired of raping and robbing and killing. I know white folks are."

"Everbody is."

"My point is that there'd be a lot of sympathy for a father who took matters into his own hands. People don't trust our judicial system. I think I could at least hang a jury. Just convince one or two that the bastard needed to die."

"Like Monroe Bowie."

"Exactly. Just like Monroe Bowie. He was a sorry nigger who needed killing and Lester took a walk. By the way, Ozzie, why do you suppose Lester drove from Chicago?"

"He's pretty close to his brother. We're watchin' him too."

The conversation changed and Ozzie finally asked about the leg. They shook hands and Jake left. He drove straight home, where Carla was waiting with her list. She didn't mind the Saturdays at the office as long as he was home by noon and pretty much followed orders thereafter.

On Sunday afternoon a crowd gathered at the hospital and followed the little Hailey girl's wheelchair as it was pushed by her father down the hall, through the doors, and into the parking lot, where he gently raised her and sat her in the front seat. As she sat between her parents, with her three brothers in the back seat, he drove away, followed by a procession of friends and relatives and strangers. The caravan moved slowly, deliberately out of town and into the country.

She sat up in the front seat like a big girl. Her father was silent, her mother tearful, and her brothers mute and rigid.

Another throng waited at the house and rushed to the porch as the cars moved up the driveway and parked on the grass on the long front yard. The crowd hushed as he carried her up the steps, through the door, and laid her on the couch. She was glad to be home, but tired of the spectators. Her mother held her feet as cousins, uncles, aunts, neighbors, and everybody walked to her and touched her and smiled, some through tears, and said nothing. Her daddy went outside and talked to Uncle Lester and the men. Her brothers were in the kitchen with the crowd devouring the pile of food.

7 Rocky Childers had been the prosecutor for Ford County for more years than he cared to remember. The job paid fifteen thousand a year and required most of his time. It also destroyed any practice he hoped to build. At forty-two he was washed up as a lawyer, stuck in a dead-end part-time, full-time job, elected permanently every four years. Thankfully, he had a wife with a good job so they could drive new Buicks and afford the country club dues and in general put on the necessary airs of educated white people in Ford County. At a younger age he had political ambitions, but the voters dissuaded him, and he was malcontent to exhaust his career prosecuting drunks, shoplifters, and juvenile delinquents, and being abused by Judge Bullard, whom he despised. Excitement crept up occasionally when people like Cobb and Willard screwed up, and Rocky, by statutory authority, handled the preliminary and other hearings before the cases were sent to the grand jury and then to Circuit Court, and then to the real prosecutor, the big prosecutor, the district attorney, Mr. Rufus Buckley, from Polk County. It was Buckley who had disposed of Rocky's political career.

Normally, a bail hearing was no big affair for Childers, but this was a bit different. Since Wednesday he had received dozens of phone calls from blacks, all registered voters or claiming to be, who were very concerned about Cobb and Willard being released from jail. They wanted the boys locked up, just like the black ones who got in trouble and could not make bail before trial. Childers promised his best, but explained the bonds would be set by County Judge Percy Bullard, whose number was also in the phone book. On Bennington Street. They promised to be in court Monday to watch him and Bullard.

At twelve-thirty Monday, Childers was summoned to the judge's chambers, where the sheriff and Bullard were waiting. The judge was so nervous he could not sit.

"How much bond do you want?" he snapped at Childers.

"I dunno, Judge. I haven't thought much about it."

"Don't you think it's about time you thought about it?" He paced rapidly back and forth behind his desk, then to the window, then back to his desk. Ozzie was amused and silent.

"Not really," Childers answered softly. "It's your decision. You're the judge."

"Thanks! Thanks! Thanks! How much will you ask for?"

"I always ask for more than I expect," replied Childers coolly, thoroughly enjoying the judge's neurosis.

"How much is that?"

"I dunno. I hadn't thought much about it."

Bullard's neck turned dark red and he glared at Ozzie. "Whatta you think, Sheriff?"

"Well," Ozzie drawled, "I would suggest pretty stiff bonds. These boys need to be in jail for their own safety. Black folk are restless out there. They might get hurt if they bond out. Better go high."

"How much money they got?"

"Willard's broke. Can't tell about Cobb. Drug money's hard to trace. He might could find twenty, thirty thousand. I hear he's hired some big-shot Memphis lawyer. Supposed to be here today. He must have some money."

"Damn, why don't I know these things. Who'd he hire?"

"Bernard. Peter K. Bernard," answered Childers. "He called me this morning."

"Never heard of him," retorted Bullard with an air of superiority, as though he memorized some kind of judicial rap sheet on all lawyers.

Bullard studied the trees outside the window as the sheriff and prosecutor exchanged winks. The bonds would be exorbitant, as always. The bail bondsmen loved Bullard for his outrageous bonds. They watched with delight as desperate families scraped and mortgaged to collect the ten percent premiums they charged to write the bonds. Bullard would be high, and he didn't care. It was politically safe to set them high and keep the criminals in jail. The blacks would appreciate it and that was important even if the county was seventy-four percent white. He owed the blacks a few favors.

"Let's go a hundred thousand on Willard and two hundred on Cobb. That oughtta satisfy them."

"Satisfy who?" asked Ozzie.

"Er, uh, the people, the people out there. Sound okay to you?"

"Fine with me," said Childers. "But what about the hearing?" he asked with a grin.

"We'll give them a hearing, a fair hearing, then I'll set the bonds at a hundred and two hundred."

"And I suppose you want me to ask for three hundred apiece so you can look fair?" asked Childers.

"I don't care what you ask for!" yelled the judge.

"Sounds fair to me," said Ozzie as he headed for the door. "Will you call me to testify?" he asked Childers.

"Naw, we don't need you. I don't guess the State will call anybody since we're having such a fair hearing."

They left the chambers and Bullard stewed. He locked the door behind them and pulled a half pint of vodka from his briefcase, and gulped it furiously. Mr. Pate waited outside the door. Five minutes later Bullard barged into the packed courtroom.

"All rise for the court!" Mr. Pate shouted.

"Be seated!" screamed the judge before anyone could stand. "Where are the defendants? Where?"

Cobb and Willard were escorted from the holding room and seated at the defense table. Cobb's new lawyer smiled at his client as the handcuffs were removed. Willard's lawyer, Tyndale, the public defender, ignored him.

The same crowd of blacks had returned from last Wednesday, and had brought some friends. They closely followed the movements of the two white boys. Lester saw them for the first time. Carl Lee was not in the courtroom.

From the bench Bullard counted deputies—nine in all. That had to be a record. Then he counted blacks—hundreds of them all bunched together, all glaring at the two rapists, who sat at the same table between their lawyers. The vodka felt good. He took a sip of what appeared to be ice water from a Styrofoam cup and managed a slight grin. It burned slowly downward and his cheeks flushed. What he ought to do was order the deputies out of the courtroom and throw Cobb and Willard to the niggers. That would be fun to watch, and justice would be served. He could just see the fat nigger women stomping up and down while their men carved on the boys with switchblades and machetes. Then, when they were finished, they would collect themselves and all march quietly from the courtroom. He smiled to himself.

He motioned for Mr. Pate, who approached the bench. "I've got a half pint of ice water in my desk drawer," he whispered. "Pour me some in a Styrofoam cup."

Mr. Pate nodded and disappeared.

"This is a bail hearing," he declared loudly, "and I don't intend for it to last long. Are the defendants ready?"

"Yes, sir," said Tyndale.

"Yes, Your Honor," said Mr. Bernard.

"The State ready?"

"Yes, sir," answered Childers without standing.

"Good. Call your first witness."

Childers addressed the judge. "Your Honor, the State will call no witnesses. His Honor is well aware of the charges against these two defendants, since His Honor held the preliminary hearing last Wednesday. It is my understanding the victim is now home, so we do not anticipate further charges. The grand jury will be asked next Monday to indict the two defendants for rape, kidnapping, and aggravated assault. Because of the violent nature of these crimes, because of the age of the victim, and because Mr. Cobb is a convicted felon, the State would ask for the maximum bonds, and not a penny less."

Bullard almost choked on his ice water. What maximum? There's no such thing as a maximum bond.

"What do you suggest, Mr. Childers?"

"Half a million apiece!" Childers announced proudly and sat down.

Half a million! Out of the question, thought Bullard. He sipped furiously and glared at the prosecutor. Half a million! Double-crossed in open court. He sent Mr. Pate after more ice water.

"The defense may proceed."

Cobb's new lawyer stood purposefully. He cleared his throat and removed his horn-rimmed, academic, go-to-hell reading glasses. "May it please the court, Your Honor, my

name is Peter K. Bernard. I am from Memphis, and I have
been retained by Mr. Cobb to represent him—"

"Do you have a license to practice in Mississippi?" interrupted Bullard.

Bernard was caught off-guard. "Well, uh, not exactly,
Your Honor."

"I see. When you say 'not exactly,' do you mean something other than no?"

Several lawyers in the jury box snickered. Bullard was
famous for this. He hated Memphis lawyers, and required
them to associate local counsel before appearing in his
court. Years before when he was practicing, a Memphis
judge had kicked him out of court because he was not licensed in Tennessee. He had enjoyed revenge since the day
he was elected.

"Your Honor, I am not licensed in Mississippi, but I am
licensed in Tennessee."

"I would hope so," came the retort from the bench.
More suppressed laughter from the jury box. "Are you familiar with our local rules here in Ford County?" His Honor
asked.

"Er, uh, yes, sir."

"Do you have a copy of these rules?"

"Yes, sir."

"And you read them carefully before you ventured into
my courtroom?"

"Uh, yes, sir, most of them."

"Did you understand Rule 14 when you read it?"

Cobb glanced up suspiciously at his new lawyer.

"Uh, I don't recall that one," Bernard admitted.

"I didn't think so. Rule 14 requires out-of-state unli-
censed attorneys to associate local counsel when appearing
in my courtroom."

"Yes, sir."

From his looks and mannerisms, Bernard was a polished attorney, at least he was known as such in Memphis.
He was, however, in the process of being totally degraded
and humbled before a small-town, redneck judge with a
quick tongue.

"Yes, sir, what?" snapped Bullard.

"Yes, sir, I think I've heard of that rule."

"Then where's the local counsel?"

"There is none, but I planned—"

"Then you drove down here from Memphis, carefully read my rules, and deliberately ignored them. Right?"

Bernard lowered his head and stared at a blank yellow legal pad on the table.

Tyndale rose slowly. "Your Honor, for the record, I show myself as associated counsel for Mr. Bernard for purposes of this hearing and for no other purpose."

Bullard smiled. Slick move, Tyndale, slick move. The ice water warmed him and he relaxed. "Very well. Call your first witness."

Bernard stood straight again. He cocked his head. "Your Honor, on behalf of Mr. Cobb, I would like to call his brother, Mr. Fred Cobb, to the stand."

"Make it brief," Bullard mumbled.

Cobb's brother was sworn and seated in the witness chair. Bernard assumed the podium and began a long, detailed direct examination. He was well prepared. He elicited proof that Billy Ray Cobb was gainfully employed, owned real estate in Ford County, grew up there, had most of his family there, and friends, and had no reason to leave. A solid citizen with deep roots with much to lose if he fled. A man who could be trusted to show up for court. A man worthy of a low bond.

Bullard sipped, tapped his pen, and searched the black faces in the audience.

Childers had no questions. Bernard called Cobb's mother, Cora, who repeated what her son Fred said about her son Billy Ray. She managed a couple of tears at an awkward moment, and Bullard shook his head.

Tyndale was next. He went through the same motions with Willard's family.

Half a million dollars bond! Anything less would be too little, and the blacks wouldn't like it. The judge had new reason to hate Childers. But he liked the blacks because they elected him last time. He received fifty-one percent of the vote countywide, but he got all the nigger vote.

"Anything else?" he asked when Tyndale finished.

The three lawyers looked blankly at each other, then at the judge. Bernard stood. "Your Honor, I would like to summarize my client's position in regard to a reasonable bond—"

"Forget it, pal. I've heard enough from you and your client. Sit down."

Bullard hesitated, then rapidly announced: "Bond is hereby set at one hundred thousand for Pete Willard, and two hundred thousand for Billy Ray Cobb. Defendants will remain in the custody of the sheriff until they are able to make bail. Court's adjourned." He rapped the gavel and disappeared into his chambers, where he finished the half pint and opened another one.

Lester was pleased with the bonds. His had been fifty thousand for the murder of Monroe Bowie. Of course, Bowie was black, and bonds were generally lower for those cases.

The crowd inched toward the rear door, but Lester did not move. He watched closely as the two white boys were handcuffed and taken through the door into the holding room. When they were out of sight, he placed his head in his hands and said a short prayer. Then he listened.

———————

At least ten times a day Jake walked through the French doors and onto the balcony to inspect downtown Clanton. He sometimes puffed a cheap cigar and blew smoke over Washington Street. Even in the summer he left the windows open in the big office. The sounds of the busy small town made good company as he worked quietly. At times he was amazed at the volume of noise generated on the streets around the courthouse, and at other times he walked to the balcony to see why things were so quiet.

Just before 2:00 P.M., Monday, May 20, he walked to the balcony and lit a cigar. A heavy silence engulfed downtown Clanton, Mississippi.

———————

Cobb went first down the stairs, cautiously, with his hands cuffed behind him, then Willard, then Deputy Looney. Ten steps down, then the landing, turn right, then ten steps to the first floor. Three other deputies waited outside by the patrol cars smoking cigarettes and watching reporters.

When Cobb reached the second step from the floor, and Willard was three steps behind, and Looney was one step off the landing, the small, dirty, neglected, unnoticed door to the janitor's closet burst open and Mr. Carl Lee Hailey sprung from the darkness with an M-16. At point-blank range he opened fire. The loud, rapid, clapping, popping gunfire shook the courthouse and exploded the silence. The rapists froze, then screamed as they were hit—Cobb first, in the stomach and chest, then Willard in the face, neck, and throat. They twisted vainly up the stairs, handcuffed and helpless, stumbling over each other as their skin and blood splashed together.

Looney was hit in the leg but managed to scramble up the stairs into the holding room, where he crouched and listened as Cobb and Willard screamed and moaned and the crazy nigger laughed. Bullets ricocheted between the walls of the narrow stairway, and Looney could see, looking down toward the landing, blood and flesh splashing on the walls and dripping down.

In short, sudden bursts of seven or eight rounds each, the enormous booming sound of the M-16 echoed through the courthouse for an eternity. Through the gunfire and the sounds of the bullets rattling around the walls of the stairway, the high-pitched, shrill, laughing voice of Carl Lee could be plainly heard.

When he stopped, he threw the rifle at the two corpses and ran. Into the restroom, he jammed the door with a chair, crawled out a window into the bushes, then onto the sidewalk. Nonchalantly, he walked to his pickup and drove home.

Lester froze when the shooting started. The gunfire was heard loudly in the courtroom. Willard's mother screamed and Cobb's mother screamed, and the deputies raced into the holding room, but did not venture down the stairs. Lester listened intently for the sounds of handguns, and hearing none, he left the courtroom.

With the first shot, Bullard grabbed the half pint and crawled under his desk while Mr. Pate locked the door.

Cobb, or what was left of him, came to rest on Willard. Their blood mixed and puddled on each step, then it overflowed and dripped to the next step, where it puddled before overflowing and dripping to the next. Soon the foot of the stairway was flooded with the mixture.

––––––––––––

Jake sprinted across the street to the rear door of the courthouse. Deputy Prather crouched in front of the door, gun drawn, and cursed the reporters who pressed forward. The other deputies knelt fearfully on the doorsteps next to the patrol cars. Jake ran to the front of the courthouse, where more deputies were guarding the door and evacuating the county employees and courtroom spectators. A mass of bodies poured onto the front steps. Jake fought through the stampede and into the rotunda and found Ozzie directing people and yelling in all directions. He motioned for Jake, and they walked down the hall to the rear doors, where a half dozen deputies stood, guns in hand, gazing silently at the stairway. Jake felt nauseated. Willard had almost made it to the landing. The front of his head was missing, and his brains rolled out like jelly covering his face. Cobb had been able to twist over and absorb the bullets with his back. His face was buried in Willard's stomach, and his feet touched the fourth step from the floor. The blood continued from the lifeless bodies, and it covered completely the bottom six steps. The crimson pool on the floor inched quickly toward the deputies, who slowly backed away. The weapon was between Cobb's legs on the fifth step, and it too was covered with blood.

The group stood silently, mesmerized by the two bodies, which, though dead, continued to spew blood. The thick smell of gunfire hung over the stairway and drifted toward the hall into the rotunda, where the deputies continued to move people toward the front door.

"Jake, you'd better leave," Ozzie said without looking from the bodies.

"Why?"

"Just leave."

"Why?"

" 'Cause we gotta take pictures and collect evidence and stuff, and you don't need to be here."

"Okay. But you don't interrogate him out of my presence. Understand?"

Ozzie nodded.

The photographs were taken, the mess cleaned, the evidence gathered, the bodies removed, and two hours later Ozzie left town followed by five patrol cars. Hastings drove and led the convoy into the country, toward the lake, past Bates Grocery, onto Craft Road. The Hailey driveway was empty except for Gwen's car, Carl Lee's pickup, and the red Cadillac from Illinois.

Ozzie expected no trouble as the patrol cars parked in a row across the front yard, and the deputies crouched behind the open doors, watching as the sheriff walked alone to the house. He stopped. The front door opened slowly and the Hailey family emerged. Carl Lee walked to the edge of the porch with Tonya in his arms. He looked down at his friend the sheriff, and behind him at the row of cars and deputies. To his right was Gwen, and to his left were his three sons, the smallest one crying softly but the older ones brave and proud. Behind them stood Lester.

The two groups watched each other, each waiting for the other to say or do something, each wanting to avoid what was about to happen. The only sounds were the soft sniffles of the little girl, her mother, and the youngest boy.

The children had tried to understand. Their daddy had explained to them what he had just done, and why. They understood that, but they could not comprehend why he had to be arrested and taken to jail.

Ozzie kicked at a clod of dirt, occasionally glancing at the family, then at his men.

Finally, he said, "You better come with me."

Carl Lee nodded slightly, but did not move. Gwen and the boy cried louder as Lester took the girl from her daddy. Then Carl Lee knelt before the three boys and whispered to them again that he must leave but wouldn't be gone long. He hugged them, and they all cried and clutched him. He turned and kissed his wife, then walked down the steps to the sheriff.

"You wanna handcuff me, Ozzie?"

"Naw, Carl Lee, just get in the car."

8 Moss Junior Tatum, the chief deputy, and Jake talked quietly in Ozzie's office while deputies, reserves, trusties, and other jailhouse regulars gathered in the large, cluttered workroom next to the office and waited anxiously for the arrival of the new prisoner. Two of the deputies peered through the blinds at the reporters and cameramen waiting in the parking lot between the jail and the highway. The television vans were from Memphis, Jackson, and Tupelo, and they were parked in various directions throughout the crowded lot. Moss did not like this, so he walked slowly down the sidewalk and ordered the press to regroup in a certain area, and to move the vans.

"Will you make a statement?" yelled a reporter.

"Yeah, move the vans."

"Can you say anything about the murders?"

"Yeah, two people got killed."

"How about the details?"

"Nope. I wasn't there."

"Do you have a suspect?"

"Yep."

"Who is it?"

"I'll tell you when the vans are moved."

The vans were immediately moved and the cameras and microphones were bunched together near the sidewalk. Moss pointed and directed until he was satisfied, then stepped to the crowd. He calmly chewed on a toothpick and stuck both thumbs in the front belt loops, just under the overlapping belly.

"Who did it?"

"Is he under arrest?"

"Was the girl's family involved?"

"Are both dead?"

Moss smiled and shook his head. "One at a time. Yes we have a suspect. He's under arrest and will be here in a minute. Keep the vans outta the way. That's all I have."

Moss walked back to the jail as they continued to call at him. He ignored them and entered the crowded workroom.

"How's Looney?" he asked.

"Prather's with him at the hospital. He's fine—slight wound to the leg."

"Yeah, that and a slight heart attack," Moss said with a smile. The others laughed.

"Here they come!" a trusty shouted, and everyone inside moved to the windows as the line of blue lights rolled slowly into the parking lot. Ozzie drove the first car with Carl Lee seated, unhandcuffed, in the front. Hastings reclined in the back and waved at the cameras as the car passed them and continued through the crowd, past the vans and around to the rear of the jail, where Ozzie parked and the three walked casually inside. Carl Lee was given to the jailer, and Ozzie walked down the hall to his office where Jake was waiting.

"You can see him in a minute, Jake," he said.

"Thanks. You sure he did it?"

"Yeah, I'm sure."

"He didn't confess, did he?"

"No, he didn't say much of nothin'. I guess Lester coached him."

Moss walked in. "Ozzie, them reporters wanna talk to you. I said you'd be out in a minute."

"Thanks, Moss," Ozzie sighed.

"Anybody see it?" Jake asked.

Ozzie wiped his forehead with a red handkerchief. "Yeah, Looney can I.D. him. You know Murphy, the little crippled man who sweeps floors in the courthouse?"

"Sure. Stutters real bad."

"He saw the whole thing. He was sittin' on the east stairs, directly across from where it happened. Eatin' his lunch. Scared him so bad he couldn't talk for an hour." Ozzie paused and eyed Jake. "Why am I tellin' you all this?"

"What difference does it make? I'll find out sooner or later. Where's my man?"

"Down the hall in the jail. They gotta take his picture and all that. Be 'bout thirty minutes."

Ozzie left and Jake used his phone to call Carla and remind her to watch the news and record it.

Ozzie faced the microphones and cameras. "I ain't an-swerin' no questions. We have a suspect in custody. Name of Carl Lee Hailey from Ford County. Arrested for two counts of murder."

"Is he the girl's father?"

"Yes, he is."

"How do you know he did it?"

"We're very smart."

"Any eyewitnesses?"

"None that we know of."

"Has he confessed?"

"No."

"Where'd you find him?"

"At his house."

"Was a deputy shot?"

"Yes."

"How is he?"

"He's fine. He's in the hospital, but he's okay."

"What's his name?"

"Looney. DeWayne Looney."

"When's the preliminary hearing?"

"I'm not the judge."

"Any idea?"

"Maybe tomorrow, maybe Wednesday. No more ques-tions, please. I have no further information to release at this time."

The jailer took Carl Lee's wallet, money, watch, keys, ring, and pocketknife and listed the items on an inventory form that Carl Lee signed and dated. In a small room next to the jailer's station, he was photographed and fingerprinted, just as Lester said. Ozzie waited outside the door and led him down the hall to a small room where the drunks were taken to blow into the Intoxilyzer. Jake sat at a small table next to the machine. Ozzie excused himself.

The lawyer and client sat across the table and analyzed each other carefully. They grinned admiringly but neither spoke. They had last talked five days before, on Wednesday after the preliminary hearing, the day after the rape.

Carl Lee was not as troubled now. His face was relaxed and his eyes were clear. Finally he said: "You didn't think I'd do it, Jake."

"Not really. You did do it?"

"You know I did."

Jake smiled, nodded, and crossed his arms. "How do you feel?"

Carl Lee relaxed and sat back in the folding chair. "Well, I feel better. I don't feel good 'bout the whole thing. I wish it didn't happen. But I wish my girl was okay too, you know. I didn't have nothin' against them boys till they messed with her. Now they got what they started. I feel sorry for their mommas and daddies, if they got daddies, which I doubt."

"Are you scared?"

"Of what?"

"How about the gas chamber?"

"Naw, Jake, that's why I got you. I don't plan to go to no gas chamber. I saw you get Lester off, now just get me off. You can do it, Jake."

"It's not quite that easy, Carl Lee."

"Say what?"

"You just don't shoot a person, or persons, in cold blood, and then tell the jury they needed killing, and expect to walk out of the courtroom."

"You did with Lester."

"But every case is different. And the big difference here is that you killed two white boys and Lester killed a nigger. Big difference."

"You scared, Jake?"

"Why should I be scared? I'm not facing the gas chamber."

"You don't sound too confident."

You big stupid idiot, thought Jake. How could he be confident at a time like this. The bodies were still warm. Sure, he was confident before the killings, but now it was different. His client was facing the gas for a crime which he admits he committed.

"Where'd you get the gun?"

"A friend in Memphis."

"Okay. Did Lester help?"

"Nope. He knew 'bout what I's gonna do, and he wanted to help, but I wouldn't let him."

"How's Gwen?"

"She's pretty crazy right now, but Lester's with her. She didn't know a thing about it."

"The kids?"

"You know how kids are. They don't want their daddy in jail. They upset, but they'll make it. Lester'll take care of them."

"Is he going back to Chicago?"

"Not for a while. Jake, when do we go to court?"

"The preliminary should be tomorrow or Wednesday, depends on Bullard."

"Is he the judge?"

"He will be for the preliminary hearing. But he won't hear the trial. That'll be in Circuit Court."

"Who's the judge there?"

"Omar Noose from Van Buren County; same judge who tried Lester."

"Good. He's okay, ain't he?"

"Yeah, he's a good judge."

"When will the trial be?"

"Late summer or early fall. Buckley will push for a quick trial."

"Who's Buckley?"

"Rufus Buckley. District attorney. Same D.A. who prosecuted Lester. You remember him. Big, loud guy—"

"Yeah, yeah, I remember. Big bad Rufus Buckley. I'd forgot all about him. He's pretty mean, ain't he?"

"He's good, very good. He's corrupt and ambitious, and he'll eat this up because of the publicity."

"You've beat him, ain't you?"

"Yeah, and he's beat me."

Jake opened his briefcase and removed a file. Inside was a contract for legal services, which he studied although he had it memorized. His fees were based on the ability to pay, and the blacks generally could pay little unless there was a close and generous relative in St. Louis or Chicago with a good-paying job. Those were rare. In Lester's trial there had been a brother in California who worked for the post office but he'd been unwilling or unable to help. There were some sisters scattered around but they had their own problems and had offered only moral support for Lester. Gwen had a big family, and they stayed out of trouble, but they were not prosperous. Carl Lee owned a few acres around his house and had mortgaged it to help Lester pay Jake before.

He had charged Lester five thousand for his murder trial; half was paid before trial and the rest in installments over three years.

Jake hated to discuss fees. It was the most difficult part of practicing law. Clients wanted to know up front, immediately, how much he would cost, and they all reacted differently. Some were shocked, some just swallowed hard, a few had stormed out of his office. Some negotiated, but most paid or promised to pay.

He studied the file and the contract and thought desperately of a fair fee. There were other lawyers out there who would take such a case for almost nothing. Nothing but publicity. He thought about the acreage, and the job at the paper mill, and the family, and finally said, "My fee is ten thousand."

Carl Lee was not moved. "You charged Lester five thousand."

Jake anticipated this. "You have three counts; Lester had one."

"How many times can I go to the gas chamber?"

"Good point. How much can you pay?"

"I can pay a thousand now," he said proudly. "And I'll borrow as much as I can on my land and give it all to you."

Jake thought a minute. "I've got a better idea. Let's agree on a fee. You pay a thousand now and sign a note for the rest. Borrow on your land and pay against the note."

"How much you want?" asked Carl Lee.

"Ten thousand."

"I'll pay five."

"You can pay more than that."

"And you can do it for less than ten."

"Okay, I can do it for nine."

"Then I can pay six."

"Eight?"

"Seven."

"Can we agree on seventy-five hundred?"

"Yeah, I think I can pay that much. Depends on how

much they'll loan me on my land. You want me to pay a
thousand now and sign a note for sixty-five hundred?"

"That's right."

"Okay, you got a deal."

Jake filled in the blanks in the contract and promissory
note, and Carl Lee signed both.

"Jake, how much would you charge a man with plenty
of money?"

"Fifty thousand."

"Fifty thousand! You serious?"

"Yep."

"Man, that's a lotta money. You ever get that much?"

"No, but I haven't seen too many people on trial for
murder with that kind of money."

Carl Lee wanted to know about his bond, the grand
jury, the trial, the witnesses, who would be on the jury, when
could he get out of jail, could Jake speed up the trial, when
could he tell his version, and a thousand other questions.
Jake said they would have plenty of time to talk. He promised to call Gwen and his boss at the paper mill.

He left and Carl Lee was placed in his cell, the one next
to the cell for state prisoners.

———————————

The Saab was blocked by a television van. Jake inquired as
to who owned it. Most of the reporters had left but a few
loitered about, expecting something. It was almost dark.

"Are you with the sheriff's department?" asked a reporter.

"No, I'm a lawyer," Jake answered nonchalantly, attempting to seem disinterested.

"Are you Mr. Hailey's attorney?"

Jake turned and stared at the reporter as the others
listened. "Matter of fact, I am."

"Will you answer some questions?"

"You can ask some. I won't promise any answers."

"Will you step over here?"

Jake walked to the microphones and cameras and tried
to act annoyed by the inconvenience. Ozzie and the deputies
watched from inside. "Jake loves cameras," he said.

"All lawyers do," added Moss.

"What is your name, sir?"

"Jake Brigance."

"You're Mr. Hailey's attorney."

"Correct," Jake answered coolly.

"Mr. Hailey is the father of the young girl raped by the two men who were killed today?"

"Correct."

"Who killed the two men?"

"I don't know."

"Was it Mr. Hailey?"

"I said I don't know."

"What's your client been charged with?"

"He's been arrested for the murders of Billy Ray Cobb and Pete Willard. He hasn't formally been charged with anything."

"Do you expect Mr. Hailey to be indicted for the two murders?"

"No comment."

"Why no comment?"

"Have you talked with Mr. Hailey?" asked another reporter.

"Yes, just a moment ago."

"How is he?"

"What do you mean?"

"Well, uh, how is he?"

"You mean, how does he like jail?" Jake asked with a slight grin.

"Uh, yeah."

"No comment."

"When will he be in court?"

"Probably tomorrow or Wednesday."

"Will he plead guilty?"

Jake smiled and replied, "Of course not."

After a cold supper, they sat in the swing on the front porch and watched the lawn sprinkler and talked about the case. The killings were big news across the country, and Carla recorded as many television reports as possible. Two of the networks covered the story live through their Memphis affiliates, and the Memphis, Jackson, and Tupelo stations replayed footage of Cobb and Willard being led into the courthouse surrounded by deputies, and seconds later, being carried from the courthouse under white sheets. One of the stations played the actual audio of the gunfire over film of the deputies scrambling for cover.

Jake's interview was too late for the evening news, so he and Carla waited, with the recorder, for the ten o'clock, and there he was, briefcase in hand, looking trim, fit, handsome, and arrogant, and very disgusted with the reporters for the inconvenience. Jake thought he looked great on TV, and he was excited to be there. There had been one other brief appearance, after Lester's acquittal, and the regulars at the Coffee Shop had kidded him for months.

He felt good. He relished the publicity and anticipated much more. He could not think of another case, another set of facts, another setting which could generate as much publicity as the trial of Carl Lee Hailey. And the acquittal of Carl Lee Hailey, for the murder of the two white men who raped his daughter, before an all-white jury in rural Mississippi—

"What're you smiling about?" Carla interrupted.

"Nothing."

"Sure. You're thinking about the trial, and the cameras, the reporters, the acquittal, and walking out of the courthouse, arm around Carl Lee, reporters chasing you with the cameras rolling, people slapping you on the back, congratulations everywhere. I know exactly what you're thinking about."

"Then why'd you ask?"

"To see if you'd admit it."

"Okay, I admit it. This case could make me famous and make us a million bucks, in the long run."

"If you win."

"Yes, if I win."

"And if you lose?"

"I'll win."

"But if you don't?"

"Think positive."

The phone rang and Jake spent ten minutes with the editor, owner, and only reporter of *The Clanton Chronicle*. It rang again, and Jake talked with a reporter with the Memphis morning paper. He hung up and called Lester and Gwen, then the foreman at the paper mill.

At eleven-fifteen it rang again, and Jake received his first death threat, anonymous of course. He was called a nigger-loving son of a bitch, one who would not live if the nigger walked.

9 Dell Perkins served more coffee and grits than usual Tuesday morning after the killings. All the regulars and some extras had gathered early to read the papers and talk about the killings, which had taken place less than three hundred feet from the front door of the Coffee Shop. Claude's and the Tea Shoppe were also crowded earlier than usual. Jake's picture made the front page of the Tupelo paper, and the Memphis and Jackson papers had front-page photos of Cobb and Willard, both before the shootings and afterward as the bodies were loaded into the ambulance. There were no pictures of Carl Lee. All three papers ran detailed accounts of the past six days in Clanton.

It was widely accepted around town that Carl Lee had done the killing, but rumors of additional gunmen surfaced and flourished until one table at the Tea Shoppe had a whole band of wild niggers in on the attack. However, the deputies in the Coffee Shop, though not talkative, throttled the gossip and kept it pretty much under control. Deputy Looney was a regular, and there was concern for his wounds, which appeared to be more serious than originally reported. He remained in the hospital, and he had identified the gunman as Lester Hailey's brother.

Jake entered at six and sat near the front with some farmers. He nodded at Prather and the other deputy, but they pretended not to see him. They'll be okay once Looney is released, he thought. There were some remarks about the front-page picture, but no one questioned Jake about his new client or the killings. He detected a certain coolness among some of the regulars. He ate quickly and left.

At nine Ethel called Jake. Bullard was holding.

"Hello, Judge. How are you?"

"Terrible. You represent Carl Lee Hailey?"

"Yes, sir."

"When do you want the preliminary?"

"Why are you asking me, Judge?"

"Good question. Look, the funerals are tomorrow

morning sometime, and I think it would be best to wait till
they bury those bastards, don't you?"

"Yeah, Judge, good idea."

"How 'bout tomorrow afternoon at two?"

"Fine."

Bullard hesitated. "Jake, would you consider waiving
the preliminary and letting me send the case straight to the
grand jury?"

"Judge, I never waive a preliminary, you know that."

"Yeah, I know. Just thought I'd ask a favor. I won't hear
this trial, and I have no desire to get near it. See you tomorrow."

———————

An hour later Ethel squawked through the intercom again:
"Mr. Brigance, there are some reporters here to see you."

Jake was ecstatic. "From where?"

"Memphis and Jackson, I believe."

"Seat them in the conference room. I'll be down in a
minute."

He straightened his tie and brushed his hair, and
checked the street below for television vans. He decided to
make them wait, and after a couple of meaningless phone
calls he walked down the stairs, ignored Ethel, and entered
the conference room. They asked him to sit at one end of
the long table, because of the lighting. He declined, told
himself he would control things, and sat at one side with his
back to the rows of thick, expensive law books.

The microphones were placed before him and the camera lights adjusted, and finally an attractive lady from Memphis with streaks of bright orange across her forehead and
under her eyes cleared her throat and asserted herself. "Mr.
Brigance, you represent Carl Lee Hailey?"

"Yes, I do."

"And he's been charged with the murders of Billy Ray
Cobb and Pete Willard?"

"That's correct."

"And Cobb and Willard were charged with raping Mr.
Hailey's daughter?"

"Yes, that's correct."

"Does Mr. Hailey deny killing Cobb and Willard?"

"He will plead not guilty to the charges."

"Will he be charged for the shooting of the deputy, Mr. Looney?"

"Yes. We anticipate a third charge of aggravated assault against the officer."

"Do you anticipate a defense of insanity?"

"I'm not willing to discuss the defense at this time because he has not been indicted."

"Are you saying there's a chance he may not be indicted?"

A fat pitch, one Jake was hoping for. The grand jury would either indict him or not, and the grand jurors would not be selected until Circuit Court convened on Monday, May 27. So the future members of the grand jury were walking the streets of Clanton, tending their shops, working in the factories, cleaning house, reading newspapers, watching TV, and discussing whether or not he should be indicted.

"Yes, I think there's a chance he may not be indicted. It's up to the grand jury, or will be after the preliminary hearing."

"When's the preliminary hearing?"

"Tomorrow. Two P.M."

"You're assuming Judge Bullard will bind him over to the grand jury?"

"That's a pretty safe assumption," replied Jake, knowing Bullard would be thrilled with the answer.

"When will the grand jury meet?"

"A new grand jury will be sworn in Monday morning. It could look at the case by Monday afternoon."

"When do you anticipate a trial?"

"Assuming he's indicted, the case could be tried in late summer or early fall."

"Which court?"

"Circuit Court of Ford County."

"Who would be the judge?"

"Honorable Omar Noose."

"Where's he from?"

"Chester, Mississippi. Van Buren County."

"You mean the case will be tried here in Clanton?"

"Yes, unless venue is changed."

"Will you request a change of venue?"

"Very good question, and one I'm not prepared to answer at this time. It's a bit premature to talk defense strategy."

"Why would you want a change of venue?"

To find a blacker county, Jake thought. He answered thoughtfully, "The usual reasons. Pretrial publicity, etc."

"Who makes the decision to change venue?"

"Judge Noose. The decision is within his sole discretion."

"Has bond been set?"

"No, and it probably won't be until after the indictments come down. He's entitled to a reasonable bond now, but as a matter of practice in this county bonds are not set in capital murder cases until after the indictment and arraignment in Circuit Court. At that point the bond will be set by Judge Noose."

"What can you tell us about Mr. Hailey?"

Jake relaxed and reflected a minute while the cameras continued. Another fat pitch, with a golden chance to plant some seeds. "He's thirty-seven years old. Married to the same woman for twenty years. Four kids—three boys and a girl. Nice guy with a clean record. Never been in trouble before. Decorated in Vietnam. Works fifty hours a week at the paper mill in Coleman. Pays his bills and owns a little land. Goes to church every Sunday with his family. Minds his own business and expects to be left alone."

"Will you allow us to talk to him?"

"Of course not."

"Wasn't his brother tried for murder several years ago?"

"He was, and he was acquitted."

"You were his attorney?"

"Yes, I was."

"You've handled several murder trials in Ford County, haven't you?"

"Three."

"How many acquittals?"

"All of them," he answered slowly.

"Doesn't the jury have several options in Mississippi?" asked the lady from Memphis.

"That's right. With a capital murder indictment, the jury

at trial can find the defendant guilty of manslaughter, which
carries twenty years, or capital murder, which carries life or
death as determined by the jury. And the jury can find the
defendant not guilty." Jake smiled at the cameras. "Again,
you're assuming he'll be indicted."

"How's the Hailey girl?"

"She's at home. Went home Sunday. She's expected to
be fine."

The reporters looked at each other and searched for
other questions. Jake knew this was the dangerous part,
when they ran out of things to ask and began serving up
screwball questions.

He stood and buttoned his coat. "Look, I appreciate
you folks stopping by. I'm usually available, just give a little
more notice and I'll be glad to talk to you anytime."

They thanked him and left.

At ten Wednesday morning, in a no-frills double service at
the funeral home, the rednecks buried their dead. The minister, a freshly ordained Pentecostal, struggled desperately
for comforting and reassuring thoughts to lay upon the small
crowd and over the two closed caskets. The service was brief
with few tears.

The pickups and dirty Chevrolets moved slowly behind
the single hearse as the procession left town and crawled
into the country. They parked behind a small red brick
church. The bodies were laid to rest one at a time at opposite ends of the tiny, overgrown cemetery. After a few additional words of inspiration, the crowd dispersed.

Cobb's parents had divorced when he was small, and his
father drove from Birmingham for the funeral. After the
burial he disappeared. Mrs. Cobb lived in a small, clean
white frame house near the settlement of Lake Village, ten
miles south of Clanton. Her other two sons and their cousins
and friends gathered under an oak tree in the backyard
while the women made a fuss over Mrs. Cobb. The men
talked about niggers in general, and chewed Red Man and
sipped whiskey, and reminisced about the other days when
niggers knew their place. Now they were just pampered and
protected by the government and courts. And there was

nothing white people could do. One cousin knew a friend or someone who used to be active in the Klan, and he might give him a call. Cobb's grandfather had been in the Klan long before his death, the cousin explained, and when he and Billy Ray were kids the old man would tell stories about hanging niggers in Ford and Tyler counties. What they should do was the same thing the nigger had done, but there were no volunteers. Maybe the Klan would be interested. There was a chapter farther down south near Jackson, near Nettles County, and the cousin was authorized to contact them.

The women prepared lunch. The men ate quietly, then returned to the whiskey under the shade tree. The nigger's hearing at 2:00 P.M. was mentioned, and they loaded up and drove to Clanton.

There was a Clanton before the killings, and there was a Clanton after the killings, and it would be months before the two resembled each other. One tragic, bloody event, the duration of which was less than fifteen seconds, transformed the quiet Southern town of eight thousand into a mecca for journalists, reporters, camera crews, photographers, some from neighboring towns, others from the national news organizations. Cameramen and TV reporters bumped into one another on the sidewalks around the square as they asked the man in the street for the hundredth time how he or she felt about the Hailey event and how he or she would vote if he or she was on the jury. There was no clear verdict from the man on the street. Television vans followed small, marked, imported television cars around the square and down the streets chasing leads, stories, and interviews. Ozzie was a favorite at first. He was interviewed a half dozen times the day after the shooting, then found other business and delegated the interviewing to Moss Junior, who enjoyed bantering with the press. He could answer twenty questions and not divulge one new detail. He also lied a lot, and the ignorant foreigners could not tell his lies from his truth.

"Sir, is there any evidence of additional gunmen?"

"Yes."

"Really! Who?"

"We have evidence that the shootin's were authorized and financed by an offshoot of the Black Panthers," Moss Junior replied with a straight face.

Half the reporters would either stutter or stare blankly while the other half repeated what he said and scribbled furiously.

Bullard refused to leave his office or take calls. He called Jake again and begged him to waive the preliminary. Jake refused. Reporters waited in the lobby of Bullard's office on the first floor of the courthouse, but he was safe with his vodka behind the locked door.

There was a request to film the funeral. The Cobb boys said yes, for a fee, but Mrs. Willard vetoed the proposal. The reporters waited outside the funeral home and filmed what they could. Then they followed the procession to the grave sites, and filmed the burials, and followed the mourners to Mrs. Cobb's, where Freddie, the oldest, cursed them and made them leave.

The Coffee Shop on Wednesday was silent. The regulars, including Jake, eyed the strangers who had invaded their sanctuary. Most of them had beards, spoke with unusual accents, and did not order grits.

"Aren't you Mr. Hailey's attorney?" shouted one from across the room.

Jake worked on his toast and said nothing.

"Aren't you? Sir?"

"What if I am?" shot Jake.

"Will he plead guilty?"

"I'm eating breakfast."

"Will he?"

"No comment."

"Why no comment?"

"No comment."

"But why?"

"I don't comment during breakfast. No comment."

"May I talk to you later?"

"Yeah, make an appointment. I talk at sixty bucks an hour."

The regulars hooted, but the strangers were undaunted.

Jake consented to an interview, without charge, with a Memphis paper Wednesday, then barricaded himself in the war room and prepared for the preliminary hearing. At noon he visited his famous client at the jail. Carl Lee was rested and relaxed. From his cell he could see the coming and going of the reporters in the parking lot.

"How's jail?" Jake asked.

"Not that bad. Food's good. I eat with Ozzie in his office."

"You what!"

"Yep. Play cards too."

"You're kidding, Carl Lee."

"Nope. Watch TV too. Saw you on the news last night. You looked real good. I'm gonna make you famous, Jake, ain't I?"

Jake said nothing.

"When do I get on TV? I mean, I did the killin' and you and Ozzie gettin' famous for it." The client was grinning—the lawyer was not.

"Today, in about an hour."

"Yeah, I heard we's goin' to court. What for?"

"Preliminary hearing. It's no big deal, at least it's not supposed to be. This one will be different because of the cameras."

"What do I say?"

"Nothing! You don't say a word to anyone. Not to the judge, the prosecutor, the reporters, anyone. We just listen. We listen to the prosecutor and see what kind of case he's got. They're supposed to have an eyewitness, and he might testify. Ozzie will testify and tell the judge about the gun, the fingerprints, and Looney—"

"How's Looney?"

"Don't know. Worse than they thought."

"Man, I feel bad 'bout shootin' Looney. I didn't even see the man."

"Well, they're going to charge you with aggravated assault for shooting Looney. Anyway, the preliminary is just a formality. Its purpose is to allow the judge to determine if there's enough evidence to bind you over to the grand jury. Bullard always does that, so it's just a formality."

"Then why do it?"

"We could waive it," replied Jake, thinking of all the

cameras he would miss. "But I don't like to. It's a good chance to see what kind of case the State has."

"Well, Jake, I'd say they gotta pretty good case, wouldn't you?"

"I would think so. But let's just listen. That's the strategy of a preliminary hearing. Okay?"

"Sounds good to me. You talked to Gwen or Lester today?"

"No, I called them Monday night."

"They were here yesterday in Ozzie's office. Said they'd be in court today."

"I think everyone will be in court today."

Jake left. In the parking lot he brushed by some of the reporters who were awaiting Carl Lee's departure from jail. He had no comments for them and no comments for the reporters waiting outside his office. He was too busy at the moment for questions, but he was very aware of the cameras. At one-thirty he went to the courthouse and hid in the law library on the third floor.

Ozzie and Moss Junior and the deputies watched the parking lot and quietly cursed the mob of reporters and cameramen. It was one forty-five, time to transport the prisoner to court.

"Kinda reminds me of a buncha vultures waitin' for a dead dog beside the highway," Moss Junior observed as he gazed through the blinds.

"Rudest buncha folks I ever saw," added Prather. "Won't take no for an answer. They expect the whole town to cater to them."

"And that's only half of them—other half's waitin' at the courthouse."

Ozzie hadn't said much. One newspaper had criticized him for the shooting, implying the security around the courthouse was intentionally relaxed. He was tired of the press. Twice Wednesday he had ordered reporters out of the jail.

"I got an idea," he said.

"What?" asked Moss Junior.

"Is Curtis Todd still in jail?"

"Yep. Gets out next week."

"He sorta favors Carl Lee, don't he?"

"Whatta you mean?"

"Well, I mean, he's 'bout as black as Carl Lee, roughly the same height and weight, ain't he?"

"Yeah, well, so what?" asked Prather.

Moss Junior grinned and looked at Ozzie, whose eyes never left the window. "Ozzie, you wouldn't."

"What?" asked Prather.

"Let's go. Get Carl Lee and Curtis Todd," Ozzie ordered. "Drive my car around back. Bring Todd here for some instructions."

Ten minutes later the front door of the jail opened and a squad of deputies escorted the prisoner down the sidewalk. Two deputies walked in front, two behind, and one on each side of the man with the thick sunglasses and handcuffs, which were not fastened. As they approached the reporters, the cameras clicked and rolled. The questions flew:

"Sir, will you plead guilty?"

"Sir, will you plead not guilty?"

"Sir, how will you plead?"

"Mr. Hailey, will you plead insanity?"

The prisoner smiled and continued the slow walk to the waiting patrol cars. The deputies smiled grimly and ignored the mob. The photographers scrambled about trying to get the perfect shot of the most famous vigilante in the country.

Suddenly, with the nation watching, with deputies all around him, with dozens of reporters recording his every move, the prisoner broke and ran. He jolted, jumped, twisted, and squirmed, running wildly across the parking lot, over a ditch, across the highway, into some trees and out of sight. The reporters shouted and broke ranks and several even chased him for a moment. Curiously, the deputies ran back to the jail and slammed the door, leaving the vultures roaming in circles of disarray. In the woods, the prisoner removed the handcuffs and walked home. Curtis Todd had just been paroled one week early.

Ozzie, Moss Junior, and Carl Lee quickly left through the rear of the jail and drove down a back street to the courthouse, where more deputies waited to escort him into the courthouse.

"How many niggers out there?" Bullard screamed at Mr. Pate.

"A ton."

"Wonderful! A ton of niggers. I guess there's a ton of rednecks too?"

"Quite a few."

"Is the courtroom full?"

"Packed."

"My God—it's only a preliminary!" Bullard screamed. He finished a half pint of vodka as Mr. Pate handed him another one.

"Take it easy, Judge."

"Brigance. It's all his fault. He could waive this if he wanted to. I asked him to. Asked him twice. He knows I'll send it to the grand jury. He knows that. All lawyers know that. But now I gotta make all the niggers mad because I won't turn him loose, and I'll make all the rednecks mad because I won't execute him today in the courtroom. I'll get Brigance for this. He's playing for the cameras. I have to get reelected, but he doesn't, does he?"

"No, Judge."

"How many officers out there?"

"Plenty. Sheriff's called in the reserves. You're safe."

"How about the press?"

"They're lined up on the front rows."

"No cameras!"

"No cameras."

"Is Hailey here?"

"Yes, sir. He's in the courtroom with Brigance. Everbody's ready, just waitin' on you."

His Honor filled a Styrofoam cup with straight vodka. "Okay, let's go."

Just like in the old days before the sixties, the courtroom was neatly segregated with the blacks and whites separated by the center aisle. The officers stood solemnly in the aisle and around the walls of the courtroom. Of particular concern was an assemblage of slightly intoxicated whites sitting together in two rows near the front. A couple were recognized as brothers or cousins of the late Billy Ray Cobb.

They were watched closely. The two front rows, the one on the right in front of the blacks and the one on the left in front of the whites, were occupied by two dozen journalists of various sorts. Some took notes while some sketched the defendant, his lawyer, and now finally, the judge.

"They gonna make this nigger a hero," mumbled one of the rednecks, loud enough for the reporters.

When Bullard assumed the bench, the deputies locked the rear door.

"Call your first witness," he ordered in the direction of Rocky Childers.

"The State calls Sheriff Ozzie Walls."

The sheriff was sworn and took the stand. He relaxed and began a long narrative describing the scene of the shooting, the bodies, the wounds, the gun, the fingerprints on the gun and the fingerprints of the defendant. Childers produced an affidavit signed by Officer Looney and witnessed by the sheriff and Moss Junior. It identified the gunman as Carl Lee. Ozzie verified Looney's signature and read the affidavit into the record.

"Sheriff, do you know of any other eyewitness?" asked Childers with no enthusiasm.

"Yes, Murphy, the janitor."

"What's his first name?"

"Nobody knows. He's just Murphy."

"Okay. Have you talked to him?"

"No, but my investigator did."

"Who is your investigator?"

"Officer Rady."

Rady was sworn and seated in the witness chair. Mr. Pate fetched the judge another cup of ice water from chambers. Jake took pages of notes. He would call no witnesses, and he chose not to cross-examine the sheriff. Occasionally, the State's witnesses would get their lies confused in a preliminary, and Jake would ask a few questions on cross-examination to nail down, for the record, the discrepancies. Later at trial when the lying started again, Jake would produce the testimony from the preliminary to further confuse the liars. But not today.

"Sir, have you had an occasion to talk with Murphy?"
Childers asked.

"Murphy who?"

"I don't know—just Murphy, the janitor."

"Oh him. Yes, sir."

"Good. What did he say?"

"About what?"

Childers hung his head. Rady was new, and had not
testified much. Ozzie thought this would be good practice.

"About the shooting! Tell us what he told you about the
shooting."

Jake stood. "Your Honor. I object. I know hearsay is
admissible in a preliminary, but this Murphy fella is available. He works here in the courthouse. Why not let him
testify?"

"Because he stutters," replied Bullard.

"What!"

"He stutters. And I don't want to hear him stutter for
the next thirty minutes. Objection overruled. Continue, Mr.
Childers."

Jake sat in disbelief. Bullard snickered at Mr. Pate, who
left for more ice water.

"Now, Mr. Rady, what did Murphy tell you about the
shooting?"

"Well, he's hard to understand because he was so excited, and when he gets excited he stutters real bad. I mean
he stutters anyway, but—"

"Just tell us what he said!" Bullard shouted.

"Okay. He said he saw a male black shoot the two white
boys and the deputy."

"Thank you," said Childers. "Now where was he when
this took place?"

"Who?"

"Murphy!"

"He was sittin' on the stairs directly opposite the stairs
where they got shot."

"And he saw it all?"

"Said he did."

"Has he identified the gunman?"

"Yes, we showed him photos of ten male blacks, and he identified the defendant, sittin' over there."

"Good. Thank you. Your Honor, we have nothing further."

"Any questions, Mr. Brigance?" asked the judge.

"No, sir," Jake said as he stood.

"Any witnesses?"

"No, sir."

"Any requests, motions, anything?"

"No, sir."

Jake knew better than to request bail. First, it would do no good. Bullard would not set bail for capital murder. Second, it would make the judge look bad.

"Thank you, Mr. Brigance. The court finds sufficient evidence exists to hold this defendant for action by the Ford County grand jury. Mr. Hailey shall remain in the custody of the sheriff, without bond. Court's adjourned."

Carl Lee was quickly handcuffed and escorted from the courtroom. The area around the rear door downstairs was sealed and guarded. The cameras outside caught a glimpse of the defendant between the door and the waiting patrol car. He was in jail before the spectators cleared the courtroom.

The deputies directed the whites on one side to leave first, followed by the blacks.

The reporters requested some of Jake's time, and they were instructed to meet him in the rotunda in a few minutes. He made them wait by first going to chambers and giving his regards to the judge. Then he walked to the third floor to check on a book. When the courtroom was empty and they had waited long enough, he walked through the rear door, into the rotunda and faced the cameras.

A microphone with red letters on it was thrust into his face. "Why didn't you request bond?" a reporter demanded.

"That comes later."

"Will Mr. Hailey plead an insanity defense?"

"As I've stated, it's too early to answer that question. We must now wait for the grand jury—he may not be indicted. If he is, we'll start planning his defense."

"Mr. Buckley, the D.A., has stated he expects easy convictions. Any comment?"

"I'm afraid Mr. Buckley often speaks when he shouldn't. It's asinine for him to make any comment on this case until it is considered by the grand jury."

"He also said he would vigorously oppose any request for a change of venue."

"That request hasn't been made yet. He really doesn't care where the trial is held. He'd try it in the desert as long as the press showed up."

"Can we assume there are hard feelings between you and the D.A.?"

"If you want to. He's a good prosecutor and a worthy adversary. He just talks when he shouldn't."

He answered a few other assorted questions and excused himself.

———————————

Late Wednesday night the doctors cut below Looney's knee and removed the lower third of his leg. They called Ozzie at the jail, and he told Carl Lee.

10 Rufus Buckley scanned the Thursday morning papers and read with great interest the accounts of the preliminary hearing in Ford County. He was delighted to see his name mentioned by the reporters and by Mr. Brigance. The disparaging remarks were greatly outweighed by the fact that his name was in print. He didn't like Brigance, but he was glad Jake mentioned his name before the cameras and reporters. For two days the spotlight had been on Brigance and the defendant; it was about time the D.A. was mentioned. Brigance should not criticize anyone for seeking publicity. Lucien Wilbanks wrote the book on manipulating the press both before and during a trial, and he had taught Jake well. But Buckley held no grudge. He was pleased. He relished the thought of a long, nasty trial with his first opportunity at real, meaningful exposure. He looked forward to Monday, the first day of the May term of court in Ford County.

He was forty-one, and when he was first elected nine years earlier he had been the youngest D.A. in Mississippi. Now he was one year into his third term and his ambitions were calling. It was time to move on to another public office, say, attorney general, or possibly governor. And then to Congress. He had it all planned, but he was not well known outside the Twenty-second Judicial District (Ford, Tyler, Polk, Van Buren, and Milburn counties). He needed to be seen, and heard. He needed publicity. What Rufus needed more than anything else was a big, nasty, controversial, well-publicized conviction in a murder trial.

Ford County was directly north of Smithfield, the county seat of Polk County, where Rufus lived. He had grown up in Tyler County, near the Tennessee line, north of Ford County. He had a good base, politically. He was a good prosecutor. During elections he boasted of a ninety percent conviction rate, and of sending more men to death row than any prosecutor in the state. He was loud, abrasive, sanctimonious. His client was the people of the State of Mississippi, by God, and he took that obligation seriously. The people hated crime, and he hated crime, and together they could eliminate it.

He could talk to a jury; oh, how he could talk to a jury. He could preach, pray, sway, plead, beg. He could inflame a jury to the point it couldn't wait to get back to that jury room and have a prayer meeting, then vote and return with a rope to hang the defendant. He could talk like the blacks and he could talk like the rednecks, and that was enough to satisfy most of the jurors in the Twenty-second. And the juries were good to him in Ford County. He liked Clanton.

When he arrived at his office in the Polk County Courthouse, Rufus was delighted to see a camera crew waiting in his reception room. He was very busy, he explained, looking at his watch, but he might have a minute for a few questions.

He arranged them in his office and sat splendidly in his leather swivel behind the desk. The reporter was from Jackson.

"Mr. Buckley, do you have any sympathy for Mr. Hailey?"

He smiled seriously, obviously in deep thought. "Yes, I do. I have sympathy for any parent whose child is raped. I certainly do. But what I cannot condone, and what our system cannot tolerate, is this type of vigilante justice."

"Are you a parent?"

"I am. I have one small son and two daughters, one the age of the Hailey girl, and I'd be outraged if one of my daughters were raped. But I would hope our judicial system would deal effectively with the rapist. I have that much confidence in the system."

"So you anticipate a conviction?"

"Certainly. I normally get a conviction when I go after one, and I intend to get a conviction in this case."

"Will you ask for the death penalty?"

"Yes, it looks like a clear case of premeditated murder. I think the gas chamber would be appropriate."

"Do you predict a death penalty verdict?"

"Of course. Ford County jurors have always been willing to apply the death penalty when I ask for it and it's appropriate. I get very good juries up there."

"Mr. Brigance, the defendant's attorney, has stated the grand jury may not indict his client."

Buckley chuckled at this. "Well, Mr. Brigance should not be so foolish. The case will be presented to the grand jury Monday, and we'll have our indictments Monday afternoon. I promise you that. Really, he knows better."

"You think the case will be tried in Ford County?"

"I don't care where it's tried. I'll get a conviction."

"Do you anticipate the insanity defense?"

"I anticipate everything. Mr. Brigance is a most capable criminal defense attorney. I don't know what ploy he will use, but the State of Mississippi will be ready."

"What about a plea bargain?"

"I don't much believe in plea negotiating. Neither does Brigance. I wouldn't expect that."

"He said he's never lost a murder case to you."

The smile disappeared instantly. He leaned forward on the desk and looked harshly at the reporter. "True, but I bet he didn't mention a number of armed robberies and grand larcenies, did he? I've won my share. Ninety percent to be exact."

The camera was turned off and the reporter thanked him for his time. No problem, said Buckley. Anytime.

———

Ethel waddled up the stairs and stood before the big desk. "Mr. Brigance, my husband and I received an obscene phone call last night, and I've just taken the second one here at the office. I don't like this."

He motioned to a chair. "Sit down, Ethel. What did these people say?"

"They weren't really obscene. They were threatening. They threatened me because I work for you. Said I'd be sorry because I worked for a nigger lover. The ones here threaten to harm you and your family. I'm just scared."

Jake was worried too, but shrugged it off for Ethel. He had called Ozzie on Wednesday and reported the calls to his house.

"Change your number, Ethel. I'll pay for it."

"I don't want to change my number. I've had it for seventeen years."

"Good, then don't. I've had my home number changed, and it's no big deal."

"Well, I'll not do it."

"Fine. What else do you want?"

"Well, I don't think you should have taken that case. I—"

"And I don't care what you think! You're not paid to think about my cases. If I want to know what you think, I'll ask. Until I do, keep quiet."

She huffed and left. Jake called Ozzie again.

An hour later Ethel announced through the intercom: "Lucien called this morning. He asked me to copy some recent cases, and he wants you to deliver them this afternoon. Said it had been five weeks since your last visit."

"Four weeks. Copy the cases, and I'll take them this afternoon."

Lucien stopped by the office or called once a month. He read cases and kept abreast of current developments in the law. He had little else to do except drink Jack Daniel's and play the stock market, both of which he did recklessly. He was a drunk, and he spent most of his time on the front porch of his big white house on the hill, eight blocks off the square, overlooking Clanton, sipping Jack in the Black and reading cases.

He had deteriorated since the disbarment. A full-time maid doubled as a nurse who served drinks on the porch from noon until midnight. He seldom ate or slept, preferring instead to rock away the hours.

Jake was expected to visit at least once a month. The visits were made out of some sense of duty. Lucien was a bitter, sick old man who cursed lawyers, judges, and especially the State Bar Association. Jake was his only friend, the only audience he could find and keep captive long enough to hear his sermons. Along with the preaching he also freely dispensed unsolicited advice on Jake's cases, a most annoying habit. He knew about the cases, although Jake never knew how Lucien knew so much. He was seldom seen downtown or anywhere in Clanton except at the package store in the black section.

The Saab parked behind the dirty, dented Porsche, and Jake handed the cases to Lucien. There were no hellos or other greetings, just the handing of the copies to Lucien, who said nothing. They sat in the wicker rockers on the long porch and looked out over Clanton. The top floor of the courthouse stood above the buildings and houses and trees around the square.

Finally he offered whiskey, then wine, then beer. Jake declined. Carla frowned on drinking, and Lucien knew it.

"Congratulations."

"For what?" Jake asked.

"For the Hailey case."

"Why am I to be congratulated?"

"I never had a case that big, and I had some big ones."

"Big in terms of what?"

"Publicity. Exposure. That's the name of the game for lawyers, Jake. If you're unknown, you starve. When people get in trouble they call a lawyer, and they call someone they've heard of. You must sell yourself to the public, if you're a street lawyer. Of course it's different if you're in a big corporate or insurance firm where you sit on your ass and bill a hundred bucks an hour, ten hours a day, ripping off little people and—"

"Lucien," Jake interrupted quietly, "we've talked about this many times. Let's talk about the Hailey case."

"All right, all right. I'll bet Noose refuses to change venue."

"Who said I would request it?"

"You're stupid if you don't."

"Why?"

"Simple statistics! This county is twenty-six percent black. Every other county in the Twenty-second is at least thirty percent black. Van Buren County is forty percent. That means more black jurors, potential jurors. If you get it moved, you have a better chance for blacks in the jury box. If it's tried here, you run the risk of an all-white jury, and believe me, I've seen enough all-white juries in this county. All you need is one black to hang it and get a mistrial."

"But then it'll be retried."

"Then hang it again. They'll give up after three trials. A hung jury is the same as a loss on Buckley's scorecard. He'll quit after the third trial."

"So I simply tell Noose I want the trial moved to a blacker county so I can get a blacker jury."

"You can if you want to, but I wouldn't. I'd go through

the usual crap about pretrial publicity, a biased community, and on and on."

"And you don't think Noose'll buy it."

"Naw. This case is too big, and it'll get bigger. The press has intervened and already started the trial. Everyone's heard of it, and not just in Ford County. You couldn't find a person in this state without a preconceived notion of guilt or innocence. So why move it to another county?"

"Then why should I request it?"

"Because when that poor man is convicted, you'll need something to argue on appeal. You can claim he was denied a fair trial because venue was not changed."

"Thanks for the encouragement. What're the chances of getting it moved to another district, say somewhere in the delta?"

"Forget it. You can request a change of venue, but you cannot request a certain location."

Jake didn't know that. He usually learned something during these visits. He nodded confidently and studied the old man with the long, dirty gray beard. There had never been a time when he stumped Lucien on a point of criminal law.

"Sallie!" Lucien screamed, throwing his ice cubes into the shrubs.

"Who's Sallie?"

"My maid," he replied as a tall, attractive black lady opened the screen door and smiled at Jake.

"Yeah, Lucien?" she answered.

"My glass is empty."

She walked elegantly across the porch and took his glass. She was under thirty, shapely, pretty, and very dark. Jake ordered iced tea.

"Where'd you find her?" he asked.

Lucien stared at the courthouse.

"Where'd you find her?"

"I dunno."

"How old is she?"

Lucien was silent.

"She live here?"

No response.

"How much do you pay her?"

"Why is it any of your business? More than you pay Ethel. She's a nurse too, you know."

Sure, Jake thought with a grin. "I'll bet she does a lot of things."

"Don't worry about it."

"I take it you're not thrilled with my chances for an acquittal."

Lucien reflected a moment. The maid/nurse returned with the whiskey and tea.

"Not really. It will be difficult."

"Why?"

"Looks like it was premeditated. From what I gather it was well planned. Right?"

"Yes."

"I'm sure you'll plead insanity."

"I don't know."

"You must plead insanity," Lucien lectured sternly. "There is no other possible defense. You can't claim it was an accident. You can't say he shot those two boys, handcuffed and unarmed, with a machine gun in self-defense, can you?"

"No."

"You won't create an alibi and tell the jury he was at home with his family?"

"Of course not."

"Then what other defense do you have? You must say he was crazy!"

"But, Lucien, he was not insane, and there's no way I can find some bogus psychiatrist to say he was. He planned it meticulously, every detail."

Lucien smiled and took a drink. "That's why you're in trouble, my boy."

Jake sat his tea on the table and rocked slowly. Lucien savored the moment. "That's why you're in trouble," he repeated.

"What about the jury? You know they'll be sympathetic."

"That's exactly why you must plead insanity. You must give the jury a way out. You must show them a way to find him not guilty, if they are so inclined. If they're sympathetic, if they want to acquit, you must provide them with a defense

they can use to do it. It makes no difference if they believe
the insanity crap. That's not important in the jury room.
What's important is that the jury have a legal basis for an
acquittal, assuming they want to acquit."

"Will they want to acquit?"

"Some will, but Buckley will make an awfully strong
case of premeditated murder. He's good. He'll take away
their sympathy. Hailey'll be just another black on trial for
killing a white man when Buckley gets through with him."

Lucien rattled his ice cubes and stared at the brown
liquid. "And what about the deputy? Assault with intent to
kill a peace officer carries life, no parole. Talk your way out
of that one."

"There was no intent."

"Great. That'll be real convincing when the poor guy
hobbles to the witness stand and shows the jury his nub."

"Nub?"

"Yes. Nub. They cut his leg off last night."

"Looney!"

"Yes, the one Mr. Hailey shot."

"I thought he was okay."

"Oh he's fine. Just minus a leg."

"How'd you find out?"

"I've got sources."

Jake walked to the edge of the porch and leaned on a
column. He felt weak. The confidence was gone, taken away
again by Lucien. He was an expert at poking holes in every
case Jake tried. It was sport to him, and he was usually right.

"Look, Jake, I don't mean to sound so hopeless. The
case can be won—it's a long shot, but it can be won. You can
walk him out of there, and you need to believe you can. Just
don't get too cocky. You've said enough to the press for a
while. Back off, and go to work."

Lucien walked to the edge of the porch and spat in the
shrubs. "Always keep in mind that Mr. Hailey is guilty, guilty
as hell. Most criminal defendants are, but especially this one.
He took the law into his own hands, and he murdered two
people. Planned it all, very carefully. Our legal system does
not permit vigilante justice. Now, you can win the case, and
if you do, justice will prevail. But if you lose it, justice will

also prevail. Kind of a strange case, I guess. I just wish I had it."

"You serious?"

"Sure I'm serious. It's a trial lawyer's dream. Win it and you're famous. The biggest gun in these parts. It could make you rich."

"I'll need your help."

"You've got it. I need something to do."

After dinner, and after Hanna was asleep, Jake told Carla about the calls at the office. They had received a strange call before during one of the other murder trials, but no threats were made, just some groaning and breathing. But these were different. They mentioned Jake's name and his family, and promised revenge if Carl Lee was acquitted.

"Are you worried?" she asked.

"Not really. It's probably just some kids, or some of Cobb's friends. Does it scare you?"

"I would prefer they didn't call."

"Everybody's getting calls. Ozzie's had hundreds. Bullard, Childers, everybody. I'm not worried about it."

"What if it becomes more serious?"

"Carla, I would never endanger my family. It's not worth it. I'll withdraw from the case if I think the threats are legitimate. I promise."

She was not impressed.

Lester peeled off nine one-hundred-dollar bills and laid them majestically on Jake's desk.

"That's only nine hundred," Jake said. "Our agreement was a thousand."

"Gwen needed groceries."

"You sure Lester didn't need some whiskey?"

"Come on, Jake, you know I wouldn't steal from my own brother."

"Okay, okay. When's Gwen going to the bank to borrow the rest?"

"I'm goin' right now to see the banker. Atcavage?"

"Yeah, Stan Atcavage, next door at Security Bank.

Good friend of mine. He loaned it before on your trial. You got the deed?"

"In my pocket. How much you reckon he'll give us?"

"No idea. Why don't you go find out."

Lester left, and ten minutes later Atcavage was on the phone.

"Jake, I can't loan the money to these people. What if he's convicted—no offense, I know you're a good lawyer—my divorce, remember—but how's he gonna pay me sitting on death row?"

"Thanks. Look Stan, if he defaults you own ten acres, right?"

"Right, with a shack on it. Ten acres of trees and kudzu plus an old house. Just what my new wife wants. Come on, Jake."

"It's a nice house, and it's almost paid for."

"It's a shack, a clean shack. But it's not worth anything, Jake."

"It's gotta be worth something."

"Jake, I don't want it. The bank does not want it."

"You loaned it before."

"And he wasn't in jail before; his brother was, remember. He was working at the paper mill. Good job, too. Now he's headed for Parchman."

"Thanks, Stan, for the vote of confidence."

"Come on, Jake, I've got confidence in your ability, but I can't loan money on it. If anybody can get him off, you can. And I hope you do. But I can't make this loan. The auditors would scream."

Lester tried the Peoples Bank and Ford National, with the same results. They hoped his brother was acquitted, but what if he wasn't.

Wonderful, thought Jake. Nine hundred dollars for a capital murder case.

11 Claude had never seen the need for printed menus in his cafe. Years before when he first opened he couldn't afford menus, and now that he could he didn't need them because most folks knew what he served. For breakfast he cooked everything but rice and toast, and the prices varied. For Friday lunch he barbecued pork shoulder and spare ribs, and everybody knew it. He had few white customers during the week, but at noon Friday, every Friday, his small cafe was half white. Claude had known for some time that whites enjoyed barbecue as much as blacks; they just didn't know how to prepare it.

Jake and Atcavage found a small table near the kitchen. Claude himself delivered two plates of ribs and slaw. He leaned toward Jake and said softly, "Good luck to you. Hope you get him off."

"Thanks, Claude. I hope you're on the jury."

Claude laughed and said louder, "Can I volunteer?"

Jake attacked the ribs and chewed on Atcavage for not making the loan. The banker was steadfast, but did offer to lend five thousand if Jake would cosign. That would be unethical, Jake explained.

On the sidewalk a line formed and faces squinted through the painted letters on the front windows. Claude was everywhere, taking orders, giving orders, cooking, counting money, shouting, swearing, greeting customers, and asking them to leave. On Friday, the customers were allotted twenty minutes after the food was served, then Claude asked and sometimes demanded that they pay and leave so he could sell more barbecue.

"Quit talkin' and eat!" he would yell.

"I've got ten more minutes, Claude."

"You got seven."

On Wednesday he fried catfish, and allowed thirty minutes because of the bones. The white folks avoided Claude's on Wednesday, and he knew why. It was the grease, a secret recipe grease handed down by his grandmother, he said. It

was heavy and sticky and wreaked havoc with the lower in-
testines of white people. It didn't faze the blacks, who piled
in by the carloads every Wednesday.

Two foreigners sat near the cash register and watched
Claude fearfully as he directed lunch. Probably reporters,
thought Jake. Each time Claude drew nigh and glared, they
obediently picked up and gnawed a rib. They had not experienced ribs before, and it was obvious to everyone they were
from the North. They had wanted chef salads, but Claude
cursed them, and told them to eat barbecue or leave. Then
he announced to the crowd these silly fools wanted chef
salads.

"Here's your food. Hurry up and eat it," he had demanded when he served them.

"No steak knives?" one had asked crisply.

Claude rolled his eyes and staggered away mumbling.

One noticed Jake, and, after staring for a few minutes,
finally walked over and knelt by the table. "Aren't you Jake
Brigance, Mr. Hailey's attorney?"

"Yes, I am. Who are you?"

"I'm Roger McKittrick, with *The New York Times*."

"Nice to meet you," Jake said with a smile and a new
attitude.

"I'm covering the Hailey case, and I'd like to talk with
you sometime. As soon as possible, really."

"Sure. I'm not too busy this afternoon. It's Friday."

"I could do it late."

"How about four?"

"Fine," said McKittrick, who noticed Claude approaching from the kitchen. "I'll see you then."

"Okay, buddy," Claude yelled at McKittrick. "Time's
up. Get your check and leave."

Jake and Atcavage finished in fifteen minutes, and
waited for the verbal assault from Claude. They licked their
fingers and mopped their faces and commented on the ten-
derness of the ribs.

"This case'll make you famous, won't it?" asked Atcavage.

"I hope. Evidently it won't make any money."

"Seriously, Jake, won't it help your practice?"

"If I win, I'll have more clients than I can handle. Sure

it'll help. I can pick and choose my cases, pick and choose my clients."

"Financially, what'll it mean?"

"I have no idea. There's no way to predict who or what it might attract. I'll have more cases to choose from, so that means more money. I could quit worrying about the overhead."

"Surely you don't worry about the overhead."

"Look, Stan, we're not all filthy rich. A law degree is not worth what it once was—too many of us. Fourteen in this little town. Competition is tough, even in Clanton—not enough good cases and too many lawyers. It's worse in the big towns, and the law schools graduate more and more, many of whom can't find jobs. I get ten kids a year knocking on my door looking for work. A big firm in Memphis laid off some lawyers a few months ago. Can you imagine? Just like a factory, they laid them off. I suppose they went down to the unemployment office and stood in line with the 'dozer operators. Lawyers now, not secretaries or truck drivers, but lawyers."

"Sorry I asked."

"Sure I worry about the overhead. It runs me four thousand a month, and I practice alone. That's fifty thousand a year before I clear a dime. Some months are good, others slow. They're all unpredictable. I wouldn't dare estimate what I'll gross next month. That's why this case is so important. There will never be another one like it. It's the biggest. I'll practice the rest of my life and never have another reporter from *The New York Times* stop me in a cafe and ask for an interview. If I win, I'll be the top dog in this part of the state. I can forget about the overhead."

"And if you lose?"

Jake paused and glanced around for Claude. "The publicity will be abundant regardless of the outcome. Win or lose, the case will help my practice. But a loss will really hurt. Every lawyer in the county is secretly hoping I blow it. They want him convicted. They're jealous, afraid I might get too big and take away their clients. Lawyers are extremely jealous."

"You too?"

"Sure. Take the Sullivan firm. I despise every lawyer in

that firm, but I'm jealous to an extent. I wish I had some of
their clients, some of their retainers, some of their security.
They know that every month they'll get a nice check, it's
guaranteed almost, and every Christmas they'll get a big bonus. They represent old money, steady money. That would
be enjoyable for a change. Me, I represent drunks, thugs,
wife beaters, husband beaters, injured people, most of whom
have little or no money. And I never know from one month
to the next how many of these people will show up at my
office."

"Look, Jake," Atcavage interrupted. "I would really
like to finish this discussion, but Claude just looked at his
watch and then looked at us. I think our twenty minutes are
up."

Jake's check was seventy-one cents more than Atcavage's, and since both orders were identical, Claude was
interrogated. No problem, he explained, Jake got an extra
rib.

McKittrick was personable and precise, thorough and pushy.
He had arrived in Clanton on Wednesday to investigate and
write about what was billed as the most famous murder in
the country, at the moment. He talked to Ozzie and Moss
Junior, and they suggested he talk to Jake. He talked to
Bullard, through the door, and the judge suggested he talk
to Jake. He interviewed Gwen and Lester, but was not per-
mitted to meet the girl. He visited with the regulars at the
Coffee Shop and the Tea Shoppe, and he visited with the
regulars at Huey's and Ann's Lounge. He talked to Willard's
ex-wife and mother, but Mrs. Cobb was through with reporters. One of Cobb's brothers offered to talk for a fee. McKittrick declined. He drove to the paper mill and talked to the
co-workers, and he drove to Smithfield to interview the D.A.
He would be in town for a few more days, then return for
the trial.

He was from Texas, and retained, when convenient, a
slight drawl, which impressed the locals and opened them
up. He even said "you all" and "y'all" occasionally, and this
distinguished him from most of the other reporters who

clung to their crisp, precise, modern American pronunciation.

"What's that?" McKittrick pointed to the center of Jake's desk.

"That's a tape recorder," Jake answered.

McKittrick sat his own recorder on the desk and looked at Jake's. "May I ask why?"

"You may. It's my office, my interview, and if I want to record it, I will."

"Are you expecting trouble?"

"I'm trying to prevent it. I hate to be misquoted."

"I'm not known for misquoting."

"Good. Then you won't mind if both of us record everthing."

"You don't trust me, do you, Mr. Brigance?"

"Hell no. And my name is Jake."

"Why don't you trust me?"

"Because you're a reporter, you're from a New York paper, you're looking for a sensational story, and if you're true to form, you'll write some well-informed, moralistic piece of trash depicting us all as racist, ignorant rednecks."

"You're wrong. First of all, I'm from Texas."

"Your paper is from New York."

"But I consider myself a Southerner."

"How long have you been gone?"

"About twenty years."

Jake smiled and shook his head, as if to say: That's too long.

"And I don't work for a sensational newspaper."

"We'll see. The trial is several months away. We'll have time to read your stories."

"Fair enough."

Jake punched the play button on his tape recorder, and McKittrick did likewise.

"Can Carl Lee Hailey receive a fair trial in Ford County?"

"Why couldn't he?" Jake asked.

"Well, he's black. He killed two white men, and he will be tried by a white jury."

"You mean he will be tried by a bunch of white racists."

"No, that's not what I said, nor what I implied. Why do

you automatically assume I think you are all a bunch of racists?"

"Because you do. We're stereotyped, and you know it."

McKittrick shrugged and wrote something on his steno pad. "Will you answer the question?"

"Yes. He can receive a fair trial in Ford County, if he's tried here."

"Do you want it tried here?"

"I'm sure we'll try to move it."

"To where?"

"We won't suggest a place. That's up to the judge."

"Where did he get the M-16?"

Jake chuckled and stared at the tape recorder. "I do not know."

"Would he be indicted if he were white?"

"He's black, and he has not been indicted."

"But if he were white, would there be an indictment?"

"Yes, in my opinion."

"Would he be convicted?"

"Would you like a cigar?" Jake opened a desk drawer and found a Roi-Tan. He unwrapped it, then lit it with a butane lighter.

"No thanks."

"No, he would not be convicted if he were white. In my opinion. Not in Mississippi, not in Texas, not in Wyoming. I'm not sure about New York."

"Why not?"

"Do you have a daughter?"

"No."

"Then you wouldn't understand."

"I think I do. Will Mr. Hailey be convicted?"

"Probably."

"So the system does not work as fairly for blacks?"

"Have you talked with Raymond Hughes?"

"No. Who is he?"

"He ran for sheriff last time, and had the misfortune of making the runoff against Ozzie Walls. He's white. Ozzie, of course, is not. If I'm not mistaken, he got thirty-one percent of the vote. In a county that's seventy-four percent white. Why don't you ask Mr. Hughes if the system treats blacks fairly?"

"I was referring to the judicial system."

"It's the same system. Who do you think sits in the jury box? The same registered voters who elected Ozzie Walls."

"Well, if a white man would not be convicted, and Mr. Hailey will probably be convicted, explain to me how the system treats both fairly."

"It doesn't."

"I'm not sure I'm following you."

"The system reflects society. It's not always fair, but it's as fair as the system in New York, or Massachusetts, or California. It's as fair as biased, emotional humans can make it."

"And you think Mr. Hailey will be treated as fairly here as he would be in New York?"

"I'm saying there's as much racism in New York as in Mississippi. Look at our public schools—they're as desegregated as any."

"By court order."

"Sure, but what about the courts in New York. For years you pious bastards pointed your fingers and noses at us down here and demanded that we desegregate. It happened, and it has not been the end of the world. But you've conveniently ignored your own schools and neighborhoods, your own voting irregularities, your own all-white juries and city councils. We were wrong, and we've paid dearly for it. But we learned, and although the change has been slow and painful, at least we're trying. Y'all are still pointing fingers."

"I didn't intend to refight Gettysburg."

"I'm sorry. What defense will we use? I do not know at this point. Honestly, it's just too early. He hasn't even been indicted."

"Of course he will?"

"Of course we don't know yet. More than likely. When will this be printed?"

"Maybe Sunday."

"Makes no difference. No one here takes your paper. Yes, he will be indicted."

McKittrick glanced at his watch, and Jake turned off his recorder.

"Look, I'm not a bad guy," McKittrick said. "Let's drink a beer sometime and finish this."

"Off the record, I don't drink. But I accept your invitation."

———————

The First Presbyterian Church of Clanton was directly across the street from the First United Methodist Church of Clanton, and both churches were within sight of the much larger First Baptist Church. The Baptists had more members and money, but the Presbyterians and Methodists adjourned earlier on Sunday and outraced the Baptists to the restaurants for Sunday dinner. The Baptists would arrive at twelve-thirty and stand in line while the Presbyterians and Methodists ate slowly and waved at them.

Jake was content not to be a Baptist. They were a bit too narrow and strict, and they were forever preaching about Sunday night church, a ritual Jake had always struggled with. Carla was raised as a Baptist, Jake a Methodist, and during the courtship a compromise was negotiated, and they became Presbyterians. They were happy with their church and its activities, and seldom missed.

On Sunday, they sat in their usual pew, with Hanna asleep between them, and ignored the sermon. Jake ignored it by watching the preacher and picturing his confronting Buckley, in court, before twelve good and lawful citizens, as the nation watched and waited, and Carla ignored it by watching the preacher and mentally redecorating the dining room. Jake caught a few inquisitive stares during the worship service, and he figured his fellow church members were somewhat awed to have a celebrity among them. There were some strange faces in the congregation, and they were either long-lost repentant members or reporters. Jake was unsure until one persisted in staring at him—then he knew they were all reporters.

"Enjoyed your sermon, Reverend," Jake lied as he shook hands with the minister on the steps outside the sanctuary.

"Good to see you, Jake," replied the reverend. "We've watched you all week on TV. My kids get excited every time they see you."

"Thanks. Just pray for us."

They drove to Karaway for Sunday lunch with Jake's

parents. Gene and Eva Brigance lived in the old family house, a sprawling country home on five acres of wooded land in downtown Karaway, three blocks from Main Street and two blocks from the school where Jake and his sister put in twelve years. Both were retired, but young enough to travel the continent in a mobile home each summer. They would leave Monday for Canada and return after Labor Day. Jake was their only son. An older daughter lived in New Orleans.

Sunday lunch on Eva's table was a typical Southern feast of fried meats, fresh garden vegetables—boiled, battered, baked, and raw, homemade rolls and biscuits, two gravies, watermelon, cantaloupe, peach cobbler, lemon pie, and strawberry shortcake. Little of it would be eaten, and the leftovers would be neatly packaged by Eva and Carla and sent to Clanton, where it would last for a week.

"How are your parents, Carla?" Mr. Brigance asked as he passed the rolls.

"They're fine. I talked to Mother yesterday."

"Are they in Knoxville?"

"No, sir. They're already in Wilmington for the summer."

"Will y'all be going to visit them?" asked Eva as she poured the tea from a one-gallon ceramic pitcher.

Carla glanced at Jake, who was dipping butterbeans onto Hanna's plate. He did not want to discuss Carl Lee Hailey. Every meal since Monday night had centered around the case, and Jake was in no mood to answer the same questions.

"Yes, ma'am. We plan to. It depends on Jake's schedule. It could be a busy summer."

"So we've heard," Eva said flatly, slowly as if to remind her son he had not called since the killings.

"Is something wrong with your phone, son?" asked Mr. Brigance.

"Yes. We've had the number changed."

The four adults ate slowly, apprehensively, while Hanna looked at the shortcake.

"Yes, I know. That's what the operator told us. To an unlisted number."

"Sorry. I've been very busy. It's been hectic."

"So we've read," said his father.

Eva stopped eating and cleared her throat. "Jake, do you really think you can get him off?"

"I'm worried about your family," said his father. "It could be a very dangerous case."

"He shot them in cold blood," Eva said.

"They raped his daughter, Mother. What would you do if someone raped Hanna?"

"What's rape?" asked Hanna.

"Never mind, dear," Carla said. "Could we please change the subject." She looked firmly at the three Brigances, and they started eating again. The daughter-in-law had spoken, with wisdom, as usual.

Jake smiled at his mother without looking at Mr. Brigance. "I just don't want to talk about the case, Mother. I'm tired of it."

"I guess we'll have to read about it," said Mr. Brigance.

They talked about Canada.

At about the time the Brigances finished lunch, the sanctuary of the Mt. Zion Chapel CME rocked and swayed as the Right Reverend Ollie Agee whipped the devotees into a glorified frenzy. Deacons danced. Elders chanted. Women fainted. Grown men screamed and raised their arms toward the heavens as the small children looked upward in holy terror. Choir members lurched and lunged and jerked, then broke down and shrieked different stanzas of the same song. The organist played one song, the pianist another, and the choir sang whatever came over it. The reverend hopped around the pulpit in his long white robe with purple trim, yelling, praying, screaming at God, and perspiring.

The bedlam rose and fell, rising it seemed with each new fainting, and falling with fatigue. Through years of experience Agee knew precisely when the fury reached its peak, when the delirium gave way to weariness, and when the flock needed a break. At that precise moment, he jigged to the pulpit and slapped it with the power of God Almighty. Instantly the music died, the convulsions ceased, the fainters awoke, the children stopped crying, and the multitude settled submissively into the pews. It was time for the sermon.

As the reverend was about to preach, the rear doors opened and the Haileys entered the sanctuary. Little Tonya walked by herself, limping, holding her mother's hand. Her brothers marched behind, and Uncle Lester followed. They moved slowly down the aisle and found a seat near the front. The reverend nodded at the organist, who began to play softly, then the choir began to hum and sway. The deacons stood and swayed with the choir. Not to be outdone, the elders stood and began to chant. Then, of all things, Sister Crystal fainted violently. Her fainting was contagious, and the other sisters began dropping like flies. The elders chanted louder than the choir, so the choir got excited. The organist could not be heard, so she increased the volume. The pianist joined in with a clanging rendition of a hymn unlike the hymn being played by the organist. The organist thundered back. Reverend Agee fluttered down from the podium and danced his way toward the Haileys. Everyone followed—the choir, the deacons, the elders, the women, the crying children—everyone followed the reverend to greet the little Hailey girl.

Jail did not bother Carl Lee. Home was more pleasant, but under the circumstances, he found jail life tolerable. It was a new jail, built with federal money under the mandate of a prisoners' rights lawsuit. The food was cooked by two huge black women who knew how to cook and write bad checks. They were eligible for early release, but Ozzie had not bothered to tell them. The food was served to forty prisoners, give or take a few, by the trusties. Thirteen of the prisoners belonged at Parchman, but it was full. So they waited, never knowing if the next day would be their day for the dreaded trip to the sprawling, enclosed delta farm where the food was not as good, the beds were not as soft, the air conditioning was nonexistent, the mosquitoes immense, plentiful, and vicious, and where toilets were scarce and clogged.

Carl Lee's cell was next to Cell Two, where the state prisoners waited. With two exceptions, they were black, and with no exceptions, they were violent. But they were all afraid of Carl Lee. He shared Cell One with two shoplifters who were not just scared, but downright terrified of their famous cellmate. Each evening he was escorted to Ozzie's office, where he and the sheriff ate dinner and watched the news. He was a celebrity, and he liked that almost as much as did his lawyer and the D.A. He wanted to explain things to the reporters, tell them about his daughter and why he should not be in jail, but his lawyer said no.

After Gwen and Lester left late Sunday afternoon, Ozzie, Moss Junior, and Carl Lee sneaked out the rear of the jail and went to the hospital. It was Carl Lee's idea, and Ozzie saw no harm. Looney was alone in a private room when the three entered. Carl Lee took one look at the leg, then stared at Looney. They shook hands. With watery eyes and a breaking voice Carl Lee said he was sorry, that he had no intention of hurting anyone but the two boys, that he wished and prayed he could undo what he had done to Looney. Without hesitation, Looney accepted the apology.

Jake was waiting in Ozzie's office when they sneaked back into the jail. Ozzie and Moss Junior excused themselves, leaving the defendant with his lawyer.

"Where have y'all been?" Jake asked suspiciously.

"Went to the hospital to see Looney."

"You what!"

"Nothin' wrong, is it?"

"I wish you would check with me before you make any more visits."

"What's wrong with seein' Looney?"

"Looney will be the star witness for the State when they attempt to send you to the gas chamber. That's all. He ain't on our side, Carl Lee, and any talking you do with Looney should be with your attorney present. Understand?"

"Not really."

"I can't believe Ozzie would do that," Jake mumbled.

"It was my idea," Carl Lee admitted.

"Well, if you get any more ideas, please let me know about them. Okay?"

"Okay."

"You talked to Lester lately?"

"Yeah, him and Gwen came by today. Brought me goodies. Told me 'bout the banks."

Jake planned to play hardball about his fee; no way he could represent Carl Lee for nine hundred dollars. The case would consume his practice for the next three months at least, and nine hundred would be less than minimum wage. It would not be fair to him or his family to work for nothing. Carl Lee would simply have to raise the money. There were plenty of relatives. Gwen had a big family. They would just have to sacrifice, maybe sell a few automobiles, maybe some land, but Jake would get his fee. If not, Carl Lee could find another lawyer.

"I'll give you the deed to my place," Carl Lee offered.

Jake melted. "I don't want your place, Carl Lee. I want cash. Sixty-five hundred dollars."

"Show me how, and I'll do it. You the lawyer, you figure out a way. I'm with you."

Jake was beat and he knew it. "I can't do it for nine hundred dollars, Carl Lee. I can't let this case bankrupt me. I'm a lawyer. I'm supposed to make money."

"Jake, I'll pay you the money. I promise. It may take a long time, but I'll pay you. Trust me."

Not if you're on death row, thought Jake. He changed the subject. "You know the grand jury meets tomorrow, and it'll take up your case."

"So I go to court?"

"Naw, it means you'll be indicted tomorrow. The courthouse will be full of people and reporters. Judge Noose will be here to open the May term of court. Buckley'll be running around chasing cameras and blowing smoke. It's a big day. Noose starts an armed robbery trial in the afternoon. If you're indicted tomorrow, we'll be in court Wednesday or Thursday for the arraignment."

"The what?"

"The arraignment. In a capital murder case, the judge is required by law to read the indictment to you in open court in front of God and everybody. They'll make a big deal out of it. We'll enter a plea of not guilty, and Noose sets the trial date. We ask for a reasonable bond, and he says no. When I mention bond Buckley'll scream and turn cartwheels. The more I think of him the more I hate him. He'll be a large pain in the ass."

"Why don't I get a bond?"

"For capital murder, the judge does not have to set a bond. He can if he wants to, but most don't. Even if Noose set a bond, you couldn't pay it, so don't worry about it. You'll be in jail until trial."

"I lost my job, you know."

"When?"

"Gwen drove over Friday and got my paycheck. They told her. Nice, ain't it. Work there eleven years, miss five days, and they fire me. Guess they think I ain't comin' back."

"I'm sorry to hear that, Carl Lee. Real sorry."

12 The Honorable Omar Noose had not always been so honorable. Before he became the circuit judge for the Twenty-second Judicial District, he was a lawyer with meager talent and few clients, but he was a politician of formidable skills. Five terms in the Mississippi Legislature had corrupted him and taught him the art of political swindling and manipulation. Senator Noose prospered handsomely as chairman of the Senate Finance Committee, and few people in Van Buren County questioned how he and his family lived so affluently on his legislative salary of seven thousand dollars a year.

Like most members of the Mississippi Legislature, he ran for reelection one time too many, and in the summer of 1971 he was humiliated by an unknown opponent. A year later, Judge Loopus, his predecessor on the bench, died, and Noose persuaded his friends in the Legislature to persuade the governor to appoint him to serve the unexpired term. That's how ex–State Senator Noose became Circuit Judge Noose. He was elected in 1975, and reelected in 1979 and 1983.

Repentant, reformed, and very humbled by his rapid descent from power, Judge Noose applied himself to the study of the law, and after a shaky start, grew to the job. It paid sixty thousand a year, so he could afford to be honest. Now, at sixty-three, he was a wise old judge, well respected by most lawyers and by the state Supreme Court, which seldom reversed his rulings. He was quiet but charming, patient but strict, and he had a huge monument of a nose that was very long and very pointed and served as a throne for his black-rimmed, octagon-shaped reading glasses, which he wore constantly but never used. His nose, plus his tall, gawky frame, plus his wild, untamed, dense gray hair, plus his squeaky voice, had given rise to his secret nickname, whispered among lawyers, of Ichabod. Ichabod Noose. The Honorable Ichabod Noose.

He assumed the bench, and the crowded courtroom stood as Ozzie mumbled incoherently a statutorily required paragraph to officially open the May term of the Ford County Circuit Court. A long, flowery prayer was offered by a local minister, and the congregation sat down. Prospective jurors filled one side of the courtroom. Criminals and other litigants, their families and friends, the press, and the curious filled the other side. Noose required every lawyer in the county to attend the opening of the term, and the members of the bar sat in the jury box, all decked out in full regalia, all looking important. Buckley and his assistant, D. R. Musgrove, sat at the prosecution's table, splendidly representing the State. Jake sat by himself in a wooden chair in front of the railing. The clerks and court reporters stood behind the large red docket books on the workbench, and with everyone else watched intently as Ichabod situated himself in his chair upon the bench, straightened his robe, adjusted his hideous reading glasses, and peered over them at the assemblage.

"Good morning," he squeaked loudly. He pulled the microphone closer and cleared his throat. "It's always nice to be in Ford County for the May term of court. I see most members of the bar found time to appear for the opening of court, and as usual, I will request Madam Clerk to note those absent attorneys so that I may personally contact them. I see a large number of potential jurors present, and I thank each of you for being here. I realize you had no choice, but your presence is vital to our judicial process. We will empanel a grand jury momentarily, and then we will select several trial juries to serve this week and next. I trust each member of the bar has a copy of the docket, and you will note it looks somewhat crowded. My calendar reveals at least two cases set for trial each day this week and next, but it's my understanding most of the criminal cases set for trial will go off on negotiated plea bargains. Nonetheless, we have many cases to move, and I request the diligent cooperation of the bar. Once the new grand jury is empaneled and goes to work, and once the indictments start coming down, I will schedule arraignments and first appearances. Let's quickly call the docket, criminal first, then civil; then the attorneys may be excused as we select a grand jury.

"State versus Warren Moke. Armed robbery, set for trial this afternoon."

Buckley rose slowly, purposefully. "The State of Mississippi is ready for trial, Your Honor," he announced gloriously for the spectators.

"So's the defense," said Tyndale, the court-appointed lawyer.

"How long do you anticipate for trial?" asked the judge.

"Day and a half," answered Buckley. Tyndale nodded in agreement.

"Good. We'll select the trial jury this morning and start the trial at one P.M. today. State versus William Daal, forgery, six counts, set for tomorrow."

"Your Honor," answered D.R. Musgrove, "there will be a plea in that case."

"Good. State versus Roger Hornton, grand larceny, two counts, set for tomorrow."

Noose continued through the docket. Each case drew the same response. Buckley would stand and proclaim the State ready for trial, or Musgrove would quietly inform the court that a plea had been negotiated. The defense attorneys would stand and nod. Jake had no cases in the May term, and although he tried his best to look bored, he enjoyed the call of the docket because he could learn who had the cases and what the competition was doing. It was also a chance to look good before some of the local folks. Half the members of the Sullivan firm were present, and they too looked bored as they sat arrogantly together in the front row of the jury box. The older partners of the Sullivan firm would not dare make an appearance at docket call, and they would lie and tell Noose they were in trial in Federal Court over in Oxford or perhaps before the Supreme Court in Jackson. Dignity prevented their mingling with the ordinary members of the bar, so the firm's younger lieutenants were sent to satisfy Noose and request that all the firm's civil cases be continued, postponed, delayed, stalled, or acted upon in such a way that the firm could drag them on forever and continue to bill by the hour. Their clients were insurance companies who generally preferred not to go to trial and would pay by the hour for legal maneuvering designed solely to keep the cases away from the juries. It would be cheaper and fairer to pay a reasonable settlement and avoid both litigation and the parasitic defense firms like Sullivan & O'Hare, but the insurance companies and their adjusters were too stupid and cheap, so street lawyers like Jake Brigancc carned their live-lihoods suing insurance companies and forcing them to pay more than what they would have paid had they dealt fairly from the beginning. Jake hated insurance companies, and he hated insurance defense attorneys, and he especially hated the Sullivan firm's younger members, all of whom were his age, and all of whom would gladly cut his throat, their asso-ciates' throats, their partners' throats, anyone's throat to make partner and earn two hundred thousand a year and skip docket calls.

Jake particularly hated Lotterhouse, or L. Winston Lot-terhouse, as the letterhead proclaimed him, a little four-eyed wimp with a Harvard degree and a bad case of haughty self-importance who was next in line to make partner and thus had been especially indiscriminate with his throat cutting during the past year. He sat smugly between two other Sulli-van associates and held seven files, each of which was being charged a hundred dollars per hour while he answered the docket call.

Noose began the civil docket. "Collins versus Royal Consolidated General Mutual Insurance Company."

Lotterhouse stood slowly. Seconds meant minutes. Min-utes meant hours. Hours meant fees, retainers, bonuses, partnerships.

"Your Honor, sir, that case is set prime for a week from Wednesday."

"I realize that," Noose said.

"Yes, sir. Well, sir, I'm afraid I must ask for a continu-ance. A conflict has developed in my trial calendar for that Wednesday, and I have a pretrial conference in Federal Court in Memphis that the judge has refused to continue. I regret this. I filed a motion this morning asking for a contin-uance."

Gardner, the plaintiff's attorney, was furious. "Your Honor, that case has been set prime for two months. It was set for trial in February, and Mr. Lotterhouse had a death in his wife's family. It was set for trial last November, and an uncle died. It was set for trial last August, and there was another funeral. I guess we should be thankful that this time no one has died."

There were pockets of light laughter in the courtroom. Lotterhouse blushed.

"Enough is enough, Your Honor," Gardner continued. "Mr. Lotterhouse would prefer to postpone this trial forever. The case is ripe for trial, and my client is entitled to one. We strenuously oppose any motion for a continuance."

Lotterhouse smiled at the judge and removed his glasses. "Your Honor, if I may respond—"

"No, you may not, Mr. Lotterhouse," interrupted Noose. "No more continuances. The case is set for trial next Wednesday. There will be no more delays."

Hallelujah, thought Jake. Noose was generally soft on the Sullivan firm. Jake smiled at Lotterhouse.

Two of Jake's civil cases were continued to the August term. When Noose finished the civil docket, he dismissed the attorneys, and turned his attention to the pool of prospective jurors. He explained the role of the grand jury, its importance and procedure. He distinguished it from the trial juries, equally important but not as time consuming. He began asking questions, dozens of questions, most of them required by law, all dealing with ability to serve as jurors, physical and moral fitness, exemptions, and age. A few were useless, but nonetheless required by some ancient statute. "Are any of you common gamblers or habitual drunkards?"

There were laughs but no volunteers. Those over sixty-five were automatically excused, at their option. Noose granted the usual exemptions for illnesses, emergencies, and hardships, but he excused only a few of the many who requested pardons for economic reasons. It was amusing to watch the jurors stand, one at a time, and meekly explain to the judge how a few days of jury duty would cause irreparable damage to the farm, or the body shop, or the pulpwood cutting. Noose took a hard line and delivered several lectures on civic responsibility to the flimsier excuses.

From the venire of ninety or so prospects, eighteen would be selected for the grand jury, and the rest would remain available for selection as trial jurors. When Noose completed his questioning, the clerk drew eighteen names from a box and laid them on the bench before His Honor, who began calling names. The jurors, one by one, rose and walked slowly toward the front of the courtroom, through the gate in the railing, and into the cushioned, swivel rocking seats in the jury box. There were fourteen such seats, twelve for the jurors and two for the alternates. When the box was filled, Noose called four more who joined their colleagues in wooden chairs placed in front of the jury box.

"Stand and take the oath," instructed Noose as the clerk stood before them holding and reading from a little black book that contained all the oaths. "Raise your right hands," she directed. "Do you solemnly swear or affirm that you will faithfully discharge your duties as grand jurors; that you will fairly hear and decide all issues and matters brought before you, so help you God?"

A chorus of assorted "I do's" followed, and the grand jury was seated. Of the five blacks, two were women. Of the thirteen whites, eight were women, and most were rural. Jake recognized seven of the eighteen.

"Ladies and gentlemen," Noose began his usual speech, "you have been selected and duly sworn as grand jurors for Ford County, and you will serve in that capacity until the next grand jury is empaneled in August. I want to stress that your duties will not be time consuming. You will meet every day this week, then several hours each month until September. You have the responsibility of reviewing criminal cases, listening to law enforcement officials and victims, and determining whether or not reasonable grounds exist to believe the accused has committed the crime. If so, you issue an indictment, which is a formal charge placed against the accused. There are eighteen of you, and when at least twelve believe a person should be indicted, the indictment is issued, or returned, as we say. You have considerable power. By law, you can investigate any criminal act, any citizen suspected of wrongdoing, any public official; really anybody or anything that smells bad. You may convene yourself whenever you choose, but normally you meet whenever the district attorney, Mr. Buckley, wants you. You have the power to subpoena witnesses to testify before you, and you may also subpoena their records. Your deliberations are extremely private, with no one being present but yourselves, the D.A. and his staff, and the witnesses. The accused is not allowed to appear before you. You are expressly forbidden to discuss anything that is said or transpires in the grand jury room.

"Mr. Buckley, would you please stand. Thank you. This is Mr. Rufus Buckley, the district attorney. He's from Smithfield, in Polk County. He will sort of act as your supervisor while you deliberate. Thank you, Mr. Buckley. Mr. Musgrove, will you stand. This is D.R. Musgrove, assistant district attorney, also from Smithfield. He will assist Mr. Buckley while you are in session. Thank you, Mr. Musgrove. Now, these gentlemen represent the State of Mississippi, and they will present the cases to the grand jury.

"One final matter: the last grand jury in Ford County was empaneled in February, and the foreman was a white male. Therefore, in keeping with tradition and following the wishes of the Justice Department, I will appoint a black female as foreman of this grand jury. Let's see. Laverne Gossett. Where are you, Mrs. Gossett? There you are, good. I believe you are a schoolteacher, correct? Good. I'm sure you'll be able to handle your new duties. Now, it's time for you to get to work. I understand there are over fifty cases waiting on you. I will ask that you follow Mr. Buckley and Mr. Musgrove down the hall to the small courtroom that we use for a grand jury room. Thank you and good luck."

Buckley proudly marched his new grand jury out of the courtroom and down the hall. He waved at reporters and had no comments—for the time being. In the small courtroom they seated themselves around two long, folding tables. A secretary rolled in boxes of files. An ancient halfcrippled, half-deaf, long-retired deputy in a faded uniform took his position by the door. The room was secure. Buckley had second thoughts, excused himself, and met with the reporters in the hall. Yes, he said, the Hailey case would be presented that afternoon. In fact, he was calling a press conference for 4:00 P.M. on the front steps of the courthouse, and he would have the indictments at that time.

After lunch, the chief of the Karaway Police Department sat at one end of the long table and shuffled nervously through his files. He avoided looking at the grand jurors, who anxiously awaited their first case.

"State your name!" barked the D.A.

"Chief Nolan Earnhart, Karaway City Police."

"How many cases do you have, Chief?"

"We have five from Karaway."

"Let's hear the first one."

"Okay, let's see, all right," the chief mumbled and stuttered as he flipped through his paperwork. "Okay, the first case is Fedison Bulow, male black, age twenty-five, got caught red-handed in the rear of Griffin's Feed Store in Karaway at two o'clock in the mornin', April 12. Silent alarm went off and we caught him in the store. Cash register had been broken into, and some fertilizer was gone. We found the cash and the goods in a car registered in his name parked behind the store. He gave a three-page confession at the jail, and I've got copies here."

Buckley walked casually around the room smiling at everyone. "And you want this grand jury to indict Fedison Bulow on one count of breaking and entering a commercial building, and one count of grand larceny?" Buckley asked helpfully.

"Yes, sir, that's right."

"Now, members of the grand jury, you have the right to ask any questions. This is your hearing. Any questions?"

"Yes, does he have a record?" asked Mack Loyd Crowell, an unemployed truck driver.

"No," replied the chief. "This is his first offense."

"Good question, always ask that question because if they have prior records we may need to indict them as habitual criminals," lectured Buckley. "Any more questions? None? Good. Now at this point, someone needs to make a motion that the grand jury return a true bill of indictment against Fedison Bulow."

Silence. The eighteen stared at the table and waited for someone else to make a motion. Buckley waited. Silence. This is great, he thought. A soft grand jury. A bunch of timid souls afraid to speak. Liberals. Why couldn't he have a bloodthirsty grand jury eager to make motions to indict everybody for everything?

"Mrs. Gossett, would you like to make the first motion, since you're the foreman?"

"I so move," she said.

"Thank you," said Buckley. "Now let's vote. How many vote to indict Fedison Bulow on one count of breaking and entering a commercial building and one count of grand larceny? Raise your hands."

Eighteen hands went up, and Buckley was relieved.

The chief presented the other four cases from Karaway. Each involved defendants equally guilty as Bulow, and each received unanimous true bills. Buckley slowly taught the grand jury how to operate itself. He made them feel important, powerful, and laden with the heavy burden of justice. They became inquisitive:

"Does he have a record?"

"How much time does that carry?"

"When will he get out?"

"How many counts can we give him?"

"When will he be tried?"

"Is he out of jail now?"

With five indictments out of the way, with five true bills and no dissension, with the grand jury eager for the next case, whatever it might be, Buckley decided the mood was ripe. He opened the door and motioned for Ozzie, who was standing in the hall talking quietly with a deputy and watching the reporters.

"Present Hailey first," Buckley whispered as the two met in the door.

"Ladies and gentlemen, this is Sheriff Walls. I'm sure most of you know him. He has several cases to present. What's first, Sheriff?"

Ozzie scrambled through his files, lost whatever he was looking for, and finally blurted, "Carl Lee Hailey."

The jurors became quiet again. Buckley watched them closely to gauge their reactions. Most of them stared at the table again. No one spoke while Ozzie reviewed the file, then excused himself to get another briefcase. He had not planned to present the Hailey case first.

Buckley prided himself on reading jurors, of watching their faces and knowing precisely their thoughts. He watched the jury constantly during a trial, always predicting to himself what each was thinking. He would cross-examine a witness and never take his eyes off the jury. He would sometimes stand and face the jury box and interrogate a witness and watch the faces react to the answers. After hundreds of trials he was good at reading jurors, and he knew instantly he was in trouble with Hailey. The five blacks grew tense and arrogant as if they welcomed the case and the inevitable argument. The foreman, Mrs. Gossett, looked particularly pious as Ozzie mumbled to himself and flipped papers. Most of the whites looked noncommittal, but Mack Loyd Crowell, a hard-looking middle-aged rural type, appeared as arrogant as the blacks. Crowell pushed back his chair and walked to the window, which looked over the north side of the courtyard. Buckley could not read him precisely, but he knew Crowell was trouble.

"Sheriff, how many witnesses do you have for the Hailey case?" Buckley asked, somewhat nervously.

Ozzie stopped shuffling paper and said, "Well, uh, just me. We can get another if we need one."

"All right, all right," replied Buckley. "Just tell us about the case."

Ozzie reared back, crossed his legs, and said, "Shoot, Rufus, everbody knows about this case. Been on TV for a week."

"Just give us the evidence."

"The evidence. Okay, one week ago today, Carl Lee Hailey, male black, age thirty-seven, shot and killed one Billy Ray Cobb and one Pete Willard, and he shot a peace officer, one DeWayne Looney, who's still in the hospital with his leg cut off. The weapon was an M-16 machine gun, illegal, which we recovered and matched the fingerprints with those of Mr. Hailey. I have an affidavit signed by Deputy Looney, and he states, under oath, that the man who did the shootin' was Carl Lee Hailey. There was an eyewitness, Murphy, the little crippled man that sweeps the courthouse and stutters real bad. I can get him here if you want."

"Any questions?" interrupted Buckley.

The D.A. nervously watched the jurors, who nervously watched the sheriff. Crowell stood with his back to the others, looking through the window.

"Any questions?" Buckley repeated.

"Yeah," answered Crowell as he turned and glared at the D.A., then at Ozzie. "Those two boys he shot, they raped his little girl, didn't they, Sheriff?"

"We're pretty sure they did," answered Ozzie.

"Well, one confessed, didn't he?"

"Yep."

Crowell walked slowly, boldly, arrogantly across the room, and stood at the other end of the tables. He looked down at Ozzie. "You got kids, Sheriff?"

"Yep."

"You got a little girl?"

"Yep."

"Suppose she got raped and you got your hands on the man who did it. What would you do?"

Ozzie paused and looked anxiously at Buckley, whose neck had turned a deep red.

"I don't have to answer that," Ozzie replied.

"Is that so. You came before this grand jury to testify, didn't you? You're a witness, ain't you? Answer the question."

"I don't know what I'd do."

"Come on, Sheriff. Give us a straight answer. Tell the truth. What would you do?"

Ozzie felt embarrassed, confused, and angry at this stranger. He would like to tell the truth, and explain in detail how he would gladly castrate and mutilate and kill any pervert who touched his little girl. But he couldn't. The grand jury might agree and refuse to indict Carl Lee. Not that he wanted him indicted, but he knew the indictment was necessary. He looked sheepishly at Buckley, who was perspiring and seated now.

Crowell zeroed in on the sheriff with the zeal and fervor of a lawyer who had just caught a witness in an obvious lie.

"Come on, Sheriff," he taunted. "We're all listenin'. Tell the truth. What would you do to the rapist? Tell us. Come on."

Buckley was near panic. The biggest case of his wonderful career was about to be lost, not at trial, but in the grand jury room, in the first round, at the hands of an unemployed truck driver. He stood and struggled for words. "The witness does not have to answer."

Crowell turned and shouted at Buckley, "You sit down and shut up! We don't take orders from you. We can indict you if we want to, can't we?"

Buckley sat and looked blankly at Ozzie. Crowell was a ringer. He was too smart to be on a grand jury. Someone must have paid him. He knew too much. Yes, the grand jury could indict anyone.

Crowell retreated and returned to the window. They watched him until it appeared he was finished.

"Are you absolutely sure he done it, Ozzie?" asked Lemoyne Frady, an illegitimate distant cousin to Gwen Hailey.

"Yes, we're sure," Ozzie answered slowly, with both eyes on Crowell.

"And you want us to indict him for what?" asked Mr. Frady, the admiration for the sheriff obvious.

"Two counts of capital murder, and one count of assault on a peace officer."

"How much time you talkin' about?" asked Barney Flaggs, another black.

"Capital murder carries the gas chamber. Assault on a deputy carries life with no parole."

"And that's what you want, Ozzie?" asked Flaggs.

"Yeah, Barney, I say this grand jury should indict Mr. Hailey. I sure do."

"Any more questions?" interrupted Buckley.

"Not so fast," replied Crowell as he turned from the window. "I think you're tryin' to ram this case down our throats, Mr. Buckley, and I resent it. I wanna talk about it some. You sit down and if we need you, we'll ask you."

Buckley glared fiercely and pointed his finger. "I don't have to sit, and I don't have to stay quiet!" he yelled.

"Yes. Yes, you do," Crowell answered coolly with a caustic grin. "Because if you don't, we can make you leave, can't we, Mr. Buckley? We can ask you to leave this room, and if you refuse, we'll go ask the judge. He'll make you leave, won't he, Mr. Buckley?"

Rufus stood motionless, speechless, and stunned. His stomach turned flips and his knees were spongy, but he was frozen in place.

"So, if you would like to hear the rest of our deliberations, sit down and shut up."

Buckley sat next to the bailiff, who was now awake.

"Thank you," said Crowell. "I wanna ask you folks a question. How many of you would do or wanna do what Mr. Hailey did if someone raped your daughter, or maybe your wife, or what about your mother? How many? Raise your hands."

Seven or eight hands shot up, and Buckley dropped his head. Crowell smiled and continued, "I admire him for what he did. It took guts. I'd hope I'd have the courage to do what he did, 'cause Lord knows I'd want to. Sometimes a man's just gotta do what he's gotta do. This man deserves a trophy, not an indictment."

Crowell walked slowly around the tables, enjoying the attention. "Before you vote, I want you to do one thing. I want you to think about that poor little girl. I think she's ten. Try to picture her layin' there, hands tied behind her, cryin', beggin' for her daddy. And think of those two outlaws, drunk, doped up, takin' turns rapin' and beatin' and kickin' her. Hell, they even tried to kill her. Think of your own daughter. Put her in the place of the little Hailey girl.

"Now, wouldn't you say they got pretty much what they deserved? We should be thankful they're dead. I feel safer just knowin' those two bastards are no longer here to rape and kill other children. Mr. Hailey has done us a great service. Let's don't indict him. Let's send him home to his family, where he belongs. He's a good man who's done a good thing."

Crowell finished and returned to the window. Buckley watched him fearfully, and when he was certain he was finished, he stood. "Sir, are you finished?" There was no response.

"Good. Ladies and gentlemen of the grand jury. I would like to explain a few things. A grand jury is not supposed to try the case. That's what a trial jury is for. Mr. Hailey will get a fair trial before twelve fair and impartial jurors, and if he's innocent, he'll be acquitted. But his guilt or innocence is not supposed to be determined by the grand jury. You're supposed to decide, after listening to the State's version of the evidence, if there is a strong possibility a crime has been committed. Now, I submit to you that a crime has been committed by Carl Lee Hailey. Three crimes actually. He killed two men, and he wounded another. We have eye-witnesses."

Buckley was warming as he circled the tables. The confidence was back. "The duty of this grand jury is to indict him, and if he has a valid defense, he'll have a chance to present it at trial. If he has a legal reason for doing what he did, let him prove it at trial. That's what trials are for. The State charges him with a crime, and the State must prove at trial he committed the crime. If he has a defense, and if he can convince the trial jury, he will be acquitted, I assure you. Good for him. But it's not the duty of this grand jury to decide today that Mr. Hailey should go free. There'll be another day for that, right, Sheriff?"

Ozzie nodded and said, "That's right. The grand jury is to indict if the evidence is presented. The trial jury will not convict him if the State can't prove its case, or if he puts a good defense. But the grand jury don't worry 'bout things like that."

"Anything further from the grand jury?" Buckley asked anxiously. "Okay, we need a motion."

"I make a motion we don't indict him for anything," yelled Crowell.

"Second," mumbled Barney Flaggs.

Buckley's knees quivered. He tried to speak, but nothing came forth. Ozzie suppressed his joy.

"We have a motion and a second," announced Mrs. Gossett. "All in favor raise your hands."

Five black hands went up, along with Crowell's. Six votes. The motion failed.

"Whatta we do now?" asked Mrs. Gossett.

Buckley spoke rapidly: "Someone make a motion to indict Mr. Hailey for two counts of capital murder and one count of assault on a peace officer."

"So move," said one of the whites.

"Second," said another.

"All in favor, raise your hands," said Mrs. Gossett. "I count twelve hands. All opposed—I count five plus mine makes six. Twelve to six. What does that mean?"

"That means he's been indicted," Buckley replied proudly. He breathed normally again, and the color returned to his face. He whispered to a secretary, then addressed the grand jury. "Let's take a ten-minute recess. We have about forty more cases to work on, so please don't be gone long. I would like to remind you of something Judge Noose said this morning. These deliberations are extremely confidential.

You are not to discuss any of your work outside this room—"

"What he's tryin' to say," interrupted Crowell, "is that we can't tell anybody that he came within one vote of not gettin' the indictments. Ain't that right, Buckley?"

The D.A. quickly left the room and slammed the door.

Surrounded by dozens of cameras and reporters, Buckley stood on the front steps of the courthouse and waved copies of the indictments. He preached, lectured, moralized, praised the grand jury, sermonized against crime and vigilantes, and condemned Carl Lee Hailey. Bring on the trial. Put the jury in the box. He guaranteed a conviction. He guaranteed a death penalty. He was obnoxious, offensive, arrogant, self-righteous. He was himself. Vintage Buckley. A few of the reporters left, but he labored on. He extolled himself and his trial skills and his ninety, no, ninety-five percent conviction rate. More reporters left. More cameras were turned off. He praised Judge Noose for his wisdom and fairness. He acclaimed the intelligence and good judgment of Ford County jurors.

He outlasted them. They grew weary of him and they all left.

13 Stump Sisson was the Klan's Imperial Wizard for Mississippi, and he had called the meeting at the small cabin deep in the pine forests of Nettles County, two hundred and thirty miles south of Ford County. There were no robes, rituals, or speeches. The small group of Klansmen discussed the events in Ford County with a Mr. Freddie Cobb, brother of Billy Ray Cobb, deceased. Freddie had called a friend who called Stump to arrange the meeting.

Had they indicted the nigger? Cobb was not sure, but he had heard the trial would be in late summer, or early fall. What concerned him most was all the talk about the nigger pleading insanity and getting off. It wasn't right. The nigger killed his brother in cold blood, planned the shooting. He hid in a closet and waited for his brother. It was cold-blooded murder, and now there was talk of the nigger walking free. What could the Klan do about it? The niggers have plenty of protection nowadays—the NAACP, ACLU, a thousand other civil rights groups, plus the courts and the government. Hell, white folks ain't got a chance, except for the Klan. Who else would march and stand up for white people. All the laws favor the niggers, and the liberal nigger-loving politicians keep making more laws against white people. Somebody's got to stand up for them. That's why he called the Klan.

Is the nigger in jail? Yes, and he's treated like a king. Got a nigger sheriff up there, Walls, and he likes this nigger. Gives him special privileges and extra protection. The sheriff's another story. Someone said Hailey might get out of jail this week on bond. Just a rumor. They hoped he got out.

What about your brother? Did he rape her? We're not sure, probably not. Willard, the other guy, confessed to rape, but Billy Ray never confessed. He had plenty of women. Why would he rape a little nigger girl? And if he did, what was the big deal?

Who's the nigger's lawyer? Brigance, a local boy in Clanton. Young, but pretty good. Does a lot of criminal work and has a good reputation. Won several murder trials. He told some reporters the nigger would plead insanity and get off.

Who's the judge? Don't know yet. Bullard was the county judge, but someone said he would not hear the case. There's talk of moving the case to another county, so who knows who will be the judge.

Sisson and the Kluxers listened intently to this ignorant redneck. They liked the part about the NAACP and the government and the politicians, but they had also read the papers and watched TV and they knew his brother had received justice. But at the hands of a nigger. It was unthinkable.

The case had real potential. With the trial several months away, there was time to plan a rebellion. They could march during the day around the courthouse in their white robes and pointed, hooded masks. They could make speeches to a captive audience and parade in front of the cameras. The press would love it—hate them, but love the altercations, the disruptions. And at night they could intimidate with burning crosses and threatening phone calls. The targets would be easy and unsuspecting. Violence would be unavoidable. They knew how to provoke it. They fully appreciated what the sight of marching white robes did to crowds of angry niggers.

Ford County could be their playground for hide and seek, search and destroy, and hit and run. They had time to organize and call in comrades from other states. What Kluxer would miss this golden moment? And new recruits? Why, this case could fuel the fires of racism and bring nigger haters out of the woods and onto the streets. Membership was down. Hailey would be their new battle cry, the rallying point.

"Mr. Cobb, can you get us the names and addresses of the nigger, his family, his lawyer, the judge, and the jurors?" asked Sisson.

Cobb pondered this task. "Everbody but the jurors. They ain't been picked yet."

"When will you know them?"

"Damned if I know. I guess at trial. What're y'all thinkin'?"

"We're not sure, but the Klan most likely will get involved. We need to flex our muscle a bit, and this could be a good opportunity."

"Can I help?" Cobb asked eagerly.

"Sure, but you need to be a member."

"We ain't got no Klan up there. It folded a long time ago. My granddaddy used to be a member."

"You mean the grandfather of the victim was a Klansman?"

"Yep," Cobb answered proudly.

"Well, then, we must get involved." The Klansmen shook their heads in disbelief and vowed revenge. They explained to Cobb that if he could get five or six friends of similar thinking and motivation to agree to join, they would have a big, secret ceremony deep in the woods of Ford County with a huge burning cross and all sorts of rituals. They would be inducted as members, full-fledged members, of the Ku Klux Klan. Ford County Klavern. And they would all join in and make a spectacle of the trial of Carl Lee Hailey. They would raise so much hell in Ford County this summer that no juror with any common sense would consider voting to acquit the nigger. Just recruit half a dozen more, and they would make him the leader of the Ford County Klavern.

Cobb said he had enough cousins to start a klavern. He left the meeting drunk with excitement of being a Klansman, just like his grandfather.

———————

Buckley's timing was a little off. His 4:00 P.M. press show was ignored by the evening news. Jake flipped the channels on a small black and white in his office, and laughed out loud when the networks and then Memphis, then Jackson, then Tupelo signed off with no news of the indictments. He could see the Buckley family in their den glued to the set, turning knobs and searching desperately for their hero while he yelled at them all to be quiet. And then at seven, after the Tupelo weather, the last weather, they backed away and left him alone in his recliner. Maybe at ten, he probably said.

At ten, Jake and Carla laid cross-legged and tangled in the dark on the sofa, waiting on the news. Finally, there he was, on the front steps, waving papers and shouting like a street preacher while the Channel 4 man on the scene explained that this was Rufus Buckley, the D.A. who would prosecute Carl Lee Hailey now that he had been indicted. After an awful glimpse of Buckley, the report panned around the square for a wonderful view of downtown Clanton, and then finally back to the reporter for two sentences about a trial in late summer.

"He's offensive," Carla said. "Why would he call a press conference to announce the indictments?"

"He's a prosecutor. We defense lawyers hate the press."

"I've noticed. My scrapbook is rapidly filling up."

"Be sure and make copies for Mom."

"Will you autograph it for her?"

"Only for a fee. Yours, I will autograph for free."

"Fine. And if you lose, I'll send you a bill for clipping and pasting."

"I remind you, dear, that I have never lost a murder case. Three and oh, as a matter of fact."

Carla punched the remote control and the weatherman remained but his volume disappeared. "You know what I dislike most about your murder trials?" She kicked the cushions from her thin, bronze, almost perfect legs.

"The blood, the carnage, the gruesomeness?"

"No." She unfolded her shoulder-length hair and let it fall around her on the arm of the sofa.

"The loss of life, regardless of how insignificant?"

"No." She was wearing one of his old, starched-out, sixteen-by-thirty-four, pinpoint Oxford button-downs, and she began to play with the buttons.

"The horrible specter of an innocent man facing the gas chamber?"

"No." She was unbuttoning it. The bluish gray rays from the television flashed like a strobe in the dark room as the anchorperson smiled and mouthed good night.

"The fear of a young family as the father walks into the courtroom and faces a jury of his peers?"

"No." It was unbuttoned, and under it a thin, fluorescent band of white silk glittered against the brown skin.

"The latent unfairness of our judicial system?"

"No." She slid an almost perfect bronze leg up, up, up to the back of the sofa where it gently came to rest.

"The unethical and unscrupulous tactics employed by cops and prosecutors to nail innocent defendants?"

"No." She unsnapped the band of silk between the two almost perfect breasts.

"The fervor, the fury, the intensity, the uncontrolled emotions, the struggle of the human spirit, the unbridled passion?"

"Close enough," she said. Shirts and shorts ricocheted off the lamps and coffee tables as the bodies meshed deep under the cushions. The old sofa, a gift from her parents, rocked and squeaked on the ancient hardwood floor. It was sturdy, and accustomed to the rocking and squeaking. Max the mix-breed instinctively ran down the hall to stand guard by Hanna's door.

14 Harry Rex Vonner was a huge slob of a lawyer who specialized in nasty divorce cases and perpetually kept some jerk in jail for back child support. He was vile and vicious, and his services were in great demand by divorcing parties in Ford County. He could get the children, the house, the farm, the VCR, and microwave, everything. One wealthy farmer kept him on retainer just so the current wife couldn't hire him for the next divorce. Harry Rex sent his criminal cases to Jake, and Jake sent his nasty divorces to Harry Rex. They were friends and disliked the other lawyers, especially the Sullivan firm.

Tuesday morning he barged in and growled at Ethel: "Jake in?" He lumbered toward the stairs, glaring at her and daring her to speak. She nodded, knowing better than to ask if he was expected. He had cursed her before. He had cursed everybody before.

The stairway shook as he thundered upward. He was gasping for air as he entered the big office.

"Morning, Harry Rex. You gonna make it?"

"Why don't you get an office downstairs?" he demanded between breaths.

"You need the exercise. If it weren't for those stairs your weight would be over three hundred."

"Thanks. Say, I just came from the courtroom. Noose wants you in chambers at ten-thirty if possible. Wants to talk about Hailey with you and Buckley. Set up arraignment, trial date, all that crap. He asked me to tell you."

"Good. I'll be there."

"I guess you heard about the grand jury?"

"Sure. I've got a copy of the indictment right here."

Harry Rex smiled. "No. No, I mean the vote on the indictment."

Jake froze and looked at him curiously. Harry Rex moved in silent and dark circles like a cloud over the county. He was an endless source of gossip and rumor, and took great pride in spreading only the truth—most of the time. He was the first to know almost everything. The legend of

Harry Rex began twenty years earlier with his first jury trial. The railroad he had sued for millions refused to offer a dime, and after three days of trial the jury retired to deliberate. The railroad lawyers became concerned when the jury failed to return with a quick verdict in their favor. They offered Harry Rex twenty-five thousand to settle when the deliberations went into the second day. With nerves of steel, he told them to go to hell. His client wanted the money. He told his client to go to hell. Hours later a weary and fatigued jury returned with a verdict for one hundred fifty thousand. Harry Rex shot the bird at the railroad lawyers, snubbed his clients and went to the bar at the Best Western. He bought drinks for everyone, and during the course of the long evening explained in detail exactly how he had wired the jury room and knew exactly what the jury was up to. Word spread, and Murphy found a series of wires running through the heating ducts to the jury room. The State Bar Association snooped around, but found nothing. For twenty years the judges had ordered the bailiffs to inspect the jury room when Harry Rex was in any way connected with a case.

"How do you know the vote?" Jake asked, suspicion hanging on every syllable.

"I got sources."

"Okay, what was the vote?"

"Twelve to six. One fewer vote and you wouldn't be holding that indictment."

"Twelve to six," Jake repeated.

"Buckley near 'bout died. A guy named Crowell, white guy, took charge and almost convinced enough of them not to indict your man."

"Do you know Crowell?"

"I handled his divorce two years ago. He lived in Jackson until his first wife was raped by a nigger. She went crazy and they got a divorce. She took a steak knife and sliced her wrists. Then he moved to Clanton and married some sleazebag out in the county. Lasted about a year. He ate Buckley's lunch. Told him to shut up and sit down. I wish I could've seen it."

"Sounds like you did."

"Naw. Just got a good source."

"Who?"

"Jake, come on."

"You been wiring rooms again?"

"Nope. I just listen. That's a good sign, ain't it?"

"What?"

"The close vote. Six outta eighteen voted to let him walk. Five niggers and Crowell. That's a good sign. Just get a couple of niggers on the jury and hang it. Right?"

"It's not that easy. If it's tried in this county there's a good chance we'll have an all-white jury. They're common here, and as you know, they're still very constitutional. Plus this guy Crowell sounds like he came outta nowhere."

"That's what Buckley thought. You should see that ass. He's in the courtroom strutting around ready to sign autographs over his big TV splash last night. No one wants to talk about it, so he manages to work it into every conversation. He's like a kid begging for attention."

"Be sweet. He may be your next governor."

"Not if he loses Hailey. And he's gonna lose Hailey, Jake. We'll pick us a good jury, twelve good and faithful citizens, then we'll buy them."

"I didn't hear that."

"Works every time."

A few minutes after ten-thirty, Jake entered the judge's chamber behind the courtroom and coolly shook hands with Buckley, Musgrove, and Ichabod. They had been waiting on him. Noose waved him toward a seat and sat behind the desk.

"Jake, this will take just a few minutes." He peered down that nose. "I would like to arraign Carl Lee Hailey in the morning at nine. Any problems with that?"

"No. That'll be fine," replied Jake.

"We'll have some other arraignments in the morning, then we start a burglary case at ten. Right, Rufus?"

"Yes, sir."

"Okay. Now let's discuss a trial date for Mr. Hailey. As you know, the next term of court here is in late August— third Monday—and I'm sure the docket will be just as crowded then. Because of the nature of this case and, frankly, because of the publicity, I think it would be best if we had a trial as soon as practical."

"The sooner the better," inserted Buckley.

"Jake, how long will you need to prepare for trial?"

"Sixty days."

"Sixty days!" Buckley repeated in disbelief. "Why so long?"

Jake ignored him and watched Ichabod adjust his reading glasses and study his calendar. "Would it be safe to anticipate a request for a change of venue?" he asked.

"Yes."

"Won't make any difference," Buckley said. "We'll get a conviction anywhere."

"Save it for the cameras, Rufus," Jake said quietly.

"You shouldn't talk about cameras," Buckley shot back. "You seem to enjoy them yourself."

"Gentlemen, please," Noose said. "What other pretrial motions can we expect from the defense?"

Jake thought for a moment. "There will be others."

"May I inquire about the others?" asked Noose with a hint of irritation.

"Judge, I really don't care to discuss my defense at this time. We just received the indictment and I haven't discussed it with my client. We obviously have some work to do."

"How much time do you need?"

"Sixty days."

"Are you kidding!" Buckley shouted. "Is this a joke? The State could try it tomorrow, Judge. Sixty days is ridiculous."

Jake began to burn but said nothing. Buckley walked to the window and mumbled to himself in disbelief.

Noose studied his calendar. "Why sixty days?"

"It could be a complicated case."

Buckley laughed and continued shaking his head.

"Then we can expect a defense of insanity?" asked the judge.

"Yes, sir. And it will take time to have Mr. Hailey examined by a psychiatrist. Then the State will of course want him examined by its doctors."

"I see."

"And we may have other pretrial matters. It's a big case, and I want to make sure we have time to adequately prepare."

"Mr. Buckley?" said the judge.

"Whatever. It makes no difference to the State. We'll be ready. We could try it tomorrow."

Noose scribbled on his calendar and adjusted his reading glasses, which were perched on the tip of that nose and held in place by a tiny wart located perfectly at the foot of the beak. Due to the size of the nose and the odd shape of the head, specially built reading glasses with extra long stems were required for His Honor, who never used them for reading or any other purpose except in a vain effort to distract from the size and shape of the nose. Jake had always suspected this, but lacked the courage to inform His Honor that the ridiculous, orange-tinted hexagonal glasses diverted attention from everything else directly to the nose.

"How long do you anticipate for trial, Jake?" Noose asked.

"Three or four days. But it could take three days to pick the jury."

"Mr. Buckley?"

"Sounds about right. But I don't understand why it takes sixty days to prepare for a three-day trial. I think it should be tried sooner."

"Relax, Rufus," Jake said calmly. "The cameras will be here in sixty days, even ninety days. They won't forget about you. You can give interviews, hold press conferences, preach sermons, everything. The works. But don't worry so much. You'll get your chance."

Buckley's eyes narrowed and his face reddened. He took three steps in Jake's direction. "If I'm not mistaken, Mr. Brigance, you've given more interviews and seen more cameras than I have during the past week."

"I know, and you're jealous, aren't you?"

"No, I'm not jealous! I don't care about the cameras—"

"Since when?"

"Gentlemen, please," Noose interrupted. "This promises to be a long, emotional case. I expect my attorneys to act like professionals. Now, my calendar is congested. The only opening I have is the week of July 22. Does that present a problem?"

"We can try it that week," said Musgrove.

Jake smiled at Buckley and flipped through his pocket calendar. "Looks good to me."

"Fine. All motions must be filed and pretrial matters disposed of by Monday, July 8. Arraignment is set for tomorrow at nine. Any questions?"

Jake stood and shook hands with Noose and Musgrove, and left.

After lunch he visited his famous client in Ozzie's office at the jail. A copy of the indictment had been served on Carl Lee in his cell. He had some questions for his lawyer.

"What's capital murder?"

"The worst kind."

"How many kinds are there?"

"Basically three. Manslaughter, regular murder, and capital murder."

"What's manslaughter?"

"Twenty years."

"What's regular murder?"

"Twenty to life."

"What's capital murder?"

"Gas chamber."

"What's aggravated assault on an officer?"

"Life. No parole."

Carl Lee studied the indictment carefully. "You mean I got two gas chambers and a life sentence."

"Not yet. You're entitled to a trial first. Which, by the way, has been set for July 22."

"That's two months away! Why so long?"

"We need the time. It'll take that long to find a psychiatrist who'll say you were crazy. Then Buckley gets to send you to Whitfield to be examined by the State's doctors, and they'll all say you were not crazy at the time. We file motions, Buckley files motions, we have a bunch of hearings. It takes time."

"No way to have it sooner?"

"We don't want it sooner."

"What if I do?" Carl Lee snapped.

Jake studied him carefully. "What's the matter, big man?"

"I gotta get outta here, and fast."

"I thought you said jail wasn't so bad."

"It ain't, but I need to get home. Gwen's outta money, can't find a job. Lester's in trouble with his wife. She's callin' all the time, so he won't last much longer. I hate to ask my folk for help."

"But they will, won't they?"

"Some. They got their own problems. You gotta get me outta here, Jake."

"Look, you'll be arraigned in the morning at nine. The trial is July 22, and the date won't be changed, so forget about that. Have I explained the arraignment to you?"

Carl Lee shook his head.

"It won't last twenty minutes. We appear before Judge Noose in the big courtroom. He'll ask you some questions, then ask me some questions. He'll read the indictment to you in open court, and ask if you've received a copy. Then he'll ask you to plead guilty or not guilty. When you answer not guilty, he'll set the trial date. You'll sit down, and me and Buckley will get into a big fight over your bond. Noose will refuse to set a bond, then they'll bring you back to the jail, where you'll stay until the trial."

"What about after the trial?"

Jake smiled. "Naw, you won't be in jail after the trial."

"You promise?"

"Nope. No promises. Any questions about tomorrow?"

"No. Say, Jake, uh, how much money did I pay you?"

Jake hesitated and smelled trouble. "Why do you ask?"

"Just thinkin'."

"Nine hundred, plus a note."

Gwen had less than a hundred dollars. Bills were due and food was low. She had visited on Sunday and cried for an hour. Panic was a part of her life, her makeup, her composition. But he knew they were broke and she was scared. Her family would be of little help, maybe some vegetables from the garden and a few bucks for milk and eggs. When it came to funerals and hospital stays they were very dependable. They were generous and gave of their time freely to wail and moan and put on a show. But when real money was needed they scattered like chickens. He had little use for her family, and his wasn't much better.

He wanted to ask Jake for a hundred dollars, but decided to wait until Gwen was completely broke. It would be easier then.

Jake flipped through his legal pad and waited for Carl Lee to ask for money. Criminal clients, especially the blacks, always asked for some of the fee back after it was paid. He doubted he would ever see more than nine hundred dollars, and he was not about to return any. Besides, the blacks always took care of their own. The families would be there and the churches would get involved. No one would starve.

He waited and placed the legal pad and file in his briefcase. "Any questions, Carl Lee?"

"Yeah. What can I say tomorrow?"

"What do you want to say?"

"I wanna tell that judge why I shot them boys. They raped my daughter. They needed shootin'."

"And you want to explain that to the judge tomorrow?"

"Yeah."

"And you think he'll turn you loose once you explain it all?"

Carl Lee said nothing.

"Look, Carl Lee, you hired me to be your lawyer. And you hired me because you have confidence in me, right? And if I want you to say something tomorrow, I'll tell you. If I don't, you stay quiet. When you go to trial in July you'll have the chance to tell your side. But in the meantime, I'll do the talking."

"You got that right."

———————————

Lester and Gwen piled the boys and Tonya in the red Cadillac and drove to the doctor's building next to the hospital. The rape was two weeks in the past. Tonya walked with a slight limp and wanted to run and climb steps with her brothers. But her mother held her hand. The soreness in her legs and buttocks was almost gone, the bandages on her wrists and ankles had been removed by the doctor last week, and the cuts were healing nicely. The gauze and cotton between her legs remained.

In a small room she undressed and sat next to her mother on a padded table. Her mother hugged her and helped her stay warm. The doctor poked in her mouth and rubbed her jaw. He held her wrists and ankles and inspected them. He laid her on the table and touched between her legs. She cried and clutched her mother, who leaned over her.

She was hurting again.

15 At five Wednesday morning, Jake sipped coffee in his office and stared through the French doors across the dark courtyard square. He had slept fitfully, and several hours earlier had given up and left his warm bed in a desperate effort to find a nameless Georgia case that, as he thought he remembered from law school, required the judge to allow bail in a capital murder case if the defendant had no prior criminal record, owned property in the county, had a stable job, and had plenty of relatives nearby. It had not been found. He did find a battery of recent, well-reasoned, clear, and unambiguous Mississippi cases allowing the judge complete discretion in denying bail to such defendants. That was the law and Jake now knew it well, but he needed something to argue to Ichabod. He dreaded asking bail for Carl Lee. Buckley would scream and preach and cite those wonderful cases, and Noose would smile and listen, then deny bail. Jake would get his tail kicked in the first skirmish.

"You're here early this morning, sweetheart," Dell said to her favorite customer as she poured his coffee.

"At least I'm here." He had missed a few mornings since the amputation. Looney was popular, and there was resentment at the Coffee Shop and around town for Hailey's lawyer. He was aware of it and tried to ignore it.

There was resentment among many for any lawyer who would defend a nigger for killing two white men.

"You got a minute?" Jake asked.

"Sure," Dell said, looking around. At five-fifteen, the cafe was not yet full. She sat across from Jake in a small booth and poured coffee.

"What's the talk in here?" he asked.

"The usual. Politics, fishing, farming. It never changes. I've been here for twenty-one years, serving the same food to the same people, and they're still talking about the same things."

"Nothing new?"

"Hailey. We get a lotta talk about that. Except when the strangers are here, then it goes back to the usual."

"Why?"

"Because if you act like you know anything about the case, some reporter will follow you outside with a bunch of questions."

"That bad, huh?"

"No. It's great. Business has never been better."

Jake smiled and buttered his grits, then added Tabasco.

"How do you feel about the case?"

Dell scratched her nose with long, red, fake fingernails and blew into her coffee. She was famous for her bluntness, and he was hoping for a straight answer.

"He's guilty. He killed them. It's cut and dried. But he had the best damned excuse I've ever seen. There's some sympathy for him."

"Let's say you're on the jury. Guilty or innocent?"

She watched the front door and waved at a regular. "Well, my instinct is to forgive anyone who kills a rapist. Especially a father. But, on the other hand, we can't allow people to grab guns and hand out their own justice. Can you prove he was crazy when he did it?"

"Let's assume I can."

"Then I would vote not guilty, even though I don't think he was crazy."

He smeared strawberry preserves on dry toast and nodded his approval.

"But what about Looney?" she asked. "He's a friend of mine."

"It was an accident."

"Is that good enough?"

"No. No, it's not. The gun did not go off by accident. Looney was accidentally shot, but I doubt if that's a valid defense. Would you convict him for shooting Looney?"

"Maybe," she answered slowly. "He lost a leg."

How could he be insane when he shot Cobb and Willard, and not when he shot Looney, Jake thought, but didn't ask. He changed the subject.

"What's the gossip on me?"

"About the same. Someone was asking where you were the other day, and said you don't have time for us now that you're a celebrity. I've heard some mumbling, about you and the nigger, but it's pretty quiet. They don't criticize you loudly. I won't let them."

"You're a sweetheart."

"I'm a mean bitch and you know it."

"No. You just try to be."

"Yeah, watch this." She jumped from the booth and shouted abuse at a table of farmers who had motioned for more coffee. Jake finished alone, and returned to the office.

When Ethel arrived at eight-thirty, two reporters were loitering on the sidewalk outside the locked door. They followed Ethel inside and demanded to see Mr. Brigance. She refused, and asked them to leave. They refused, and repeated their demand. Jake heard the commotion downstairs and locked his door. Let Ethel fight with them.

From his office he watched a camera crew set up by the rear door of the courthouse. He smiled and felt a wonderful surge of adrenaline. He could see himself on the evening news walking briskly, stern, businesslike, across the street followed by reporters begging for dialogue but getting no comments. And this was just the arraignment. Imagine the trial! Cameras everywhere, reporters yelling questions, front page stories, perhaps magazine covers. An Atlanta paper had called it the most sensational murder in the South in twenty years. He would have taken the case for free, almost.

Moments later he interrupted the argument downstairs, and warmly greeted the reporters. Ethel disappeared into the conference room.

"Could you answer some questions?" one of them asked.

"No," Jake answered politely. "I have to meet with Judge Noose."

"Just a couple of questions?"

"No. But there will be a press conference at three P.M." Jake opened the door, and the reporters followed him onto the sidewalk.

"Where's the press conference?"

"In my office."

"What's the purpose?"

"To discuss the case."

Jake walked slowly across the street and up the short

driveway to the courthouse answering questions along the way.

"Will Mr. Hailey be at the press conference?"

"Yes, along with his family."

"The girl, too?"

"Yes, she will be there."

"Will Mr. Hailey answer questions?"

"Maybe. I haven't decided."

Jake said good day, and disappeared into the courthouse, leaving the reporters to chat and gossip about the press conference.

Buckley entered the courthouse through the huge wooden front doors, amid no fanfare. He had hoped for a camera or two, but was dismayed to learn they were gathering at the rear door to catch a glimpse of the defendant. He would use the rear door in the future.

Judge Noose parked by a fire hydrant in front of the post office and loped along the east sidewalk across the courtyard square and into the courthouse. He, too, attracted no attention, except for a few curious stares.

Ozzie peered through the front windows of the jail and watched the mob waiting for Carl Lee in the parking lot. The ploy of another end run crossed his mind, but he dismissed it. His office had received two dozen death threats on Carl Lee, and Ozzie took a few seriously. They were specific, with dates and places. But most were just general, everyday death threats. And this was just the arraignment. He thought of the trial, and mumbled something to Moss Junior. They surrounded Carl Lee with uniformed bodies and marched him down the sidewalk, past the press and into a rented step van. Six deputies and a driver piled in. Escorted by Ozzie's three newest patrol cars, the van drove quickly to the courthouse.

Noose had scheduled a dozen arraignments for 9:00 A.M., and when he settled into the chair on the bench he shifted through the files until he found Hailey's. He looked to the front row in the courtroom and saw a somber group of suspicious-looking men, all newly indicted. At the far end of the front row, two deputies sat next to a handcuffed defendant, and Brigance was whispering to him. Must be Hailey.

Noose picked up a red court file and adjusted his reading glasses so they would not hinder his reading. "State versus Carl Lee Hailey, case number 3889. Will Mr. Hailey come forward?"

The handcuffs were removed, and Carl Lee followed his attorney to the bench, where they stood looking up to His Honor, who quietly and nervously scanned the indictment in the file. The courtroom grew silent. Buckley rose and strutted slowly to within a few feet of the defendant. The artists near the railing busily sketched the scene.

Jake glared at Buckley, who had no reason to stand before the bench during the arraignment. The D.A. was dressed in his finest black three-piece polyester suit. Every hair on his huge head had been meticulously combed and plastered in place. He had the appearance of a television evangelist.

Jake walked to Buckley and whispered, "That's a nice suit, Rufus."

"Thanks," he replied, somewhat off-guard.

"Does it glow in the dark?" Jake asked, then returned to the side of his client.

"Are you Carl Lee Hailey?" asked the judge.

"Yes."

"Mr. Brigance your attorney?"

"Yes."

"I'm holding here a copy of an indictment returned against you by the grand jury. Have you been served a copy of this?"

"Yes."

"Have you read it?"

"Yes."

"Have you discussed it with your attorney?"

"Yes."

"Do you understand it?"

"Yes."

"Good. I'm required by law to read it to you in open court." Noose cleared his throat. " 'The grand jurors of the State of Mississippi, taken from the body of good and lawful citizens of Ford County thereof, duly elected, empaneled, sworn, and charged to inquire in and for said county and state aforesaid, in the name and under the authority of the State of Mississippi, upon their oaths present that Carl Lee

Hailey, late of the county and state aforesaid, within the jurisdiction of this court, did unlawfully, willfully, and feloniously and intentionally and with malice aforethought, kill and murder Billy Ray Cobb, a human being, and Pete Willard, a human being, and did shoot and attempt to kill DeWayne Looney, a peace officer, in direct violation of the Mississippi Code, and against the peace and dignity of the State of Mississippi. A true bill. Signed, Laverne Gossett, foreman of the grand jury."

Noose caught his breath. "Do you understand the charges against you?"

"Yes."

"Do you understand that if convicted you could be put to death in the gas chamber at the state penitentiary at Parchman?"

"Yes."

"Do you wish to plead guilty or not guilty?"

"Not guilty."

Noose reviewed his calendar as the audience watched intently. The reporters took notes. The artists focused on the principals, including Buckley, who had managed to enter the picture and stand sideways, allowing for a profile shot. He was anxious to say something. He scowled contemptuously at the rear of Carl Lee's head, as if he could not wait to fry this murderer. He swaggered to the table where Musgrove was sitting and the two whispered importantly. He marched across the courtroom and engaged in hushed conversation with one of the clerks. Then he returned to the bench where the defendant stood motionless next to his attorney, who was aware of Buckley's show and was trying desperately to ignore it.

"Mr. Hailey," Noose squeaked, "your trial is set for Monday, July 22. All pretrial motions and matters must be filed by June 24, and disposed of by July 8."

Carl Lee and Jake nodded.

"Anything further?"

"Yes, Your Honor," Buckley boomed loud enough for the reporters in the rotunda. "The State opposes any request for bail by this defendant."

Jake gripped his fists and wanted to scream. "Your Honor, the defendant has not yet asked for bail. Mr. Buckley, as usual, is confused about the procedure. He cannot oppose a request until it is made. He should've learned that in law school."

Buckley was stung, but continued. "Your Honor, Mr. Brigance always requests bail, and I'm sure he'll request it today. The State will oppose any such request."

"Well, why don't you wait until he makes his request?" Noose asked the D.A. with a touch of irritation.

"Very well," Buckley said. His face had reddened and he glared at Jake.

"Do you plan to request bail?" Noose asked.

"I had planned to at the proper time, but before I got a chance Mr. Buckley intervened with his theatrics—"

"Never mind Mr. Buckley," Noose interrupted.

"I know, Judge, he's just confused."

"Bail, Mr. Brigance?"

"Yes, I had planned to request it."

"I thought so, and I've already considered whether bail should be allowed in this case. As you know, it is completely within my discretion, and I never allow bail in a capital murder case. I don't feel as though an exception is in order in this case."

"You mean you've decided to deny bail?"

"Yes."

Jake shrugged his shoulders and laid a file on the table. "Good enough."

"Anything further?" Noose asked.

"No, Your Honor," Jake said.

Buckley shook his head in silence.

"Good. Mr. Hailey, you are hereby ordered to remain in the custody of the Ford County sheriff until trial. You are dismissed."

Carl Lee returned to the front row, where a deputy waited with the handcuffs. Jake opened his briefcase, and was stuffing it with files and papers when Buckley grabbed his arm.

"That was a cheap shot, Brigance," he said through clenched teeth.

"You asked for it," Jake replied. "Let go of my arm."

Buckley released his arm. "I don't appreciate it."

"Too bad, big man. You shouldn't talk so much. Big mouths get burned."

Buckley had three inches and fifty pounds on Jake, and his irritation was growing. The exchange had drawn attention, and a deputy moved between them. Jake winked at Buckley and left the courtroom.

———————

At two the Hailey clan, led by Uncle Lester, entered Jake's office through the rear door. Jake met them in a small office next to the conference room downstairs. They talked about the press conference. Twenty minutes later, Ozzie and Carl Lee strolled nonchalantly through the rear door, and Jake led them to the office, where Carl Lee was reunited with his family. Ozzie and Jake left the room.

The press conference was carefully orchestrated by Jake, who marveled at his ability to manipulate the press and its willingness to be manipulated. On one side of the long conference table he sat with the three Hailey boys standing behind him. Gwen was seated to his left, Carl Lee to his right holding Tonya.

Legal etiquette forbade revealing the identity of a child rape victim, but Tonya was different. Her name, face, and age were well known because of her daddy. She had already been exposed to the world, and Jake wanted her to be seen and photographed in her best white Sunday dress sitting on her daddy's knee. The jurors, whoever they were and wherever they lived, would be watching.

Reporters crammed into the room, which overflowed and trailed down the hall to the reception area, where Ethel rudely ordered them to sit and leave her alone. A deputy guarded the front door, and two others sat on the rear steps. Sheriff Walls and Lester stood awkwardly behind the Haileys and their lawyer. Microphones were clustered on the table in front of Jake, and the cameras clicked and flashed under the warm television lights.

"I have a few prefatory remarks," Jake began. "First, all questions will be answered by me. No questions are to be directed to Mr. Hailey or any member of his family. If he is asked a question, I will instruct him not to answer. Second, I would like to introduce his family. To my left is his wife,

Gwen Hailey. Standing behind us are his sons, Carl Lee, Jr., Jarvis, and Robert. Behind the boys is Mr. Hailey's brother, Lester Hailey."

Jake paused and smiled at Tonya. "Sitting in her daddy's lap is Tonya Hailey. Now I'll answer questions."

"What happened in court this morning?"

"Mr. Hailey was arraigned, he pled not guilty, and his trial was set for July 22."

"Was there an altercation between you and the district attorney?"

"Yes. After the arraignment, Mr. Buckley approached me, grabbed my arm, and looked as if he planned to assault me when a deputy intervened."

"What caused it?"

"Mr. Buckley has a tendency to crack under pressure."

"Are you and Mr. Buckley friends?"

"No."

"Will the trial be in Clanton?"

"A motion to change venue will be filed by the defense. The location of the trial will be determined by Judge Noose. No predictions."

"Could you describe what this has done to the Hailey family?"

Jake thought a minute while the cameras rolled. He glanced at Carl Lee and Tonya. "You're looking at a very nice family. Two weeks ago life was good and simple. There was a job at the paper mill, a little money in the bank, security, stability, church every Sunday together, a loving family. Then, for reasons known only to God, two drunk, drugged punks committed a horrible, violent act against this little ten-year-old girl. They shocked us, and made us all feel sick. They ruined her life, and the lives of her parents and family. It was too much for her father. He snapped. He broke. Now he's in jail facing trial and the prospect of the gas chamber. The job is gone. The money is gone. The innocence is gone. The children face the possibility of growing up without their father. Their mother must now find a job to support them, and she'll have to beg and borrow from friends and relatives in order to survive.

"To answer your question, sir, the family has been devastated and destroyed."

Gwen began crying quietly, and Jake handed her a handkerchief.

"Are you hinting at a defense of insanity?"

"Yes."

"Will there in fact be a plea of insanity?"

"Yes."

"Can you prove it?"

"That will be left for the jury. We will provide them experts in the field of psychiatry."

"Have you already consulted with these experts?"

"Yes," lied Jake.

"Could you give us their names?"

"No, that would be inappropriate at this point."

"We've heard rumors of death threats against Mr. Hailey. Could you confirm?"

"There continue to be threats against Mr. Hailey, his family, my family, the sheriff, the judge, just about everyone involved. I don't know how serious they are."

Carl Lee patted Tonya on the leg and looked blankly at the table. He looked scared, pitiful, and in need of sympathy. His boys looked scared too, but, according to strict orders, they stood at attention, afraid to move. Carl Lee, Jr., the oldest at fifteen, stood behind Jake. Jarvis, the middle son at thirteen, stood behind his daddy. And Robert, age eleven, stood behind his mother. They wore identical navy suits with white shirts and little red bow ties. Robert's suit was once Carl Lee, Jr.'s, then Jarvis's, and now his, and it looked a bit more worn than the other two. But it was clean, neatly pressed, and perfectly cuffed. The boys looked sharp. How could any juror vote to force these children to live without their father?

The press conference was a hit. Segments of it ran on the networks and local stations, both on the evening and late news. The Thursday papers ran front page pictures of the Haileys and their lawyer.

16 The Swede had called several times during the two weeks her husband had been in Mississippi. She didn't trust him down there. There were old girlfriends he had confessed to. Each time she called, Lester was not around, and Gwen lied and explained that he was fishing or cutting pulpwood so they could buy groceries. Gwen was tired of lying, and Lester was tired of carousing, and they were tired of each other. When the phone rang before dawn Friday morning, Lester answered it. It was the Swede.

Two hours later the red Cadillac was parked at the jail. Moss Junior led Lester into Carl Lee's cell. The brothers whispered above the sleep of the inmates.

"Gotta go home," Lester mumbled, somewhat ashamed, somewhat timid.

"Why?" Carl Lee asked as if he had been expecting it.

"My wife called this mornin'. I gotta be at work tomorrow or I'm fired."

Carl Lee nodded approvingly.

"I'm sorry, bubba. I feel bad about goin', but I ain't got no choice."

"I understand. When you comin' back?"

"When you want me back?"

"For the trial. It'll be real hard on Gwen and the kids. Can you be back then?"

"You know I'll be here. I got some vacation time and all. I'll be here."

They sat on the edge of Carl Lee's bunk and watched each other in silence. The cell was dark and quiet. The two bunks opposite Carl Lee's were empty.

"Man, I forgot how bad this place is," Lester said.

"I just hope I ain't here much longer."

They stood and embraced, and Lester called for Moss Junior to open the cell. "I'm proud of you, bubba," he said to his older brother, then left for Chicago.

Carl Lee's second visitor of the morning was his attorney, who met him in Ozzie's office. Jake was red eyed and irritable.

"Carl Lee, I talked to two psychiatrists in Memphis yesterday. Do you know what the minimum fee is to evaluate you for trial purposes? Do you?"

"Am I supposed to know?" asked Carl Lee.

"One thousand dollars," Jake shouted. "One thousand dollars. Where can you find a thousand dollars?"

"I gave you all the money I got. I even offered—"

"I don't want the deed to your land. Why? Because nobody wants to buy it, and if you can't sell it, it's no good. We've got to have cash, Carl Lee. Not for me, but for the psychiatrists."

"Why?"

"Why!" Jake repeated in disbelief. "Why? Because I'd like to keep you away from the gas chamber, and it's only a hundred miles from here. It's not that far. And to do that, we've got to convince the jury that you were insane when you shot those boys. I can't tell them you were crazy. You can't tell them you were crazy. It takes a psychiatrist. An expert. A doctor. And they don't work for free. Understand?"

Carl Lee leaned on his knees and watched a spider crawl across the dusty carpet. After twelve days in jail and two court appearances, he had had enough of the criminal justice system. He thought of the hours and minutes before the killings. What was he thinking? Sure the boys had to die. He had no regrets. But did he contemplate jail, or poverty, or lawyers, or psychiatrists? Maybe, but only in passing. Those unpleasantries were only by-products to be encountered and endured temporarily before he was set free. After the deed, the system would process him, vindicate him, and send him home to his family. It would be easy, just as Lester's episode had been virtually painless.

But the system was not working now. It was conspiring to keep him in jail, to break him, to make orphans of his children. It seemed determined to punish him for performing an act he considered unavoidable. And now, his only ally was making demands he could not meet. His lawyer asked the impossible. His friend Jake was angry and yelling.

"Get it," Jake shouted as he headed for the door. "Get it from your brothers and sisters, from Gwen's family, get it from your friends, get it from your church. But get it. And as soon as possible."

Jake slammed the door and marched out of the jail.

———————

Carl Lee's third visitor of the morning arrived before noon in a long black limousine with a chauffeur and Tennessee plates. It maneuvered through the small parking lot and came to rest straddling three spaces. A large black bodyguard emerged from behind the wheel and opened the door to release his boss. They strutted up the sidewalk and into the jail.

The secretary stopped typing and smiled suspiciously. "Good mornin'."

"Mornin'," said the smaller one, the one with the patch. "My name is Cat Bruster, and I'd like to see Sheriff Walls."

"May I ask what for?"

"Yes ma'am. It's regardin' a Mr. Hailey, a resident of your fine facility."

The sheriff heard his name mentioned, and appeared from his office to greet this infamous visitor. "Mr. Bruster, I'm Ozzie Walls." They shook hands. The bodyguard did not move.

"Nice to meet you, Sheriff. I'm Cat Bruster, from Memphis."

"Yes. I know who you are. Seen you in the news. What brings you to Ford County?"

"Well, I gotta buddy in bad trouble. Carl Lee Hailey, and I'm here to help."

"Okay. Who's he?" Ozzie asked, looking up at the bodyguard. Ozzie was six feet four, and at least five inches shorter than the bodyguard. He weighed at least three hundred pounds, most of it in his arms.

"This here is Tiny Tom," Cat explained. "We just call him Tiny for short."

"I see."

"He's sort of like a bodyguard."

"He's not carryin' a gun, is he?"

"Naw, Sheriff, he don't need a gun."

"Fair enough. Why don't you and Tiny step into my office?"

In the office, Tiny closed the door and stood by it while his boss took a seat across from the sheriff.

"He can sit if he wants to," Ozzie explained to Cat.

"Naw, Sheriff, he always stands by the door. That's the way he's been trained."

"Sorta like a police dog?"

"Right."

"Fine. What'd you wanna talk about?"

Cat crossed his legs and laid a diamond-clustered hand on his knee. "Well, Sheriff, me and Carl Lee go way back. Fought together in 'Nam. We was pinned down near Da Nang, summer of '71. I got hit in the head, and, bam!, two seconds later he got hit in the leg. Our squad disappeared, and the gooks was usin' us for target practice. Carl Lee limped to where I's layin', put me on his shoulders, and ran through the gunfire to a ditch next to a trail. I hung on his back while he crawled two miles. Saved my life. He got a medal for it. You know that?"

"No."

"It's true. We laid next to each other in a hospital in Saigon for two months, then got our black asses outta Vietnam. Don't plan to go back."

Ozzie was listening intently.

"And now that my man is in trouble, I'd like to help."

"Did he get the M-16 from you?"

Tiny grunted and Cat smiled. "Of course not."

"Would you like to see him?"

"Why sure. It's that easy?"

"Yep. If you can move Tiny away from that door, I'll get him."

Tiny stepped aside, and two minutes later Ozzie was back with the prisoner. Cat yelled at him, hugged him, and they patted each other like boxers. Carl Lee looked awkwardly at Ozzie, who took the hint and left. Tiny again closed the door and stood guard. Carl Lee moved two chairs together so they could face each other closely and talk.

Cat spoke first. "I'm proud of you, big man, for what you did. Real proud. Why didn't you tell me that's why you wanted the gun?"

"Just didn't."

"How was it?"

"Just like 'Nam, except they couldn't shoot back."

"That's the best way."

"Yeah, I guess. I just wish none of this had to happen."

"You ain't sorry, are you?"

Carl Lee rocked in his chair and studied the ceiling. "I'd do it over, so I got no regrets about that. I just wish they hadn't messed with my little girl. I wish she was the same. I wish none of it ever happened."

"Right, right. It's gotta be tough on you here."

"I ain't worried 'bout me. I'm real concerned with my family."

"Right, right. How's the wife?"

"She's okay. She'll make it."

"I saw in the paper where the trial's in July. You been in the paper more than me here lately."

"Yeah, Cat. But you always get off. I ain't so sure 'bout me."

"You gotta good lawyer, don't you?"

"Yeah. He's good."

Cat stood and walked around the office, admiring Ozzie's trophies and certificates. "That's the main reason I came to see you, my man."

"What's that?" Carl Lee asked, unsure of what his friend had in mind, but certain his visit had a purpose.

"Carl Lee, you know how many times I been on trial?"

"Seems like all the time."

"Five! Five times they put me on trial. The federal boys. The state boys. The city boys. Dope, gamblin', bribery, guns, racketeerin', whores. You name it, and they've tried me for it. And you know somethin', Carl Lee, I've been guilty of it all. Evertime I've gone to trial, I've been guilty as hell. You know how many times I been convicted?"

"No."

"None! Not once have they got me. Five trials, five not guilties."

Carl Lee smiled with admiration.

"You know why they can't convict me?"

Carl Lee had an idea, but he shook his head anyway.

"Because, Carl Lee, I got the smartest, meanest,

crookedest criminal lawyer in these parts. He cheats, he plays dirty, and the cops hate him. But I'm sittin' here instead of some prison. He'll do whatever it takes to win a case."

"Who is he?" Carl Lee asked eagerly.

"You've seen him on television walkin' in and outta court. He's in the papers all the time. Evertime some bigshot crook gets in trouble, he's there. He gets the drug dealers, the politicians, me, all the big-time thugs."

"What's his name?"

"He handles nothin' but criminal cases, mainly dope, bribery, extortion, stuff like that. But you know what his favorite is?"

"What?"

"Murder. He loves murder cases. Ain't never lost one. Gets all the big ones in Memphis. Remember when they caught those two niggers throwin' a dude off the bridge into the Mississippi. Caught them redhanded. 'Bout five years ago?"

"Yeah, I remember."

"Had a big trial for two weeks, and they got off. He was the man. Walked them outta there. Not guilty."

"I think I remember seein' him on TV."

"Sure you did. He's a bad dude, Carl Lee. I'm tellin' you the man never loses."

"What's his name?"

Cat landed in his chair and stared solemnly into Carl Lee's face. "Bo Marsharfsky," he said.

Carl Lee gazed upward as if he remembered the name. "So what?"

Cat laid five fingers with eight carats on Carl Lee's knee. "So he wants to help you, my man."

"I already got one lawyer I can't pay. How I'm gonna pay another?"

"You ain't gotta pay, Carl Lee. That's where I come in. He's on my retainer all the time. I own him. Paid the guy 'bout a hundred thousand last year just to keep me outta trouble. You don't pay."

Suddenly, Carl Lee had a keen interest in Bo Marsharfsky. "How does he know 'bout me?"

"Because he reads the paper and watches the tube. You

know how lawyers are. I was in his office yesterday and he was studyin' the paper with your picture on the front. I told him 'bout me and you. He went crazy. Said he had to have your case. I said I would help."

"And that's why you're here?"

"Right, right. He said he knew just the folks to get you off."

"Like who?"

"Doctors, psychiatrists, folks like that. He knows them all."

"They cost money."

"I'll pay for it, Carl Lee! Listen to me! I'll pay for it all. You'll have the best lawyer and doctors money can buy, and your old pal Cat will pay the tab. Don't worry 'bout money!"

"But I gotta good lawyer."

"How old is he?"

"I guess 'bout thirty."

Cat rolled his eyes in amazement. "He's a child, Carl Lee. He ain't been outta school long enough. Marsharfsky's fifty, and he's handled more murder cases than your boy'll ever see. This is your life, Carl Lee. Don't trust it to no rookie."

Suddenly, Jake was awful young. But then there was Lester's trial when Jake had been even younger.

"Look, Carl Lee, I been in many trials, and that crap is complicated and technical. One mistake and your ass is gone. If this kid misses one trick, it might be the difference between life and death. You can't afford to have no young kid in there hopin' he don't mess up. One mistake," Cat snapped his fingers for special effect, "and you're in the gas chamber. Marsharfsky don't make mistakes."

Carl Lee was on the ropes. "Would he work with my lawyer?" he asked, seeking compromise.

"No! No way. He don't work with nobody. He don't need no help. Your boy'd be in the way."

Carl Lee placed his elbows on his knees and stared at his feet. A thousand bucks for a doctor would be impossible. He did not understand the need for one since he had not felt insanc at the time, but evidently one would be necessary. Everyone seemed to think so. A thousand bucks for a cheap doctor. Cat was offering the best money could buy.

"I hate to do this to my lawyer," he muttered quietly.

"Don't be stupid, man," Cat scolded. "You better be lookin' out for Carl Lee and to hell with this child. This ain't no time to worry 'bout hurtin' feelin's. He's a lawyer, forget him. He'll get over it."

"But I already paid him—"

"How much?" Cat demanded, snapping his fingers at Tiny.

"Nine hundred bucks."

Tiny produced a wad of cash, and Cat peeled off nine one-hundred-dollar bills and stuffed them in Carl Lee's shirt pocket. "Here's somethin' for the kids," he said as he unraveled a one-thousand-dollar bill and stuffed it with the rest.

Carl Lee's pulse jumped as he thought of the cash covering his heart. He felt it move in the pocket and press gently against his chest. He wanted to look at the big bill and hold it firmly in his hand. Food, he thought, food for his kids.

"We gotta deal?" Cat asked with a smile.

"You want me to fire my lawyer and hire yours?" he asked carefully.

"Right, right."

"And you gonna pay for everthing?"

"Right, right."

"What about this money?"

"It's yours. Lemme know if you need more."

"Mighty nice of you, Cat."

"I'm a very nice man. I'm helpin' two friends. One saved my life many years ago, and the other saves my ass ever two years."

"Why does he want my case so bad?"

"Publicity. You know how lawyers are. Look at how much press this kid's already made off you. It's a lawyer's dream. We gotta deal?"

"Yeah. It's a deal."

Cat struck him on the shoulder with an affectionate blow, and walked to the phone on Ozzie's desk. He punched the numbers. "Collect to 901-566-9800. From Cat Bruster. Person to person to Bo Marsharfsky."

On the twentieth floor in a downtown office building, Bo
Marsharfsky hung up the phone and asked his secretary if
the press release was prepared. She handed it to him, and he
read it carefully.

"This looks fine," he said. "Get it to both newspapers
immediately. Tell them to use the file photograph, the new
one. See Frank Fields at the *Post*. Tell him I want it on the
front page in the morning. He owes me a favor."

"Yes, sir. What about the TV stations?" she asked.

"Deliver them a copy. I can't talk now, but I'll hold a
news conference in Clanton next week."

Lucien called at six-thirty Saturday morning. Carla was buried deep under the blankets and did not respond to the
phone. Jake rolled toward the wall and grappled with the
lamp until he found the receiver. "Hello," he managed
weakly.

"What're you doing?" Lucien asked.

"I was sleeping until the phone rang."

"You seen the paper?"

"What time is it?"

"Go get the paper and call me after you read it."

The phone was dead. Jake stared at the receiver, then
placed it on the table. He sat on the edge of the bed, rubbed
the fog from his eyes, and tried to remember the last time
Lucien called his house. It must be important.

He made the coffee, turned out the dog, and walked
quickly in his gym shorts and sweatshirt to the edge of the
street where the three morning papers had fallen within ten
inches of each other. He rolled the rubber bands off onto
the kitchen table and spread the papers next to his coffee.
Nothing in the Jackson paper. Nothing from Tupelo. *The
Memphis Post* carried a headline of death in the Middle
East, and, then, he saw it. On the bottom half of the front
page he saw himself, and under his picture was the caption:
"Jake Brigance—Out." Next was a picture of Carl Lee, and
then a splendid picture of a face he had seen before. Under
it, the words: "Bo Marsharfsky—In." The headline announced that the noted Memphis criminal attorney had
been hired to represent the "vigilante killer."

He was stunned, weak, and confused. Surely it was a mistake. He had seen Carl Lee only yesterday. He read the story slowly. There were few details, just a history of Marsharfsky's greatest verdicts. He promised a news conference in Clanton. He said the case would present new challenges, etc. He had faith in the jurors of Ford County.

Jake slipped silently into starched khakis and a button-down. His wife was still lost somewhere deep in the bed. He would tell her later. He took the paper and drove to the office. The Coffee Shop would not be safe. At Ethel's desk he read the story again and stared at his picture on the front page.

Lucien had a few words of comfort. He knew Marsharfsky, or "The Shark," as he was known. He was a sleazy crook with polish and finesse. Lucien admired him.

———————

Moss Junior led Carl Lee into Ozzie's office, where Jake waited with a newspaper. The deputy quickly left and closed the door. Carl Lee sat on the small black vinyl couch.

Jake threw the newspaper at him. "Have you seen this?" he demanded.

Carl Lee glared at him and ignored the paper.

"Why, Carl Lee?"

"I don't have to explain, Jake."

"Yes, you do. You didn't have the guts to call me like a man and tell me. You let me read it in the paper. I demand an explanation."

"You wanted too much money, Jake. You're always gripin' over the money. Here I am sittin' in jail and you're bitchin' 'bout somethin' I can't help."

"Money. You can't afford to pay me. How can you afford Marsharfsky?"

"I ain't gotta pay him."

"What!"

"You heard me. I ain't payin' him."

"I guess he works for free."

"Nope. Somebody else is payin'."

"Who!" Jake shouted.

"I ain't tellin'. It ain't none of your business, Jake."

"You've hired the biggest criminal lawyer in Memphis, and someone else is payin' his bill?"

"Yep."

The NAACP, thought Jake. No, they wouldn't hire Marsharfsky. They've got their own lawyers. Besides, he was too expensive for them. Who else?

Carl Lee took the newspaper and folded it neatly. He was ashamed, and felt bad, but the decision had been made. He had asked Ozzie to call Jake and convey the news, but the sheriff wanted no part of it. He should have called, but he was not going to apologize. He studied his picture on the front page. He liked the part about the vigilante business.

"And you're not going to tell me who?" Jake said, somewhat quieter.

"Naw, Jake. I ain't tellin'."

"Did you discuss it with Lester?"

The glare returned to his eyes. "Nope. He ain't on trial, and it ain't none of his business."

"Where is he?"

"Chicago. Left yesterday. And don't you go call him. I've made up my mind, Jake."

We'll see, Jake said to himself. Lester would find out shortly.

Jake opened the door. "That's it. I'm fired. Just like that."

Carl Lee stared at his picture and said nothing.

———————

Carla was eating breakfast and waiting. A reporter from Jackson had called looking for Jake, and had told her about Marsharfsky.

There were no words, just motions. He filled a cup with coffee and went to the back porch. He sipped from the steaming cup and surveyed the unkempt hedges that lined the boundary of his long and narrow backyard. A brilliant sun baked the rich green Bermuda and dried the dew, creating a sticky haze that drifted upward and hung to his shirt. The hedges and grass were waiting on their weekly grooming. He kicked off his loafers—no socks—and walked through the soggy turf to inspect a broken birdbath near a scrawny crepe myrtle, the only tree of any significance.

She followed the wet footprints and stood behind him. He took her hand and smiled. "You okay?" she asked.

"Yeah, I'm fine."

"Did you talk to him?"

"Yes."

"What did he say?"

He shook his head and said nothing.

"I'm sorry, Jake."

He nodded and stared at the birdbath.

"There will be other cases," she said without confidence.

"I know." He thought of Buckley, and could hear the laughter. He thought of the guys at the Coffee Shop, and vowed not to return. He thought of the cameras and reporters, and a dull pain moved through his stomach. He thought of Lester, his only hope of retrieving the case.

"Would you like some breakfast?" she asked.

"No. I'm not hungry. Thanks."

"Look on the bright side," she said. "We won't be afraid to answer the phone."

"I think I'll cut the grass," he said.

17 The Council of Ministers was a group of black preachers that had been formed to coordinate political activities in the black communities of Ford County. It met infrequently during the off years, but during election years it met weekly, on Sunday afternoons, to interview candidates and discuss issues, and, more importantly, to determine the benevolence of each office seeker. Deals were cut, strategies developed, money exchanged. The council had proven it could deliver the black vote. Gifts and offerings to black churches rose dramatically during elections.

The Reverend Ollie Agee called a special meeting of the council for Sunday afternoon at his church. He wrapped up his sermon early, and by 4:00 P.M. his flock had scattered when the Cadillacs and Lincolns began filling his parking lot. The meetings were secret, with only ministers who were council members invited. There were twenty-three black churches in Ford County, and twenty-two members were present when Reverend Agee called the meeting to order. The meeting would be brief, since some of the ministers, especially from the Church of Christ, would begin their evening services shortly.

The purpose of the meeting, he explained, was to organize moral, political, and financial support of Carl Lee Hailey, a member in good standing of his church. A legal defense fund must be established to assure the best legal representation. Another fund must be established to provide support for his family. He, Reverend Agee, would chair the fund-raising efforts, with each minister responsible for his own congregation, as usual. A special offering would be taken during the morning and evening services, starting next Sunday. Agee would use his discretion in disbursing the money to the family. Half of the proceeds would go to the defense fund. Time was important. The trial was next month. The money had to be raised quickly while the issue was hot, and the people were in a giving mood.

The council unanimously agreed with Reverend Agee. He continued.

The NAACP must become active in the Hailey case. He would not be on trial if he was white. Not in Ford County. He was on trial only because he was black, and this must be addressed by the NAACP. The national director had been called. The Memphis and Jackson chapters had promised help. Press conferences would be held. Demonstrations and marches would be important. Maybe boycotts of white-owned businesses—that was a popular tactic at the moment, and it worked with amazing results.

This must be done immediately, while the people were willing and in a giving mood. The ministers unanimously agreed and left for their evening services.

In part due to fatigue, and in part due to embarrassment, Jake slept through church. Carla fixed pancakes, and they enjoyed a long breakfast with Hanna on the patio. He ignored the Sunday papers after he found, on the front page of the second section of *The Memphis Post*, a full-page spread on Marsharfsky and his famous new client. The story was complete with pictures and quotes from the great lawyer. The Hailey case presented his biggest challenge, he said. Serious legal and social issues would be addressed. A novel defense would be employed, he promised. He had not lost a murder case in twelve years, he boasted. It would be difficult, but he had confidence in the wisdom and fairness of Mississippi jurors.

Jake read the article without comment and laid the paper in the trash can.

Carla suggested a picnic, and although he needed to work he knew better than to mention it. They loaded the Saab with food and toys and drove to the lake. The brown, muddy waters of Lake Chatulla had crested for the year, and within days would begin their slow withdrawal to the center. The high water attracted a flotilla of skiboats, bass rigs, catamarans, and dinghies.

Carla threw two heavy quilts under an oak on the side of a hill while Jake unloaded the food and doll house. Hanna arranged her large family with pets and automobiles

on one quilt and began giving orders and setting up house.
Her parents listened and smiled. Her birth had been a har-
rowing, gut-wrenching nightmare, two and a half months
premature and shrouded with conflicting symptoms and
prognoses. For eleven days Jake sat by the incubator in ICU
and watched the tiny, purple, scrawny, beautiful three-pound
body cling to life while an army of doctors and nurses studied the monitors and adjusted tubes and needles, and shook
their heads. When he was alone he touched the incubator
and wiped tears from his cheeks. He prayed as he had never
prayed. He slept in a rocking chair near his daughter and
dreamed of a beautiful blue-eyed, dark-haired little girl playing with dolls and sleeping on his shoulder. He could hear
her voice.

After a month the nurses smiled and the doctors relented. The tubes were removed one at a time each day for a
week. Her weight ballooned to a hearty four and a half
pounds, and the proud parents took her home. The doctors
suggested no more children, unless adopted.

She was perfect now, and the sound of her voice could
still bring tears to his eyes. They ate and chuckled as Hanna
lectured her dolls on proper hygiene.

"This is the first time you've relaxed in two weeks,"
Carla said as they lay on their quilt. Wildly colored catamarans crisscrossed the lake below dodging a hundred roaring
boats pulling half-drunken skiers.

"We went to church last Sunday," he replied.

"And all you thought about was the trial."

"Still thinking about it."

"It's over, isn't it?"

"I don't know."

"Will he change his mind?"

"He might, if Lester talks to him. It's hard to say.
Blacks are so unpredictable, especially when they're in trouble. He's got a good deal, really. He's got the best criminal
lawyer in Memphis, and he's free."

"Who's paying the bill?"

"An old friend of Carl Lee's from Memphis, a guy by
the name of Cat Bruster."

"Who's he?"

"A very rich pimp, dope pusher, thug, thief. Marsharf-sky's his lawyer. A couple of crooks."

"Did Carl Lee tell you this?"

"No. He wouldn't tell me, so I asked Ozzie."

"Does Lester know?"

"Not yet."

"What do you mean by that? You're not going to call him, are you?"

"Well, yes, I had planned to."

"That's going a bit far, isn't it?"

"I don't think so. Lester has a right to know, and—"

"Then Carl Lee should tell him."

"He should, but he won't. He's made a mistake, and he does not realize it."

"But it's his problem, not yours. At least not anymore."

"Carl Lee's too embarrassed to tell Lester. He knows Lester will cuss him and tell him he's made another mistake."

"So it's up to you to intervene in their family affairs."

"No. But I think Lester should know."

"I'm sure he'll see it in the papers."

"Maybe not," Jake said without any conviction. "I think Hanna needs some more orange juice."

"I think you want to change the subject."

"The subject doesn't bother me. I want the case, and I intend to get it back. Lester's the only person who can retrieve it."

Her eyes narrowed and he could feel them. He watched a bass rig drift into a mud bar on the near shore.

"Jake, that's unethical, and you know it." Her voice was calm, yet controlled and firm. The words were slow and scornful.

"That's not true, Carla. I'm a very ethical attorney."

"You've always preached ethics. But at this moment you're scheming to solicit the case. That's wrong, Jake."

"Retrieve, not solicit."

"What's the difference?"

"Soliciting is unethical. I've never seen a prohibition against retrieving."

"It's not right, Jake. Carl Lee's hired another lawyer and it's time for you to forget it."

"And I suppose you think Marsharfsky reads ethics opinions. How do you think he got the case? He's been hired by a man who's never heard of him. He chased the case, and he's got it."

"So that makes it okay if you chase it now?"

"Retrieve, not chase."

Hanna demanded cookies, and Carla searched through the picnic basket. Jake reclined on an elbow and ignored them both. He thought of Lucien. What would he do in this situation? Probably rent a plane, fly to Chicago, get Lester, slip him some money, bring him home, and convince him to browbeat Carl Lee. He would assure Lester that Marsharfsky could not practice in Mississippi, and since he was a foreigner, the rednecks on the jury wouldn't believe him anyway. He would call Marsharfsky and curse him for chasing cases and threaten him with an ethics complaint the minute he stepped into Mississippi. He would get his black cronies to call Gwen and Ozzie and persuade them that the only lawyer with a dog's chance in hell of winning the case was Lucien Wilbanks. Finally, Carl Lee would knuckle under and send for Lucien.

That's exactly what Lucien would do. Talk about ethics.

"Why are you smiling?" Carla interrupted.

"Just thinking about how nice it is out here with you and Hanna. We don't do this enough."

"You're disappointed, aren't you?"

"Sure. There will never be another case like this one. Win it, and I'm the greatest lawyer in these parts. We would never have to worry about money again."

"And if you lost it?"

"It would still be a drawing card. But I can't lose what I don't have."

"Embarrassed?"

"A little. It's hard to accept. Every lawyer in the county is laughing about it, except maybe Harry Rex. But I'll get over it."

"What should I do with the scrapbook?"

"Save it. You might fill it up yet."

The cross was a small one, nine feet long and four feet wide, made to fit inconspicuously in the long bed of a pickup. Much larger crosses were used for the rituals, but the small ones worked better in the nocturnal raids into residential areas. They were not used often, or often enough according to their builders. In fact, it had been many years since one had been used in Ford County. The last one was planted in the yard of a nigger accused of raping a white woman.

Several hours before dawn on Monday morning, the cross was lifted quietly and quickly from the pickup and thrust into a ten-inch, freshly dug slot in the front yard of the quaint Victorian house on Adams Street. A small torch was thrown at the foot of the cross, and in seconds it was in flames. The pickup disappeared into the night and stopped at a pay phone at the edge of town, where a call was placed to the dispatcher.

Moments later, Deputy Marshall Prather turned down Adams and instantly saw the blazing cross in Jake's front yard. He turned into the driveway and parked behind the Saab. He punched the doorbell and stood on the porch watching the flames. It was almost three-thirty. He punched it again. Adams was dark and silent except for the glow of the cross and the snapping and crackling of the wood burning fifty feet away. Finally, Jake stumbled through the front door and froze, wild-eyed and stunned, next to the deputy. The two stood side by side on the porch, mesmerized not only by the burning cross, but by its purpose.

"Mornin', Jake," Prather finally said without looking from the fire.

"Who did it?" Jake asked with a scratchy, dry throat.

"Don't know. They didn't leave a name. Just called and told us about it."

"When did they call?"

"Fifteen minutes ago."

Jake ran his fingers through his hair in an effort to keep it from blowing wild in the soft breeze. "How long will it burn?" he asked, knowing Prather knew as little or even less than he about burning crosses.

"No tellin'. Probably soaked in kerosene. Smells like it anyway. Might burn for a couple of hours. You want me to call a fire truck?"

Jake looked up and down the street. Every house was silent and dark.

"Naw. No need to wake everybody. Let it burn. It won't hurt anything, will it?"

"It's your yard."

Prather never moved; just stood there, hands in his pockets, his belly hanging over his belt. "Ain't had one of these in a long time around here. Last one I remember was in Karaway, nineteen-sixty—"

"Nineteen sixty-seven."

"You remember?"

"Yeah. I was in high school. We drove out and watched it burn."

"What was that nigger's name?"

"Robinson, something Robinson. Said he raped Velma Thayer."

"Did he?" asked Prather.

"The jury thought so. He's in Parchman chopping cotton for the rest of his life."

Prather seemed satisfied.

"Let me get Carla," Jake mumbled as he disappeared. He returned with his wife behind him.

"My God, Jake! Who did it?"

"Who knows."

"Is it the KKK?" she asked.

"Must be," answered the deputy. "I don't know anybody else who burns crosses, do you, Jake?"

Jake shook his head.

"I thought they left Ford County years ago," said Prather.

"Looks like they're back," said Jake.

Carla stood frozen, her hand over her mouth, terrified. The glow of the fire reddened her face. "Do something, Jake. Put it out."

Jake watched the fire and again glanced up and down the street. The snapping and popping grew louder and the orange flames reached higher into the night. For a moment he hoped it would die quickly without being seen by anyone other than the three of them, and that it would simply go away and be forgotten and no one in Clanton would ever know. Then he smiled at his foolishness.

Prather grunted, and it was obvious he was tired of standing on the porch. "Say, Jake, uh, I don't mean to bring this up, but accordin' to the papers they got the wrong lawyer. That true?"

"I guess they can't read," Jake muttered.

"Probably not."

"Tell me, Prather, do you know of any active Klan members in this county?"

"Not a one. Got some in the southern part of the state, but none around here. Not that I know of. FBI told us the Klan was a thing of the past."

"That's not very comforting."

"Why not?"

"Because these guys, if they're Klan members, are not from around here. Visitors from parts unknown. It means they're serious, don't you think, Prather?"

"I don't know. I'd worry more if it was local people workin' with the Klan. Could mean the Klan's comin' back."

"What does it mean, the cross?" Carla asked the deputy.

"It's a warnin'. Means stop what you're doin', or the next time we'll do more than burn a little wood. They used these things for years to intimidate whites who were sympathetic to niggers and all that civil rights crap. If the whites didn't stop their nigger lovin', then violence followed. Bombs, dynamite, beatings, even murder. But that was a long time ago, I thought. In your case, it's their way of tellin' Jake to stay away from Hailey. But since he ain't Hailey's lawyer no more, I don't know what it means."

"Go check on Hanna," Jake said to Carla, who went inside.

"If you got a water hose, I'll be glad to put it out," offered Prather.

"That's a good idea," Jake said. "I'd hate for the neighbors to see it."

Jake and Carla stood on the porch in their bathrobes and watched the deputy spray the burning cross. The wood fizzed and smoked as the water covered the cross and snuffed out the flames. Prather soaked it for fifteen minutes, then neatly rolled the hose and placed it behind the shrubs in the flower bed next to the front steps.

"Thanks, Marshall. Let's keep this quiet, okay?"

Prather wiped his hands on his pants and straightened his hat. "Sure. Y'all lock up good. If you hear anything, call the dispatcher. We'll keep a close watch on it for the next few days."

He backed from the driveway and drove slowly down Adams Street toward the square. They sat in the swing and watched the smoking cross.

"I feel like I'm looking at an old issue of *Life* magazine," Jake said.

"Or a chapter from a Mississippi history textbook. Maybe we should tell them you got fired."

"Thanks."

"Thanks?"

"For being so blunt."

"I'm sorry. Should I say discharged, or terminated, or—"

"Just say he found another lawyer. You're really scared aren't you?"

"You know I'm scared. I'm terrified. If they can burn a cross in our front yard, what's to stop them from burning the house? It's not worth it, Jake. I want you to be happy and successful and all that wonderful stuff, but not at the expense of our safety. No case is worth this."

"You're glad I got fired?"

"I'm glad he found another lawyer. Maybe they'll leave us alone now."

Jake put his arm around her, and pulled her into his lap. The swing rocked gently. She was beautiful, at three-thirty in the morning in her bathrobe.

"They won't be back, will they?" she asked.

"Naw. They're through with us. They'll find out I'm off the case, then they'll call and apologize."

"It's not funny, Jake."

"I know."

"Do you think people will know?"

"Not for another hour. When the Coffee Shop opens at five, Dell Perkins will know every detail before she pours the first cup of coffee."

"What're you going to do with it?" she asked, nodding at the cross, now barely visible under the half moon.

"I've got an idea. Let's load it up, take it to Memphis, and burn it in Marsharfsky's yard."

"I'm going to bed."

———————————

By 9:00 A.M. Jake had finished dictating his motion to withdraw as counsel of record. Ethel was typing it with zest when she interrupted him: "Mr. Brigance, there's a Mr. Marsharfsky on the phone. I told him you were in conference, and he said he would hold."

"I'll talk to him." Jake gripped the receiver. "Hello."

"Mr. Brigance, Bo Marsharfsky in Memphis. How are you?"

"Terrific."

"Good. I'm sure you saw the morning paper Saturday and Sunday. You do get the paper in Clanton?"

"Yes, and we have telephones and mail."

"So you saw the stories on Mr. Hailey?"

"Yes. You write some very nice articles."

"I'll ignore that. I wanted to discuss the Hailey case if you have a minute."

"I would love to."

"As I understand Mississippi procedure, out-of-state counsel must associate local counsel for trial purposes."

"You mean you don't have a Mississippi license?" Jake asked incredulously.

"Well, no, I don't."

"That wasn't mentioned in your articles."

"I'll ignore that too. Do the judges require local counsel in all cases?"

"Some do, some don't."

"I see. What about Noose?"

"Sometimes."

"Thanks. Well, I usually associate local counsel when I try cases out in the country. The locals feel better with one of their own sitting there at counsel table with me."

"That's real nice."

"I don't suppose you'd be interested in—"

"You must be kidding!" Jake yelled. "I've just been fired and now you want me to carry your briefcase. You're crazy. I wouldn't have my name associated with yours."

"Wait a minute, hayseed—"

"No, you wait a minute, counselor. This may come as a surprise to you, but in this state we have ethics and laws against soliciting litigation and clients. Champerty—ever hear of it? Of course not. It's a felony in Mississippi, as in most states. We have canons of ethics that prohibit ambulance chasing and solicitation. Ethics, Mr. Shark, ever hear of them?"

"I don't chase cases, sonny. They come to me."

"Like Carl Lee Hailey. I'm supposed to believe he picked your name out of the yellow pages. I'm sure you have a full-page ad, next to the abortionists."

"He was referred to me."

"Yeah, by your pimp. I know exactly how you got him. Outright solicitation. I may file a complaint with the bar. Better yet, I might have your methods reviewed by the grand jury."

"Yeah, I understand you and the D.A. are real close. Good day, counselor."

Marsharfsky got the last word before he hung up. Jake fumed for an hour before he could concentrate on the brief he was writing. Lucien would have been proud of him.

Just before lunch Jake received a call from Walter Sullivan, of the Sullivan firm.

"Jake, my boy, how are you?"

"Wonderful."

"Good. Listen, Jake, Bo Marsharfsky is an old friend of mine. We defended a couple of bank officials years ago on fraud charges. Got them off, too. He's quite a lawyer. He's associated me as local counsel for Carl Lee Hailey. I was just wanting to know—"

Jake dropped the receiver and walked out of his office. He spent the afternoon on Lucien's front porch.

18 Gwen did not have Lester's number. Neither did Ozzie, nor did anyone else. The operator said there were two pages of Haileys in the Chicago phone book, at least a dozen Lester Haileys, and several L. S.'s. Jake asked for the first five Lester Haileys and called each one. They were all white. He called Tank Scales, the owner of one of the safer and finer black honky tonks in the county. Tank's Tonk, as it was known. Lester was especially fond of the place. Tank was a client and often provided Jake with valuable and confidential information on various blacks, their dealings and whereabouts.

Tank stopped by the office Tuesday morning on the way to the bank.

"Have you seen Lester Hailey in the past two weeks?" Jake asked.

"Sure. Spent several days at the place shootin' pool, drinkin' beer. Went back to Chicago last weekend, I heard. Must've, I didn't see him all weekend."

"Who was he with?"

"Hisself mostly."

"What about Iris?"

"Yeah, he brung her a couple of times when Henry was outta town. Makes me nervous when he brings her. Henry's a bad dude. He'd cut them both if he knew they's datin'."

"They've been doing it for ten years, Tank."

"Yeah, she got two kids by Lester. Everbody knows it but Henry. Poor old Henry. He'll find out one day, and you'll have another murder case."

"Listen, Tank, can you talk to Iris?"

"She don't come in too often."

"That's not what I asked. I need Lester's phone number in Chicago. I figure Iris knows it."

"I'm sure she does. I think he sends her money."

"Can you get it for me? I need to talk to Lester."

"Sure, Jake. If she's got it, I'll get it."

————

By Wednesday Jake's office had returned to normal. Clients
began to reappear. Ethel was especially sweet, or as sweet as
possible for a cranky old nag. He went through the motions
of practicing law, but the pain showed. He skipped the Coffee Shop each morning and avoided the courthouse by making Ethel do the filing or checking or whatever business required his presence across the street. He was embarrassed,
humiliated, and troubled. It was difficult to concentrate on
other cases. He contemplated a long vacation, but couldn't
afford it. Money was tight, and he was not motivated to
work. He spent most of his time in his office doing little but
watching the courthouse and the town square below.

He dwelt on Carl Lee, sitting in his cell a few blocks
away, and asked himself a thousand times why he had been
betrayed. He had pushed too hard for money, and forgot
there were other lawyers willing to take the case for free. He
hated Marsharfsky. He recalled the many times he had seen
Marsharfsky parade in and out of Memphis courtrooms pro-
claiming the innocence and mistreatment of his pitiful, oppressed clients. Dope dealers, pimps, crooked politicians,
and slimy corporate thugs. All guilty, all deserving of long
prison terms, or perhaps even death. He was a yankee, with
an obnoxious twang from somewhere in the upper Midwest.
It would irritate anybody south of Memphis. An accomplished actor, he would look directly into the cameras and
whine: "My client has been horribly abused by the Memphis
police." Jake had seen it a dozen times. "My client is completely, totally, absolutely innocent. He should not be on
trial. My client is a model citizen, a taxpayer." What about
his four prior convictions for extortion? "He was framed by
the FBI. Set up by the government. Besides, he's paid his
debt. He's innocent this time." Jake hated him, and to his
recollection, he had lost as many as he had won.

By Wednesday afternoon, Marsharfsky had not been
seen in Clanton. Ozzie promised to notify Jake if he showed
up at the jail.

Circuit Court would be in session until Friday, and it
would be respectful to meet briefly with Judge Noose and
explain the circumstances of his departure from the case.
His Honor was presiding over a civil case, and there was a

good chance Buckley would be absent. He had to be absent. He could not be seen or heard.

Noose usually recessed for ten minutes around three-thirty, and precisely at that time Jake entered chambers through the side door. He had not been seen. He sat patiently by the window waiting for Ichabod to descend from the bench and stagger into the room. Five minutes later the door flung open, and His Honor walked in.

"Jake, how are you?" he asked.

"Fine, Judge. Can I have a minute?" Jake asked as he closed the door.

"Sure, sit down. What's on your mind?" Noose removed his robe, threw it over a chair, and lay on top of the desk, knocking off books, files, and the telephone in the process. Once his gawky frame had ceased moving, he slowly folded his hands over his stomach, closed his eyes, and breathed deeply. "It's my back, Jake. My doctor tells me to rest on a hard surface when possible."

"Uh, sure, Judge. Should I leave?"

"No, no. What's on your mind?"

"The Hailey case."

"I thought so. I saw your motion. Found a new lawyer, huh?"

"Yes, sir. I had no idea it was coming. I expected to try the case in July."

"You owe no apologies, Jake. The motion to withdraw will be granted. It's not your fault. Happens all the time. Who's the new guy Marsharfsky?"

"Yes, sir. From Memphis."

"With a name like that he should be a hit in Ford County."

"Yes, sir." Almost as bad as Noose, thought Jake.

"He has no Mississippi license," Jake explained, helpfully.

"That's interesting. Is he familiar with our procedure?"

"I'm not sure he's ever tried a case in Mississippi. He told me he normally associates a local boy when he's out in the country."

"In the country?"

"That's what he said."

"Well, he'd better associate if he comes into my court.

I've had some bad experiences with out-of-state attorneys, especially from Memphis."

"Yes, sir."

Noose was breathing harder, and Jake decided to leave. "Judge, I need to go. If I don't see you in July, I'll see you during the August term of court. Take care of your back."

"Thanks, Jake. Take care."

Jake almost made it to the rear door of the small office when the main door from the courtroom opened and the Honorable L. Winston Lotterhouse and another hatchet man from the Sullivan firm strutted into chambers.

"Well, hello, Jake," Lotterhouse announced. "You know K. Peter Otter, our newest associate."

"Nice to meet you K. Peter," replied Jake.

"Are we interrupting anything?"

"No, I was just leaving. Judge Noose is resting his back, and I was on my way out."

"Sit down, gentlemen," Noose said.

Lotterhouse smelled blood. "Say, Jake, I'm sure Walter Sullivan has informed you that our firm will serve as local counsel for Carl Lee Hailey."

"I have heard."

"I'm sorry it happened to you."

"Your grief is overwhelming."

"It does present an interesting case for our firm. We don't get too many criminal cases, you know."

"I know," Jake said, looking for a hole to crawl in. "I need to run. Nice chatting with you, L. Winston. Nice meeting you, K. Peter. Tell J. Walter and F. Robert and all the boys I said hello."

Jake slid out of the rear door of the courthouse and cursed himself for showing his face where he could get it slapped. He ran to his office.

"Has Tank Scales called?" he asked Ethel as he started up the stairs.

"No. But Mr. Buckley is waiting."

Jake stopped on the first step. "Waiting where?" he asked without moving his jaws.

"Upstairs. In your office."

He walked slowly to her desk and leaned across to within inches of her face. She had sinned, and she knew it.

He glared at her fiercely. "I didn't know he had an appointment." Again, the jaws did not move.

"He didn't," she replied, her eyes glued to the desk.

"I didn't know he owned this building."

She didn't move, didn't answer.

"I didn't know he had a key to my office."

Again, no movement, no answer.

He leaned closer. "I should fire you for this."

Her lip quivered and she looked helpless.

"I'm sick of you, Ethel. Sick of your attitude, your voice, your insubordination. Sick of the way you treat people, sick of everything about you."

Her eyes watered. "I'm sorry."

"No you're not. You know, and have known for years, that no one, no one in the world, not even my wife, goes up those stairs into my office if I'm not here."

"He insisted."

"He's an ass. He gets paid for pushing people around. But not in this office."

"Shhh. He can hear you."

"I don't care. He knows he's an ass."

He leaned even closer until their noses were six inches apart. "Would you like to keep your job, Ethel?"

She nodded, unable to speak.

"Then do exactly as I say. Go upstairs to my office, fetch Mr. Buckley, and lead him into the conference room, where I'll meet him. And don't ever do it again."

Ethel wiped her face and ran up the stairs. Moments later the D.A. was seated in the conference room with the door closed. He waited.

Jake was next door in the small kitchen drinking orange juice and assessing Buckley. He drank slowly. After fifteen minutes he opened the door and entered the room. Buckley was seated at one end of the long conference table. Jake sat at the other end, far away.

"Hello, Rufus. What do you want?"

"Nice place you have here. Lucien's old offices, I believe."

"That's right. What brings you here?"

"Just wanted to visit."

"I'm very busy."

"And I wanted to discuss the Hailey case."

"Call Marsharfsky."

"I was looking forward to the battle, especially with you on the other side. You're a worthy adversary, Jake."

"I'm honored."

"Don't get me wrong. I don't like you, and I haven't for a long time."

"Since Lester Hailey."

"Yeah, I guess you're right. You won, but you cheated."

"I won, that's all that counts. And I didn't cheat. You got caught with your pants down."

"You cheated and Noose let you by with it."

"Whatever. I don't like you either."

"Good. That makes me feel better. What do you know about Marsharfsky?"

"Is that the reason you're here?"

"Could be."

"I've never met the man, but if he was my father I wouldn't tell you anything. What else do you want?"

"Surely you've talked to him."

"We had some words on the phone. Don't tell me you're worried about him."

"No. Just curious. He's got a good reputation."

"Yes, he does. You didn't come here to discuss his reputation."

"No, not really. I wanted to talk about the case."

"What about it?"

"Chances for an acquittal, possible defenses, was he really insane. Things like that."

"I thought you guaranteed a conviction. In front of the cameras, remember? Just after the indictment. One of your press conferences."

"Do you miss the cameras already, Jake?"

"Relax, Rufus. I'm out of the game. The cameras are all yours, at least yours and Marsharfsky's, and Walter Sullivan's. Go get them, tiger. If I've stolen some of your spotlight, then I'm deeply sorry. I know how it hurts you."

"Apology accepted. Has Marsharfsky been to town?"

"I don't know."

"He promised a press conference this week."

"And you came here to talk about his press conference, right?"

"No, I wanted to discuss Hailey, but obviously you're too busy."

"That's right. Plus I have nothing to discuss with you, Mr. Governor."

"I resent that."

"Why? You know it's true. You'd prosecute your mother for a couple of headlines."

Buckley stood and began pacing back and forth behind his chair. "I wish you were still on this case, Brigance," he said, the volume increasing.

"So do I."

"I'd teach you a few things about prosecuting murderers. I really wanted to clean your plow."

"You haven't been too successful in the past."

"That's why I wanted you on this one, Brigance. I wanted you so bad." His face had returned to the deep red that was so familiar.

"There'll be others, Governor."

"Don't call me that," he shouted.

"It's true, isn't it, Governor. That's why you chase the cameras so hard. Everybody knows it. There goes old Rufus, chasing cameras, running for governor. Sure it's true."

"I'm doing my job. Prosecuting thugs."

"Carl Lee Hailey's no thug."

"Watch me burn him."

"It won't be that easy."

"Watch me."

"It takes twelve out of twelve."

"No problem."

"Just like your grand jury?"

Buckley froze in his tracks. He squinted his eyes and frowned at Jake. Three huge wrinkles creased neatly across his mammoth forehead. "What do you know about the grand jury?"

"As much as you do. One vote less and you'd have sucked eggs."

"That's not true!"

"Come on, Governor. You're not talking to a reporter. I know exactly what happened. Knew it within hours."

"I'll tell Noose."

"And I'll tell the newspapers. That'll look good before the trial."

"You wouldn't dare."

"Not now. I have no reason to. I've been fired, remember? That's the reason you're here, right, Rufus? To remind me that I'm no longer on the case, but you are. To rub a little salt in the wounds. Okay, you've done it. Now I wish you'd leave. Go check on the grand jury. Or maybe there's a reporter hanging around the courthouse. Just leave."

"Gladly. I'm sorry I bothered."

"Me too."

Buckley opened the door leading into the hall, then stopped. "I lied, Jake. I'm tickled to death you're not on this case."

"I know you lied. But don't count me out."

"What does that mean?"

"Good day, Rufus."

The Ford County grand jury had been busy, and by Thursday of the second week of the term Jake had been retained by two freshly indicted defendants. One was a black who cut another black at Massey's Tonk back in April. Jake enjoyed the stabbings because acquittals were possible; just get an all-white jury full of rednecks who could care less if all niggers stabbed each other. They were just having a little fun down at the tonk, things got out of hand, one got stabbed, but didn't die. No harm, no conviction. It was similar to the strategy Jake had learned with Lester Hailey. The new client promised fifteen hundred dollars, but first had to post bond.

The other new indictee was a white kid caught driving a stolen pickup. It was the third time he'd been caught in a stolen pickup, and there was no way to keep him out of Parchman for seven years.

Both were in jail, and their presence there afforded Jake the opportunity, and duty, to visit them and check with Ozzie. Late Thursday afternoon he found the sheriff in his office.

"Are you busy?" Jake asked. A hundred pounds of paper was strewn over the desk and onto the floor.

"No, just paperwork. Any more burnin' crosses?"

"No, thank God. One's enough."

"I haven't seen your friend from Memphis."

"That's strange," said Jake. "I thought he would be here by now. Have you talked to Carl Lee?"

"Every day. He's gettin' nervous. The lawyer ain't even called, Jake."

"Good. Let him sweat. I don't feel sorry for him."

"You think he made a mistake?"

"I know he did. I know these rednecks around here, Ozzie, and I know how they act when you put them on a jury. They won't be impressed by some slick-talking foreigner. You agree?"

"I don't know. You're the lawyer. I don't doubt what you say, Jake. I've seen you work."

"He's not even licensed to practice in Mississippi. Judge Noose is laying for him. He hates out-of-state lawyers."

"You're kiddin'?"

"Nope. I talked to him yesterday."

Ozzie looked disturbed and eyed Jake carefully. "You wanna see him?"

"Who?"

"Carl Lee."

"No! I have no reason to see him." Jake glanced in his briefcase. "I need to see Leroy Glass, aggravated assault."

"You got Leroy?"

"Yeah. His folks came in this morning."

"Follow me."

Jake waited in the Intoxilyzer room while a trusty went for the new client. Leroy wore the standard Ford County jail issue of glow-in-the-dark orange coveralls. Pink sponge rollers shot in all directions from his scalp, and two long greasy cornrows clung to the back of his neck. His black leathery feet were protected from the dirty linoleum by a pair of lime green terrycloth slides. No socks. A wicked, aged scar started next to his right ear lobe, made the ridge over his cheekbone, and connected neatly with his right nostril. It proved beyond a reasonable doubt that Leroy was no stranger to stabbings and carvings. He wore it like a medal. He smoked Kools.

"Leroy, I'm Jake Brigance," the lawyer introduced him-

self and pointed to a folding chair next to the Pepsi machine.
"Your momma and brother hired me this morning."

"Good to know you, Mr. Jake."

A trusty waited in the hall by the door as Jake asked
questions. He filled three pages of notes on Leroy Glass. Of
primary interest, at least at this point, was money. How
much did he have, and where could he find more. They
would talk about the stabbing later. Aunts, uncles, brothers,
sisters, friends, anyone with a job who might be able to make
a loan. Jake took phone numbers.

"Who referred you to me?" Jake asked.

"Saw you on TV, Mr. Jake. You and Carl Lee Hailey."

Jake was proud, but did not smile. Television was just
part of his job. "You know Carl Lee?"

"Yeah, know Lester too. You's Lester's lawyer, wasn't
you?"

"Yes."

"Me and Carl Lee in the same cell. Moved me last
night."

"You don't say."

"Yeah. He don't talk much. He said you's a real good
lawyer and all, but he found somebody else from Memphis."

"That's right. What does he think of his new lawyer?"

"I don't know, Mr. Jake. He was fussin' this mornin'
cause the new lawyer ain't been to see him yet. He say you
come to see him all the time and talk 'bout the case, but the
new lawyer, some funny name, ain't even been down to meet
him yet."

Jake concealed his delight with a grim face, but it was
difficult. "I'll tell you something if you promise you won't tell
Carl Lee."

"Okay."

"His new lawyer can't come to see him."

"No! Why not?"

"Because he doesn't have a license to practice law in
Mississippi. He's a Tennessee lawyer. He'll get thrown out of
court if he comes down here by himself. I'm afraid Carl
Lee's made a big mistake."

"Why don't you tell him?"

"Because he's already fired me. I can't give him advice
anymore."

"Somebody ought to."

"You just promised you won't, okay?"

"Okay. I won't."

"Promise?"

"I swear."

"Good. I gotta go. I'll meet with the bondsman in the morning, and maybe we'll have you out in a day or so. Not a word to Carl Lee, right?"

"Right."

Tank Scales was leaning on the Saab in the parking lot when Jake left the jail. He stepped on a cigarette butt and pulled a piece of paper from his shirt pocket. "Two numbers. Top one's for home, bottom for work. But don't call at work unless you have to."

"Good work, Tank. Did you get them from Iris?"

"Yeah. She didn't want to. She stopped by the tonk last night and I got her drunk."

"I owe you one."

"I'll get it, sooner or later."

It was dark, almost eight o'clock. Dinner was cold, but that was not unusual. That's why he had bought her a microwave. She was accustomed to the hours and the warmed-over dinners, and she did not complain. They would eat when he came home, whether it was six or ten.

Jake drove from the jail to his office. He wouldn't dare call Lester from home, not with Carla listening. He settled behind his desk and stared at the numbers Tank had located. Carl Lee had told him not to make this call. Why should he do it? Would it be solicitation? Unethical? Would it be unethical to call Lester and tell him that Carl Lee had fired him and hired another lawyer? No. And to answer Lester's questions about the new lawyer? No. And to express concern? No. And to criticize the new lawyer? Probably not. Would it be unethical to encourage Lester to talk to his brother? No. And convince him to fire Marsharfsky? Probably so. And to rehire Jake? Yes, no doubt about it. That would be very unethical. What if he just called Lester and talked about Carl Lee and allowed the conversation to follow its own course.

"Hello."

"Is there a Lester Hailey there?"

"Yes. Who's calling?" came the accented reply from the Swede.

"Jake Brigance, from Mississippi."

"One moment."

Jake checked his watch. Eight-thirty. It was the same time in Chicago, wasn't it?

"Jake!"

"Lester, how are you?"

"Fine, Jake. Tired, but fine. How 'bout you?"

"Great. Listen, have you talked to Carl Lee this week?"

"No. I left Friday, and I've been workin' two shifts since Sunday. I ain't had time for nothin'."

"You seen the newspapers?"

"No. What's happened?"

"You won't believe it, Lester."

"What is it, Jake?"

"Carl Lee fired me and hired a big-shot lawyer from Memphis."

"What! You're kiddin'? When?"

"Last Friday. I guess after you left. He didn't bother to tell me. I read it in the Memphis paper Saturday morning."

"He's crazy. Why'd he do it, Jake? Who'd he hire?"

"You know a guy named Cat Bruster from Memphis?"

"Of course."

"It's his lawyer. Cat's paying for it. He drove down from Memphis last Friday and saw Carl Lee at the jail. Next morning I saw my picture in the paper and read where I've been fired."

"Who's the lawyer?"

"Bo Marsharfsky."

"He any good?"

"He's a crook. He defends all the pimps and drug dealers in Memphis."

"Sounds like a Polack."

"He is. I think he's from Chicago."

"Yeah, bunch of Polacks up here. Does he talk like these?"

"Like he's got a mouthful of hot grease. He'll go over big in Ford County."

"Stupid, stupid, stupid. Carl Lee never was too bright. I always had to think for him. Stupid, stupid."

"Yeah, he's made a mistake, Lester. You know what a murder trial is like because you've been there. You realize how important that jury is when they leave the courtroom and go to the jury room. Your life is in their hands. Twelve local people back there fighting and arguing over your case, your life. The jury's the most important part. That's why you gotta be able to talk to the jury."

"That's right, Jake. You can do it too."

"I'm sure Marsharfsky can do it in Memphis, but not Ford County. Not in rural Mississippi. These people won't trust him."

"You're right, Jake. I can't believe he did it. He's screwed up again."

"He did it, Lester, and I'm worried about him."

"Have you talked to him?"

"Last Saturday, after I saw the newspaper, I went straight to the jail. I asked him why, and he could not answer. He felt bad about it. I haven't talked to him since then. But neither has Marsharfsky. He hasn't found Clanton yet, and I understand Carl Lee's upset. As far as I can tell, nothing has been done on the case this week."

"Has Ozzie talked to him?"

"Yeah, but you know Ozzie. He's not gonna say too much. He knows Bruster's a crook and Marsharfsky's a crook, but he won't lean on Carl Lee."

"Man oh man. I can't believe it. He's stupid if he thinks those rednecks'll listen to some shyster from Memphis. Hell, Jake, they don't trust the lawyers from Tyler County and it's next door. Man oh man."

Jake smiled at the receiver. So far, nothing unethical.

"What should I do, Jake?"

"I don't know, Lester. He needs some help, and you're the only one he'll listen to. You know how headstrong he is."

"I guess I'd better call him."

No, thought Jake, it would be easier for Carl Lee to say no over the phone. Confrontation was needed between the brothers. A drive from Chicago would make an impact.

"I don't think you'll get very far over the phone. His

mind's made up. Only you can change it, and you can't do it over the phone."

Lester paused a few seconds while Jake waited anxiously. "What's today?"

"Thursday, June 6."

"Let's see," Lester mumbled. "I'm ten hours away. I work the four-to-midnight shift tomorrow and again Sunday. I could leave here midnight tomorrow, and be in Clanton by ten Saturday mornin'. Then I could leave early Sunday mornin' and be back by four. That's a lot of drivin', but I can handle it."

"It's very important, Lester. I think it's worth the trip."

"Where will you be Saturday, Jake?"

"Here at the office."

"Okay. I'll go to the jail, and if I need you I'll call the office."

"Sounds good. One other thing, Lester. Carl Lee told me not to call you. Don't mention it."

"What'll I tell him?"

"Tell him you called Iris, and she gave you the story."

"Iris who?"

"Come on, Lester. It's been common knowledge around here for years. Everybody knows it but her husband, and he'll find out."

"I hope not. We'll have us another murder. You'll have another client."

"Please. I can't keep the ones I've got. Call me Saturday."

He ate from the microwave at ten-thirty. Hanna was asleep. They talked about Leroy Glass and the white kid in the stolen pickup. About Carl Lee, but not about Lester. She felt better, safer now that Carl Lee Hailey was behind them. No more calls. No more burning crosses. No more stares at church. There would be other cases, she promised. He said little; just ate and smiled.

19 Just before the courthouse closed on Friday, Jake called the clerk to see if a trial was in progress. No, she said, Noose was gone. Buckley, Musgrove, everybody was gone. The courtroom was deserted. Secure with that knowledge, Jake eased across the street, through the rear door of the courthouse, and down the hall to the clerk's office. He flirted with the clerks and secretaries while he located Carl Lee's file. He held his breath as he flipped through the pages. Good! Just as he had hoped. Nothing had been added to the file all week, with the exception of his motion to withdraw as counsel. Marsharfsky and his local counsel had not touched the file. Nothing had been done. He flirted some more and eased back to his office.

Leroy Glass was still in jail. His bond was ten thousand dollars, and his family couldn't raise the thousand-dollar premium to pay a bondsman. So he continued to share the cell with Carl Lee. Jake had a friend who was a bondsman and who took care of Jake's clients. If a client needed out of jail, and there was little danger of him disappearing once he was sprung, the bond would be written. Terms were available for Jake's clients. Say, five percent down and so much a month. If Jake wanted Leroy Glass out of jail, the bond could be written anytime. But Jake needed him in jail.

"Look, Leroy, I'm sorry. I'm working with the bondsman," Jake explained to his client in the Intoxilyzer room.

"But you said I'd be out by now."

"Your folks don't have the money, Leroy. I can't pay it myself. We'll get you out, but it'll take a few days. I want you out so you can go to work, make some money and pay me."

Leroy seemed satisfied. "Okay, Mr. Jake, just do what you can."

"Food's pretty good here, isn't it?" Jake asked with a smile.

"It ain't bad. Better at home."

"We'll get you out," Jake promised.

"How's the nigger I stabbed?"

"Not sure. Ozzie said he's still in the hospital. Moss

Tatum says he's been released. Who knows. I don't think he's hurt too bad."

"Who was the woman?" Jake asked, unable to remember the details.

"Willie's woman."

"Willie who?"

"Willie Hoyt."

Jake thought for a second and tried to recall the indictment. "That's not the man you stabbed."

"Naw, he's Curtis Sprawling."

"You mean, y'all were fighting over another man's woman?"

"That's right."

"Where was Willie?"

"He was fightin' too."

"Who was he fighting?"

"Some other dude."

"You mean the four of you were fighting over Willie's woman?"

"Yeah, you got it."

"What caused the fight?"

"Her husband was outta town."

"She's married?"

"That's right."

"What's her husband's name?"

"Johnny Sands. When he's outta town, there's normally a fight."

"Why is that?"

"'Cause she ain't got no kids, can't have any, and she likes to have company. Know what I mean? When he leaves, everybody knows it. If she shows up at a tonk, look out for a fight."

What a trial, thought Jake. "But I thought you said she showed up with Willie Hoyt?"

"That's right. But that don't mean nothin' because everybody at the tonk starts easin' up on her, buyin' drinks, wantin' to dance. You can't help it."

"Some woman, huh?"

"Oh, Mr. Jake, she looks so good. You oughtta see her."

"I will. On the witness stand."

Leroy gazed at the wall, smiling, dreaming, lusting after the wife of Johnny Sands. Never mind that he stabbed a man and could get twenty years. He had proven, in hand-to-hand combat, that he was worthy.

"Listen, Leroy, you haven't talked to Carl Lee, have you?"

"Sure. I'm still in his cell. We talk all the time. Ain't much else to do."

"You haven't told him what we discussed yesterday?"

"Oh no. I told you I wouldn't."

"Good."

"But I'll tell you this, Mr. Jake, he's some kinda worried. He ain't heard from his new lawyer. He's bad upset. I had to bite my tongue to keep from tellin' him, but I didn't. I did tell him you were my lawyer."

"That's okay."

"He said you was good 'bout comin' by the jail and talkin' 'bout the case and all. He said I hired a good lawyer."

"Not good enough for him, though."

"I think Carl Lee's confused. He ain't sure who to trust or anything. He's a good dude."

"Well, don't be telling him what we discussed, right? It's confidential."

"Right. But somebody needs to."

"He didn't consult with me or anyone else before he fired me and hired his new lawyer. He's a grown man. He made the decision. It's his baby." Jake paused and moved closer to Leroy. He lowered his voice. "And I'll tell you something else, but you can't tell it. I checked his court file thirty minutes ago. His new lawyer hasn't touched the case all week. Not one thing has been filed. Nothing."

Leroy frowned and shook his head. "Man oh man."

His lawyer continued. "These big shots operate like that. Talk a lot, blow a lot of smoke, fly by the seat of their pants. Take more cases than they can handle, and end up losing more than they win. I know them. I watch them all the time. Most are overrated."

"Is that why he ain't been to see Carl Lee?"

"Sure. He's too busy. Plus he's got plenty of other big cases. He don't care about Carl Lee."

"That's bad. Carl Lee deserves better."

"It was his choice. He'll have to live with it."

"You think he'll be convicted, Mr. Jake?"

"No doubt about it. He's looking at the gas chamber. He's hired a bogus big-shot lawyer who doesn't have time to work on his case, doesn't even have the time to talk to him in jail."

"Are you sayin' you could get him off?"

Jake relaxed and crossed his legs. "No, I never make that promise, and I won't make it for your trial. A lawyer is stupid if he promises an acquittal. Too many things can go wrong at trial."

"Carl Lee said his lawyer promised a not guilty in the newspaper."

"He's a fool."

———————

"Where you been?" Carl Lee asked his cellmate as the jailer locked the door.

"Talkin' to my lawyer."

"Jake?"

"Yeah."

Leroy sat on his bunk directly across the cell from Carl Lee, who was rereading a newspaper. He folded the paper and laid it under his bunk.

"You look worried," Carl Lee said. "Bad news about your case?"

"Naw. Just can't make my bail. Jake says it'll be a few days."

"Jake talk about me?"

"Naw. Not much."

"Not much? What'd he say?"

"Just ask how you was."

"That all?"

"Yeah."

"He's not mad at me?"

"Naw. He might be worried about you, but I don't think he's mad."

"Why's he worried about me?"

"I don't know," Leroy answered as he stretched out on his bunk, folding his hands behind his head.

"Come on, Leroy. You know somethin' you ain't tellin'. What'd Jake say about me?"

"Jake said I can't tell you what we talk about. He says it's confidential. You wouldn't want your lawyer repeatin' what y'all talk about, would you?"

"I ain't seen my lawyer."

"You had a good lawyer till you fired him."

"I gotta good one now."

"How do you know? You ain't ever met him. He's too busy to come talk to you, and if he's that busy, he ain't got time to work on your case."

"How do you know about him?"

"I asked Jake."

"Yeah. What'd he say?"

Leroy was silent.

"I wanna know what he said," demanded Carl Lee as he sat on the edge of Leroy's bunk. He glared at his smaller, weaker cellmate. Leroy decided he was frightened and now had a good excuse to tell Carl Lee. Either talk or get slapped.

"He's a crook," Leroy said. "He's a big-shot crook who'll sell you out. He don't care about you or your case. He just wants the publicity. He hasn't touched your case all week. Jake knows, he checked in the courthouse this afternoon. Not a sign of Mr. Big Shot. He's too busy to leave Memphis and check on you. He's got too many other crooked clients in Memphis, includin' your friend Mr. Bruster."

"You're crazy, Leroy."

"Okay, I'm crazy. Wait and see who pleads insaneness. Wait and see how hard he works on your case."

"What makes you such an expert?"

"You asked me and I'm tellin' you."

Carl Lee walked to the door and grabbed the bars, gripping them tightly with his huge hands. The cell had shrunk in three weeks, and the smaller it became the harder it was for him to think, to reason, to plan, to react. He could not concentrate in jail. He knew only what was told to him and had no one to trust. Gwen was irrational. Ozzie was noncommittal. Lester was in Chicago. There was no other person he trusted except Jake, and for some reason he had found a new lawyer. Money, that was the reason. Nineteen hundred dollars cash, paid by the biggest pimp and dope dealer in Memphis, whose lawyer specialized in defending pimps and dope dealers, and all kinds of cutthroats and hoodlums. Did Marsharfsky represent decent people? What would the jury think when they watched Carl Lee sit at the defense table next to Marsharfsky? He was guilty, of course. Why else would he hire a famous, big-city crook like Marsharfsky?

"You know what them rednecks on the jury'll say when they see Marsharfsky?" Leroy asked.

"What?"

"They're gonna think this poor nigger is guilty, and he's sold his soul to hire the biggest crook in Memphis to tell us he ain't guilty."

Carl Lee mumbled something through the bars.

"They're gonna fry you, Carl Lee."

——————

Moss Junior Tatum was on duty at six-thirty Saturday morning when the phone rang in Ozzie's office. It was the sheriff.

"What're you doing awake?" asked Moss.

"I'm not sure I'm awake," answered the sheriff. "Listen, Moss, do you remember an old black preacher named Street, Reverend Isaiah Street?"

"Not really."

"Yeah you do. He preached for fifty years at Springdale Church, north of town. First member of the NAACP in Ford County. He taught all the blacks around here how to march and boycott back in the sixties."

"Yeah, now I remember. Didn't the Klan catch him once?"

"Yeah, they beat him and burned his house, but nothin' serious. Summer of '65."

"I thought he died a few years back."

"Naw, he's been half dead for ten years, but he still moves a little. He called me at five-thirty and talked for an hour. Reminded me of all the political favors I owe him."

"What's he want?"

"He'll be there at seven to see Carl Lee. Why, I don't know. But treat him nice. Put them in my office and let them talk. I'll be in later."

"Sure, Sheriff."

In his heyday in the sixties, the Reverend Isaiah Street had been the moving force behind civil rights activity in Ford County. He walked with Martin Luther King in Memphis and Montgomery. He organized marches and protests in Clanton and Karaway and other towns in north Mississippi. In the summer of '64 he greeted students from the North and coordinated their efforts to register black voters. Some had lived in his home that memorable summer, and they still visited him from time to time. He was no radical. He was quiet, compassionate, intelligent, and had earned the respect of all blacks and most whites. His was a calm, cool voice in the midst of hatred and controversy. He unofficially offici- ated the great public school desegregation in '69, and Ford County saw little trouble.

A stroke in '75 deadened the right side of his body but left his mind untouched. Now, at seventy-eight, he walked by himself, slowly and with a cane. Proud, dignified, erect as possible. He was ushered into the sheriff's office and seated. He declined coffee, and Moss Junior left to get the defen- dant.

"You awake, Carl Lee?" he whispered loudly, not want- ing to wake the other prisoners, who would begin screaming for breakfast, medicine, lawyers, bondsmen, and girlfriends.

Carl Lee sat up immediately. "Yeah, I didn't sleep much."

"You have a visitor. Come on." Moss quietly unlocked the cell.

Carl Lee had met the reverend years earlier when he addressed the last senior class at East High, the black school. Desegregation followed, and East became the junior high. He had not seen the reverend since the stroke.

"Carl Lee, do you know Reverend Isaiah Street?" Moss asked properly.

"Yes, we met years ago."

"Good, I'll close the door and let y'all talk."

"How are you, sir?" Carl Lee asked. They sat next to each other on the couch.

"Fine, my son, and you?"

"As good as possible."

"I've been in jail too, you know. Years ago. It's a terrible place, but I guess it's necessary. How are they treating you?"

"Fine, just fine. Ozzie lets me do as I please."

"Yes, Ozzie. We're very proud of him, aren't we?"

"Yes, suh. He's a good man." Carl Lee studied the frail, feeble old man with the cane. His body was weak and tired, but his mind was sharp, his voice strong.

"We're proud of you too, Carl Lee. I don't condone violence, but at times it's necessary too, I guess. You did a good deed, my son."

"Yes, suh," answered Carl Lee, uncertain of the appropriate response.

"I guess you wonder why I'm here."

Carl Lee nodded. The reverend tapped his cane on the floor.

"I'm concerned about your acquittal. The black community is concerned. If you were white, you would most likely go to trial, and most likely be acquitted. The rape of a child is a horrible crime, and who's to blame a father for rectifying the wrong? A white father, that is. A black father evokes the same sympathy among blacks, but there's one problem: the jury will be white. So a black father and a white father would not have equal chances with the jury. Do you follow me?"

"I think so."

"The jury is all important. Guilt versus innocence. Freedom versus prison. Life versus death. All to be determined by the jury. It's a fragile system, this trusting of lives to twelve average, ordinary people who do not understand the law and are intimidated by the process."

"Yes, suh."

"Your acquittal by a white jury for the killings of two white men will do more for the black folk of Mississippi than any event since we integrated the schools. And it's not just Mississippi; it's black folk everywhere. Yours is a most famous case, and it's being watched carefully by many people."

"I just did what I had to do."

"Precisely. You did what you thought was right. It was right; although it was brutal and ugly, it was right. And most folks, black and white, believe that. But will you be treated as though you were white? That's the question."

"And if I'm convicted?"

"Your conviction would be another slap at us; a symbol of deep-seated racism; of old prejudices, old hatreds. It would be a disaster. You must not be convicted."

"I'm doin' all I can do."

"Are you? Let's talk about your attorney, if we may."

Carl Lee nodded.

"Have you met him?"

"No." Carl Lee lowered his head and rubbed his eyes. "Have you?"

"Yes, I have."

"You have? When?"

"In Memphis in 1968. I was with Dr. King. Marsharfsky was one of the attorneys representing the garbage workers on strike against the city. He asked Dr. King to leave Memphis, claimed he was agitating the whites and inciting the blacks, and that he was impeding the contract negotiations. He was arrogant and abusive. He cursed Dr. King—in private, of course. We thought he was selling out the workers and getting money under the table from the city. I think we were right."

Carl Lee breathed deeply and rubbed his temples.

"I've followed his career," the reverend continued. "He's made a name for himself representing gangsters, thieves, and pimps. He gets some of them off, but they're always guilty. When you see one of his clients, you know he's guilty. That's what worries me most about you. I'm afraid you'll be considered guilty by association."

Carl Lee sunk lower, his elbows resting on his knees. "Who told you to come here?" he asked softly.

"I had a talk with an old friend."

"Who?"

"Just an old friend, my son. He's concerned about you too. We're all concerned about you."

"He's the best lawyer in Memphis."

"This isn't Memphis, is it?"

"He's an expert on criminal law."

"That could be because he's a criminal."

Carl Lee stood abruptly and walked across the room, his back to the reverend.

"He's free. He's not costin' me a dime."

"His fee won't seem important when you're on death row, my son."

Moments passed and neither spoke. Finally, the reverend lowered his cane and struggled to his feet. "I've said enough. I'm leaving. Good luck, Carl Lee."

Carl Lee shook his hand. "I do appreciate your concern and I thank you for visitin'."

"My point is simply this, my son. Your case will be difficult enough to win. Don't make it more difficult with a crook like Marsharfsky."

Lester left Chicago just before midnight Friday. He headed south alone, as usual. Earlier his wife went north to Green Bay for a weekend with her family. He liked Green Bay much less than she liked Mississippi, and neither cared to visit the other's family. They were nice people, the Swedes, and they would treat him like family if he allowed it. But they were different, and it wasn't just their whiteness. He grew up with whites in the South and knew them. He didn't like them all and didn't like most of their feelings toward him, but at least he knew them. But the Northern whites, especially the Swedes, were different. Their customs, speech, food, almost everything was foreign to him, and he would never feel comfortable with them.

There would be a divorce, probably within a year. He was black, and his wife's older cousin had married a black in the early seventies and received a lot of attention. Lester was a fad, and she was tired of him. Luckily, there were no kids. He suspected someone else. He had someone else too, and Iris had promised to marry him and move to Chicago once she ditched Henry.

Both sides of Interstate 57 looked the same after midnight—scattered lights from the small, neat farms strewn over the countryside, and occasionally a big town like Champaign or Effingham. The north was where he lived and worked, but it wasn't home. Home was where Momma was, in Mississippi, although he would never live there again. Too much ignorance and poverty. He didn't mind the racism; it wasn't as bad as it once was and he was accustomed to it. It would always be there, but gradually becoming less visible.

The whites still owned and controlled everything, and that in itself was not unbearable. It was not about to change. What he found intolerable was the ignorance and stark poverty of many of the blacks; the dilapidated, shotgun houses, the high infant mortality rate, the hopelessly unemployed, the unwed mothers and their unfed babies. It was depressing to the point of being intolerable, and intolerable to the point he fled Mississippi like thousands of others and migrated north in search of a job, any decent-paying job which could ease the pain of poverty.

It was both pleasant and depressing to return to Mississippi. Pleasant in that he would see his family; depressing because he would see their poverty. There were bright spots. Carl Lee had a decent job, a clean house, and well-dressed kids. He was an exception, and now it was all in jeopardy because of two drunk, low-bred pieces of white trash. Blacks had an excuse for being worthless, but for whites in a white world, there were no excuses. They were dead, thank God, and he was proud of his big brother.

Six hours out of Chicago the sun appeared as he crossed the river at Cairo. Two hours later he crossed it again at Memphis. He drove southeast into Mississippi, and an hour later circled the courthouse in Clanton. He'd been awake for twenty hours.

"Carl Lee, you have a visitor," Ozzie said through the iron bars in the door.

"I'm not surprised. Who is it?"

"Just follow me. I think you better use my office. This could take a while."

Jake loitered at his office waiting on the phone to ring. Ten o'clock. Lester should be in town, if he's coming. Eleven. Jake riffled through some stale files and made notes for Ethel. Noon. He called Carla and lied about meeting a new client at one o'clock, so forget lunch. He would work in the yard later. One o'clock. He found an ancient case from Wyoming where a husband was acquitted after tracking down the man who raped his wife. In 1893. He copied the case, then threw it in the garbage. Two o'clock. Was Lester in town? He could go visit Leroy and snoop around the jail. No, that didn't feel right. He napped on the couch in the big office.

At two-fifteen the phone rang. Jake bolted upright and scrambled from the couch. His heart was pounding as he grabbed the phone. "Hello!"

"Jake, this is Ozzie."

"Yeah, Ozzie, what's up?"

"Your presence is requested here at the jail."

"What?" Jake asked, feigning innocence.

"You're needed down here."

"By who?"

"Carl Lee wants to talk to you."

"Is Lester there?"

"Yeah. He wants you too."

"Be there in a minute."

———————

"They've been in there for over four hours," Ozzie said, pointing to the office door.

"Doing what?" asked Jake.

"Talkin', cussin', shoutin'. Things got quiet about thirty minutes ago. Carl Lee came out and asked me to call you."

"Thanks. Let's go in."

"No way, man. I ain't goin' in there. They didn't send for me. You're on your own."

Jake knocked on the door.

"Come in!"

He opened it slowly, walked inside and closed it. Carl Lee was sitting behind the desk. Lester was lying on the couch. He stood and shook Jake's hand. "Good to see you, Jake."

"Good to see you, Lester. What brings you home?"

"Family business."

Jake looked at Carl Lee, then walked to the desk and shook his hand. The defendant was clearly irritated.

"Y'all sent for me?"

"Yeah, Jake, sit down. We need to talk," said Lester. "Carl Lee's got somethin' to tell you."

"You tell him," Carl Lee said.

Lester sighed and rubbed his eyes. He was tired and

frustrated. "I ain't sayin' another word. This is between you and Jake." Lester closed his eyes and relaxed on the couch. Jake sat in a padded, folding chair that he leaned against the wall opposite the couch. He watched Lester carefully, but did not look at Carl Lee, who rocked slowly in Ozzie's swivel chair. Carl Lee said nothing. Lester said nothing. After three minutes of silence, Jake was annoyed.

"Who sent for me?" he demanded.

"I did," answered Carl Lee.

"Well, what do you want?"

"I wanna give you my case back."

"You assume I want it back."

"What!" Lester sat up and looked at Jake.

"It's not a gift you give or take away. It's an agreement between you and your attorney. Don't act as though you're doing me a great favor." Jake's voice was rising, his anger apparent.

"Do you want the case?" asked Carl Lee.

"Are you trying to rehire me, Carl Lee?"

"That's right."

"Why do you want to rehire me?"

" 'Cause Lester wants me to."

"Fine, then I don't want your case." Jake stood and started for the door. "If Lester wants me and you want Marsharfsky, then stick with Marsharfsky. If you can't think for yourself, you need Marsharfsky."

"Wait, Jake. Be cool, man," Lester said as he met Jake at the door. "Sit down, sit down. I don't blame you for bein' mad at Carl Lee for firin' you. He was wrong. Right, Carl Lee?"

Carl Lee picked at his fingernails.

"Sit down, Jake, sit down and let's talk," Lester pleaded as he led him back to the folding chair. "Good. Now, let's discuss this situation. Carl Lee, do you want Jake to be your lawyer?"

Carl Lee nodded. "Yeah."

"Good. Now, Jake—"

"Explain why." Jake asked Carl Lee.

"What?"

"Explain why you want me to handle your case. Explain why you're firing Marsharfsky."

"I don't have to explain."

"Yes! Yes, you do. You at least owe me an explanation. You fired me a week ago and didn't have the guts to call me. I read it in the newspaper. Then I read about your new high-priced lawyer who evidently can't find his way to Clanton. Now you call me and expect me to drop everything because you might change your mind again. Explain, please."

"Explain, Carl Lee. Talk to Jake," Lester said.

Carl Lee leaned forward and placed his elbows on the desk. He buried his face in his hands and spoke between his palms. "I'm just confused. This place is drivin' me crazy. My nerves are shot. I'm worried about my little girl. I'm worried about my family. I'm worried about my own skin. Everbody's tellin' me to do somethin' different. I ain't ever been in a situation like this and I don't know what to do. All I can do is trust people. I trust Lester, and I trust you, Jake. That's all I can do."

"You trust my advice?" asked Jake.

"I always have."

"And you trust me to handle your case?"

"Yeah, Jake, I want you to handle it."

"Good enough."

Jake relaxed, and Lester eased into the couch. "You'll need to notify Marsharfsky. Until you do, I can't work on your case."

"We'll do that this afternoon," Lester said.

"Good. Once you talk to him, give me a call. There's a lot of work to do, and the time will disappear."

"What about the money?" asked Lester.

"Same fee. Same arrangements. Is that satisfactory?"

"Okay with me," replied Carl Lee. "I'll pay you any way I can."

"We'll discuss that later."

"What about the doctors?" asked Carl Lee.

"We'll make some arrangements. I don't know. It'll work out."

The defendant smiled. Lester snored loudly and Carl Lee laughed at his brother. "I figured you called him, but he swears you didn't."

Jake smiled awkwardly but said nothing. Lester was a

smooth liar, a talent which had proved extremely beneficial during his murder trial.

"I'm sorry, Jake. I was wrong."

"No apologies. There's too much work to spend time apologizing."

———————

Next to the parking lot outside the jail, a reporter stood under a shade tree waiting for something to happen.

"Excuse me, sir, aren't you Mr. Brigance?"

"Who wants to know?"

"I'm Richard Flay, with *The Jackson Daily*. You're Jake Brigance."

"Yes."

"Mr. Hailey's ex-lawyer."

"No. Mr. Hailey's lawyer."

"I thought he had retained Bo Marsharfsky. In fact, that's why I'm here. I heard a rumor Marsharfsky would be here this afternoon."

"If you see him, tell him he's too late."

———————

Lester slept hard on the couch in Ozzie's office. The dispatcher woke him at 4:00 A.M. Sunday, and after filling a tall Styrofoam cup with black coffee, he left for Chicago. Late Saturday night he and Carl Lee had called Cat in his office above the club and informed him of Carl Lee's conversion. Cat was indifferent and busy. He said he would call Marsharfsky. There was no mention of the money.

20 Not long after Lester disappeared, Jake staggered down his driveway in his bathrobe to get the Sunday papers. Clanton was an hour southeast of Memphis, three hours north of Jackson, and forty-five minutes from Tupelo. All three cities had daily papers with fat Sunday editions that were available in Clanton. Jake had long subscribed to all three, and was now glad he did so Carla would have plenty of material for her scrapbook. He spread the papers and began the task of plowing through five inches of print.

Nothing in the Jackson paper. He hoped Richard Flay had reported something. He should have spent more time with him outside the jail. Nothing from Memphis. Nothing from Tupelo. Jake was not surprised, just hopeful that somehow the story had been discovered. But it happened too late yesterday. Maybe Monday. He was tired of hiding; tired of feeling embarrassed. Until it was in the papers and read by the boys at the Coffee Shop, and the people at church, and the other lawyers, including Buckley and Sullivan and Lotterhouse, until everybody knew it was his case again, he would stay quiet and out of view. How should he tell Sullivan? Carl Lee would call Marsharfsky, or the pimp, probably the pimp, who would then call Marsharfsky with the news. What kind of press release would Marsharfsky write for that? Then the great lawyer would call Walter Sullivan with the wonderful news. That should happen Monday morning, if not sooner. Word would spread quickly throughout the Sullivan firm, and the senior partners, junior partners, and little associates would all gather in the long, mahogany-laced conference room and curse Brigance and his low ethics and tactics. The associates would try to impress their bosses by spouting rules and code numbers of ethics Brigance probably violated. Jake hated them, every one of them. He would send Sullivan a short, curt letter with a copy to Lotterhouse.

He wouldn't call or write Buckley. He would be in shock after he saw the paper. A letter to Judge Noose with a copy to Buckley would work fine. He would not honor him with a personal letter.

Jake had a thought, then hesitated, then dialed Lucien's number. It was a few minutes after seven. The nurse/maid/bartender answered the phone.

"Sallie?"

"Yes."

"This is Jake. Is Lucien awake?"

"Just a moment." She rolled over and handed the phone to Lucien.

"Hello."

"Lucien, it's Jake."

"Yeah, whatta you want?"

"Good news. Carl Lee Hailey rehired me yesterday. The case is mine again."

"Which case?"

"The Hailey case!"

"Oh, the vigilante. He's yours?"

"As of yesterday. We've got work to do."

"When's the trial? July sometime?"

"Twenty-second."

"That's pretty close. What's priority?"

"A psychiatrist. A cheap one who'll say anything."

"I know just the man," said Lucien.

"Good. Get busy. I'll call in a couple of days."

Carla awoke at a decent hour and found her husband in the kitchen with newspapers strewn over and under the breakfast table. She made fresh coffee and, without a word, sat across the table. He smiled at her and continued reading.

"What time did you get up?" she asked.

"Five-thirty."

"Why so early? It's Sunday."

"I couldn't sleep."

"Too excited?"

Jake lowered the paper. "As a matter of fact, I am excited. Very excited. It's too bad the excitement will not be shared."

"I'm sorry about last night."

"You don't have to apologize. I know how you feel. Your problem is that you only look at the negative, never the positive. You have no idea what this case can do for us."

"Jake, this case scares me. The phone calls, the threats, the burning cross. If the case means a million dollars, is it worth it if something happens?"

"Nothing will happen. We'll get some more threats and they'll stare at us at church and around town, but nothing serious."

"But you can't be sure."

"We went through this last night and I don't care to rehash it this morning. I do have an idea, though."

"I can't wait to hear it."

"You and Hanna fly to North Carolina and stay with your parents until after the trial. They'd love to have you, and we wouldn't worry about the Klan or whoever likes to burn crosses."

"But the trial is six weeks away! You want us to stay in Wilmington for six weeks?"

"Yes."

"I love my parents, but that's ridiculous."

"You don't see enough of them, and they don't see enough of Hanna."

"And we don't see enough of you. I'm not leaving for six weeks."

"There's a ton of preparation. I'll eat and sleep this case until the trial is over. I'll work nights, weekends—"

"What else is new?"

"I'll ignore y'all and think of nothing but this case."

"We're used to that."

Jake smiled at her. "You're saying you can handle it?"

"I can handle you. It's those crazies out there that scare me."

"When the crazies get serious, I'll back off. I will run from this case if my family is in danger."

"You promise?"

"Of course I promise. Let's send Hanna."

"If we're not in danger, why do you want to send anybody?"

"Just for safety. She'd have a great time spending the summer with her grandparents. They'd love it."

"She wouldn't last a week without me."

"And you wouldn't last a week without her."

"That's true. It's out of the question. I don't worry about her as long as I can hold her and squeeze her."

The coffee was ready and Carla filled their cups. "Anything in the paper?"

"No. I thought the Jackson paper might run something, but it happened too late, I guess."

"I guess your timing is a little rusty after a week's lay-off."

"Just wait till in the morning."

"How do you know?"

"I promise."

She shook her head and searched for the fashion and food sections. "Are you going to church?"

"No."

"Why not? You've got the case. You're a star again."

"Yeah, but no one knows it yet."

"I see. Next Sunday."

"Of course."

———————————

At Mount Hebron, Mount Zion, Mount Pleasant, and at Brown's Chapel, Green's Chapel, and Norris Road, Section Line Road, Bethel Road, and at God's Temple, Christ's Temple, and Saints' Temple, the buckets and baskets and plates were passed and re-passed and left at the altars and front doors to collect the money for Carl Lee Hailey and his family. The large, family-size Kentucky Fried Chicken buckets were used in many of the churches. The bigger the bucket, or basket, the smaller the individual offerings appeared as they fell to the bottom, thus allowing the minister just cause to order another passing through the flock. It was a special offering, separate from the regular giving, and was preceded in virtually every church with a heart-wrenching account of what happened to the precious little Hailey girl, and what would happen to her daddy and family if the buckets were not filled. In many instances the sacred name of the NAACP was invoked and the effect was a loosening of the wallets and purses.

It worked. The buckets were emptied, the money counted, and the ritual repeated during the evening services. Late Sunday night the morning offerings and evening offer-

ings were combined and counted by each minister, who
would then deliver a great percentage of the total to the
Reverend Agee sometime Monday. He would keep the
money somewhere in his church, and a great percentage of it
would be spent for the benefit of the Hailey family.

From two to five each Sunday afternoon, the prisoners in the
Ford County jail were turned out into a large fenced yard
across the small back street behind the jail. A limit of three
friends and/or relatives for each prisoner was allowed inside
for no more than an hour. There were a couple of shade
trees, some broken picnic tables, and a well-maintained basketball hoop. Deputies and dogs watched carefully from the
other side of the fence.

    A routine was established. Gwen and the kids would
leave church after the benediction around three, and drive
to the jail. Ozzie allowed Carl Lee early entrance to the
recreation area so he could assume the best picnic table, the
one with four legs and a shade tree. He would sit there by
himself, speaking to no one, and watch the basketball skirmish until his family arrived. It wasn't basketball, but a hy-
brid of rugby, wrestling, judo, and basketball. No one dared
officiate. No blood, no foul. And, surprisingly, no fights. A
fight meant quick admittance to solitary and no recreation
for a month.

    There were a few visitors, some girlfriends and wives,
and they would sit in the grass by the fence with their men
and quietly watch the mayhem under the basketball hoop.
One couple asked Carl Lee if they could use his table for
lunch. He shook his head, and they ate in the grass.

    Gwen and the kids arrived before three. Deputy Has-
tings, her cousin, unlocked the gate and the children ran to
meet their daddy. Gwen spread the food. Carl Lee was
aware of the stares from the less fortunate, and he enjoyed
the envy. Had he been white, or smaller and weaker, or
perhaps charged with a lesser crime, he would have been
asked to share his food. But he was Carl Lee Hailey, and no
one stared too long. The game returned to its fury and violence, and the family ate in peace. Tonya always sat next to
her daddy.

"They started an offerin' for us this mornin'," Gwen said after lunch.

"Who did?"

"The church. Reverend Agee said all the black churches in the county are gonna take up money ever Sunday for us and for the lawyer fees."

"How much?"

"Don't know. He said they gonna pass the bucket ever Sunday until the trial."

"That's mighty nice. What'd he say 'bout me?"

"Just talked about your case and all. Said how expensive it would be, and how we'd need help from the churches. Talked about Christian givin' and all that. Said you're a real hero to your people."

What a pleasant surprise, thought Carl Lee. He expected some help from his church, but nothing financial. "How many churches?"

"All the black ones in the county."

"When do we get the money?"

"He didn't say."

After he got his cut, thought Carl Lee. "Boys, y'all take your sister and go play over there by the fence. Me and Momma needs to talk. Be careful now."

Carl Lee, Jr., and Robert took their little sister by the hand and did exactly as ordered.

"What does the doctor say?" Carl Lee asked as he watched the children walk away.

"She's doin' good. Her jaw's healin' good. He might take the wire off in a month. She can't run and jump and play yet, but it won't be long. Still some soreness."

"What about the, uh, the other?"

Gwen shook her head and covered her eyes. She began crying and wiping her eyes. She spoke and her voice cracked. "She'll never have kids. He told me . . ." She stopped, wiped her face and tried to continue. She began sobbing loudly, and buried her face in a paper towel.

Carl Lee felt sick. He placed his forehead in his palms. He ground his teeth together as his eyes watered. "What'd he say?"

Gwen raised her head and spoke haltingly, fighting back tears. "He told me Tuesday there was too much damage . . ." She wiped her wet face with her fingers. "But he wants to send her to a specialist in Memphis."

"He's not sure?"

She shook her head. "Ninety percent sure. But he thinks she should be examined by another doctor in Memphis. We're supposed to take her in a month."

Gwen tore off another paper towel and wiped her face. She handed one to her husband, who quickly dabbed his eyes.

Next to the fence, Tonya sat listening to her brothers argue about which one would be a deputy and which one would be in jail. She watched her parents talk and shake their heads and cry. She knew something was wrong with her. She rubbed her eyes and started crying too.

"The nightmares are gettin' worse," Gwen said, interrupting the silence. "I have to sleep with her ever night. She dreams about men comin' to get her, men hidin' in the closets, chasin' her through the woods. She wakes up screamin' and sweatin'. The doctor says she needs to see a psychiatrist. Says it'll get worse before it gets better."

"How much will it cost?"

"I don't know. I haven't called yet."

"Better call. Where is this psychiatrist?"

"Memphis."

"Figures."

"How are the boys treatin' her?"

"They've been great. They treat her special. But the nightmares keep them scared. When she wakes up screamin' she wakes everybody. The boys run to her bed and try to help, but it scares them. Last night she wouldn't go back to sleep unless the boys slept on the floor next to her. We all laid there wide awake with the lights on."

"The boys'll be all right."

"They miss their daddy."

Carl Lee managed a forced smile. "It won't be much longer."

"You really think so?"

"I don't know what to think anymore. But I don't plan to spend the rest of my life in jail. I hired Jake back."

"When?"

"Yesterday. That Memphis lawyer never showed up, never even called. I fired him and hired Jake again."

"But you said Jake is too young."

"I was wrong. He is young, but he's good. Ask Lester."

"It's your trial."

Carl Lee walked slowly around the yard, never leaving the fence. He thought of the two boys, somewhere out there, dead and buried, their flesh rotting by now, their souls burning in hell. Before they died, they met his little girl, only briefly, and within two hours wrecked her little body and ruined her mind. So brutal was their attack that she could never have children; so violent the encounter that she now saw them hiding for her, waiting in closets. Could she ever forget about it, block it out, erase it from her mind so her life would be normal? Maybe a psychiatrist could do that. Would other children allow her to be normal?

She was just a little nigger, they probably thought. Somebody's little nigger kid. Illegitimate, of course, like all of them. Rape would be nothing new.

He remembered them in court. One proud, the other scared. He remembered them coming down the stairs as he awaited the execution. Then, the looks of horror as he stepped forward with the M-16. The sound of the gunfire, the cries for help, the screams as they fell backward together, one on top of the other, handcuffed, screaming and twisting, going nowhere. He remembered smiling, even laughing, as he watched them struggle with their heads half blown away, and when their bodies were still, he ran.

He smiled again. He was proud of it. The first gook he killed in Vietnam had bothered him more.

The letter to Walter Sullivan was to the point:

Dear J. Walter:
By now it's safe to assume Mr. Marsharfsky has informed you that his employment by Carl Lee Hailey has been terminated. Your services as local counsel will, of course, no longer be needed. Have a nice day.
Sincerely,
Jake

A copy was sent to L. Winston Lotterhouse. The letter to Noose was just as short:

> Dear Judge Noose:
> Please be advised that I have been retained by Carl Lee Hailey. We are preparing for trial on July 22. Please show me as counsel of record.
> Sincerely,
> Jake

A copy was sent to Buckley.

Marsharfsky called at nine-thirty Monday. Jake watched the hold button blink for two minutes before he lifted the receiver. "Hello."

"How'd you do it?"

"Who is this?"

"Your secretary didn't tell you? This is Bo Marsharfsky, and I want to know how you did it."

"Did what?"

"Hustled my case."

Stay cool, thought Jake. He's an agitator. "As I recall, it was hustled from me," replied Jake.

"I never met him before he hired me."

"You didn't have to. You sent your pimp, remember?"

"Are you accusing me of chasing cases?"

"Yes."

Marsharfsky paused and Jake braced for the obscenities.

"You know something, Mr. Brigance, you're right. I chase cases everyday. I'm a pro at hustling cases. That's how I make so much money. If there's a big criminal case, I intend to get it. And I'll use whatever method I find necessary."

"Funny, that wasn't mentioned in the paper."

"And if I want the Hailey case, I'll get it."

"Come on down." Jake hung up and laughed for ten minutes. He lit a cheap cigar, and began working on his motion for a change of venue.

Two days later Lucien called and instructed Ethel to instruct Jake to come see him. It was important. He had a visitor Jake needed to meet.

The visitor was Dr. W.T. Bass, a retired psychiatrist from Jackson. He had known Lucien for years, and they had collaborated on a couple of insane criminals during their friendship. Both of the criminals were still in Parchman. His retirement had been one year before the disbarment and had been precipitated by the same thing that contributed heavily to the disbarment, to wit, a strong affection for Jack Daniel's. He visited Lucien occasionally in Clanton, and Lucien visited him more frequently in Jackson, and they enjoyed their visits because they enjoyed staying drunk together. They sat on the big porch and waited on Jake.

"Just say he was insane," instructed Lucien.

"Was he?" asked the doctor.

"That's not important."

"What is important?"

"It's important to give the jury an excuse to acquit the man. They won't care if he's crazy or not. But they'll need some reason to acquit him."

"It would be nice to examine him."

"You can. You can talk to him all you want. He's at the jail just waiting on someone to talk to."

"I'll need to meet with him several times."

"I know that."

"What if I don't think he was insane at the time of the shooting?"

"Then you won't get to testify at trial, and you won't get your name and picture in the paper, and you won't be interviewed on TV."

Lucien paused long enough to take a long drink. "Just do as I say. Interview him, take a bunch of notes. Ask stupid questions. You know what to do. Then say he was crazy."

"I'm not so sure about this. It hasn't worked too well in the past."

"Look, you're a doctor, aren't you? Then act proud, vain, arrogant. Act like a doctor's supposed to act. Give your opinion and dare anyone to question it."

"I don't know. It hasn't worked too well in the past."

"Just do as I say."

"I've done that before, and they're both at Parchman."

"They were hopeless. Hailey's different."

"Does he have a chance?"

"Slim."

"I thought you said he was different."

"He's a decent man with a good reason for killing."

"Then why are his chances slim?"

"The law says his reason is not good enough."

"That's par for the law."

"Plus he's black, and this is a white county. I have no confidence in these bigots around here."

"And if he were white?"

"If he were white and he killed two blacks who raped his daughter, the jury would give him the courthouse."

Bass finished one glass and poured another. A fifth and a bucket of ice sat on the wicker table between the two.

"What about his lawyer?" he asked.

"He should be here in a minute."

"He used to work for you?"

"Yeah, but I don't think you met him. He was in the firm about two years before I left. He's young, early thirties. Clean, aggressive, works hard."

"And he used to work for you?"

"That's what I said. He's got trial experience for his age. This is not his first murder case, but, if I'm not mistaken, it's his first insanity case."

"That's nice to hear. I don't want someone asking a lot of questions."

"I like your confidence. Wait till you meet the D.A."

"I just don't feel good about this. We tried it twice, and it didn't work."

Lucien shook his head in bewilderment. "You've got to be the humblest doctor I've known."

"And the poorest."

"You're supposed to be pompous and arrogant. You're the expert. Act like one. Who's gonna question your professional opinion in Clanton, Mississippi?"

"The State will have experts."

"They will have one psychiatrist from Whitfield. He'll examine the defendant for a few hours, and then drive up for trial and testify that the defendant is the sanest man he's ever met. He's never seen a legally insane defendant. To him no one is insane. Everybody's blessed with perfect mental health. Whitfield is full of sane people, except when it applies for government money, then half the state's crazy. He'd get fired if he started saying defendants are legally insane. So that's who you're up against."

"And the jury will automatically believe me?"

"You act as though you've never been through one of these before."

"Twice, remember. One rapist, one murderer. Neither was insane, in spite of what I said. Both are now locked away where they belong."

Lucien took a long drink and studied the light brown liquid and the floating ice cubes. "You said you would help me. God knows you owe me the favor. How many divorces did I handle for you?"

"Three. And I got cleaned out every time."

"You deserved it every time. It was either give in or go to trial and have your habits discussed in open court."

"I remember."

"How many clients, or patients, have I sent you over the years?"

"Not enough to pay my alimony."

"Remember the malpractice case by the lady whose treatment consisted primarily of weekly sessions on your couch with the foldaway bed? Your malpractice carrier refused to defend, so you called your dear friend Lucien who settled it for peanuts and kept it out of court."

"There were no witnesses."

"Just the lady herself. And the court files showing where your wives had sued for divorce on the grounds of adultery."

"They couldn't prove it."

"They didn't get a chance. We didn't want them to try, remember?"

"All right, enough, enough. I said I would help. What about my credentials?"

"Are you a compulsive worrier?"

"No. I just get nervous when I think of courtrooms."

"Your credentials are fine. You've been qualified before as an expert witness. Don't worry so much."

"What about this?" He waved his drink at Lucien.

"You shouldn't drink so much," he said piously.

The doctor dropped his drink and exploded in laughter. He rolled out of his chair and crawled to the edge of the porch, holding his stomach and shaking in laughter.

"You're drunk," Lucien said as he left for another bottle.

———

When Jake arrived an hour later, Lucien was rocking slowly in his huge wicker rocker. The doctor was asleep in the swing at the far end of the porch. He was barefoot, and his toes had disappeared into the shrubbery that lined the porch. Jake walked up the steps and startled Lucien.

"Jake, my boy, how are you?" he slurred.

"Fine, Lucien. I see you're doing quite well." He looked at the empty bottle and one not quite empty.

"I wanted you to meet that man," he said, trying to sit up straight.

"Who is he?"

"He's our psychiatrist. Dr. W.T. Bass, from Jackson. Good friend of mine. He'll help us with Hailey."

"Is he good?"

"The best. We've worked together on several insanity cases."

Jake took a few steps in the direction of the swing and stopped. The doctor was lying on his back with his shirt unbuttoned and his mouth wide open. He snored heavily, with an unusual guttural gurgling sound. A horsefly the size of a small sparrow buzzed around his nose and retreated to the top of the swing with each thunderous exhalation. A rancid vapor emanated with the snoring and hung like an invisible fog over the end of the porch.

"He's a doctor?" Jake asked as he sat next to Lucien.

"Psychiatry," Lucien said proudly.

"Did he help you with those?" Jake nodded at the bottles.

"I helped him. He drinks like a fish, but he's always sober at trial."

"That's comforting."

"You'll like him. He's cheap. Owes me a favor. Won't cost a dime."

"I like him already."

Lucien's face was as red as his eyes. "Wanna drink?"

"No. It's three-thirty in the afternoon."

"Really! What day is it?"

"Wednesday, June 12. How long have y'all been drinking?"

" 'Bout thirty years." Lucien laughed and rattled his ice cubes.

"I mean today."

"We drank our breakfast. What difference does it make?"

"Does he work?"

"Naw, he's retired."

"Was his retirement voluntary?"

"You mean, was he disbarred, so to speak?"

"That's right, so to speak."

"No. He still has his license, and his credentials are impeccable."

"He looks impeccable."

"Booze got him a few years ago. Booze and alimony. I handled three of his divorces. He reached the point where all of his income went for alimony and child support, so he quit working."

"How does he manage?"

"We, uh, I mean, he stashed some away. Hid it from his wives and their hungry lawyers. He's really quite comfortable."

"He looks comfortable."

"Plus he peddles a little dope, but only to a rich clientele. Not really dope, but narcotics which he can legally prescribe. It's not really illegal; just a little unethical."

"What's he doing here?"

"He visits occasionally. He lives in Jackson but hates it. I called him Sunday after I talked to you. He wants to meet Hailey as soon as possible, tomorrow if he can."

The doctor grunted and rolled to his side, causing the swing to move suddenly. It swung a few times, and he moved again, still snoring. He stretched his right leg, and his foot caught a thick branch in the shrubbery. The swing jerked sideways and threw the good doctor onto the porch. His head crashed onto the wooden floor while his right foot remained lodged through the end of the swing. He grimaced and coughed, then began snoring again. Jake instinctively started toward him, but stopped when it was apparent he was unharmed and still asleep.

"Leave him alone!" ordered Lucien between laughs.

Lucien slid an ice cube down the porch and just missed the doctor's head. The second cube landed perfectly on the tip of his nose. "Perfect shot!" Lucien roared. "Wake up, you drunk!"

Jake walked down the steps toward his car, listening to his former boss laugh and curse and throw ice cubes at Dr. W.T. Bass, psychiatrist, witness for the defense.

———————

Deputy DeWayne Looney left the hospital on crutches, and drove his wife and three children to the jail, where the sheriff, the other deputies, the reserves, and a few friends waited with a cake and small gifts. He would be a dispatcher now, and would retain his badge and uniform and full salary.

21 The fellowship hall of the Springdale Church had been thoroughly cleaned and shined, and the folding tables and chairs dusted and placed in perfect rows around the room. It was the largest black church in the county and it was in Clanton, so the Reverend Agee deemed it necessary to meet there. The purpose of the press conference was to get vocal, to show support of the local boy who made good, and to announce the establishment of the Carl Lee Hailey Legal Defense Fund. The national director of the NAACP was present with a five-thousand-dollar check and a promise of serious money later. The executive director of the Memphis branch brought five thousand and grandly laid it on the table. They sat with Agee behind the two folding tables in the front of the room with every member of the council seated behind them and two hundred black church members in the crowded audience. Gwen sat next to Agee. A few reporters and cameras, much fewer than expected, grouped in the center of the room and filmed away.

Agee spoke first and was inspired by the cameras. He talked of the Haileys and their goodness and innocence, and of baptizing Tonya when she was only eight. He talked of a family wrecked by racism and hatred. There were sniffles in the audience. Then he got mean. He tore into the judicial system and its desire to prosecute a good and decent man who had done no wrong; a man, who, if white, would not be on trial; a man who was on trial only because he was black and that was what was so wrong with the prosecution and persecution of Carl Lee Hailey. He found his rhythm and the crowd joined in, and the press conference took on the fervor of a tent revival. He lasted for forty-five minutes.

He was a hard act to follow. But the national director did not hesitate. He delivered a thirty-minute oratorical condemnation of racism. He seized the moment and spouted national statistics on crime and arrests and convictions and inmate population and summed it all up by declaring that the criminal justice system was controlled by white people

who unfairly persecuted black people. Then in a bewildering
flurry of rationale he brought the national statistics to Ford
County and pronounced the system unfit to deal with Carl
Lee Hailey. The lights from the TV cameras produced a line
of sweat above his eyebrows and he warmed to the task. He
got angrier than Reverend Agee and pounded the podium
and made the cluster of microphones jump and shake. He
exhorted the blacks of Ford County and of Mississippi to
give until it hurt. He promised demonstrations and marches.
The trial would be a battle cry for black and oppressed folk
everywhere.

He answered questions. How much money would be
raised? At least fifty thousand, they hoped. It would be expensive to defend Carl Lee Hailey and fifty thousand may
not be enough, but they would raise whatever it took. But
time was running short. Where would the money go? Legal
fees and litigation expenses. A battery of lawyers and doctors would be needed. Would NAACP lawyers be used? Of
course. The legal staff in Washington was already at work on
the case. The capital defense unit would handle all aspects
of the trial. Carl Lee Hailey had become their top priority
and all available resources would be devoted to his defense.

When he finished, Reverend Agee retook the podium
and nodded at a piano player in the corner. The music
started. They all stood, hand in hand, and sang a stirring
rendition of "We Shall Overcome."

Jake read about the defense fund in Tuesday's paper. He
had heard rumors of the special offering being administered
by the council, but was told the money was for the support of
the family. Fifty thousand for legal fees! He was angry, but
interested. Would he be fired again? Suppose Carl Lee refused to hire the NAACP lawyers, what would happen to the
money? The trial was five weeks away, plenty of time for the
capital defense team to descend on Clanton. He had read
about these guys; a team of six capital murder specialists
who toured the South defending blacks accused of heinous
and notorious crimes. "The Death Squad" was their nickname. They were very bright, very talented, very educated
lawyers dedicated to rescuing black murderers from the vari-

ous gas chambers and electric chairs around the South. They handled nothing but capital murder cases and were very, very good at their work. The NAACP ran their interference, raising money, organizing local blacks, and generating publicity. Racism was their best, and sometimes only, defense and though they lost much more than they won, their record was not bad. The cases they handled were supposed to be lost, all of them. Their goal was to martyr the defendant before the trial and hopefully hang the jury.

Now they were coming to Clanton.

———————————

A week earlier Buckley had filed the proper motions to have Carl Lee examined by the State's doctors. Jake requested the doctors be required to conduct their examinations in Clanton, preferably in Jake's office. Noose declined, and ordered the sheriff to transport Carl Lee to the Mississippi State Mental Hospital at Whitfield. Jake requested that he be allowed to accompany his client and be present during the examinations. Again, Noose declined.

Early Wednesday morning, Jake and Ozzie sipped coffee in the sheriff's office and waited for Carl Lee to shower and change clothes. Whitfield was three hours away, and he was to check in at nine. Jake had final instructions for his client.

"How long will y'all be there?" Jake asked Ozzie.

"You're the lawyer. How long will it take?"

"Three or four days. You've been there before, haven't you?"

"Sure, we've had to transport plenty of crazy people. But nothin' like this. Where do they keep him?"

"They've got all kinds of cells."

Deputy Hastings casually entered the office, sleepy-eyed and crunching on a stale doughnut. "How many cars we takin'?"

"Two," answered Ozzie. "I'll drive mine and you drive yours. I'll take Pirtle and Carl Lee, you take Riley and Nesbit."

"Guns?"

"Three shotguns in each car. Plenty of shells. Everbody

wears a vest, includin' Carl Lee. Get the cars ready. I'd like to leave by five-thirty."

Hastings mumbled something and disappeared.

"Are you expecting trouble?" Jake asked.

"We've had some phone calls. Two in particular mentioned the trip to Whitfield. Lot of highway between here and there."

"How are you going?"

"Most folks take 22 to the interstate, wouldn't you say? It might be safer to take some smaller highways. We'll probably run 14 south to 89."

"That would be unexpected."

"Good. I'm glad you approve."

"He's my client, you know."

"For right now, anyway."

Carl Lee quickly devoured the eggs and biscuits as Jake briefed him on what to expect during the stay at Whitfield.

"I know, Jake. You want me to act crazy, right?" Carl Lee said with a laugh. Ozzie thought it was funny too.

"This is serious, Carl Lee. Listen to me."

"Why? You said yourself it won't matter what I say or do down there. They won't say I was insane when I shot them. Them doctors work for the State, right? The State's prosecutin' me, right? What difference does it make what I say or do? They've already made up their minds. Ain't that right, Ozzie?"

"I'm not gettin' involved. I work for the State."

"You work for the County," said Jake.

"Name, rank, and serial number. That's all they're gettin' outta me," Carl Lee said as he emptied a small paper sack.

"Very funny," said Jake.

"He's crackin' up, Jake," Ozzie said.

Carl Lee stuck two straws up his nose and began tiptoeing around the office, staring at the ceiling and then grabbing at something above his head. He put it in the sack. He lunged at another one and put it in the sack. Hastings returned and stopped in the door. Carl Lee grinned at him with wild eyes, then grabbed at another one toward the ceiling.

"What the hell he's doin'?" Hastings asked.

"Catchin' butterflies," Carl Lee said.

Jake grabbed his briefcase and headed for the door. "I think you should leave him at Whitfield." He slammed the door and left the jail.

Noose had scheduled the venue hearing for Monday, June 24, in Clanton. The hearing would be long and well publicized. Jake had requested the change of venue, and he had the burden of proving Carl Lee could not receive a fair and impartial trial in Ford County. He needed witnesses. Persons with credibility in the community who were willing to testify that a fair trial was not possible. Atcavage said he might do it as a favor, but the bank might not want him involved. Harry Rex had eagerly volunteered. Reverend Agee said he would be glad to testify, but that was before the NAACP announced its lawyers would be handling the case. Lucien had no credibility, and Jake did not seriously consider asking him.

Buckley, on the other hand, would line up a dozen credible witnesses—elected officials, lawyers, businessmen, maybe other sheriffs—all of whom would testify that they had vaguely heard of Carl Lee Hailey and he could most certainly receive a fair trial in Clanton.

Jake personally preferred the trial to be in Clanton, in his courthouse across the street from his office, in front of his people. Trials were pressure-filled, tedious, sleepless ordeals. It would be nice to have this one in a friendly arena, three minutes from his driveway. When the trial recessed, he could spend the free moments in his office doing research, preparing witnesses or relaxing. He could eat at the Coffee Shop or Claude's, or even run home for a quick lunch. His client could remain in the Ford County jail, near his family.

And, of course, his media exposure would be much greater. The reporters would gather in front of his office each morning of the trial and follow him as he walked slowly toward the courthouse. That thought was exciting.

Did it matter where they tried Carl Lee Hailey? Lucien was correct: the publicity had reached every resident of every county in Mississippi. So why change venue? His guilt or innocence had already been prejudged by every prospective juror in the state.

Sure it mattered. Some prospective jurors were white and some were black. Percentage-wise, there would be more white ones in Ford County than the surrounding counties. Jake loved black jurors, especially in criminal cases and especially when the criminal was black. They were not as anxious to convict. They were open minded. He preferred them in civil cases, too. They felt for the underdog against the big corporation or insurance company, and they were more liberal with other people's money. As a rule, he picked all the black jurors he could find, but they were scarce in Ford County.

It was imperative the case be tried in another county, a blacker county. One black could hang the jury. A majority could force, maybe, an acquittal. Two weeks in a motel and strange courthouse was not appealing, but the small discomforts were greatly outweighed by the need to have black faces in the jury box.

The venue question had been thoroughly researched by Lucien. As instructed, Jake arrived promptly, although reluctantly, at 8:00 A.M. Sallie served breakfast on the porch. Jake drank coffee and orange juice; Lucien, bourbon and water. For three hours they covered every aspect of a change of venue. Lucien had copies of every Supreme Court case for the past eighty years, and lectured like a professor. The pupil took notes, argued once or twice, but mainly listened.

Whitfield was located a few miles from Jackson in a rural part of Rankin County. Two guards waited by the front gate and argued with reporters. Carl Lee was scheduled to arrive at nine, that was all the guards knew. At eight-thirty two patrol cars with Ford County insignia rolled to a stop at the gate. The reporters and their cameramen ran to the driver of the first car. Ozzie's window was down.

"Where's Carl Lee Hailey?" a reporter shouted in a panic.

"He's in the other car," Ozzie drawled, winking at Carl Lee in the back seat.

"He's in the second car!" someone shouted, and they ran to Hastings' car.

"Where's Hailey?" they demanded.

Pirtle, in the front seat, pointed to Hastings, the driver. "That's him."

"Are you Carl Lee Hailey?" a reporter screamed at Hastings.

"Yep."

"Why are you driving?"

"What's with the uniform?"

"They made me a deputy," answered Hastings with a straight face. The gate opened, and the two cars sped through.

Carl Lee was processed in the main building and led, along with Ozzie and the deputies, to another building where he was checked into his cell, or room, as it was called. The door was locked behind him. Ozzie and his men were excused and returned to Clanton.

After lunch, an assistant of some sort with a clipboard and white jacket arrived and began asking questions. Starting with birth, he asked Carl Lee about every significant event and person in his life. It lasted two hours. At 4:00 P.M., two security guards handcuffed Carl Lee and rode him in a golf cart to a modern brick building a half mile from his room. He was led to the office of Dr. Wilbert Rodeheaver, head of staff. The guards waited in the hall by the door.

22 It had been five weeks since the shootings of Billy Ray Cobb and Pete Willard. The trial was four weeks away. The three motels in Clanton were booked solid for the week of the trial and the week before. The Best Western was the largest and nicest, and had attracted the Memphis and Jackson press. The Clanton Court had the best bar and restaurant, and was booked by reporters from Atlanta, Washington, and New York. At the less than elegant East Side Motel the rates had curiously doubled for the month of July but it had nonetheless sold out.

The town had been friendly at first to these outsiders, most of whom were rude and spoke with different accents. But some of the descriptions of Clanton and its people had been less than flattering, and most of the locals now honored a secret code of silence. A noisy cafe would become instantly silent when a stranger walked in and took a seat. Merchants around the square offered little assistance to anyone they did not recognize. The employees in the courthouse had become deaf to questions asked a thousand times by nosy intruders. Even the Memphis and Jackson reporters had to struggle to extract anything new from the locals. The people were tired of being described as backward, redneck, and racist. They ignored the outsiders whom they could not trust and went about their business.

The bar at the Clanton Court became the watering hole for the reporters. It was the one place in town they could go to find a friendly face and good conversation. They sat in the booths under the big-screen TV and gossiped about the small town and the upcoming trial. They compared notes and stories and leads and rumors, and drank until they were drunk because there was nothing else to do in Clanton after dark.

The motels filled Sunday night, June 23, the night before the venue hearing. Early Monday morning they gathered in the restaurant at the Best Western to drink coffee and speculate. The hearing was the first major skirmish, and could likely be the only courtroom action until the trial. A rumor surfaced that Noose was ill and did not want to hear the case, and that he would ask the Supreme Court to appoint another judge. Just a rumor, with no source and nothing more definite, said a reporter from Jackson. At eight they packed their cameras and microphones and left for the square. One group set up outside the jail, another at the rear of the courthouse, but most headed for the courtroom. By eight-thirty it was filled.

From the balcony of his office, Jake watched the activity around the courthouse. His heart beat faster than normal, and his stomach tingled. He smiled. He was ready for Buckley, ready for the cameras.

Noose looked down past the end of his nose, over his reading glasses, and around the packed courtroom. Everyone was in place.

"The court has before it," he began, "the defendant's motion for a change of venue. The trial in this matter has been set for Monday, July 22. That's four weeks from today, according to my calendar. I have set a deadline for filing motions and disposing of same, and I believe those are the only two deadlines between now and trial."

"That's correct, Your Honor," thundered Buckley, half standing behind his table. Jake rolled his eyes and shook his head.

"Thank you, Mr. Buckley," Noose said dryly. "The defendant has filed the proper notice that he intends to use an insanity defense. Has he been examined at Whitfield?"

"Yes sir, Your Honor, last week," Jake answered.

"Will he employ his own psychiatrist?"

"Of course, Your Honor."

"Has he been examined by his own?"

"Yes, sir."

"Good. So that's out of the way. What other motions do you anticipate filing?"

"Your Honor, we expect to file a motion requesting the clerk to summons more than the usual number of prospective jurors—"

"The State will oppose that motion," Buckley yelled as he jumped to his feet.

"Sit down, Mr. Buckley!" Noose said sternly, ripping off his glasses and glaring at the D.A. "Please don't yell at me again. Of course you will oppose it. You will oppose any motion filed by the defense. That's your job. Don't interrupt again. You'll have ample opportunity after we adjourn to perform for the media."

Buckley slumped in his chair and hid his red face. Noose had never screamed at him before.

"Continue, Mr. Brigance."

Jake was startled by Ichabod's meanness. He looked tired and ill. Perhaps it was the pressure.

"We may have some written objections to anticipated evidence."

"Motions *in limine*?"

"Yes, sir."

"We'll hear those at trial. Anything else?"

"Not at this time."

"Now, Mr. Buckley, will the State file any motions?"

"I can't think of any," Buckley answered meekly.

"Good. I want to make sure there are no surprises between now and trial. I will be here one week before trial to hear and decide any pretrial matters. I expect any motions to be filed promptly, so that we can tie up any loose ends well before the twenty-second."

Noose flipped through his file and studied Jake's motion for a change of venue. Jake whispered to Carl Lee, whose presence was not required for the hearing, but he insisted. Gwen and the three boys sat in the first row behind their daddy. Tonya was not in the courtroom.

"Mr. Brigance, your motion appears to be in order. How many witnesses?"

"Three, Your Honor."

"Mr. Buckley, how many will you call?"

"We have twenty-one," Buckley said proudly.

"Twenty-one!" yelled the judge.

Buckley cowered and glanced at Musgrove. "B-but, we probably won't need them all. In fact, I know we won't call all of them."

"Pick your best five, Mr. Buckley. I don't plan to be here all day."

"Yes, Your Honor."

"Mr. Brigance, you've asked for a change of venue. It's your motion. You may proceed."

Jake stood and walked slowly across the courtroom, behind Buckley, to the wooden podium in front of the jury box. "May it please the court, Your Honor, Mr. Hailey has requested that his trial be moved from Ford County. The reason is obvious: the publicity in this case will prevent a fair trial. The good people of this county have prejudged the guilt or innocence of Carl Lee Hailey. He is charged with killing two men, both of whom were born here and left families here. Their lives were not famous, but their deaths certainly have been. Mr. Hailey was known by few outside his community until now. Now everyone in this county knows who he is, knows about his family and his daughter and what happened to her, and knows most of the details of his alleged crimes. It will be impossible to find twelve people in Ford County who have not already prejudged this case. This trial should be held in another part of the state where the people are not so familiar with the facts."

"Where would you suggest?" interrupted the judge.

"I wouldn't recommend a specific county, but it should be as far away as possible. Perhaps the Gulf Coast."

"Why?"

"Obvious reasons, Your Honor. It's four hundred miles away, and I'm sure the people down there do not know as much as the people around here."

"And you think the people in south Mississippi haven't heard about it?"

"I'm sure they have. But they are much further away."

"But they have televisions and newspapers, don't they, Mr. Brigance?"

"I'm sure they do."

"Do you believe you could go to any county in this state and find twelve people who haven't heard the details of this case?"

Jake looked at his legal pad. He could hear the artists sketching on their pads behind him. He could see Buckley grinning out of the corner of his eye. "It would be difficult," he said quietly.

"Call your first witness."

Harry Rex Vonner was sworn in and took his seat on the witness stand. The wooden swivel chair popped and creaked under the heavy load. He blew into the microphone and a loud hiss echoed around the courtroom. He smiled at Jake and nodded.

"Would you state your name?"

"Harry Rex Vonner."

"And your address?"

"Eighty-four ninety-three Cedarbrush, Clanton, Mississippi."

"How long have you lived in Clanton?"

"All my life. Forty-six years."

"Your occupation?"

"I'm a lawyer. I've had my license for twenty-two years."

"Have you ever met Carl Lee Hailey?"

"Once."

"What do you know about him?"

"He supposedly shot two men, Billy Ray Cobb and Pete Willard, and he wounded a deputy, DeWayne Looney."

"Did you know either of those boys?"

"Not personally. I knew of Billy Ray Cobb."

"How did you learn of the shootings?"

"Well, it happened on a Monday, I believe. I was in the courthouse, on the first floor, checking title on some land in the clerk's office, when I heard the gunshots. I ran out into the hall and bedlam had broken loose. I asked a deputy and he told me that the boys had been killed near the back door of the courthouse. I hung around here for a while, and pretty soon there was a rumor that the killer was the father of the little girl who got raped."

"What was your initial reaction?"

"I was shocked, like most people. But I was shocked when I first heard of the rape too."

"When did you learn that Mr. Hailey had been arrested?"

"Later that night. It was all over the television."

"What did you see on TV?"

"Well, I watched as much of it as I could. There were news reports from the local stations in Memphis and Tupelo. We've got the cable, you know, so I watched the news out of New York, Chicago, and Atlanta. Just about every channel had something about the shootings and the arrest. There was footage from the courthouse and jail. It was a big deal. Biggest thing that ever happened in Clanton, Mississippi."

"How did you react when you learned that the girl's father had supposedly done the shooting?"

"It was no big surprise to me. I mean, we all sort of figured it was him. I admired him. I've got kids, and I sympathize with what he did. I still admire him."

"How much do you know about the rape?"

Buckley leapt to his feet. "Objection! The rape is irrelevant!"

Noose ripped off his glasses again and stared angrily at the D.A. Seconds passed and Buckley glanced at the table. He shifted his weight from one foot to the next, then sat down. Noose leaned forward and glared down from the bench.

"Mr. Buckley, don't yell at me. If you do it again, so help me God, I will hold you in contempt. You may be correct, the rape may be irrelevant. But this is not the trial, is it? This is simply a hearing, isn't it? We don't have a jury in the box, do we? You're overruled and out of order. Now stay in your seat. I know it's hard with this sort of audience, but I instruct you to stay in your seat unless you have something truly worthy to say. At that point, you may stand and politely and quietly tell me what's on your mind."

"Thank you, Your Honor," Jake said as he smiled at Buckley. "Now, Mr. Vonner, as I was saying, how much do you know about the rape?"

"Just what I've heard."

"And what's that?"

Buckley stood and bowed like a Japanese sumo wrestler. "If Your Honor please," he said softly and sweetly, "I would like to object at this point, if it pleases the court. The witness may testify to only what he knows from first-hand knowledge, not from what he's heard from other people."

Noose answered just as sweetly. "Thank you, Mr. Buckley. Your objection is noted, and you are overruled. Please continue, Mr. Brigance."

"Thank you, Your Honor."

"What have you heard about the rape?"

"Cobb and Willard grabbed the little Hailey girl and took her out in the woods somewhere. They were drunk, they tied her to a tree, raped her repeatedly and tried to hang her. They even urinated on her."

"They what!" asked Noose.

"They pissed on her, Judge."

The courtroom buzzed at this revelation. Jake had never heard it, Buckley hadn't heard it, and evidently no one knew it but Harry Rex. Noose shook his head and lightly rapped his gavel.

Jake scribbled something on his legal pad and marveled at his friend's esoteric knowledge. "Where did you learn about the rape?"

"All over town. It's common knowledge. The cops were giving the details the next morning at the Coffee Shop. Everybody knows it."

"Is it common knowledge throughout the county?"

"Yes. I haven't talked to anybody in a month who did not know the details of the rape."

"Tell us what you know about the shootings."

"Well, like I said, it was a Monday afternoon. The boys were here in this courtroom for a bail hearing, I believe, and when they left the courtroom they were handcuffed and led by the deputies down the back stairs. When they got down the stairs, Mr. Hailey jumped out of a closet with an M-16. They were killed and DeWayne Looney was shot. Part of his leg was amputated."

"Exactly where did this take place?"

"Right below us here, at the rear entrance of the courthouse. Mr. Hailey was hiding in a janitor's closet and just stepped out and opened fire."

"Do you believe this to be true?"

"I know it's true."

"Where did you learn all this?"

"Here and there. Around town. In the newspapers. Everybody knows about it."

"Where have you heard it discussed?"

"Everywhere. In bars, in churches, at the bank, at the cleaners, at the Tea Shoppe, at the cafes around town, at the liquor store. Everywhere."

"Have you talked to anyone who believes Mr. Hailey did not kill Billy Ray Cobb and Pete Willard?"

"No. You won't find a single person in this county who believes he didn't do it."

"Have most folks around here made up their minds about his guilt or innocence?"

"Every single one of them. There are no fence strad-dlers on this one. It's a hot topic, and everyone has an opin-ion."

"In your opinion, could Mr. Hailey receive a fair trial in Ford County?"

"No, sir. You couldn't find three people in this county of thirty thousand who have not already made up their minds, one way or the other. Mr. Hailey has been judged already. There's just no way to find an impartial jury."

"Thank you, Mr. Vonner. No further questions, Your Honor." Buckley patted his pompadour and ran his fingers over his ears to make sure every hair was in place. He walked purposefully to the podium.

"Mr. Vonner," he bellowed magnificently, "have you al-ready prejudged Carl Lee Hailey?"

"Damn right I have."

"Your language, please," said Noose.

"And what would your judgment be?"

"Mr. Buckley, let me explain it this way. And I'll do so very carefully and slowly so that even you will understand it. If I was the sheriff, I would not have arrested him. If I was on the grand jury, I would not have indicted him. If I was the judge, I would not try him. If I was the D.A., I would not prosecute him. If I was on the trial jury, I would vote to give him a key to the city, a plaque to hang on his wall, and I would send him home to his family. And, Mr. Buckley, if my daughter is ever raped, I hope I have the guts to do what he did."

"I see. You think people should carry guns and settle their disputes in shootouts?"

"I think children have a right not to be raped, and their parents have the right to protect them. I think little girls are special, and if mine was tied to a tree and gang raped by two dopeheads I'm sure it would make me crazy. I think good and decent fathers should have a constitutional right to execute any pervert who touches their children. And I think you're a lying coward when you claim you would not want to kill the man who raped your daughter."

"Mr. Vonner, please!" Noose said.

Buckley struggled, but kept his cool. "You obviously feel very strongly about this case, don't you?"

"You're very perceptive."

"And you want to see him acquitted, don't you?"

"I would pay money, if I had any."

"And you think he stands a better chance of acquittal in another county, don't you?"

"I think he's entitled to a jury made up of people who don't know everything about the case before the trial starts."

"You would acquit him, wouldn't you?"

"That's what I said."

"And you've no doubt talked to other people who would acquit him?"

"I have talked to many."

"Are there folks in Ford County who would vote to convict him?"

"Of course. Plenty of them. He's black, isn't he?"

"In all your discussions around the county, have you detected a clear majority one way or the other?"

"Not really."

Buckley looked at his legal pad and made a note. "Mr. Vonner, is Jake Brigance a close friend of yours?"

Harry Rex smiled and rolled his eyes at Noose. "I'm a lawyer, Mr. Buckley, my friends are few and far between. But he is one of them. Yes, sir."

"And he asked you to come testify?"

"No. I just happened to stumble through the courtroom a few moments ago and landed here in this chair. I had no idea you guys were having a hearing this morning."

Buckley threw his legal pad on the table and sat down. Harry Rex was excused.

"Call your next witness," Noose ordered.

"Reverend Ollie Agee," Jake said.

The reverend was led from the witness room and seated

in the witness stand. Jake had met him at his church the day before with a list of questions. He wanted to testify. They did not discuss the NAACP lawyers.

The reverend was an excellent witness. His deep, graveled voice needed no microphone as it carried around the courtroom. Yes, he knew the details of the rape and the shooting. They were members of his church. He had known them for years, they were family almost, and he had held their hands and suffered with them after the rape. Yes, he had talked to countless people since it happened and everyone had an opinion on guilt or innocence. He and twenty-two other black ministers were members of the council and they had all talked about the Hailey case. And, no, there were no unmade minds in Ford County. A fair trial was not possible in Ford County, in his opinion.

Buckley asked one question. "Reverend Agee, have you talked to any black who would vote to convict Carl Lee Hailey?"

"No, suh, I have not."

The reverend was excused. He took a seat in the courtroom between two of his brethren on the council.

"Call your next witness," Noose said.

Jake smiled at the D.A., and announced, "Sheriff Ozzie Walls."

Buckley and Musgrove immediately locked heads and whispered. Ozzie was on their side, the side of law and order, the prosecution's side. It was not his job to help the defense. Proves you can't trust a nigger, thought Buckley. They take up for each other when they know they're guilty.

Jake led Ozzie through a discussion of the rape and the backgrounds of Cobb and Willard. It was boring and repetitious, and Buckley wanted to object. But he'd been embarrassed enough for one day. Jake sensed that Buckley would remain in his seat so he dwelt on the rape and the gory details. Finally, Noose had enough.

"Move on please, Mr. Brigance."

"Yes, Your Honor. Sheriff Walls, did you arrest Carl Lee Hailey?"

"I did."

"Do you believe he killed Billy Ray Cobb and Pete Willard?"

"I do."

"Have you met anybody in this county who believes he did not shoot them?"

"No, sir."

"Is it widely believed in this county that Mr. Hailey killed them?"

"Yes. Everbody believes it. At least everbody I've talked to."

"Sheriff, do you circulate in this county?"

"Yes, sir. It's my job to know what's goin' on."

"And you talk to a lot of people?"

"More than I would like."

"Have you run across anyone who hasn't heard of Carl Lee Hailey?"

Ozzie paused and answered slowly. "A person would have to be deaf, dumb, and blind not to know of Carl Lee Hailey."

"Have you met anyone without an opinion on his guilt or innocence?"

"There's no such person in this county."

"Can he get a fair trial here?"

"I don't know about that. I do know you can't find twelve people who don't know all about the rape and the shootin'."

"No further questions," Jake said to Noose.

"Is he your last witness?"

"Yes, sir."

"Any cross-examination, Mr. Buckley?"

Buckley remained in his seat and shook his head.

"Good," said His Honor. "Let's take a short recess. I would like to see the attorneys in chambers."

The courtroom erupted in conversation as the attorneys followed Noose and Mr. Pate through the door beside the bench. Noose closed the door to his chambers and removed his robe. Mr. Pate brought him a cup of black coffee.

"Gentlemen, I am considering imposing a gag order from now until the trial is over. I am disturbed by the publicity, and I don't want this case tried by the press. Any comments?"

Buckley looked pale and shaken. He opened his mouth, but nothing happened.

"Good idea, Your Honor," Jake said painfully. "I had considered requesting such an order."

"Yes, I'm sure you have. I've noticed how you run from publicity. What about you, Mr. Buckley?"

"Uh, who would it apply to?"

"You, Mr. Buckley. You, and Mr. Brigance, would be ordered not to discuss any aspect of the case or the trial with the press. It would apply to everyone, at least everyone under the control of this court. The attorneys, the clerks, the court officials, the sheriff."

"But why?" asked Buckley.

"I don't like the idea of the two of you trying this case through the media. I'm not blind. You've both fought for the spotlight, and I can only imagine what the trial will be like. A circus, that's what it will be. Not a trial, but a three-ring circus." Noose walked to the window and mumbled something to himself. He paused for a moment, then continued mumbling. The attorneys looked at each other, then at the awkward frame standing in the window.

"I'm imposing a gag order, effective immediately, from now until the trial is over. Violation of the order will result in contempt of court proceedings. You are not to discuss any aspect of this case with any member of the press. Any questions?"

"No, sir," Jake said quickly.

Buckley looked at Musgrove and shook his head.

"Now, back to this hearing. Mr. Buckley, you said you have over twenty witnesses. How many do you really need?"

"Five or six."

"That's much better. Who are they?"

"Floyd Loyd."

"Who's he?"

"Supervisor, First District, Ford County."

"What's his testimony?"

"He's lived here for fifty years, been in office ten years or so. In his opinion a fair trial is possible in this county."

"I suppose he's never heard of this case?" Noose said sarcastically.

"I'm not sure."

"Who else?"

"Nathan Baker. Justice of the Peace, Third District, Ford County."

"Same testimony?"

"Well, basically, yes."

"Who else?"

"Edgar Lee Baldwin, former supervisor, Ford County."

"He was indicted a few years back, wasn't he?" Jake asked.

Buckley's face turned redder than Jake had ever seen it. His huge mouth dropped open and his eyes glazed over.

"He was not convicted," shot Musgrove.

"I didn't say he was. I simply said he was indicted. FBI, wasn't it?"

"Enough, enough," said Noose. "What will Mr. Baldwin tell us?"

"He's lived here all his life. He knows the people of Ford County, and thinks Mr. Hailey can receive a fair trial here," Musgrove answered. Buckley remained speechless as he stared at Jake.

"Who else?"

"Sheriff Harry Bryant, Tyler County."

"Sheriff Bryant? What'll he say?"

Musgrove was talking for the State now. "Your Honor, we have two theories we are submitting in opposition to the motion for a change of venue. First, we contend a fair trial is possible here in Ford County. Second, if the court is of the opinion that a fair trial is not possible here, the State contends that the immense publicity has reached every prospective juror in this state. The same prejudices and opinions, for and against, which exist in this county exist in every county. Therefore, nothing will be gained by moving the trial. We have witnesses to support this second theory."

"That's a novel concept, Mr. Musgrove. I don't think I've heard it before."

"Neither have I," added Jake.

"Who else do you have?"

"Robert Kelly Williams, district attorney for the Ninth District."

"Where's that?"

"Southwestern tip of the state."

"He drove all the way up here to testify that everyone in his neck of the woods has already prejudged the case?"

"Yes, sir."

"Who else?"

"Grady Liston, district attorney, Fourteenth District."

"Same testimony?"

"Yes, sir."

"Is that all?"

"Well, Your Honor, we have several more. But their testimony will pretty much follow the other witnesses'."

"Good, then we can limit your proof to these six witnesses?"

"Yes, sir."

"I will hear your proof. I will allow each of you five minutes to conclude your arguments, and I will rule on this motion within two weeks. Any questions?"

23 It hurt to say no to the reporters. They followed Jake across Washington Street, where he excused himself, offered his no comments, and sought refuge in his office. Undaunted, a photographer from *Newsweek* pushed his way inside and asked if Jake would pose for a photograph. He wanted one of those important ones with a stern look and thick leather books in the background. Jake straightened his tie and showed the photographer into the conference room, where he posed in court-ordered silence. The photographer thanked him and left.

"May I have a few minutes of your time?" Ethel asked politely as her boss headed for the stairs.

"Certainly."

"Why don't you sit down. We need to talk."

She's finally quitting, Jake thought as he took a seat by the front window.

"What's on your mind?"

"Money."

"You're the highest-paid legal secretary in town. You got a raise three months ago."

"Not my money. Please listen. You don't have enough in the bank to pay this month's bills. June is almost gone, and we've grossed seventeen hundred dollars."

Jake closed his eyes and rubbed his forehead.

"Look at these bills," she said, waving a stack of invoices. "Four thousand dollars worth. How am I supposed to pay these?"

"How much is in the bank?"

"Nineteen hundred dollars, as of Friday. Nothing came in this morning."

"Nothing?"

"Not a dime."

"What about the settlement on the Liford case? That's three thousand in fees."

Ethel shook her head. "Mr. Brigance, that file has not been closed. Mr. Liford has not signed the release. You were to take it by his house. Three weeks ago, remember?"

"No, I don't remember. What about Buck Britt's retainer? That's a thousand dollars."

"His check bounced. The bank returned it, and it's been on your desk for two weeks."

She paused and took a deep breath. "You've stopped seeing clients. You don't return phone calls, and—"

"Don't lecture me, Ethel!"

"And you're a month behind on everything."

"That's enough."

"Ever since you took the Hailey case. That's all you think about. You're obsessed with it. It's going to break us."

"Us! How many paychecks have you missed, Ethel? How many of those bills are past due? Huh?"

"Several."

"But no more than usual, right?"

"Yes, but what about next month? The trial is four weeks away."

"Shut up, Ethel. Just shut up. If you can't take the pressure, then quit. If you can't keep your mouth shut, then you're fired."

"You'd like to fire me, wouldn't you?"

"I could care less."

She was a tough, hard woman. Fourteen years with Lucien had toughened her skin and hardened her conscience, but she was a woman nonetheless, and at this moment her lip started to quiver, and her eyes watered. She dropped her head.

"I'm sorry," she muttered. "I'm just worried."

"Worried about what?"

"Me and Bud."

"What's wrong with Bud?"

"He's a very sick man."

"I know that."

"His blood pressure keeps acting up. Especially after the phone calls. He's had three strokes in five years, and he's due for another one. He's scared; we're both scared."

"How many phone calls?"

"Several. They threaten to burn our house or blow it up. They always tell us they know where we live, and if Hailey is acquitted, then they'll burn it or stick dynamite under it while we are asleep. A couple have threatened to kill us. It's just not worth it."

"Maybe you should quit."

"And starve? Bud hasn't worked in ten years, you know that. Where else would I work?"

"Look, Ethel, I've had threats too. I don't take them seriously. I promised Carla I'd give up the case before I endangered my family, and you should be comforted by that. You and Bud should relax. The threats are not serious. There are a lot of nuts out there."

"That's what worries me. People are crazy enough to do something."

"Naw, you worry too much. I'll tell Ozzie to watch your house a bit closer."

"Will you do that?"

"Sure. They've been watching mine. Take my word, Ethel, there's nothing to worry about. Probably just some young punks."

She wiped her eyes. "I'm sorry for crying, and I'm sorry for being so irritable lately."

You've been irritable for forty years, Jake thought. "That's okay."

"What about these?" she asked, pointing to the invoices.

"I'll get the money. Don't worry about it."

———————

Willie Hastings finished the second shift at 10:00 P.M. and punched the clock next to Ozzie's office. He drove straight to the Hailey house. It was his night to sleep on the couch. Someone slept on Gwen's couch every night; a brother, a cousin, or a friend. Wednesday was his night.

It was impossible to sleep with the lights on. Tonya refused to go near the bed unless every light in the house was on. Those men could be in the dark, waiting for her. She had seen them many times crawling along the floor toward her bed, and lurking in the closets. She had heard their voices outside her window, and she had seen their bloodshot eyes peering in, watching her as she got ready for bed. She heard noises in the attic, like the footsteps of the bulky cowboy boots they had kicked her with. She knew they were up there, waiting for everyone to go to sleep so they could come down and take her back to the woods. Once a week her mother and oldest brother climbed the folding stairs and inspected the attic with a flashlight and a pistol.

Not a single room in the house could be dark when she went to bed. One night, as she lay wide awake next to her mother, a light in the hall burned out. She screamed violently until Gwen's brother drove to Clanton to an all-night quick shop for more bulbs.

She slept with her mother, who held her firmly for hours until the demons faded into the night and she drifted away. At first, Gwen had trouble with the lights, but after five weeks she napped periodically through the night. The small body next to her wiggled and jerked even while it slept.

Willie said good night to the boys and kissed Tonya. He showed her his gun and promised to stay awake on the couch. He walked through the house and checked the closets. When Tonya was satisfied, she lay next to her mother and stared at the ceiling. She cried softly.

Around midnight, Willie took off his boots and relaxed on the couch. He removed his holster and placed the gun on the floor. He was almost asleep when he heard the scream. It was the horrible, high-pitched cry of a child being tortured. He grabbed his gun and ran to the bedroom. Tonya was sitting on the bed, facing the wall, screaming and shaking. She had seen them in the window, waiting for her. Gwen hugged her. The three boys ran to the foot of the bed and watched helplessly. Carl Lee, Jr., went to the window and saw nothing. They had been through it many times in five weeks, and knew there was little they could do.

Gwen soothed her and laid her head gently on the pillow. "It's okay, baby, Momma's here and Uncle Willie's here. Nobody's gonna get you. It's okay, baby."

She wanted Uncle Willie to sit under the window with his gun and the boys to sleep on the floor around the bed. They took their positions. She moaned pitifully for a few moments, then grew quiet and still.

Willie sat on the floor by the window until they were all asleep. He carried the boys one at a time to their beds and tucked them in. He sat under her window and waited for the morning sun.

Jake and Atcavage met for lunch at Claude's on Friday. They ordered ribs and slaw. The place was packed as usual, and for the first time in four weeks there were no strange faces. The regulars talked and gossiped like old times. Claude was in fine form—ranting and scolding and cursing his loyal customers. Claude was one of those rare people who could curse a man and make him enjoy it.

Atcavage had watched the venue hearing, and would have testified had he been needed. The bank had discouraged his testifying, and Jake did not want to cause trouble. Bankers have an innate fear of courtrooms, and Jake admired his friend for overcoming this paranoia and attending the hearing. In doing so, he became the first banker in the history of Ford County to voluntarily appear in a courtroom without a subpoena while court was in session. Jake was proud of him.

Claude raced by and told them they had ten minutes, so shut up and eat. Jake finished a rib and mopped his face. "Say, Stan, speaking of loans, I need to borrow five thousand for ninety days, unsecured."

"Who said anything about loans?"

"You said something about banks."

"I thought we were condemning Buckley. I was enjoying it."

"You shouldn't criticize, Stan. It's an easy habit to acquire and an impossible one to break. It robs your soul of character."

"I'm terribly sorry. How can you ever forgive me?"

"About the loan?"

"Okay. Why do you need it?"

"Why is that relevant?"

"What do you mean, 'Why is that relevant?'"

"Look Stan, all you should worry about is whether or not I can repay the money in ninety days."

"Okay. Can you repay the money in ninety days?"

"Good question. Of course I can."

The banker smiled. "Hailey's got you bogged down, huh?"

The lawyer smiled. "Yeah," he admitted. "It's hard to

concentrate on anything else. The trial is three weeks from Monday, and until then I won't concentrate on anything else."

"How much will you make off this case?"

"Nine hundred minus ten thousand."

"Nine hundred dollars!"

"Yeah, he couldn't borrow on his land, remember?"

"Cheap shot."

"Of course, if you'd loan Carl Lee the money on his land, then I wouldn't have to borrow any."

"I prefer to loan it to you."

"Great. When can I get a check?"

"You sound desperate."

"I know how long you guys take, with your loan committees and auditors and vice-presidents here and vice-presidents there, and maybe a vice-president will finally approve my loan in a month or so, if the manual says he can and if the home office is in the right mood. I know how you operate."

Atcavage looked at his watch. "Three o'clock soon enough?"

"I guess."

"Unsecured?"

Jake wiped his mouth and leaned across the table. He spoke quietly. "My house is a landmark with landmark mortgages, and you've got the lien cn my car, remember? I'll give you the first mortgage on my daughter, but if you try to foreclose I'll kill you. Now what security do you have in mind?"

"Sorry I asked."

"When can I get the check?"

"Three P.M."

Claude appeared and refilled the tea glasses. "You got five minutes," he said loudly.

"Eight," replied Jake.

"Listen Mr. Big Shot," Claude said with a grin. "This ain't no courtroom, and your picturc in the paper ain't worth two cents in here. I said five minutes."

"Just as well. My ribs were tough anyway."

"I notice you didn't leave any."

"Might as well eat them, as much as they cost."

"They cost more if you complain."

"We're leaving," Atcavage said as he stood and threw a dollar on the table.

———

Sunday afternoon the Haileys picnicked under the tree away from the violence under the basketball goal. The first heat wave of the summer had settled in, and the heavy, sticky humidity hung close to the ground and penetrated the shade. Gwen swatted flies as the children and their daddy ate warm fried chicken and sweated. The children ate hurriedly and ran to a new swing Ozzie had installed for the children of his inmates.

"What'd they do at Whitfield?" Gwen asked.

"Nothin' really. Asked a bunch of questions, made me do some tests. Bunch of crap."

"How'd they treat you?"

"With handcuffs and padded walls."

"No kiddin'. They put you in a room with padded walls?" Gwen was amused and managed a rare giggle.

"Sure did. They watched me like I was some animal. Said I was famous. My guards told me they was proud of me —one was white and one was black. Said that I did the right thing and they hoped I got off. They was nice to me."

"What'd the doctors say?"

"They won't say nothin' till we get to trial, and then they'll say I'm fine."

"How do you know what they'll say?"

"Jake told me. He ain't been wrong yet."

"Has he found you a doctor?"

"Yeah, some crazy drunk he drug up somewhere. Says he's a psychiatrist. We've talked a couple of times in Ozzie's office."

"What'd he say?"

"Not much. Jake said he'll say whatever we want him to say."

"Must be a real good doctor."

"He'd fit in good with those folks in Whitfield."

"Where's he from?"

"Jackson, I think. He wasn't too sure of anything. He acted like I was gonna kill him too. I swear he was drunk both times we talked. He asked some questions that neither one of us understood. Took some notes like a real big shot. Said he thought he could help me. I asked Jake about him. Jake said not to worry, that he would be sober at the trial. But I think Jake's worried too."

"Then why are we usin' him?"

" 'Cause he's free. Owes somebody some favors. A real shrink'd cost over a thousand dollars just to evaluate me, and then another thousand or so to come testify at trial. A cheap shrink. Needless to say, I can't pay it."

Gwen lost her smile and looked away. "We need some money around the house," she said without looking at him.

"How much?"

"Coupla hundred for groceries and bills."

"How much you got?"

"Less than fifty."

"I'll see what I can do."

She looked at him. "What does that mean? What makes you think you can get money while you're in jail?"

Carl Lee raised his eyebrows and pointed at his wife. She was not to question him. He still wore the pants, even though he put them on in jail. He was the boss.

"I'm sorry," she whispered.

24 Reverend Agee peered through a crack in one of the huge stained glass windows of his church and watched with satisfaction as the clean Cadillacs and Lincolns arrived just before five Sunday afternoon. He had called a meeting of the council to assess the Hailey situation and plan strategy for the final three weeks before the trial, and to prepare for the arrival of the NAACP lawyers. The weekly collections had gone well—over seven thousand dollars had been gathered throughout the county and almost six thousand had been deposited by the reverend in a special account for the Carl Lee Hailey Legal Defense Fund. None had been given to the family. Agee was waiting for the NAACP to direct him in spending the money, most of which, he thought, should go to the defense fund. The sisters in the church could feed the family if they got hungry. The cash was needed elsewhere.

The council talked of ways to raise more money. It was not easy getting money from poor people, but the issue was hot and the time was right, and if they didn't raise it now it would not be raised. They agreed to meet the following day at the Springdale Church in Clanton. The NAACP people were expected in town by morning. No press; it was to be a work session.

Norman Reinfeld was a thirty-year-old genius in criminal law who held the record for finishing Harvard's law school at the age of twenty-one, and after graduation declined a most generous offer to join his father and grandfather's prestigious Wall Street law factory, opting instead to take a job with the NAACP and spend his time fighting furiously to keep Southern blacks off death row. He was very good at what he did although, through no fault of his own, he was not very successful at what he did. Most Southern blacks along with most Southern whites who faced the gas chamber deserved the gas chamber. But Reinfeld and his team of capital murder defense specialists won more than their share, and even in the ones they lost they usually managed to keep the convicts alive through a myriad of exhausting delays and appeals. Four of his former clients had either been gassed, electrocuted, or lethally injected, and that was four too many for Reinfeld. He had watched them all die, and with each execution he renewed his vow to break any law, violate any ethic, contempt any court, disrespect any judge, ignore any mandate, or do whatever it took to prevent a human from legally killing another human. He didn't worry much about the illegal killings of humans, such as those killings so artfully and cruelly achieved by his clients. It wasn't his business to think about those killings, so he didn't. Instead he vented his righteous and sanctimonious anger and zeal at the legal killings.

He seldom slept more than three hours a night. Sleep was difficult with thirty-one clients on death row. Plus seventeen clients awaiting trial. Plus eight egotistical attorneys to supervise. He was thirty and looked forty-five. He was old, abrasive, and ill-tempered. In the normal course of his business, he would have been much too busy to attend a gathering of local black ministers in Clanton, Mississippi. But this was not the normal case. This was Hailey. The vigilante. The father driven to revenge. The most famous criminal case in the country at the moment. This was Mississippi, where for years whites shot blacks for any reason or no reason and no one cared; where whites raped blacks and it was considered sport; where blacks were hanged for fighting back. And now a black father had killed two white men who raped his daughter, and faced the gas chamber for something that thirty years earlier would have gone unnoticed had he been white. This was the case, his case, and he would handle it personally.

On Monday he was introduced to the council by Reverend Agee, who opened the meeting with a lengthy and detailed review of the activities in Ford County. Reinfeld was brief. He and his team could not represent Mr. Hailey because he had not been hired by Mr. Hailey, so a meeting was imperative. Today, preferably. Tomorrow morning at the latest, because he had a flight out of Memphis at noon. He was needed in a murder trial somewhere in Georgia. Reverend Agee promised to arrange a meeting with the defendant as soon as possible. He was friends with the sheriff. Fine, said Reinfeld, just get it done.

"How much money have you raised?" Reinfeld asked.

"Fifteen thousand from you folks," Agee answered.

"I know that. How much locally?"

"Six thousand," Agee said proudly.

"Six thousand!" repeated Reinfeld. "Is that all? I thought you people were organized. Where's all this great local support you were talking about? Six thousand! How much more can you raise? We've only got three weeks."

The council members were silent. This Jew had a lot of nerve. The only white man in the group and he was on the attack.

"How much do we need?" asked Agee.

"That depends, Reverend, on how good a defense you want for Mr. Hailey. I've only got eight other attorneys on my staff. Five are in trial at this very moment. We've got thirty-one capital murder convictions at various stages of appeal. We've got seventeen trials scheduled in ten states over the next five months. We get ten requests each week to represent defendants, eight of which we turn down because we simply don't have the staff or the money. For Mr. Hailey, fifteen thousand has been contributed by two local chapters and the home office. Now you tell me that only six thousand has been raised locally. That's twenty-one thousand. For that amount you'll get the best defense we can afford. Two attorneys, at least one psychiatrist, but nothing fancy. Twenty-one thousand gets a good defense, but not what I had in mind."

"What exactly did you have in mind?"

"A first-class defense. Three or four attorneys. A battery of psychiatrists. Half dozen investigators. A jury psychologist, just to name a few. This is not your run-of-the-mill murder case. I want to win. I was led to believe that you folks wanted to win."

"How much?" asked Agee.

"Fifty thousand, minimum. A hundred thousand would be nice."

"Look, Mr. Reinfeld, you're in Mississippi. Our people are poor. They've given generously so far, but there's no way we can raise another thirty thousand here."

Reinfeld adjusted his horn-rimmed glasses and

scratched his graying beard. "How much more can you raise?"

"Another five thousand, maybe."

"That's not much money."

"Not to you, but it is to the black folk of Ford County."

Reinfeld studied the floor and continued stroking his beard. "How much has the Memphis chapter given?"

"Five thousand," answered someone from Memphis.

"Atlanta?"

"Five thousand."

"How about the state chapter?"

"Which state?"

"Mississippi."

"None."

"None?"

"None."

"Why not?"

"Ask him," Agee said, pointing at Reverend Henry Hillman, the state director.

"Uh, we tryin' to raise some money now," Hillman said weakly. "But—"

"How much have you raised so far?" asked Agee.

"Well, uh, we got—"

"Nothin', right? You ain't raised nothin', have you, Hillman?" Agee said loudly.

"Come on, Hillman, tell us how much you raised," chimed in Reverend Roosevelt, vice-chairman of the council.

Hillman was dumbfounded and speechless. He had been sitting quietly on the front pew minding his own business, half asleep. Suddenly he was under attack.

"The state chapter will contribute."

"Sure you will, Hillman. You folks at state are constantly badgerin' us locals to contribute here and donate there for this cause and that cause, and we never see any of the money. You always cryin' about bein' so broke, and we're always sendin' money to state. But when we need help, state don't do a thing but show up here and talk."

"That's not true."

"Don't start lyin', Hillman."

Reinfeld was embarrassed and immediately aware that

a nerve had been touched. "Gentlemen, gentlemen, let's move on," he said diplomatically.

"Good idea," Hillman said.

"When can we meet with Mr. Hailey?" Reinfeld asked.

"I'll arrange a meetin' for in the mornin'," Agee said.

"Where can we meet?"

"I suggest we meet in Sheriff Walls' office in the jail. He's black, you know, the only black sheriff in Mississippi."

"Yes, I've heard."

"I think he'll let us meet in his office."

"Good. Who is Mr. Hailey's attorney?"

"Local boy. Jake Brigance."

"Make sure he's invited. We'll ask him to help us on the case. It'll ease the pain."

Ethel's obnoxious, high-pitched, bitchy voice broke the tranquility of the late afternoon and startled her boss. "Mr. Brigance, Sheriff Walls is on line two," she said through the intercom.

"Okay."

"Do you need me for anything else, sir?"

"No. See you in the morning."

Jake punched line two. "Hello, Ozzie. What's up?"

"Listen Jake, we've got a bunch of NAACP big shots in town."

"What else is new?"

"No, this is different. They wanna meet with Carl Lee in the mornin'."

"Why?"

"Some guy named Reinfeld."

"I've heard of him. He heads up their capital murder team. Norman Reinfeld."

"Yeah, that's him."

"I've been waiting for this."

"Well, he's here, and he wants to talk to Carl Lee."

"Why are you involved?"

"Reverend Agee called me. He wants a favor, of course. He asked me to call you."

"The answer is no. Emphatically no."

Ozzie paused a few seconds. "Jake, they want you to be present."

"You mean I'm invited?"

"Yes. Agee said Reinfeld insisted on it. He wants you to be here."

"Where?"

"In my office. Nine A.M."

Jake breathed deeply and replied slowly. "Okay, I'll be there. Where's Carl Lee?"

"In his cell."

"Get him in your office. I'll be there in five minutes."

"What for?"

"We need to have a prayer meeting."

Reinfeld and Reverends Agee, Roosevelt, and Hillman sat in a perfect row of folding chairs and faced the sheriff, the defendant, and Jake, who puffed a cheap cigar in a determined effort to pollute the small office. He puffed mightily and stared nonchalantly at the floor, trying his best to show nothing but absolute contempt for Reinfeld and the reverends. Reinfeld was no pushover when it came to arrogance, and his disdain for this simple, small-time lawyer was not well hidden because he made no attempt to hide it. He was arrogant and insolent by nature. Jake had to work at it.

"Who called this meeting?" Jake asked impatiently, after a long, uncomfortable silence.

"Uh, well, I guess we did," answered Agee as he searched Reinfeld for guidance.

"Well, get on with it. What do you want?"

"Take it easy now, Jake," Ozzie said. "Reverend Agee asked me to arrange the meeting so Carl Lee could meet Mr. Reinfeld here."

"Fine. They've met. Now what, Mr. Reinfeld?"

"I'm here to offer my services, and the services of my staff and the entire NAACP to Mr. Hailey," said Reinfeld.

"What type of services?" asked Jake.

"Legal, of course."

"Carl Lee, did you ask Mr. Reinfeld to come here?" asked Jake.

"Nope."

"Sounds like solicitation to me, Mr. Reinfeld."

"Skip the lecture, Mr. Brigance. You know what I do, and you know why I'm here."

"So you chase all your cases?"

"We don't chase anything. We're called in by local NAACP members and other civil rights activists. We handle only capital murder cases, and we're very good at what we do."

"I suppose you're the only attorney competent to handle a case of this magnitude?"

"I've handled my share."

"And lost your share."

"Most of my cases are supposed to be lost."

"I see. Is that your position on this case? Do you expect to lose it?"

Reinfeld picked at his beard and glared at Jake. "I didn't come here to argue with you, Mr. Brigance."

"I know. You came here to offer your formidable legal skills to a defendant who's never heard of you and happens to be satisfied with his attorney. You came here to take my client. I know exactly why you're here."

"I'm here because the NAACP invited me. Nothing more or less."

"I see. Do you get all your cases from the NAACP?"

"I work for the NAACP, Mr. Brigance. I'm in charge of its capital murder defense team. I go where the NAACP sends me."

"How many clients do you have?"

"Several dozen. Why is that important?"

"Did they all have attorneys before you pushed yourself into their cases?"

"Some did, some didn't. We always try to work with the local attorney."

Jake smiled. "That's marvelous. You're offering me a chance to carry your briefcase and chauffeur you around Clanton. I might even get to fetch you a sandwich during the noon recess. What a thrill."

Carl Lee sat frozen with arms crossed and his eyes fixed on a spot in the rug. The reverends watched him closely, waiting for him to say something to his lawyer, to tell him to shut up, that he was fired and the NAACP lawyers would handle the case. They watched and waited, but Carl Lee just sat calmly and listened.

"We have a lot to offer, Mr. Hailey," Reinfeld said. It was best to stay calm until the defendant decided who would represent him. A tantrum might ruin things.

"Such as?" Jake asked.

"Staff, resources, expertise, experienced trial lawyers who do nothing but capital defense. Plus we have a number of highly competent doctors we use in these cases. You name it, we have it."

"How much money do you have to spend?"

"That's none of your business."

"Is that so? Is it Mr. Hailey's business? After all, it's his case. Perhaps Mr. Hailey would like to know how much you have to spend in his defense. Would you, Mr. Hailey?"

"Yep."

"All right, Mr. Reinfeld, how much do you have to spend?"

Reinfeld squirmed and looked hard at the reverends, who looked hard at Carl Lee.

"Approximately twenty thousand, so far," Reinfeld admitted sheepishly.

Jake laughed and shook his head in disbelief. "Twenty thousand! Y'all are really serious about this, aren't you? Twenty thousand! I thought you guys played in the big leagues. You raised a hundred and fifty thousand for the cop killer in Birmingham last year. And he was convicted, by the way. You spent a hundred thousand for the whore in Shreveport who killed her customer. And she, too, was convicted, I might add. And you think this case is worth only twenty thousand."

"How much do you have to spend?" asked Reinfeld.

"If you can explain to me how that's any of your business, I'll be glad to discuss it with you."

Reinfeld started to speak, then leaned forward and rubbed his temples. "Why don't you talk to him, Reverend Agee."

The reverends stared at Carl Lee. They wished they were alone with him, with no white folks around. They could talk to him like he was a nigger. They could explain things to him; tell him to fire this young white boy and get him some real lawyers. NAACP lawyers. Lawyers who knew how to fight for blacks. But they were not alone with him, and they couldn't curse him. They had to show respect for the white folks present. Agee spoke first.

"Look here, Carl Lee, we tryin' to help you. We brought in Mr. Reinfeld here, and he's got all his lawyers and everbody at your disposal, to help you now. We ain't got nothin' against Jake here; he's a fine young lawyer. But he can work with Mr. Reinfeld. We don't want you to fire Jake; we just want you to hire Mr. Reinfeld too. They can all work together."

"Forget that," said Jake.

Agee paused and looked helplessly at Jake.

"Come on, Jake. We ain't got nothin' against you. It's a big chance for you. You can work with some real big lawyers. Get some real good experience. We—"

"Let me make it real clear, Reverend. If Carl Lee wants your lawyers, fine. But I'm not playing gofer for anyone. I'm either in or out. Nothing in between. My case or your case. The courtroom is not big enough for me, Reinfeld, and Rufus Buckley."

Reinfeld rolled his eyes and looked at the ceiling, shaking his head slowly and grinning with an arrogant little smirk.

"You sayin' it's up to Carl Lee?" asked Reverend Agee.

"Of course it's up to him. He's hired me. He can fire me. He's already done it once. I'm not the one facing the gas chamber."

"How 'bout it, Carl Lee?" asked Agee.

Carl Lee uncrossed his arms and stared at Agee. "This twenty thousand, what's it for?"

"Really, it's more like thirty thousand," answered Reinfeld. "The local folks have pledged another ten thousand. The money will be used for your defense. None of it's attorney fees. We'll need two or three investigators. Two, maybe three, psychiatric experts. We often use a jury psychologist to assist us in selecting the jury. Our defenses are very expensive."

"Uh huh. How much money has been raised by local people?" asked Carl Lee.

"About six thousand," answered Reinfeld.

"Who collected this money?"

Reinfeld looked at Agee. "The churches," answered the reverend.

"Who collected the money from the churches?" asked Carl Lee.

"We did," answered Agee.

"You mean, you did," said Carl Lee.

"Well, uh, right. I mean, each church gave the money to me, and I deposited it in a special bank account."

"Yeah, and you deposited every nickel you received?"

"Of course I did."

"Of course. Let me ask you this. How much of the money have you offered to my wife and kids?"

Agee looked a bit pale, or as pale as possible, and quickly searched the faces of the other reverends, who, at the moment, were preoccupied with a stink bug on the carpet. They offered no help. Each knew Agee had been taking his cut, and each knew the family had received nothing. Agee had profited more than the family. They knew it, and Carl Lee knew it.

"How much, Reverend?" repeated Carl Lee.

"Well, we thought the money—"

"How much, Reverend?"

"The money is gonna be spent on lawyer fees and stuff like that."

"That ain't what you told your church, is it? You said it was for the support of the family. You almost cried when you talked about how my family might starve to death if the folks didn't donate all they could. Didn't you, Reverend?"

"The money's for you, Carl Lee. You and your family. Right now we think it could be better spent on your defense."

"And what if I don't want your lawyers? What happens to the twenty thousand?"

Jake chuckled. "Good question. What happens to the money if Mr. Hailey doesn't hire you, Mr. Reinfeld?"

"It's not my money," answered Reinfeld.

"Reverend Agee?" asked Jake.

The reverend had had enough. He grew defiant and belligerent. He pointed at Carl Lee. "Listen here, Carl Lee. We busted our butts to raise this money. Six thousand bucks from the poor people of this county, people who didn't have it to give. We worked hard for this money, and it was given by poor people, your people, people on food stamps and welfare and Medicaid, people who couldn't afford to donate a dime. But they gave for one reason, and only one reason: they believe in you and what you did, and they want you to walk outta that courtroom a free man. Don't say you don't want the money."

"Don't preach to me," Carl Lee replied softly. "You say the poor folks of this county gave six thousand?"

"Right?"

"Where'd the rest of the money come from?"

"NAACP. Five thousand from Atlanta, five from Memphis, and five from national. And it's strictly for your defense fees."

"If I use Mr. Reinfeld here?"

"Right."

"And if I don't use him, the fifteen thousand disappears?"

"Right."

"What about the other six thousand?"

"Good question. We ain't discussed that yet. We thought you'd appreciate us for raisin' money and tryin' to help. We're offerin' the best lawyers and obviously you don't care."

The room was silent for an eternity as the preachers, the lawyers, and the sheriff waited for some message from the defendant. Carl Lee chewed on his lower lip and stared at the floor. Jake lit another cigar. He had been fired before, and he could handle it again.

"You gotta know right now?" Carl Lee asked finally.

"No," said Agee.

"Yes," said Reinfeld. "The trial is less than three weeks away, and we're two months behind already. My time is too valuable to wait on you, Mr. Hailey. Either you hire me now or forget it. I've got a plane to catch."

"Well, I'll tell you what you do, Mr. Reinfeld. You go and catch your plane and don't ever worry 'bout comin' back to Clanton on my behalf. I'll take my chances with my friend

25 The Ford County Klavern was founded at midnight, Thursday, July 11, in a small pasture next to a dirt road deep in a forest somewhere in the northern part of the county. The six inductees stood nervously before the huge burning cross and repeated strange words offered by a wizard. A dragon and two dozen white-robed Klansmen watched and chanted when appropriate. A guard with a gun stood quietly down the road, occasionally watching the ceremony but primarily watching for uninvited guests. There were none.

Precisely at midnight the six fell to their knees and closed their eyes as the white hoods were ceremoniously placed onto their heads. They were Klansmen now, these six. Freddie Cobb, brother of the deceased, Jerry Maples, Clifton Cobb, Ed Wilburn, Morris Lancaster, and Terrell Grist. The grand dragon hovered above each one and chanted the sacred vows of klanhood. The flames from the cross scorched the faces of the new members as they knelt and quietly suffocated under the heavy robes and hoods. Sweat dripped from their red faces as they prayed fervently for the dragon to shut up with his nonsense and finish the ceremony. When the chanting stopped, the new members rose and quickly retreated from the cross. They were embraced by their new brothers, who grabbed their shoulders firmly and pounded primal incantations onto their sweaty collarbones. The heavy hoods were removed, and the Klansmen, both new members and old, walked proudly from the pasture and into the rustic cabin across the dirt road. The same guard sat on the front steps as the whiskey was poured around the table and plans were made for the trial of Carl Lee Hailey.

———

Deputy Pirtle pulled the graveyard shift, ten to six, and had stopped for coffee and pie at Gurdy's all-night diner on the highway north of town when his radio blared out the news that he was wanted at the jail. It was three minutes after midnight, Friday morning.

Pirtle left his pie and drove a mile south to the jail. "What's up?" he asked the dispatcher.

"We got a call a few minutes ago, anonymous, from someone lookin' for the sheriff. I explained that he was not on duty, so they asked for whoever was on duty. That's you. They said it was very important, and they'd call back in fifteen minutes."

Pirtle poured some coffee and relaxed in Ozzie's big chair. The phone rang. "It's for you," yelled the dispatcher.

"Hello," answered Pirtle.

"Who's this?" asked the voice.

"Deputy Joe Pirtle. Who's this?"

"Where's the sheriff?"

"Asleep, I reckon."

"Okay listen, and listen real good because this is important and I ain't callin' again. You know that Hailey nigger?"

"Yeah."

"You know his lawyer, Brigance?"

"Yeah."

"Then listen. Sometime between now and three A.M., they're gonna blow up his house."

"Who?"

"Brigance."

"No, I mean who's gonna blow up his house?"

"Don't worry about that, Deputy, just listen to me. This ain't no joke, and if you think it's a joke, just sit there and wait for his house to go up. It may happen any minute."

The voice became silent but did not disappear. Pirtle listened. "You still there?"

"Good night, Deputy." The receiver clicked.

Pirtle jumped to his feet and ran to the dispatcher. "Did you listen?"

"Of course I did."

"Call Ozzie and tell him to get down here. I'll be at the Brigance house."

Pirtle hid his patrol car in a driveway on Monroe Street and walked across the front lawns to Jake's house. He saw nothing. It was 12:55 A.M. He walked around the house with his flashlight and noticed nothing unusual. Every house on the street was dark and asleep. He unscrewed the light bulb on the front porch and took a seat in a wicker chair. He waited. The odd-looking foreign car was parked next to the Oldsmobile under the veranda. He would wait and ask Ozzie about notifying Jake.

Headlights appeared at the end of the street. Pirtle slumped lower in the chair, certain he could not be seen. A red pickup moved suspiciously toward the Brigance house but did not stop. He sat up and watched it disappear down the street.

Moments later he noticed two figures jogging from the direction of the square. He unbuttoned his holster and removed his service revolver. The first figure was much larger than the second, and seemed to run with more ease and grace. It was Ozzie. The other was Nesbit. Pirtle met the two in the driveway and they retreated into the darkness of the front porch. They whispered and watched the street.

"What exactly did he say?" asked Ozzie.

"Said someone's gonna blow up Jake's house between now and three A.M. Said it was no joke."

"Is that all?"

"Yep. He wasn't real friendly."

"How long you been here?"

"Twenty minutes."

Ozzie turned to Nesbit. "Give me your radio and go hide in the backyard. Stay quiet and keep your eyes open."

Nesbit scurried to the rear of the house and found a small opening between the shrubs along the back fence. Crawling on all fours, he disappeared into the shrubs. From his nest he could see the entire rear of the house.

"You gonna tell Jake?" asked Pirtle.

"Not yet. We might in a minute. If we knock on the door, they'll be turnin' on lights and we don't need that right now."

"Yeah, but what if Jake hears us and comes through the door firin' away. He might think we're just a couple of niggers tryin' to break in."

Ozzie watched the street and said nothing.

"Look, Ozzie, put yourself in his place. The cops have

your house surrounded at one o'clock in the mornin' waitin' for somebody to throw a bomb. Now, would you wanna stay in bed asleep or would you wanna know about it?"

Ozzie studied the houses in the distance.

"Listen, Sheriff, we better wake them up. What if we don't stop whoever's plannin' this, and somebody inside the house gets hurt? We get blamed, right?"

Ozzie stood and punched the doorbell. "Unscrew that light bulb," he ordered, pointing at the porch ceiling.

"I already did."

Ozzie punched the doorbell again. The wooden door swung open, and Jake walked to the storm door and stared at the sheriff. He was wearing a wrinkled nightshirt that fell just below his knees, and he held a loaded .38 in his right hand. He slowly opened the storm door.

"What is it, Ozzie?" he asked.

"Can I come in?"

"Yeah. What's going on?"

"Stay here on the porch," Ozzie told Pirtle. "I'll be just a minute."

Ozzie closed the front door behind them and turned off the light in the foyer. They sat in the dark living room overlooking the porch and the front yard.

"Start talking," Jake said.

" 'Bout a half hour ago we took an anonymous call from someone who said that someone planned to blow up your house between now and three A.M. We're takin' it serious."

"Thanks."

"I've got Pirtle on the front porch and Nesbit in the backyard. 'Bout ten minutes ago Pirtle saw a pickup drive by real interested like, but that's all we've seen."

"Have you searched around the house?"

"Yeah, nothin'. They ain't been here yet. But somethin' tells me this is the real thing."

"Why?"

"Just a hunch."

Jake laid the .38 beside him on the couch and rubbed his temples. "What's your suggestion?"

"Sit and wait. That's all we can do. You got a rifle?"

"I've got enough guns to invade Cuba."

"Why don't you get it and get dressed. Take a position

in one of those cute little windows upstairs. We'll hide outside and wait."

"Have you got enough men?"

"Yeah, I figure there'll only be one or two of them."

"Who's them?"

"Don't know. Could be the Klan, could be some freelancers. Who knows?"

Both men sat in deep thought and stared at the dark street. They could see the top of Pirtle's head as he slumped in the wicker chair just outside the window.

"Jake, you remember those three civil rights workers killed by the Klan back in '64? Found them buried in a levee down around Philadelphia."

"Sure. I was a kid, but I remember."

"Those boys would've never been found if someone hadn't told where they was. That someone was in the Klan. An informant. Seems like that always happened to the Klan. Somebody on the inside was always squealin'."

"You think it's the Klan?"

"Sure looks like it. If it was just one or two freelancers, then who else would know about it? The bigger the group, the better the chance of someone tippin' us off."

"That makes sense, but for some reason I'm not comforted by it."

"Of course, it could be a joke."

"Nobody's laughing."

"You gonna tell your wife?"

"Yeah. I'd better go do that."

"I would too. But don't be turnin' on lights. You might scare them off."

"But I would like to scare them off."

"And I'd like to catch them. If we don't catch them now, they'll try again, and next time they might forget to call us ahead of time."

Carla dressed hurriedly in the dark. She was terrified. Jake laid Hanna on the couch in the den, where she mumbled something and went back to sleep. Carla held her head and watched Jake load a rifle.

"I'll be upstairs·in the guest room. Don't turn on any lights. The cops have the place surrounded, so don't worry."

"Don't worry! Are you crazy?"

"Try to go back to sleep."

"Sleep! Jake, you've lost your mind."

They didn't wait long. From his vantage point somewhere deep in the shrubs in front of the house, Ozzie saw him first: a lone figure walking casually down the street from the direction opposite the square. He had in his hand a small box or case of some sort. When he was two houses away, he left the street and cut through the front lawns of the neighbors. Ozzie pulled his revolver and nightstick and watched the man walk directly toward him. Jake had him in the scope of his deer rifle. Pirtle crawled like a snake across the porch and into the shrubs, ready to strike.

Suddenly, the figure darted across the front lawn next door and to the side of Jake's house. He carefully laid the small suitcase under Jake's bedroom window. As he turned to run, a huge black nightstick crashed across the side of his head, ripping his right ear in two places, each barely hanging to his head. He screamed and fell to the ground.

"I got him!" Ozzie yelled. Pirtle and Nesbit sprinted to the side of the house. Jake calmly walked down the stairs.

"I'll be back in a minute," he told Carla.

Ozzie grabbed the suspect by the neck and sat him next to the house. He was conscious but dazed. The suitcase was inches away.

"What's your name?" Ozzie demanded.

He moaned and clutched his head and said nothing.

"I asked you a question," Ozzie said as he hovered over his suspect. Pirtle and Nesbit stood nearby, guns drawn, too frightened to speak or move. Jake stared at the suitcase.

"I ain't sayin'," came the reply.

Ozzie raised the nightstick high over his head and drove it solidly against the man's right ankle. The crack of the bone was sickening.

He howled and grabbed his leg. Ozzie kicked him in the face. He fell backward and his head smashed into the side of the house. He rolled to his side and groaned in pain.

Jake knelt above the suitcase and put his ear next to it. He jumped and retreated. "It's ticking," he said weakly.

Ozzie bent over the suspect and laid the nightstick softly against his nose. "I've got one more question before I break ever bone in your body. What's in the box?"

No answer.

Ozzie recoiled the nightstick and broke the other ankle. "What's in the box!" he shouted.

"Dynamite!" came the anguished reply.

Pirtle dropped his gun. Nesbit's blood pressure shot through his cap and he leaned on the house. Jake turned white and his knees vibrated. He ran through the front door yelling at Carla. "Get the car keys! Get the car keys!"

"What for?" she asked nervously.

"Just do as I say. Get the car keys and get in the car."

He lifted Hanna and carried her through the kitchen, into the carport, and laid her in the back seat of Carla's Cutlass. He took Carla by the arm and helped her into the car. "Leave, and don't come back for thirty minutes."

"Jake, what's going on?" she demanded.

"I'll tell you later. There's no time now. Just leave. Go drive around for thirty minutes. Stay away from this street."

"But why, Jake? What have you found?"

"Dynamite."

She backed out of the driveway and disappeared.

When Jake returned to the side of the house, the suspect's left hand had been handcuffed to the gas meter next to the window. He was moaning, mumbling, cursing. Ozzie carefully lifted the suitcase by the handle and sat it neatly between the suspect's broken legs. Ozzie kicked both legs to spread them. He groaned louder. Ozzie, the deputies, and Jake backed away slowly and watched him. He began to cry.

"I don't know how to defuse it," he said through clenched teeth.

"You'd better learn fast," Jake said, his voice somewhat stronger.

The suspect closed his eyes and lowered his head. He bit his lip and breathed loudly and rapidly. Sweat dripped from his chin and eyebrows. His ear was shredded and hung like a falling leaf. "Give me a flashlight."

Pirtle handed him a flashlight.

"I need both hands," he said.

"Try it with one," Ozzie said.

He placed his fingers gently on the latch and closed his eyes.

"Let's get outta here," Ozzie said. They ran around the corner of the house and into the carport, as far away as possible.

"Where's your family?" Ozzie asked.

"Gone. Recognize him?"

"Nope," said Ozzie.

"I never seen him," said Nesbit.

Pirtle shook his head.

Ozzie called the dispatcher, who called Deputy Riley, the self-trained explosives man for the county.

"What if he passes out and the bomb goes off?" Jake asked.

"You got insurance, don't you, Jake?" asked Nesbit.

"That's not funny."

"We'll give him a few minutes, then Pirtle can go check on him," said Ozzie.

"Why me?"

"Okay, Nesbit can go."

"I think Jake should go," said Nesbit. "It's his house."

"Very funny," said Jake.

They waited and chatted nervously. Nesbit made another stupid remark about insurance. "Quiet!" Jake said. "I heard something."

They froze. Seconds later the suspect yelled again. They ran back across the front yard, then slowly turned the corner. The empty suitcase had been tossed a few feet away. Next to the man was a neat pile of a dozen sticks of dynamite. Between his legs was a large, round-faced clock with wires bound together with silver electrical tape.

"Is it defused?" Ozzie asked anxiously.

"Yeah," he replied between heavy, rapid breaths.

Ozzie knelt before him and removed the clock and the wires. He did not touch the dynamite. "Where are your buddies?"

No response.

He removed his nightstick and moved closer to the man. "I'm gonna start breakin' ribs one at a time. You better start talkin'. Now where are your buddies?"

"Kiss my ass."

Ozzie stood and quickly looked around, not at Jake and the deputies, but at the house next door. Seeing nothing, he raised the nightstick. The suspect's left arm hung from the gas meter, and Ozzie planted the stick just below the left armpit. He squealed and jerked to the left. Jake almost felt sorry for him.

"Where are they?" Ozzie demanded.

No response.

Jake turned his head as the sheriff landed another blow to the ribs.

"Where are they?"

No response.

Ozzie raised the nightstick.

"Stop . . . please stop," the suspect begged.

"Where are they?"

"Down that way. A couple of blocks."

"How many?"

"One."

"What vehicle?"

"Pickup. Red GMC."

"Get the patrol cars," Ozzie ordered.

Jake waited impatiently under the carport for his wife to return. At two-fifteen she drove slowly into the driveway and parked.

"Is Hanna asleep?" Jake asked as he opened the door.

"Yes."

"Good. Leave her there. We'll be leaving in a few minutes."

"Where are we going?"

"We'll discuss it inside."

Jake poured the coffee and tried to act calm. Carla was scared and shaking and angry and making it difficult to act calm. He described the bomb and suspect and explained that Ozzie was searching for the accomplice.

"I want you and Hanna to go to Wilmington and stay with your parents until after the trial," he said.

She stared at the coffee and said nothing.

"I've already called your dad and explained everything.

They're scared too, and they insist you stay with them until this thing is over."

"And what if I don't want to go?"

"Please, Carla. How can you argue at a time like this?"

"What about you?"

"I'll be fine. Ozzie will give me a bodyguard and they'll watch the house around the clock. I'll sleep at the office some. I'll be safe, I promise."

She was not convinced.

"Look, Carla, I've got a thousand things on my mind right now. I've got a client facing the gas chamber and his trial is ten days away. I can't lose it. I'll work night and day from now until the twenty-second, and once the trial starts you won't see me anyway. The last thing I need is to be worried about you and Hanna. Please go."

"They were going to kill us, Jake. They tried to kill us."

He couldn't deny it.

"You promised to withdraw if the danger became real."

"It's out of the question. Noose would never allow me to withdraw at this late date."

"I feel as though you've lied to me."

"That's not fair. I think I underestimated this thing, and now it's too late."

She walked to the bedroom and began packing.

"The plane leaves Memphis at six-thirty. Your father will meet you at the Raleigh airport at nine-thirty."

"Yes, sir."

Fifteen minutes later they left Clanton. Jake drove and Carla ignored him. At five, they ate breakfast in the Memphis airport. Hanna was sleepy but excited about seeing her grandparents. Carla said little. She had much to say, but as a rule, they didn't argue in front of Hanna. She ate quietly and sipped her coffee and watched her husband casually read the paper as if nothing had happened.

Jake kissed them goodbye and promised to call every day. The plane left on time. At seven-thirty he was in Ozzie's office.

"Who is he?" Jake asked the sheriff.

"We have no idea. No wallet, no identification, nothin'. And he ain't talkin'."

"Does anybody recognize him?"

Ozzie thought for a second. "Well, Jake, he's kinda hard to recognize right now. Got a lot of bandages on his face."

Jake smiled. "You play rough, don't you, big guy?"

"Only when I have to. I didn't hear you object."

"No, I wanted to help. What about his friend?"

"We found him sleepin' in a red GMC 'bout a half a mile from your house. Terrell Grist. Local redneck. Lives out from Lake Village. I think he's a friend of the Cobb family."

Jake repeated the name a few times. "Never heard of him. Where is he?"

"Hospital. Same room with the other."

"My God, Ozzie, did you break his legs too?"

"Jake, my friend, he resisted arrest. We had to subdue him. Then we had to interrogate him. He didn't want to cooperate."

"What did he say?"

"Not much. Don't know nothin'. I'm convinced he doesn't know the guy with the dynamite."

"You mean they brought in a professional?"

"Could be. Riley looked at the firecrackers and timin' device and said it was pretty good work. We'd have never found you, your wife, your daughter, probably never found your house. It was set for two A.M. Without the tip, you'd be dead, Jake. So would your family."

Jake felt dizzy and sat on the couch. Reaction set in like a hard kick to the groin. A case of diarrhea almost manifested itself, and he was nauseated.

"You get your family off?"

"Yeah," he said weakly.

"I'm gonna assign a deputy to you full-time. Got a preference?"

"Not really."

"How 'bout Nesbit?"

"Fine. Thanks."

"One other thing. I guess you want this kept quiet?"

"If possible. Who knows about it?"

"Just me and the deputies. I think we can keep it under wraps until after the trial, but I can't guarantee anything."

"I understand. Try your best."

"I will, Jake."

"I know you will, Ozzie. I appreciate you."

———————

Jake drove to the office, made the coffee and lay on the
couch in his office. He wanted a quick nap, but sleep was
impossible. His eyes burned, but he could not close them.
He stared at the ceiling fan.

"Mr. Brigance," Ethel called over the intercom.

No response.

"Mr. Brigance!"

Somewhere in the deep recesses of his subconscious,
Jake heard himself being paged. He bolted upright. "Yes!"
he yelled.

"Judge Noose is on the phone."

"Okay, okay," he mumbled as he staggered to his desk.
He checked his watch. Nine A.M. He had slept for an hour.

"Good morning, Judge," he said cheerfully, trying to
sound alert and awake.

"Good morning, Jake. How are you?"

"Just fine, Judge. Busy getting ready for the big trial."

"I thought so. Jake, what is your schedule today?"

What's today, he thought. He grabbed his appointment
book. "Nothing but office work."

"Good. I would like to have lunch with you at my home.
Say around eleven-thirty."

"I would be delighted, Judge. What's the occasion?"

"I want to discuss the Hailey case."

"Fine, Judge. I'll see you at eleven-thirty."

———————

The Nooses lived in a stately antebellum home off the town
square in Chester. The home had been in the wife's family
for over a century, and although it could stand some maintenance and repair, it was in decent condition. Jake had never
been a guest in the house, and had never met Mrs. Noose,
although he had heard she was a snobby blue blood whose
family at one time had money but lost it. She was as unattractive as Ichabod, and Jake wondered what the children
looked like. She was properly polite when she met Jake at

the door and attempted small talk as she led him to the patio, where His Honor was drinking iced tea and reviewing correspondence. A maid was preparing a small table nearby.

"Good to see you, Jake," Ichabod said warmly. "Thanks for coming over."

"My pleasure, Judge. Beautiful place you have here."

They discussed the Hailey trial over soup and chicken salad sandwiches. Ichabod was dreading the ordeal, although he didn't admit it. He seemed tired, as if the case was already a burden. He surprised Jake with an admission that he detested Buckley. Jake said he felt the same way.

"Jake, I'm perplexed over this venue ruling," he said. "I've studied your brief and Buckley's brief, and I've researched the law myself. It's a tough question. Last weekend I attended a judges' conference on the Gulf Coast, and I had a few drinks with Judge Denton on the Supreme Court. He and I were in law school together, and we were colleagues in the state senate. We're very close. He's from Dupree County in south Mississippi, and he says that everybody down there talks about the case. People on the street ask him how he's gonna rule if the case winds up on appeal. Everybody's got an opinion, and that's almost four hundred miles away. Now, if I agree to change venue, where do we go? We can't leave the state, and I'm convinced that everyone has not only heard about your client, but already prejudged him. Would you agree?"

"Well, there's been a lot of publicity," Jake said carefully.

"Talk to me, Jake. We're not in court. That's why I invited you here. I want to pick your brain. I know there's been a lot of publicity. If we move it, where do we go?"

"How about the delta?"

Noose smiled. "You'd like that, wouldn't you?"

"Of course. We could pick us a good jury over there. One that would truly understand the issues."

"Yeah, and one that would be half black."

"I hadn't thought about that."

"Do you really believe those folks haven't already prejudged this defendant?"

"I suppose so."

"So where do we go?"

"Did Judge Denton have a suggestion?"

"Not really. We discussed the court's traditional refusal to allow changes of venue except in the most heinous of cases. It's a difficult issue with a notorious crime that arouses passion both for and against the defendant. With television and all the press nowadays, these crimes are instant news, and everyone knows the details long before the trial. And this case tops them all. Even Denton admitted he'd never seen a case with this much publicity, and he admitted it would be impossible to find a fair and impartial jury anywhere in Mississippi. Suppose I leave it in Ford County and your man is convicted. Then you appeal claiming venue should have been changed. Denton indicated he would be sympathetic with my decision not to move it. He thinks a majority of the court would uphold my denial of the venue change. Of course, that's no guarantee, and we discussed it over several long drinks. Would you like a drink?"

"No thanks."

"I just don't see any reason to move the trial from Clanton. If we did, we'd be fooling ourselves if we thought we could find twelve people who are undecided about Mr. Hailey's guilt."

"Sounds like you've already made up your mind, Judge."

"I have. We're not changing venue. The trial will be held in Clanton. I'm not comfortable with it, but I see no reason to move the trial. Besides, I like Clanton. It's close to home and the air conditioning works in the courthouse."

Noose reached for a file and found an envelope. "Jake, this is an order, dated today, overruling the request to change venue. I've sent a copy to Buckley, and there's a copy for you. The original is in here, and I would appreciate you filing this with the clerk in Clanton."

"I'll be glad to."

"I just hope I'm doing the right thing. I've really struggled with this."

"It's a tough job," Jake offered, attempting sympathy.

Noose called the maid and ordered a gin and tonic. He insisted that Jake view his rose garden, and they spent an hour in the sprawling rear lawn admiring His Honor's flow-crs. Jake thought of Carla, and Hanna, and his home, and the dynamite, but gallantly remained interested in Ichabod's handiwork.

Friday afternoons often reminded Jake of law school, when, depending on the weather, he and his friends would either group in their favorite bar in Oxford and guzzle happy-hour beer and debate their new-found theories of law or curse the insolent, arrogant, terroristic law professors, or, if the weather was warm and sunny, pile the beer in Jake's well-used convertible Beetle and head for the beach at Sardis Lake, where the women from sorority row plastered their beautiful, bronze bodies with oil and sweated in the sun and coolly ignored the catcalls from the drunken law students and fraternity rats. He missed those innocent days. He hated law school—every law student with any sense hated law school—but he missed the friends and good times, especially the Fridays. He missed the pressureless lifestyle, although at times the pressure had seemed unbearable, especially during the first year when the professors were more abusive than normal. He missed being broke, because when he had nothing he owed nothing and most of his classmates were in the same boat. Now that he had an income he worried constantly about mortgages, the overhead, credit cards, and realizing the American dream of becoming affluent. Not wealthy, just affluent. He missed his Volkswagen because it had been his first new car, a gift at high school graduation, and it was paid for, unlike the Saab. He missed being single, occasionally, although he was happily married. And he missed beer, either from a pitcher, can, or bottle. It didn't matter. He had been a social drinker, only with friends, and he spent as much time as possible with his friends. He didn't drink every day in law school, and he seldom got drunk. But there had been several painful, memorable hangovers.

    Then came Carla. He met her at the beginning of his last semester, and six months later they married. She was beautiful, and that's what got his attention. She was quiet, and a little snobby at first, like most of the wealthy sorority girls at Ole Miss. But he found her to be warm and personable and lacking in self-confidence. He had never understood how someone as beautiful as Carla could be insecure. She was a Dean's List scholar in liberal arts with no intention of ever doing more than teaching school for a few years. Her family had money, and her mother had never worked. This appealed to Jake—the family money and the absence of a career ambition. He wanted a wife who would stay home and stay beautiful and have babies and not try to wear the pants. It was love at first sight.

But she frowned on drinking, any type of drinking. Her father drank heavily when she was a child, and there were painful memories. So Jake dried out his last semester in law school and lost fifteen pounds. He looked great, felt great, and he was madly in love. But he missed beer.

There was a country grocery a few miles out of Chester with a Coors sign in the window. Coors had been his favorite in law school, although at that time it was not for sale east of the river. It was a delicacy at Ole Miss, and the bootlegging of Coors had been profitable around the campus. Now that it was available everywhere most folks had returned to Budweiser.

It was Friday, and hot. Carla was nine hundred miles away. He had no desire to go to the office, and anything there could wait until tomorrow. Some nut just tried to kill his family and remove his landmark from the National Register of Historic Places. The biggest trial of his career was ten days away. He was not ready and the pressure was mounting. He had just lost his most critical pretrial motion. And he was thirsty. Jake stopped and bought a six-pack of Coors.

It took almost two hours to travel the sixty miles from Chester to Clanton. He enjoyed the diversion, the scenery, the beer. He stopped twice to relieve himself and once to get another six-pack. He felt great.

There was only one place to go in his condition. Not home, not the office, certainly not the courthouse to file Ichabod's villainous order. He parked the Saab behind the nasty little Porsche and glided up the sidewalk with cold beer in hand. As usual, Lucien was rocking slowly on the front porch, drinking and reading a treatise on the insanity defense. He closed the book and, noticing the beer, smiled at his former associate. Jake just grinned at him.

"What's the occasion, Jake?"

"Nothing, really. Just got thirsty."

"I see. What about your wife?"

"She doesn't tell me what to do. I'm my own man. I'm the boss. If I want beer, I'll drink some beer, and she'll say nothing." Jake took a long sip.

"She must be outta town."

"North Carolina."

"When did she leave?"

"Six this morning. Flew from Memphis with Hanna. She'll stay with her parents in Wilmington until the trial's over. They've got a fancy little beach house where they spend their summers."

"She left this morning, and you're drunk by mid-afternoon."

"I'm not drunk," Jake answered. "Yet."

"How long you been drinkin'?"

"Coupla hours. I bought a six-pack when I left Noose's house around one-thirty. How long have you been drinking?"

"I normally drink my breakfast. Why were you at his house?"

"We discussed the trial over lunch. He refused to change venue."

"He what?"

"You heard me. The trial will be in Clanton."

Lucien took a drink and rattled his ice. "Sallie!" he screamed.

"Did he give any reason?"

"Yeah. Said it would be impossible to find jurors anywhere who hadn't heard of the case."

"I told you so. That's a good common sense reason not to move it, but it's a poor legal reason. Noose is wrong."

Sallie returned with a fresh drink and took Jake's beer to the refrigerator. Lucien took a slug and smacked his lips. He wiped his mouth with his arm, and took another long drink.

"You know what that means, don't you?" he asked.

"Sure. An all-white jury."

"That, plus a reversal on appeal if he's convicted."

"Don't bet on it. Noose has already consulted with the Supreme Court. He thinks the Court will affirm him if challenged. He thinks he's on solid ground."

"He's an idiot. I can show him twenty cases that say the trial should be moved. I think he's afraid to move it."

"Why would Noose be afraid?"

"He's taking some heat."

"From who?"

Lucien admired the golden liquid in his large glass and slowly stirred the ice cubes with a finger. He grinned and looked as though he knew something but wouldn't tell unless he was begged.

"From who?" Jake demanded, glaring at his friend with shiny, pink eyes.

"Buckley," Lucien said smugly.

"Buckley," Jake repeated. "I don't understand."

"I knew you wouldn't."

"Do you mind explaining?"

"I guess I could. But you can't repeat it. It's very confidential. Came from good sources."

"Who?"

"Can't tell."

"Who are your sources?" Jake insisted.

"I said I can't tell. Won't tell. Okay?"

"How can Buckley put pressure on Noose?"

"If you'll listen, I'll tell you."

"Buckley has no influence over Noose. Noose despises him. Told me so himself. Today. Over lunch."

"I realize that."

"Then how can you say Noose is feeling some heat from Buckley?"

"If you'll shut up, I'll tell you."

Jake finished a beer and called for Sallie.

"You know what a cutthroat and political whore Buckley is."

Jake nodded.

"You know how bad he wants to win this trial. If he wins, he thinks it will launch his campaign for attorney general."

"Governor," said Jake.

"Whatever. He's ambitious, okay?"

"Okay."

"Well, he's been getting political chums throughout the district to call Noose and suggest that the trial be held in Ford County. Some have been real blunt with Noose. Like, move the trial, and we'll get you in the next election. Leave it in Clanton, and we'll help you get reelected."

"I don't believe that."

"Fine. But it's true."

"How do you know?"

"Sources."

"Who's called him?"

"One example. Remember that thug that used to be sheriff in Van Buren County? Motley? FBI got him, but he's out now. Still a very popular man in that county."

"Yeah, I remember."

"I know for a fact he went to Noose's house with a couple of sidekicks and suggested very strongly that Noose leave the trial here. Buckley put them up to it."

"What did Noose say?"

"They all cussed each other real good. Motley told Noose he wouldn't get fifty votes in Van Buren County next election. They promised to stuff ballot boxes, harass the blacks, rig the absentee ballots, the usual election practices in Van Buren County. And Noose knows they'll do it."

"Why should he worry about it?"

"Don't be stupid, Jake. He's an old man who can do nothing but be a judge. Can you imagine him trying to start a law practice. He makes sixty thousand a year and would starve if he got beat. Most judges are like that. He's got to keep that job. Buckley knows it, so he's talking to the local bigots and pumping them up and telling how this no-good nigger might be acquitted if the trial is moved and that they should put a little heat on the judge. That's why Noose is feeling some pressure."

They drank for a few minutes in silence, both rocking quietly in the tall wooden rockers. The beer felt great.

"There's more," Lucien said.

"To what?"

"To Noose."

"What is it?"

"He's had some threats. Not political threats, but death threats. I hear he's scared to death. Got the police over there guarding his house. Carries a gun now."

"I know the feeling," Jake mumbled.

"Yeah, I heard."

"Heard what?"

"About the dynamite. Who was he?"

Jake was flabbergasted. He stared blankly at Lucien, unable to speak.

"Don't ask. I got connections. Who was he?"

"No one knows."

"Sounds like a pro."

"Thanks."

"You're welcome to stay here. I've got five bedrooms."

———————

The sun was gone by eight-fifteen when Ozzie parked his patrol car behind the Saab, which was still parked behind the Porsche. He walked to the foot of the steps leading up to the porch. Lucien saw him first.

"Hello, Sheriff," he attempted to say, his tongue thick and ponderous.

"Evenin', Lucien. Where's Jake?"

Lucien nodded toward the end of the porch, where Jake lay sprawled on the swing.

"He's taking a nap," Lucien explained helpfully.

Ozzie walked across the squeaking boards and stood above the comatose figure snoring peacefully. He punched him gently in the ribs. Jake opened his eyes, and struggled desperately to sit up.

"Carla called my office lookin' for you. She's worried sick. She's been callin' all afternoon and couldn't find you. Nobody's seen you. She thinks you're dead."

Jake rubbed his eyes as the swing rocked gently. "Tell her I'm not dead. Tell her you've seen me and talked to me and you are convinced beyond a shadow of a doubt that I am not dead. Tell her I'll call her tomorrow. Tell her, Ozzie, please tell her."

"No way, buddy. You're a big boy, you call her and tell her." Ozzie walked off the porch. He was not amused.

Jake struggled to his feet and staggered into the house. "Where's the phone?" he yelled at Sallie. As he dialed, he could hear Lucien on the porch laughing uncontrollably.

26 The last hangover had been in law school, six or seven years earlier; he couldn't remember. The date, that is. He couldn't remember the date, but the pounding head, dry mouth, short breath, and burning eyes brought back painful, vivid memories of long and unforgettable bouts with the tasty brown stuff.

He knew he was in trouble immediately, when his left eye opened. The eyelids on the right one were matted firmly together, and they would not open, unless manually opened with fingers, and he did not dare move. He lay there in the dark room on a couch, fully dressed, including shoes, listening to his head pound and watching the ceiling fan rotate slowly. He felt nauseated. His neck ached because there was no pillow. His feet throbbed because of the shoes. His stomach rolled and flipped and promised to erupt. Death would have been welcome.

Jake had problems with hangovers because he could not sleep them off. Once his eyes opened and his brain awoke and began spinning again, and the throbbing between his temples set in, he could not sleep. He had never understood this. His friends in law school could sleep for days with a hangover, but not Jake. He never managed more than a few hours after the last can or bottle was empty.

Why? That was always the question the next morning. Why did he do it? A cold beer was refreshing. Maybe two or three. But ten, fifteen, even twenty? He had lost count. After six, beer lost its taste, and from then on the drinking was just for the sake of drinking and getting drunk. Lucien had been very helpful. Before dark he had sent Sallie to the store for a whole case of Coors, which he gladly paid for, then encouraged Jake to drink. There were a few cans left. It was Lucien's fault.

Slowly he lifted his legs, one at a time, and placed his feet on the floor. He gently rubbed his temples, to no avail. He breathed deeply, but his heart pounded rapidly, pumping more blood to his brain and fueling the small jackhammers at work on the inside of his head. He had to have water. His tongue was dehydrated and puffed to the point where it was easier to leave his mouth open like a dog in heat. Why, oh why?

He stood, carefully, slowly, retardedly, and crept into the kitchen. The light above the stove was shielded and dim, but it penetrated the darkness and pierced his eyes. He rubbed his eyes and tried to clean them with his smelly fingers. He drank the warm water slowly and allowed it to run from his mouth and drip on the floor. He didn't care. Sallie would clean it. The clock on the counter said it was two-thirty.

Gaining momentum, he walked awkwardly yet quietly through the living room, past the couch with no pillow, and out the door. The porch was littered with empty cans and bottles. Why?

He sat in the hot shower in his office for an hour, unable to move. It relieved some of the aches and soreness, but not the violence swirling around his brain. Once in law school, he had managed to crawl from his bed to the refrigerator for a beer. He drank it, and it helped; then he drank another, and felt much better. He remembered this now while sitting in the shower, and the thought of another beer made him vomit.

He lay on the conference table in his underwear and tried his best to die. He had plenty of life insurance. They would leave his house alone. The new lawyer could get a continuance.

Nine days to trial. Time was scarce, precious, and he had just wasted one day with a massive hangover. Then he thought of Carla, and his head pounded harder. He had tried to sound sober. Told her he and Lucien had spent the afternoon reviewing insanity cases, and he would have called earlier but the phones weren't working, at least Lucien's weren't. But his tongue was heavy and his speech slow, and she knew he was drunk. She was furious—a controlled fury. Yes, her house was still standing. That was all she believed.

At six-thirty he called her again. She might be impressed if she knew he was at the office by dawn working diligently. She wasn't. With great pain and fortitude, he sounded cheerful, even hyper. She was not impressed.

"How do you feel?" she insisted.

"Great!" he answered with closed eyes.

"What time did you go to bed?"

What bed, thought Jake. "Right after I called you."

She said nothing.

"I got to the office at three o'clock this morning," he said proudly.

"Three o'clock!"

"Yeah, I couldn't sleep."

"But you didn't sleep any Thursday night." A touch of concern edged through her icy words, and he felt better.

"I'll be okay. I may stay with Lucien some this week and next. It might be safer over there."

"What about the bodyguard?"

"Yeah, Deputy Nesbit. He's parked outside asleep in his car."

She hesitated and Jake could feel the phone lines thawing. "I'm worried about you," she said warmly.

"I'll be fine, dear. I'll call tomorrow. I've got work to do."

He replaced the receiver, ran to the restroom and vomited again.

———————————

The knocking persisted at the front door. Jake ignored it for fifteen minutes, but whoever it was knew he was there and kept knocking.

He walked to the balcony. "Who is it?" he yelled at the street.

The woman walked from the sidewalk under the balcony and leaned on a black BMW parked next to the Saab. Her hands were thrust deep into the pockets of faded, starched, well-fitting jeans. The noon sun burned brightly and blinded her as she looked up in his direction. It also illuminated her light, goldish red hair.

"Are you Jake Brigance?" she asked, shielding her eyes with a forearm.

"Yeah. Whatta you want?"

"I need to talk to you."

"I'm very busy."

"It's very important."

"You're not a client, are you?" he asked, focusing his

eyes on the slender figure and knowing she was indeed not a client.

"No. I just need five minutes of your time."

Jake unlocked the door. She walked in casually as if she owned the place. She shook his hand firmly.

"I'm Ellen Roark."

He pointed to a seat by the door. "Nice to meet you. Sit down."

Jake sat on the edge of Ethel's desk. "One syllable or two?"

"I beg your pardon."

She had a quick, cocky Northeast accent, but tempered with some time in the South.

"Is it Rork or Row Ark?"

"R-o-a-r-k. That's Rork in Boston, and Row Ark in Mississippi."

"Mind if I call you Ellen?"

"Please do, with two syllables. Can I call you Jake?"

"Yes, please."

"Good, I hadn't planned to call you Mister."

"Boston, huh?"

"Yeah, I was born there. Went to Boston College. My dad is Sheldon Roark, a notorious criminal lawyer in Boston."

"I guess I've missed him. What brings you to Mississippi?"

"I'm in law school at Ole Miss."

"Ole Miss! How'd you wind up down here?"

"My mother's from Natchez. She was a sweet little sorority girl at Ole Miss, then moved to New York, where she met my father."

"I married a sweet little sorority girl from Ole Miss."

"They have a great selection."

"Would you like coffee?"

"No thanks."

"Well, now that we know each other, what brings you to Clanton?"

"Carl Lee Hailey."

"I'm not surprised."

"I'll finish law school in December, and I'm killing time

in Oxford this summer. I'm taking criminal procedure under Guthrie, and I'm bored."

"Crazy George Guthrie."

"Yeah, he's still crazy.

"He flunked me in constitutional law my first year."

"Anyway, I'd like to help you with the trial."

Jake smiled and took a seat in Ethel's heavy-duty, rotating secretarial chair. He studied her carefully. Her black cotton polo shirt was fashionably weathered and neatly pressed. The outlines and subtle shadows revealed a healthy bustline, no bra. The thick, wavy hair fell perfectly on her shoulders.

"What makes you think I need help?"

"I know you practice alone, and I know you don't have a law clerk."

"How do you know all this?"

"*Newsweek.*"

"Ah, yes. A wonderful publication. It was a good picture, wasn't it?"

"You looked a bit stuffy, but it was okay. You look better in person."

"What credentials do you bring with you?"

"Genius runs in my family. I finished *summa cum laude* at BC, and I'm second in my law class. Last summer I spent three months with the Southern Prisoners Defense League in Birmingham and played gofer in seven capital trials. I watched Elmer Wayne Doss die in the Florida electric chair and I watched Willie Ray Ash get lethally injected in Texas. In my spare time at Ole Miss I write briefs for the ACLU and I'm working on two death penalty appeals for a law firm in Spartanburg, South Carolina. I was raised in my father's law office, and I was proficient in legal research before I could drive. I've watched him defend murderers, rapists, embezzlers, extortionists, terrorists, assassins, child abusers, child fondlers, child killers, and children who killed their parents. I worked forty hours a week in his office when I was in high school and fifty when I was in college. He has eighteen lawyers in his firm, all very bright, very talented. It's a great training ground for criminal lawyers, and I've been there for fourteen years. I'm twenty-five years old, and when I grow up I want to be a radical criminal lawyer like my dad and spend a glorious career stamping out the death penalty."

"Is that all?"

"My dad's filthy rich, and even though we're Irish Catholic I'm an only child. I've got more money than you do so I'll work for free. No charge. A free law clerk for three weeks. I'll do all the research, typing, answering the phone. I'll even carry your briefcase and make the coffee."

"I was afraid you'd want to be a law partner."

"No. I'm a woman, and I'm in the South. I know my place."

"Why are you so interested in this case?"

"I want to be in the courtroom. I love criminal trials, big trials where there's a life on the line and pressure so thick you can see it in the air. Where the courtroom's packed and security is tight. Where half the people hate the defendant and his lawyers and the other half pray he gets off. I love it. And this is the trial of all trials. I'm not a Southerner and I find this place bewildering most of the time, but I have developed a perverse love for it. It'll never make sense to me, but it is fascinating. The racial implications are enormous. The trial of a black father for killing two white men who raped his daughter—my father said he would take the case for free."

"Tell him to stay in Boston."

"It's a trial lawyer's dream. I just want to be there. I'll stay out of the way, I promise. Just let me work in the background and watch the trial."

"Judge Noose hates women lawyers."

"So does every male lawyer in the South. Besides, I'm not a lawyer, I'm a law student."

"I'll let you explain that to him."

"So I've got the job."

Jake stopped staring at her and breathed deeply. A minor wave of nausea vibrated through his stomach and lungs and took his breath. The jackhammers had returned with a fury and he needed to be near the restroom.

"Yes, you've got the job. I could use some free research. These cases are complicated, as I'm sure you are aware."

She flashed a comely, confident smile. "When do I start?"

"Now."

Jake led her through a quick tour of the office, and assigned her to the war room upstairs. They laid the Hailey file on the conference table and she spent an hour copying it.

At two-thirty Jake awoke from a nap on his couch. He walked downstairs to the conference room. She had removed half the books from the shelves and had them scattered the length of the table with page markers sticking up every fifty or so pages. She was busy taking notes.

"Not a bad library," she said.

"Some of these books haven't been used in twenty years."

"I noticed the dust."

"Are you hungry?"

"Yes. I'm starving."

"There's a little cafe around the corner where the specialty is grease and fried corn meal. My system needs a shot of grease."

"Sounds delicious."

They walked around the square to Claude's, where the crowd was thin for a Saturday afternoon. There were no other whites in the place. Claude was absent and the silence was deafening. Jake ordered a cheeseburger, onion rings, and three headache powders.

"Got a headache?" Ellen asked.

"Massive."

"Stress?"

"Hangover."

"Hangover? I thought you were a teetotaler."

"And where'd you hear that?"

"*Newsweek*. The article said you were a clean-cut family man, workaholic, devout Presbyterian who drank nothing and smoked cheap cigars. Remember? How could you forget, right?"

"You believe everything you read?"

"No."

"Good, because last night I got plastered, and I've puked all morning."

The law clerk was amused. "What do you drink?"

"I don't—remember. At least I didn't until last night.

This is my first hangover since law school, and I hope it's my last. I'd forgotten how terrible these things are."

"Why do lawyers drink so much?"

"They learn how in law school. Does your dad drink?"

"Are you kidding? We're Catholic. He's careful, though."

"Do you drink?"

"Sure, all the time," she said proudly.

"Then you'll make a great lawyer."

Jake carefully mixed the three powders in a glass of ice water and slugged it down. He grimaced and wiped his mouth. She watched intently with an amused smile.

"What'd your wife say?"

"About what?"

"The hangover, from such a devout and religious family man."

"She doesn't know about it. She left me early yesterday morning."

"I'm sorry."

"She went to stay with her parents until the trial is over. We've had anonymous phone calls and death threats for two months now, and early yesterday morning they planted dynamite outside our bedroom window. The cops found it in time and they caught the men, probably the Klan. Enough dynamite to level the house and kill all of us. That was a good excuse to get drunk."

"I'm sorry to hear that."

"The job you've just taken could be very dangerous. You should know that at this point."

"I've been threatened before. Last summer in Dothan, Alabama, we defended two black teenagers who had sodomized and strangled an eighty-year-old woman. No lawyer in the state would take the case so they called the Defense League. We rode into town on black horses and the mere sight of us would cause lynch mobs to form instantly on street corners. I've never felt so hated in my life. We hid in a motel in another town and felt safe, until one night two men cornered me in the motel lounge and tried to abduct me."

"What happened?"

"I carry a snub-nosed .38 in my purse and I convinced them I knew how to use it."

"A snub-nosed .38?"

"My father gave it to me for my fifteenth birthday. I have a license."

"He must be a hell of a guy."

"He's been shot at several times. He takes very controversial cases, the kind you read about in the papers where the public is outraged and demanding that the defendant be hanged without a trial or a lawyer. Those are the cases he likes best. He has a full-time bodyguard."

"Big deal. So do I. His name is Deputy Nesbit, and he couldn't hit the side of a barn with a shotgun. He was assigned to me yesterday."

The food arrived. She removed the onions and tomatoes from her Claudeburger, and offered him the french fries. She cut it in half and nibbled around the edges like a bird. Hot grease dripped to her plate. With each small bite, she carefully wiped her mouth.

Her face was gentle and pleasant with an easy smile that belied the ACLU, ERA, burn-the-bra, I-can-outcuss-you bitchiness Jake knew was lurking somewhere near the surface. There was not a trace of makeup anywhere on the face. None was needed. She was not beautiful, not cute, and evidently determined not to be so. She had the pale skin of a redhead, but it was healthy skin with seven or eight freckles splattered about the small, pointed nose. With each frequent smile, her lips spread wonderfully and folded her cheeks into neat, transient, hollow dimples. The smiles were confident, challenging, and mysterious. The metallic green eyes radiated a soft fury and were fixed and unblinking when she talked.

It was an intelligent face, attractive as hell.

Jake chewed on his burger and tried to nonchalantly ignore her eyes. The heavy food settled his stomach, and for the first time in ten hours he began to think he might live.

"Seriously, why'd you choose Ole Miss?" he asked.

"It's a good law school."

"It's my school. But we don't normally attract the brightest students from the Northeast. That's Ivy League country. We send our smartest kids up there."

"My father hates every lawyer with an Ivy League degree. He was dirt poor and scratched his way through law school at night. He's endured the snubs from rich, well-educated, and incompetent lawyers all his life. Now he laughs at them. He told me I could go to law school anywhere in the country, but if I chose an Ivy League school he would not pay for it. Then there's my mother. I was raised on these enchanting stories of life in the Deep South, and I had to see for myself. Plus, the Southern states seemed determined to practice the death penalty, so I think I'll end up here."

"Why are you so opposed to the death penalty?"

"And you're not?"

"No, I'm very much in favor of it."

"That's incredible! Coming from a criminal defense lawyer."

"I'd like to go back to public hangings on the courthouse lawn."

"You're kidding, aren't you? I hope. Tell me you are."

"I am not."

She stopped chewing and smiling. The eyes glowed fiercely and watched him for a signal of weakness. "You are serious."

"I am very serious. The problem with the death penalty is that we don't use it enough."

"Have you explained that to Mr. Hailey?"

"Mr. Hailey does not deserve the death penalty. But the two men who raped his daughter certainly did."

"I see. How do you determine who gets it and who doesn't?"

"That's very simple. You look at the crime and you look at the criminal. If it's a dope dealer who guns down an undercover narcotics officer, then he gets the gas. If it's a drifter who rapes a three-year-old girl, drowns her by holding her little head in a mudhole, then throws her body off a bridge, then you take his life and thank God he's gone. If it's an escaped convict who breaks into a farmhouse late at night and beats and tortures an elderly couple before burning them with their house, then you strap him in a chair, hook up a few wires, pray for his soul, and pull the switch. And if it's two dopeheads who gang-rape a ten-year-old girl and kick her with pointed-toe cowboy boots until her jaws break, then you happily, merrily, thankfully, gleefully lock them in a gas chamber and listen to them squeal. It's very simple."

"It's barbaric."

"Their crimes were barbaric. Death is too good for them, much too good."

"And if Mr. Hailey is convicted and sentenced to die?"

"If that happens, I'm sure I'll spend the next ten years cranking out appeals and fighting furiously to save his life. And if they ever strap him in the chair, I'm sure I'll be outside the prison with you and the Jesuits and a hundred other kindly souls marching and holding candles and singing hymns. And then I'll stand beside his grave behind his church with his widow and children and wish I'd never met him."

"Have you ever witnessed an execution?"

"Not that I recall."

"I've watched two. You'd change your mind if you saw one."

"Good. I won't see one."

"It's a horrible thing to watch."

"Were the victims' families there?"

"Yes, in both instances."

"Were they horrified? Were their minds changed? Of course not. Their nightmares were over."

"I'm surprised at you."

"And I'm bewildered by people like you. How can you be so zealous and dedicated in trying to save people who have begged for the death penalty and according to the law should get it?"

"Whose law? It's not the law in Massachusetts."

"You don't say. What do you expect from the only state McGovern carried in 1972? You folks have always been tuned in with the rest of the country."

The Claudeburgers were being ignored and their voices had grown too loud. Jake glanced around and caught a few stares. Ellen smiled again, and took one of his onion rings.

"What do you think of the ACLU?" she asked, crunching.

"I suppose you've got a membership card in your purse."

"I do."

"Then you're fired."

"I joined when I was sixteen."

"Why so late? You must've been the last one in your Girl Scout troop to join."

"Do you have any respect for the Bill of Rights?"

"I adore the Bill of Rights. I despise the judges who interpret them. Eat."

They finished the burgers in silence, watching each other carefully. Jake ordered coffee and two more headache powders.

"So how do we plan to win this case?" she asked.

"We?"

"I still have the job, don't I?"

"Yes. Just remember that I'm the boss and you're the clerk."

"Sure, boss. What's your strategy?"

"How would you handle it?"

"Well, from what I gather, our client carefully planned the killings and shot them in cold blood, six days after the rape. It sounds exactly like he knew what he was doing."

"He did."

"So we have no defense and I think you should plead him guilty for a life sentence and avoid the gas chamber."

"You're a real fighter."

"Just kidding. Insanity is our only defense. And it sounds impossible to prove."

"You're familiar with the M'Naghten Rule?" Jake asked.

"Yes. Do we have a psychiatrist?"

"Sort of. He'll say anything we want him to say; that is, if he's sober at trial. One of your more difficult tasks as my new law clerk will be to make sure he is sober at trial. It won't be easy, believe me."

"I live for new challenges in the courtroom."

"All right Row Ark, take a pen. Here's a napkin. Your boss is about to give you instructions."

She began making notes on a paper napkin.

"I want a brief on the M'Naghten decisions rendered by the Mississippi Supreme Court in the past fifty years. There's probably a hundred. There's a big case from 1976, *State vs. Hill*, where the court was bitterly divided five to four, with the dissenters opting for a more liberal definition of insanity. Keep the brief short, less than twenty pages. Can you type?"

"Ninety words a minute."

"I should've known. I'd like it by Wednesday."

"You'll have it."

"There are some evidentiary points I need researched. You saw those gruesome pictures of the two bodies. Noose normally allows the jury to see the blood and gore, but I'd like to keep them away from the jury. See if there's a way."

"It won't be easy."

"The rape is crucial to his defense. I want the jury to know details. This needs to be researched thoroughly. I've got two or three cases you can start from, and I think we can prove to Noose that the rape is very relevant."

"Okay. What else?"

"I don't know. When my brain is alive again I'll think of more, but that will do it for now."

"Do I report Monday morning?"

"Yes, but no sooner than nine. I like my quiet time."

"What's the dress code?"

"You look fine."

"Jeans and no socks?"

"I have one other employee, a secretary by the name of Ethel. She's sixty-four, top heavy, and thankfully she wears a bra. It wouldn't be a bad idea for you."

"I'll think about it."

"I don't need the distraction."

27 Monday, July 15. One week until trial. Over the weekend word spread quickly that the trial would be in Clanton, and the small town braced for the spectacle. The phones rang steadily at the three motels as the journalists and their crews confirmed reservations. The cafes buzzed with anticipation. A county maintenance crew swarmed around the courthouse after breakfast and began painting and polishing. Ozzie sent the yardboys from the jail with their mowers and weed-eaters. The old men under the Vietnam monument whittled cautiously and watched all this activity. The trusty who supervised the yard work asked them to spit their Red Man in the grass, not on the sidewalk. He was told to go to hell. The thick, dark Bermuda was given an extra layer of fertilizer, and a dozen lawn sprinklers were hissing and splashing by 9:00 A.M.

By 10:00 A.M. the temperature was ninety-two. The merchants in the small shops around the square opened their doors to the humidity and ran their ceiling fans. They called Memphis and Jackson and Chicago for inventory to be sold at special prices next week.

Noose had called Jean Gillespie, the Circuit Court clerk, late Friday and informed her that the trial would be in her courtroom. He instructed her to summon one hundred and fifty prospective jurors. The defense had requested an enlarged panel from which to select the twelve, and Noose agreed. Jean and two deputy clerks spent Saturday combing the voter registration books randomly selecting potential jurors. Following Noose's specific instructions, they culled those over sixty-five. One thousand names were chosen, and each name along with its address was written on a small index card and thrown into a cardboard box. The two deputy clerks then took turns drawing cards at random from the box. One clerk was white, one black. Each would pull a card blindly from the box and arrange it neatly on a folding table with the other cards. When the count reached one hundred and fifty, the drawing ceased and a master list was typed. These were the jurors for State *vs*. Hailey. Each step of their

selection had been carefully dictated by the Honorable
Omar Noose, who knew exactly what he was doing. If there
was an all-white jury, and a conviction, and a death sentence,
every single elementary step of the jury selection procedure
would be attacked on appeal. He had been through it before, and had been reversed. But not this time.

From the master list, the name and address of each
juror was typed on a separate jury summons. The stack of
summonses was kept in Jean's office under lock until eight
Monday morning when Sheriff Ozzie Walls arrived. He
drank coffee with Jean and received his instructions.

"Judge Noose wants these served between four P.M. and
midnight tonight," she said.

"Okay."

"The jurors are to report to the courtroom promptly by
nine next Monday."

"Okay."

"The summons does not indicate the name or nature of
the trial, and the jurors are not to be told anything."

"I reckon they'll know."

"Probably so, but Noose was very specific. Your men
are to say nothing about the case when the summonses are
served. The names of the jurors are very confidential, at
least until Wednesday. Don't ask why—Noose's orders."

Ozzie flipped through the stack. "How many do we
have here?"

"One fifty."

"A hundred and fifty! Why so many?"

"It's a big case. Noose's orders."

"It'll take ever man I've got to serve these papers."

"I'm sorry."

"Oh well. If that's what His Honor wants."

Ozzie left, and within seconds Jake was standing at the
counter flirting with the secretaries and smiling at Jean Gillespie. He followed her back to her office. He closed the
door. She retreated behind her desk and pointed at him. He
kept smiling.

"I know why you're here," she said sternly, "and you
can't have it."

"Give me the list, Jean."

"Not until Wednesday. Noose's orders."

"Wednesday? Why Wednesday?"

"I don't know. But Omar was very specific."

"Give me the list, Jean."

"Jake, I can't. Do you want me to get in trouble?"

"You won't get in trouble because no one will know it. You know how well I can keep a secret." He was not smiling now. "Jean, give me the damned list."

"Jake, I just can't."

"I need it, and I need it now. I can't wait until Wednesday. I've got work to do."

"It wouldn't be fair to Buckley," she said weakly.

"To hell with Buckley. Do you think he plays fair? He's a snake and you dislike him as much as I do."

"Probably more."

"Give me the list, Jean."

"Look, Jake, we've always been close. I think more of you than any lawyer I know. When my son got in trouble I called you, right? I trust you and I want you to win this case. But I can't defy a judge's orders."

"Who helped you get elected last time, me or Buckley?"

"Come on, Jake."

"Who kept your son out of jail, me or Buckley?"

"Please."

"Who tried to put your son in jail, me or Buckley?"

"That's not fair, Jake."

"Who stood up for your husband when everybody, and I mean everybody, in the church wanted him gone when the books didn't balance?"

"It's not a question of loyalty, Jake. I love you and Carla and Hanna, but I just can't do it."

Jake slammed the door and stormed out of the office. Jean sat at her desk and wiped tears from her cheeks.

———

At 10:00 A.M. Harry Rex barged into Jake's office and threw a copy of the jury list on his desk. "Don't ask," he said. Beside each name he had made notes, such as "Don't know" or "Former client—hates niggers" or "Works at the shoe factory, might be sympathetic."

Jake read each name slowly, trying to place it with a

face or a reputation. There was nothing but names. No addresses, ages, occupations. Nothing but names. His fourth-grade schoolteacher from Karaway. One of his mother's friends from the Garden Club. A former client, shoplifting, he thought. A name from church. A regular at the Coffee Shop. A prominent farmer. Most of the names sounded white. There was a Willie Mae Jones, Leroy Washington, Roosevelt Tucker, Bessie Lou Bean, and a few other black names. But the list looked awfully pale. He recognized thirty names at most.

"Whatta you think?" asked Harry Rex.

"Hard to tell. Mostly white, but that's to be expected. Where'd you get this?"

"Don't ask. I made notes by twenty-six names. That's the best I can do. The rest I don't know."

"You're a true friend, Harry Rex."

"I'm a prince. Are you ready for trial?"

"Not yet. But I've found a secret weapon."

"What?"

"You'll meet her later."

"Her?"

"Yeah. You busy Wednesday night?"

"I don't think so. Why?"

"Good. Meet here at eight. Lucien will be here. Maybe one or two others. I want to take a couple of hours and talk about the jury. Who do we want? Let's get a profile of the model juror, and go from there. We'll cover each name and hopefully identify most of these people."

"Sounds like fun. I'll be here. What's your model juror?"

"I'm not sure. I think the vigilante would appeal to rednecks. Guns, violence, protection of women. The rednecks would eat it up. But my man is black, and a bunch of rednecks would fry him. He killed two of their own."

"I agree. I'd stay away from women. They would have no sympathy for the rapists, but they place a higher value on life. Taking an M-16 and blowing their heads off is something women just don't understand. You and I understand it because we're fathers. It appeals to us. The violence and blood doesn't bother us. We admire him. You've got to pick some admirers on that jury. Young fathers with some education."

"That's interesting. Lucien said he would stick with women because they're more sympathetic."

"I don't think so. I know some women who'd cut your throat if you crossed them."

"Some of your clients?"

"Yeah, and one is on that list. Frances Burdeen. Pick her, and I'll tell her how to vote."

"You serious?"

"Yep. She'll do anything I tell her."

"Can you be in court Monday? I want you to watch the jury during the selection process, then help me decide on the twelve."

"I wouldn't miss it."

Jake heard voices downstairs and pressed his finger to his lips. He listened, then smiled and motioned for Harry Rex to follow him. They tiptoed to the top of the stairs and listened to the commotion around Ethel's desk.

"You most certainly do not work here," Ethel insisted.

"I most certainly do. I was hired Saturday by Jake Brigance, who I believe is your boss."

"Hired for what?" Ethel demanded.

"As a law clerk."

"Well, he didn't discuss it with me."

"He discussed it with me, and gave me the job."

"How much is he paying you?"

"A hundred bucks an hour."

"Oh my God! I'll have to speak with him first."

"I've already spoken with him, Ethel."

"It's Mrs. Twitty to you." Ethel studied her carefully from head to toe. Acid-washed jeans, penny loafers, no socks, an oversized white cotton button-down with, evidently, nothing on underneath. "You're not dressed appropriately for this office. You're, you're indecent."

Harry Rex raised his eyebrows and smiled at Jake. They watched the stairs and listened.

"My boss, who happens to be your boss, said I could dress like this."

"But you forgot something, didn't you?"

"Jake said I could forget it. He told me you hadn't worn

a bra in twenty years. He said most of the women in Clanton go braless, so I left mine at home."

"He what?" Ethel screamed with arms crossed over her chest.

"Is he upstairs?" Ellen asked coolly.

"Yes, I'll call him."

"Don't bother."

Jake and Harry Rex retreated into the big office and waited for the law clerk. She entered carrying a large briefcase.

"Good morning, Row Ark," Jake said. "I want you to meet a good friend, Harry Rex Vonner."

Harry Rex shook her hand and stared at her shirt. "Nice to meet you. What was your first name?"

"Ellen."

"Just call her Row Ark," Jake said. "She'll clerk here until Hailey's over."

"That's nice," said Harry Rex, still staring.

"Harry Rex is a local lawyer, Row Ark, and one of the many you cannot trust."

"What'd you hire a female law clerk for, Jake?" he asked bluntly.

"Row Ark's a genius in criminal law, like most third-year law students. And she works very cheap."

"You have something against females, sir?" Ellen asked.

"No ma'am. I love females. I've married four of them."

"Harry Rex is the meanest divorce lawyer in Ford County," Jake explained. "In fact, he's the meanest lawyer, period. Come to think of it, he's the meanest man I know."

"Thanks," said Harry Rex. He had stopped staring at her.

She looked at his huge, dirty, scuffed, worn wingtips, his ribbed nylon socks that had drooped into thick wads around his ankles, his soiled and battered khaki pants, his frayed navy blazer, his brilliant pink wool tie that fell eight inches above his belt, and she said, "I think he's cute."

"I might make you wife number five," Harry Rex said.

"The attraction is purely physical," she said.

"Watch it," Jake said. "There's been no sex in this office since Lucien left."

"A lot of things left with Lucien," said Harry Rex.

"Who's Lucien?"

Jake and Harry Rex looked at each other. "You'll meet him soon enough," Jake explained.

"Your secretary is very sweet," Ellen said.

"I knew y'all would hit it off. She's really a doll once you get to know her."

"How long does that take?"

"I've known her for twenty years," said Harry Rex, "and I'm still waiting."

"How's the research coming?" Jake asked.

"Slow. There are dozens of M'Naghten cases, and they are all very long. I'm about half through. I planned to work on it all day here; that is, if that pit bull downstairs doesn't attack me."

"I'll take care of her," Jake said.

Harry Rex headed for the door. "Nice meetin' you, Row Ark. I'll see you around."

"Thanks, Harry Rex," said Jake. "See you Wednesday night."

———————

The dirt and gravel parking lot of Tank's Tonk was full when Jake finally found it after dark. There had been no reason to visit Tank's before, and he was not thrilled about seeing the place now. It was well hidden off a dirt road, six miles out of Clanton. He parked far away from the small cinderblock building and toyed with the idea of leaving the engine running in case Tank was not there and a quick escape became necessary. But he quickly dismissed the stupid idea because he liked his car, and theft was not only likely but highly probable. He locked it, then double-checked it, almost certain that all or part of it would be missing when he returned.

The juke box blasted from the open windows, and he thought he heard a bottle crash on the floor, or across a table or someone's head. He hesitated beside his car and decided to leave. No, it was important. He sucked in his stomach, held his breath, and opened the ragged wooden door.

Forty sets of black eyes immediately focused on this poor lost white boy with a coat and tie who was squinting and trying to focus inside the vast blackness of their tonk. He stood there awkwardly, desperately searching for a friend. There were none. Michael Jackson conveniently finished his song on the juke box, and for an eternity the tonk was silent. Jake stayed close to the door. He nodded and smiled and tried to act like one of the gang. There were no other smiles.

Suddenly, there was movement at the bar and Jake's knees began vibrating. "Jake! Jake!" someone shouted. It was the sweetest two words he had ever heard. From behind the bar he saw his friend Tank removing his apron and heading for him. They shook hands warmly.

"What brings you here?"

"I need to talk to you for a minute. Can we step outside?"

"Sure. What's up?"

"Just business."

Tank flipped on a light switch by the front door. "Say, everbody, this here is Carl Lee Hailey's lawyer, Jake Brigance. A good friend of mine. Let's hear it for him."

The small room exploded in applause and bravos. Several of the boys at the bar grabbed Jake and shook his hand. Tank reached in a drawer under the bar and pulled out a handful of Jake's cards, which he passed out like candy. Jake was breathing again and the color returned to his face.

Outside, they leaned on the hood of Tank's yellow Cadillac. Lionel Richie echoed through the windows and the crowd returned to normal. Jake handed Tank a copy of the list.

"Look at each name. See how many of these folks you know. Ask around and find out what you can."

Tank held the list near his eyes. The light from the Michelob sign in the window glowed over his shoulder. "How many are black?"

"You tell me. That's one reason I want you to look at it. Circle the black ones. If you're not sure, find out. If you know any of the white folks, make a note."

"I'll be glad to, Jake. This ain't illegal, is it?"

"Naw, but don't tell anybody. I need it back by Wednesday morning."

"You're the boss."

Tank got the last list, and Jake headed for the office. It was almost ten. Ethel had retyped the list from the initial one provided by Harry Rex, and a dozen copies had been hand-delivered to selected, trusted friends. Lucien, Stan Atcavage, Tank, Dell at the Coffee Shop, a lawyer in Karaway named Roland Isom, and a few others. Even Ozzie got a list.

Less than three miles from the tonk was a small, neat white-framed country house where Ethel and Bud Twitty had lived for almost forty years. It was a pleasant house with pleasant memories of raising children who were now scattered up North. The retarded son, the one who greatly resembled Lucien, lived in Miami for some reason. The house was quieter now. Bud hadn't worked in years, not since his first stroke in '75. Then a heart attack, followed by two more major strokes and several small ones. His days were numbered, and he had long since accepted the fact that he would most likely catch the big one and die on his front porch shelling butterbeans. That's what he hoped for, anyway.

Monday night he sat on the porch shelling butterbeans and listening to the Cardinals on the radio. Ethel was working in the kitchen. In the bottom of the eighth with the Cards at bat and two on, he heard a noise from the side of the house. He turned the volume down. Probably just a dog. Then another noise. He stood and walked to the end of the porch. Suddenly, a huge figure dressed in solid black with red, white, and black war paint smeared wickedly across his face jumped from the bushes, grabbed Bud and yanked him off the porch. Bud's anguished cry was not heard in the kitchen. Another warrior joined in and they dragged the old man to the foot of the steps leading up to the front porch. One maneuvered him into a half-nelson while the other pounded his soft belly and bloodied his face. Within seconds, he was unconscious.

Ethel heard noises and scurried through the front door. She was grabbed by a third member of the gang, who twisted her arm tightly behind her and wrapped a huge arm around her throat. She couldn't scream or talk or move, and was held there on the porch, terrified, watching below as the two thugs took turns with her husband. On the front sidewalk ten feet behind the violence stood three figures, each garbed in a full, flowing, white robe with red garnishment, each with a tall, white, pointed headdress from which fell a red and white mask that loosely covered each face. They emerged from the darkness and watched over the scene as though they were the three wise men attending the manger.

After a long, agonizing minute, the beating grew monotonous. "Enough," said the ruler in the middle. The three terrorists in black ran. Ethel rushed down the steps and slumped over her battered husband. The three in white disappeared.

———

Jake left the hospital after midnight with Bud still alive but everyone pessimistic. Along with the broken bones he had suffered another major heart attack. Ethel had made a scene and blamed it all on Jake.

"You said there was no danger!" she screamed. "Tell that to my husband! It's all your fault!"

He had listened to her rant and rave, and the embarrassment turned to anger. He glanced around the small waiting room at the friends and relatives. All eyes were on him. Yes, they seemed to say, it was all his fault.

28 Gwen called the office early Tuesday morning and the new secretary, Ellen Roark, answered the phone. She fumbled with the intercom until she broke it, then walked to the stairs and yelled: "Jake, it's Mr. Hailey's wife."

He slammed a book shut and angrily picked up the receiver. "Hello."

"Jake, are you busy?"

"Very. What's on your mind?"

She started crying. "Jake, we need money. We're broke, and the bills are past due. I haven't paid the house note in two months and the mortgage company is callin'. I don't know who else to turn to."

"What about your family?"

"They're poor folks, Jake, you know that. They'll feed us and do what they can, but they can't make our house notes and pay the utilities."

"Have you talked to Carl Lee?"

"Not about money. Not lately. There's not much he can do except worry, and Lord knows he's got enough to worry about."

"What about the churches?"

"Ain't seen a dime."

"How much do you need?"

"At least five hundred, just to catch up. I don't know 'bout next month. I'll guess I'll worry then."

Nine hundred minus five hundred left Jake with four hundred dollars for a capital murder defense. That had to be a record. Four hundred dollars! He had an idea.

"Can you be at my office at two this afternoon?"

"I'll have to bring the kids."

"That's okay. Just be here."

"I'll be there."

He hung up and quickly searched the phone book for Reverend Ollie Agee. He found him at the church. Jake fed him a line about meeting to discuss the Hailey trial and covering Agee's testimony. Said the reverend would be an important witness. Agee said he would be there at two.

The Hailey clan arrived first, and Jake seated them around the conference table. The kids remembered the room from the press conference and were awed by the long table, thick swivel chairs, and impressive rows of books. When the reverend arrived he hugged Gwen and made a fuss over the kids, especially Tonya.

"I'll be very brief, Reverend," started Jake. "There are some things we need to discuss. For several weeks now, you and the other black ministers in this county have been raising money for the Haileys. And you've done a real good job. Over six thousand, I believe. I don't know where the money is, and it's none of my business. You offered the money to the NAACP lawyers to represent Carl Lee, but as you and I know, those lawyers won't be involved in this case. I'm the lawyer, the only lawyer, and so far none of the money has been offered to me. I don't expect any of it. Evidently you don't care about what kind of defense he gets if you can't pick his lawyer. That's fine. I can live with that. What really bothers me, Reverend, is the fact that none, and I repeat none, of the money has been given to the Haileys. Right, Gwen?"

The empty look on her face had turned to one of amazement, then disbelief, then anger as she glared at the reverend.

"Six thousand dollars," she repeated.

"Over six thousand, at last reported count," said Jake. "And the money is lying in some bank while Carl Lee sits in jail, Gwen's not working, the bills are past due, the only food comes from friends, and foreclosure is a few days away. Now, tell us, Reverend, what're your plans with the money?"

Agee smiled and said with an oily voice, "That's none of your business."

"But it's my business!" Gwen said loudly. "You used my name and my family's name when you raised that money, didn't you, Reverend. I heard it myself. Told all the church folk that the love offerin', as you called it, was for my family. I figured you had done spent the money on lawyers' fee or somethin' like that. And now, today, I find out you've got it stuck in the bank. I guess you plan to keep it."

Agee was unmoved. "Now wait a minute, Gwen. We thought the money could best be spent on Carl Lee. He declined the money when he refused to hire the NAACP lawyers. So I asked Mr. Reinfeld, the head lawyer, what to do with the money. He told me to save it because Carl Lee will need it for his appeal."

Jake cocked his head sideways and clenched his teeth. He started to rebuke this ignorant fool, but realized Agee did not understand what he was saying. Jake bit his lip.

"I don't understand," said Gwen.

"It's simple," said the reverend with an accommodating smile. "Mr. Reinfeld said that Carl Lee would be convicted because he didn't hire him. So then we've got to appeal, right? And after Jake here loses the trial, you and Carl Lee will of course be lookin' for another lawyer who can save his life. That's when we'll need Reinfeld and that's when we'll need the money. So you see, it's all for Carl Lee."

Jake shook his head and silently cursed. He cursed Reinfeld more than Agee.

Gwen's eyes flooded and she clenched her fists. "I don't understand all that, and I don't want to understand it. All I know is that I'm tired of beggin' for food, tired of dependin' on others, and tired of worryin' about losin' my house."

Agee looked at her sadly. "I understand, Gwen, but—"

"And if you got six thousand dollars of our money in the bank, you're wrong not to give it to us. We've got enough sense to spend it right."

Carl Lee, Jr., and Jarvis stood next to their mother and comforted her. They stared at Agee.

"But it's for Carl Lee," the reverend said.

"Good," Jake said. "Have you asked Carl Lee how he wants his money spent?"

The dirty little grin left Agee's face and he squirmed in his chair. "Carl Lee understands what we're doin'," he said without much conviction.

"Thank you. That's not what I asked. Listen to me carefully. Have you asked Carl Lee how he wants his money spent?"

"I think it's been discussed with him," Agee lied.

"Let's see," Jake said. He stood and walked to the door leading to the small office next to the conference room. The reverend watched nervously, almost in panic. Jake opened the door and nodded to someone. Carl Lee and Ozzie casually walked in. The kids yelled and ran to their father. Agee looked devastated.

After a few awkward minutes of hugs and kisses, Jake moved in for the kill. "Now, Reverend, why don't you ask Carl Lee how he wants to spend his six thousand dollars."

"It ain't exactly his," said Agee.

"And it ain't exactly yours," shot Ozzie.

Carl Lee removed Tonya from his knee and walked to the chair where Agee was sitting. He sat on the edge of the table, above the reverend, poised and ready to strike if necessary. "Let me make it real simple, preacher, so you won't have trouble understandin' it. You raised that money in my name, for the benefit of my family. You took it from the black folk of this county, and you took it with the promise that it'd go to help me and my family. You lied. You raised it so you could impress the NAACP, not to help my family. You lied in church, you lied in the newspapers, you lied everwhere."

Agee looked around the room and noticed that everyone, including the kids, was staring at him and nodding slowly.

Carl Lee put his foot in Agee's chair and leaned closer. "If you don't give us that money, I'll tell ever nigger I know that you're a lyin' crook. I'll call ever member of your church, and I'm one too, remember, and tell them we ain't got a dime from you, and when I get through you won't be able to raise two dollars on Sunday mornin'. You'll lose your fancy Cadillacs and your fancy suits. You may even lose your church, 'cause I'll ask everbody to leave."

"You finished?" Agee asked. "If you are, I just wanna say that I'm hurt. Hurt real bad that you and Gwen feel this way."

"That's the way we feel, and I don't care how hurt you are."

Ozzie stepped forward. "I agree with them, Reverend Agee, you ain't done right, and you know it."

"That hurts, Ozzie, comin' from you. It really hurts."

"Lemme tell you what's gonna hurt a whole lot worse than that. Next Sunday me and Carl Lee will be in your church. I'll sneak him outta the jail early Sunday and we'll take a little drive. Just about the time you get ready to preach, we'll walk in the front door, down the aisle and up to the pulpit. If you get in my way, I'll put handcuffs on you. Carl Lee will do the preachin'. He'll tell all your people that the money they've given so generously has so far not left your pocket, that Gwen and the kids are about to lose their house 'cause you're tryin' to big-shot with the NAACP. He'll tell them that you lied to them. He may preach for an hour or so. And when he gets through, I'll say a few words. I'll tell them what a lyin', sleazy nigger you are. I'll tell them about the time you bought that stolen Lincoln in Memphis for a hundred dollars and almost got indicted. I'll tell them about the kickbacks from the funeral home. I'll tell them about the DUI charge in Jackson I got dismissed for you two years ago. And, Reverend, I'll tell—"

"Don't say it, Ozzie," Agee begged.

"I'll tell them a dirty little secret that only you and me and a certain woman of ill repute know about."

"When do y'all want the money?"

"How soon can you get it?" Carl Lee demanded.

"Awfully damned quick."

Jake and Ozzie left the Haileys to themselves and went upstairs to the big office, where Ellen was buried in law books. Jake introduced Ozzie to his law clerk, and the three sat around the big desk.

"How are my buddies?" Jake asked.

"The dynamite boys? They're recuperatin' nicely. We'll keep them in the hospital until the trial's over. We fixed a lock on the door, and I keep a deputy in the hall. They ain't goin' anywhere."

"Who's the main man?"

"We still don't know. Fingerprint tests haven't come back yet. There may be no prints to match. He ain't talkin'."

"The other is a local boy, isn't he?" asked Ellen.

"Yeah. Terrell Grist. He wants to sue because he got hurt during the arrest. Can you imagine?"

"I can't believe it's been kept quiet so far," Jake said.

"Me neither. Of course, Grist and Mr. X ain't talkin'. My men are quiet. That leaves you and your clerk here."

"And Lucien, but I didn't tell him."

"Figures."

"When will you process them?"

"After the trial we'll move them to the jail and start the paperwork. It's up to us."

"How's Bud?" Jake asked.

"I stopped by this mornin' to check on the other two, and I went downstairs to see Ethel. He's still critical. No changes."

"Any suspects?"

"Gotta be the Klan. With the white robes and all. It all adds up. First there was the burnin' cross in your yard, then the dynamite, and now Bud. Plus all the death threats. I figure it's them. And we got an informant."

"You what!"

"You heard me. Calls himself Mickey Mouse. He called me at home Sunday and told me that he saved your life. 'That nigger's lawyer' is what he called you. Said the Klan has officially arrived in Ford County. They've set up a klavern, whatever that is."

"Who's in it?"

"He ain't much on details. He promised to call me only if someone is about to get hurt."

"How nice. Can you trust him?"

"He saved your life."

"Good point. Is he a member?"

"Didn't say. They've got a big march planned Thursday."

"The Klan?"

"Yep. NAACP has a rally tomorrow in front of the courthouse. Then they're gonna march for a while. The Klan's supposed to show up for a peaceful march on Thursday."

"How many?"

"The Mouse didn't say. Like I said, he ain't much on details."

"The Klan, marching in Clanton. I can't believe it."

"This is heavy stuff," Ellen said.

"It'll get heavier," Ozzie replied. "I've asked the governor to keep the highway patrol on standby. It could be a rough week."

"Can you believe Noose is willing to try this case in this town?" asked Jake.

"It's too big to move, Jake. It would draw marches, and protests, and Klansmen anywhere you tried it."

"Maybe you're right. How about your jury list?"

"I'll have it tomorrow."

————————

After supper Tuesday Joe Frank Perryman sat on his front porch with the evening paper and a fresh chew of Red Man, and spat carefully, neatly through a small hand-carved hole in the porch. This was the evening ritual. Lela would finish the dishes and fix them a tall glass of iced tea, and they would sit on the porch until dark and talk about the crops, the grandchildren, the humidity. They lived out from Karaway on eighty acres of neatly trimmed and cultivated farmland that Joe Frank's father had stolen during the Depression. They were quiet, hardworking Christian folks.

After a few discharges through the hole, a pickup slowed out on the highway and turned into the Perrymans' long gravel driveway. It parked next to the front lawn, and a familiar face emerged. It was Will Tierce, former president of the Ford County Board of Supervisors. Will had served his district for twenty-four years, six consecutive terms, but had lost the last election in '83 by seven votes. The Perrymans had always supported Tierce because he took care of them with an occasional load of gravel or a culvert for the driveway.

"Evenin', Will," said Joe Frank as the ex-supervisor walked across the lawn and up the steps.

"Evenin', Joe Frank." They shook hands and relaxed on the porch.

"Gimme a chew," Tierce said.

"Sure. What brings you around here?"

"Just passin' by. Thought about Lela's iced tea and got real thirsty. Hadn't seen you folks in a while."

They sat and talked, chewed and spat, and drank iced tea until it was dark and time for the mosquitoes. The drought required most of their time and Joe Frank talked at length of the dry spell and how it was the worst in ten years. Hadn't had a drop of rain since the third week of June. And if it didn't let up, he could forget the cotton crop. The beans might make it, but he was worried about the cotton.

"Say, Joe Frank, I hear you got one of those jury summons for the trial next week."

"Yeah, afraid so. Who told you?"

"I don't know. I just heard it around."

"I didn't know it was public knowledge."

"Well, I guess I must've heard it in Clanton today. I had business at the courthouse. That's where I heard it. It's that nigger's trial, you know."

"That's what I figured."

"How do you feel about that nigger shootin' them boys like he did?"

"I don't blame him," inserted Lela.

"Yeah, but you can't take the law into your own hands," explained Joe Frank to his wife. "That's what the court system is for."

"I'll tell you what bothers me," said Tierce, "is this insanity crap. They're gonna say the nigger was crazy and try to get him off by insanity. Like that nut who shot Reagan. It's a crooked way to get off. Plus it's a lie. That nigger planned to kill them boys, and just sat there and waited on them. It was cold-blooded murder."

"What if it was your daughter, Will?" asked Lela.

"I'd let the courts handle it. When we catch a rapist around here, especially a nigger, we generally lock him up. Parchman's full of rapists who'll never get out. This ain't New York or California or some crazy place where criminals go free. We've got a good system, and old Judge Noose hands down tough sentences. You gotta let the courts handle it. Our system won't survive if we allow people, especially niggers, to take the law into their own hands. That's what really scares me. Suppose this nigger gets off, walks out of the courthouse a free man. Everbody in the country will know it, and the niggers will go crazy. Evertime somebody crosses a nigger, he'll just kill him, then say he was insane, and try to get off. That's what's dangerous about this trial."

"You gotta keep the niggers under control," agreed Joe Frank.

"You better believe it. And if Hailey gets off, none of us will be safe. Ever nigger in this county'll carry a gun and just look for trouble."

"I hadn't really thought about that," admitted Joe Frank.

"I hope you do the right thing, Joe Frank. I just hope they put you in that jury box. We need some people with some sense."

"Wonder why they picked me?"

"I heard they fixed up a hundred and fifty summonses. They're expectin' about a hundred to show up."

"What're my chances of gettin' picked?"

"One in a hundred," said Lela.

"I feel better then. I really ain't got time to serve, what with my farmin' and all."

"We sure need you on that jury," said Tierce.

The conversation drifted to local politics and the new supervisor and what a sorry job he was doing with the roads. Darkness meant bedtime for the Perrymans. Tierce said good night and drove home. He sat at his kitchen table with a cup of coffee and reviewed the jury list. His friend Rufus would be proud. Six names had been circled on Will's list, and he had talked to all six. He put an okay by each name. They would be good jurors, people Rufus could count on to keep law and order in Ford County. A couple had been noncommittal at first, but their good and trusted friend Will Tierce had explained justice to them and they were now ready to convict.

Rufus would be real proud. And he had promised that young Jason Tierce, a nephew, would never be tried on those dope charges.

Jake picked at the greasy pork chops and butterbeans, and watched Ellen across the table do the same thing. Lucien sat at the head of the table, ignored his food, fondled his drink, and flipped through the jury list offering comments on every name he recognized. He was drunker than normal. Most of the names he didn't recognize, but he commented on them anyway. Ellen was amused and winked repeatedly at her boss.

He dropped the list, and knocked his fork off the table. "Sallie!" he yelled.

"Do you know how many ACLU members are in Ford County?" he asked Ellen.

"At least eighty percent of the population," she said.

"One. Me. I was the first in history and evidently the last. These people are fools around here, Row Ark. They don't appreciate civil liberties. They're a bunch of right-wing knee-jerk conservative Republican fanatics, like our friend Jake here."

"That's not true. I eat at Claude's at least once a week," Jake said.

"So that makes you progressive?" asked Lucien.

"It makes me a radical."

"I still think you're a Republican."

"Look, Lucien, you can talk about my wife, or my mother, or my ancestors, but don't call me a Republican."

"You look like a Republican," said Ellen.

"Does he look like a Democrat?" Jake asked, pointing at Lucien.

"Of course. I knew he was a Democrat the moment I saw him."

"Then I'm a Republican."

"See! See!" yelled Lucien. He dropped his glass on the floor and it shattered.

"Sallie!"

"Row Ark, guess who was the third white man in Mississippi to join the NAACP?"

"Rufus Buckley," said Jake.

"Me. Lucien Wilbanks. Joined in 1967. White people thought I was crazy."

"Can you imagine," Jake said.

"Of course, black folks, or Negroes as we called them back then, thought I was crazy too. Hell, everybody thought I was crazy back then."

"Have they ever changed their minds?" Jake asked.

"Shut up, Republican. Row Ark, why don't you move to Clanton and we'll start us a law firm handling nothing but ACLU cases. Hell, bring your old man down from Boston and we'll make him a partner."

"Why don't you just go to Boston?" Jake asked.

"Why don't you just go to hell?"

"What will we call it?" asked Ellen.

"The nut house," said Jake.

"Wilbanks, Row and Ark. Attorneys at law."

"None of whom have licenses," said Jake.

Lucien's eyelids weighed several pounds each. His head nodded forward involuntarily. He slapped Sallie on the rear as she cleaned up his mess.

"That was a cheap shot, Jake," he said seriously.

"Row Ark," Jake said, imitating Lucien, "guess who was the last lawyer permanently disbarred by the Mississippi Supreme Court?"

Ellen gracefully smiled at both men and said nothing.

"Row Ark," Lucien said loudly, "guess who will be the next lawyer in this county to be evicted from his office?" He roared with laughter, screaming and shaking. Jake winked at her.

When he settled down, he asked, "What's this meeting tomorrow night?"

"I want to cover the jury list with you and a few others."

"Who?"

"Harry Rex, Stan Atcavage, maybe one other."

"Where?"

"Eight o'clock. My office. No alcohol."

"It's my office, and I'll bring a case of whiskey if I want to. My grandfather built the building, remember?"

"How could I forget."

"Row Ark, let's get drunk."

"No thanks, Lucien. I've enjoyed dinner, and the conversation, but I need to get back to Oxford."

They stood and left Lucien at the table. Jake declined the usual invitation to sit on the porch. Ellen left, and he went to his temporary room upstairs. He had promised Carla he would not sleep at home. He called her. She and Hanna were fine. Worried, but fine. He didn't mention Bud Twitty.

29 A convoy of converted school buses, each with an original paint job of white and red or green and black or a hundred other combinations and the name of a church emblazoned along the sides under the windows, rolled slowly around the Clanton square after lunch Wednesday. There were thirty-one in all, each packed tightly with elderly black people who waved paper fans and handkerchiefs in a futile effort to overcome the stifling heat. After three trips around the courthouse, the lead bus stopped by the post office and thirty-one doors flew open. The buses emptied in a frenzy. The people were directed to a gazebo on the courthouse lawn, where Reverend Ollie Agee was shouting orders and handing out blue and white FREE CARL LEE placards.

The side streets leading into the square became congested as cars from all directions inched toward the courthouse and finally parked when they could move no closer. Hundreds of blacks left their vehicles in the streets and walked solemnly toward the square. They mingled around the gazebo and waited for their placards, then wandered through the oaks and magnolias looking for shade and greeting friends. More church buses arrived and were unable to circle the square because of the traffic. They unloaded next to the Coffee Shop.

For the first time that year the temperature hit a hundred and promised to go higher. The sky produced no clouds for protection, and there were no winds or breezes to weaken the burning rays or to blow away the humidity. A man's shirt would soak and stick to his back in fifteen minutes under a shade tree; five minutes without shade. Some of the weaker old folks found refuge inside the courthouse.

The crowd continued to grow. It was predominantly elderly, but there were many younger, militant, angry-looking blacks who had missed the great civil rights marches and demonstrations of the sixties and now realized that this might be a rare opportunity to shout and protest and sing "We Shall Overcome," and in general celebrate being black and oppressed in a white world. They meandered about waiting for someone to take charge. Finally, three students marched to the front steps of the courthouse, lifted their placards, and shouted, "Free Carl Lee. Free Carl Lee."

Instantly, the mob repeated the war cry:

"Free Carl Lee!"

"Free Carl Lee!"

"Free Carl Lee!"

They left the shade trees and courthouse and moved closer together near the steps where a makeshift podium and PA system had been set up. They yelled in unison at no one or no place or nothing in particular, just howled the newly established battle cry in a perfect chorus:

"Free Carl Lee!"

"Free Carl Lee!"

The windows of the courthouse flew open as the clerks and secretaries gawked at the happening below. The roar could be heard for blocks and the small shops and offices around the square emptied. The owners and customers filled the sidewalks and watched in astonishment. The demonstrators noticed their spectators, and the attention fueled the chanting, which increased in tempo and volume. The vultures had loitered about waiting and watching, and the noise excited them. They descended upon the front lawn of the courthouse with cameras and microphones.

Ozzie and his men directed traffic until the highway and the streets were hopelessly gridlocked. They maintained a presence, although there was no hint they would be needed.

Agee and every full-time, part-time, retired, and prospective black preacher in three counties paraded through the dense mass of black screaming faces and made their way to the podium. The sight of the ministers pumped up the celebrants, and their unified chants reverberated around the square, down the side streets into the sleepy residential districts and out into the countryside. Thousands of blacks waved their placards and yelled their lungs out. Agee swayed with the crowd. He danced across the small podium. He slapped hands with the other ministers. He led the rhythmic noise like a choir director. He was a sight.

"Free Carl Lee!"

"Free Carl Lee!"

For fifteen minutes, Agee whipped the crowd into a frenzied, coalescent mob. Then, when with his finely trained ear he detected the first hint of fatigue, he walked to the microphones and asked for quiet. The panting, sweating faces yelled on but with less volume. The chants of freedom died quickly. Agee asked for room near the front so the press could congregate and do its job. He asked for stillness so they could go to the Lord in prayer. Reverend Roosevelt offered a marathon to the Lord, an eloquent, alliterative oratorical fiesta that brought tears to the eyes of many.

When he finally said "Amen," an enormous black woman with a sparkling red wig stepped to the microphones and opened her vast mouth. The opening stanza of "We Shall Overcome" flowed forth in a deep, rich, mellow river of glorious a cappella. The ministers behind her immediately clasped hands and began to sway. Spontaneity swept the crowd and two thousand voices joined her in surprising harmony. The mournful, promising anthem rose above the small town.

When they finished, someone shouted "Free Carl Lee!" and ignited another round of chanting. Agee quieted them again, and stepped to the microphones. He pulled an index card from his pocket, and began his sermon.

As expected, Lucien arrived late and half loaded. He brought a bottle and offered a drink to Jake, Atcavage, and Harry Rex, and each declined.

"It's a quarter till nine, Lucien," Jake said. "We've been waiting for almost an hour."

"I'm being paid for this, am I?" he asked.

"No, but I asked you to be here at eight sharp."

"And you also told me not to bring a bottle. And I informed you this was my building, built by my grandfather, leased to you as my tenant, for a very reasonable rent I might add, and I will come and go as I please, with or without a bottle."

"Forget it. Did you—"

"What're those blacks doing across the street walking around the courthouse in the dark?"

"It's called a vigil," explained Harry Rex. "They've

vowed to walk around the courthouse with candles, keeping a vigil until their man is free."

"That could be an awfully long vigil. I mean, those poor people could be walking until they die. I mean, this could be a twelve-, fifteen-year vigil. They might set a record. They might have candle wax up to their asses. Evenin', Row Ark."

Ellen sat at the rolltop desk under William Faulkner. She looked at a well-marked copy of the jury list. She nodded and smiled at Lucien.

"Row Ark," Lucien said, "I have all the respect in the world for you. I view you as an equal. I believe in your right to equal pay for equal work. I believe in your right to choose whether to have a child or abort. I believe in all that crap. You are a woman and entitled to no special privileges because of your gender. You should be treated just like a man." Lucien reached in his pocket and pulled out a clip of cash. "And since you are a law clerk, genderless in my eyes, I think you should be the one to go buy a case of cold Coors."

"No, Lucien," Jake said.

"Shut up, Jake."

Ellen stood and stared at Lucien. "Sure, Lucien. But I'll pay for the beer."

She left the office.

Jake shook his head and fumed at Lucien. "This could be a long night."

Harry Rex changed his mind and poured a shot of whiskey into his coffee cup.

"Please don't get drunk," Jake begged. "We've got work to do."

"I work better when I'm drunk," said Lucien.

"Me too," said Harry Rex.

"This could be interesting," said Atcavage.

Jake laid his feet on his desk and puffed on a cigar. "Okay, the first thing I want to do is decide on a model juror."

"Black," said Lucien.

"Black as old Coaly's ass," said Harry Rex.

"I agree," said Jake. "But we won't get a chance. Buckley will save his peremptory challenges for the blacks. We know that. We've got to concentrate on white people."

"Women," said Lucien. "Always pick women for criminal trials. They have bigger hearts, bleeding hearts, and they're much more sympathetic. Always go for women."

"Naw," said Harry Rex. "Not in this case. Women don't understand things like taking a gun and blowing people away. You need fathers, young fathers who would want to do the same thing Hailey did. Daddies with little girls."

"Since when did you get to be such an expert on picking juries?" asked Lucien. "I thought you were a sleazy divorce lawyer."

"I am a sleazy divorce lawyer, but I know how to pick juries."

"And listen to them through the wall."

"Cheap shot."

Jake raised his arms. "Fellas, please. How about Victor Onzell? You know him, Stan?"

"Yeah, he banks with us. He's about forty, married, three or four kids. White. From somewhere up North. Runs the truck stop on the highway north of town. He's been here about five years."

"I wouldn't take him," Lucien said. "If he's from up North, he doesn't think like we do. Probably in favor of gun control and all that crap. Yankees always scare me in criminal cases. I've always thought we should have a law in Mississippi that no certified yankee could sit on a jury down here regardless of how long he's lived here."

"Thank you so much," said Jake.

"I'd take him," said Harry Rex.

"Why?"

"He's got kids, probably a daughter. If he's from the North he's probably not as prejudiced. Sounds good to me."

"John Tate Aston."

"He's dead," said Lucien.

"What?"

"I said he's dead. Been dead for three years."

"Why's he on the list?" asked Atcavage, the non-lawyer.

"They don't purge the voter registration list," explained Harry Rex, between drinks. "Some die and some move away, and it's impossible to keep the list up to date. They've issued a hundred and fifty summons, and you can expect a hundred to a hundred and twenty to show up. The rest have died or moved away."

"Caroline Baxter. Ozzie says she's black," Jake said flipping through his notes. "Works at the carburetor plant in Karaway."

"Take her," said Lucien.

"I wish," said Jake.

Ellen returned with the beer. She dropped it in Lucien's lap and tore a sixteen-ounce can out of a six-pack. She popped the top and returned to the rolltop desk. Jake declined, but Atcavage decided he was thirsty. Jake remained the non-drinker.

"Joe Kitt Shepherd."

"Sounds like a redneck," said Lucien.

"Why do you say that?" asked Harry Rex.

"The double first name," Lucien explained. "Most rednecks have double first names. Like Billy Ray, Johnny Ray, Bobby Lee, Harry Lee, Jesse Earl, Billy Wayne, Jerry Wayne, Eddie Mack. Even their women have double first names. Bobbie Sue, Betty Pearl, Mary Belle, Thelma Lou, Sally Faye."

"What about Harry Rex?" asked Harry Rex.

"Never heard of a woman named Harry Rex."

"I mean for a male redneck."

"I guess it'll do."

Jake interrupted. "Dell Perry said he used to own a bait shop down by the lake. I take it no one knows him."

"No, but I bet he's a redneck," said Lucien. "Because of his name. I'd scratch him."

"Aren't you given their addresses, ages, occupations, basic information like that?" asked Atcavage.

"Not until the day of trial. On Monday each prospective juror fills out a questionnaire in the courtroom. But until then we have only the names."

"What kind of juror are we looking for, Jake?" Ellen asked.

"Young to middle-aged men with families. I would prefer to have no one over fifty."

"Why?" Lucien asked belligerently.

"Younger whites are more tolerant of blacks."

"Like Cobb and Willard," Lucien said.

"Most of the older folks will always dislike blacks, but

the younger generation has accepted an integrated society. Less bigotry, as a rule, with youth."

"I agree," said Harry Rex, "and I would stay away from women and rednecks."

"That's my plan."

"I think you're wrong," said Lucien. "Women are more sympathetic. Just look at Row Ark. She's sympathetic toward everyone. Right, Row Ark?"

"Right, Lucien."

"She has sympathy for criminals, child pornographers, atheists, illegal immigrants, gays. Don't you, Row Ark?"

"Right, Lucien."

"She and I hold the only two ACLU cards existing at this very moment in Ford County, Mississippi."

"That's sick," said Atcavage, the banker.

"Clyde Sisco," Jake said loudly, trying to minimize controversy.

"He can be bought," Lucien said smugly.

"What do you mean 'He can be bought'?" Jake asked.

"Just what I said. He can be bought."

"How do you know?" asked Harry Rex.

"Are you kidding? He's a Sisco. Biggest bunch of crooks in the eastern part of the county. They all live around the Mays community. They're professional thieves and insurance defrauders. They burn their houses every three years. You've never heard of them?" He was shouting at Harry Rex.

"No. How do you know he can be bought?"

"Because I bought him once. In a civil case, ten years ago. He was on the jury list, and I got word to him that I'd give him ten percent of the jury verdict. He's very persuasive."

Jake dropped the jury lists and rubbed his eyes. He knew this was probably true, but didn't want to believe it.

"And?" asked Harry Rex.

"And he was selected for the jury, and I got the largest verdict in the history of Ford County. It's still the record."

"Stubblefield?" Jake asked in disbelief.

"That's it, my boy. Stubblefield versus North Texas Pipeline. September 1974. Eight hundred thousand dollars. Appealed and affirmed by the Supreme Court."

"Did you pay him?" asked Harry Rex.

Lucien finished a long drink and smacked his lips. "Eighty thousand cash, in one-hundred-dollar bills," he said proudly. "He built a new house, then burned it down."

"What was your cut?" asked Atcavage.

"Forty percent, minus eighty thousand."

The room was silent as everybody but Lucien made the calculation.

"Wow," Atcavage mumbled.

"You're kidding, aren't you, Lucien?" Jake asked half-heartedly.

"You know I'm serious, Jake. You know I lie compulsively, but never about things like this. I'm telling the truth, and I'm telling you this guy can be bought."

"How much?" asked Harry Rex.

"Forget it!" said Jake.

"Five thousand cash, just guessing."

"Forget it!"

There was a pause as each one looked at Jake to make sure he was not interested in Clyde Sisco, and when it was obvious he was not interested, they took a drink and waited for the next name. Around ten-thirty Jake had his first beer, and an hour later the case was gone and forty names remained. Lucien staggered to the balcony and watched the blacks carry their candles along the sidewalks next to the streets around the courthouse.

"Jake, why is this deputy sitting in his car in front of my office?" he asked.

"That's my bodyguard."

"What's his name?"

"Nesbit."

"Is he awake?"

"Probably not."

Lucien leaned dangerously over the railing. "Hey, Nesbit," he yelled.

Nesbit opened the door of his patrol car. "Yeah, what is it?"

"Jake here wants you to go to the store and get us some more beer. He's very thirsty. Here's a twenty. He'd like a case of Coors."

"I can't buy it when I'm on duty," Nesbit protested.

"Since when?" Lucien laughed at himself.

"I can't do it."

"It's not for you, Nesbit. It's for Mr. Brigance, and he really needs it. He's already called the sheriff, and it's okay."

"Who called the sheriff?"

"Mr. Brigance," lied Lucien. "Sheriff said he didn't care what you did as long as you didn't drink any."

Nesbit shrugged and appeared satisfied. Lucien dropped a twenty from the balcony. Within minutes Nesbit was back with a case minus one which had been opened and was sitting on his radar gun. Lucien ordered Atcavage to fetch the beer from below and distribute the first six-pack.

An hour later the list was finished and the party was over. Nesbit loaded Harry Rex, Lucien, and Atcavage into his patrol car and took them home. Jake and his clerk sat on the balcony, sipping and watching the candles flicker and move slowly around the courthouse. Several cars were parked on the west side of the square, and a small group of blacks sat nearby in lawn chairs waiting to take their turns with the candles.

"We didn't do bad," Jake said quietly, staring at the vigil. "We made notes on all but twenty of the hundred and fifty."

"What's next?"

"I'll try to find something on the other twenty, then we'll make an index card for each juror. We'll know them like family by Monday."

Nesbit returned to the square and circled twice, watching the blacks. He parked between the Saab and the BMW.

"The M'Naghten brief is a masterpiece. Our psychiatrist, Dr. Bass, will be here tomorrow, and I want you to review M'Naghten with him. You need to outline in detail the necessary questions to ask him at trial, and cover these with him. He worries me. I don't know him, and I'm relying on Lucien. Get his résumé and investigate his background. Make whatever phone calls are necessary. Check with the state medical association to make sure he has no history of disciplinary problems. He is very important to our case, and I don't want any surprises."

"Okay, boss."

Jake finished his last beer. "Look, Row Ark, this is a

very small town. My wife left five days ago, and I'm sure people will know it soon. You look suspicious. People love to talk, so be discreet. Stay in the office and do your research and tell anyone who asks that you're Ethel's replacement."

"That's a big bra to fill."

"You could do it if you wanted to."

"I hope you know that I'm not nearly as sweet as I'm being forced to act."

"I know that."

They watched the blacks change shifts and a new crew take up the candles. Nesbit threw an empty beer can onto the sidewalk.

"You're not driving home are you?" Jake asked.

"It would not be a good idea. I'd register at least .20."

"You can sleep on the couch in my office."

"Thanks. I will."

Jake said good night, locked the office, and spoke briefly to Nesbit. Then he placed himself carefully behind the wheel of the Saab. Nesbit followed him to his home on Adams. He parked under the carport, next to Carla's car, and Nesbit parked in the driveway. It was 1:00 A.M., Thursday, July 18.

30 They arrived in groups of two and three and came from all over the state. They parked along the gravel road by the cabin deep in the woods. They entered the cabin dressed as normal working men, but once inside they slowly and meticulously changed into their neatly pressed and neatly folded robes and head-dresses. They admired one another's uniforms and helped each other into the bulky outfits. Most of them knew each other, but a few introductions were necessary. They were forty in number; a good turnout.

Stump Sisson was pleased. He sipped whiskey and moved around the room like a head coach reassuring his team before the kickoff. He inspected the uniforms and made adjustments. He was proud of his men, and told them so. It was the biggest meeting of its kind in years, he said. He admired them and their sacrifices in being there. He knew they had jobs and families, but this was important. He talked about the glory days when they were feared in Mississippi and had clout. Those days must return, and it was up to this very group of dedicated men to take a stand for white people. The march could be dangerous, he explained. Niggers could march and demonstrate all day long and no one cared. But let white folks try and march and it was dangerous. The city had issued a permit, and the nigger sheriff promised order, but most Klan marches nowadays were disrupted by roving bands of young wild nigger punks. So be careful, and keep ranks. He, Stump, would do the talking.

They listened intently to Stump's pep talk, and when he finished they loaded into a dozen cars and followed him to town.

Few if any people in Clanton had ever seen the Klan march, and as 2:00 P.M. approached a great wave of excitement rippled around the square. The merchants and their customers found excuses to inspect the sidewalks. They milled about importantly and watched the side streets. The vultures were out in full force and had congregated near the gazebo on the front lawn. A group of young blacks gathered nearby under a massive oak. Ozzie smelled trouble. They assured him they had only come to watch and listen. He threatened them with jail if trouble started. He stationed his men at various points around the courthouse.

"Here they come!" someone yelled, and the spectators strained to get a glimpse of the marching Klansmen as they strutted importantly from a small street onto Washington Avenue, the north border of the square. They walked cautiously, but arrogantly, their faces hidden by the sinister red and white masks hanging from the royal headdresses. The spectators gawked at the faceless figures as the procession moved slowly along Washington, then south along Caffey Street, then east along Jackson Street. Stump waddled proudly in front of his men. When he neared the front of the courthouse, he made a sharp left turn and led his troops down the long sidewalk in the center of the front lawn. They closed ranks in a loose semicircle around the podium on the courthouse steps.

The vultures had scrambled and fallen over themselves following the march, and when Stump stopped his men the podium was quickly adorned with a dozen microphones trailing wires in all directions to the cameras and recorders. Under the tree the group of blacks had grown larger, much larger, and some of them walked to within a few feet of the semicircle. The sidewalks emptied as the merchants and shopkeepers, their customers, and the other curious streamed across the streets onto the lawn to hear what the leader, the short fat one, was about to say. The deputies walked slowly through the crowd, paying particular attention to the group of blacks. Ozzie placed himself under the oak, in the midst of his people.

Jake watched intently from the window in Jean Gillespie's second floor office. The sight of the Klansmen, in full regalia, their cowardly faces hidden behind the ominous masks, gave him a sick feeling. The white hood, for decades a symbol of hatred and violence in the South, was back. Which one of those men had burned the cross in his yard? Were they all active in planning the bombing of his home? Which one would try something next? From the second floor, he could see the blacks inch closer.

"You niggers were not invited to this rally!" Stump

screamed into the microphone, pointing at the blacks. "This is a Klan meetin', not a meetin' for a buncha niggers!"

From the side streets and small alleys behind the rows of red brick buildings, a steady stream of blacks moved toward the courthouse. They joined the others, and in seconds Stump and his boys were outnumbered ten to one. Ozzie radioed for backup.

"My name's Stump Sisson," he said as he removed his mask. "And I'm proud to say I'm the Mississippi Imperial Wizard for the Invisible Empire of the Ku Klux Klan. I'm here to say that the law-abidin' white folks of Mississippi are sick and tired of niggers stealin', rapin', killin', and gettin' by with it. We demand justice, and we demand that this Hailey nigger be convicted and his black ass sent to the gas chamber!"

"Free Carl Lee!" screamed one of the blacks.

"Free Carl Lee!" they repeated in unison.

"Free Carl Lee!"

"Shut up, you wild niggers!" Stump shrieked back. "Shut up, you animals!" His troops stood facing him, frozen, with their backs to the screaming crowd. Ozzie and six deputies moved between the groups.

"Free Carl Lee!"

"Free Carl Lee!"

Stump's naturally colorful face had turned an even deeper red. His teeth nearly touched the microphones. "Shut up, you wild niggers! You had your rally yesterday and we didn't disturb you. We have a right to assemble in peace, just like you do! Now, shut up!"

The chanting intensified. "Free Carl Lee! Free Carl Lee!"

"Where's the sheriff? He's supposed to keep law and order. Sheriff, do your job. Shut those niggers up so we can assemble in peace. Can't you do your job, Sheriff? Can't you control your own people? See, folks, that's what you get when you elect niggers to public office."

The shouting continued and Stump stepped back from the microphones and watched the blacks. The photographers and TV crews spun in circles trying to record it all. No one noticed a small window on the third floor of the courthouse. It opened slowly, and from the darkness within a crude firebomb was thrown onto the podium below. It landed perfectly at Stump's feet and exploded, engulfing the wizard in flames.

The riot was on. Stump screamed and rolled wildly down the front steps. Three of his men shed their heavy robes and masks and attempted to cover him and smother the flames. The wooden podium and platform burned with the thick, unmistakable smell of gasoline. The blacks charged, wielding sticks and knives and hacking at anything with a white face or white robe. Under each white robe was a short black nightstick, and the Klansmen proved ready for the assault. Within seconds of the explosion, the front lawn of the Ford County Courthouse was a battlefield as men screamed and cursed and howled in pain through thick, heavy smoke. The air was filled with rocks and stones and nightsticks as the two groups brawled in hand-to-hand combat.

Bodies began falling on the lush, green grass. Ozzie fell first; the victim of a wicked smash to the base of his skull with a wrecking bar. Nesbit, Prather, Hastings, Pirtle, Tatum, and other deputies ran here and there attempting unsuccessfully to separate various combatants before they killed each other. Instead of running for cover, the vultures darted crazily through the midst of the smoke and violence valiantly trying to capture yet a better shot of the blood and gore. They were sitting ducks. One cameraman, his right eye buried deep in his camera, caught a jagged piece of brick with his left eye. He and his camera dropped quickly to the sidewalk, where, after a few seconds, another cameraman appeared and filmed his fallen comrade. A fearless, busy female reporter from a Memphis station charged into the melee with her microphone in hand and her cameraman at her heels. She dodged a brick, then maneuvered too close to a large Klansman who was just finishing off a couple of black teenagers, when, with a loud piercing scream, he slapped her pretty head with his nightstick, kicked her as she fell, then brutally attacked her cameraman.

Fresh troops from the Clanton City Police arrived. In the center of the battle, Nesbit, Prather, and Hastings came together, stood with their backs to each other, and began firing their Smith & Wesson .357 magnum service revolvers into the air. The sound of the gunfire quelled the riot. The warriors froze and searched for the gunfire, then quickly separated and glared at each other. They retreated slowly to their own groups. The officers formed a dividing line between the blacks and the Klansmen, all of whom were thankful for the truce.

A dozen wounded bodies were unable to retreat. Ozzie sat dazed, rubbing his neck. The lady from Memphis was unconscious and bleeding profusely from the head. Several Klansmen, their white robes soiled and bloody, lay sprawled near the sidewalk. The fire continued to burn.

The sirens drew closer and finally the fire trucks and ambulances arrived and drove onto the battlefield. Firemen and medics attended the wounded. None were dead. Stump Sisson was taken away first. Ozzie was half dragged and half carried to a patrol car. More police arrived and broke up the crowd.

———————

Jake, Harry Rex, and Ellen ate a lukewarm pizza and watched intently as the small television in the conference room broadcasted the day's events in Clanton, Mississippi. CBS ran the story halfway through the news. The reporter had apparently escaped the riot unscathed, and he narrated the video with a play by play of the march, the shouting, the firebomb, and the melee. "As of late this afternoon," he reported, "the exact number of casualties is unknown. The most serious injuries are believed to be the extensive burns suffered by a Mr. Sisson, who identified himself as an imperial wizard of the Ku Klux Klan. He is listed in serious condition at the Mid South Burn Hospital in Memphis."

The video showed a closeup of Stump burning while all hell broke loose. He continued: "The trial of Carl Lee Hailey is scheduled to start Monday here in Clanton. It is unknown at this time what effect, if any, today's riot will have on this trial. There is some speculation the trial will be postponed and/or moved to another county."

"That's news to me," said Jake.

"You haven't heard anything?" asked Harry Rex.

"Not a word. And I presume I would be notified before CBS."

The reporter disappeared and Dan Rather said he would return in a moment.

"What does this mean?" asked Ellen.

"It means Noose is stupid for not changing venue."

"Be glad he didn't," said Harry Rex. "It'll give you something to argue on appeal."

"Thanks, Harry Rex. I appreciate your confidence in my ability as a trial lawyer."

The phone rang. Harry Rex grabbed it and said hello to Carla. He handed it to Jake. "It's your wife. Can we listen?"

"No! Go get another pizza. Hello dear."

"Jake, are you all right?"

"Of course I'm all right."

"I just saw it on the news. It's awful. Where were you?"

"I was wearing one of those white robes."

"Jake, please. This is not funny."

"I was in Jean Gillespie's office on the second floor. We had wonderful seats. Saw the whole thing. It was very exciting."

"Who are those people?"

"Same ones who burned the cross in our front yard and tried to blow up the house."

"Where are they from?"

"Everywhere. Five are in the hospital and their addresses are scattered all over the state. One is a local boy. How's Hanna?"

"She's fine. She wants to come home. Will the trial be postponed?"

"I doubt it."

"Are you safe?"

"Sure. I've got a full-time bodyguard and I carry a .38 in my briefcase. Don't worry."

"But I'm worried, Jake. I need to be home with you."

"No."

"Hanna can stay here until it's over, but I want to come home."

"No, Carla. I know you're safe out there. You won't be safe if you're here."

"Then you're not safe either."

"I'm as safe as I can get. But I'm not taking chances

with you and Hanna. It's out of the question. That's final.
How are your parents?"

"I didn't call to talk about my parents. I called because
I'm scared and I want to be with you."

"And I want to be with you, but not now. Please understand."

She hesitated. "Where are you staying?"

"At Lucien's most of the time. Occasionally at home,
with my bodyguard in the driveway."

"How's my house?"

"It's still there. Dirty, but still there."

"I miss it."

"Believe me, it misses you."

"I love you, Jake, and I'm scared."

"I love you, and I'm not scared. Just relax and take care
of Hanna."

"Goodbye."

"Goodbye."

Jake handed the receiver to Ellen. "Where is she?"

"Wilmington, North Carolina. Her parents spend the
summers there."

Harry Rex had left for another pizza.

"You miss her, don't you?" asked Ellen.

"In more ways than you can imagine."

"Oh, I can imagine."

At midnight they were in the cabin drinking whiskey, cussing
niggers, and comparing wounds. Several had returned from
the hospital in Memphis where they had visited briefly with
Stump Sisson. He told them to proceed as planned. Eleven
had been released from the Ford County Hospital with various cuts and bruises, and the others admired their wounds as
each took his turn describing to the last detail how he had
gallantly battled multiple niggers before being wounded,
usually from the rear or blind side. They were the heroes,
the ones with the bandages. Then the others told their stories and the whiskey flowed. They heaped praise upon the
largest one when he told of his attack on the pretty television
reporter and her nigger cameraman.

After a couple of hours of drinking and storytelling the

talk turned to the task at hand. A map of the county was produced, and one of the locals pinpointed the targets. There were twenty homes this night—twenty names taken from the list of prospective jurors someone had furnished.

Five teams of four each left the cabin in pickups and headed into the darkness to further their mischief. In each pickup were four wooden crosses, the smaller models, nine feet by four feet, each soaked with kerosene. They avoided Clanton and the small towns in the county and instead kept to the dark countryside. The targets were in isolated areas, away from traffic and neighbors, out in the country where things go unnoticed and people go to bed early and sleep soundly.

The plan of attack was simple: a truck would stop a few hundred feet down the road, out of sight, no headlights, and the driver remained with engine running while the other three carried the cross to the front yard, stuck it in the ground, and threw a torch on it. The pickup then met them in front of the house for a quiet getaway and joyride to the next target.

The plan worked simply and with no complications at nineteen of the twenty targets. But at Luther Pickett's residence a strange noise earlier in the night had aroused Luther, and he sat in the darkness of his front porch waiting for nothing in particular when he saw a strange pickup move suspiciously along the gravel road out beyond his pecan tree. He grabbed his shotgun and listened as the truck turned around and stopped down the road. He heard voices, and then saw three figures carrying a pole or something into his front yard, next to the gravel road. Luther crouched behind a shrub next to the porch, and aimed.

The driver took a slug of cold beer and watched to see the cross go up in flames. He heard a shotgun instead. His buddies abandoned the cross and the torch and the front yard, and jumped into a small ditch next to the road. Another shotgun blast. The driver could hear the screams and obscenities. They had to be rescued! He threw down his beer and stepped on the gas.

Old Luther fired again as he came off the porch, and again as the truck appeared and stopped by the shallow ditch. The three scrambled desperately from the mud, stumbling and sliding, cussing and yelling as they attacked the truck and furiously fought to jump into the bed.

"Hang on!" yelled the driver just as old Luther fired again, this time spraying the pickup. He watched with a smile as the truck sped away, spinning gravel and fishtailing from ditch to ditch. Just a bunch of drunk kids, he thought.

From a pay phone, a Kluxer held the list of twenty names and twenty phone numbers. He called them all, simply to ask them to take a look in their front yards.

31 Friday morning Jake phoned the Noose home and was informed by Mrs. Ichabod that His Honor was presiding over a civil trial in Polk County. Jake gave instructions to Ellen and left for Smithfield, an hour away. He nodded at His Honor as he entered the empty courtroom and sat on the front row. Except for the jurors, there were no other spectators. Noose was bored, the jurors were bored, the lawyers were bored, and after two minutes Jake was bored. After the witness finished Noose called for a short recess, and Jake went to his chambers.

"Hello, Jake. Why're you here?"

"You heard what happened yesterday."

"I saw it on the news last night."

"Have you heard what happened this morning?"

"No."

"Evidently someone gave the Klan a list of the prospective jurors. Last night they burned crosses in the yards of twenty of the jurors."

Noose was shocked. "Our jurors!"

"Yes, sir."

"Did they catch anybody?"

"Of course not. They were too busy putting out fires. Besides, you don't catch these people."

"Twenty of our jurors," Noose repeated.

"Yes, sir."

Noose pawed at his mangled mass of brilliant gray hair and walked slowly around the small room, shaking his head and occasionally scratching his crotch.

"Sounds like intimidation to me," he muttered.

What a mind, thought Jake. A real genius. "I would say so."

"So what am I supposed to do?" he asked with a touch of frustration.

"Change venue."

"To where?"

"Southern part of the state."

"I see. Perhaps Carey County. I believe it's sixty percent

black. That would generate at least a hung jury, wouldn't it? Or maybe you would like Brower County. I think it's even blacker. You'd probably get an acquittal there, wouldn't you?"

"I don't care where you move it. It's not fair to try him in Ford County. Things were bad enough before the war yesterday. Now the white folks are really in a lynching mood, and my man's got the nearest available neck. The situation was terrible before the Klan started decorating the county with Christmas trees. Who knows what else they'll try before Monday. There's no way to pick a fair and impartial jury in Ford County."

"You mean black jury?"

"No, sir! I mean a jury that hasn't prejudged this case. Carl Lee Hailey is entitled to twelve people who haven't already decided his guilt or innocence."

Noose lumbered toward his chair and fell into it. He removed those glasses from that nose and picked at the end of it.

"We could excuse the twenty," he wondered aloud.

"That won't help. The entire county knows about it or will know about it within a few hours. You know how fast word travels. The entire panel will feel threatened."

"Then we could disqualify the entire panel and summon a new one."

"Won't work," Jake answered sharply, frustrated by Noose's stubbornness. "All jurors must come from Ford County, and everybody in the county knows about it. And how do you keep the Klan from harassing the next panel? It won't work."

"What makes you so confident the Klan won't follow the case if I move it to another county?" The sarcasm dripped from every word.

"I think they will follow it," Jake admitted. "But we don't know that for sure. What we do know is that the Klan is already in Ford County, that it's quite active now, and that it has already intimidated some potential jurors. That's the issue. The question is, what will you do about it?"

"Nothing," Noose said bluntly.

"Sir?"

"Nothing. I will do nothing but dismiss the twenty. I will

carefully interrogate the panel next Monday, when the trial starts in Clanton."

Jake stared in disbelief. Noose had a reason, a motive, a fear, something he was not telling. Lucien was right—someone had gotten to him.

"May I ask why?"

"I don't think it matters where we try Carl Lee Hailey. I don't think it matters who we put in the jury box. I don't think it matters what color they are. Their minds are made up. All of them, wherever and whoever they are. They've already made up their minds, Jake, and it's your job to pick those who think your man is a hero."

That's probably true, thought Jake, but he wouldn't admit it. He continued staring at the trees outside. "Why are you afraid to move it?"

Ichabod's eyes narrowed, and he glared at Jake. "Afraid? I'm not afraid of any ruling I make. Why are you afraid to try it in Ford County?"

"I thought I just explained it."

"Mr. Hailey will be tried in Ford County starting Monday. That's three days from today. And he will be tried there not because I'm afraid to move it, but because it wouldn't do any good to move it. I've considered all this very carefully, Mr. Brigance, many times, and I feel comfortable with the trial in Clanton. It will not be moved. Anything further?"

"No, sir."

"Good. See you Monday."

———

Jake entered his office through the rear door. The front door had been locked for a week now, and there was always someone banging on it and yelling at it. Most of them were reporters, but many were friends just stopping by to gossip and find out what they could about the big trial. Clients were a thing of the past. The phone rang constantly. Jake never touched it and Ellen grabbed it if she was nearby.

He found her in the conference room up to her elbows in law books. The M'Naghten brief was a masterpiece. He had requested no more than twenty pages. She gave him seventy-five perfectly typed and plainly worded pages, and explained there was no way to cover the Mississippi version of M'Naghten in fewer words. Her research was painstaking and detailed. She had started with the original M'Naghten case in England in the 1800's and worked through a hundred and fifty years of insanity law in Mississippi. She discarded insignificant or confusing cases, and explained in wonderful simplicity the complicated, major cases. The brief concluded with a summary of current law, and applied it to the trial of Carl Lee Hailey.

In a smaller brief, only fourteen pages, she had reached the unmistakable conclusion that the jury would see the sickening pictures of Cobb and Willard with their brains splattered about the stairway. Mississippi admitted such inflammatory evidence, and she had found no way around it.

She had typed thirty-one pages of research on the defense of justifiable homicide, something Jake had considered briefly after the killings. She reached the same conclusion Jake had reached—it wouldn't work. She had found an old Mississippi case where a man had caught and killed an escaped convict who was armed. He had been acquitted, but the differences in that case and Carl Lee's case were enormous. Jake had not asked for the brief, and was irritated that so much energy had been spent on it. He said nothing, however, since she had produced everything he had asked for.

The most pleasant surprise had been her work with Dr. W.T. Bass. She had met with him twice during the week, and they had covered M'Naghten in great detail. She prepared a twenty-five-page script of the questions to be asked by Jake and the answers to be given by Bass. It was a skillfully crafted dialogue, and he marveled at her seasoning. When he was her age, he was an average student more concerned with romance than research. She, on the other hand, as a third-year law student was writing briefs that read like treatises.

"How'd it go?" she asked.

"As expected. He did not budge. The trial will start here Monday with the same panel, minus the twenty who received their subtle warnings."

"He's crazy."

"What're you working on?"

"I'm finishing the brief to support our position that the

details of the rape should be discussed before the jury. It
looks good, at this point."

"When will you finish it?"

"Is there some hurry?"

"By Sunday, if possible. I've got another chore, something a little different."

She slid her legal pad away and listened.

"The State's psychiatrist will be Dr. Wilbert Rodeheaver, head of staff at Whitfield. He's been there forever,
and has testifed in hundreds of cases. I want you to dig a
little and see how often his name appears in court decisions."

"I've already run across his name."

"Good. As you know, the only cases we read about
from the Supreme Court are the ones where the defendant
at trial was convicted and has appealed. The acquittals are
not reported. I'm more interested in these."

"Where are you coming from?"

"I have a hunch Rodeheaver is very reluctant to give an
opinion that a defendant was legally insane. There's a
chance he's never done it. Even in cases where the defendant was clearly crazy and did not know what he was doing.
I'd like to ask Rodeheaver, on cross-examination, about
some of the cases in which he's said there's nothing wrong
with an obviously sick man, and the jury acquitted him."

"Those cases will be very hard to find."

"I know, but you can do it, Row Ark. I've watched you
work for a week now, and I know you can do it."

"I'm flattered, boss."

"You may have to make phone calls to attorneys around
the state who've crossed Rodeheaver before. It'll be hard,
Row Ark, but get it done."

"Yes, boss. I'm sure you wanted it yesterday."

"Not really. I doubt if we'll get to Rodeheaver next
week, so you have some time."

"I don't know how to act. You mean it's not urgent?"

"No, but that rape brief is."

"Yes, boss."

"Have you had lunch?"

"I'm not hungry."

"Good. Don't make any plans for dinner."

"What does that mean?"

"It means I've got an idea."

"Sort of like a date?"

"No, sort of like a business lunch with two professionals."

Jake packed two briefcases and left. "I'll be at Lucien's," he told her, "but don't call unless it's a dire emergency. Don't tell anyone where I am."

"What are you working on?"

"The jury."

Lucien had passed out drunk in the swing on the porch, and Sallie was not around. Jake helped himself to the spacious study upstairs. Lucien had more law books in his home than most lawyers had in their offices. He unpacked his mess in a chair, and on the desk he placed an alphabetical list of the jurors, a stack of three-by-five notecards, and several Magic Markers.

The first name was Acker, Barry Acker. The last name was written in large print across the top of a notecard with a blue Magic Marker. Blue for men, red for women, black for blacks, regardless of gender. Under Acker's name he made notes with a pencil. Age, about forty. Married to his second wife, three children, two daughters. Runs a small unprofitable hardware store on the highway in Clanton. Wife, secretary at a bank. Drives a pickup. Likes to hunt. Wears cowboy boots. Pretty nice guy. Atcavage had gone to the hardware store Thursday to get a look at Barry Acker. Said he looked okay, talked like he had some education. Jake wrote the number nine by the name Acker.

Jake was impressed with his research. Surely Buckley would not be as thorough.

The next name was Bill Andrews. What a name. There were six of them in the phonebook. Jake knew one, Harry Rex knew another one, and Ozzie knew a black one, but nobody knew which one got the summons. He put a question mark by the name.

Gerald Ault. Jake smiled when he wrote the name on the notecard. Ault had passed through his office a few years back when the bank foreclosed on his house in Clanton. His wife was stricken with kidney disease, and the medical bills broke them. He was an intellectual, educated at Princeton, where he met his wife. She was from Ford County, the only child of a once prominent family of fools who had invested all their money in railroads. He arrived in Ford County just in time for his in-laws to go under, and the easy life he had married dissolved into one of struggle. He taught school for a while, then ran the library, then worked as a clerk in the courthouse. He developed an aversion to hard work. Then his wife got sick, and they lost their modest house. He now worked in a convenience store.

Jake knew something about Gerald Ault that no one else knew. As a child in Pennsylvania, his family lived in a farmhouse near the highway. One night while they slept, the house caught fire. A passing motorist stopped, kicked in the front door and began rescuing the Aults. The fire spread quickly, and when Gerald and his brother awoke they were trapped in their upstairs bedroom. They ran to the window and screamed. Their parents and siblings yelled helplessly from the front lawn. Flames poured from every window in the house except for their bedroom. Suddenly, the rescuer soaked himself with water from the garden hose, dashed into the burning house, fought the flames and smoke as he raced upstairs, then bolted through the bedroom door. He kicked out the window, grabbed Gerald and his brother, and jumped to the ground. Miraculously, they were not hurt. They thanked him, through tears and embraces. They thanked this stranger, whose skin was black. He was the first Negro the children had ever seen.

Gerald Ault was one of the few white people in Ford County who truly loved black people. Jake put a ten by his name.

For six hours he went through the jury list, making note-cards, concentrating on each name, envisioning each juror in the box and in deliberation, talking to each one. He rated them. Every black got an automatic ten; the whites were not so easy. The men rated higher than the women; the young men higher than the old men; the educated slightly higher than the uneducated; the liberals, both of them, received the highest ratings.

He eliminated the twenty Noose planned to exclude. He knew something about one hundred and eleven of the prospective jurors. Surely, Buckley could not know so much.

Ellen was typing on Ethel's machine when Jake returned from Lucien's. She turned it off, closed the law books she was typing from, and watched him.

"Where's dinner?" she asked with a wicked smile.

"We're taking a road trip."

"All right! Where to?"

"Have you ever been to Robinsonville, Mississippi?"

"No, but I'm ready. What's there?"

"Nothing but cotton, soybeans, and a great little restaurant."

"What's the dress code?"

Jake inspected her. She wore the usual—jeans, neatly starched and faded, no socks, a navy button-down that was four sizes too big but tucked in nicely above her slender hips.

"You look fine," he said.

They turned off the copier and the lights and left Clanton in the Saab. Jake stopped at a liquor store in the black section of town and bought a six-pack of Coors and a tall, cold bottle of Chablis.

"You have to bring your own bottle to this place," he explained as they left town. The sun was setting into the highway ahead, and Jake flipped down the sun visors. Ellen played bartender and opened two cans.

"How far is this place?" she asked.

"Hour and a half."

"Hour and a half! I'm starving."

"Then fill up on beer. Believe me it's worth it."

"What's on the menu?"

"Barbecued, sauteed shrimp, frog legs, and charbroiled catfish."

She sipped on the beer. "We'll see."

Jake stepped on the gas, and they raced across bridges over the countless tributaries of Lake Chatulla. They climbed steep hills covered with layers of dark green kudzu. They flew around corners and dodged pulpwood trucks making their last runs of the day. Jake opened the sunroof, lowered the windows and let the wind blow. Ellen leaned back in the seat and closed her eyes. Her thick, wavy hair swirled around her face.

"Look, Row Ark, this dinner is strictly business—"

"Sure, sure."

"I mean it. I'm the employer, you're the employee, and this is a business meal. Nothing more or less. So don't get any lustful ideas in your ERA, sexually liberated brain."

"Sounds like you're the one with the ideas."

"Nope. I just know what you're thinking."

"How do you know what I'm thinking? Why do you assume you're so irresistible and that I'm planning a big seduction scene?"

"Just keep your hands to yourself. I'm a wonderfully happily married man with a gorgeous wife who'd kill if she thought I was fooling around."

"Okay, let's pretend to be friends. Just two friends having dinner."

"That doesn't work in the South. A male friend cannot have dinner with a female friend if the male friend has a wife. It just doesn't work down here."

"Why not?"

"Because men don't have female friends. No way. I don't know of a single man in the entire South who is married and has a female friend. I think it goes back to the Civil War."

"I think it goes back to the Dark Ages. Why are Southern women so jealous?"

"Because that's the way we've trained them. They learned from us. If my wife met a male friend for lunch or dinner, I'd tear his head off and file for divorce. She learned it from me."

"That makes absolutely no sense."

"Of course it doesn't."

"Your wife has no male friends?"

"None that I know of. If you learn of any, let me know."

"And you have no female friends?"

"Why would I want female friends? They can't talk about football, or duck hunting, or politics, or lawsuits, or anything that I want to talk about. They talk about kids, clothes, recipes, coupons, furniture, stuff I know nothing about. No, I don't have any female friends. Don't want any."

"That's what I love about the South. The people are so tolerant."

"Thank you."

"Do you have any Jewish friends?"

"I don't know of any in Ford County. I had a real good friend in law school, Ira Tauber, from New Jersey. We were very close. I love Jews. Jesus was a Jew, you know. I've never understood anti-Semitism."

"My God, you are a liberal. How about, uh, homosexuals?"

"I feel sorry for them. They don't know what they're missing. But that's their problem."

"Could you have a homosexual friend?"

"I guess, as long as he didn't tell me."

"Nope, you're a Republican."

She took his empty can and threw it in the back seat. She opened two more. The sun was gone, and the heavy, humid air felt cool at ninety miles an hour.

"So we can't be friends?" she said.

"Nope."

"Nor lovers."

"Please. I'm trying to drive."

"So what are we?"

"I'm the lawyer, you're the law clerk. I'm the employer, you're the employee. I'm the boss, you're the gofer."

"You're the male, I'm the female."

Jake admired her jeans and bulky shirt. "There's not much doubt about that."

Ellen shook her head and stared at the mountains of kudzu flying by. Jake smiled, drove faster, and sipped his beer. He negotiated a series of intersections on the rural, deserted highways and, suddenly, the hills disappeared and the land became flat.

"What's the name of the restaurant?" she asked.

"The Hollywood."

"The what?"

"The Hollywood."

"Why is it called that?"

"It was once located in a small town a few miles away by the name of Hollywood, Mississippi. It burned, and they moved it to Robinsonville. They still call it the Hollywood."

"What's so great about it?"

"Great food, great music, great atmosphere, and it's a

thousand miles from Clanton and no one will see me having dinner with a strange and beautiful woman."

"I'm not a woman, I'm a gofer."

"A strange and beautiful gofer."

Ellen smiled to herself and ran her fingers through her hair. At another intersection, he turned left and headed west until they found a settlement near a railroad. A row of wooden buildings sat empty on one side of the road, and across the street, all by itself, was an old dry goods store with a dozen cars parked around it and music rolling softly out the windows. Jake grabbed the bottle of Chablis and escorted his law clerk up the steps, onto the front porch, and inside the building.

Next to the door was a small stage, where a beautiful old black lady, Merle, sat at her piano and sang "Rainy Night in Georgia." Three long rows of tables ran to the front and stopped next to the stage. The tables were half full, and a waitress in the back poured beer from a pitcher and motioned for them to come on in. She seated them in the rear, at a small table with a red-checkered tablecloth.

"Y'all want some fried dill pickles, honey?" she asked Jake.

"Yes! Two orders."

Ellen frowned and looked at Jake. "Fried dill pickles?"

"Yes, of course. They don't serve them in Boston?"

"Do you people fry everything?"

"Everything that's worth eating. If you don't like them, I'll eat them."

A yell went up from the table across the aisle. Four couples toasted something or somebody, then broke into riotous laughing. The restaurant maintained a constant roar of yelling and talking.

"The good thing about the Hollywood," Jake explained, "is that you can make all the noise you want and stay as long as you want, and nobody cares. When you get a table here, it's yours for the night. They'll start singing and dancing in a minute."

Jake ordered sauteed shrimp and charbroiled catfish for both of them. Ellen passed on the frog legs. The waitress hurried back with the Chablis and two chilled glasses. They toasted Carl Lee Hailey and his insane mind.

"Whatta you think of Bass?" Jake asked.

"He's the perfect witness. He'll say anything we want him to say."

"Does that bother you?"

"It would if he was a fact witness. But he's an expert, and he can get by with his opinions. Who will challenge him?"

"Is he believable?"

"When he's sober. We talked twice this week. On Tuesday he was lucid and helpful. On Wednesday, he was drunk and indifferent. I think he'll be as helpful as any psychiatrist we could find. He doesn't care what the truth is, and he'll tell us what we want to hear."

"Does he think Carl Lee was legally insane?"

"No. Do you?"

"No. Row Ark, Carl Lee told me five days before the killings that he would do it. He showed me the exact place where he would ambush them, although at the time I didn't realize it. Our client knew exactly what he was doing."

"Why didn't you stop him?"

"Because I didn't believe him. His daughter had just been raped and was fighting for her life."

"Would you have stopped him if you could?"

"I did tell Ozzie. But at the time neither of us dreamed it could happen. No, I would not have stopped him if I knew for certain. I would have done the same thing."

"How?"

"Exactly as he did it. It was very easy."

Ellen approached a fried dill pickle with her fork and played with it suspiciously. She cut it in half, pierced it with the fork, and sniffed it carefully. She put it in her mouth and chewed slowly. She swallowed, then pushed her pile of pickles across the table toward Jake.

"Typical yankee," he said. "I don't understand you, Row Ark. You don't like fried dill pickles, you're attractive, very bright, you could go to work with any blue-chip law firm in the country for megabucks, yet you want to spend your career losing sleep over cutthroat murderers who are on death row and about to get their just rewards. What makes you tick, Row Ark?"

"You lose sleep over the same people. Now it's Carl

Lee Hailey. Next year it'll be some other murderer who everybody hates but you'll lose sleep over him because he happens to be your client. One of these days, Brigance, you'll have a client on death row, and you'll learn how terrible it is. When they strap him in the chair and he looks at you for the last time, you'll be a changed man. You'll know how barbaric the system is, and you'll remember Row Ark."

"Then I'll grow a beard and join the ACLU."

"Probably, if they would accept you."

The sauteed shrimp arrived in a small black skillet. It simmered in butter and garlic and barbeque sauce. Ellen dipped spoonfuls onto her plate and ate like a refugee. Merle lit into a stirring rendition of "Dixie," and the crowd sang and clapped along.

The waitress ran by and threw a platter of battered and crunchy frog legs on the table. Jake finished a glass of wine and grabbed a handful of the frog legs. Ellen tried to ignore them. When they were full of appetizers, the catfish was served. The grease popped and fizzed and they did not touch the china. It was charbroiled to a deep brown crisp with black squares from the grill burned on each side. They ate and drank slowly, watching each other and savoring the delicious entree.

At midnight, the bottle was empty and the lights were dimmed. They said good night to the waitress and to Merle. They walked carefully down the steps and to the car. Jake buckled his seat belt.

"I'm too drunk to drive," he said.

"So am I. I saw a little motel not far down the road."

"I saw it too, and there were no vacancies. Nice try, Row Ark. Get me drunk and try to take advantage of me."

"I would if I could, mister."

For a moment their eyes met. Ellen's face reflected the red light cast by the neon sign that flashed HOLLYWOOD atop the restaurant.

The moment grew longer and then the sign was turned off. The restaurant had closed.

Jake started the Saab, let it warm, and raced away into the darkness.

Mickey Mouse called Ozzie early Saturday morning at his home and promised more trouble from the Klan. The riot on Thursday had not been their fault, he explained, yet they were being blamed for it. They had marched in peace, and now their leader lay near death with seventy percent of his body covered with third-degree burns. There would be retaliation; it had been ordered from above. Reinforcements were on the way from other states, and there would be violence. No specifics now, but he would call later when he knew more.

Ozzie sat on the side of his bed, rubbed the swollen hump on the back of his neck and called the mayor. And he called Jake. An hour later they met in Ozzie's office.

"The situation is about to get outta hand," Ozzie said, holding an ice pack to his neck and grimacing with every word. "I've got it from a reliable informant that the Klan plans to retaliate for what happened Thursday. They're supposed to bring fresh troops from other states."

"Do you believe it?" asked the mayor.

"I'm afraid not to believe it."

"Same informant?" asked Jake.

"Yep."

"Then I believe it."

"Somebody said there was talk of movin' or postponin' the trial," Ozzie said. "Any chance of it?"

"No. I met with Judge Noose yesterday. It won't be moved and it'll start Monday."

"Did you tell him about the burnin' crosses?"

"I told him everything."

"Is he crazy?" asked the mayor.

"Yes, and stupid. But don't quote me on that."

"Is he on solid legal ground?" asked Ozzie.

Jake shook his head. "More like quicksand."

"What have you got in mind?" asked the mayor.

Ozzie changed ice packs and carefully rubbed his neck. He spoke with pain. "I have a strong desire to prevent another riot. Our hospital is not big enough to allow this crap to continue. We must do something. The blacks are angry and volatile, and it wouldn't take much to ignite them. Some

blacks are just lookin' for a reason to start shootin', and
those white robes are good targets. I've got a hunch the Klan
may do somethin' really stupid, like try to kill somebody.
They're gettin' more national exposure off this than they've
had in ten years. The informant told me that after Thursday
they've had calls from all over the country from volunteers
wantin' to come down here and join the fun."

He slowly rolled his head around his shoulders and
changed ice packs again. "I hate to say it, Mayor, but I think
you should call the governor and ask for the National
Guard. I know it's a drastic step, but I'd hate to get someone
killed."

"The National Guard!" the mayor repeated in disbelief.

"That's what I said."

"Occupying Clanton?"

"Yep. Protectin' your people."

"Patrolling the streets?"

"Yep. With guns and everthing."

"Oh my, this is drastic. Aren't you overreacting a bit?"

"No. It's evident I don't have enough men to keep
peace around here. We couldn't even stop a riot that happened right in front of us. The Klan's burnin' crosses all over
the county, and we can't do anything about it. What will we
do when the blacks decide to start some trouble? I don't
have enough men, Mayor. I need some help."

Jake thought it was a marvelous idea. How could a fair
and impartial jury be chosen when the National Guard had
the courthouse surrounded? He thought of the jurors arriving for court Monday and walking past the soldiers with guns
and jeeps and maybe even a tank or two parked in front of
the courthouse. How could they be fair and impartial? How
could Noose insist on trying the case in Clanton? How could
the Supreme Court refuse to reverse if, heaven forbid, there
was a conviction? It was a great idea.

"Whatta you think, Jake?" asked the mayor, looking for
help.

"I don't think you have a choice, Mayor. We can't stand
another riot. It could hurt you politically."

"I'm not worried about politics," the mayor replied angrily, knowing Jake and Ozzie knew better. The mayor had
been reelected last time by less than fifty votes and did not

make a move without weighing the political fallout. Ozzie caught a grin from Jake as the mayor squirmed with the thought of having his quiet little town occupied by the army.

After dark Saturday, Ozzie and Hastings led Carl Lee out the rear door of the jail and into the sheriff's patrol car. They talked and laughed as Hastings drove in slow motion out into the country, past Bates Grocery and onto Craft Road. The Haileys' front yard was covered with cars when they arrived, so he parked in the road. Carl Lee walked through his front door like a free man and was immediately embraced by a mob of kinfolks, friends, and his children. They had not been told he was coming. He hugged them desperately, all four at the same time in one long bear hug as if there might be no more for a long time. The crowd watched in silence as this huge man knelt on the floor and buried his head among his weeping children. Most of those in the crowd wept too.

The kitchen was covered with food, and the guest of honor was seated in his usual chair at the head of the table with his wife and children seated around him. Reverend Agee returned thanks with a short prayer of hope and homecoming. A hundred friends waited on the family. Ozzie and Hastings filled their plates and retreated to the front porch, where they swatted mosquitoes and planned strategy for the trial. Ozzie was deeply concerned about Carl Lee's safety while they moved him from the jail to court and back each day. The defendant himself had proven clearly that such journeys are not always safe.

After supper the crowd spilled out into the front yard. The children played while the adults stayed on the porch, as close as possible to Carl Lee. He was their hero, the most famous man most of them would ever see, and they knew him personally. To his people he was on trial for one reason only. Sure he killed those boys, but that wasn't the issue. If he was white, he would receive civic awards for what he did. They would half-heartedly prosecute him, but with a white jury the trial would be a joke. Carl Lee was on trial because he was black. And if they convicted him, it would be because he was black. No other reason. They believed that. They

listened carefully as he talked about the trial. He wanted
their prayers and support, and wanted them all to be there
and watch it and to protect his family.

They sat for hours in the sweltering humidity; Carl Lee
and Gwen in the swing rocking slowly, surrounded by admirers all wanting to be near this great man. When they began
to leave they all embraced him and promised to be there
Monday. They wondered if they would see him again sitting
on his front porch.

At midnight Ozzie said it was time to go. Carl Lee
hugged Gwen and the kids one last time, then took his seat
in Ozzie's car.

Bud Twitty died during the night. The dispatcher called Nesbit, who told Jake. He made a note to send flowers.

32 Sunday. One day before trial. Jake awoke at 5:00 A.M. with a knot in his stomach that he attributed to the trial, and a headache that he attributed to the trial and a late Saturday night session on Lucien's porch with his law clerk and former boss. Ellen had decided to sleep in a guest room at Lucien's, so Jake spent the night on his couch in the office.

He lay on the couch and heard voices from the street below. He staggered in the dark to the balcony, and stopped in amazement at the scene around the courthouse. D-Day! The war was on! Patton had arrived! The streets around the square were lined with transport trucks, jeeps, and soldiers busy running here and there in an effort to get organized and look military. Radios squawked, and potbellied commanders yelled to their men to hurry and get organized. A command post was set up near the gazebo on the front lawn. Three squads of soldiers hammered on stakes and pulled ropes and strung up three enormous canvas camouflage pavilions. Barricades were set up on the four corners of the square, and sentries took their positions. They smoked cigarettes and leaned on the street lights.

Nesbit sat on the trunk of his car and watched the fortifying of downtown Clanton. He chatted with a few of the guardsmen. Jake made coffee and took him a cup. He was awake now, safe and secure, and Nesbit could go home and rest until dark. Jake returned to the balcony and watched the activity until dawn. Once the troops were unloaded, the transport trucks were moved to the National Guard armory north of town, where the men would sleep. He estimated their number at two hundred. They piddled around the courthouse and walked in small groups around the square, looking in shops, waiting for daylight and the hope of some excitement.

Noose would be furious. How dare they call the National Guard without asking him. It was his trial. The mayor had mentioned this, and Jake had explained that it was the mayor's responsibility to keep Clanton safe, not the trial judge's. Ozzie concurred, and Noose was not called.

The sheriff and Moss Junior Tatum arrived and met with the colonel in the gazebo. They walked around the courthouse, inspecting troops and pavilions. Ozzie pointed in various directions and the colonel seemed to agree with whatever he wanted. Moss Junior unlocked the courthouse so the troops would have drinking water and toilet facilities. It was after nine before the first of the vultures stumbled onto the occupation of downtown Clanton. Within an hour they were running everywhere with cameras and microphones gathering important words from a sergeant or a corporal.

"What is your name, sir?"

"Sergeant Drumwright."

"Where are you from?"

"Booneville."

"Where's that?"

" 'Bout a hundred miles from here."

"Why are you here?"

"Governor called us."

"Why did he call you?"

"Keep things under control."

"Are you expecting trouble?"

"No."

"How long will you be here?"

"Don't know."

"Will you be here until the trial's over?"

"Don't know."

"Who knows?"

"The governor, I reckon."

And so on.

Word of the invasion spread quickly through the quiet Sunday morning, and after church the townfolk streamed to the square to verify for themselves that the army had indeed captured the courthouse. The sentries removed the barricades and allowed the curious to drive around their square and gawk at the real live soldiers with their rifles and jeeps. Jake sat on the balcony, drinking coffee and memorizing the notecards of his jurors.

He called Carla and explained that the National Guard

had been deployed, but he was still safe. In fact, he had
never felt so safe. As he talked to her, he explained, there
were hundreds of heavily armed army militiamen across
Washington Street just waiting to protect him. Yes, he still
had his bodyguard. Yes, the house was still standing. He
doubted if the death of Bud Twitty had been reported yet, so
he did not tell her. Maybe she would not hear of it. They
were going fishing on her father's boat, and Hanna wanted
her daddy to go. He said goodbye, and missed the two
women in his life more than ever.

———————

Ellen Roark unlocked the rear door of the office and placed
a small grocery sack on the table in the kitchen. She pulled a
file out of her briefcase and began looking for her boss. He
was on the balcony, staring at notecards and watching the
courthouse. "Evenin', Row Ark."

"Good evening, boss." She handed him a brief an inch
thick. "It's the research you requested on the admissibility of
the rape. It's a tough issue, and it got involved. I apologize
for the size of it."

It was as neat as her other briefs, complete with a table
of contents, bibliography, and numbered pages. He flipped
through it. "Damn, Row Ark, I didn't ask for a textbook."

"I know you're intimidated by scholarly work, so I made
a conscious effort to use words with fewer than three syllables."

"My, aren't we frisky today. Could you summarize this
in a dissertation of, say, thirty pages or so?"

"Look, it's a thorough study of the law by a gifted law
student with a remarkable ability to think and write clearly.
It's a work of genius, and it's yours, and it's absolutely free.
So quit bitching."

"Yes, ma'am. Does your head hurt?"

"Yes. It's been aching since I woke up this morning. I've
typed on that brief for ten hours, and I need a drink. Do you
have a blender?"

"A what?"

"Blender. It's a new invention we have up North.
They're kitchen appliances."

"There's one in the shelves next to the microwave."

She disappeared. It was almost dark, and the traffic had thinned around the square as the Sunday drivers had grown bored with the sight of soldiers guarding their courthouse. After twelve hours of suffocating heat and foglike humidity in downtown Clanton, the troops were weary and homesick. They sat under trees and on folding canvas chairs, and cursed the governor. As it grew darker, they strung wires from inside the courthouse and hung floodlights around the pavilions. By the post office a carload of blacks arrived with lawn chairs and candles to start the nightly vigil. They began pacing the sidewalk along Jackson Street under the suddenly aroused stares of two hundred heavily armed guardsmen. The lead walker was Miss Rosia Alfie Gatewood, a two-hundred-pound widow who had raised eleven children and sent nine to college. She was the first black known to have sipped cold water from the public fountain on the square and live to tell about it. She glared at the soldiers. They did not speak.

Ellen returned with two Boston College beer mugs filled with a pale green liquid. She sat them on the table and pulled up a chair.

"What's that?"

"Drink it. It'll help you relax."

"I'll drink it. But I'd like to know what it is."

"Margaritas."

Jake studied the top of his mug. "Where's the salt?"

"I don't like salt on mine."

"Well, I don't either then. Why margaritas?"

"Why not?"

Jake closed his eyes and took a long drink. And then another. "Row Ark, you are a talented woman."

"Gofer."

He took another long drink. "I haven't had a margarita in eight years."

"I'm very sorry." Her twenty-ounce mug was half empty.

"What kind of rum?"

"I would call you a dumbass if you weren't my boss."

"Thank you."

"It's not rum. It's tequila, with lime juice and Cointreau. I thought every law student knew that."

"How can you ever forgive me? I'm sure I knew it when I was a law student."

She gazed around the square.

"This is incredible! It looks like a war zone."

Jake drained his glass and licked his lips. Under the pavilions they played cards and laughed. Others sought refuge from the mosquitoes in the courthouse. The candles turned the corner and made a pass down Washington Street.

"Yes," Jake said with a smile. "It's beautiful, isn't it? Think of our fair and impartial jurors as they arrive in the morning and are confronted with that. I'll renew my motion for a change of venue. It'll be denied. I'll ask for a mistrial, and Noose will say no. And then I'll make sure the court reporter records the fact that this trial is being conducted in the middle of a three-ring circus."

"Why are they here?"

"The sheriff and the mayor called the governor, and convinced him the National Guard was needed to preserve peace in Ford County. They told him our hospital is not large enough for this trial."

"Where are they from?"

"Booneville and Columbus. I counted two hundred and twenty around lunch."

"They've been here all day?"

"They woke me at five this morning. I've followed their movements all day. They were pinned down a couple of times, but reinforcements arrived. A few minutes ago they met the enemy when Miss Gatewood and her friends arrived with their candles. She stared them down, so now they're playing cards."

Ellen finished her drink and left for more. Jake picked up the stack of notecards for the hundredth time and flashed them on the table. Name, age, occupation, family, race, education—he had read and repeated the information since early morning. Round Two arrived with haste, and she took the cards.

"Correen Hagan," she said, sipping.

He thought a second. "Age, about fifty-five. Secretary for an insurance agent. Divorced, two grown children. Education, probably high school, no more. Native of Florida, for what that's worth."

"Rating?"

"I think I gave her a six."

"Very good. Millard Sills."

"Owns a pecan orchard near Mays. About seventy years old. His nephew was shot in the head by two blacks during a robbery in Little Rock several years ago. Hates blacks. He will not be on the jury."

"Rating?"

"Zero, I believe."

"Clay Bailey."

"Age, about thirty. Six kids. Devout Pentecostal. Works at the furniture plant west of town."

"You've given him a ten."

"Yeah. I'm sure he's read that part in the Bible about an eye for an eye, etc. Plus, out of six kids, I'd think at least two would be daughters."

"Do you have all of them memorized?"

He nodded and took a drink. "I feel like I've known them for years."

"How many will you recognize?"

"Very few. But I'll know more about them than Buckley."

"I'm impressed."

"What! What did you say! I have impressed you with my intellect!"

"Among other things."

"I feel so honored. I've impressed a genius in criminal law. The daughter of Sheldon Roark, whoever he is. A real live *summa cum laude.* Wait'll I tell Harry Rex."

"Where is that elephant? I miss him. I think he's cute."

"Go call him. Ask him to join us for a patio party as we watch the troops prepare for the Third Battle of Bull Run."

She headed for the phone on Jake's desk. "What about Lucien?"

"No! I'm tired of Lucien."

———————

Harry Rex brought a fifth of tequila he found somewhere deep in his liquor cabinet. He and the law clerk argued violently over the proper ingredients of a good margarita. Jake voted with his clerk.

They sat on the balcony, calling names from index
cards, drinking the tangy concoction, yelling at the soldiers,
and singing Jimmy Buffet songs. At midnight, Nesbit loaded
Ellen in his patrol car and took her to Lucien's. Harry Rex
walked home. Jake slept on the couch.

33 Monday, July 22. Not long after the last margarita Jake bolted from the couch and stared at the clock on his desk. He had slept for three hours. A swarm of wild butterflies fought violently in his stomach. A nervous pain shot through his groin. He had no time for a hangover.

Nesbit slept like an infant behind the wheel. Jake roused him and jumped in the back seat. He waved at the sentries, who watched curiously from across the street. Nesbit drove two blocks to Adams, released his passenger, and waited in the driveway as instructed. He showered and shaved quickly. He chose a charcoal worsted wool suit, a white pinpoint button-down, and a very neutral, noncontroversial, expressionless burgundy silk tie with a few narrow navy stripes for good measure. The pleated pants hung perfectly from his trim waist. He looked great, much more stylish than the enemy.

Nesbit was asleep again when Jake released the dog and jumped in the back seat.

"Everything okay in there?" Nesbit asked, wiping the saliva from his chin.

"I didn't find any dynamite, if that's what you mean."

Nesbit laughed at this, with the same irritating, laughing response he made to almost everything. They circled the square and Jake got out in front of his office. Thirty minutes after he left, he turned on the front lights and made the coffee.

He took four aspirin and drank a quart of grapefruit juice. His eyes burned and his head ached from abuse and fatigue, and the tiring part had not yet begun. On the conference table he spread out his file on Carl Lee Hailey. It had been organized and indexed by his law clerk, but he wanted to break it down and put it back together. If a document or case can't be found in thirty seconds, it's no good. He smiled at her talent for organization. She had files and sub-files on everything, all ten seconds away at a fingertip. In a one-inch, three-ring notebook she had a summary of Dr. Bass's qualifi-

cations and the outline of his testimony. She had made notes
on anticipated objections from Buckley, and provided case
authority to fight his objections. Jake took great pride in his
trial preparation, but it was humbling to learn from a third-
year law student.

He repacked the file in his trial briefcase, the heavy
black leather one with his initials in gold on the side. Nature
called, and he sat on the toilet flipping through the index
cards. He knew them all. He was ready.

A few minutes after five, Harry Rex knocked on the
door. It was dark and he looked like a burglar.

"Whatta you doing up so early?" Jake asked.

"I couldn't sleep. I'm kinda nervous." He thrust forward a loaded paper sack with grease spots. "Dell sent these
over. They're fresh and hot. Sausage biscuits, bacon and
cheese biscuits, chicken and cheese biscuits, you name it.
She's worried about you."

"Thanks, Harry Rex, but I'm not hungry. My system is
in revolt."

"Nervous?"

"As a whore in church."

"You look pretty haggard."

"Thanks."

"Nice suit though."

"Carla picked it out."

Harry Rex reached into the sack and produced a handful of biscuits wrapped in foil. He piled them on the conference table and fixed his coffee. Jake sat across from him and
flipped through Ellen's brief on M'Naghten.

"She write that?" Harry Rex asked with both cheeks full
and his jaws grinding rapidly.

"Yeah, it's a seventy-five-page summary of the insanity
defense in Mississippi. It took her three days."

"She seems very bright."

"She's got the brains, and she writes fluidly. The intellect is there, but she has trouble applying what she knows to
the real world."

"Whatta you know about her?" Crumbs fell from his
mouth and bounced on the table. He brushed them onto the
floor with a sleeve.

"She's solid. Number two in her class at Ole Miss. I

called Nelson Battles, Assistant Dean of the Law School, and she checked out fine. She has a good chance of finishing number one."

"I finished ninety-third outta ninety-eight. I would've finished ninety-second but they caught me cheating on an exam. I started to protest, but I figured ninety-third was just as good. Hell, I figured, who cares in Clanton. These people were just glad I came back here to practice when I graduated instead of going to Wall Street or some place like that."

Jake smiled at the story he had heard a hundred times.

Harry Rex unwrapped a chicken and cheese biscuit. "You look nervous, buddy."

"I'm okay. The first day is always the hardest. The preparation has been done. I'm ready. It's just a matter of waiting now."

"What time does Row Ark make her entrance?"

"I don't know."

"Lord, I wonder what she'll wear."

"Or not wear. I just hope she's decent. You know what a prude Noose is."

"You're not gonna let her sit at counsel table are you?"

"I don't think so. She'll stay in the background, sort of like you. She might offend some of the women jurors."

"Yeah, keep her there, but outta sight."

Harry Rex wiped his mouth with a huge paw. "You sleeping with her?"

"No! I'm not crazy, Harry Rex."

"You're crazy if you don't. That woman could be had."

"Then have her. I've got enough on my mind."

"She thinks I'm cute, don't she?"

"She says she does."

"I think I'll give it a shot," he said with a straight face, then he smiled, then he burst into laughter with crumbs spraying the bookshelves.

The phone rang. Jake shook his head, and Harry Rex picked up the receiver. "He's not here, but I'll be glad to give him the message." He winked at Jake. "Yes sir, yes sir, uh huh, yes sir. It's a terrible thing, ain't it. Can you believe a man would do it? Yes sir, yes sir, I agree one hundred percent. Yes sir, and what's your name, sir? Sir?" Harry Rex smiled at the receiver and laid it down.

"What'd he want?"

"Said you was a shame to the white race for being that nigger's lawyer, and that he didn't see how any lawyer could represent a nigger such as Hailey. And that he hoped the Klan got ahold of you, and if they didn't he hoped the bar association looked into it and took away your license for helping niggers. Said he knew you were no 'count because you were trained by Lucien Wilbanks who lives with a nigger woman."

"And you agreed with him!"

"Why not? He was really sincere, not hateful, and he feels better now that it's off his chest."

The phone rang again. Harry Rex snatched the receiver. "Jake Brigance, Attorney, Counselor, Consultant, Adviser, and Guru at Law."

Jake left for the restroom. "Jake, it's a reporter!" Harry Rex yelled.

"I'm on the potty."

"He's got the runs!" Harry Rex told the reporter.

At six—seven in Wilmington—Jake called Carla. She was awake, reading the paper, drinking coffee. He told her about Bud Twitty, and Mickey Mouse, and the promise of more violence. No, he wasn't afraid of that. It did not bother him. He was afraid of the jury, of the twelve who would be chosen, and their reaction to him and his client. His only fear, at the moment, was of what the jury might do to his client. Everything else was irrelevant. For the first time, she did not mention coming home. He promised to call that night.

When he hung up, he heard a commotion downstairs. Ellen had arrived, and Harry Rex was talking loudly. She's wearing a see-through blouse with a miniskirt, thought Jake as he walked downstairs. She was not. Harry Rex was congratulating her on dressing like a Southern woman with all the accessories. She was wearing a gray glen plaid suit with a V-necked jacket and short slim skirt. The silk blouse was black, and apparently the necessary garment was underneath. Her hair was pulled back and braided in some fashion. Incredibly, traces of mascara, eyeliner, and lipstick were visible. In the words of Harry Rex, she looked as much like a lawyer as a woman could look.

"Thanks, Harry Rex," she said. "I wish I had your taste in clothes."

"You look nice, Row Ark," Jake said.

"So do you," she said. She looked at Harry Rex, but said nothing.

"Please forgive us, Row Ark," Harry Rex said. "We're impressed because we had no idea you owned so many types of garments. We apologize for admiring you and we know how much this infuriates your little liberated heart. Yes, we're sexist pigs, but you chose to come to the South. And in the South we, as a rule, drool over well-dressed attractive females, liberated or not."

"What's in the sack?" she said.

"Breakfast."

She tore it open and unwrapped a sausage and biscuit. "No bagels?" she asked.

"What's that?" asked Harry Rex.

"Forget it."

Jake rubbed his hands together and tried to sound enthusiastic. "Well, now that we've gathered here three hours before trial, what would y'all like to do?"

"Let's make some margaritas," said Harry Rex.

"No!" said Jake.

"It'll take the edge off."

"Not me," said Ellen. "This is business."

Harry Rex unwrapped a biscuit, the last of the sack. "What happens first today?"

"After the sun comes up, we start the trial. At nine, Noose will say a few words to the jurors and we start the selection process."

"How long will it take?" asked Ellen.

"Two or three days. In Mississippi, we have the right to interrogate each juror individually in chambers. That takes time."

"Where do I sit and what do I do?"

"She certainly sounds experienced," Harry Rex said to Jake. "Does she know where the courthouse is?"

"You do not sit at counsel table," said Jake. "Just me and Carl Lee."

She wiped her mouth. "I see. Just you and the defendant sitting alone, surrounded by the forces of evil, facing death alone."

"Something like that."

"My father uses that tactic occasionally."

"I'm glad you approve. You'll sit behind me, next to the railing. I'll ask Noose to allow you into chambers for the private discussions."

"What about me?" asked Harry Rex.

"Noose doesn't like you, Harry Rex. He never has. He'd have a stroke if I asked if you could go in chambers. It'd be best if you pretended we'd never met."

"Thanks."

"But we do appreciate your assistance," Ellen said.

"Up yours, Ellie Mae."

"And you can still drink with us," she said.

"And furnish the tequila."

"There will be no more alcohol in this office," Jake said.

"Until the noon recess," said Harry Rex.

"I want you to stand behind the clerk's table, just loiter about like you always do, and take notes on the jury. Try to match them with the notecards. There'll probably be a hundred and twenty."

"Whatever you say."

Daybreak brought the army out in force. The barricades were reinstalled, and on each corner of the square soldiers clustered around the orange and white barrels blocking the street. They were poised and anxious, watching every car intently, waiting for the enemy to attack, wanting some excitement. Things stirred a little when a few of the vultures in their compact wagons and minivans with fancy logos on the doors appeared at seven-thirty. The troops surrounded the vehicles and informed everyone there would be no parking around the courthouse during the trial. The vultures disappeared down the side streets, then moments later reappeared on foot with their bulky cameras and equipment. Some set up camp on the front steps of the courthouse, others by the back door, and another group in the rotunda outside the main door of the courtroom on the second floor.

Murphy, the janitor and only real eyewitness to the killings of Cobb and Willard, informed the press, as best he could, that the courtroom would be opened at eight, and not a minute before. A line formed and soon circled the rotunda.

The church buses parked somewhere off the square, and the marchers were led slowly down Jackson Street by the ministers. They carried FREE CARL LEE signs and sang "We Shall Overcome" in a perfect chorus. As they neared the square, the soldiers heard them and the radios began squawking. Ozzie and the colonel conferred quickly, and the soldiers relaxed. The marchers were led by Ozzie to a section of the front lawn where they milled about and waited under the watchful eyes of the Mississippi National Guard.

At eight, a metal detector was moved to the front doors of the courtroom, and a trio of heavily armed deputies began slowly searching and admitting the crowd of spectators that now filled the rotunda and trailed off into the halls. Inside the courtroom, Prather directed traffic, seating people on the long pews on one side of the aisle while reserving the other side for the jurors. The front pew was reserved for the family, and the second row was filled with courtroom artists who immediately began sketching the bench and the bar and the portraits of Confederate heroes.

The Klan felt obligated to make its presence known on opening day, especially to the prospective jurors as they arrived. Two dozen Kluxers in full parade dress walked quietly onto Washington Street. They were immediately stopped and surrounded by soldiers. The potbellied colonel swaggered across the street and for the first time in his life came face to face with a white-robed and white-hooded Ku Klux Klansman, who happened to be a foot taller. He then noticed the cameras, which had gravitated to this confrontation, and the bully in him vanished. His usual bark and growl was instantly replaced by a high-pitched, nervous, trembling stutter that was incomprehensible even to himself.

Ozzie arrived and saved him. "Good mornin', fellas," he said coolly as he stepped beside the faltering colonel. "We've got you surrounded, and we've got you outnumbered. We also know we can't keep you from being here."

"That's right," said the leader.

"If you'll just follow me and do as I say, we won't have any trouble."

They followed Ozzie and the colonel to a small area on the front lawn, where it was explained that this was their turf for the trial. Stay there and stay quiet, and the colonel would personally keep the troops off them. They agreed.

As expected, the sight of the white robes aroused the blacks who were some two hundred feet away. They began shouting: "Free Carl Lee! Free Carl Lee! Free Carl Lee!"

The Klansmen shook their fists and shouted back:

"Fry Carl Lee!"

"Fry Carl Lee!"

"Fry Carl Lee!"

Two rows of troops lined the main sidewalk that divided the lawn and led to the front steps. Another row stood between the sidewalk and the Klansmen, and one between the sidewalk and the blacks.

As the jurors began arriving, they walked briskly through the rows of soldiers. They clutched their summonses and listened in disbelief as the two groups screamed at each other.

The Honorable Rufus Buckley arrived in Clanton and politely informed the guardsmen of who he was and what that meant, and he was allowed to park in his spot marked RESERVED FOR D.A. next to the courthouse. The reporters went wild. This must be important, someone had broken through the barricade. Buckley sat in his well-used Cadillac for a moment to allow the reporters to catch him. They surrounded him as he slammed the door. He smiled and smiled and made his way ever so slowly to the front door of the courthouse. The rapid fire of questions proved irresistible, and Buckley violated the gag order at least eight times, each time smiling and explaining that he could not answer the question he had just answered. Musgrove trailed behind carrying the great man's briefcase.

Jake paced nervously in his office. The door was locked. Ellen was downstairs working on another brief. Harry Rex was at the Coffee Shop eating another breakfast and gossiping. The notecards were scattered on his desk, and he was tired of them. He flipped through a brief, then walked to the French doors. The shouting echoed through the open windows. He returned to the desk and studied the outline of his opening comments to the prospective jurors. The first impression was critical.

He lay on the couch, closed his eyes, and thought of a thousand things he'd rather be doing. For the most part, he enjoyed his work. But there were moments, frightening moments like this one, when he wished he'd become an insurance agent or a stockbroker. Or maybe even a tax lawyer. Surely those guys didn't regularly suffer from nausea and diarrhea at critical moments in their careers.

Lucien had taught him that fear was good; fear was an ally; that every lawyer was afraid when he stood before a new jury and presented his case. It was okay to be afraid—just don't show it. Jurors would not follow the lawyer with the quickest tongue or prettiest words. They would not follow the sharpest dresser. They would not follow a clown or court jester. They would not follow the lawyer who preached the loudest or fought the hardest. Lucien had convinced him that jurors followed the lawyer who told the truth, regardless of his looks, words, or superficial abilities. A lawyer had to be himself in the courtroom, and if he was afraid, so be it. The jurors were afraid too.

Make friends with fear, Lucien always said, because it will not go away, and it will destroy you if left uncontrolled.

The fear hit deep in his bowels, and he walked carefully downstairs to the rest room.

"How are you, boss?" Ellen asked when he checked on her.

"Ready, I guess. We'll leave in a minute."

"There are some reporters waiting outside. I told them you had withdrawn from the case and left town."

"At this moment, I wish I had."

"Have you heard of Wendall Solomon?"

"Not right off hand."

"He's with the Southern Prisoner Defense Fund. I worked under him last summer. He's tried over a hundred capital cases all over the South. He gets so nervous before a trial he can neither eat nor sleep. His doctor gives him sedatives, but he's still so jumpy no one speaks to him on opening day. And that's after a hundred of these trials."

"How does your father handle it?"

"He has a couple of martinis with a Valium. Then he lies on his desk with the door locked and the lights off until it's time for court. His nerves are ragged and he's ill-tempered. Of course, a lot of that is natural."

"So you know the feeling?"

"I know it well."

"Do I look nervous?"

"You look tired. But you'll do."

Jake checked his watch. "Let's go."

The reporters on the sidewalk pounced on their prey. "No comment" he insisted as he moved slowly across the street toward the courthouse. The barrage continued.

"Is it true you plan to ask for a mistrial?"

"I can't do that until the trial starts."

"Is it true the Klan has threatened you?"

"No comment."

"Is it true you sent your family out of town until after the trial?"

Jake hesitated and glanced at the reporter. "No comment."

"What do you think of the National Guard?"

"I'm proud of them."

"Can your client get a fair trial in Ford County?"

Jake shook his head, then added, "No comment."

A deputy stood guard a few feet from where the bodies had come to rest. He pointed at Ellen. "Who's she, Jake?"

"She's harmless. She's with me."

They ran up the rear stairs. Carl Lee sat alone at the defense table, his back to the packed courtroom. Jean Gillespie was busy checking in jurors while deputies roamed the aisles looking for anything suspicious. Jake greeted his client warmly, taking special care to shake his hand, smile broadly at him, and put his hand on his shoulder. Ellen unpacked the briefcases and neatly arranged the files on the table.

Jake whispered to his client and looked around the courtroom. All eyes were on him. The Hailey clan sat handsomely in the front row. Jake smiled at them and nodded at Lester. Tonya and the boys were decked out in their Sunday clothes, and they sat between Lester and Gwen like perfect little statues. The jurors sat across the aisle, and they were carefully studying Hailey's lawyer. Jake thought this would be a good time for the jurors to see the family, so he walked through the swinging gate in the railing and went to speak to the Haileys. He patted Gwen on the shoulder, shook hands with Lester, pinched each of the boys, and, finally, hugged Tonya, the little Hailey girl, the one who had been raped by the two rednecks who got what they deserved. The jurors watched every move of this production, and paid special attention to the little girl.

"Noose wants us in chambers," Musgrove whispered to Jake as he returned to the defense table.

Ichabod, Buckley, and the court reporter were chatting when Jake and Ellen entered chambers. Jake introduced his clerk to His Honor and Buckley and Musgrove, and to Norma Gallo, the court reporter. He explained that Ellen Roark was a third-year law student at Ole Miss who was clerking in his office, and requested that she be allowed to sit near counsel table and participate in the proceedings in chambers. Buckley had no objections. It was common practice, Noose explained, and he welcomed her.

"Preliminary matters, gentlemen?" Noose asked.

"None," said the D.A.

"Several," said Jake as he opened a file. "I want this on the record."

Norma Gallo started writing.

"First of all, I want to renew my motion for a change of venue—"

"We object," interrupted Buckley.

"Shut up, Governor!" Jake yelled. "I'm not through, and don't interrupt me again!"

Buckley and the others were startled by this loss of composure. It's all those margaritas, thought Ellen.

"I apologize, Mr. Brigance," Buckley said calmly. "Please don't refer to me as governor."

"Let me say something at this point," Noose started. "This trial will be a long and arduous ordeal. I can appreciate the pressure you're both under. I've been in your shoes many times myself, and I know what you're going through. You're both excellent lawyers, and I'm thankful that I have two fine lawyers for a trial of this magnitude. I can also detect a certain amount of ill will between you. That's certainly not uncommon, and I will not ask you to shake hands and be good friends. But I will insist that when you're in my courtroom or in these chambers that you refrain from interrupting each other, and that the shouting be held to a bare minimum. You will refer to each other as Mr. Brigance, and Mr. Buckley, and Mr. Musgrove. Now do each of you understand what I'm saying?"

"Yes, sir."

"Yes, sir."

"Good. Then continue, Mr. Brigance."

"Thank you, Your Honor, I appreciate that. As I was saying, the defendant renews his motion for a change of venue. I want the record to reflect that as we sit here now in chambers, at nine-fifteen, July twenty-second, as we are about to select a jury, the Ford County Courthouse is surrounded by the Mississippi National Guard. On the front lawn a group of Ku Klux Klansmen, in white robes, is at this very moment yelling at a group of black demonstrators, who are, of course, yelling back. The two groups are separated by heavily armed National Guardsmen. As the jurors arrived for court this morning, they witnessed this circus on the courthouse lawn. It will be impossible to select a fair and impartial jury."

Buckley watched with a cocky grin on his huge face, and when Jake finished he said, "May I respond, Your Honor?"

"No," Noose said bluntly. "Motion is overruled. What else do you have?"

"The defense moves to strike this entire panel."

"On what grounds?"

"On the grounds that there has been an overt effort by the Klan to intimidate this panel. We know of at least twenty cross burnings."

"I intend to excuse those twenty, assuming they all showed up," said Noose.

"Fine," Jake replied sarcastically. "What about the threats we don't know about? What about the jurors who've heard of the cross burnings?"

Noose wiped his eyes and said nothing. Buckley had a speech but didn't want to interrupt.

"I've got a list here," Jake said, reaching into a file, "of the twenty jurors who received visits. I've also got copies of the police reports, and an affidavit from Sheriff Walls in which he details the acts of intimidation. I am submitting these to the court in support of my motion to strike this panel. I want this made a part of the record so the Supreme Court can see it in black and white."

"Expecting an appeal, Mr. Brigance?" asked Mr. Buckley.

Ellen had just met Rufus Buckley, and now, seconds later, she understood exactly why Jake and Harry Rex hated him.

"No, Governor, I'm not expecting an appeal. I'm trying to insure that my man gets a fair trial from a fair jury. You should understand that."

"I'm not going to strike this panel. That would cost us a week," Noose said.

"What's time when a man's life is at stake? We're talking about justice. The right to a fair trial, remember, a most basic constitutional right. It's a travesty not to strike this panel when you know for a fact that some of these people have been intimidated by a bunch of goons in white robes who want to see my client hanged."

"Your motion is overruled," Noose said flatly. "What else do you have?"

"Nothing, really. I request that when you do excuse the twenty, you so do in such a way that the other jurors don't know the reason."

"I can handle that, Mr. Brigance."

Mr. Pate was sent to find Jean Gillespie. Noose handed her a list of the twenty names. She returned to the courtroom and read the list. They were not needed for jury duty, and were free to go. She returned to chambers.

"How many jurors do we have?" Noose asked her.

"Ninety-four."

"That's enough. I'm sure we can find twelve who are fit to serve."

"You couldn't find two," Jake mumbled to Ellen, loud enough for Noose to hear and Norma Gallo to record. His Honor excused them and they took their places in the courtroom.

Ninety-four names were written on small strips of paper that were placed in a short wooden cylinder. Jean Gillespie spun the cylinder, stopped it, and picked a name at random. She handed it to Noose, who sat above her and everyone else on his throne, or bench, as it was called. The courtroom watched in dead silence as he squinted down that nose and looked at the first name.

"Carlene Malone, juror number one," he shrieked in his loudest voice. The front row had been cleared, and Mrs. Malone took her seat next to the aisle. Each pew would seat ten, and there were ten pews, all to be filled with jurors. The ten pews on the other side of the aisle were packed with family, friends, spectators, but mainly reporters who scribbled down the name of Carlene Malone. Jake wrote her name too. She was white, fat, divorced, lower income. She was a two on the Brigance scale. Zero for one, he thought.

Jean spun again.

"Marcia Dickens, juror number two," yelled Noose. White, fat, over sixty with a rather unforgiving look. Zero for two.

"Jo Beth Mills, number three."

Jake sank a little in his seat. She was white, about fifty, and worked for minimum wage at a shirt factory in Karaway. Thanks to affirmative action, she had a black boss who was ignorant and abusive. She had a zero by her name on the Brigance notecard. Zero for three.

Jake stared desperately at Jean as she spun again. "Reba Betts, number four."

He sunk lower and began pinching his forehead. Zero for four. "This is incredible," he mumbled in the direction of Ellen. Harry Rex shook his head.

"Gerald Ault, number five."

Jake smiled as his number-one juror took a seat next to Reba Betts. Buckley placed a nasty black mark by his name.

"Alex Summers, number six."

Carl Lee managed a weak smile as the first black emerged from the rear and took a seat next to Gerald Ault. Buckley smiled too as he neatly circled the name of the first black.

The next four were white women, none of whom rated above three on the scale. Jake was worried as the first pew filled. By law he had twelve peremptory challenges, free strikes with no reason required. The luck of the draw would force him to use at least half of his peremptories on the first pew.

"Walter Godsey, number eleven," announced Noose, his voice declining steadily in volume. Godsey was a middle-aged sharecropper with no compassion and no potential.

When Noose finished the second row, it contained seven white women, two black men, and Godsey. Jake sensed a disaster. Relief didn't come until the fourth row when Jean hit a hot streak and pulled the names of seven men, four of whom were black.

It took almost an hour to seat the entire panel. Noose recessed for fifteen minutes to allow Jean time to type a numerical list of names. Jake and Ellen used the break to review their notes and place the names with the faces. Harry Rex had sat at the counter behind the red docket books and feverishly taken notes while Noose called the names. He huddled with Jake and agreed things were not going well.

At eleven, Noose reassumed the bench, and the courtroom was silenced. Someone suggested he should use the mike, and he placed it within inches of his nose. He spoke loudly, and his fragile, obnoxious voice rattled violently around the courtroom as he asked a lengthy series of statutorily required questions. He introduced Carl Lee and asked if any juror was kin to him or knew him. They all knew of him, and Noose assumed that, but only two of the panel admitted knowing him prior to May. Noose introduced the lawyers, then explained briefly the nature of the charges. Not a single juror confessed to being ignorant of the Hailey case.

Noose rambled on and on, and mercifully finished at twelve-thirty. He recessed until two.

———————

Dell delivered hot sandwiches and iced tea to the conference room. Jake hugged and thanked her, and told her to send him the bill. He ignored his food, and laid the notecards on the table in the order the jurors had been seated. Harry Rex attacked a roast beef and cheddar sandwich. "We got a terrible draw," he kept repeating with both cheeks stretched to the limit. "We got a terrible draw."

When the ninety-fourth card was in place, Jake stood back and studied them. Ellen stood beside him and nibbled on a french fry. She studied the cards.

"We got a terrible draw," Harry Rex said, washing it all down with a pint of tea.

"Would you shut up," Jake snapped.

"Of the first fifty, we have eight black men, three black women, and thirty white women. That leaves nine white men, and most are unattractive. Looks like a white female jury," Ellen said.

"White females, white females," Harry Rex said. "The worst possible jurors in the world. White females!"

Ellen stared at him. "I think fat white men are the worst jurors."

"Don't get me wrong, Row Ark, I love white females. I've married four of them, remember. I just hate white female jurors."

"I wouldn't vote to convict him."

"Row Ark, you're an ACLU communist. You wouldn't vote to convict anybody of anything. In your little demented mind you think child pornographers and PLO terrorists are really swell people who've been abused by the system and should be given a break."

"And in your rational, civilized, and compassionate mind, what do you think we should do with them?"

"Hang them by their toes, castrate them, and let them bleed to death, without a trial."

"And the way you understand the law, that would be constitutional?"

"Maybe not, but it'd stop a lot of child pornography and terrorism. Jake, are you gonna eat this sandwich?"

"No."

Harry Rex unwrapped a ham and cheese. "Stay away from number one, Carlene Malone. She's one of those Malones from Lake Village. White trash and mean as hell."

"I'd like to stay away from this entire panel," Jake said, still staring at the table.

"We got a terrible draw."

"Whatta you think, Row Ark?" Jake asked.

Harry Rex swallowed quickly. "I think we oughtta plead

him guilty and get the hell outta there. Run like a scalded dog."

Ellen stared at the cards. "It could be worse."

Harry Rex forced a loud laugh. "Worse! The only way it could be worse would be if the first thirty were sitting there wearing white robes with pointed hats and little masks."

"Harry Rex, would you shut up," Jake said.

"Just trying to help. Do you want your french fries?"

"No. Why don't you put all of them in your mouth and chew on them for a long time?"

"I think you're wrong about some of these women," Ellen said. "I'm inclined to agree with Lucien. Women, as a very general rule, will have more sympathy. We're the ones who get raped, remember?"

"I have no response to that," Harry Rex said.

"Thanks," replied Jake. "Which one of these girls is your former client who'll supposedly do anything for you if you'll simply wink at her?"

Ellen snickered. "Must be number twenty-nine. She's five feet tall and weighs four hundred pounds."

Harry Rex wiped his mouth with a sheet of paper. "Very funny. Number seventy-four. She's too far back. Forget her."

Noose rapped his gavel at two and the courtroom came to order.

"The State may examine the panel," he said.

The magnificent district attorney rose slowly and walked importantly to the bar, where he stood and gazed pensively at the spectators and jurors. He realized the artists were sketching him, and he seemed to pose for just a moment. He smiled sincerely at the jurors, then introduced himself. He explained that he was the people's lawyer; his client, the State of Mississippi. He had served as their prosecutor for nine years now, and it was an honor for which he would always be grateful to the fine folks of Ford County. He pointed at them and told them that they, the very ones sitting there, were the folks who had elected him to represent them. He thanked them, and hoped he did not let them down.

Yes, he was nervous and frightened. He had prosecuted

thousands of criminals, but he was always scared with each trial. Yes! He was scared, and not ashamed to admit it. Scared because of the awesome responsibility the people had bestowed upon him as the man responsible for sending criminals to jail and protecting the people. Scared because he might fail to adequately represent his client, the people of this great state.

Jake had heard all this crap many times before. He had it memorized. Buckley the good guy, the state's lawyer, united with the people to seek justice, to save society. He was a smooth, gifted orator who one moment could chat softly with a jury, much like a grandfather giving advice to his grandchildren. The next moment he would launch into a tirade and deliver a sermon that any black preacher would envy. A split second later, in a fluid burst of eloquence, he could convince a jury that the stability of our society, yes, even the future of the human race, depended upon a guilty verdict. He was at his best in big trials, and this was his biggest. He spoke without notes, and held the courtroom captivated as he portrayed himself as the underdog, the friend and partner of the jury, who, together with him, would find the truth, and punish this man for his monstrous deed.

After ten minutes, Jake had enough. He stood with a frustrated look. "Your Honor, I object to this. Mr. Buckley is not selecting a jury. I'm not sure what he's doing, but he's not interrogating the panel."

"Sustained!" Noose yelled into the mike. "If you don't have any questions for the panel, Mr. Buckley, then please sit down."

"I apologize, Your Honor," Buckley said awkwardly, pretending to be hurt. Jake had drawn first blood.

Buckley picked up a legal pad and launched into a list of a thousand questions. He asked if anyone on the panel had ever served on a jury before. Several hands went up. Civil or criminal? Did you vote to acquit or convict? How long ago? Was the defendant black or white? Victim, black or white? Had anyone been the victim of a violent crime? Two hands. When? Where? Was the assailant caught? Convicted? Black or white? Jake, Harry Rex, and Ellen took pages of notes. Any member of your family been the victim of a violent crime? Several more hands. When? Where? What happened to the criminal? Any member of your family ever been charged with a crime? Indicted? Put on trial? Convicted? Any friends or family members employed in law enforcement? Who? Where?

For three nonstop hours Buckley probed and picked like a surgeon. He was masterful. The preparation was obvious. He asked questions that Jake had not considered. And he asked virtually every question Jake had written in his outline. He delicately pried details of personal feelings and opinions. And when the time was right, he would say something funny so everyone could laugh and relieve the tension. He held the courtroom in his palm, and when Noose stopped him at five o'clock he was in full stride. He would finish in the morning.

His Honor adjourned until nine the next morning. Jake talked to his client for a few moments while the crowd moved toward the rear. Ozzie stood nearby with the handcuffs. When Jake finished, Carl Lee knelt before his family on the front row and hugged them all. He would see them tomorrow, he said. Ozzie led him into the holding room and down the stairs, where a swarm of deputies waited to take him to jail.

34 For Day Two the sun rose quickly in the east and in seconds burned the dew off the thick green Bermuda around the Ford County Courthouse. A sticky, invisible fog smoldered from the grass and clung to the heavy boots and bulky pants of the soldiers. The sun baked them as they nonchalantly paced the sidewalks of downtown Clanton. They loitered under shade trees and the canopies of small shops. By the time breakfast was served under the pavilions, the soldiers had stripped to their pale green undershirts and were drenched in sweat.

The black preachers and their followers went directly to their spot and set up camp. They unfolded lawn chairs under oak trees and placed coolers of ice water on card tables. Blue and white FREE CARL LEE placards were tacked on tomato stakes and stuck in the ground like neat fencerows. Agee had printed some new posters with an enlarged black and white photo of Carl Lee in the center and a red, white, and blue border. They were slick and professional.

The Klansmen went obediently to their section of the front lawn. They brought their own placards—white backgrounds with bold red letters screaming FRY CARL LEE, FRY CARL LEE. They waved them at the blacks across the lawn, and the two groups started shouting. The soldiers formed neat lines along the sidewalk, and stood armed but casual as obscenities and chants flew over their heads. It was 8:00 A.M. of Day Two.

The reporters were giddy with all the newsworthiness. They rushed to the front lawn when the yelling started. Ozzie and the colonel walked around and around the courthouse, pointing here and there and yelling into their radios.

At nine, Ichabod said good morning to the standing-room-only crowd. Buckley stood slowly and with great animation informed His Honor that he had no further questions for the panel.

Lawyer Brigance rose from his seat with rubber knees

and turbulence in his stomach. He walked to the railing and gazed into the anxious eyes of ninety-four prospective jurors.

The crowd listened intently to this young, cocky mouthpiece who had once boasted of never having lost a murder case. He appeared relaxed and confident. His voice was loud, yet warm. His words were educated, yet colloquial. He introduced himself again, and his client, then his client's family, saving the little girl for last. He complimented the D.A. for such an exhaustive interrogation yesterday afternoon, and confessed that most of his questions had already been asked. He glanced at his notes. His first question was a bombshell.

"Ladies and gentlemen, do any of you believe that the insanity defense should not be used under any circumstances?"

They squirmed a little, but no hands. He caught them off-guard, right off the bat. Insanity! Insanity! The seed had been planted.

"If we prove Carl Lee Hailey was legally insane when he shot Billy Ray Cobb and Pete Willard, is there a person on this panel who cannot find him not guilty?"

The question was hard to follow—intentionally so. There were no hands. A few wanted to respond, but they were not certain of the appropriate response.

Jake eyed them carefully, knowing most of them were confused, but also knowing that for this moment every member of the panel was thinking about his client being insane. That's where he would leave them.

"Thank you," he said with all the charm he had ever mustered in his life. "I have nothing further, Your Honor."

Buckley looked confused. He stared at the judge, who was equally bewildered.

"Is that all?" Noose asked incredulously. "Is that all, Mr. Brigance?"

"Yes, sir, Your Honor, the panel looks fine to me," Jake said with an air of trust, as opposed to Buckley, who had grilled them for three hours. The panel was anything but acceptable to Jake, but there was no sense repeating the same questions Buckley had asked.

"Very well. Let me see the attorneys in chambers."

Buckley, Musgrove, Jake, Ellen, and Mr. Pate followed

Ichabod through the door behind the bench and sat around the desk in chambers. Noose spoke: "I assume, gentlemen, that you want each juror questioned individually on the death penalty."

"Yes, sir," said Jake.

"That's correct, Your Honor," said Buckley.

"Very well. Mr. Bailiff, would you bring in juror number one, Carlene Malone."

Mr. Pate left, walked to the courtroom and yelled for Carlene Malone. Moments later she followed him into chambers. She was terrified. The attorneys smiled but said nothing: Noose's instructions.

"Please have a seat," Noose offered as he removed his robe. "This will only take a minute, Mrs. Malone. Do you have any strong feelings one way or the other about the death penalty?" asked Noose.

She shook her head nervously and stared at Ichabod. "Uh, no, sir."

"You realize that if you're selected for this jury and Mr. Hailey is convicted, you will be called upon to sentence him to death?"

"Yes, sir."

"If the State proves beyond a reasonable doubt that the killings were premeditated, and if you believe Mr. Hailey was not legally insane at the time of the killings, could you consider imposing the death penalty?"

"Certainly. I think it should be used all the time. Might stop some of this meanness. I'm all for it."

Jake continued smiling and nodding politely at juror number one. Buckley smiled too, and winked at Musgrove.

"Thank you, Mrs. Malone. You may return to your seat in the courtroom," Noose said.

"Bring in number two," Noose ordered Mr. Pate. Marcia Dickens, an elderly white woman with a hard frown, was led to chambers. Yes, sir, she said, she was very much in favor of the death penalty. Would have no problems voting for it. Jake sat there and smiled. Buckley winked again. Noose thanked her and called for number three.

Three and four were equally unforgiving, ready to kill if the proof was there. Then number five, Gerald Ault, Jake's secret weapon, was seated in chambers.

"Thank you Mr. Ault, this will only take a minute," Noose repeated. "First of all, do you have strong feelings for or against the death penalty?"

"Oh, yes, sir." Ault answered eagerly, his voice and face radiating compassion. "I'm very much against it. It's cruel and unusual. I'm ashamed I live in a society which permits the legal killing of a human being."

"I see. Could you, under any circumstances, if you were a juror, vote to impose the death penalty?"

"Oh, no, sir. Under no circumstances. Regardless of the crime. No, sir."

Buckley cleared his throat and somberly announced, "Your Honor, the State would challenge Mr. Ault for cause and move to excuse him under the authority of State vs. Witherspoon."

"Motion sustained. Mr. Ault, you are excused from jury duty," Noose said. "You may leave the courtroom if you wish. If you choose to remain in the courtroom, I ask that you not sit with the other jurors."

Ault was puzzled and looked helplessly at his friend Jake, who at the moment was staring at the floor with a tight mouth.

"May I ask why?" Gerald asked.

Noose removed his glasses and became the professor. "Under the law, Mr. Ault, the court is required to excuse any potential juror who admits he or she cannot consider, and the key word is consider, the death penalty. You see, whether you like it or not, the death penalty is a legal method of punishment in Mississippi and in most states. Therefore, it is unfair to select jurors who cannot follow the law."

The curiosity of the crowd was piqued when Gerald Ault emerged from behind the bench, walked through the small gate in the railing, and left the courtroom. The bailiff fetched number six, Alex Summers, and led him to chambers. He returned moments later and took his seat on the first row. He lied about the death penalty. He opposed it as did most blacks, but he told Noose he had no objections to it. No problem. Later during a recess, he quietly met with other black jurors and explained how the questions in chambers should be answered.

The slow process continued until mid-afternoon, when the last juror left chambers. Eleven had been excused due to reservations about capital punishment. Noose recessed at three-thirty and gave the lawyers until four to review their notes.

In the library on the third floor, Jake and his team stared at the jury lists and notecards. It was time to decide. He had dreamed about names written in blue and red and black with numbers beside them. He had watched them in the courtroom for two full days now. He knew them. Ellen wanted women. Harry Rex wanted men.

Noose stared at his master list, with the jurors renumbered to reflect the dismissals for cause, and looked at his lawyers. "Gentlemen, are you ready? Good. As you know this is a capital case, so each of you have twelve peremptory challenges. Mr. Buckley, you are required to submit a list of twelve jurors to the defense. Please start with juror number one and refer to each juror only by number."

"Yes sir. Your Honor, the State will accept jurors number one, two, three, four, use our first challenge on number five, accept numbers six, seven, eight, nine, use our second challenge on number ten, accept numbers eleven, twelve, thirteen, use our third challenge on number fourteen, and accept number fifteen. That's twelve, I believe."

Jake and Ellen circled and made notes on their lists. Noose methodically recounted. "Yes, that's twelve. Mr. Brigance."

Buckley submitted twelve white females. Two blacks and a white male had been stricken.

Jake studied his list and scratched names. "The defense will strike jurors number one, two, three, accept four, six, and seven, strike eight, nine, eleven, twelve, accept thirteen, strike fifteen. I believe that's eight of our challenges."

His Honor drew lines and check marks down his list, calculating slowly as he went. "Both of you have accepted jurors number four, six, seven, and thirteen. Mr. Buckley, it's back to you. Give us eight more jurors."

"The State will accept sixteen, use our fourth challenge on seventeen, accept eighteen, nineteen, twenty, strike twenty-one, accept twenty-two, strike twenty-three, accept twenty-four, strike twenty-five and twenty-six, and accept twenty-seven and twenty-eight. That's twelve with four challenges remaining."

Jake was flabbergasted. Buckley had again stricken all the blacks and all the men. He was reading Jake's mind.

"Mr. Brigance, it's back to you."

"May we have a moment to confer, Your Honor?"

"Five minutes," Noose replied.

Jake and his clerk stepped next door to the coffee room, where Harry Rex was waiting. "Look at this," Jake said as he laid the list on a table and the three huddled around it. "We're down to twenty-nine. I've got four challenges left and so does Buckley. He's struck every black and every male. It's an all-white female jury right now. The next two are white females, thirty-one is Clyde Sisco, and thirty-two is Barry Acker."

"Then four of the next six are black," Ellen said.

"Yeah, but Buckley won't take it that far. In fact, I'm surprised he's let us get this close to the fourth row."

"I know you want Acker. What about Sisco?" asked Harry Rex.

"I'm afraid of him. Lucien said he's a crook who could be bought."

"Great! Let's get him, then go buy him."

"Very funny. How do you know Buckley hasn't already bought him?"

"I'd take him."

Jake studied the list, counting and recounting. Ellen wanted to strike both men—Acker and Sisco.

They returned to chambers and sat down. The court reporter was ready. "Your Honor, we will strike number twenty-two and number twenty-eight, with two challenges remaining."

"Back to you, Mr. Buckley. Twenty-nine and thirty."

"The State will take them both. That's twelve with four challenges left."

"Back to you, Mr. Brigance."

"We will strike twenty-nine and thirty."

"And you're out of challenges, correct?" Noose asked.

"Correct."

"Very well. Mr. Buckley, thirty-one and thirty-two."

"The State will take them both," Buckley said quickly,
looking at the names of the blacks coming after Clyde Sisco.

"Good. That's twelve. Let's select two alternates. You
will both have two challenges for the alternates. Mr. Buckley, thirty-three and thirty-four."

Juror thirty-three was a black male. Thirty-four was a
white female Jake wanted. The next two were black males.

"We'll strike thirty-three, accept thirty-four and thirty-
five."

"The defense will accept both," Jake said.

Mr. Pate brought the courtroom to order as Noose and
the lawyers took their places. His Honor called the names of
the twelve and they slowly, nervously made their way to the
jury box, where they were seated in order by Jean Gillespie.
Ten women, two men, all white. The blacks in the courtroom
mumbled and eyed each other in disbelief.

"Did you pick that jury?" Carl Lee whispered to Jake.

"I'll explain later," Jake said.

The two alternates were called and seated next to the
jury box.

"What's the black dude for?" Carl Lee whispered, nodding at the alternate.

"I'll explain later," Jake said.

Noose cleared his throat and looked down at his new
jury. "Ladies and gentlemen, you have been carefully selected to serve as jurors in this case. You have been sworn to
fairly try all issues presented before you and to follow the
law as I instruct. Now, according to Mississippi law, you will
be sequestered until this trial is over. This means you will be
housed in a motel and will not be allowed to return home
until it's over. I realize this is an extreme hardship, but it's
one the law requires. In just a few moments we will recess
until in the morning, and you will be given the chance to call
home and order your clothes, toiletries, and whatever else
you need. Each night you will stay in a motel at an undis-
closed location outside of Clanton. Any questions?"

The twelve appeared dazed, bewildered by the thought
of not going home for several days. They thought of families,
kids, jobs, laundry. Why them? Out of all those people in the
courtroom, why them?

With no response, Noose banged his gavel and the

courtroom began to empty. Jean Gillespie escorted the first juror to the judge's chambers, where she called home and ordered clothes and a toothbrush.

"Where are we going?" she asked Jean.

"It's confidential," Jean said.

"It's confidential," she repeated over the phone to her husband.

By seven, the families had responded with a wild assortment of luggage and boxes. The chosen ones loaded a chartered Greyhound bus outside the rear door. Preceded by two patrol cars and an army jeep and followed by three state troopers, the bus circled the square and left Clanton.

Stump Sisson died Tuesday night at the burn hospital in Memphis. His short, fat body had been neglected over the years and proved itself deficient in resisting the complications bred by the serious burns. His death brought to four the number of fatalities related to the rape of Tonya Hailey. Cobb, Willard, Bud Twitty, and now Sisson.

Immediately, word of his death reached the cabin deep in the woods where the patriots met, ate, and drank each night after the trial. Revenge, they vowed, an eye for an eye and so on. There were new recruits from Ford County—five in all—making a total of eleven local boys. They were eager and hungry, and wanted some action.

The trial had been too quiet so far. It was time for excitement.

Jake paced in front of the couch and delivered his opening statement for the hundredth time. Ellen listened intently. She had listened, interrupted, objected, criticized, and argued for two hours. She was tired now. He had it perfect. The margaritas had calmed him and plated his tongue silver. The words flowed smoothly. He was gifted. Especially after a drink or two.

When he finished they sat on the balcony and watched the candles inch slowly in the darkness around the square. The laughter from the poker games under the pavilions echoed softly through the night. There was no moon.

Ellen left for the final round of drinks. She returned with her same beer mugs filled with ice and margaritas. She sat them on the table and stood behind her boss. She placed her hands on his shoulders and began rubbing the lower part of his neck with her thumbs. He relaxed and moved his head from side to side. She massaged his shoulders and upper back, and pressed her body against his.

"Ellen, it's ten-thirty, and I'm sleepy. Where are you staying tonight?"

"Where do you think I should stay?"

"I think you should stay at your apartment at Ole Miss."

"I'm too drunk to drive."

"Nesbit will drive you."

"Where, may I ask, are you staying?"

"At the house my wife and I own on Adams Street."

She stopped rubbing and grabbed her drink. Jake stood and leaned over the rail and yelled at Nesbit. "Nesbit! Wake up! You're driving to Oxford!"

35 Carla found the story on the second page of the front section. "All White Jury Chosen for Hailey" read the headline. Jake had not called Tuesday night. She read the story and ignored her coffee.

The beach house sat by itself in a semisecluded area of the beach. The nearest neighbor was two hundred yards away. Her father owned the land in between and had no plans to sell it. He had built the house ten years earlier when he sold his company in Knoxville and retired wealthy. Carla was the only child, and now Hanna would be the only grandchild. The house—with four bedrooms and four bathrooms scattered over three levels—had room for a dozen grandchildren.

She finished the article and walked to the bay windows in the breakfast room overlooking the beach, and then the ocean. The brilliant orange mass of the sun had just cleared the horizon. She preferred the warmth of the bed until well after daybreak, but life with Jake had brought new adventure to the first seven hours of each day. Her body was conditioned to at least wake up at five-thirty. He once told her his goal was to go to work in the dark and return from work in the dark. He usually achieved this goal. He took great pride in working more hours each day than any lawyer in Ford County. He was different, but she loved him.

Forty-eight miles northeast of Clanton, the Milburn county seat of Temple lay peacefully beside the Tippah River. It had three thousand people and two motels. The Temple Inn was deserted, there being no moral reason to be there this time of year. At the end of one secluded wing, eight rooms were occupied and guarded by soldiers and a couple of state troopers. The ten women had paired off nicely, as had Barry Acker and Clyde Sisco. The black alternate, Ben Lester Newton, was awarded a room to himself, as was the other alternate, Francie Pitts. The televisions had been disconnected and no newspapers were allowed. Supper Tuesday night had been delivered to the rooms, and Wednesday's breakfast arrived promptly at seven-thirty while the Greyhound warmed and blew diesel fumes all over the parking lot. Thirty minutes later the fourteen loaded aboard and the entourage set out for Clanton.

They talked on the bus about their families and jobs. Two or three had known each other prior to Monday; most were strangers. They awkwardly avoided any mention of why they were all together and the task before them. Judge Noose had been very plain on this point; no discussions about the case. They wanted to talk about many things: the rape, the rapists, Carl Lee, Jake, Buckley, Noose, the Klan, lots of things. Everyone knew of the burning crosses, but they weren't discussed, at least they weren't discussed on the bus. There had been many discussions back in the motel rooms.

The Greyhound arrived at the courthouse five minutes before nine, and the jurors stared through dark windows to see how many blacks and how many Klansmen and how many others were being separated by the guardsmen. It eased past the barricades and parked at the rear of the courthouse, where the deputies were waiting to escort them upstairs as soon as possible. They went up the back stairs to the jury room, where coffee and doughnuts were waiting. The bailiff informed them it was nine, and His Honor was ready to start. He led them into the crowded courtroom and into the jury box, where they sat in their designated seats.

"All rise for the court," Mr. Pate yelled.

"Please be seated," Noose said as he fell into the tall leather chair behind the bench. "Good morning, ladies and gentlemen," he said warmly to the jurors. "I trust you're all feeling well this morning, and ready to go."

They all nodded.

"Good. I'm going to ask you this question every morning: Did anybody attempt to contact you, talk to you, or influence you in any way last night?"

They all shook their heads.

"Good. Did you discuss this case among yourselves?"

They all lied and shook their heads.

"Good. If anyone attempts to contact you and discuss

this case or influence you in any way, I expect you to notify me as soon as possible. Do you understand?"

They nodded.

"Now at this time we are ready to start the trial. The first order of business is to allow the attorneys to make opening statements. I want to caution you that nothing the attorneys say is testimony and is not to be taken as evidence. Mr. Buckley, do you wish to make an opening statement?"

Buckley rose and buttoned his shiny polyester coat. "Yes, Your Honor."

"I thought so. You may proceed."

Buckley lifted the small, wooden podium and moved it squarely in front of the jury box, where he stood behind it and breathed deeply and slowly flipped through some notes on a legal pad. He enjoyed the brief period of quietness with all eyes on him and all ears anxious for his words. He started by thanking the jurors for being there, for their sacrifices, for their citizenship (as if they had a choice, thought Jake). He was proud of them and honored to be associated with them in this most important case. Again, he was their lawyer. His client, the State of Mississippi. He expressed fear at this awesome responsibility that they, the people, had given to him, Rufus Buckley, a simple country lawyer from Smithfield. He rambled on about himself and his thoughts on the trial, and his hopes and prayers that he would do a good job for the people of this state.

He gave pretty much the same spiel in all of his opening statements, but this was a better performance. It was refined and polished garbage, and objectionable. Jake wanted to burn him, but from experience he knew Ichabod would not sustain an objection during an opening statement unless the offense was flagrant, and Buckley's rhetoric did not qualify —yet. All this fake sincerity and gushiness irritated Jake to no end, primarily because the jury listened to it and, more often than not, fell for it. The prosecutor was always the good guy, seeking to right an injustice and punish a criminal for some heinous crime; to lock him away forever so he could sin no more. Buckley was master at convincing a jury, right off the mark, during the opening statement, that it was up to them, He and The Twelve Chosen Ones, to search diligently for the truth, together as a team, united against evil. It was the truth they were after, nothing but the truth. Find the truth and justice would win. Follow him, Rufus Buckley, the people's lawyer, and they would find the truth.

The rape was a terrible deed. He was a father, in fact had a daughter the same age of Tonya Hailey, and when he first heard of the rape he was sick at his stomach. He grieved for Carl Lee and his wife. Yes, he thought of his own little girls and had thoughts of retribution.

Jake smiled quickly at Ellen. This was interesting. Buckley had chosen to confront the rape instead of keeping it from the jury. Jake was expecting a critical confrontation with him on the admissibility of any testimony regarding the rape. Ellen's research found the law to be clear that the lurid details were inadmissible, but it wasn't so clear as to whether it could be mentioned or referred to. Evidently Buckley felt it was better to acknowledge the rape than try to hide it. Good move, thought Jake, since all twelve and the rest of the world knew the details anyway.

Ellen smiled too. The rape of Tonya Hailey was about to be tried for the first time.

Buckley explained it would be natural for any parent to want revenge. He would too, he admitted. But, he continued with his voice growing heavier, there is a mighty distinction between wanting revenge and getting revenge.

He was warming up now as he paced deliberately back and forth, ignoring the podium, getting his rhythm. He launched himself into a twenty-minute discourse on the criminal justice system and how it was practiced in Mississippi, and how many rapists that he, Rufus Buckley, had personally sent to Parchman, for life, most of them. The system worked because Mississippians had enough good common sense to make it work, and it would collapse if people like Carl Lee Hailey were allowed to short-circuit the system and dispense justice according to their own terms. Imagine that. A lawless society where vigilantes roamed at will. No police, no jails, no courts, no trials, no juries. Every man for himself.

It was sort of ironic, he said, winding down for a moment. Carl Lee Hailey now sat before them asking for due process and a fair trial, yet he did not believe in such things.

Ask the mothers of Billy Ray Cobb and Pete Willard. Ask them what kind of fair trials their sons received.

He paused to allow the jury and the courtroom to absorb and ponder that last thought. It sunk in heavy, and every person in the jury box looked at Carl Lee Hailey. They were not looks of compassion. Jake cleaned his fingernails with a small knife and looked thoroughly bored. Buckley pretended to review his notes at the podium, then checked his watch. He started again, this time in a most confident businesslike tone of voice. The State would prove that Carl Lee Hailey carefully planned the killings. He waited for almost an hour in a small room next to the stairs where he knew the boys would eventually be led as they were taken back to jail. He somehow managed to sneak an M-16 into the courthouse. Buckley walked to a small table by the court reporter and hoisted the M-16. "This is the M-16!" he announced to the jury, waving it wildly about with one hand. He sat it on the podium and talked about how it was carefully selected by Carl Lee Hailey because he had used one before in close combat, and he knew how to kill with it. He had been trained with an M-16. It's an illegal weapon. You can't buy one down at the Western Auto. He had to go find it. He planned it.

The proof would be clear: premeditated, carefully planned, cold-blooded murder.

And then there was Deputy DeWayne Looney. A fourteen-year veteran of the Sheriff's Department. A family man —one of the finest law enforcement officers he had ever known. Gunned down in the line of duty by Carl Lee Hailey. His leg was partially amputated. What was his sin? Perhaps the defense would say it was accidental, that it shouldn't count. That's no defense in Mississippi.

There's no excuse, ladies and gentlemen, for any of this violence. The verdict must be guilty.

They each had an hour for their openings, and the lure of that much time proved irresistible for the D.A., whose remarks were becoming repetitive. He lost himself twice during his condemnation of the insanity ruse. The jurors began to look bored and searched for other points of interest around the courtroom. The artists quit sketching, the reporters quit writing, and Noose cleaned his glasses seven or eight times. It was a known fact that Noose cleaned the glasses to stay awake and fight boredom, and he usually cleaned them throughout the trial. Jake had seen him rub them with a handkerchief or tie or shirttail while witnesses broke down and cried and lawyers screamed and flailed their arms at each other. He didn't miss a word or objection or trick; he was just bored with it all, even a case of this magnitude. He never slept on the bench, although he was sorely tempted at times. Instead he removed his glasses, held them upward in the light, blew on them, rubbed them as though they were caked with grease, then remounted them just north of the wart. No more than five minutes later they would be dirty again. The longer Buckley droned on, the more they were cleaned.

Finally, after an hour and a half, Buckley shut up and the courtroom sighed.

"Ten-minute recess," Noose announced, and lunged off the bench, through the door, past chambers to the men's room.

Jake had planned a brief opening, and after Buckley's marathon, he decided to make it even shorter. Most people don't like lawyers to begin with, especially long-winded, tall-talking, wordy lawyers who feel that every insignificant point must be repeated at least three times, and the major ones have to be hammered and drilled by constant repetition into whoever happened to be listening. Jurors especially dislike lawyers who waste time, for two very good reasons. First, they can't tell the lawyers to shut up. They're captives. Outside the courtroom a person can curse a lawyer and shut him up, but in the jury box they become trapped and forbidden to speak. Thus, they must resort to sleeping, snoring, glaring, squirming, checking their watches, or any one of a dozen signals which boring lawyers never recognize. Second, jurors don't like long trials. Cut the crap and get it over with. Give us the facts and we'll give you a verdict.

He explained this to his client during the recess.

"I agree. Keep it short," said Carl Lee.

He did. Fourteen minutes worth of opening statement, and the jury appreciated every word. He began by talking about daughters and how special they are. How they are different from little boys and need special protection. He told them of his own daughter and the special bond that exists between father and daughter, a bond that could not be explained and should not be tampered with. He admitted admiration for Mr. Buckley and his alleged ability to be so forgiving and compassionate to any drunken pervert who might rape his daughter. He was a big man indeed. But in reality, could they, as jurors, as parents, be so tender and trusting and indulging if their daughter had been raped—by two drunk, stoned, brutal animals who tied her to a tree and—"

"Objection!" shouted Buckley.

"Sustained," Noose shouted back.

He ignored the shouting and continued softly. He asked them to try to imagine, throughout the trial, how they would feel had it been their daughter. He asked them not to convict Carl Lee but to send him home to his family. He didn't mention insanity. They knew it was coming.

He finished shortly after he started, and left the jury with a marked contrast in the two styles.

"Is that all?" Noose asked in amazement.

Jake nodded as he sat by his client.

"Very well. Mr. Buckley, you may call your first witness."

"The State calls Cora Cobb."

The bailiff went to the witness room and fetched Mrs. Cobb. He led her through the door by the jury box, into the courtroom where she was sworn by Jean Gillespie, and then he seated her in the witness chair.

"Speak into the microphone," he instructed.

"You are Cora Cobb?" Buckley asked with full volume as he situated the podium near the railing.

"Yes, sir."

"Where do you live?"

"Route 3, Lake Village, Ford County."

"You are the mother of Billy Ray Cobb, deceased?"

"Yes, sir," she said as her eyes watered. She was a rural woman whose husband had left when the boys were small. They had raised themselves while she worked two shifts at a cheap furniture factory between Karaway and Lake Village. She lost control over them at an early age. She was about fifty, tried to look forty with hair dye and makeup, but could easily pass for early sixties.

"How old was your son at the time of his death?"

"Twenty-three."

"When did you last see him alive?"

"Just a few seconds before he was kilt."

"Where did you see him?"

"Here in this courtroom."

"Where was he killed?"

"Downstairs."

"Did you hear the shots that killed your son?"

She began to cry. "Yes, sir."

"Where did you last see him?"

"At the funeral home."

"And what was his condition?"

"He was dead."

"Nothing further," Buckley announced.

"Cross-examination, Mr. Brigance?"

She was a harmless witness, called to establish that the victim was indeed dead, and to evoke a little sympathy. Nothing could be gained by cross-examination, and normally she would have been left alone. But Jake saw an opportunity he couldn't pass. He saw a chance to set the tone for the trial, to wake Noose and Buckley and the jury; to just get everyone aroused. She was not really that pitiful; she was faking some. Buckley had probably instructed her to cry if possible.

"Just a few questions," Jake said as he walked behind Buckley and Musgrove to the podium. The D.A. was immediately suspicious.

"Mrs. Cobb, is it true that your son was convicted of selling marijuana?"

"Objection!" Buckley roared, springing to his feet. "The criminal record of the victim is inadmissible!"

"Sustained!"

"Thank you, Your Honor," Jake said properly, as if Noose had done him a favor.

She wiped her eyes and cried harder.

"You say your son was twenty-three when he died?"

"Yes."

"In his twenty-three years, how many other children did he rape?"

"Objection! Objection!" yelled Buckley, waving his arms and looking desperately at Noose, who was yelling, "Sustained! Sustained! You're out of order, Mr. Brigance! You're out of order!"

Mrs. Cobb burst into tears and bawled uncontrollably as the shouting erupted. She managed to keep the microphone in her face, and her wailing and carrying on resounded through the stunned courtroom.

"He should be admonished, Your Honor!" Buckley demanded, his face and eyes glowing with violent anger and his neck a deep purple.

"I'll withdraw the question," Jake replied loudly as he returned to his seat.

"Cheap shot, Brigance," Musgrove mumbled.

"Please admonish him," Buckley begged, "and instruct the jury to disregard."

"Any redirect?" asked Noose.

"No," answered Buckley as he dashed to the witness stand with a handkerchief to rescue Mrs. Cobb, who had buried her head in her hands and was sobbing and shaking violently.

"You are excused, Mrs. Cobb," Noose said. "Bailiff, please assist the witness."

The bailiff lifted her by the arm, with Buckley's assistance, and led her down from the witness stand, in front of the jury box, through the railing, down the center aisle. She shrieked and whined every step of the way, and her noises increased as she neared the back door until she was roaring at full throttle when she made her exit.

Noose glared at Jake until she was gone and the courtroom was quiet again. Then he turned to the jury and said: "Please disregard the last question by Mr. Brigance."

"What'd you do that for?" Carl Lee whispered to his lawyer.

"I'll explain later."

"The State calls Earnestine Willard," Buckley announced in a quieter tone and with much more hesitation.

Mrs. Willard was brought from the witness room above the courtroom. She was sworn and seated.

406 JOHN GRISHAM

"You are Earnestine Willard?" asked Buckley.

"Yes, sir," she said in a fragile voice. Life had been rough on her too, but she had a certain dignity that made her more pitiful and believable than Mrs. Cobb. The clothes were inexpensive, but clean and neatly pressed. The hair was minus the cheap black dye that Mrs. Cobb relied on so heavily. The face was minus the layers of makeup. When she began crying, she cried to herself.

"And where do you live?"

"Out from Lake Village."

"Pete Willard was your son?"

"Yes, sir."

"When did you last see him alive?"

"Right here in this room, just before he was killed."

"Did you hear the gunfire that killed him?"

"Yes, sir."

"Where did you last see him?"

"At the funeral home."

"And what was his condition?"

"He was dead," she said, wiping tears with a Kleenex.

"I'm very sorry," Buckley offered. "No further questions," he added, eyeing Jake carefully.

"Any cross-examination?" Noose asked, also eyeing Jake suspiciously.

"Just a couple," Jake said.

"Mrs. Willard, I'm Jake Brigance." He stood behind the podium and looked at her without compassion.

She nodded.

"How old was your son when he died?"

"Twenty-seven."

Buckley pushed his chair from the table and sat on its edge, ready to spring. Noose removed his glasses and leaned forward. Carl Lee lowered his head.

"During his twenty-seven years, how many other children did he rape?"

Buckley bolted upright. "Objection! Objection! Objection!"

"Sustained! Sustained! Sustained!"

The yelling frightened Mrs. Willard, and she cried louder.

"Admonish him, Judge! He must be admonished!"

"I'll withdraw the question," Jake said on his way back to his seat.

Buckley pleaded with his hands. "But that's not good enough, Judge! He must be admonished!"

"Let's go into chambers," Noose ordered. He excused the witness and recessed until one.

Harry Rex was waiting on the balcony of Jake's office with sandwiches and a pitcher of margaritas. Jake declined and drank grapefruit juice. Ellen wanted just one, a small one she said to calm her nerves. For the third day, lunch had been prepared by Dell and personally delivered to Jake's office. Compliments of the Coffee Shop.

They ate and relaxed on the balcony and watched the carnival around the courthouse. What happened in chambers? Harry Rex demanded. Jake nibbled on a Reuben. He said he wanted to talk about something other than the trial.

"What happened in chambers, dammit?"

"Cardinals are three games out, did you know that, Row Ark?"

"I thought it was four."

"What happened in chambers!"

"Do you really want to know?"

"Yes! Yes!"

"Okay. I've got to go use the rest room. I'll tell you when I get back." Jake left.

"Row Ark, what happened in chambers?"

"Not much. Noose rode Jake pretty good, but no permanent damage. Buckley wanted blood, and Jake said he was sure some was forthcoming if Buckley's face got any redder. Buckley ranted and screamed and condemned Jake for intentionally inflaming the jury, as he called it. Jake just smiled at him and said he was sorry, Governor. Every time he would say governor, Buckley would scream at Noose, 'He's calling me governor, Judge, do something.' And Noose would say, 'Please, gentlemen, I expect you to act like professionals.' And Jake would say, 'Thank you, Your Honor.' Then he would wait a few minutes and call him governor again."

"Why did he make those two old ladies cry?"

"It was a brilliant move, Harry Rex. He showed the jury, Noose, Buckley, everybody, that it's his courtroom and he's not afraid of a damned person in it. He drew first blood. He's got Buckley so jumpy right now he'll never relax. Noose respects him because he's not intimidated by His Honor. The jurors were shocked, but he woke them up and told them in a not so subtle way that this is war. A brilliant move."

"Yeah, I thought so myself."

"It didn't hurt us. Those women were asking for sympathy, but Jake reminded the jury of what their sweet little boys did before they died."

"The scumbags."

"If there's any resentment by the jury, they'll forget by the time the last witness testifies."

"Jake's pretty smooth, ain't he?"

"He's good. Very good. He's the best I've seen for his age."

"Wait till his closing argument. I've heard a couple. He could get sympathy out of a drill sergeant."

Jake returned and poured a small margarita. Just a very small one, for his nerves. Harry Rex drank like a sailor.

Ozzie was the first State witness after lunch. Buckley produced large, multicolored plats of the first and second floors of the courthouse, and together they traced the precise, last movements of Cobb and Willard.

Then Buckley produced a set of ten 16 × 24 color photographs of Cobb and Willard lying freshly dead on the stairs. They were gruesome. Jake had seen lots of pictures of dead bodies, and although none were particularly pleasant given their nature, some weren't so bad. In one of his cases, the victim had been shot in the heart with a .357 and simply fell over dead on his porch. He was a large, muscular old man, and the bullet never found its way out of the body. So there was no blood, just a small hole in his overalls, and then a small sealed hole in his chest. He looked as though he could have fallen asleep and slumped over, or passed out drunk on the porch, like Lucien. It was not a spectacular scene, and Buckley had not been proud of those photographs. They had not been enlarged. He had just handed the small Polaroids to the jury and looked disgusted because they were so clean.

But most murder pictures were grisly and sickening, with blood splashed on walls and ceilings, and parts of bodies blown free and scattered everywhere. Those were always enlarged by the D.A. and entered into evidence with great fanfare, then waved around the courtroom by Buckley as he and the witness described the scenes in the pictures. Finally, with the jurors fidgeting with curiosity, Buckley would politely ask the judge for permission to show the photographs to the jury, and the judge would always consent. Then Buckley and everybody else would watch their faces intently as they were shocked, horrified, and occasionally nauseated. Jake had actually seen two jurors vomit when handed photos of a badly slashed corpse.

Such pictures were highly prejudicial and highly inflammatory, and also highly admissible. "Probative" was the word used by the Supreme Court. Such pictures could aid the jury, according to ninety years of decisions from the Court. It was well settled in Mississippi that murder pictures, regardless of their impact on the jury, were always admissible.

Jake had seen the Cobb and Willard photographs weeks earlier, and had filed the standard objection and received the standard denial.

These were mounted professionally on heavy posterboard, something the D.A. had not done before. He handed the first one into the jury box to Reba Betts. It was the one of Willard's head and brains taken at close range.

"My God!" she gasped, and shoved it to the next juror, who gawked in horror, and passed it on. They handed it to one another, then to the alternates. Buckley took it, and gave Reba another one. The ritual continued for thirty minutes until all the pictures were returned to the D.A.

Then he grabbed the M-16 and thrust it at Ozzie. "Can you identify this?"

"Yes, it's the weapon found at the scene."

"Who picked it up at the scene?"

"I did."

"And what did you do with it?"

"Wrapped it in a plastic bag and placed it in the vault at the jail. Kept it locked up until I handed it to Mr. Laird with the crime lab in Jackson."

"Your Honor, the State would offer the weapon, Exhibit S-13, into evidence," Buckley said, waving it wildly.

"No objections," Jake said.

"We have nothing further of this witness," Buckley announced.

"Cross-examination?"

Jake flipped through his notes as he walked slowly to the podium. He had just a few questions for his friend.

"Sheriff, did you arrest Billy Ray Cobb and Pete Willard?"

Buckley pushed his chair back and perched his ample frame on the edge, poised to leap and scream if necessary.

"Yes I did," answered the sheriff.

"For what reason?"

"For the rape of Tonya Hailey," he answered perfectly.

"And how old was she at the time she was raped by Cobb and Willard?"

"She was ten."

"Is it true, Sheriff, that Pete Willard signed a written confession in—"

"Objection! Objection! Your Honor! That's inadmissible and Mr. Brigance knows it."

Ozzie nodded affirmatively during the objection.

"Sustained."

Buckley was shaking. "I ask that the question be stricken from the record and the jury be instructed to disregard it."

"I'll withdraw the question," Jake said to Buckley with a smile.

"Please disregard the last question from Mr. Brigance," Noose instructed the jury.

"No further questions," said Jake.

"Any redirect examination, Mr. Buckley?"

"No, sir."

"Very well. Sheriff, you may step down."

Buckley's next witness was a fingerprint man from Washington who spent an hour telling the jurors what they had known for weeks. His dramatic final conclusion unmistakably linked the prints on the M-16 to those of Carl Lee Hailey. Then came the ballistics expert from the state crime lab whose testimony was as boring and uninformative as his predecessor on the stand. Yes, without a doubt, the fragments recovered from the crime scene were fired from the M-16 lying there on the table. That was his final opinion, and with the charts and diagrams, it took Buckley an hour to get it to the jury. Prosecutorial overkill, as Jake called it; a debility suffered by all prosecutors.

The defense had no questions for either expert, and at five-fifteen Noose said goodbye to the jurors with strict instructions against discussing the case. They nodded politely as they filed from the courtroom. Then he banged his gavel and adjourned until nine in the morning.

36 The great civic duty of jury service had grown old rapidly. The second night in the Temple Inn had seen the telephones removed—judge's orders. Some old magazines donated by the Clanton library were circulated and quickly discarded, there being little interest among the group in *The New Yorker, The Smithsonian,* and *Architectural Digest.*

"Got any *Penthouses*?" Clyde Sisco had whispered to the bailiff as he made the rounds. He said no, but he'd see what he could do.

Confined to their rooms with no television, newspapers, or phones, they did little but play cards and talk about the trial. A trip to the end of the hall for ice and a soft drink became a special occasion, something the roommates planned and rotated. The boredom descended heavily.

At each end of the hall two soldiers guarded the darkness and solitude, the stillness interrupted only by the systematic emergence of the jurors with change for the drink machine.

Sleep came early, and when the sentries knocked on the doors at 6:00 A.M., all the jurors were awake, some even dressed. They devoured Thursday's breakfast of pancakes and sausage, and eagerly boarded the Greyhound at eight for the trip back home.

For the fourth straight day the rotunda was crowded by eight o'clock. The spectators had learned that all seats were taken by eight-thirty. Prather opened the door and the crowd filed slowly through the metal detector, past the careful eyes of the deputies and finally into the courtroom, where the blacks filled the left side and the whites the right. The front row was again reserved by Hastings for Gwen, Lester, the kids, and other relatives. Agee and other council members sat in the second row with the kinfolks who couldn't fit up front. Agee was in charge of alternating courtroom duty and outside demonstration duty for the ministers. Personally, he preferred the courtroom duty, where he felt safer, but he did miss the cameras and reporters which were so abundant on the front lawn. To his right, across the aisle, sat the families and friends of the victims. They had behaved so far.

A few minutes before nine, Carl Lee was escorted from the small holding room. The handcuffs were removed by one of the many officers surrounding him. He flashed a big smile at his family and sat in his chair. The lawyers took their places and the courtroom grew quiet. The bailiff poked his head through the door beside the jury box, and, satisfied with whatever he saw, opened the door and released the jurors to their assigned seats. Mr. Pate was watching all this from the door leading to chambers, and when all was perfect, he stepped forward and yelled: "All rise for the Court!"

Ichabod, draped in his favorite wrinkled and faded black robe, loped to the bench and instructed everyone to have a seat. He greeted the jury and questioned them about what happened or didn't happen since yesterday's adjournment.

He looked at the lawyers. "Where's Mr. Musgrove?"

"He's running a bit late, Your Honor. We are ready to proceed," Buckley announced.

"Call your next witness," Noose ordered Buckley.

The pathologist from the state crime lab was located in the rotunda and entered the courtroom. Normally, he would have been much too busy for a simple trial and would have sent one of his underlings to explain to the jury precisely what killed Cobb and Willard. But this was the Hailey case, and he felt compelled to do the job himself. It was actually the simplest case he had seen in a while; the bodies were found as they were dying, the weapon was with the bodies, and there were enough holes in the boys to kill them a dozen times. Everybody in the world knew how those boys died. But the D.A. had insisted on the most thorough pathological workup, so the doctor took the stand Thursday morning laden with photos of the autopsies and multicolored anatomy charts.

Earlier in chambers, Jake had offered to stipulate to the causes of death, but Buckley would have no part of it. No sir, he wanted the jury to hear and know how they died.

"We will admit that they died by multiple wounds from bullets fired from the M-16," Jake had stated precisely.

"No, sir. I have a right to prove it," Buckley said stubbornly.

"But he's offering to stipulate to the causes of death," Noose said incredulously.

"I have the right to prove it," Buckley hung on.

So he proved it. In a classic case of prosecutorial overkill, Buckley proved it. For three hours the pathologist talked about how many bullets hit Cobb and how many hit Willard, and what each bullet did upon penetration, and the ghastly damage thereafter. The anatomy charts were placed on easels before the jury, and the expert took a plastic, numbered pellet that represented a bullet, and moved it ever so slowly through the body. Fourteen pellets for Cobb and eleven for Willard. Buckley would ask a question, elicit a response, then interrupt to belabor a point.

"Your Honor, we would be glad to stipulate as to the causes of death," Jake announced with great frustration every thirty minutes.

"We won't," Buckley replied tersely, and moved to the next pellet.

Jake fell into his chair, shook his head, and looked at the jurors, those who were awake.

The doctor finished at noon and Noose, tired and numb with boredom, awarded a two-hour lunch break. The jurors were awakened by the bailiff and led to the jury room where they dined on barbeque specials on plastic plates, then struck up card games. They were forbidden to leave the courthouse.

———

In every small Southern town there's a kid who was born looking for the quick buck. He was the kid who at the age of five set up the first lemonade stand on his street and charged twenty-five cents a cup for four ounces of artificially flavored water. He knew it tasted awful, but he knew the adults thought he was adorable. He was the first kid on the street to purchase a lawn mower on credit at the Western Auto and knock on doors in February to line up yard work for the summer. He was the first kid to pay for his own bike, which he used for morning and afternoon paper routes. He sold Christmas cards to old ladies in August. He sold fruitcakes door to door in November. On Saturday mornings when his friends were watching cartoons, he was at the flea markets at the courthouse selling roasted peanuts and corn dogs. At the age of twelve he bought his first certificate of deposit. He had his own banker. At fifteen, he paid cash for his new pickup the same day he passed his driver's license exam. He bought a trailer to follow the truck and filled it with lawn equipment. He sold T-shirts at high school football games. He was a hustler; a millionaire to be.

In Clanton, his name was Hinky Myrick, age sixteen. He waited nervously in the rotunda until Noose broke for lunch, then moved past the deputies and entered the courtroom. Seating was so precious that almost none of the spectators left for lunch. Some would stand, glare at their neighbors, point at their seats and make sure everybody knew it was theirs for the day, then leave for the rest room. But most of them sat in their highly treasured spaces on the pews, and suffered through lunch.

Hinky could smell opportunity. He could sense people in need. On Thursday, just as he had on Wednesday, he rolled a shopping cart down the aisle to the front of the courtroom. It was filled with a wide assortment of sand-wiches and plate lunches in plastic containers. He began yelling toward the far end of the rows, then passing food down to his customers. He worked his way slowly toward the rear of the courtroom. He was a vicious scalper. A tuna salad on white bread went for two dollars; his cost, eighty cents. A plate lunch of cold chicken with a few peas went for three dollars; his cost, a buck twenty-five. A canned soft drink was one-fifty. But they gladly paid his prices and kept their seats. He sold out before he reached the fourth row from the front, and began taking orders from the rest of the courtroom. Hinky was the man of the hour.

With a fistful of orders, he raced from the courthouse, across the lawn, through the crowd of blacks, across Caffey Street and into Claude's. He ran to the kitchen, shoved a twenty-dollar bill at the cook and handed him the orders. He waited and watched his watch. The cook moved slowly. Hinky gave him another twenty.

The trial ushered a wave of prosperity Claude had never dreamed of. Breakfast and lunch in his small cafe became happenings as demand greatly exceeded the number of chairs and the hungry lined the sidewalk, waiting in the heat and haze for a table. After the lunch recess on Monday, he had dashed around Clanton buying every folding card table and matching chair set he could find. At lunch the aisles disappeared, forcing his waitresses to maneuver nimbly among and between the rows of people, virtually all of whom were black.

The trial was the only topic of conversation. On Wednesday, the composition of the jury had been hotly condemned. By Thursday, the talk centered on the growing dislike for the prosecutor.

"I hear tell he wants to run for governor."

"He Democrat or Republican?"

"Democrat."

"He can't win without the black vote, not in this state."

"Yeah, and he ain't likely to get much after this trial."

"I hope he tries."

"He acts more like a Republican."

In pretrial Clanton, the noon hour began ten minutes before twelve when the young, tanned, pretty, coolly dressed secretaries from the banks, law offices, insurance agencies, and courthouse left their desks and took to the sidewalks. During lunch they ran errands around the square. They went to the post office. They did their banking. They shopped. Most of them bought their food at the Chinese Deli and ate on the park benches under the shade trees around the courthouse. They met friends and gossiped. At noon the gazebo in front of the courthouse attracted more beautiful women than the Miss Mississippi pageant. It was an unwritten rule in Clanton that an office girl on the square got a headstart on lunch and did not have to return until one. The men followed at twelve, and watched the girls.

But the trial changed things. The shade trees around the courthouse were in a combat zone. The cafes were full from eleven to one with soldiers and strangers who couldn't get seats in the courtroom. The Chinese Deli was packed with foreigners. The office girls ran their errands and ate at their desks.

At the Tea Shoppe the bankers and other white collars discussed the trial more in terms of its publicity and how the town was being perceived. Of particular concern was the Klan. Not a single customer knew anyone connected with the Klan, and it had long been forgotten in north Mississippi. But the vultures loved the white robes, and as far as the outside world knew, Clanton, Mississippi, was the home of the Ku Klux Klan. They hated the Klan for being there. They cussed the press for keeping them there.

For lunch Thursday, the Coffee Shop offered the daily special of country-fried pork chops, turnip greens, and either candied yams, creamed corn, or fried okra. Dell served the specials to a packed house that was evenly divided among locals, foreigners, and soldiers. The unwritten but firmly established rule of not speaking to anyone with a beard or funny accent was strictly enforced, and for a friendly people it was awkward not to smile and carry on with those from the outside. A tight-lipped arrogance had long since replaced the warm reception given to the visitors in the first few days after the shootings. Too many of the press hounds had betrayed their hosts and printed unkind, unflattering, and unfair words about the county and its people. It was amazing how they could arrive in packs from all over and within twenty-four hours become experts on a place they had never heard of and a people they had never met.

The locals had watched them as they scrambled like idiots around the square chasing the sheriff, the prosecutor, the defense lawyer, or anybody who might know anything. They watched them wait at the rear of the courthouse like hungry wolves to pounce on the defendant, who was invariably surrounded by cops, and who invariably ignored them as they yelled the same ridiculous questions at him. The locals watched with distaste as they kept their cameras on the Kluxers and the rowdier blacks, always searching for the most radical elements, and then making those elements appear to be the norm.

They watched them, and they hated them.

"What's that orange crap all over her face?" Tim Nunley asked, looking at a reporter sitting in a booth by the window. Jack Jones crunched on his okra and studied the orange face.

"I think it's something they use for the cameras. Makes her face look white on TV."

"But it's already white."

"I know, but it don't look white on TV unless it's painted orange."

Nunley was not convinced. "Then what do the niggers use on TV?" he asked.

No one could answer.

"Did you see her on TV last night?" asked Jack Jones.

"Nope. Where's she from?"

"Channel Four, Memphis. Last night she interviewed Cobb's mother, and of course she kept on pushing till the old woman broke down. All they showed on TV was the cryin'. It was sickenin'. Night before she had some Klansmen from Ohio talkin' about what we need here in Mississippi. She's the worst."

The State finished its case against Carl Lee Thursday afternoon. After lunch Buckley put Murphy on the stand. It was gut-wrenching, nerve-wracking testimony as the poor little man stuttered uncontrollably for an hour.

"Calm down, Mr. Murphy," Buckley said a hundred times.

He would nod, and take a drink of water. He nodded affirmatively and shook negatively as much as possible, but the court reporter had an awful time picking up the nods and shakes.

"I didn't get that," she would say, her back to the witness stand. So he would try to answer and get hung, usually on a hard consonant like a "P" or "T." He would blurt out something, then stutter and spit incoherently.

"I didn't get that," she would say helplessly when he finished. Buckley would sigh. The jurors rocked furiously. Half the spectators chewed their fingernails.

"Could you repeat that?" Buckley would say with as much patience as he could find.

"I'm s-s-s-s-s-s-s-s-sorry," he would say frequently. He was pitiful.

Through it all, it was determined that he had been drinking a Coke on the rear stairs, facing the stairs where the boys were killed. He had noticed a black man peeking out of a small closet some forty feet away. But he didn't think much about it. Then when the boys came down, the black man just stepped out and opened fire, screaming and laughing. When he stopped shooting, he threw down the gun and took off. Yes, that was him, sitting right there. The black one.

Noose rubbed holes in his glasses listening to Murphy. When Buckley sat down, His Honor looked desperately at Jake. "Any cross-examination?" he asked painfully.

Jake stood with a legal pad. The court reporter glared at him. Harry Rex hissed at him. Ellen closed her eyes. The jurors wrung their hands and watched him carefully.

"Don't do it," Carl Lee whispered firmly.

"No, Your Honor, we have no questions."

"Thank you, Mr. Brigance," Noose said, breathing again.

The next witness was Officer Rady, the investigator for the Sheriff's Department. He informed the jury that he found a Royal Crown Cola can in the closet next to the stairs, and the prints on the can matched those of Carl Lee Hailey.

"Was it empty or full?" Buckley asked dramatically.

"It was completely empty."

Big deal, thought Jake, so he was thirsty. Oswald had a chicken dinner waiting on Kennedy. No, he had no questions for this witness.

"We have one final witness, Your Honor," Buckley said with great finality at 4:00 P.M. "Officer DeWayne Looney."

Looney limped with a cane into the courtroom and to the witness stand. He removed his gun and handed it to Mr. Pate.

Buckley watched him proudly. "Would you state your name, please, sir?"

"DeWayne Looney."

"And your address?"

"Fourteen sixty-eight Bennington Street, Clanton, Mississippi."

"How old are you?"

"Thirty-nine."

"Where are you employed?"

"Ford County Sheriff's Department."

"And what do you do there?"

"I'm a dispatcher."

"Where did you work on Monday, May 20?"

"I was a deputy."

"Were you on duty?"

"Yes. I was assigned to transport two subjects from the jail to court and back."

"Who were those two subjects?"

"Billy Ray Cobb and Pete Willard."

"What time did you leave court with them?"

"Around one-thirty, I guess."

"Who was on duty with you?"

"Marshall Prather. He and I were in charge of the two subjects. There were some other deputies in the courtroom helpin' us, and we had two or three men outside waitin' on us. But me and Marshall were in charge."

"What happened when the hearing was over?"

"We immediately handcuffed Cobb and Willard and got them outta here. We took them to that little room over there and waited a second or two, and Prather walked on down the stairs."

"Then what happened?"

"We started down the back stairs. Cobb first, then Willard, then me. Like I said, Prather had already gone on down. He was out the door."

"Yes, sir. Then what happened?"

"When Cobb was near 'bout to the foot of the stairs, the shootin' started. I was on the landing, fixin' to go on down. I didn't see anybody at first for a second, then I seen Mr. Hailey with the machine gun firin' away. Cobb was blown backward into Willard, and they both screamed and fell in a heap, tryin' to get back up where I was."

"Yes, sir. Describe what you saw."

"You could hear the bullets bouncin' off the walls and hittin' everywhere. It was the loudest gun I ever heard and seemed like he kept shootin' forever. The boys just twisted and thrashed about, screamin' and squealin'. They were handcuffed, you know."

"Yes, sir. What happened to you?"

"Like I said, I never made it past the landing. I think

one of the bullets ricocheted off the wall and caught me in the leg. I was tryin' to get back up the steps when I felt my leg burn."

"And what happened to your leg?"

"They cut it off," Looney answered matter-of-factly, as if an amputation happened monthly. "Just below the knee."

"Did you get a good look at the man with the gun?"

"Yes, sir."

"Can you identify him for the jury?"

"Yes, sir. It's Mr. Hailey, the man sittin' over there."

That answer would have been a logical place to end Looney's testimony. He was brief, to the point, sympathetic and positive of the identification. The jury had listened to every word so far. But Buckley and Musgrove retrieved the large diagrams of the courthouse and arranged them before the jury so that Looney could limp around for a while. Under Buckley's direction, he retraced everybody's exact movements just before the killings.

Jake rubbed his forehead and pinched the bridge of his nose. Noose cleaned and recleaned his glasses. The jurors fidgeted.

"Any cross-examination, Mr. Brigance?" Noose asked at last.

"Just a few questions," Jake said as Musgrove cleared the debris from the courtroom.

"Officer Looney, who was Carl Lee looking at when he was shooting?"

"Them boys, as far as I could tell."

"Did he ever look at you?"

"Well, now, I didn't spend a lotta time tryin' to make eye contact with him. In fact, I was movin' in the other direction."

"So he didn't aim at you?"

"Oh, no, sir. He just aimed at those boys. Hit them too."

"What did he do when he was shooting?"

"He just screamed and laughed like he was crazy. It was the weirdest thing I ever heard, like he was some kinda madman or something. And you know, what I'll always remember is that with all the noise, the gun firin', the bullets

whistlin', the boys screamin' as they got hit, over all the noise
I could hear him laughin' that crazy laugh."

The answer was so perfect Jake had to fight off a smile.
He and Looney had worked on it a hundred times, and it
was a thing of beauty. Every word was perfect. Jake busily
flipped through his legal pad and glanced at the jurors. They
all stared at Looney, enthralled by his answer. Jake scribbled
something, anything, nothing, just to kill a few more seconds
before the most important questions of the trial.

"Now, Deputy Looney, Carl Lee Hailey shot you in the
leg."

"Yes, sir, he did."

"Do you think it was intentional?"

"Oh, no, sir. It was an accident."

"Do you want to see him punished for shooting you?"

"No, sir. I have no ill will toward the man. He did what
I would've done."

Buckley dropped his pen and slumped in his chair. He
looked sadly at his star witness.

"What do you mean by that?"

"I mean I don't blame him for what he did. Those boys
raped his little girl. I gotta little girl. Somebody rapes her
and he's a dead dog. I'll blow him away, just like Carl Lee
did. We oughtta give him a trophy."

"Do you want the jury to convict Carl Lee?"

Buckley jumped and roared, "Objection! Objection!
Improper question!"

"No!" Looney yelled. "I don't want him convicted. He's
a hero. He—"

"Don't answer, Mr. Looney!" Noose said loudly. "Don't
answer!"

"Objection! Objection!" Buckley continued, on his
tiptoes.

"He's a hero! Turn him loose!" Looney yelled at Buckley.

"Order! Order!" Noose banged his gavel.

Buckley was silent. Looney was silent. Jake walked to
his chair and said, "I'll withdraw the question."

"Please disregard," Noose instructed the jury.

Looney smiled at the jury and limped from the courtroom.

"Call your next witness," Noose said, removing his glasses.

Buckley rose slowly and with a great effort at drama, said, "Your Honor, the State rests."

"Good," Noose replied, looking at Jake. "I assume you have a motion or two, Mr. Brigance."

"Yes, Your Honor."

"Very well, we'll take those up in chambers."

Noose excused his jury with the same parting instructions and adjourned until nine Friday.

37 Jake awoke in the darkness with a slight hangover, a headache due to fatigue and Coors, and the distant but unmistakable sound of his doorbell ringing continually as if held firmly in place by a large and determined thumb. He opened the front door in his nightshirt and tried to focus on the two figures standing on the porch. Ozzie and Nesbit, it was finally determined.

"Can I help you?" he asked as he opened the door. They followed him into the den.

"They're gonna kill you today," Ozzie said.

Jake sat on the couch and massaged his temples. "Maybe they'll succeed."

"Jake, this is serious. They plan to kill you."

"Who?"

"The Klan."

"Mickey Mouse?"

"Yeah. He called yesterday and said something was up. He called back two hours ago and said you're the lucky man. Today is the big day. Time for some excitement. They bury Stump Sisson this morning in Loydsville, and it's time for the eye-for-an-eye, tooth-for-a-tooth routine."

"Why me? Why don't they kill Buckley or Noose or someone more deserving?"

"We didn't get a chance to talk about that."

"What method of execution?" Jake asked, suddenly feeling awkward sitting there in his nightshirt.

"He didn't say."

"Does he know?"

"He ain't much on details. He just said they'd try to do it sometime today."

"So what am I supposed to do? Surrender?"

"What time you goin' to the office?"

"What time is it?"

"Almost five."

"As soon as I can shower and dress."

"We'll wait."

At five-thirty, they rushed him into his office and locked

the door. At eight, a platoon of soldiers gathered on the sidewalk under the balcony and waited for the target. Harry Rex and Ellen watched from the second floor of the courthouse. Jake squeezed between Ozzie and Nesbit, and the three of them crouched in the center tight formation. Off they went across Washington Street in the direction of the courthouse. The vultures sniffed something and surrounded the entourage.

———————

The abandoned feed mill sat near the abandoned railroad tracks halfway down the tallest hill in Clanton, two blocks north and east of the square. Beside it was a neglected asphalt and gravel street that ran downhill and intersected Cedar Street, after which it became much smoother and wider and continued downward until finally it terminated and merged into Quincy Street, the eastern boundary of the Clanton square.

From his position inside an abandoned silo, the marksman had a clear but distant view of the rear of the courthouse. He crouched in the darkness and aimed through a small opening, confident no one in the world could see him. The whiskey helped the confidence, and the aim, which he practiced a thousand times from seven-thirty until eight, when he noticed activity around the nigger's lawyer's office.

A comrade waited in a pickup hidden in a run-down warehouse next to the silo. The engine was running and the driver chain-smoked Lucky Strikes, waiting anxiously to hear the clapping sounds from the deer rifle.

As the armored mass stepped its way across Washington, the marksman panicked. Through the scope he could barely see the head of the nigger's lawyer as it bobbed and weaved awkwardly among the sea of green, which was surrounded and chased by a dozen reporters. Go ahead, the whiskey said, create some excitement. He timed the bobbing and weaving as best he could, and pulled the trigger as the target approached the rear door of the courthouse.

The rifle shot was clear and unmistakable.

Half the soldiers hit the ground rolling and the other half grabbed Jake and threw him violently under the veranda. A guardsman screamed in anguish. The reporters and

TV people crouched and stumbled to the ground, but valiantly kept the cameras rolling to record the carnage. The soldier clutched his throat and screamed again. Another shot. Then another.

"He's hit!" someone yelled. The soldiers scrambled on all fours across the driveway to the fallen one. Jake escaped through the doors to the safety of the courthouse. He fell onto the floor of the rear entrance and buried his head in his hands. Ozzie stood next to him, watching the soldiers through the door.

The gunman dropped from the silo, threw his gun behind the back seat, and disappeared with his comrade into the countryside. They had a funeral to attend in south Mississippi.

"He's hit in the throat!" someone screamed as his buddies waded around the reporters. They lifted him and dragged him to a jeep.

"Who got hit?" Jake asked without removing his palms from his eyes.

"One of the guardsmen," Ozzie said. "You okay?"

"I guess," he answered as he clasped his hands behind his head and stared at the floor. "Where's my briefcase?"

"It's out there on the driveway. We'll get it in a minute." Ozzie removed his radio from his belt and barked orders to the dispatcher, something about all men to the courthouse.

When it was apparent the shooting was over, Ozzie joined the mass of soldiers outside. Nesbit stood next to Jake. "You okay?" he asked.

The colonel rounded the corner, yelling and swearing. "What the hell happened?" he demanded. "I heard some shots."

"Mackenvale got hit."

"Where is he?" the colonel said.

"Off to the hospital," a sergeant replied, pointing at a jeep flying away in the distance.

"How bad is he?"

"Looked pretty bad. Got him in the throat."

"Throat! Why did they move him?"

No one answered.

"Did anybody see anything?" the colonel demanded.

."Sounded like it came from up the hill," Ozzie said looking up past Cedar Street. "Why don't you send a jeep up there to look around."

"Good idea." The colonel addressed his eager men with a string of terse commands, punctuated liberally with obscenities. The soldiers scattered in all directions, guns drawn and ready for combat, in search of an assassin they could not identify, who was, in fact, in the next county when the foot patrol began exploring the abandoned feed mill.

Ozzie laid the briefcase on the floor next to Jake. "Is Jake okay?" he whispered to Nesbit. Harry Rex and Ellen stood on the stairs where Cobb and Willard had fallen.

"I don't know. He ain't moved in ten minutes," Nesbit said.

"Jake, are you all right?" the sheriff asked.

"Yes," he said slowly without opening his eyes. The soldier had been on Jake's left shoulder. "This is kinda silly, ain't it?" he had just said to Jake when a bullet ripped through his throat. He fell into Jake, grabbing at his neck, gurgling blood and screaming. Jake fell, and was tossed to safety.

"He's dead, isn't he?" Jake asked softly.

"We don't know yet," replied Ozzie. "He's at the hospital."

"He's dead. I know he's dead. I heard his neck pop."

Ozzie looked at Nesbit, then at Harry Rex. Four or five coin-sized drops of blood were splattered on Jake's light gray suit. He hadn't noticed them yet, but they were apparent to everyone else.

"Jake, you've got blood on your suit," Ozzie finally said. "Let's go back to your office so you can change clothes."

"Why is that important?" Jake mumbled to the floor. They stared at each other.

Dell and the others from the Coffee Shop stood on the sidewalk and watched as they led Jake from the courthouse, across the street, and into his office, ignoring the absurdities thrown by the reporters. Harry Rex locked the front door, leaving the bodyguards on the sidewalk. Jake went upstairs and removed his coat.

"Row Ark, why don't you make some margaritas," Harry Rex said. "I'll go upstairs and stay with him."

———————

"Judge, we've had some excitement," Ozzie explained as Noose unpacked his briefcase and removed his coat.

"What is it?" Buckley asked.

"They tried to kill Jake this mornin'."

"What!"

"When?" asked Buckley.

" 'Bout an hour ago, somebody shot at Jake as he was comin' into the courthouse. It was a rifle at long range. We have no idea who did it. They missed Jake and hit a guardsman. He's in surgery now."

"Where's Jake?" asked His Honor.

"Over in his office. He's pretty shook up."

"I would be too," Noose said sympathetically.

"He wanted you to call him when you got here."

"Sure." Ozzie dialed the number and handed the phone to the judge.

"It's Noose," Harry Rex said, handing the phone to Jake.

"Hello."

"Are you okay, Jake?"

"Not really. I won't be there today."

Noose struggled for a response. "Do what?"

"I said I won't be in court today. I'm not up to it."

"Well, uh, Jake, where does that leave the rest of us?"

"I don't care, really," Jake said, sipping on his second margarita.

"Beg your pardon?"

"I said I don't care, Judge. I don't care what you do, I won't be there."

Noose shook his head and looked at the receiver. "Are you hurt?" he asked with feeling.

"You ever been shot at, Judge?"

"No, Jake."

"You ever seen a man get shot, hear him scream?"

"No, Jake."

"You ever had somebody else's blood splashed on your suit?"

"No, Jake."

"I won't be there."

Noose paused and thought for a moment. "Come on over, Jake, and let's talk about it."

"No. I'm not leaving my office. It's dangerous out there."

"Suppose we stand in recess until one. Will you feel better then?"

"I'll be drunk by then."

"What!"

"I said I'll be drunk by then,"

Harry Rex covered his eyes. Ellen left for the kitchen.

"When do you think you might be sober?" Noose asked sternly. Ozzie and Buckley looked at each other.

"Monday."

"What about tomorrow?"

"Tomorrow's Saturday."

"Yes, I know, and I'd planned to hold court tomorrow. We've got a jury sequestered, remember?"

"Okay, I'll be ready in the morning."

"That's good to hear. What do I tell the jury right now? They're sitting in the jury room waiting on us. The court-room is packed. Your client is sitting out there by himself waiting on you. What do I tell these people?"

"You'll think of something, Judge. I've got faith in you." Jake hung up. Noose listened to the unbelievable until it was evident that he had in fact been hung up on. He handed the phone to Ozzie.

His Honor looked out the window and removed his glasses. "He says he ain't comin' today."

Uncharacteristically, Buckley remained silent.

Ozzie was defensive. "It really got to him, Judge."

"Has he been drinking?"

"Naw, not Jake," Ozzie replied. "He's just tore up over that boy gettin' shot like he did. He was right next to Jake, and caught the bullet that was aimed for him. It would upset anybody, Judge."

"He wants us to remain in recess until tomorrow morn-ing," Noose said to Buckley, who shrugged and again said nothing.

As word spread, a regular carnival developed on the sidewalk outside Jake's office. The press set up camp and pawed at the front window in hopes of seeing someone or something newsworthy inside. Friends stopped by to check on Jake, but were informed by various of the reporters that he was locked away inside and would not come out. Yes, he was unhurt.

Dr. Bass had been scheduled to testify Friday morning. He and Lucien entered the office through the rear door a few minutes after ten, and Harry Rex left for the liquor store.

With all the crying, the conversation with Carla had been difficult. He called after three drinks, and things did not go well. He talked to her father, told him he was safe, unhurt, and that half of the Mississippi National Guard had been assigned to protect him. Settle her down, he said, and he would call back later.

Lucien was furious. He had fought with Bass to keep him sober Thursday night so he could testify Friday. Now that he would testify Saturday, there was no way to keep him sober two days in a row. He thought of all the drinking they had missed Thursday, and was furious.

Harry Rex returned with a gallon of liquor. He and Ellen mixed drinks and argued over the ingredients. She rinsed the coffeepot, filled it with Bloody Mary mix and a disproportionate helping of Swedish vodka. Harry Rex added a lavish dose of Tabasco. He made the rounds in the conference room and refilled each cup with the delightful mixture.

Dr. Bass gulped frantically and ordered more. Lucien and Harry Rex debated the likely identity of the gunman. Ellen silently watched Jake, who sat in the corner and stared at the bookshelves.

The phone rang. Harry Rex grabbed it and listened intently. He hung up and said, "That was Ozzie. The soldier's outta surgery. Bullet's lodged in the spine. They think he'll be paralyzed."

They all sipped in unison and said nothing. They made great efforts to ignore Jake as he rubbed his forehead with one hand and sloshed his drink with the other. The faint sound of someone knocking at the rear door interrupted the brief memorial.

"Go see who it is," Lucien ordered Ellen, who left to see who was knocking.

"It's Lester Hailey," she reported to the conference room.

"Let him in," Jake mumbled, almost incoherently.

Lester was introduced to the party and offered a Bloody Mary. He declined and asked for something with whiskey in it.

"Good idea," said Lucien. "I'm tired of light stuff. Let's get some Jack Daniel's."

"Sounds good to me," added Bass as he gulped the remnants in his cup.

Jake managed a weak smile at Lester, then returned to the study of the bookshelves. Lucien threw a hundred-dollar bill on the table, and Harry Rex left for the liquor store.

When she awoke hours later, Ellen was on the couch in Jake's office. The room was dark and deserted, with an acrid, intoxicating smell to it. She moved cautiously. She found her boss peacefully snoring away in the war room, on the floor, partially under the war desk. There were no lights to extinguish, so she carefully walked down the stairs. The conference room was littered with empty liquor bottles, beer cans, plastic cups and chicken dinner boxes. It was 9:30 P.M. She had slept five hours.

She could stay at Lucien's, but needed to change clothes. Her friend Nesbit would drive her to Oxford, but she was sober. Plus, Jake needed all the protection he could get. She locked the front door and walked to her car.

Ellen almost made it to Oxford when she saw the blue lights behind her. As usual, she was driving seventy-five. She parked on the shoulder and walked to her taillights, where she searched her purse and waited on the trooper.

Two plainsclothesmen approached from the blue lights.

"You drunk, ma'am?" one of them asked, spewing tobacco juice.

"No, sir. I'm trying to find my license."

She crouched before the taillights and fished for the

license. Suddenly, she was knocked to the ground. A heavy
quilt was thrown over her and both men held her down. A
rope was wrapped around her chest and waist. She kicked
and cursed, but could offer little resistance. The quilt covered her head and trapped her arms underneath. They
pulled the rope tightly.

"Be still, bitch! Be still!"

One of them removed her keys from the ignition and
opened the trunk. They threw her inside and slammed it
shut. The blue lights were unplugged in the old Lincoln and
it roared away, trailed by the BMW. They found a gravel
road and followed it deep into the woods. It turned into a
dirt road that led to a small pasture where a large cross was
being burned by a handful of Kluxers.

The two assailants quickly donned their robes and
masks and removed her from the trunk. She was thrown to
the ground and the quilt removed. They bound and gagged
her, and dragged her to a large pole a few feet from the
cross where she was tied, her back to the Kluxers, her face to
the pole.

She saw the white robes and pointed hats, and tried
desperately to spit out the oily, cotton rag crammed in her
mouth. She managed only to gag and cough.

The flaming cross illuminated the small pasture, dis-
charging a glowing wave of heat that began to roast her as
she wrestled with the pole and emitted strange, guttural
noises.

A hooded figure left the others and approached her.
She could hear him walking and breathing. "You nigger-
loving bitch," he said in a crisp Midwestern voice. He
grabbed the rear of her collar and ripped the white silk
blouse until it hung in shreds around her neck and shoulders. Her hands were tied firmly around the pole. He removed a bowie knife from under the robe, and began cutting
the remainder of the blouse from her body. "You nigger-
loving bitch. You nigger-loving bitch."

Ellen cursed him, but her words were muffled groans.

He unzipped the navy linen skirt on the right side. She
tried to kick, but the heavy rope around her ankles held her
feet to the pole. He placed the tip of the knife at the bottom
of the zipper, and cut downward through the hem. He

grabbed around the waist and pulled it off like a magician. The Kluxers stepped forward.

He slapped her on the butt, and said, "Nice, very nice." He stepped back to admire his handiwork. She grunted and twisted but could not resist. The slip fell to mid-thigh. With great ceremony, he cut the straps, then sliced it neatly down the back. He yanked it off and threw it at the foot of the burning cross. He cut the bra straps and removed it. She jerked and the moans became louder. The silent semicircle inched forward and stopped ten feet away.

The fire was hot now. Her bare back and legs were covered with sweat. The light red hair was drenched around her neck and shoulders. He reached under his robe again and brought out a bullwhip. He popped it loudly near her, and she flinched. He marched backward, carefully measuring the distance to the pole.

He cocked the bullwhip and aimed at the bare back. The tallest one stepped forward with his back to her. He shook his head. Nothing was said, but the whip disappeared.

He walked to her and grabbed her head. With his knife, he cut her hair. He grabbed handfuls and hacked away until her scalp was gapped and ugly. It piled gently around her feet. She moaned and did not move.

They headed for their cars. A gallon of gasoline was splashed inside the BMW with Massachusetts tags and somebody threw a match.

When he was certain they were gone, Mickey Mouse slid from the bushes. He untied her and carried her to a small clearing away from the pasture. He gathered the remains of her clothing and tried to cover her. When her car finished burning beside the dirt road, he left her. He drove to Oxford, to a pay phone, and called the Lafayette County sheriff.

38 Saturday court was unusual but not unheard of, especially in capital cases where the jury was locked up. The participants didn't mind because Saturday brought the end one day nearer.

The locals didn't mind either. It was their day off, and for most Ford Countians it was their only chance to watch the trial, or if they couldn't get a seat, at least hang around the square and see it all first-hand. Who knows, there may even be some more shooting.

By seven, the cafes downtown were at full capacity serving nonregulars. For every customer who was awarded a seat, two were turned away and left to loiter around the square and the courthouse and wait for a seat in the courtroom. Most of them paused for a moment in front of the lawyer's office, hoping to catch a glimpse of the one they tried to kill. The braggarts told of being clients of this famous man.

Upward, a few feet, the target sat at his desk and sipped a bloody concoction left from yesterday's party. He smoked a Roi-Tan, ate headache powders, and rubbed the cobwebs from his brain. Forget about the soldier, he had told himself for the past three hours. Forget about the Klan, the threats, forget everything but the trial, and specifically Dr. W.T. Bass. He uttered a short prayer, something about Bass being sober on the witness stand. The expert and Lucien had stayed through the afternoon, drinking and arguing, accusing each other of being a drunk and receiving a dishonorable discharge from their respective professions. Violence flared briefly at Ethel's desk when they were leaving. Nesbit intervened and escorted them to the patrol car for the ride home. The reporters burned with curiosity as the two blind drunks were led from Jake's office by the deputy and put in the car, where they continued to rage and cuss at each other, Lucien in the back seat, Bass in the front.

He reviewed Ellen's masterpiece on the insanity defense. Her outline of questions for Bass needed only minor changes. He studied his expert's résumé, and though unimpressive, it would suffice for Ford County. The nearest psychiatrist was eighty miles away.

Judge Noose glanced at the D.A. and looked sympathetically at Jake, who sat next to the door and watched the faded portrait of some dead judge hanging over Buckley's shoulder.

"How do you feel this morning, Jake?" Noose asked warmly.

"I'm fine."

"How's the soldier?" asked Buckley.

"Paralyzed."

Noose, Buckley, Musgrove, and Mr. Pate looked at the same spot on the carpet and grimly shook their heads in a quiet moment of respect.

"Where's your law clerk?" Noose asked, looking at the clock on the wall.

Jake looked at his watch. "I don't know. I expected her by now."

"Are you ready?"

"Sure."

"Is the courtroom ready, Mr. Pate?"

"Yes, sir."

"Very well. Let's proceed."

Noose seated the courtroom, and for ten minutes offered a rambling apology to the jurors for yesterday's delay. They were the only fourteen in the county who did not know what happened Friday morning, and it might be prejudicial to tell them. Noose droned on about emergencies and how sometimes during trials things conspire to cause delays. When he finally finished, the jurors were completely bewildered and praying that somebody would call a witness.

"You may call your first witness," Noose said in Jake's direction.

"Dr. W.T. Bass," Jake announced as he moved to the podium. Buckley and Musgrove exchanged winks and silly grins.

Bass was seated next to Lucien on the second row in the middle of the family. He stood noisily and made his way to the center aisle, stepping on feet and assaulting people with his heavy, leather, empty briefcase. Jake heard the commotion behind him and continued smiling at the jury.

"I do, I do," Bass said rapidly at Jean Gillespie during his swearing in.

Mr. Pate led him to the witness stand and delivered the standard orders to speak up and use the microphone. Though mortified and hung over, the expert looked remarkably arrogant and sober. He wore his most expensive dark gray hand-sewn wool suit, a perfectly starched white button-down, and a cute little red paisley bow tie that made him appear rather cerebral. He looked like an expert, in something. He also wore, over Jake's objections, a pair of light gray ostrich skin cowboy boots that he had paid over a thousand for and worn less than a dozen times. Lucien had insisted on the boots eleven years earlier in the first insanity case. Bass wore them, and the very sane defendant went to Parchman. He wore them in the second insanity trial, again at Lucien's behest; again, Parchman. Lucien referred to them as Bass's good luck charm.

Jake wanted no part of the damned boots. But the jury could relate to them, Lucien had argued. Not expensive ostrich skin, Jake countered. They're too dumb to know the difference, replied Lucien. Jake could not be swayed. The rednecks will trust someone with boots, Lucien had explained. Fine, said Jake, let him wear a pair of those camouflage squirrel-hunting boots with a little mud on the heels and soles, some boots they could really identify with. Those wouldn't complement his suit, Bass had inserted.

He crossed his legs, laying the right boot on his left knee, flaunting it. He grinned at it, then grinned at the jury. The ostrich would have been proud.

Jake looked from his notes on the podium and saw the boot, which was plainly visible above the rail of the witness stand. Bass was admiring it, the jurors pondering it. He choked and returned to his notes.

"State your name, please."

"Dr. W.T. Bass," he replied, his attention suddenly diverted from the boot. He looked grimly, importantly at Jake.

"What is your address?"

"Nine-oh-eight West Canterbury, Jackson, Mississippi."

"What is your profession?"

"I am a physician."

"Are you licensed to practice in Mississippi?"

"Yes."

"When were you licensed?"

"February 8, 1963."

"Are you licensed to practice medicine in any other state?"

"Yes."

"Where?"

"Texas."

"When did you obtain that license?"

"November 3, 1962."

"Where did you go to college?"

"I received my bachelor's degree from Millsaps College in 1956, and received my M.D., or Doctor of Medicine, from the University of Texas Health Science Center in Dallas, Texas, in 1960."

"Is that an accredited medical school?"

"Yes."

"By whom?"

"By the Council of Medical Education and Hospitals of the American Medical Association, the recognized accrediting agency of our profession, and by the educational authority of the State of Texas."

Bass relaxed a bit, uncrossed and recrossed his legs, and displayed his left boot. He rocked gently and turned the comfortable swivel chair partially toward the jury.

"Where did you intern and for how long?"

"After graduation from medical school, I spent twelve months as an intern at the Rocky Mountain Medical Center in Denver."

"What is your medical specialty?"

"Psychiatry."

"Explain to us what that means."

"Psychiatry is that branch of medicine concerned with the treatment of disorders of the mind. It usually, but not always, deals with mental malfunction, the organic basis of which is unknown."

Jake breathed for the first time since Bass took the stand. His man was sounding good.

"Now, Doctor," he said as he casually walked to within

a foot of the jury box, "describe to the jury the specialized training you received in the field of psychiatry."

"My specialized training in psychiatry consisted of two years as a resident in psychiatry at the Texas State Mental Hospital, an approved training center. I engaged in clinical work with psychoneurotic and psychotic patients. I studied psychology, psychopathology, psychotherapy, and the physiological therapies. This training, supervised by competent psychiatric teachers, included instruction in the psychiatric aspects of general medicine, the behavior aspects of children, adolescents, and adults."

It was doubtful if a single person in the courtroom comprehended any of what Bass had just said, but it came from the mouth of a man who suddenly appeared to be a genius, an expert, for he had to be a man of great wisdom and intelligence to pronounce those words. With the bow tie and vocabulary, and in spite of the boots, Bass was gaining credibility with each answer.

"Are you a diplomate of the American Board of Psychiatry?"

"Of course," he answered confidently.

"In which branch are you certified?"

"I am certified in psychiatry."

"And when were you certified?"

"April of 1967."

"What does it take to become certified by the American Board of Psychiatry?"

"A candidate must pass oral and practical exams, as well as a written test at the direction of the Board."

Jake glanced at his notes and noticed Musgrove winking at Buckley.

"Doctor, do you belong to any professional groups?"

"Yes."

"Name them please."

"I am a member of the American Medical Association, American Psychiatric Association, and the Mississippi Medical Association."

"How long have you been engaged in the practice of psychiatry?"

"Twenty-two years."

Jake walked three steps in the direction of the bench and eyed Noose, who was watching intently.

"Your Honor, the defense offers Dr. Bass as an expert in the field of psychiatry."

"Very well," replied Noose. "Do you wish to examine this witness, Mr. Buckley?"

The D.A. stood with his legal pad. "Yes, Your Honor, just a few questions."

Surprised but not worried, Jake took his seat next to Carl Lee. Ellen was still not in the courtroom.

"Dr. Bass, in your opinion, are you an expert in the field of psychiatry?" asked Buckley.

"Yes."

"Have you ever taught psychiatry?"

"No."

"Have you ever published any articles on psychiatry?"

"No."

"Have you ever published any books on psychiatry?"

"No."

"Now, I believe you testified that you are a member of the A.M.A., M.M.A., and the American Psychiatric Association?"

"Yes."

"Have you ever served as an officer in any of these organizations?"

"No."

"What hospital positions do you currently hold, as of today?"

"None."

"Has your experience in psychiatry included any work under the auspices of the federal government or any state government?"

"No."

The arrogance was beginning to fade from his face, and the confidence from his voice. He shot a glance at Jake, who was digging through a file.

"Dr. Bass, are you now engaged in the practice of psychiatry full-time?"

The expert hesitated, and looked briefly at Lucien on the second row. "I see patients on a regular basis."

"How many patients and how regular?" Buckley retorted with an enormous air of confidence.

"I see from five to ten patients per week."

"One or two a day?"

"Something like that."

"And you consider that a full-time practice?"

"I'm as busy as I want to be."

Buckley threw his legal pad on the table and looked at Noose. "Your Honor, the State objects to this man testifying as an expert in the field of psychiatry. It's obvious he's not qualified."

Jake was on his feet with his mouth open.

"Overruled, Mr. Buckley. You may proceed, Mr. Brigance."

Jake gathered his legal pads and returned to the podium, well aware of the suspicion the D.A. had just artfully thrown over his star witness. Bass shifted boots.

"Now, Dr. Bass, have you examined the defendant, Carl Lee Hailey?"

"Yes."

"How many times?"

"Three."

"When was your first examination?"

"June 10."

"What was the purpose of this examination?"

"I examined him to determine his current mental condition as well as his condition on May 20, when he allegedly shot Mr. Cobb and Mr. Willard."

"Where did this examination take place?"

"Ford County Jail."

"Did you conduct this examination alone?"

"Yes. Just Mr. Hailey and myself."

"How long did the examination last?"

"Three hours."

"Did you review his medical history?"

"In a roundabout way, you could say. We talked at great length about his past."

"What did you learn?"

"Nothing remarkable, except for Vietnam."

"What about Vietnam?"

Bass folded his hands over his slightly overweight stomach and frowned intelligently at the defense attorney. "Well, Mr. Brigance, like many Vietnam vets I've worked with, Mr. Hailey had some rather horrible experiences over there."

War is hell, thought Carl Lee. He listened intently. Now, Vietnam was bad. He'd been shot. He'd lost friends. He'd killed people, many people. He'd killed children, Vietnamese children carrying guns and grenades. It was bad. He wished he'd never seen the place. He dreamed about it, had flashbacks and nightmares occasionally. But he didn't feel warped or insane because of it. He didn't feel warped or insane because of Cobb and Willard. In fact, he felt quite satisfied because they were dead. Just like those in Vietnam.

He had explained all this to Bass once at the jail, and Bass had seemed unimpressed by it. And they had talked only twice, and never more than an hour.

Carl Lee eyed the jury and listened suspiciously to the expert, who talked at length of Carl Lee's dreadful experiences in the war. Bass's vocabulary jumped several octaves as he explained to the laymen in nonlaymen terms the effects of Vietnam on Carl Lee. It sounded good. There had been nightmares over the years, dreams Carl Lee had never worried much about, but to hear Bass explain it, were extremely significant events.

"Did he talk freely of Vietnam?"

"Not really," replied Bass, then explaining in great detail the tremendous task he confronted in dragging out the war from this complex, burdened, probably unstable mind. Carl Lee didn't remember it that way. But he dutifully listened with a pained expression, wondering for the first time in his life if perhaps he could be a little off.

After an hour, the war had been refought and its effects flogged thoroughly. Jake decided to move on.

"Now, Dr. Bass," Jake said, scratching his head. "Other than Vietnam, what other significant events did you note regarding his mental history?"

"None, except the rape of his daughter."

"Did you discuss the rape with Carl Lee?"

"At great length, during each of the three examinations."

"Explain to the jury what the rape did to Carl Lee Hailey."

Bass stroked his chin and looked perplexed. "Quite frankly, Mr. Brigance, it would take a great deal of time to explain what the rape did to Mr. Hailey."

Jake thought a moment, and seemed to thoroughly analyze this last statement. "Well, could you summarize it for the jury?"

Bass nodded gravely. "I'll try."

Lucien grew weary of listening to Bass, and began watching the jury in hopes of eyeing Clyde Sisco, who had also lost interest but appeared to be admiring the boots. Lucien watched intently from the corner of his eye, waiting for Sisco to gaze around the courtroom.

Finally, as Bass rambled on, Sisco left the testimony and looked at Carl Lee, then Buckley, then one of the reporters on the front row. Then his line of vision locked solidly into a wild-eyed, bearded old man who had once handed him eighty thousand cash for performing his civic duty and returning a just verdict. They focused unmistakably on each other, and both managed a slight grin. How much? was the look in Lucien's eyes. Sisco returned to the testimony, but seconds later he was staring at Lucien. How much? Lucien said, his lips actually moving but with no sound.

Sisco looked away and watched Bass, thinking of a fair price. He looked in Lucien's direction, scratched his beard, then suddenly, while staring at Bass, flashed five fingers across his face and coughed. He coughed again and studied the expert.

Five hundred or five thousand? Lucien asked himself. Knowing Sisco, it was five thousand, maybe fifty thousand. It made no difference; Lucien would pay it. He was worth a ton.

By ten-thirty, Noose had cleaned his glasses a hundred times and consumed a dozen cups of coffee. His bladder pressed forward toward the spillway. "Time for the morning recess. We'll adjourn until eleven." He rapped the gavel and disappeared.

"How'm I doing?" Bass asked nervously. He followed Jake and Lucien to the law library on the third floor.

"You're doing fine," Jake said. "Just keep those boots outta sight."

"The boots are critical," Lucien protested.

"I needa drink," Bass said desperately.

"Forget it," Jake said.

"So do I," Lucien added. "Let's run over to your office for a quick one."

"Great idea!" Bass said.

"Forget it," Jake repeated. "You're sober and you're doing great."

"We got thirty minutes," Bass said as he and Lucien were leaving the library and heading for the stairs.

"No! Don't do it, Lucien!" Jake demanded.

"Just one," Lucien replied, pointing a finger at Jake. "Just one."

"You've never had just one."

"Come with us, Jake. It'll settle your nerves."

"Just one," Bass yelled as he disappeared down the steps.

At eleven, Bass sat himself in the witness chair and looked through glazed eyes at the jury. He smiled, and almost giggled. He was aware of the artists on the front row, so he looked as expert as possible. His nerves were indeed settled.

"Dr. Bass, are you familiar with the criminal responsibility test relative to the M'Naghten Rule?" Jake asked.

"I certainly am!" Bass replied with a sudden air of superiority.

"Would you explain this rule to the jury?"

"Of course. The M'Naghten Rule is the standard for criminal responsibility in Mississippi, as in fifteen other states. It goes back to England, in the year 1843, when a man by the name of Daniel M'Naghten attempted to assassinate the prime minister, Sir Robert Peel. He mistakenly shot and killed the prime minister's secretary, Edward Drummond. During his trial the evidence plainly showed M'Naghten was suffering from what we would call paranoid schizophrenia. The jury returned a verdict of not guilty, by reason of insanity. From this the M'Naghten Rule was established. It is still followed in England and sixteen states."

"What does the M'Naghten Rule mean?"

"The M'Naghten Rule is fairly simple. Every man is presumed to be sane, and to establish a defense on the ground of insanity, it must be clearly proven that when the defendant did what he did he was laboring under such a defect of reason, from a mental disease, that he did not know the nature and quality of the act he was doing, or if he did know what he was doing, he did not know it was wrong."

"Could you simplify that?"

"Yes. If a defendant cannot distinguish right from wrong, he is legally insane."

"Define insanity, please."

"It has no significance, medically. It is strictly a legal standard for a person's mental state or condition."

Jake breathed deeply and plowed forward. "Now, Doctor, based upon your examination of the defendant, do you have an opinion as to the mental condition of Carl Lee Hailey on May 20 of this year, at the time of the shooting?"

"Yes, I do."

"And what is that opinion?"

"It is my opinion," Bass said slowly, "that the defendant had a total break with reality when his daughter was raped. When he saw her immediately after the rape he didn't recognize her, and when someone told him she'd been gangraped, and beaten, and almost hanged, something just snapped in Carl Lee's mind. That's a very elementary way of putting it, but that's what happened. Something snapped. He broke with reality.

"They had to be killed. He told me once that when he first saw them in court, he could not understand why the deputies were protecting them. He kept waiting for one of the cops to pull a gun and blow their heads off. A few days went by and nobody killed them, so he figured it was up to him. I mean, he felt as though someone in the system would execute the two for raping his little girl.

"What I'm saying, Mr. Brigance, is that, mentally, he left us. He was in another world. He was suffering from delusions. He broke."

Bass knew he was sounding good. He was talking to the jury now, not the lawyer.

"The day after the rape he spoke with his daughter in the hospital. She could barely talk, with the broken jaws and all, but she said she saw him in the woods running to save her, and she asked him why he disappeared. Now, can you imagine what that would do to a father? She later told him she begged for her daddy, and the two men laughed at her and told her she didn't have a daddy."

Jake let those words sink in. He studied Ellen's outline and saw only two more questions.

"Now, Dr. Bass, based upon your observations of Carl Lee Hailey, and your diagnosis of his mental condition at the time of the shooting, do you have an opinion, to a reasonable degree of medical certainty, as to whether Carl Lee Hailey was capable of knowing the difference between right and wrong when he shot these men?"

"I have."

"And what is that opinion?"

"That due to his mental condition, he was totally incapable of distinguishing right from wrong."

"Do you have an opinion, based upon the same factors, as to whether Carl Lee Hailey was able to understand and appreciate the nature and quality of his actions?"

"I do."

"And what is that opinion?"

"In my opinion, as an expert in the field of psychiatry, Mr. Hailey was totally incapable of understanding and appreciating the nature and quality of what he was doing."

"Thank you, Doctor. I tender the witness."

Jake gathered his legal pad and strolled confidently back to his seat. He glanced at Lucien, who was smiling and nodding. He glanced at the jury. They were watching Bass and thinking about his testimony. Wanda Womack, a young woman with a sympathetic glow about her, looked at Jake and smiled ever so slightly. It was the first positive signal he received from the jury since the trial started.

"So far so good," Carl Lee whispered.

Jake smiled at his client. "You're a real psycho, big man."

"Any cross-examination?" Noose asked Buckley.

"Just a few questions," Buckley said as he grabbed the podium.

Jake could not imagine Buckley arguing psychiatry with an expert, even if it was W.T. Bass.

But Buckley had no plans to argue psychiatry. "Dr. Bass, what is your full name?"

Jake froze. The question had an ominous hint to it. Buckley asked it with a great deal of suspicion.

"William Tyler Bass."

"What do you go by?"

"W.T. Bass."

"Have you ever been known as Tyler Bass?"

The expert hesitated. "No," he said meekly.

An immense feeling of anxiety hit Jake and felt like a hot spear tearing into his stomach. The question could only mean trouble.

"Are you positive?" Buckley asked with raised eyebrows and an enormous amount of distrust in his voice.

Bass shrugged. "Maybe when I was younger."

"I see. Now, I believe you testified that you studied medicine at the University of Texas Health Science Center?"

"That's correct."

"And where is that?"

"Dallas."

"And when were you a student there?"

"From 1956 to 1960."

"And under what name were you registered?"

"William T. Bass."

Jake was numb with fear. Buckley had something, a dark secret from the past known only to Bass and himself.

"Did you ever use the name Tyler Bass while you were a medical student?"

"No."

"Are you positive?"

"I certainly am."

"What is your social security number?"

"410-96-8585."

Buckley made a check mark beside something on his legal pad.

"And what is your date of birth?" he asked carefully.

"September 14, 1934."

"And what was your mother's name?"

"Jonnie Elizabeth Bass."

"And her maiden name?"

"Skidmore."

Another check mark. Bass looked nervously at Jake.

"And your place of birth?"

"Carbondale, Illinois."

Another check mark.

An objection to the relevance of these questions was in order and sustainable, but Jake's knees were like Jell-O and his bowels were suddenly fluid. He feared he would embarrass himself if he stood and tried to speak.

Buckley studied his check marks and waited a few seconds. Every ear in the courtroom waited for the next question, knowing it would be brutal. Bass watched the D.A. like a prisoner watching the firing squad, hoping and praying the guns would somehow misfire.

Finally, Buckley smiled at the expert. "Dr. Bass, have you ever been convicted of a felony?"

The question echoed throughout the silence and landed from all directions on the trembling shoulders of Tyler Bass. Even a cursory look at his face revealed the answer.

Carl Lee squinted and looked at his lawyer.

"Of course not!" Bass answered loudly, desperately.

Buckley just nodded and walked slowly to the table, where Musgrove, with much ceremony, handed him some important-looking papers.

"Are you certain?" Buckley thundered.

"Of course I'm certain," Bass protested as he eyed the important-looking papers.

Jake knew he needed to rise and say something or do something to stop the carnage that was seconds away, but his mind was paralyzed.

"You're certain?" Buckley asked.

"Yes," Bass answered through clenched teeth.

"You've never been convicted of a felony?"

"Of course not."

"Are you as certain of that as you are the rest of your testimony before this jury?"

That was the trap, the killer, the deadliest question of all; one Jake had used many times, and when he heard it, he knew Bass was finished. And so was Carl Lee.

"Of course," Bass answered with feigned arrogance.

Buckley moved in for the kill. "You're telling this jury that on October 17, 1956, in Dallas, Texas, you were not convicted of a felony under the name of Tyler Bass?"

Buckley asked the question while looking at the jury and reading from the important-looking documents.

"That's a lie," Bass said quietly, and unconvincingly.

"Are you sure it's a lie?" Buckley asked.

"A bald-faced lie."

"Do you know a lie from the truth, Dr. Bass?"

"Damn right I do."

Noose placed his glasses on his nose and leaned forward. The jurors quit rocking. The reporters quit scribbling. The deputies along the back wall stood still and listened.

Buckley picked out one of the important-looking documents and studied it. "You're telling this jury that on October 17, 1956, you were not convicted of statutory rape?"

Jake knew it was important, in the midst of any great courtroom crisis, even this one, to maintain a straight, poker face. It was important for the jurors, who missed nothing, to see the defendant's lawyer with a positive look about him. Jake had practiced this positive, everything's-wonderful, I'm-in-control look through many trials and many surprises, but with the "statutory rape" the positive and confident and certain look was immediately replaced by a sickly, pale, pained expression that was being scrutinized by at least half of those in the jury box.

The other half scowled at the witness on the stand.

"Were you convicted of statutory rape, Doctor?" Buckley asked again after a lengthy silence.

No answer.

Noose uncoiled and leaned downward in the direction of the witness. "Please answer the question, Dr. Bass."

Bass ignored His Honor and stared at the D.A., then said, "You've got the wrong man."

Buckley snorted and walked to Musgrove, who was holding some more important-looking papers. He opened a large white envelope and removed something that resembled an 8 × 10 photograph.

"Well, Dr. Bass, I've got some photographs of you taken by the Dallas Police Department on September 11, 1956. Would you like to see them?"

No answer.

Buckley held them out to the witness. "Would you like

to see these, Dr. Bass? Perhaps they could refresh your memory."

Bass slowly shook his head, then lowered it and stared blankly at his boots.

"Your Honor, the State would introduce into evidence these copies, certified under the Acts of Congress, of the Final Judgment and Sentencing Order in the case styled State of Texas versus Tyler Bass, said records being obtained by the State from the proper officials in Dallas, Texas, and showing that on October 17, 1956, a one Tyler Bass pled guilty to the charge of statutory rape, a felony under the laws of the State of Texas. We can prove that Tyler Bass and this witness, Dr. W.T. Bass, are one and the same."

Musgrove politely handed Jake a copy of everything Buckley was waving.

"Any objections to this introduction into evidence?" Noose asked in Jake's direction.

A speech was needed. A brilliant, emotional explanation that would touch the hearts of the jurors and make them weep with pity for Bass and his patient. But the rules of procedure did not permit one at this point. Of course the evidence was admissible. Unable to stand, Jake waved in the negative. No objections.

"We have no further questions," Buckley announced.

"Any redirect, Mr. Brigance?" Noose asked.

In the split second available, Jake could not think of a single thing he could ask Bass to improve the situation. The jury had heard enough from the defense expert.

"No," Jake said quietly.

"Very well, Dr. Bass, you are excused."

Bass made a quick exit through the small gate in the railing, down the center aisle, and out of the courtroom. Jake watched his departure intently, conveying as much hatred as possible. It was important for the jury to see how shocked the defendant and his lawyer were. The jury had to believe a convicted felon was not knowingly put on the stand.

When the door closed and Bass was gone, Jake scanned the courtroom in hopes of finding an encouraging face. There were none. Lucien stroked his beard and stared at the floor. Lester sat with his arms folded and a disgusted look on his face. Gwen was crying.

"Call your next witness," Noose said.

Jake continued searching. In the third row, between Reverend Ollie Agee and Reverend Luther Roosevelt, sat Norman Reinfeld. When his eyes met Jake's, he frowned and shook his head as if to say "I told you so." On the other side of the courtroom, most of the whites looked relaxed and a few even grinned at Jake.

"Mr. Brigance, you may call your next witness."

Against his better judgment, Jake attempted to stand. His knees buckled and he leaned forward with his palms flat against the table. "Your Honor," he said in a high-pitched, shrill, defeated voice, "could we recess till one?"

"But Mr. Brigance, it's only eleven-thirty."

A lie seemed appropriate. "Yes, Your Honor, but our next witness is not here, and will not arrive until one."

"Very well. We'll stand in recess until one. I need to see the attorneys in chambers."

Next to chambers was a coffee room where the lawyers loitered and gossiped by the hour, and next to it was a small rest room. Jake closed and locked the rest room door and removed his coat, throwing it to the floor. He knelt beside the toilet, waited momentarily, then vomited.

Ozzie stood before the judge and attempted small talk while Musgrove and the D.A. smiled at each other. They waited on Jake. Finally, he entered chambers and apologized.

"Jake, I have some bad news," Ozzie said.

"Let me sit down."

"I got a call an hour ago from the sheriff of Lafayette County. Your law clerk, Ellen Roark, is in the hospital."

"What happened!"

"The Klan got her last night. Somewhere between here and Oxford. They tied her to a tree and beat her."

"How is she?" Jake asked.

"Stable but serious."

"What happened?" Buckley asked.

"We ain't sure. They stopped her car somehow and took her out in the woods. Cut her clothes off her and cut her hair. She's got a concussion and cuts on the head, so they figure she was beat."

Jake needed to vomit again. He couldn't speak. He massaged his temples and thought how nice it would be to tie Bass to a tree and beat him.

Noose studied the defense attorney with compassion. "Mr. Brigance, are you okay?"

No response.

"Let's recess until two. I think we could all use the break," Noose said.

———————————

Jake walked slowly up the front steps with an empty Coors bottle and for a moment gave serious thought to smashing it against Lucien's head. He realized the injury would not be felt.

Lucien rattled his ice cubes and stared off in the distance, in the direction of the square, which had long been deserted except for the soldiers and the regular crowd of teenagers flocking to the theater for the Saturday night double feature.

They said nothing. Lucien stared away. Jake glared at him with the empty bottle. Bass was hundreds of miles away.

After a minute or so, Jake asked, "Where's Bass?"

"Gone."

"Gone where?"

"Gone home."

"Where's his home?"

"Why do you wanna know?"

"I'd like to see his home. I'd like to see him in his home. I'd like to beat him to death with a baseball bat in his home."

Lucien rattled some more. "I don't blame you."

"Did you know?"

"Know what?"

"About the conviction?"

"Hell no. No one knew. The record was expunged."

"I don't understand."

"Bass told me the record of the conviction in Texas was expunged three years after it was entered."

Jake placed the beer bottle on the porch beside his

chair. He grabbed a dirty glass, blew into it, then filled it with ice cubes and Jack Daniel's.

"Do you mind explaining, Lucien?"

"According to Bass, the girl was seventeen, and the daughter of a prominent judge in Dallas. They fell in heat, and the judge caught them screwing on the couch. He pressed charges, and Bass didn't have a chance. He pled guilty to the statutory rape. But the girl was in love. They kept seeing each other and she comes up pregnant. Bass married her, and gives the judge a perfect baby boy for his first grandchild. The old man has a change of heart, and the record is expunged."

Lucien drank and watched the lights from the square.

"What happened to the girl?"

"According to Bass, a week before he finished medical school, his wife, who's pregnant again, and the little boy were killed in a train wreck in Fort Worth. That's when he started drinking, and quit living."

"And he's never told you this before?"

"Don't interrogate me. I told you I knew nothing about it. I put him on the witness stand twice myself, remember. If I had known it, he would never have testified."

"Why didn't he ever tell you?"

"I guess because he thought the record was erased. I don't know. Technically, he's right. There is no record after the expungement. But he was convicted."

Jake took a long, bitter drink of whiskey. It was nasty.

They sat in silence for ten minutes. It was dark and the crickets were in full chorus. Sallie walked to the screen door and asked Jake if he wanted supper. He said no thanks.

"What happened this afternoon?" Lucien asked.

"Carl Lee testified, and we adjourned at four. Buckley didn't have his psychiatrist ready. He'll testify Monday."

"How'd he do?"

"Fair. He followed Bass, and you could feel the hatred from the jurors. He was stiff and sounded rehearsed. I don't think he scored too many points."

"What'd Buckley do?"

"Went wild. Screamed at Carl Lee for an hour. Carl Lee kept getting smart with him, and they sniped back and forth. I think they both got hurt. On redirect, I propped him up some and he came across pitiful and sympathetic. Almost cried at the end."

"That's nice."

"Yeah, real nice. But they'll convict him, won't they?"

"I would imagine."

"After we adjourned, he tried to fire me. Said I'd lost his case and he wanted a new lawyer."

Lucien walked to the edge of the porch and unzipped his pants. He leaned on a column and sprayed the shrubs. He was barefoot and looked like a flood victim. Sallie brought him a fresh drink.

"How's Row Ark?" he asked.

"Stable, they say. I called her room and a nurse said she couldn't talk. I'll go over tomorrow."

"I hope she's okay. She's a fine girl."

"She's a radical bitch, but a very smart one. I feel like it's my fault, Lucien."

"It's not your fault. It's a crazy world, Jake. Full of crazy people. Right now I think half of them are in Ford County."

"Two weeks ago, they planted dynamite outside my bedroom window. They beat to death my secretary's husband. Yesterday they shot at me and hit a guardsman. Now they grab my law clerk, tie her to a pole, rip her clothes off, cut her hair, and she's in the hospital with a concussion. I wonder what's next."

"I think you should surrender."

"I would. I would march down to the courthouse right now and surrender my briefcase, lay down my arms, give up. But to whom? The enemy is invisible."

"You can't quit, Jake. Your client needs you."

"To hell with my client. He tried to fire me today."

"He needs you. This thing ain't over till it's over."

Nesbit's head hung halfway out the window and the saliva dripped down the left side of his chin, down the door, forming a small puddle over the "O" in the Ford of the Sheriff's Department insignia on the side of the car. An empty beer can moistened his crotch. After two weeks of bodyguard duty he had grown accustomed to sleeping with the mosquitoes in his patrol car while protecting the nigger's lawyer.

Moments after Saturday turned into Sunday, the radio violated his rest. He grabbed the mike while wiping his chin on his left sleeve.

"S.O. 8," he responded.

"What's your 10-20?"

"Same place it was two hours ago."

"The Wilbanks house?"

"10-4."

"Is Brigance still there?"

"10-4."

"Get him and take him to his house on Adams. It's an emergency."

Nesbit walked past the empty bottles on the porch, through the unlocked door, where he found Jake sprawled on the couch in the front room.

"Get up, Jake! You gotta go home! It's an emergency!"

Jake jumped to his feet and followed Nesbit. They stopped on the front steps and looked past the dome of the courthouse. In the distance a boiling funnel of black smoke rose above an orange glow and drifted peacefully toward the half moon.

Adams Street was blocked with an assortment of volunteer vehicles, mostly pickups. Each had a variety of red and yellow emergency lights, at least a thousand in all. They spun and flashed and streaked through the darkness in a silent chorus, illuminating the street.

The fire engines were parked haphazardly in front of the house. The firemen and volunteers worked frantically laying lines and getting organized, responding occasionally to the commands of the chief. Ozzie, Prather, and Hastings stood near an engine. Some guardsmen lingered benignly near a jeep.

The fire was brilliant. Flames roared from every window across the front of the house, upstairs and down. The carport was completely engulfed. Carla's Cutlass burned inside and out—the four tires emitting a darker glow of their own. Curiously, another, smaller car, not the Saab, burned next to the Cutlass.

The thundering, crackling noise of the fire, plus the rumbling of the fire engines, plus the loud voices, attracted neighbors from several blocks. They crowded together in the lawns across the street and watched.

Jake and Nesbit ran down the street. The chief spotted them and came running.

"Jake! Is anybody in the house?"

"No!"

"Good. I didn't think so."

"Just a dog."

"A dog!"

Jake nodded and watched the house.

"I'm sorry," said the chief.

They gathered at Ozzie's car in front of Mrs. Pickle's house. Jake answered questions.

"That's not your Volkswagen under there, is it, Jake?"

Jake stared in stunned silence at Carla's landmark. He shook his head.

"I didn't think so. Looks like that's where it started."

"I don't understand," said Jake.

"If it ain't your car, then somebody parked it there, right? Notice how the floor of the carport is burnin'? Concrete don't normally burn. It's gasoline. Somebody loaded the VW with gasoline, parked it and ran away. Probably had some kinda device which set the thing off."

Prather and two volunteers agreed.

"How long's it been burning?" Jake asked.

"We got here ten minutes ago," the chief said, "and it was well involved. I'd say thirty minutes. It's a good fire. Somebody knew what they's doin'."

"I don't suppose we could get anything out of there, could we?" Jake asked in general, knowing the answer.

"No way, Jake. It's too involved. My men couldn't go in there if people were trapped. It's a good fire."

"Why do you say that?"

"Well, look at it. It's burnin' evenly through the house. You can see flames in every window. Downstairs and up. That's very unusual. In just a minute, it'll burn through the roof."

Two squads inched forward with the lines, shooting water in the direction of the windows by the front porch. A smaller line was aimed at a window upstairs. After watching for a minute or two as the water disappeared into the flames with no noticeable effect, the chief spat and said, "It'll burn to the ground." With that he disappeared around an engine and began shouting.

Jake looked at Nesbit. "Will you do me a favor?"

"Sure, Jake."

"Drive over to Harry Rex's and bring him back. I'd hate for him to miss this."

"Sure."

For two hours Jake, Ozzie, Harry Rex, and Nesbit sat on the patrol car and watched the fire fulfill the chief's prediction. From time to time a neighbor would stop by and extend sympathies and ask about the family. Mrs. Pickle, the sweet old woman next door, cried loudly when informed by Jake that Max had been consumed.

By three, the deputies and other curious had disappeared, and by four the quaint little Victorian had been reduced to smoldering rubble. The last of the firemen smothered any sign of smoke from the ruins. Only the chimney and burnt frames of two cars stood above the remains as the heavy rubber boots kicked and plowed through the waste looking for sparks or hidden flames that might somehow leap from the dead and burn the rest of the wreckage.

They rolled up the last of the lines as the sun began to appear. Jake thanked them when they left. He and Harry Rex walked through the backyard and surveyed the damage.

"Oh well," Harry Rex said. "It's just a house."

"Would you call Carla and tell her that?"

"No. I think you should."

"I think I'll wait."

Harry Rex looked at his watch. "It's about breakfast time, isn't it?"

"It's Sunday morning, Harry Rex. Nothing's open."

"Ah, Jake, you're an amateur, and I'm a professional. I can find hot food at any time of any day."

"The truck stop?"

"The truck stop!"

"Okay. And when we finish we'll go to Oxford to check on Row Ark."

"Great. I can't wait to see her with a butch haircut."

Sallie grabbed the phone and threw it at Lucien, who fumbled with it until it was arranged properly next to his head.

"Yeah, who is it?" he asked, squinting through the window into the darkness.

"Is this Lucien Wilbanks?"

"Yeah, who's this?"

"Do you know Clyde Sisco?"

"Yeah."

"It's fifty thousand."

"Call me back in the morning."

39 Sheldon Roark sat in the window with his feet on the back of a chair, reading the Memphis Sunday paper's version of the Hailey trial. On the bottom of the front page was a picture of his daughter and the story about her encounter with the Klan. She rested comfortably in the bed a few feet away. The left side of her head was shaved and covered with a thick bandage. The left ear was sewn with twenty-eight stitches. The severe concussion had been downgraded to a mild concussion, and the doctors had promised she could leave by Wednesday.

She had not been raped or whipped. When the doctors called him in Boston they were short on details. He had flown for seven hours not knowing what they had done to her, but expecting the worst. Late Saturday night, the doctors ran more X rays and told him to relax. The scars would fade and the hair would grow back. She had been frightened and roughed up, but it could have been much worse.

He heard a commotion in the hall. Someone was arguing with a nurse. He laid the paper on her bed and opened the door.

A nurse had caught Jake and Harry Rex sneaking down the hall. She explained that visiting hours started at 2:00 P.M., and that happened to be six hours away; that only family members were allowed; and that she would call security if they didn't leave. Harry Rex explained that he didn't give a damn about visiting hours or any other silly rules of the hospital; that it was his fiancée and that he would see her one last time before she died; and that if the nurse didn't shut up he would sue her for harassment because he was a lawyer and hadn't sued anybody in a week and was getting anxious.

"What's going on here?" Sheldon said.

Jake looked at the small man with the red hair and green eyes, and said, "You must be Sheldon Roark."

"I am."

"I'm Jake Brigance. The one—"

"Yes, I've been reading about you. It's okay, nurse, they're with me."

"Yeah," Harry Rex said. "It's okay. We're with him. Now would you please leave us alone before I garnishee your check."

She vowed to call security, and stormed down the hall.

"I'm Harry Rex Vonner," he said, shaking hands with Sheldon Roark.

"Step inside," he said. They followed him into the small room and stared at Ellen. She was still asleep.

"How bad is she?" Jake asked.

"Mild concussion. Twenty-eight stitches in her ear, and eleven in her head. She'll be fine. Doctor said she might leave by Wednesday. She was awake last night and we talked for a long time."

"Her hair looks awful," Harry Rex observed.

"They yanked it and cut it with a dull knife, she said. They also cut her clothes off, and at one time threatened to bullwhip her. The head injuries are self-inflicted. She thought they would either kill her or rape her, or both. So she banged her brains out against the pole she was tied to. Must have scared them."

"You mean they didn't beat her?"

"No. They didn't hurt her. Just scared the hell out of her."

"What did she see?"

"Not much. Burning cross, white robes, about a dozen men. Sheriff said it was a pasture eleven miles east of here. Owned by some paper company."

"Who found her?" Harry Rex asked.

"The sheriff received an anonymous phone call from a fella by the name of Mickey Mouse."

"Ah yes. My old friend."

Ellen moaned softly and stretched.

"Let's step outside," Sheldon said.

"Does this place have a cafeteria?" Harry Rex asked. "I get hungry when I get near a hospital."

"Sure. Let's have coffee."

The cafeteria on the first floor was empty. Jake and Mr. Roark drank black coffee. Harry Rex started with three sweet rolls and a pint of milk.

"According to the paper, things aren't going too well," Sheldon said.

"The paper is very kind," Harry Rex said with a mouthful. "Jake here is gettin' his ass kicked all over the courtroom. And life ain't so great outside the courtroom, either. When they're not shooting at him, or kidnapping his law clerk, they're burning his house."

"They burned your house!"

Jake nodded. "Last night. It's still smoldering."

"I thought I detected the smell of smoke."

"We watched it burn to the ground. It took four hours."

"I'm sorry to hear that. They've threatened me with that before, but the worst I've had was slashed tires. I've never been shot at either."

"I've been shot at a couple of times."

"Do y'all have the Klan in Boston?" asked Harry Rex.

"Not that I know of."

"It's a shame. Those folks add a real dimension to your law practice."

"Sounds like it. We saw the television reports of the riot around the courthouse last week. I've watched it pretty close since Ellen became involved. It's a famous case. Even up there. I wish I had it."

"It's all yours," said Jake. "I think my client is looking for a new lawyer."

"How many shrinks will the State call?"

"Just one. He'll testify in the morning, and we'll have closing arguments. The jury should get it by late tomorrow afternoon."

"I hate that Ellen will miss it. She called me every day and talked about the case."

"Where did Jake go wrong?" Harry Rex asked.

"Don't talk with your mouth full," Jake said.

"I think Jake has done a good job. It's a lousy set of facts to begin with. Hailey committed the murders, planned them carefully, and is relying on a rather weak plea of insanity. Juries in Boston would not be too sympathetic."

"Nor in Ford County," added Harry Rex.

"I hope you have a soul-stirring final summation up your sleeve," Sheldon said.

"He doesn't have any sleeves," said Harry Rex.

"They've all been burned. Along with his pants and under-wear."

"Why don't you come over tomorrow and watch?" Jake asked. "I'll introduce you to the judge and ask that you have privileges of chambers."

"He wouldn't do that for me," Harry Rex said.

"I can understand why," Sheldon said with a smile. "I might just do that. I had planned to stay until Tuesday anyway. Is it safe over there?"

"Not really."

———————

Woody Mackenvale's wife sat on a plastic bench in the hall next to his room and cried quietly while trying to be brave for her two small sons seated next to her. Each boy squeezed a well-used wad of Kleenexes, occasionally wiping their cheeks and blowing their noses. Jake knelt before her and listened intently as she described what the doctors had said. The bullet had lodged in the spine—the paralysis was severe and permanent. He was a foreman at a plant in Booneville. Good job. Good life. She didn't work, at least until now. They would make it somehow, but she wasn't sure how. He coached his sons' Little League team. He was very active.

She cried louder and the boys wiped their cheeks.

"He saved my life," Jake said to her, and looked at the boys.

She closed her eyes and nodded. "He was doing his job. We'll make it."

Jake took a Kleenex from the box on the bench and wiped his eyes. A group of relatives stood nearby and watched. Harry Rex paced nervously at the end of the hall.

Jake hugged her and patted the boys on the head. He gave her his phone number—office—and told her to call if he could do anything. He promised to visit Woody when the trial was over.

———————

The beer stores opened at noon on Sunday, as if the church folks needed it then and would stop on the way home from the Lord's house to pick up a couple of six-packs, then on to Grandmother's for Sunday dinner and an afternoon of hell-raising. Oddly, they would close again at six in the afternoon, as if the same folks should then be denied beer as they returned to church for the Sunday night services. On the other six days beer was sold from six in the morning until midnight. But on Sunday, the selling was curtailed in honor of the Almighty.

Jake bought a six-pack at Bates Grocery and directed his chauffeur toward the lake. Harry Rex's antique Bronco carried three inches of dried mud across the doors and fenders. The tires were imperceptible. The windshield was cracked and dangerous, with thousands of splattered insects caked around the edges. The inspection sticker was four years old and unseen from the outside. Dozens of empty beer cans and broken bottles littered the floorboard. The air conditioner had not worked in six years. Jake had suggested use of the Saab. Harry Rex had cursed him for his stupidity. The red Saab was an easy target for snipers. No one would suspect the Bronco.

They drove slowly in the general direction of the lake, to no place in particular. Willie Nelson wailed from the cassette. Harry Rex tapped the steering wheel and sang along. His normal speaking voice was coarse and unrefined. With song, it was heinous. Jake sipped his beer and searched for daylight through the windshield.

The heat wave was about to be broken. Dark clouds loomed to the southwest, and when they passed Huey's Lounge the rains fell and showered the parched earth. It cleansed and removed the dust from the kudzu that lined the roadbeds and hung like Spanish moss from the trees. It cooled the scorched pavement and created a sticky fog that rose three feet above the highway. The red baked gullies absorbed the water, and when full began to carry tiny streams downward to the larger field drains and road ditches. The rains drenched the cotton and soybeans, and pounded the crop rows until small puddles formed between the stalks.

Remarkably, the windshield wipers worked. They slapped back and forth furiously and removed the mud and insect collection. The storm grew. Harry Rex increased the volume of the stereo.

The blacks with their cane poles and straw hats camped

under the bridges and waited for the storm to blow over. Below them, the still creeks came to life. Muddy water from the fields and gullies rushed downward and stirred the small streams and brooks. The water rose and moved forward. The blacks ate bologna and crackers and told fishing stories.

Harry Rex was hungry. He stopped at Treadway's Grocery near the lake, and bought more beer, two catfish dinners, and a large bag of Cajun-spiced red-hot barbecue pork skins. He threw them at Jake.

They crossed the dam in a blinding downpour. Harry Rex parked next to a small pavilion over a picnic area. They sat on the concrete table and watched the rain batter Lake Chatulla. Jake drank beer while Harry Rex ate the catfish dinners.

"When you gonna tell Carla?" he asked, slurping beer.

The tin roof roared above. "About what?"

"The house."

"I'm not gonna tell her. I think I can have it rebuilt before she gets back."

"You mean by the end of the week?"

"Yeah."

"You're cracking up, Jake. You're drinking too much, and you're losing your mind."

"I deserve it. I've earned it. I'm two weeks away from bankruptcy. I'm about to lose the biggest case of my career, for which I have been paid nine hundred dollars. My beautiful home that everyone took pictures of and the old ladies from the Garden Club tried to get written up in *Southern Living* has been reduced to rubble. My wife has left me, and when she hears about the house, she'll divorce me. No question about that. So I'll lose my wife. And once my daughter learns that her damned dog died in the fire, she'll hate me forever. There's a contract on my head. I've got Klan goons looking for me. Snipers shooting at me. There's a soldier lying up in the hospital with my bullet in his spine. He'll be a vegetable, and I'll think about him every hour of every day for the rest of my life. My secretary's husband was killed because of me. My last employee is in the hospital with a punk haircut and a concussion because she worked for me. The jury thinks I'm a lying crook because of my expert witness. My client wants to fire me. When he's convicted, everybody will blame me. He'll hire another lawyer for the appeal, one of those ACLU types, and they'll sue me claiming ineffective trial counsel. And they'll be right. So I'll get my ass sued for malpractice. I'll have no wife, no daughter, no house, no practice, no clients, no money, nothing."

"You need psychiatric help, Jake. I think you should make an appointment with Dr. Bass. Here, have a beer."

"I guess I'll move in with Lucien and sit on the porch all day."

"Can I have your office?"

"Do you think she'll divorce me?"

"Probably so. I've had four divorces, and they'll file for damned near anything."

"Not Carla. I worship the ground she walks on, and she knows it."

"She'll be sleeping on the ground when she gets back to Clanton."

"Naw, we'll get a nice, cozy little double-wide trailer. It'll do us fine until the bankruptcy is over. Then we'll find another old house and start over."

"You'll probably find you another wife and start over. Why would she leave a swanky cottage on the beach and return to a house trailer in Clanton?"

"Because I'll be in the house trailer."

"That's not good enough, Jake. You'll be a drunk, bankrupt, disbarred lawyer, living in a house trailer. You will be publicly disgraced. All of your friends, except me and Lucien, will forget about you. She'll never come back. It's over, Jake. As your friend and divorce lawyer, I advise you to file first. Do it now, tomorrow, so she'll never know what hit her."

"Why would I sue her for divorce?"

"Because she's gonna sue you. We'll file first and allege that she deserted you in your hour of need."

"Is that grounds for divorce?"

"No. But we'll also claim that you're crazy, temporary insanity. Just let me handle it. The M'Naghten Rule. I'm the sleazy divorce lawyer, remember."

"How could I forget?"

Jake poured hot beer from his neglected bottle, and

opened another. The rain slackened and the clouds lightened. A cool wind blew up from the lake.

"They'll convict him, won't they, Harry Rex?" he asked, staring at the lake in the distance.

He quit chomping and wiped his mouth. He laid the paper plate on the table, and took a long drink of beer. The wind blew light drops of water onto his face. He wiped it with a sleeve.

"Yeah, Jake. Your man is about to be sent away. I can see it in their eyes. The insanity crap just didn't work. They didn't want to believe Bass to begin with, and after Buckley yanked his pants down, it was all over. Carl Lee didn't help himself any. He seemed rehearsed and too sincere. Like he was begging for sympathy. He was a lousy witness. I watched the jury while he testified. I saw no support for him. They'll convict, Jake. And quickly."

"Thanks for being so blunt."

"I'm your friend, and I think you should start preparing for a conviction and a long appeal."

"You know, Harry Rex, I wish I'd never heard of Carl Lee Hailey."

"I think it's too late, Jake."

———

Sallie answered the door and told Jake she was sorry about the house. Lucien was upstairs in his study, working and sober. He pointed to a chair and instructed Jake to sit down. Legal pads littered his desk.

"I've spent all afternoon working on a closing argument," he said, waving at the mess before him. "Your only hope of saving Hailey is with a spellbinding performance on final summation. I mean, we're talking about the greatest closing argument in the history of jurisprudence. That's what it'll take."

"And I assume you've created such a masterpiece."

"As a matter of fact, I have. It's much better than anything you could come up with. And I assumed—correctly—that you would spend your Sunday afternoon mourning the loss of your home and drowning your sorrows with Coors. I knew you would have nothing prepared. So I've done it for you."

"I wish I could stay as sober as you, Lucien."

"I was a better lawyer drunk than you are sober."

"At least I'm a lawyer."

Lucien tossed a legal pad at Jake. "There it is. A compilation of my greatest closing arguments. Lucien Wilbanks at his best, all rolled into one for you and your client. I suggest you memorize it and use it word for word. It's that good. Don't try to modify it, or improvise. You'll just screw it up."

"I'll think about it. I've done this before, remember?"

"You'd never know it."

"Dammit, Lucien! Get off my back!"

"Take it easy, Jake. Let's have a drink. Sallie! Sallie!"

Jake threw the masterpiece on the couch and walked to the window overlooking the backyard. Sallie ran up the stairs. Lucien ordered whiskey and beer.

"Were you up all night?" Lucien asked.

"No. I slept from eleven to twelve."

"You look terrible. You need a good night's rest."

"I feel terrible, and sleep will not help. Nothing will help, except the end of this trial. I don't understand, Lucien. I don't understand how everything has gone so wrong. Surely to God we're entitled to a little good luck. The case should not even be tried in Clanton. We were dealt the worst possible jury—a jury that's been tampered with. But I can't prove it. Our star witness was completely destroyed. The defendant made a lousy witness. And the jury does not trust me. I don't know what else could go wrong."

"You can still win the case, Jake. It'll take a miracle, but those things happen sometimes. I've snatched victory from the jaws of defeat many times with an effective closing argument. Zero in on one or two jurors. Play to them. Talk to them. Remember, it just takes one to hang the jury."

"Should I make them cry?"

"If you can. It's not that easy. But I believe in tears in the jury box. It's very effective."

Sallie brought the drinks, and they followed her downstairs to the porch. After dark, she fed them sandwiches and fried potatoes. At ten, Jake excused himself and went to his room. He called Carla and talked for an hour. There was no mention of the house. His stomach cramped when he heard her voice and realized that one day very soon he would be forced to tell her that the house, her house, no longer existed. He hung up and prayed she didn't read about it in the newspaper.

40 Clanton returned to normal Monday morning as the barricades were put in place around the square and the ranks of the soldiers swelled to preserve the public peace. They loitered about in loose formation, watching as the Kluxers returned to their appointed ground on one side, and the black protestors on the other. The day of rest brought renewed energy to both groups, and by eight-thirty they were in full chorus. The collapse of Dr. Bass had been big news, and the Kluxers smelled victory. Plus they had scored a direct hit on Adams Street. They appeared to be louder than normal.

At nine, Noose summoned the attorneys to chambers. "Just wanted to make sure you were all alive and well." He grinned at Jake.

"Why don't you kiss my ass, Judge?" Jake said under his breath, but loud enough to be heard. The prosecutors froze. Mr. Pate cleared his throat.

Noose cocked his head sideways as if hard of hearing. "What did you say, Mr. Brigance?"

"I said, 'Why don't we get started, Judge?'"

"Yes, that's what I thought you said. How's your clerk, Ms. Roark?"

"She'll be fine."

"Was it the Klan?"

"Yes, Judge. The same Klan that tried to kill me. Same Klan that lit up the county with crosses and who knows what else for our jury panel. Same Klan that's probably intimidated most of those jurors sitting out there. Yes, sir, it's the same Klan."

Noose ripped off his glasses. "Can you substantiate that?"

"You mean, do I have written, signed, notarized confessions from the Klansmen? No, sir. They're most uncooperative."

"If you can't prove it, Mr. Brigance, then leave it alone."

"Yes, Your Honor."

Jake left chambers and slammed the door. Seconds later Mr. Pate called the place to order and everyone rose. Noose welcomed his jury back and promised the ordeal was almost over. No one smiled at him. It had been a lonely weekend at the Temple Inn.

"Does the State have any rebuttal?" he asked Buckley.

"One witness, Your Honor."

Dr. Rodeheaver was fetched from the witness room. He carefully situated himself in the witness chair and nodded warmly at the jury. He looked like a psychiatrist. Dark suit, no boots.

Buckley assumed the podium and smiled at the jury. "You are Dr. Wilbert Rodeheaver?" he thundered, looking at the jury as if to say, "Now you'll meet a real psychiatrist."

"Yes, sir."

Buckley asked questions, a million questions, about his educational and professional background. Rodeheaver was confident, relaxed, prepared, and accustomed to the witness chair. He talked at great length about his broad educational training, his vast experience as a practicing physician, and more recently, the enormous magnitude of his job as head of staff at the state mental hospital. Buckley asked him if he had written any articles in his field. He said yes, and for thirty minutes they discussed the writings of this very learned man. He had received research grants from the federal government and from various states. He was a member of all the organizations Bass belonged to, and a few more. He had been certified by every association remotely touching the study of the human mind. He was polished, and sober.

Buckley tendered him as an expert, and Jake had no questions.

Buckley continued. "Dr. Rodeheaver, when did you first examine Carl Lee Hailey?"

The expert checked his notes. "June 19."

"Where did the examination take place?"

"In my office at Whitfield."

"How long did you examine him?"

"Couple of hours."

"What was the purpose of this examination?"

"To try and determine his mental condition at that time and also at the time he killed Mr. Cobb and Mr. Willard."

"Did you obtain his medical history?"

"Most of the information was taken by an associate at the hospital. I reviewed it with Mr. Hailey."

"What did the history reveal?"

"Nothing remarkable. He talked a lot about Vietnam, but nothing remarkable."

"Did he talk freely about Vietnam?"

"Oh yes. He wanted to talk about it. It was almost like he had been told to discuss it as much as possible."

"What else did you discuss at the first examination?"

"We covered a wide variety of topics. His childhood, family, education, various jobs, just about everything."

"Did he discuss the rape of his daughter?"

"Yes, in great detail. It was painful for him to talk about it, the same as it would have been for me had it been my daughter."

"Did he discuss with you the events leading up to the shootings of Cobb and Willard?"

"Yes, we talked about that for quite a while. I tried to ascertain the degree of knowledge and understanding he had about those events."

"What did he tell you?"

"Initially, not much. But with time, he opened up and explained how he inspected the courthouse three days before the shooting and picked a good place to attack."

"What about the shootings?"

"He never told me much about the actual killings. Said he didn't remember much, but I suspect otherwise."

Jake sprang to his feet. "Objection! The witness can only testify as to what he actually knows. He cannot speculate."

"Sustained. Please continue, Mr. Buckley."

"What else did you observe concerning his mood, attitude, and manner of speech?"

Rodeheaver crossed his legs and rocked gently. He lowered his eyebrows in deep thought. "Initially, he was distrustful of me and had difficulty looking me in the eye. He gave short answers to my questions. He was very resentful of the fact that he was guarded and sometimes handcuffed while at our facility. He questioned the padded walls. But after a while, he opened up and talked freely about most everything. He flatly refused to answer a few questions, but other than that I would say he was fairly cooperative."

"When and where did you examine him again?"

"The next day, same place."

"What was his mood and attitude?"

"About the same as the day before. Cool at first, but he opened up eventually. He discussed basically the same topics as the day before."

"How long did this examination last?"

"Approximately four hours."

Buckley reviewed something on a legal pad, then whispered to Musgrove. "Now, Dr. Rodeheaver, as a result of your examinations of Mr. Hailey on June 19 and 20, were you able to arrive at a medical diagnosis of the defendant's psychiatric condition on those dates?"

"Yes, sir."

"And what is that diagnosis?"

"On June 19 and 20, Mr. Hailey appeared to be of sound mind. Perfectly normal, I would say."

"Thank you. Based on your examinations, were you able to arrive at a diagnosis of Mr. Hailey's mental condition on the day he shot Billy Ray Cobb and Pete Willard?"

"Yes."

"And what is that diagnosis?"

"At that time his mental condition was sound, no defects of any nature."

"Upon what factors do you base this?"

Rodeheaver turned to the jury and became a professor. "You must look at the level of premeditation involved in this crime. Motive is an element of premeditation. He certainly had a motive for doing what he did, and his mental condition at that time did not prevent him from entertaining the requisite premeditation. Frankly, Mr. Hailey carefully planned what he did."

"Doctor, you are familiar with the M'Naghten Rule as a test for criminal responsibility?"

"Certainly."

"And you are aware that another psychiatrist, a Dr. W.T. Bass, has told this jury that Mr. Hailey was incapable of knowing the difference between right and wrong, and, further, that he was unable to understand and appreciate the nature and quality of his actions."

"Yes, I am aware of that."

"Do you agree with that testimony?"

"No. I find it preposterous, and I am personally offended by it. Mr. Hailey himself has testified he planned the murders. He's admitted, in effect, that his mental condition at the time did not prevent him from possessing the ability to plan. That's called premeditation in every legal and medical book. I've never heard of someone planning a murder, admitting he planned it, then claiming he did not know what he was doing. It's absurd."

At that moment, Jake felt it was absurd too, and as it echoed around the courtroom it sounded mighty absurd. Rodeheaver sounded good and infinitely credible. Jake thought of Bass and cursed to himself.

Lucien sat with the blacks and agreed with every word of Rodeheaver's testimony. When compared to Bass, the State's doctor was terribly believable. Lucien ignored the jury box. From time to time he would cut his eyes without moving his head and catch Clyde Sisco blatantly and openly staring directly at him. But Lucien would not allow their eyes to meet. The messenger had not called Monday morning as instructed. An affirmative nod or wink from Lucien would consummate the deal, with payment to be arranged later, after the verdict. Sisco knew the rules, and he watched for an answer. There was none. Lucien wanted to discuss it with Jake.

"Now, Doctor, based upon these factors and your diagnosis of his mental condition as of May 20, do you have an opinion, to a reasonable degree of medical certainty, as to whether Mr. Hailey was capable of knowing the difference between right and wrong when he shot Billy Ray Cobb, Pete Willard, and Deputy DeWayne Looney?"

"I have."

"And what is that opinion?"

"His mental condition was sound, and he was very capable of distinguishing right from wrong."

"And do you have an opinion, based upon the same factors, as to whether Mr. Hailey was able to understand and appreciate the nature and quality of his actions?"

"I have."

"And what is that opinion?"

"That he fully appreciated what he was doing."

Buckley snatched his legal pad and bowed politely. "Thank you, Doctor. I have no further questions."

"Any cross-examination, Mr. Brigance?" Noose asked.

"Just a few questions."

"I thought so. Let's take a fifteen-minute recess."

Jake ignored Carl Lee, and moved quickly out of the courtroom, up the stairs, and into the law library on the third floor. Harry Rex was waiting, and smiling.

"Relax, Jake. I've called every newspaper in North Carolina, and there's no story about the house. There's nothing about Row Ark. The Raleigh morning paper ran a story about the trial, but it was in real general terms. Nothing else. Carla doesn't know about it, Jake. As far as she knows, her pretty little landmark is still standing. Isn't that great?"

"Wonderful. Just wonderful. Thanks, Harry Rex."

"Don't mention it. Look, Jake, I sorta hate to bring this up."

"I can't wait."

"You know I hate Buckley. Hate him worse than you do. But me and Musgrove get along okay. I can talk to Musgrove. I was thinking last night that it might be a good idea to approach them—me through Musgrove—and explore the possibilities of a plea bargain."

"No!"

"Listen, Jake. What harm will it do? None! If you can plead him guilty to murder with no gas chamber, then you know you have saved his life."

"No!"

"Look, Jake. Your man is about forty-eight hours away from a death penalty conviction. If you don't believe that, then you're blind, Jake. My blind friend."

"Why should Buckley cut a deal? He's got us on the ropes."

"Maybe he won't. But let me at least find out."

"No, Harry Rex. Forget it."

Rodeheaver returned to his seat after the recess, and Jake
looked at him from behind the podium. In his brief legal
career, he had never won an argument, in court or out, with
an expert witness. And the way his luck was running, he
decided not to argue with this one.

"Dr. Rodeheaver, psychiatry is the study of the human
mind, is it not?"

"It is.".

"And it is an inexact science at best, is it not?"

"That is correct."

"You might examine a person and reach a diagnosis,
and the next psychiatrist might reach a completely different
diagnosis?"

"That's possible, yes."

"In fact, you could have ten psychiatrists examine a
mental patient, and arrive at ten different opinions about
what's wrong with the patient."

"That's unlikely."

"But it could happen, couldn't it, Doctor?"

"Yes, it could. Just like legal opinions, I guess."

"But we're not dealing with legal opinions in this case,
are we, Doctor?"

"No."

"The truth is, Doctor, in many cases psychiatry cannot
tell us what is wrong with a person's mind?"

"That is true."

"And psychiatrists disagree all the time, don't they,
Doctor?"

"Of course."

"Now, who do you work for, Doctor?"

"The State of Mississippi."

"And for how long?"

"Eleven years."

"And who is prosecuting Mr. Hailey?"

"The State of Mississippi."

"During your eleven-year career with the State, how
many times have you testified in trials where the insanity
defense was used?"

Rodeheaver thought for a moment. "I think this is my
forty-third trial."

Jake checked something in a file and eyed the doctor

with a nasty little smile. "Are you sure it's not your forty-sixth?"

"It could be, yes. I'm not certain."

The courtroom became still. Buckley and Musgrove hovered over their legal pads, but watched their witness carefully.

"Forty-six times you've testified for the State in insanity trials?"

"If you say so."

"And forty-six times you've testified that the defendant was not legally insane. Correct, Doctor?"

"I'm not sure."

"Well, let me make it simple. You've testified forty-six times, and forty-six times it has been your opinion the defendant was not legally insane. Correct?"

Rodeheaver squirmed just a little, and a hint of discomfort broke around his eyes. "I'm not sure."

"You've never seen a legally insane criminal defendant, have you, Doctor?"

"Of course I have."

"Good. Would you then, please, sir, tell us the name of the defendant and where he was tried?"

Buckley rose and buttoned his coat. "Your Honor, the State objects to these questions. Dr. Rodeheaver cannot be required to remember the names and places of the trials he has testified in."

"Overruled. Sit down. Answer the question, Doctor."

Rodeheaver breathed deeply and studied the ceiling. Jake glanced at the jurors. They were awake and waiting on an answer.

"I can't remember," he finally said.

Jake lifted a thick stack of papers and waved it at the witness. "Could it be, Doctor, that the reason you can't remember is that in eleven years, forty-six trials, you have never testified in favor of the defendant?"

"I honestly can't remember."

"Can you honestly name us one trial in which you found the defendant to be legally insane?"

"I'm sure there are some."

"Yes or no, Doctor. One trial?"

The expert looked briefly at the D.A. "No. My memory fails me. I cannot at this time."

Jake walked slowly to the defense table and picked up a thick file.

"Dr. Rodeheaver, do you recall testifying in the trial of a man by the name of Danny Booker in McMurphy County in December of 1975? A rather gruesome double homicide?"

"Yes, I recall that trial."

"And you testified to the effect that he was not legally insane, did you not?"

"That is correct."

"Do you recall how many psychiatrists testified in his behalf?"

"Not exactly. There were several."

"Do the names Noel McClacky, M.D.; O.G. McGuire, M.D.; and Lou Watson, M.D., ring a bell?"

"Yes."

"They're all psychiatrists, aren't they?"

"Yes."

"They're all qualified, aren't they?"

"Yes."

"And they all examined Mr. Booker and testified at trial that in their opinions the poor man was legally insane?"

"That's correct."

"And you testified he was not legally insane?"

"That's correct."

"How many other doctors supported your position?"

"None, that I recall."

"So it was three against one?"

"Yes, but I'm still convinced I was right."

"I see. What did the jury do, Doctor?"

"He, uh, was found not guilty by reason of insanity."

"Thank you. Now, Dr. Rodeheaver, you're the head doctor at Whitfield, aren't you?"

"Yes, so to speak."

"Are you directly or indirectly responsible for the treatment of every patient at Whitfield?"

"I'm directly responsible, Mr. Brigance. I may not personally see every patient, but their doctors are under my supervision."

"Thank you. Doctor, where is Danny Booker today?"

Rodeheaver shot a desperate look at Buckley, and immediately covered it with a warm, relaxed grin for the jury. He hesitated for a few seconds, then hesitated one second too long.

"He's at Whitfield, isn't he?" Jake asked in a tone of voice that informed everyone that the answer was yes.

"I believe so," Rodeheaver said.

"So, he's directly under your care, then, Doctor?"

"I suppose."

"And what is his diagnosis, Doctor?"

"I really don't know. I have a lot of patients and—"

"Paranoid schizophrenic?"

"It's possible, yes."

Jake walked backward and sat on the railing. He turned up the volume. "Now, Doctor, I want to make this clear for the jury. In 1975 you testified that Danny Booker was legally sane and understood exactly what he was doing when he committed his crime, and the jury disagreed with you and found him not guilty, and since that time he has been a patient in your hospital, under your supervision, and treated by you as a paranoid schizophrenic. Is that correct?"

The smirk on Rodeheaver's face informed the jury that it was indeed correct.

Jake picked up another piece of paper and seemed to review it. "Do you recall testifying in the trial of a man by the name of Adam Couch in Dupree County in May of 1977?"

"I remember that case."

"It was a rape case, wasn't it?"

"Yes."

"And you testified on behalf of the State against Mr. Couch?"

"That's correct."

"And you told the jury that he was not legally insane?"

"That was my testimony."

"Do you recall how many doctors testified on his behalf and told the jury he was a very sick man, that he was legally insane?"

"There were several."

"Have you ever heard of the following doctors: Felix Perry, Gene Shumate, and Hobny Wicker?"

"Yes."

"Are they all qualified psychiatrists?"

"They are."

"And they all testified on behalf of Mr. Couch, didn't they?"

"Yes."

"And they all said he was legally insane, didn't they?"

"They did."

"And you were the only doctor in the trial who said he was not legally insane?"

"As I recall, yes."

"And what did the jury do, Doctor?"

"He was found not guilty."

"By reason of insanity?"

"Yes."

"And where is Mr. Couch today, Doctor?"

"I think he's at Whitfield."

"And how long has he been there?"

"Since the trial, I believe."

"I see. Do you normally admit patients and keep them for several years if they are of perfectly sound mind?"

Rodeheaver shifted his weight and began a slow burn. He looked at his lawyer, the people's lawyer, as if to say he was tired of this, do something to stop it.

Jake picked up more papers. "Doctor, do you recall the trial of a man by the name of Buddy Wooddall in Cleburne County, May of 1979?"

"Yes, I certainly do."

"Murder, wasn't it?"

"Yes."

"And you testified as an expert in the field of psychiatry and told the jury that Mr. Wooddall was not insane?"

"I did."

"Do you recall how many psychiatrists testified on his behalf and told the jury the poor man was legally insane?"

"I believe there were five, Mr. Brigance."

"That's correct, Doctor. Five against one. Do you recall what the jury did?"

The anger and frustration was building in the witness

stand. The wise old grandfather/professor with all the right answers was becoming rattled. "Yes, I recall. He was found not guilty by reason of insanity."

"How do you explain that, Dr. Rodeheaver? Five against one, and the jury finds against you?"

"You just can't trust juries," he blurted, then caught himself. He fidgeted and grinned awkwardly at the jurors.

Jake stared at him with a wicked smile, then looked at the jury in disbelief. He folded his arms and allowed the last words to sink in. He waited, staring and grinning at the witness.

"You may proceed, Mr. Brigance," Noose finally said.

Moving slowly and with great animation, Jake gathered his files and notes while staring at Rodeheaver. "I think we've heard enough from this witness, Your Honor."

"Any redirect, Mr. Buckley?"

"No, sir. The State rests."

Noose addressed the jury. "Ladies and gentlemen, this trial is almost over. There will be no more witnesses. I will now meet with the attorneys to cover some technical areas, then they will be allowed to make their final arguments to you. That will begin at two o'clock and take a couple of hours. You will finally get the case around four, and I will allow you to deliberate until six. If you do not reach a verdict today, you will be taken back to your rooms until tomorrow. It is now almost eleven, and we'll recess until two. I need to see the attorneys in chambers."

Carl Lee leaned over and spoke to his lawyer for the first time since Saturday's adjournment. "You tore him up pretty good, Jake."

"Wait till you hear the closing argument."

———————

Jake avoided Harry Rex, and drove to Karaway. His childhood home was an old country house in downtown, surrounded by ancient oaks and maples and elms that kept it cool in spite of the summer heat. In the back, past the trees, was a long open field which ran for an eighth of a mile and disappeared over a small hill. A chickenwire backstop stood over the weeds in one corner. Here, Jake had taken his first steps, rode his first bike, thrown his first football and baseball. Under an oak beside the field, he had buried three dogs, a raccoon, a rabbit, and some ducks. A tire from a '54 Buick swung not far from the small cemetery.

The house had been locked and deserted for two months. A neighborhood kid cut the grass and tended the lawn. Jake checked the house once a week. His parents were somewhere in Canada in a camper—the summer ritual. He wished he were with them.

He unlocked the door and walked upstairs to his room. It would never change. The walls were covered with team pictures, trophies, baseball caps, posters of Pete Rose, Archie Manning, and Hank Aaron. A row of baseball gloves hung above the closet door. A cap and gown picture sat on the dresser. His mother still cleaned it weekly. She once told him she often went to his room and expected to find him doing homework or sorting baseball cards. She would flip through his scrapbooks, and get all teary eyed.

He thought of Hanna's room, with the stuffed animals and Mother Goose wallpaper. A thick knot formed in his throat.

He looked out the window, past the trees, and saw himself swinging in the tire near the three white crosses where he buried his dogs. He remembered each funeral, and his father's promises to get another dog. He thought of Hanna and her dog, and his eyes watered.

The bed was much smaller now. He removed his shoes and lay down. A football helmet hung from the ceiling. Eighth grade, Karaway Mustangs. He scored seven touchdowns in five games. It was all on film downstairs under the bookshelves. The butterflies floated wildly through his stomach.

He carefully placed his notes—his notes, not Lucien's—on the dresser. He studied himself in the mirror.

He addressed the jury. He began by facing his biggest problem, Dr. W.T. Bass. He apologized. A lawyer walks into a courtroom, faces a strange jury, and has nothing to offer but his credibility. And if he does anything to hurt his credibility, he has hurt his cause, his client. He asked them to believe that he would never put a convicted felon on the stand as an expert witness in any trial. He did not know of the conviction, he raised his hand and swore to this. The world is full of psychiatrists, and he could easily have found another if he had known Bass had a problem, but he simply did not know. And he was sorry.

But what about Bass's testimony. Thirty years ago he had sex with a girl under eighteen in Texas. Does that mean he is lying now in this trial? Does that mean you cannot trust his professional opinion? Please be fair to Bass the psychiatrist, forget Bass the person. Please be fair to his patient, Carl Lee Hailey. He knew nothing of the doctor's past.

There was something about Bass they might like to know. Something that was not mentioned by Mr. Buckley when he was ripping the doctor to pieces. The girl he had sex with was seventeen. She later became his wife, bore him a son, and was pregnant when she and the boy were killed in a train—

"Objection!" Buckley shouted. "Objection, Your Honor. That evidence is not in the record!"

"Sustained. Mr. Brigance, you are not to refer to facts not in evidence. The jury will disregard the last statements by Mr. Brigance."

Jake ignored Noose and Buckley and stared painfully at the jury.

When the shouting died, he continued. What about Rodeheaver? He wondered if the State's doctor had ever engaged in sex with a girl under eighteen. Seemed silly to think about such things, didn't it? Bass and Rodeheaver in their younger days—it seemed so unimportant now in this courtroom almost thirty years later.

The State's doctor is a man with an obvious bias. A highly trained specialist who treats thousands for all sorts of mental illnesses, yet when crimes are involved he cannot recognize insanity. His testimony should be carefully weighed.

They watched him, listened to every word. He was not a courtroom preacher, like his opponent. He was quiet, sincere. He looked tired, almost hurt.

Lucien was sober, and he sat with folded arms and watched the jurors, all except Sisco. It was not his closing, but it was good. It was coming from the heart.

Jake apologized for his inexperience. He had not been in many trials, not nearly as many as Mr. Buckley. And if he seemed a little green, or if he made mistakes, please don't hold it against Carl Lee. It wasn't his fault. He was just a rookie trying his best against a seasoned adversary who tried murder cases every month. He made a mistake with Bass, and he made other mistakes, and he asked the jury to forgive him.

He had a daughter, the only one he would ever have. She was four, almost five, and his world revolved around her. She was special; she was a little girl, and it was up to him to protect her. There was a bond there, something he could not explain. He talked about little girls.

Carl Lee had a daughter. Her name was Tonya. He pointed to her on the front row next to her mother and brothers. She's a beautiful little girl, ten years old. And she can never have children. She can never have a daughter because—"

"Objection," Buckley said without shouting.

"Sustained," Noose said.

Jake ignored the commotion. He talked about rape for a while, and explained how rape is much worse than murder. With murder, the victim is gone, and not forced to deal with what happened to her. The family must deal with it, but not the victim. But rape is much worse. The victim has a lifetime of coping, of trying to understand, of asking questions, and, the worst part, of knowing the rapist is still alive and may someday escape or be released. Every hour of every day, the victim thinks of the rape and asks herself a thousand questions. She relives it, step by step, minute by minute, and it hurts just as bad.

Perhaps the most horrible crime of all is the violent rape of a child. A woman who is raped has a pretty good idea why it happened. Some animal was filled with hatred, anger and violence. But a child? A ten-year-old child? Suppose you're a parent. Imagine yourself trying to explain to your child why she was raped. Imagine yourself trying to explain why she cannot bear children.

"Objection."

"Sustained. Please disregard that last statement, ladies and gentlemen."

Jake never missed a beat. Suppose, he said, your ten-year-old daughter is raped, and you're a Vietnam vet, very familiar with an M-16, and you get your hands on one while your daughter is lying in the hospital fighting for her life. Suppose the rapist is caught, and six days later you manage to maneuver to within five feet of him as he leaves court. And you've got the M-16.

What do you do?

Mr. Buckley has told you what he would do. He would mourn for his daughter, turn the other cheek, and hope the judicial system worked. He would hope the rapist would receive justice, be sent to Parchman, and hopefully never paroled. That's what he would do, and they should admire him for being such a kind, compassionate, and forgiving soul. But what would a reasonable father do?

What would Jake do? If he had the M-16? Blow the bastard's head off!

It was simple. It was justice.

Jake paused for a drink of water, then shifted gears. The pained and humble look was replaced with an air of indignation. Let's talk about Cobb and Willard. They started this mess. It was their lives the State was attempting to justify. Who would miss them except their mothers? Child rapists. Drug pushers. Would society miss such productive citizens? Wasn't Ford County safer without them? Were not the other children in the county better off now that two rapists and pushers had been removed? All parents should feel safer. Carl Lee deserves a medal, or at least a round of applause. He was a hero. That's what Looney said. Give the man a trophy. Send him home to his family.

He talked about Looney. He had a daughter. He also had one leg, thanks to Carl Lee Hailey. If anyone had a right to be bitter, to want blood, it was DeWayne Looney. And he said Carl Lee should be sent home to his family.

He urged them to forgive as Looney had forgiven. He asked them to follow Looney's wishes.

He became much quieter, and said he was almost through. He wanted to leave them with one thought. Picture this if they could. When she was lying there, beaten, bloodied, legs spread and tied to trees, she looked into the woods around her. Semiconscious and hallucinating, she saw someone running toward her. It was her daddy, running desperately to save her. In her dreams she saw him when she needed him the most. She cried out for him, and he disappeared. He was taken away.

She needs him now, as much as she needed him then. Please don't take him away. She waits on the front row for her daddy.

Let him go home to his family.

The courtroom was silent as Jake sat next to his client. He glanced at the jury, and saw Wanda Womack brush away a tear with her finger. For the first time in two days he felt a flicker of hope.

———————

At four, Noose bid farewell to his jury. He told them to elect a foreman, get organized, and get busy. He told them they could deliberate until six, maybe seven, and if no verdict was reached he would recess until nine Tuesday morning. They stood and filed slowly from the courtroom. Once out of sight, Noose recessed until six and instructed the attorneys to remain close to the courtroom or leave a number with the clerk.

The spectators held their seats and chatted quietly. Carl Lee was allowed to sit on the front row with his family. Buckley and Musgrove waited in chambers with Noose. Harry Rex, Lucien, and Jake left for the office and a liquid supper. No one expected a quick verdict.

The bailiff locked them in the jury room and instructed the two alternates to take a seat in the narrow hallway. Inside, Barry Acker was elected foreman by acclamation. He laid the jury instructions and exhibits on a small table in a corner. They sat anxiously around two folding tables placed end to end.

"I suggest we take an informal vote," he said. "Just to see where we are. Any objections to that?"

There were none. He had a list of twelve names.

"Vote guilty, not guilty, or undecided. Or you can pass for now."

"Reba Betts."

"Undecided."

"Bernice Toole."

"Guilty."

"Carol Corman."

"Guilty."

"Donna Lou Peck."

"Undecided."

"Sue Williams."

"Pass."

"Jo Ann Gates."

"Guilty."

"Rita Mae Plunk."

"Guilty."

"Frances McGowan."

"Guilty."

"Wanda Womack."

"Undecided."

"Eula Dell Yates."

"Undecided, for now. I wanna talk about it."

"We will. Clyde Sisco."

"Undecided."

"That's eleven. I'm Barry Acker, and I vote not guilty."

He tallied for a few seconds and said, "That's five guilties, five undecideds, one pass, and one not guilty. Looks like we've got our work cut out for us."

They worked through the exhibits, photographs, fingerprints, and ballistics reports. At six, they informed the judge they had not reached a verdict. They were hungry and wanted to go. He recessed until Tuesday morning.

41 They sat for hours on the porch, saying little, watching as darkness surrounded the town below and ushered in the mosquitoes. The heat wave had returned. The soggy air clung to their skin and moistened their shirts. The sounds of a hot summer night echoed softly across the front lawn. Sallie had offered to cook. Lucien declined and ordered whiskey. Jake had no appetite for food, but the Coors filled his system and satisfied any hunger pangs stirring within. When things were good and dark, Nesbit emerged from his car, walked across the porch, through the front screen door, and into the house. A moment later he slammed the door, walked past them with a cold beer, and disappeared down the driveway in the direction of his car. He never said a word.

Sallie stuck her head through the door and made one last offer of food. Both declined.

"Jake, I got a call this afternoon. Clyde Sisco wants twenty-five thousand to hang the jury, fifty thousand for an acquittal."

Jake began shaking his head.

"Before you say no, listen to me. He knows he can't guarantee an acquittal, but he can guarantee a hung jury. It just takes one. That's twenty-five thousand. I know it's a lot of money, but you know I've got it. I'll pay it and you can repay me over the years. Whenever, I don't care. If you never repay it, I don't care. I've got a bankful of C.D.'s. You know money means nothing to me. If I were you I'd do it in a minute."

"You're crazy, Lucien."

"Sure I'm crazy. You haven't been acting so good yourself. Trial work'll drive you crazy. Just take a look at what this trial has done to you. No sleep, no food, no routine, no house. Plenty of booze, though."

"But I've still got ethics."

"And I have none. No ethics, no morals, no conscience. But I won, bubba. I won more than anybody has ever won around here, and you know it."

"It's corrupt, Lucien."

"And I guess you think Buckley's not corrupt. He would lie, cheat, bribe, and steal to win this case. He's not worried about fancy ethics, rules, and opinions. He's not concerned about morality. He's concerned with one thing and only one thing—winning! And you've got a golden chance to beat him at his own game. I'd do it, Jake."

"Forget it, Lucien. Please, just forget it."

An hour passed with no words. The lights of the town below slowly disappeared. Nesbit's snoring was audible in the darkness. Sallie brought one last drink and said good night.

"This is the hardest part," Lucien said. "Waiting on twelve average, everyday people to make sense of all this."

"It's a crazy system, isn't it?"

"Yes, it is. But it usually works. Juries are right ninety percent of the time."

"I just don't feel lucky. I'm waiting on the miracle."

"Jake, my boy, the miracle happens tomorrow."

"Tomorrow?"

"Yes. Early tomorrow morning."

"Would you care to elaborate?"

"By noon tomorrow, Jake, there will be ten thousand angry blacks swarming like ants around the Ford County Courthouse. Maybe more."

"Ten thousand! Why?"

"To scream and shout and chant 'Free Carl Lee, Free Carl Lee.' To raise hell, to scare everybody, to intimidate the jury. To just disrupt the hell out of everything. There'll be so many blacks, white folks will run for cover. The governor will send in more troops."

"And how do you know all this?"

"Because I planned it, Jake."

"You?"

"Listen, Jake, when I was in my prime I knew every black preacher in fifteen counties. I've been in their churches. Prayed with them, marched with them, sang with them. They sent me clients, and I sent them money. I was the only white radical NAACP lawyer in north Mississippi. I filed more race discrimination lawsuits than any ten firms in Washington. These were my people. I've just made a few phone calls. They'll start arriving in the morning, and by noon you won't be able to stir niggers with a stick in downtown Clanton."

"Where will they come from?"

"Everywhere. You know how blacks love to march and protest. This will be great for them. They're looking forward to it."

"You're crazy, Lucien. My crazy friend."

"I win, bubba."

———————

In Room 163, Barry Acker and Clyde Sisco finished their last game of gin rummy and made preparations for bed. Acker gathered some coins and announced he wanted a soft drink. Sisco said he was not thirsty.

Acker tiptoed past a guardsman asleep in the hall. The machine informed him it was out of order, so he quietly opened the exit door and walked up the stairs to the second floor, where he found another machine next to an ice maker. He inserted his coins. The machine responded with a diet Coke. He bent over to pick it up.

Out of the darkness two figures charged. They knocked him to the floor, kicked him and pinned him in a dark corner beside the ice maker, next to a door with a chain and padlock. The large one grabbed Acker's collar and threw him against the cinder block wall. The smaller one stood by the Coke machine and watched the dark hall.

"You're Barry Acker!" said the large one through clenched teeth.

"Yeah! Let go of me!" Acker attempted to shake free, but his assailant lifted him by the throat and held him to the wall with one hand. He used the other hand to unsheathe a shiny hunting knife, which he placed next to Acker's nose. The wiggling stopped.

"Listen to me," he demanded in a loud whisper, "and listen good. We know you're married and you live at 1161 Forrest Drive. We know you got three kids, and we know where they play and go to school. Your wife works at the bank."

Acker went limp.

"If that nigger walks free, you'll be sorry. Your family will be sorry. It may take years, but you'll be awfully sorry."

He dropped him to the floor and grabbed his hair. "You breathe one word of this to anyone, and you'll lose a kid. Understand?"

They vanished. Acker breathed deeply, almost gasping for breath. He rubbed his throat and the back of his head. He sat in the darkness, too scared to move.

42 At hundreds of small black churches across north Mississippi, the faithful gathered before dawn and loaded picnic baskets, coolers, lawn chairs, and water jugs into converted school buses and church vans. They greeted friends and chatted nervously about the trial. For weeks they had read and talked about Carl Lee Hailey; now, they were about to go help. Many were old and retired, but there were entire families with children and playpens. When the buses were full, they piled into cars and followed their preachers. They sang and prayed. The preachers met other preachers in small towns and county seats, and they set out in force down the dark highways. When daylight materialized, the highways and roads leading to Ford County were filled with caravans of pilgrims.

They jammed the side streets for blocks around the square. They parked where they stopped and unloaded.

The fat colonel had just finished breakfast and stood in the gazebo watching intently. Buses and cars, many with horns honking, were coming from all directions to the square. The barricades held firm. He barked commands and the soldiers jumped into high gear. More excitement. At seven-thirty, he called Ozzie and told him of the invasion. Ozzie arrived immediately and found Agee, who assured him it was a peaceful march. Sort of like a sit-in. How many were coming? Ozzie asked. Thousands, said Agee. Thousands.

They set up camp under the stately oaks, and milled around the lawn inspecting things. They arranged tables and chairs and playpens. They were indeed peaceful, until a group began the familiar cry of "Free Carl Lee!" They cleared their throats and joined in. It was not yet eight o'clock.

A black radio station in Memphis flooded the airwaves early Tuesday with a call for help. Black bodies were needed to march and demonstrate in Clanton, Mississippi, an hour away. Hundreds of cars met at a mall and headed south.

Every civil rights activist and black politician in the city made the trip.

Agee was a man possessed. He used a bullhorn to shout orders here and there. He herded new arrivals into their places. He organized the black preachers. He assured Ozzie and the colonel everything was okay.

Everything was okay until a handful of Klansmen made their routine appearance. The sight of the white robes was new to many of the blacks, and they reacted loudly. They inched forward, screaming and jeering. The troops surrounded the robes and protected them. The Kluxers were stunned and scared, and did not yell back.

By eight-thirty, the streets of Clanton were gridlocked. Deserted cars, vans, and buses were scattered haphazardly through parking lots and along the quiet residential streets. A steady stream of blacks walked toward the square from all directions. Traffic did not move. Driveways were blocked. Merchants parked blocks away from their shops. The mayor stood in the center of the gazebo, wringing his hands and begging Ozzie to do something. Around him thousands of blacks swarmed and yelled in perfect unison. Ozzie asked the mayor if he wanted him to start arresting everybody on the courthouse lawn.

Noose parked at a service station a half mile south of the jail, and walked with a group of blacks to the courthouse. They watched him curiously, but said nothing. No one would suspect he was a person of authority. Buckley and Musgrove parked in a driveway on Adams Street. They cursed and walked toward the square. They noticed the pile of rubble that had been Jake's house but said nothing. They were too busy cursing. With state troopers leading the way, the Greyhound from Temple reached the square at twenty minutes after nine. Through the dark windows, the fourteen passengers stared in disbelief at the carnival around the courthouse.

Mr. Pate called the packed courtroom to order, and Noose welcomed his jury. He apologized for the trouble outside, but there was nothing he could do. If there were no problems to report, they could continue deliberations.

"Very well, you may retire to the jury room and get to work. We will meet again just before lunch."

The jurors filed out and went to the jury room. The Hailey children sat with their father at the defense table. The spectators, now predominantly black, remained seated and struck up conversations. Jake returned to his office.

Foreman Acker sat at the end of the long, dusty table and thought of the hundreds, perhaps thousands, of Ford Countians who had served in this room and sat around this table and argued about justice over the past century. Any pride he may have felt for serving on the jury of the most famous case was greatly overshadowed by what happened last night. He wondered how many of his predecessors had been threatened with death. Probably a few, he decided.

The others fixed their coffee and slowly found seats around the tables. The room brought back fond memories for Clyde Sisco. Prior jury duty had proved lucrative for him, and he relished the thought of another handsome payoff for another just and true verdict. His messenger had not contacted him.

"How would y'all like to proceed?" the foreman asked.

Rita Mae Plunk had an especially hard and unforgiving look about her. She was a rough woman with a house trailer, no husband, and two outlaws for sons, both of whom had expressed hatred for Carl Lee Hailey. She had a few things she wanted to get off her large chest.

"I got a few things I wanna say," she informed Acker.

"Fine. Why don't we start with you, Miss Plunk, and go around the table."

"I voted guilty yesterday in the first vote, and I'll vote guilty next time. I don't see how anybody could vote not guilty, and I want just one of you to explain to me how you could vote in favor of this nigger!"

"Don't say that word again!" yelled Wanda Womack.

"I'll say 'nigger' if I wanna say 'nigger,' and there ain't a damned thing you can do," replied Rita Mae.

"Please don't use that word," said Frances McGowan.

"I find it personally offensive," said Wanda Womack.

"Nigger, Nigger, Nigger, Nigger, Nigger, Nigger," Rita Mae yelled across the table.

"Come on," said Clyde Sisco.

"Oh boy," said the foreman. "Look, Miss Plunk, let's be honest, okay. Most of us use that word, from time to time.

I'm sure some of us use it more than others. But it's offensive to many people, and I think it'd be a good idea not to use it during our deliberations. We've got enough to worry about as it is. Can we all agree not to use that word?"

Everyone nodded but Rita Mae.

Sue Williams decided to answer. She was well dressed, attractive, about forty. She worked for the county welfare department. "I didn't vote yesterday. I passed. But I tend to sympathize with Mr. Hailey. I have a daughter, and if she was raped, it would greatly affect my mental stability. I can understand how a parent might crack in that situation, and I think it's unfair for us to judge Mr. Hailey as if he was supposed to act completely rational."

"You think he was legally insane?" asked Reba Betts, an undecided.

"I'm not sure. But I know he wasn't stable. He couldn't have been."

"So you believe that nut of a doctor who testified for him?" asked Rita Mae.

"Yes. He was as believable as the State's doctor."

"I liked his boots," said Clyde Sisco. No one laughed.

"But he's a convict," said Rita Mae. "He lied and tried to cover it up. You can't believe a word he said."

"He had sex with a girl under eighteen," Clyde said. "If that's a crime, then a bunch of us should've been indicted."

Again, no one appreciated the attempt at humor. Clyde decided to stay quiet for a while.

"He later married the girl," said Donna Lou Peck, an undecided.

They went around the table, one at a time, expressing opinions and answering questions. The N word was carefully avoided by those wanting a conviction. The battle lines became clearer. Most of the undecideds leaned toward guilty, it seemed. The careful planning by Carl Lee, knowing the exact movements of the boys, the M-16—it all seemed so premeditated. If he had caught them in the act and killed them on the spot, he would not be held accountable. But to plan it so carefully for six days did not indicate an insane mind.

Wanda Womack, Sue Williams, and Clyde Sisco leaned

toward acquittal—the rest toward conviction. Barry Acker was noticeably noncommittal.

Agee unfurled a long blue and white FREE CARL LEE banner. The ministers gathered fifteen abreast behind it, and waited for the parade to form behind them. They stood in the center of Jackson Street, in front of the courthouse, while Agee screamed instructions to the masses. Thousands of blacks packed tightly behind them, and off they went. They inched down Jackson, and turned left on Caffey, up the west side of the square. Agee led the marchers in their now familiar battle cry of "Free Carl Lee! Free Carl Lee!" They screamed it in an endless, repetitive, numbing chorus. As the crowd moved around the square, it grew in number and volume.

Smelling trouble, the merchants locked up and headed for home and safety. They checked their policies to see if they were insured for riot damage. The green soldiers were lost in a sea of black. The colonel, sweating and nervous, ordered his troops to circle the courthouse and stand firm. While Agee and the marchers were turning onto Washington Street, Ozzie met with the handful of Kluxers. In a sincere and diplomatic way, he convinced them things could get out of hand, and he could no longer guarantee their safety. He acknowledged their right to assemble, said they had made their point, and asked them to get away from the square before there was trouble. They huddled quickly, and disappeared.

When the banner passed under the jury room, all twelve gaped from the window. The incessant chanting rattled the glass panes. The bullhorn sounded like a loudspeaker hanging from the ceiling. The jurors stared in disbelief at the mob, the black mob which filled the street and trailed around the corner onto Caffey. A varied assortment of homemade signs bobbed above the masses and demanded that the man be freed.

"I didn't know there were this many niggers in Ford County," Rita Mae Plunk said. At that moment, the other eleven held the same thought.

Buckley was furious. He and Musgrove watched from a third-floor window in the library. The roar below had disrupted their quiet conversation.

"I didn't know there were this many niggers in Ford County," Musgrove said.

"There ain't. Somebody shipped these niggers in here. I wonder who put them up to it."

"Probably Brigance."

"Yeah, probably so. It's mighty convenient that they start all this hell-raising when the jury is deliberating. There must be five thousand niggers down there."

"At least."

———————————

Noose and Mr. Pate watched and listened from a second-floor window in chambers. His Honor was not happy. He worried about his jury. "I don't see how they can concentrate on much with all this going on."

"Pretty good timing, ain't it, Judge?" Mr. Pate said.

"It certainly is."

"I didn't know we had that many blacks in the whole county."

———————————

It took twenty minutes for Mr. Pate and Jean Gillespie to find the attorneys and bring the courtroom to order. When it was quiet, the jurors filed into their seats. There were no smiles.

Noose cleared his throat. "Ladies and gentlemen, it is time for lunch. I don't suppose you have anything to report."

Barry Acker shook his head.

"That's what I figured. Let's break for lunch, until one-thirty. I realize you cannot leave the courthouse, but I want you to eat for a while without working on the case. I apologize for the disturbance outside, but, frankly, I can't do anything about it. We'll be in recess until one-thirty."

In chambers, Buckley went wild. "This is crazy, Judge! There's no way the jury can concentrate on this case with all that noise out there. This is a deliberate effort to intimidate the jury."

"I don't like it," Noose said.

"It was planned, Judge! It's intentional!" Buckley yelled.

"It looks bad," Noose added.

"I'm almost ready for a mistrial!"

"I won't grant one. What do you say, Jake?"

Jake grinned for a moment, and said, "Free Carl Lee."

"Very funny," Buckley growled. "You probably planned all this."

"No. If you will recall, Mr. Buckley, I tried to prevent it. I have repeatedly asked for a change of venue. I have repeatedly said the trial should not be held in this courthouse. You wanted it here, Mr. Buckley, and you kept it here, Judge Noose. You both now look foolish complaining."

Jake was impressed with his arrogance. Buckley growled and stared out the window. "Look at them. Wild niggers. Must be ten thousand out there."

During lunch the ten thousand grew to fifteen thousand. Cars from a hundred miles away—some with Tennessee plates—parked on the shoulders of the highways outside the city limits. The people hiked for two and three miles under a blistering sun to join the festivities around the courthouse. Agee broke for lunch, and the square quieted.

The blacks were peaceful. They opened their coolers and picnic baskets, and shared with each other. They congregated in the shade, but there were not enough trees to go around. They filled the courthouse in search of cold water and rest rooms. They walked the sidewalks and gazed in the windows of the closed shops and stores. Fearing trouble from the horde, the Coffee Shop and the Tea Shoppe closed during lunch. Outside of Claude's, they lined the sidewalk for a block and a half.

Jake, Harry Rex, and Lucien relaxed on the balcony and enjoyed the circus below. A pitcher of fresh, slushy margaritas sat on the table and slowly disappeared. At times they participated in the rally, yelling "Free Carl Lee" or humming along with "We Shall Overcome." No one knew the words but Lucien. He had learned them during the glorious civil rights days of the sixties, and still claimed to be the only white in Ford County who knew all the words to every stanza. He had even joined a black church back then, he explained between drinks, after his church voted to exclude

black members. He dropped out after a three-hour sermon
ruptured a disc. He had decided white people were not cut
out for that kind of worship. He still contributed, however.

Occasionally, a crew of TV people would stray near
Jake's office and serve up a question. Jake would pretend
not to hear, then finally yell "Free Carl Lee."

Precisely at one-thirty, Agee found his bullhorn, unfurled his banner, lined up the ministers and gathered his
marchers. He started with the hymn, sung directly into the
bullhorn, and the parade crawled down Jackson, then onto
Caffey, and around and around the square. Each lap attracted more people and made more noise.

———————————

The jury room was silent for fifteen minutes after Reba Betts
was converted from an undecided to a not guilty. If a man
raped her, she just might blow his head off if she got the
chance. It was now five to five with two undecideds, and a
compromise looked hopeless. The foreman continued to
straddle the fence. Poor old Eula Dell Yates had cried one
way, then cried the other, and everyone knew she would
eventually go with the majority. She had burst into tears at
the window, and was led to her seat by Clyde Sisco. She
wanted to go home. Said she felt like a prisoner.

The shouting and marching had taken its toll. When the
bullhorn passed nearby, the anxiety level in the small room
reached a frenzied peak. Acker would ask for quiet, and they
would wait impatiently until the racket faded to the front of
the courthouse. It never disappeared completely. Carol
Corman was the first to inquire about their safety. For the
first time in a week, the quiet motel was awfully attractive.

Three hours of nonstop chanting had unraveled whatever nerves were left. The foreman suggested they talk about
their families and wait until Noose sent for them at five.

Bernice Toole, a soft guilty, suggested something they
had all thought about but no one had mentioned. "Why
don't we just tell the judge we are hopelessly deadlocked?"

"He'd declare a mistrial, wouldn't he?" asked Jo Ann
Gates.

"Yes," answered the foreman. "And he would be retried in a few months. Why don't we call it a day, and try again tomorrow?"

They agreed. They were not ready to quit. Eula Dell cried softly.

At four, Carl Lee and the kids walked to one of the tall windows lining each side of the courtroom. He noticed a small knob. He turned it, and the windows swung open to a tiny platform hanging over the west lawn. He nodded at a deputy, and stepped outside. He held Tonya and watched the crowd.

They saw him. They yelled his name and rushed to the building under him. Agee led the marchers off the street and across the lawn. A wave of black humanity gathered under the small porch and pressed forward for a closer look at their champion.

"Free Carl Lee!"

"Free Carl Lee!"

"Free Carl Lee!"

He waved at his fans below him. He kissed his daughter and hugged his sons. He waved and told the kids to wave.

Jake and his small band of hombres used the diversion to stagger across the street to the courthouse. Jean Gillespie had called. Noose wanted to see the lawyers in chambers. He was disturbed. Buckley was raging.

"I demand a mistrial! I demand a mistrial!" he yelled at Noose the second Jake walked in.

"You move for a mistrial, Governor. You don't demand," Jake said through glassy eyes.

"You go to hell, Brigance! You planned all this. You plotted this insurrection. Those are your niggers out there."

"Where's the court reporter?" Jake asked. "I want this on the record."

"Gentlemen, gentlemen," Noose said. "Let's be professionals."

"Judge, the State moves for a mistrial," Buckley said, somewhat professionally.

"Overruled."

"All right, then. The State moves to allow the jury to deliberate at someplace other than the courthouse."

"Now that's an interesting idea," Noose said.

"I see no reason why they can't deliberate at the motel. It's quiet and few people know where it is," Buckley said confidently.

"Jake?" Noose said.

"Nope, it won't work. There is no statutory provision giving you the authority to allow deliberations outside the courthouse." Jake reached in his pocket and found several folded papers. He threw them on the desk. "State versus Dubose, 1963 case from Linwood County. The air conditioning in the Linwood County Courthouse quit during a heat wave. The circuit judge allowed the jury to deliberate in a local library. The defense objected. Jury convicted. On appeal, the Supreme Court ruled the judge's decision was improper and an abuse of discretion. The court went on to hold that the jury deliberations must take place in the jury room in the courthouse where the defendant is being tried. You can't move them."

Noose studied the case and handed it to Musgrove.

"Get the courtroom ready," he said to Mr. Pate.

With the exception of the reporters, the courtroom was solid black. The jurors looked haggard and strained.

"I take it you do not have a verdict," Noose said.

"No, sir," replied the foreman.

"Let me ask you this. Without indicating any numerical division, have you reached a point where you can go no further?"

"We've talked about that, Your Honor. And we'd like to leave, get a good night's rest, and try again tomorrow. We're not ready to quit."

"That's good to hear. I apologize for the distractions, but, again, there's nothing I can do. I'm sorry. You'll just have to do your best. Anything further?"

"No, sir."

"Very well. We'll stand adjourned until nine A.M. tomorrow."

Carl Lee pulled Jake's shoulder. "What does all this mean?"

"It means they're deadlocked. It could be six to six, or eleven to one against you, or eleven to one for acquittal. So don't get excited."

Barry Acker cornered the bailiff and handed him a folded sheet of paper. It read:

.Luann:
     Pack the kids and go to your mother's. Don't tell anyone. Stay there until this thing is over. Just do as I say. Things are dangerous.
                                   Barry

     "Can you get this to my wife today? Our number is 881–0774."
     "Sure," said the bailiff.

————————

Tim Nunley, mechanic down at the Chevrolet place, former client of Jake Brigance, and Coffee Shop regular, sat on a couch in the cabin deep in the woods and drank a beer. He listened to his Klan brothers as they got drunk and cursed niggers. Occasionally, he cursed them too. He had noticed whispering for the past two nights now, and felt something was up. He listened carefully.

He stood to get another beer. Suddenly, they jumped him. Three of his comrades pinned him against the wall and pounded him with fists and feet. He was beaten badly, then gagged, bound, and dragged outside, across the gravel road, and into the field where he had been inducted as a member. A cross was lit as he was tied to a pole and stripped. A bullwhip lashed him until his shoulders, back, and legs were solid crimson.

Two dozen of his ex-brethren watched in mute horror as the pole and limp body were soaked with kerosene. The leader, the one with the bullwhip, stood next to him for an eternity. He pronounced the death sentence, then threw a match.

Mickey Mouse had been silenced.

They packed their robes and belongings, and left for home. Most would never return to Ford County.

43 Wednesday. For the first time in weeks Jake slept more than eight hours. He had fallen asleep on the couch in his office, and he awoke at five to the sounds of the military preparing for the worst. He was rested, but the nervous throbbing returned with the thought that this day would probably be the big day. He showered and shaved downstairs, and ripped open a new pack of Fruit of the Loom he had purchased at the drug store. He dressed himself in Stan Atcavage's finest navy all-season suit, which was an inch too short and a bit loose, but not a bad fit under the circumstances. He thought of the rubble on Adams Street, then Carla, and the knot in his stomach began to churn. He ran for the newspapers.

On the front pages of the Memphis, Jackson, and Tupelo papers were identical photos of Carl Lee standing on the small porch over the mob, holding his daughter and waving to his people. There was nothing about Jake's house. He was relieved, and suddenly hungry.

Dell hugged him like a lost child. She removed her apron and sat next to him in a corner booth. As the regulars arrived and saw him, they stopped by and patted him on the back. It was good to see him again. They had missed him, and they were for him. He looked gaunt, she said, so he ordered most of the menu.

"Say, Jake, are all those blacks gonna be back today?" asked Bert West.

"Probably," he said as he stabbed a chunk of pancakes.

"I heard they's plannin' to bring more folks this mornin'," said Andy Rennick. "Ever nigger radio station in north Mississippi is tellin' folks to come to Clanton."

Great, thought Jake. He added Tabasco to his scrambled eggs.

"Can the jury hear all that yellin'?" asked Bert.

"Sure they can," Jake answered. "That's why they're doing it. They're not deaf."

"That's gotta scare them."

Jake certainly hoped so.

"How's the family?" Dell asked quietly.

"Fine, I guess. I talked to Carla every night."

"She scared?"

"Terrified."

"What have they done to you lately?"

"Nothing since Sunday morning."

"Does Carla know?"

Jake chewed and shook his head.

"I didn't think so. You poor thing."

"I'll be okay. What's the talk in here?"

"We closed at lunch yesterday. There were so many blacks outside, and we were afraid of a riot. We'll watch it close this morning, and we may close again. Jake, what if there's a conviction?"

"It could get hairy."

He stayed for an hour and answered their questions. Strangers arrived, and Jake excused himself.

There was nothing to do but wait. He sat on the balcony, drank coffee, smoked a cigar, and watched the guardsmen. He thought of the clients he once had; of a quiet little Southern law office with a secretary and clients waiting to see him. Of docket calls and interviews at the jail. Of normal things, like a family, a home, and church on Sunday mornings. He was not meant for the big time.

The first church bus arrived at seven-thirty and was halted by the soldiers. The doors flew open and an endless stream of blacks with lawn chairs and food baskets headed for the front lawn. For an hour Jake blew smoke into the heavy air and watched with great satisfaction as the square filled beyond capacity with noisy yet peaceful protestors. The reverends were out in full force, directing their people and assuring Ozzie and the colonel they were nonviolent folk. Ozzie was convinced. The colonel was nervous. By nine, the streets were crammed with demonstrators. Someone spotted the Greyhound. "Here they come!" Agee screamed into the loudspeaker. The mob pushed to the corner of Jackson and Quincy, where the soldiers, troopers, and deputies formed a mobile barricade around the bus and walked it through the crowd to the rear of the courthouse.

Eula Dell Yates cried openly. Clyde Sisco sat next to the window and held her hand. The others stared in fear as the bus inched around the square. A heavily armed passageway was cleared from the bus to the courthouse, and Ozzie came aboard. The situation was under control, he assured them over the roar. Just follow him and walk as fast as possible.

The bailiff locked the door as they gathered around the coffeepot. Eula Dell sat by herself in the corner crying softly and flinching as each "Free Carl Lee!'" boomed from below.

"I don't care what we do," she said. "I really don't care, but I just can't take any more of this. I haven't seen my family in eight days, and now this madness. I didn't sleep any last night." She cried louder. "I think I'm close to a nervous breakdown. Let's just get outta here."

Clyde handed her a Kleenex and rubbed her shoulder.

Jo Ann Gates was a soft guilty who was ready to crack. "I didn't sleep either last night. I can't take another day like yesterday. I wanna go home to my kids."

Barry Acker stood by the window and thought of the riot that would follow a guilty verdict. There wouldn't be a building left downtown, including the courthouse. He doubted if anybody would protect the jurors in the aftermath of a wrong verdict. They probably wouldn't make it back to the bus. Thankfully, his wife and kids had fled to safety in Arkansas.

"I feel like a hostage," said Bernice Toole, a firm guilty. "That mob would storm the courthouse in a split second if we convict him. I feel intimidated."

Clyde handed her a box of Kleenexes.

"I don't care what we do," Eula Dell whined in desperation. "Let's just get outta here. I honestly don't care if we convict him or cut him loose, let's just do something. My nerves can't take it."

Wanda Womack stood at the end of the table and nervously cleared her throat. She asked for attention. "I have a proposal," she said slowly, "that just might settle this thing."

The crying stopped, and Barry Acker returned to his seat. She had their complete attention.

"I thought of something last night when I couldn't sleep, and I want you to consider it. It may be painful. It may cause you to search your heart and take a long look at your soul. But I'll ask you to do it anyway. And if each of you will be honest with yourself, I think we can wrap this up before noon."

The only sounds came from the street below.

"Right now we are evenly divided, give or take a vote. We could tell Judge Noose that we are hopelessly dead-locked. He would declare a mistrial, and we would go home. Then in a few months this entire spectacle would be re-peated. Mr. Hailey would be tried again in this same court-room, with the same judge, but with a different jury, a jury drawn from this county, a jury of our friends, husbands, wives, and parents. The same kind of people who are now in this room. That jury will be confronted with the same issues before us now, and those people will not be any smarter than we are.

"The time to decide this case is now. It would be mor-ally wrong to shirk our responsibilities and pass the buck to the next jury. Can we all agree on that?"

They silently agreed.

"Good. This is what I want you to do. I want you to pretend with me for a moment. I want you to use your imagi-nations. I want you to close your eyes and listen to nothing but my voice."

They obediently closed their eyes. Anything was worth a try.

Jake lay on the couch in his office and listened to Lucien tell stories about his prestigious father and grandfather, and their prestigious law firm, and all the people they screwed out of money and land.

"My inheritance was built by my promiscuous ances-tors!" he yelled. "They screwed everybody they could!"

Harry Rex laughed uncontrollably. Jake had heard the stories before, but they were always funny, and different.

"What about Ethel's retarded son?" Jake asked.

"Don't talk that way about my brother," Lucien pro-tested. "He's the brightest one in the family. Sure he's my brother. Dad hired her when she was seventeen, and believe it or not, she looked good back then. Ethel Twitty was the hottest thing in Ford County. My dad couldn't keep his hands off her. Sickening to think about now, but it's true."

"It's disgusting," Jake said.

"She had a houseful of kids, and two of them looked just like me, especially the dunce. It was very embarrassing back then."

"What about your mother?" asked Harry Rex.

"She was one of those dignified old Southern ladies whose main concern was who had blue blood and who didn't. There's not much blue blood around here, so she spent most of her time in Memphis trying to impress and be accepted by the cotton families. I spent a good part of my childhood at the Peabody Hotel all starched out with a little red bow tie, trying to act polished around the rich kids from Memphis. I hated it, and I didn't care much for my mother either. She knew about Ethel, but she accepted it. She told the old man to be discreet and not embarrass the family. He was discreet, and I wound up with a retarded half-brother."

"When did she die?"

"Six months before my father was killed in the plane crash."

"How'd she die?" asked Harry Rex.

"Gonorrhea. Caught it from the yard boy."

"Lucien! Seriously?"

"Cancer. Carried it for three years, but she was dignified to the very end."

"Where'd you go wrong?" Jake asked.

"I think it started in the first grade. My uncle owned the big plantation south of town, and he owned several black families. This was in the Depression, right? I spent most of my childhood there because my father was too busy right here in this office and my mother was too busy with her hot-tea-drinkers clubs. All of my playmates were black. I'd been raised by black servants. My best friend was Willie Ray Wilbanks. No kidding. My great-grandfather purchased his great-grandfather. And when the slaves were freed, most of them just kept the family name. What were they supposed to do? That's why you've got so many black Wilbankses around here. We owned all the slaves in Ford County, and most of them became Wilbankses."

"You're probably kin to some," Jake said.

"Given the proclivities of my forefathers, I'm probably kin to all of them."

The phone rang. They froze and stared at it. Jake sat up and held his breath. Harry Rex picked up the receiver, then hung up. "Wrong number," he said.

They studied each other, then smiled.

"Anyway, back to the first grade," Jake said.

"Okay. When it came time to start school, Willie Ray and the rest of my little buddies got on the bus headed for the black school. I jumped on the bus too, and the driver very carefully took my hand and made me get off. I cried and screamed, and my uncle took me home and told my mother, 'Lucien got on the nigger school bus.' She was horrified, and beat my little ass. The old man beat me too, but years later admitted it was funny. So I went to the white school where I was always the little rich kid. Everybody hated the little rich kid, especially in a poor town like Clanton. Not that I was lovable to begin with, but everyone got a kick out of hating me just because we had money. That's why I've never thought much of money. That's where the nonconformity started. In the first grade. I decided not to be like my mother because she frowned all the time and looked down on the world. And my old man was always too busy to enjoy himself. I said piss on it. I'm gonna have some fun."

Jake stretched and closed his eyes.

"Nervous?" Lucien asked.

"I just want it to be over."

The phone rang again, and Lucien grabbed it. He listened, then hung up.

"What is it?" Harry Rex demanded.

Jake sat up and glared at Lucien. The moment had arrived.

"Jean Gillespie. The jury is ready."

"Oh my God," Jake said as he rubbed his temples.

"Listen to me, Jake," Lucien lectured. "Millions of people will see what is about to happen. Keep your cool. Be careful what you say."

"What about me?" Harry Rex moaned. "I need to go vomit."

"That's strange advice coming from you, Lucien," Jake said as he buttoned Stan's coat.

"I've learned a lot. Show your class. If you win, watch what you say to the press. Be sure and thank the jury. If you lose—"

"If you lose," Harry Rex said, "run like hell, because those niggers will storm the courthouse."

"I feel weak," Jake admitted.

———————————

Agee took the platform on the front steps and announced the jury was ready. He asked for quiet, and instantly the mob grew still. They moved toward the front columns. Agee asked them to fall to their knees and pray. They knelt obediently and prayed earnestly. Every man, woman, and child on the front lawn bowed before God and begged him to let their man go.

The soldiers stood bunched together and also prayed for an acquittal.

Ozzie and Moss Junior seated the courtroom and lined deputies and reserves around the walls and down the aisle. Jake entered from the holding room and stared at Carl Lee at the defense table. He glanced at the spectators. Many were praying. Many were biting their fingers. Gwen was wiping tears. Lester looked fearfully at Jake. The children were confused and scared.

Noose assumed the bench and an electrified silence engulfed the courtroom. There was no sound from the outside. Twenty thousand blacks knelt on the ground like Muslims. Perfect stillness inside the courtroom and out.

"I have been advised that the jury has reached a verdict, is that correct, Mr. Bailiff? Very well. We will soon seat the jury, but before we do so I have some instructions. I will not tolerate any outbursts or displays of emotion. I will direct the sheriff to remove any person who creates a disturbance. If need be, I will clear the courtroom. Mr. Bailiff, will you seat the jury."

The door opened, and it seemed like an hour before Eula Dell Yates appeared first with tears in her eyes. Jake dropped his head. Carl Lee stared gamely at the portrait of Robert E. Lee above Noose. They awkwardly filled the jury box. They seemed jittery, tense, scared. Most had been crying. Jake felt sick. Barry Acker held a piece of paper that attracted the attention of everyone.

"Ladies and gentlemen, have you reached a verdict?"

"Yes, sir, we have," answered the foreman in a high-pitched, nervous voice.

"Hand it to the clerk, please."

Jean Gillespie took it and handed it to His Honor, who studied it forever. "It is technically in order," he finally said.

Eula Dell was flooding, and her sniffles were the only sounds in the courtroom. Jo Ann Gates and Bernice Toole padded their eyes with handkerchiefs. The crying could mean only one thing. Jake had vowed to ignore the jury before the verdict was read, but it was impossible. In his first criminal trial, the jurors had smiled as they took their seats. At that moment, Jake had become confident of an acquittal. Seconds later he learned that the smiles were because a criminal was about to be removed from the streets. Since that trial, he had vowed never to look at the jurors. But he always did. It would be nice to see a wink or a thumbs up, but that never happened.

Noose looked at Carl Lee. "Will the defendant please rise."

Jake knew there were probably more terrifying requests known to the English tongue, but to a criminal lawyer that request at that particular moment had horrible implications. His client stood awkwardly, pitifully. Jake closed his eyes and held his breath. His hands shook and his stomach ached.

Noose handed the verdict back to Jean Gillespie. "Please read it, Madam Clerk."

She unfolded it and faced the defendant. "As to each count of the indictment, we the jury find the defendant not guilty by reason of insanity."

Carl Lee turned and bolted for the railing. Tonya and the boys sprang from the front pew and grabbed him. The courtroom exploded in pandemonium. Gwen screamed and burst into tears. She buried her head in Lester's arms. The reverends stood, looked upward, and shouted "Hallelujah!" and "Praise Jesus!" and "Lord! Lord! Lord!"

Noose's admonition meant nothing. He rapped the gavel half-heartedly and said, "Order, order, order in the courtroom." He was inaudible in the midst of the roar, and seemed content to allow a little celebration.

Jake was numb, lifeless, paralyzed. His only movement was a weak smile in the direction of the jury box. His eyes watered and his lip quivered, and he decided not to make a spectacle of himself. He nodded at Jean Gillespie, who was crying, and just sat at the defense table nodding and trying to smile, unable to do anything else. From the corner of his eye he could see Musgrove and Buckley removing files, legal pads, and important-looking papers, and throwing it all into their briefcases. Be gracious, he told himself.

A teenager darted between two deputies, through the door, and ran through the rotunda screaming "Not guilty! Not guilty!" He ran to a small balcony over the front steps and screamed to the masses below *"Not guilty! Not guilty!"* Bedlam erupted.

"Order, order in the court," Noose was saying when the delayed reaction from the outside came thundering through the windows.

"Order, order in the courtroom." He tolerated the excitement for another minute, then asked the sheriff to restore order. Ozzie raised his hands and spoke. The clapping, hugging and praising died quickly. Carl Lee released his children and returned to the defense table. He sat close to his attorney and put his arm around him, grinning and crying at the same time.

Noose smiled at the defendant. "Mr. Hailey, you have been tried by a jury of your peers and found not guilty. I do not recall any expert testimony that you are now dangerous or in need of further psychiatric treatment. You are a free man."

His Honor looked at the attorneys. "If there is nothing further, this court will stand adjourned until August 15."

Carl Lee was smothered by his family and friends. They hugged him, hugged each other, hugged Jake. They wept unashamedly and praised the Lord. They told Jake they loved him.

The reporters pressed against the railing and began firing questions at Jake. He held up his hands, and said he would have no comment. But there would be a full-blown press conference in his office at 2:00 P.M.

Buckley and Musgrove left through a side door. The jurors were locked in the jury room to await the last bus ride to the motel. Barry Acker asked to speak to the sheriff. Ozzie met him in the hallway, listened intently, and promised to escort him home and provide protection around the clock.

The reporters assaulted Carl Lee. "I just wanna go home," he said over and over. "I just wanna go home."

The celebration kicked into high gear on the front lawn. There was singing, dancing, crying, back-slapping, hugging, thanks-giving, congratulating, outright laughing, cheering, chanting, high fives, low fives, and soul brother shakes. The heavens were praised in one glorious, tumultuous, irreverent jubilee. They packed closer together in front of the courthouse and waited impatiently for their hero to emerge and bask in his much deserved adulation.

Their patience grew thin. After thirty minutes of screaming "We Want Carl Lee! We Want Carl Lee!" their man appeared at the door. An ear-splitting, earth-shaking roar greeted him. He inched forward through the mass with his lawyer and family, and stopped on the top step under the pillars where the plywood platform held a thousand microphones. The whooping and yelling of twenty thousand voices was deafening. He hugged his lawyer, and they waved to the sea of screaming faces.

The shouting from the army of reporters was completely inaudible. Occasionally, Jake would stop waving and yell something about a press conference in his office at two.

Carl Lee hugged his wife and children, and they waved. The crowd roared its approval. Jake slid away and into the courthouse, where he found Lucien and Harry Rex waiting in a corner, away from the mad rush of spectators. "Let's get out of here," Jake yelled. They pushed through the mob, down the hall and out the rear door. Jake spotted a swarm of reporters on the sidewalk outside his office.

"Where are you parked?" he asked Lucien. He pointed to a side street, and they disappeared behind the Coffee Shop.

Sallie fried pork chops and green tomatoes, and served them on the porch. Lucien produced a bottle of expensive champagne, and swore he had saved it just for the occasion. Harry Rex ate with his fingers, gnawing on the bones as if he hadn't seen food in a month. Jake played with his food and worked on the ice-cold champagne. After two glasses, he smiled into the distance. He savored the moment.

"You look silly as hell," Harry Rex said with a mouthful of pork.

"Shut up, Harry Rex," Lucien said. "Let him enjoy his finest hour."

"He's enjoying it. Look at that smirk."

"What should I tell the press?" Jake asked.

"Tell them you need some clients," Harry Rex said.

"Clients will be no problem," Lucien said. "They'll line the sidewalks waiting for appointments."

"Why didn't you talk to the reporters in the courthouse? They had their cameras running and everything. I started to say something for them," Harry Rex said.

"I'm sure it would've been a gem," Lucien said.

"I've got them at my fingertips," Jake said. "They're not going anywhere. We could sell tickets to the press conference and make a fortune."

"Can I sit and watch, please, Jake, please," Harry Rex said.

44 They argued over whether they should take the antique Bronco or the nasty little Porsche. Jake said he was not driving. Harry Rex cursed the loudest, and they loaded into the Bronco. Lucien found a spot in the rear seat. Jake rode shotgun and gave instructions. They hit the back streets, and missed most of the traffic from the square. The highway was crowded, and Jake directed his driver through a myriad of gravel roads. They found blacktop, and Harry Rex raced away in the direction of the lake.

"I have one question, Lucien," Jake said.

"What?"

"And I want a straight answer."

"What?"

"Did you cut a deal with Sisco?"

"No, my boy, you won it on your own."

"Do you swear?"

"I swear to God. On a stack of Bibles."

Jake wanted to believe him, so he dropped it. They rode in silence, in the sweltering heat, and listened as Harry Rex sang along with the stereo. Suddenly, Jake pointed and yelled. Harry Rex slammed on the brakes, made a wild left turn, and sped down another gravel road.

"Where are we going?" Lucien demanded.

"Just hang on," Jake said as he looked at a row of houses approaching on the right. He pointed to the second one, and Harry Rex pulled into the driveway and parked under a shade tree. Jake got out, looked around the front yard, and walked onto the porch. He knocked on the screen door.

A man appeared. A stranger. "Yeah, whatta you want?"

"I'm Jake Brigance, and—"

The door flew open, and the man rushed onto the porch and grabbed Jake's hand. "Nice to meet you, Jake. I'm Mack Loyd Crowell. I was on the grand jury that almost didn't indict. You done a real good job. I'm proud of you."

Jake shook his hand and repeated his name. Then he

remembered. Mack Loyd Crowell, the man who told Buckley to shut up and sit down in the grand jury. "Yeah, Mack Loyd, now I remember. Thanks."

Jake looked awkwardly through the door.

"You lookin' for Wanda?" Crowell asked.

"Well, yes. I was just passing by, and remembered her address from the jury research."

"You've come to the right place. She lives here, and I do too most of the time. We ain't married or nothing, but we go together. She's layin' down takin' a nap. She's pretty wore out."

"Don't wake her," Jake said.

"She told me what happened. She won it for you."

"How? What happened?"

"She made them all close their eyes and listen to her. She told them to pretend that the little girl had blond hair and blue eyes, that the two rapists were black, that they tied her right foot to a tree and her left foot to a fence post, that they raped her repeatedly and cussed her because she was white. She told them to picture the little girl layin' there beggin' for her daddy while they kicked her in the mouth and knocked out her teeth, broke both jaws, broke her nose. She said to imagine two drunk blacks pouring beer on her and pissing in her face, and laughing like idiots. And then she told them to imagine that the little girl belonged to them —their daughter. She told them to be honest with themselves and to write on a piece of paper whether or not they would kill those black bastards if they got the chance. And they voted, by secret ballot. All twelve said they would do the killing. The foreman counted the votes. Twelve to zero. Wanda said she'd sit in that jury room until Christmas before she'd vote to convict, and if they were honest with themselves, then they ought to feel the same way. Ten of them agreed with her, and one lady held out. They all started cryin' and cussin' her so bad, she finally caved in. It was rough in there, Jake."

Jake listened to every word without breathing. He heard a noise. Wanda Womack walked to the screen door. She smiled at him and began crying. He stared at her through the screen, but could not talk. He bit his lip and nodded. "Thanks," he managed weakly. She wiped her eyes and nodded.

On Craft Road, a hundred cars lined both shoulders east and west of the Hailey driveway. The long front yard was packed with vehicles, children playing, and parents sitting under shade trees and on car hoods. Harry Rex parked in a ditch by the mailbox. A crowd rushed to greet Carl Lee's lawyer. Lester grabbed him and said, "You done it again, you done it again."

They shook hands and slapped backs across the yard and up to the porch. Agee hugged him and praised God. Carl Lee left the swing and walked down the steps, followed by his family and admirers. They gathered around Jake as the two great men came face to face. They clutched hands and smiled at each other, both searching for words. They embraced. The crowd clapped and shouted.

"Thank you, Jake," Carl Lee said softly.

The lawyer and client sat in the swing and answered questions about the trial. Lucien and Harry Rex joined Lester and some of his friends under a shade tree for a little drink. Tonya ran and jumped around the yard with a hundred other kids.

At two-thirty, Jake sat at his desk and talked to Carla. Harry Rex and Lucien drank the last of the margaritas, and quickly got drunk. Jake drank coffee and told his wife he would leave Memphis in three hours and be in North Carolina by ten. Yes, he was fine, he said. Everything was okay, and everything was over. There were dozens of reporters packed into his conference room, so be sure and watch the evening news. He would meet with them briefly, then drive to Memphis. He said he loved her, missed her body, and would be there soon. He hung up.

Tomorrow, he'd call Ellen.

"Why are you leaving today!" Lucien demanded.

"You're stupid, Jake, just stupid. You've got a thousand reporters in the palm of your hand, and you're leaving town. Stupid, just stupid," Harry Rex shouted.

Jake stood. "How do I look, fellas?"

"Like a dumbass if you leave town," Harry Rex said.

"Hang around for a couple of days," Lucien pleaded. "This is an opportunity you'll never have again. Please, Jake."

"Relax, fellas. I'm going to meet with them now, let them take my picture, answer a few of their stupid questions, then I'm leaving town."

"You're crazy, Jake," Harry Rex said.

"I agree," said Lucien.

Jake checked the mirror, adjusted Stan's tie, and smiled at his friends. "I appreciate you guys. I really do. I got paid nine hundred dollars for this trial, and I plan to share it with y'all."

They poured the last of the margaritas, gulped it down, and followed Jake Brigance down the stairs to face the reporters.